I0612044

The critics have spoken:
(continued from back cover)

Prime Minister Margaret Thatcher:
Berserkley is the light at the end of the Chunnel.

Norman Mailer:
With Berserkley, Roth has succeeded where the rest of us have failed. He has not only knocked Hemingway out of the ring. He has knocked him senseless.

Julia Child:
There is only one word to describe *Berserkley* — "Delicious".

Amazon.com:
Berserkley, by Robert Roth, is a NOVEL.

J.D. Salinger:
I tip my hunting cap to Roth (Robert, not Philip).

Truman Capote:
Roth's *Berserkley* is a novel far superior to *To Kill A Mockingbird*.

i

President Donald J. Trump:
The most important book published since *The Art Of The Deal* — no collusion, no obstruction, no quid pro quo, perfect.

Dorothy Parker:
…a novel…with great force.

Carlo Gambino:
On the advice of counsel, I invoke my Fifth Amendment privilege against self-incrimination and respectfully decline to comment.

Harold Bloom (a relatively positive review from a notoriously hard to please critic):
When I was a young man, I often heard supposedly intelligent people claim that if you locked 100 monkeys in a room with 100 typewriters for 100 years, they would reproduce every book ever written. I myself found this idea ridiculous and reeking of monkey excrement. However, while reading *Berserkley*, it occurred to me that, without a doubt, this was one book those monkeys would have written, and quite likely improved upon, and done so in far less than 100 years.

Berserkley

by Robert Roth

Publisher's note: There are numerous places in this book where the author decided logic trumped common usage as to punctuation, most often concerning the placement of quotation marks.

BERSERKLEY

ISBN: 978-0-99-11690-2-3

The Periphery Press

peripherypress.com

Sanibel, Florida

Robert Roth is also the author of *Sand In The Wind*, widely considered the finest novel to come out of the Vietnam War

This book is dedicated to the memory of my darling little brother, Jerold. He is not actually dead yet, but eventually, God willing, he will be.

Though the author is a survivor of Berkeley, this book is fiction, neither personal account nor history. Any resemblance of the characters, events, or institutions described herein, to actual people, events, or institutions is completely coincidental (and surely pales by comparison).

ACKNOWLEDGMENTS

DESPITE THEIR BRUTAL HONESTY, THEIR LACK OF FAITH IN THIS NOVEL, AND THEIR VISCERAL DISLIKE FOR ITS AUTHOR, I AM FORCED TO THANK THE ENTIRE EDITORIAL STAFF OF THE PERIPHERY PRESS (YES, I RAN THROUGH ALL OF THEM): RON WOGAMAN, WILLIAM J. SMITH, STEVE GROGAN, PHYLLIS WEISBERG, WILLIAM R. BUTLER, LORETTA BRESH, RICHARD ARNOLD, DAVID ROEMER, MANNY KLIBANER, VLADIMIR SHKOLNIKOV, AND, BOTH LAST AND BY FAR THE LEAST, ALEX TARGONSKY.

Berserkley

"Unbelievable", he mumbled to himself. Everywhere he looked, almost all that he saw, was not just new, not just outrageous, not just mind blowing. It was, he repeated, "Unbelievable".

Smitty had expected Berkeley, California to be different from Columbus, Ohio, very different. Yet as he walked its streets, the word different failed pathetically to describe the scene engulfing him. Different city? This had to be a different galaxy. The street sign said "Telegraph Avenue", but the sidewalks said Fantasy Land Over the Rainbow Through the Looking Glass On Acid. A phantasmagorical horde of hippies had swarmed the town, inundated and overwhelmed it, magically taken root. The Freak Nation had set up shop, turned Berkeley into its fairgrounds, strewn its sidewalks with tables and blankets offering old fashioned clothing, dashikis, tie-dyed shirts, woven shoulder bags, belts of every material and color, leather crafts, handmade jewelry, strings of beads, hash pipes, hookahs, psychedelic day-glo posters, weird paintings, wood carvings, sculptures, porcelain, pottery, blown glass, lava lamps, kaleidoscopes, roach clips, wineskin canteens, and every other newly discovered necessity of the turned-on Sixties.

Beards were "in", the preference being full and shaggy. Sandals and boots fought it out for footwear of choice. Clothing ran the gamut from biblical to science fiction, with an emphasis on brilliant colors and outlandish frills. The sidewalks were flowing, blending rainbows of shoppers, walkers, and even a few wide-eyed gawkers such as Smitty. His own clothing, seemingly counterculture that morning, paled to conservative by comparison. Wearing a plain white T-shirt and faded Levis, he felt certifiably alien. Luckily, his colorful Mexican peasant poncho added a little flash. Still, it was his hair that saved him — straight shiny black, shoulder length, parted down the middle, and pinned back with a red headband American Indian style. For sure, none of the freaks around him were making Smitty for an FBI agent. Those who weren't smiling were laughing, everyone grooving on everyone else at this perpetual block party where colors rioted and anarchy ruled.

As he walked, Smitty glanced down a side street to see a traffic stopping mural half a block long. Painted upon a brick wall, the vibrant colors jumped out at him — blood red, Negro black, sun orange, sky blue. It was more than a depiction of Berkeley's streets. It was a primitive, violent statement that screamed, "Revolution!"

Smitty got his head back around barely in time to stop dead. He stood nose to nose with as zonked-out a mug as he had ever seen. Beneath a set of flying saucer eyes and an Errol Flynn mustache, hung a sloppily hand-rolled joint the thickness of a cigar and an inch short of poking him in the eye.

"Hey, Man, got a light?"

Smitty glanced left and right. Merely looking at that much marijuana had to be grounds for arrest. No telling what they could do to you for actually lighting it up for someone. Fortunately, no decision — moral, legal, or practical — would be necessary. The serene, patient face before him weaved around like a snake charmer's cobra.

"Sorry, Man, don't smoke."

The face moved in and back, aiding its spaced-out eyes in an attempt to focus, to study Smitty as if he were a Martian. Finally, its owner staggered back a step, asking in disbelief, "Not even weed?"

Smitty took another paranoid glance to each side before dodging the question with, "No matches." It was then that he noticed the pointed green cap, the primitive green shirt laced in front with rawhide, and then the weird green ballet tights, and finally the pointy, rawhide moccasins. 'What the—' wondered Smitty. The man in green turned and stumbled away, thus revealing a bow and quiver of arrows slung across his back. 'Oh,' Smitty realized in a flash of insight, 'Robin Hood.' Things were beginning to make sense.

Adrift in an alien present, Smitty turned to start walking again. He barely managed to lift his foot before a healthy, happy hippie asked, "Hey Man, you got a quarter?"

"Think so," said Smitty, digging into his Levis as some far from pedestrian pedestrians brushed by him. Sure enough, he found a quarter and handed it over.

The panhandler, smiling with satisfaction, nodded thanks. He then raised his hand, showing Smitty a two fingered V. "Peace, Brother."

Smitty started walking and kept walking, right to the end of Telegraph Avenue where it intersected Bancroft Way. Across the street stood the austere, impressive main entrance to the University of California at Berkeley. This huge, open gate seemed to promise a world unto itself. Smitty smiled confidently, ready and eager to cross that street, go through that gate, and finally enter that world. He had spent his first two years of college at Ohio State, reading about Berkeley in the newspapers. Reading was not good enough. He had sweated the last three months on a raucous loading dock to scrape up the needed cash. Now he'd finish college here, getting his news live and firsthand. Berkeley — where it always happens first.

The wide sidewalk in front of the university was crowded with large pushcarts. Smitty walked quickly past the one selling donuts. You could buy those in Ohio. Stone-ground muffins sounded good, whatever they were. Still, the cart doing the best business was selling something called quiche. Smitty, in no hurry, joined the line. People strolled the area smiling, enjoying themselves. Their mood was contagious. He caught it.

Just outside the gate stood a lean, agitated, gesticulating man in an ill-fitting black suit and a tieless white shirt. He was surrounded by a dozen smiling spectators. "You know what's inside this gate?"

"Freedom!" yelled a heckler, drawing laughs from the crowd.

"Freedom?" the preacher exclaimed, "Freedom to sin against the Lord. These are gates to debauchery, depravity, and fornication. These are the gates to hell."

"Let me in!" the same heckler yelled.

'Me too,' thought Smitty, now even more anxious to crash that gate and see if UC Berkeley was really as advertised. The person in line behind him gave a jerk of his head, indicating that it was Smitty's turn. He ordered, "One quiche", pronouncing it to rhyme with "cliché".

The girl tending the cart raised her nose and dropped her smile before replying, "Quiche", pronouncing it "keesh".

Quiche in hand, Smitty walked away repeating the proper pronunciation. He would not make that mistake again. His first bite enlightened him as to another mistake not to make again. Quiche tasted like vulcanized eggs laced with spinach and laminated onto soggy cardboard. His luck took a sudden turn for the better. A garbage can stood a handy few steps away. Halfway there, he heard the words, "Hey Man, can you spare some change for a bite to eat?" This time the panhandler was more Skid Row than Flower Power.

Faced with real need, Smitty shifted his snack to his left hand so he could search his pocket. The panhandler's eyes followed the quiche. "Oh," said Smitty as he dug for a quarter, "Here, finish it."

The insulted panhandler recoiled at the thought. "Hippy puke?...I'm hungry, Man, not starving."

Smitty handed over a quarter.

The panhandler, still eyeing him suspiciously, took the quarter and nodded thanks.

'Right-on,' thought Smitty. 'You gotta be desperate.' He flipped the quiche into the trash.

Smitty continued across Sproul Plaza. So did the carnival. A band of saffron robed, shaved-headed Hare Krishnas banged away on their drums and tambourines while hopping around in a circle, singing, "Hare Krishna, Hare Krishna, Hare Krishna, Hare Rama." He noticed some pasty-white Caucasians among them, then noticed they were all Caucasians, some less pasty. No one besides himself seemed to pay them any mind.

Up ahead, a dozen people gathered around and obscured something. Smitty politely weaved his way to the front, where a young girl sang "Kumbaya". She was good. At Ohio State she would have been a star attraction. Yet Berkeley offered so much more to see.

A long row of booths was gathering quite a bit of attention, including Smitty's. The first one belonged to Vietnam Veterans Opposing the War. Wearing their old military bush jackets, they looked with satisfaction on the two long lines of students waiting patiently to sign a petition to, "Free the Presidio Six". Smitty had no idea who exactly were the Presidio Six, or why they weren't free. This provided excuse enough not to stand in line. A large sign above the next stall proved more enticing — "KISSING BOOTH". Two students, one outside, leaning over the front of the table, one inside leaning over its back, embraced in a passionate, opened mouthed kiss. Smitty, feeling a pleasant twinge in the immediate area of his groin, mused, 'Wouldn't mind some of that.' This thought was quickly banished from his mind as he read the banner — "Gay Students' Organization — Kisses $1". His eyes shot back towards the kissers. 'Yup.' Sure enough, both were male.

Further on, in front of two crossed Viet Cong flags, a uniformed nurse stood soliciting blood donations. Two people were heeding her call. The next table, attended by students not farm workers, urged him to boycott grapes. 'I'm easy,' Smitty said to himself without stopping. After all, he couldn't remember the last time he'd had an urge for a grape. The "Down With The Shah" booth itself didn't draw a second glance from him, though one of the girls in it sure did.

In front of the "Fight The Draft" booth, a dozen people chanted, "Hell, no! We won't go!" A sign advertised, "Complimentary Lighters To Burn Your Draft Card". To Smitty, the draft was a noose hanging over him. One serious academic misstep, and the noose would be cinched tight around his neck, a thought he preferred not to contemplate. The "Legalize Pot" booth was enough to take his mind off of that. Legalization, sure to happen soon, was something to look forward to.

Smitty decided to take the remaining tables at a fast walk. A very serious young lady decided otherwise. She stepped sideways, right into his path. This small yet formidable roadblock wore a military green T-shirt beneath a set of baggy denim overalls. She demanded to know, "You don't think the university's custodians deserve the right to unionize?"

About to ask agreeably, "What makes you say that?" Smitty perceived that this woman would not be into small talk. He just shrugged.

"Then sign our petition," she commanded.

Smitty glanced to the side, seeing that he stood in front of the Union of Communist Workers booth. A huge red star with Chairman Mao's head emblazoned upon its center hung between the back posts. Smitty glanced at the petition on the front table, up at Mao, back at the unsmiling roadblock, then again at the petition. 'What the hell.' He signed, failing to effect the slightest change in the girl's expression.

Smitty walked away asking himself, 'Why'd I do that?' Still, it was no big thing. He had already regained his amused expression by the time three cold, belligerent stares wiped it from his face. Smitty glanced over his shoulder to be sure they weren't glaring at someone in back of him. The stares belonged to three members of the Black Panther Party. The sign across their booth demanded, "Free Huey Newton". They stood motionless, in the at-ease position, wearing black quasi-military pants, black leather jackets over black T-shirts, topped off with black berets to match. Despite their aviator sunglasses, Smitty could tell they were staring at him. They talked to no one as the passing white students dropped money into their fish bowl. Smitty walked by, fighting the urge to stare back. 'Kids' stuff.'

"Charlie," one of the Black Panther called after him.

Smitty turned back, his own stare giving no quarter.

"You owe black people reparations."

Here he was again, back in grade school, fighting to keep his lunch money. "That right?"

"Bet your white ass it is."

Smitty shrugged. "Send me the bill." He turned away, asking himself, 'Does that crap work around here?' then answering himself, 'It must.'

At the next booth stood two burly students, the burlier one female. They wore straw sombreros and loose white peasants' clothing, with red cloth sashes for belts. Yet it was their long, mean looking machetes that held his gaze.

The male student asked challengingly, "You ready to join the Venceramos?"

"Venceramos?" he asked, no smile on his face and making no move to approach the machete wielders. 'What is this, Intimidation Day?'

"Come to Cuba with us, to harvest sugar cane."

"Man, I just got here," Smitty replied, already on his way.

The female student called coyly after him, "C'mon, you got the muscles."

Flattery got her somewhere. Those three months on the loading dock had made a difference. Smitty fought an urge to look back.

The girl added, "We'll be here all week."

This time he did glance back, a smile on his face.

Smitty headed through Sather Gate, his pumped up ego adding bounce to his step. To him, the unbelievable part was that all this was probably the believable part, which they'd still never believe back home. Of course, that was no reflection upon Cleveland. Smitty saw no damn need to be ashamed of being from Cleveland, Ohio. Never had. He liked the place, felt at home there, and rightfully so, having been born and raised within its city limits. In fact, he and some high school friends had once decided, over a few six packs, that Cleveland's motto should be, "Better Than Most Places".

There was at least one real advantage to being from there, and Smitty appreciated it. Outside of Ohio, people didn't prejudge a person from Cleveland. New Yorkers were loud mouthed wise guys. Mississippians were drawling, racist rednecks. Californians were bleach brained surf bums. People from Cleveland — "Who knows?"

Up ahead, Smitty saw something that made him forget about home — long, shiny chestnut hair adorning a very attractive face. The young lady was hawking something, calling out, "Get your Slate here."

The closer Smitty approached, the prettier she appeared. From a few feet away, he asked, "What's a slate?"

She laughed, showing off a gorgeous, bright-white smile, and cheek bones that left shadows. "Come here. I'll show you."

9

Smitty was glad to obey.

"You a student?" she asked.

Smitty nodded.

"Freshman?"

"Transfer."

"Then you need this."

With his eyes still locked on hers, Smitty reached into his pocket, saying ingenuously, "I'll take your word for it."

She winked, replying, "The Slate's a student magazine that tells you which instructors to choose....What courses do you need?"

"English," Smitty replied, still gazing into her eyes.

She smiled, getting off on him. "You stoned?"

Smitty shook his head as he handed her fifty cents.

"Look, you find out which instructors are teaching the course you want, then you check them out in The Slate." She held up the page to him. "Here, Anderson — 'Ask him what time it is, and he'll explain how to build a watch.'"

Smitty's expression remained the same.

"You're stoned."

He shook his head, saying innocently, "No."

"A bummer," she sympathized. "I can't turn you on to anything except a Slate right now." She switched her attention back to the magazine. "Here, Castellano — 'His lectures cure insomnia.'"

Smitty nodded.

"Here's another, Constance Dusenberry — 'Easy grader. Her Hemingway heroine wardrobe is an education in itself, but stinks worse than your roommate's laundry bag. Taught a generation of English majors how to breathe through their mouths'". She looked up at Smitty for his reaction.

His attention was elsewhere. Distracted by the graceful curves of her breasts, Smitty had just noticed that she wasn't wearing anything beneath her fishnet sweater. One pale pink, beautifully formed nipple had him close to hypnotized. No, his eyes are not deceiving him. The nipple was poking its way through the mesh. It did not stop until a good quarter inch of its tip had periscoped outside the sweater. He nodded, saying absentmindedly, "Okay, I'll take her."

She laughed, knowing damn well where his eyes were. "First you have to make sure she's teaching a course you want."

Smitty stood mute, mesmerized.

Handing him The Slate, she said coyly, "I like the way it feels…and it helps me sell."

He heard someone beside him say, "I'll take a Slate."

Another person, squeezing in front of Smitty, said, "Me too."

'Helps her sell,' thought Smitty as he walked away. 'She'll make her first million in no time.' Could he assume credit for that seductively erect nipple? If so, how the hell had he done it?

Someone called out, "Black Panther Eldridge Cleaver charged with murder. It's all in The Badger. Get your Badger right here." He was a lanky, barefoot kid, a few feet away.

Smitty had been meaning to pick up a copy of The Berkeley Badger, the local counterculture tabloid.

The hawker, a few years younger than Smitty, continued his spiel. "Read all about it — The Revolution. Get your Badger right here — fifteen cents." His worn Levis and yellow pocket T-shirt appeared recently laundered, his face freshly scrubbed, but his brown wavy hair looked as if it had lost a fight with an egg beater. Still, nothing could detract from the kid's winning, teeth flashing smile.

Smitty, thinking about his need for an apartment, held out a quarter. "It has classifieds?"

"Outa sight classifieds!" He took the coin and handed over the paper and a dime. "Whatever's your trip, Man, it's for sale in The Badger — single white females, black males, Asian, straight, homo, bi, sadists, masochists, sadomasochists, they'll whip you, strip you, and—"

Smitty, noticing a passerby giving them the eye, cut in, "I mean apartments for rent."

This stopped the vendor cold. He pondered the question. "Not sure, Man….Check it out."

Smitty nodded and started to walk off when—

"Hey Man, you new here?"

Again Smitty nodded.

The vendor, his grin even larger, held his arms out to his sides. "Ain't it a trip — The Revolution? We're winning!" He flashed Smitty a peace sign and a contagious smile. "Hey, there's some vacant apartments in my building — 2441 Burgess Street. Check 'em out."

"2441 Burgess Street," Smitty repeated mechanically, checking out the kid's bare feet. He seemed agreeable, yet not quite next door neighbor material. As Smitty started to turn away—

The vendor held out his hand. "Hey man, what's your name?"

Smitty offered his own hand. "Smitty'll do."

"I'm Screw. See you around."

Smitty nodded before turning away, this time actually getting away.

Screw called out, "We're winning! Get your Badger right here."

Smitty scanned the tabloid as he walked. 'Screw? What kinda nickname? Screw as in loose? Screw as in lay? Screw as in screwball?' The Badger's cover photo showed a demonstration against police brutality. A large freaked-out crowd surrounded a big bonfire built in the street, right in front of police headquarters. 'Without a permit,' Smitty guessed. A half dozen hippies, some female, were dancing their naked asses around the fire. 'My kind of demonstration.' Still, his real interest lay in the classifieds, apartment rentals. Instead, he found the Personals. Now here was something you could take in at a walk.

"W female, 32, requires two Blk males for Oreo cookie. Send photos of necessary parts."

"W couple, 20's, wants Asian couple for creative sex."

"Blk female, 40, offers long, warm golden showers."

The ads seemed to cover all the perversion he had ever heard of — and a surprisingly large number he hadn't — solicited by every race and color of both sexes in all their variations and preferences. If The Badger contained a single personal ad that The Cleveland Plain Dealer would be willing to run, Smitty had yet to come across it. Smile on his face, going from ad to ad like a ten year old kid glued to his first Playboy magazine, he asked himself, 'God, why the hell did I waste two years at Ohio State?'

Before he could answer his own question, Smitty crashed into the top of a large bush that extended out over the pavement. He extracted himself, and immediately folded up The Berkeley Badger. Right now he would concentrate upon where he was going. It then dawned on him that not only was he failing to look where he was going, he didn't even know where he was going. He would have to check out the Off Campus Housing Office. Why not do that first? The question was, where was it? The only way to find out was to ask someone. Here came a nice looking Asian girl. That someone might as well be female. Smitty stopped walking and started glancing this way and that as if lost, which he more or less was. He timed his question perfectly to allow the young lady just enough time to come to a comfortable stop. "Excuse me, can you point me towards the Off-Campus Housing Office?"

Without stopping, slowing down, or changing the serious expression on her face, the Asian girl pointed in the direction Smitty had come.

Smitty turned to look. He sure hadn't noticed it on the way. Neither could he spot it from where he stood. Apparently he'd need more than a point. Now appearing even more lost without even trying, Smitty would have settled for either sex. Yet another young girl was walking right towards him. "Excuse me, can you tell me where the Off-Campus Housing Office is?"

Stopping, she replied with a smile, "Off campus."

Taking her reply as a question, Smitty answered, "Yes, off-campus."

"No," she replied, "It's off campus."

Smitty's expression switched from lost to confused. He had to be missing something. "Yes, off-campus housing is off campus."

The girl peered into his eyes. "Are you stoned?"

"No," Smitty replied. Where the hell would off-campus housing be if not off campus? And why did everyone think he was stoned? He felt like the transfer student from outer space.

She decided to try speaking more slowly, carefully enunciating each word. "The Off-Campus Housing Office is off campus, not off-campus housing." Daring Smitty to misunderstand that, she stared right at him before quickly correcting herself, "Well, off-campus housing is off campus too, of course."

"Oh," Smitty said with relief. It all became so clear.

Head still tilted sideways, she studied him. "You sure you're not stoned?"

Now Smitty would not have felt disgraced if he were stoned, but he was damn tired of being asked that question. In fact, he didn't feel it deserved another answer.

She did not wait long for one, asking with polite patience, "Would you like to know exactly where the Off-Campus Housing Office is?"

"Yes," Smitty assured her, reminded that he did, reminded that that was the reason he now found himself in this awkward, uncomfortable conversation.

With sincere sweetness, she explained as she would to a child, "You go out the front gate, cross the street, make a left at the second or third block, I'm not sure which, and go about three blocks down. You'll find it. Ask anybody." She smiled nicely.

"Thanks," he replied, assuring himself that he'd damn well find it without asking anyone else, now aware of what that could lead to.

"Good luck," she said with a little laugh, as if he would need some.

"Thanks," he repeated, watching her walk away. Had the last few minutes been a weird dream? Was he still in it? Well, if his pants suddenly fell down and he wasn't wearing any underwear, that would settle the question.

Smitty walked towards the Off-Campus Housing Office. He weaved his way through merging swarms of students, freaks, and student-freaks, feeling good again, feeling alive. He quickened his pace until his long black hair flopped rhythmically against the back of his neck. Smitty increased his stride, for no other reason than to make his hair bounce higher. The sensation made him feel like an Indian, and it was a sensation he loved. To him, this was the greatest feeling in the feelingest decade. Ever since the Saturday morning he had sat in his local movie theatre, watching in black and white The Jim Thorpe Story, himself a boy no older than the boy playing Thorpe in the movie, watching that boy being dropped off at school by buckboard, only to immediately slip away, run like a deer, across the fields and foothills, his Indian hair flopping on his neck. Ever since that afternoon, as a little boy staring up at that huge movie screen, this had been Smitty's vision of freedom. It took the Sixties to place him within that scene. He'd grown his hair as long as the Indian boy's, pinned it back with a similar headband, let it bounce against the back of his neck. The Sixties — "drugs, sex, and rock and roll" — freedom defined!

*****

The headquarters of The Berkeley Badger was a four alarm fire waiting for one measly spark. The only entrance, a dark narrow stairway between two storefronts, led up to a second story loft. The office was a single unpartitioned room. Its floor of soft, unfinished planks was tattooed slick with fifty years of filth and fluids, some no doubt bodily. The place looked like an office turned into a paper recycling dump without bothering to first remove the desks. Every stationary object was at least half covered with haphazard stacks of papers. Every filing cabinet, and there were plenty, was topped with overstuffed cardboard boxes. The lights that hung over most of the desks ran the gamut from florescent to naked bulbs. They were needed. The dust on the windows was half as thick as the panes themselves.

Moe Schwartzman, Red Diaper son of labor organizers, was born and bred to be founder/owner/publisher/editor of a left wing anti-establishment rag such as The Berkeley Badger. In his brawler's stance, a mere foot shy of six foot eight, Moe's broad shoulders would have done justice to a man a good foot taller.

Schwartzman was no neatness freak. From a distance, he appeared to be wearing a full beard. Within ten feet, the "beard" proved to be no more than a face full of befouled, matted hair containing traces of just about everything except soap and water. Analyzing its contents would be work better suited to an archaeologist than a chemist. Moe couldn't wear a shirt five minutes before it looked as if he'd been born in it, afterbirth and all. And no shirt he ever wore managed to completely cover the hairy pot belly that hung over his baggy, low slung pants. Moe was one of those men who never saw need to buy a larger belt. For every inch his waist expanded, he'd merely let his old belt slide down another inch or so below his hanging blob of a gut.

Schwartzman always had a cigar in his mouth, usually unlit, half smoked, and a third chewed. It stayed there, even when he talked, except, on rare occasions, when he removed it for emphasis. The permanent scowl on Moe's face made clear that he would rather be chewing his cigar than talking, especially to whomever he happened to be talking at the time.

Moe was now scowling at Screw. He handed him a stack of Badgers. "Here, kid, make us both some gelt."

Screw gave Moe a nod and a smile. He headed for the exit without bothering to ask what exactly was "gelt".

Moe watched him leave. There was something about the kid he liked. There had to be. Moe was rarely able to distinguish one vendor from another. No reason to. Street people were street people. A few would make it off the streets, but most would rot and die there. Moe had seen enough of them to know. Hawking The Badger was not a step up the ladder to anything. It was more like a step on the down escalator. The first time Moe had seen Screw, he had a face right off a Corn Flakes box — wholesome All American Boy. The kid had gotten freakier, that's for sure. He'd ditched his shoes in no time. Yet none of the damage seemed permanent. Watching this barefoot boy head out the door, Moe hoped this would be the last time he would see him, thinking, 'Get out of Berkeley, Kid….Before it's too late.'

Moe caught himself, and was embarrassed for giving a damn. That was no way to run a newspaper. The best and easiest way to do that was to get yourself in a bad mood and stay that way. Moe usually had that down to an art. Rarely did it take much effort. Today it took no effort at all. He had just finished a book, one he'd been avoiding — The True Believer by Eric Hoffer. The thing that unnerved him about the book, the reason he had been avoiding it, was that Hoffer was not one of these effete, ivory tower intellectuals like Marcuse. He was a hardworking union man, a longshoreman who did his writing during his off hours. What he wrote made him a traitor to his class. Hoffer's argument was that the man of the Left and the man of the Right, extremists he branded both, were interchangeable. They shared the same personality traits. Chance could have sent them to either extreme. It often did, switching them from one to the other. Moe knew this had to be false, because it meant that he himself could just as easily be a fascist. The idea was ridiculous. Someone had to counter Hoffer's insidious theories. Moe himself had always wanted to write a book, one book. Yet Hoffer was no pushover. It would take some skill to punch holes in his arguments. These days, he wasn't sure he still had that skill. If only he were ten years younger.

The Badger's office was now just the way Moe liked it — empty except for himself. His attitude stemmed from the first years of the paper, when he and half his staff had nowhere else to sleep. Of course, this had practically eliminated the need for a payroll. Still, he had felt as if he were putting out a newspaper in an overcrowded flophouse, which, as a matter of fact, was very close to the truth. There had always been at least one staffer passed out and sleeping something off at his, hers, or someone else's desk, and at least one or two more doing the same under a desk. Still, Moe could have put up with this, and also with the occasional urine reeking corner or anonymous puddle of vomit. The final straw had been two fatal overdoses within a week, the first going undetected in a room full of so-called reporters. Moe alone exhibited nose enough to recognize the not so subtle aroma of decaying flesh. As soon as The Badger showed a profit sufficient to cover rent for his own apartment, Schwartzman evicted the entire staff-in-residence, dead and alive.

Moe now handled or ignored most of the office work himself. Only on Friday, when the paper was actually put out, did he want his staff around. The rest of the week they had to call in a few times a day for assignments, errands, and occasional office work. To his mind, the key to being a good reporter was legwork. The key to being a good editor was making sure the "worthless fuckoffs" did their legwork.

The Berkeley Badger, up until recently, had always been Moe's pride and joy. Now, some of the pride and most of the joy had fallen victim to diminishing returns. This was not to say that Moe wasn't proud of what he had accomplished against such stiff odds. It was just that he, like many of us, had seen himself as the hero of his own autobiography. Lately, he did not feel like a hero. Far from it.

Moe was now wandering around his office, not just looking for something, but also trying like hell to remember what exactly it was that he was looking for. Not being able to find something was in itself bad enough. This was worse, and it had been happening more often lately. Maybe the fascists were right. Maybe marijuana could destroy your memory. Yet if this were true, why was it so difficult to forget the things you wanted to forget? Moe was confident that if he had to, he could cut down to two or three joints a day. Admittedly, he did not relish that thought. Perhaps he was just getting senile — 'At fifty?' That would be even worse.

Moe gradually became aware of an odor that took his mind off his search — a horrendous fart. Or at least that was what it smelled like. But he was alone in the office and didn't remember farting.

Could his memory be that bad? It sure as hell smelled that way, at least until Moe spotted a pair of feet, one of them bare, sticking out from behind some filing cabinets.

By reflex, Schwartzman took his fighter's stance. Yet only for a second. The foul air forced a quick retreat. Moe just stood staring at the visible body parts of this prime candidate for one of The Badger's most cherished traditions — Ye Olde Stair Toss.

This tradition started quite by accident in the very early days of The Badger. His best reporter had asked for a raise. Moe, instead, granted him the meaningless title of Assistant Editor. Meaningless or not, this new title inflated that reporters ego to the extent that he actually took a swing a Moe before the day was out. By reflex, Moe's straight right hand sent his new Assistant Editor flying down the stairs. Moe followed behind with visions of himself standing in the dock on a manslaughter charge. Fortunately for Moe and his Assistant Editor, there were only about a half dozen steps between the top of those stairs and the landing, enough to knock him senseless yet not quite enough to break his neck. Not only did Moe's new Assistant Editor show up on time the next day, the improvement in his work habits was almost as substantial as the improvement in his manners. Thus started The Badger's cherished tradition of Ye Olde Stair Toss.

Now relieved in the knowledge that he could still remember not having farted, Moe decided to forgo tradition. He then remembered that he still couldn't remember what the hell he had been looking for in the first place. He'd compromise — just drag the foul smelling fuck-off down the stairs.

Moe approached the body at rest. He grabbed the booted ankle with one hand and the bare one with the other, and dragged the sleeper out from behind the cabinets. A hypodermic needle slid out with him. Moe recognized the drug ravaged face as that of a former journalism student from Oregon. Months ago, he had come into the office, looking a damn sight healthier and wanting to do an article on the local heroin scene. Moe never found out if the kid could write, but he obviously took his research seriously.

A few sharp slaps from Moe brought the would be reporter around, barely. One handed, he hauled the kid to his feet and towards the stairs by his jacket front. Just before reaching them, the kid made a serious mistake. He farted again. Worse yet, Moe noticed a stolen box of his own cheap pens in the kid's top pocket. Moe, furious, flung him down the steps.

Roger Basil Straughton VI, halfway up, just below the landing, knew what was coming. He jumped to the side and out of the way as the kid came to rest in a sitting position upon the landing.

Straughton's arrival surprised Moe. He concealed this with the words, "Help the gentleman out." Moe's mood took a turn for the better. He could use that louse Straughton. Despite himself, Moe had a lot of respect for the slimeball. Straughton's complete lack of character made him a natural newspaperman.

Moe hadn't always thought so highly of Straughton. No, at first Moe had pegged him for the most egregious bull artist he had ever met, which in itself was certainly no black mark against a reporter, not as long as he saved most of his bull for where it belonged — in his writing. Yet all the seemingly farfetched personal particulars that had dribbled out of Straughton, mostly about his family, had turned out to be true. There remained only one thing that Moe still found disturbingly hard to believe. Straughton not only claimed not to drive, he swore he had never even learned. Driving was something you picked up by osmosis. How the hell did he survive, especially in California? On the other hand, why would he lie about this?

As Straughton reached the top of the stairs, Moe, not wanting to seem happy to see him, asked gruffly, "What happened, your fascist old man wouldn't buy you a job on some eastern paper?"

Straughton, like all good reporters, is hard to insult. "Roger Basil Straughton The Fifth does not have to buy influence. He was born with it." Tall and slender, Roger The Sixth was himself born with what could be called, at first glance, patrician good looks. A second, more careful glance, would reveal a few flaws, mostly around the eyes and mouth, caused no doubt by some mild inbreeding. Roger's features were not helped by his sallow, unhealthy complexion, nor by the greasy sheen of his lank, dirty-blond, shoulder-length hair, and even less so by the unctuous, almost permanent smile on his lips. Though his clothes were Ivy League, including a leather elbowed sport jacket and loosened tie, he wore them so sloppily they almost qualified as counterculture. Still, Straughton was far from a freak. In fact, his only obvious qualification for freakdom was his long hair.

"Then why the hell are you back here for chicken feed?" Moe demanded to know.

"I assumed you'd pay a conscionable wage this time."

Moe was reminded that the 'arrogant twit' standing before him had managed to leave The Badger without ever experiencing Ye Olde Stair Toss. This fact had gnawed at Moe ever since. Now Straughton was giving him another chance, and another reason to be glad he had returned. "When your old man starts paying real taxes, then I'll start paying real wages." As was his habit, Moe dismissively flicked the bottom of his beard with the back of his hand, as if clearing dangling cobwebs.

"My father spends more on polo pony feed than you spend on your payroll."

Schwartzman stared Straughton in the eye. "Horses are hard working animals....Get the hell out of here and get me a story." Blond blonde

*****

Roger Basil Straughton VI strode the sidewalks of Berkeley as if he lorded over them. The masses surrounding him were his subjects, literally. He recorded their struggles and celebrated their triumphs, grossly exaggerating both. He wrote to give them their view of the world, and to give the world his view of them. And if these views differed from reality, little matter. Reality could be changed. Straughton himself could change it, merely by inventing it. Long ago, a flash of insight had brought to him the abiding principle of his calling — Great Journalism Rises Far Above The Truth.

As Straughton approached the street corner, he heard someone call out, "Eldridge Cleaver goes underground. The Revolution, read all about it."

Since his return, Straughton had been viewing Berkeley from a slight distance, not as an expat, yet not quite as a resident either. The name Eldridge Clever evaporated that distance, bringing with it pleasant memories. Straughton now saw Berkeley, related to it, just as he had on the day he had left, as his milieu. His path had only crossed that of Cleaver's one single time, yet since then, Straughton had carried the odd feeling that their fates were entwined. From that chance meeting, he had wangled an interview from the man. It was Straughton's most extensively circulated, most widely read, most often quoted, though seldom attributed, piece of writing — the sparkling diamond of his portfolio, proving without a doubt that he could handle more than just straight news.

Eldridge himself may have been little more than a thuggish, personable dolt, yet this dolt had somehow accumulated a résumé so extensive and varied as to indicate powers of imagination at least the equal of this world's finest writers of fiction. Cleaver was a murderous street thug turned rapist turned convict turned Black Muslim turned ex-con turned revolutionary turned Black Panther. As if all that were not enough, he had written a book, Soul On Ice, which turned him once again, this time into a best selling author and instant intellectual icon of the New Left, and from there the presidential standard bearer of the Peace and Freedom Party. Now it was the government's turn to turn Cleaver once again, this time back into an indicted defendant on his way back to being a convict. Would this be the chameleon's last turn? Straughton doubted it. Cleaver's imagination would surely reign triumphant yet again. The fugitive was probably hiding out right here in Berkeley. 'Have to put out some feelers.' The man was so much more than an acclaimed author now. He had transcended even that. The dolt/genius was presently a criminally indicted author — 'The very best kind!' A second interview with this most wanted fugitive could mean that magic word — "syndication".

Again Straughton heard, "Eldridge Cleaver, charged with murder, goes underground. The Revolution, read all about it." There stood Screw, hawking The Badger. Straughton felt a twinge of pride, of power, at the sight of him. Next week the kid would be working for him, hustling his stories. The name Eldridge Cleaver and the sight of Screw combined to remind Straughton of the myriad possibilities Berkeley offered.

'Read all about it,' thought Straughton. Did some forgotten newsboy get that phrase turned cliché from some forgotten book or movie, or did some forgotten book or movie get the phrase from some forgotten newsboy? Where did this particular newsboy get it? And where did his source get it? And more important, what possible difference did it make? 'Ah, Berkeley,' thought Straughton, 'merely walking her streets stoned you out of your mind.'

Straughton had really missed Berkeley. The two months at the family's summer home in Rhode Island had been pleasant, and the month on Cape Cod had been more so. Still, it took Berkeley to get his adrenalin flowing, and adrenalin was one of Straughton's favorite chemical substances. Only in Berkeley did he have the permanent feeling that, at any second, anything was possible, and also that every second, something was happening. All he had to do was keep moving and sniff it out. Doing so was Straughton's God given talent, his birthright, that of a born newspaperman.

Straughton had graduated from Berkeley with a degree in journalism the previous year. Working for The Californian, the campus daily, had turned out to be over-supervised homework, with sparse opportunity for profit or mischief. During his last two years of college, he had switched to The Badger.

Three months previously, Straughton had left Berkeley with an inch thick portfolio of articles under his arm. If he ever returned, it would be triumphantly on assignment for some big eastern paper. For the first time in his life, he knew that he would get exactly what he wanted without drawing upon his father's influence. He was wrong. The jealous skeptics had been right. A man needed real pull to get a job with one of those overrated newspapers. His portfolio never got high enough up the ladder to reach anyone aware of his lineage. Next time he would let his father manage the job hunt, from the top of the ladder down. At the very least, one more year in Berkeley, polishing his craft and expanding his mind, with the assistance of the finest chemical additives available, would not be boring.

Straughton had never considered drugs a social problem. However, he did consider the lack of them a personal problem, a serious one, and his stash was down to dangerous levels. It had been so long since he had gone an entire day without smoking a few joints, he had lost all memory and curiosity as to how that might feel. Straughton found it imperative to score and score fast. Still, this newspaperman had his pride. Roger Basil Straughton VI would never stoop to actually paying for drugs if he could help it. To a man of his talents, the very idea seemed absurd. The problem was that during Straughton's absence, all his former sources, with a single exception, had gone under, two literally. The only reason he had yet to visit that remaining source, was the necessity of a long car or bus ride to get there. Not only did Roger lack a car of his own, the one time he had asked his father for driving lessons earned him the rebuke, "A Straughton would no more drive a car than unclog a commode." This reprimand ended, as most of them did, with the words, "I would like to remind you, Young Man, you are a Straughton, not a Kennedy." Roger saw his father's point, himself having been contentedly chauffeured about all his life. Still, even as a passenger, it was difficult not to take every stop sign and red light as an insult to your station. The problem was that when Roger was away from home, he was also away from chauffeured rides. This necessitated honing his skill at having others satisfy his transportation needs. Unfortunately, since his return, he had yet to ingratiate himself with anyone who did own a car. Straughton had no doubt that he would, but managing to do so before his stash ran out was no certainty.

Though Straughton usually championed the masses in print, he had no desire to undergo the painful degradation of sharing public transport with them. Nor would his allowance support hiring a taxi for this length of a trip. Truth be told, Roger's father tossed around nickels as if they were manhole covers, and the boy's lack of a car did save the old man money. Roger tried desperately to rationalize the indignity of public transport as research that would someday come in handy. He couldn't. No, for the sake of his dwindling stash, he would suffer the inefficient, time consuming hippie rite of hitchhiking to his supplier. This would involve at least two, possibly three rides, and, starting in town, the first ride would be the hardest to catch. Then again, experience told him that in almost every other car a joint would be passed around.

*****

Marcia sat on a stool at the Power To The People Pizza Parlor. Her glistening, dark brown hair, parted in the middle, fell halfway down her back. Delicate features and large eyes combined to give her the appearance of a serious child.

She had her back to the narrow counter that lined the rear wall. The front of the restaurant was completely open to the street except for one center column. Marcia looked out towards the busy sidewalk, searching for a sign of her friend. She glanced at her watch. Heather was almost an hour late. She was usually late, a trait Marcia found quite inconsiderate. Still, Heather's heart was in the right place. Some day she might learn to deliver the rest of herself to the right place, which, at the moment, was the Power To The People Pizza Parlor.

They were supposed to be looking for an apartment right now. In fact, Heather was supposed to have been looking for the last month, while Marcia was still working her summer job. Heather had gone up to Berkeley ahead of her. Marcia had even helped pay her rent at a rooming house. Whenever Marcia had phoned, Heather had claimed to be on the verge of signing a rental contract. Marcia had believed her every time, right down to the day she arrived in Berkeley only to join Heather at the rooming house. Now, if they didn't find a place in a few days, they would have to waste another week's room rent. And here Marcia was, instead of looking for an apartment, waiting for Heather, and this after hunting all morning by herself.

Heather didn't seem to have much time for apartment hunting. There were always the meetings and the demonstrations she had to attend. Marcia refused to fault her for that. She herself was determined to get more involved during her sophomore year. Marcia had spent her freshman year as a bookworm dorm rat. Her grades showed it. Upon returning to Santa Monica for the summer, she had been barraged with questions about all the wild happenings at Berkeley. Marcia rarely had an answer. More embarrassing, she usually ended up asking the questioners specifics about what she had missed. This was a relief only to her father. Two magazine articles that he had saved to ask her about actually served to heighten her determination to get more involved. After all, the way she spent her freshman year, she might as well have lived at home and attended Santa Monica Junior College. This was where Heather had come in.

Heather had been her dorm roommate. Though they had gotten along great in their room, Heather had actually gotten outside of it, moving in spheres well beyond Marcia's consciousness. To Heather, academics were merely a nuisance, a set of inconvenient distractions hampering her struggle to change the world. She always knew what was happening, on and off campus. A congenital activist, she could easily drag half her dorm section along with her. Marcia had never been part of these groups. During the summer, the more she thought about this, the more she regretted it. When Heather telephoned, asking if Marcia could put her up in Santa Monica for a few days, Marcia found out she had not yet made any housing plans for the coming year. It was she who asked Heather to share an apartment. Heather would be Marcia's ticket to all that was "happening" at Berkeley.

Marcia's ticket, wearing a broad, self-assured smile, came bursting into Power To The People Pizza Parlor. "Sorry I'm a few minutes late."

Marcia was already off her stool and headed outside. "Let's go," she said, too relieved to quibble over Heather's "few minutes".

Heather grabbed her arm. "Wait, I'm starved." She didn't look starved. Her pretty, smiling face came with a teddy bear figure. Yet, there was a playfulness about Heather that men found attractive, and she usually had more than her share of admirers. The only time she really gave her weight a thought was when she was buying or getting into clothes. Right now she couldn't care less. Heather was starved, and it was a pizza slice she was buying.

Marcia objected, "We have to get started."

"It'll only take a minute."

It took a few of them, long ones for Marcia. Heather hopped off her stool still chewing the last bite of her Power To The People pizza. "How many addresses do you have?"

"Six," Marcia replied.

"We won't have time for that many. I have a Venceramos meeting." She reached over and took Marcia's arm to get a look at her watch. "Oh my God! I'm late." Heather was already backing out of the pizza parlor. "I'll meet you at the custodian's rally."

"That's tonight!" Marcia objected, taking a step forward.

Heather kept moving backwards. "I'll help you tomorrow, promise."

Marcia stood stunned. "That's what you said yesterday."

Just before she turned away, Heather reminded, "Well don't forget, I've been doing this by myself for a month."

Even if Heather had given her the time, Marcia was not the type who would have asked what exactly it was that Heather had been doing for the last month. No, Marcia had the feeling that if she and Heather did find an apartment, this would not be due to even the slightest effort on the part of her roommate. In any case, this was no tragedy. Marcia could certainly find them an apartment by herself. After all, she was a woman now, a woman taking charge of her own life.

*****

Twelve Gauge was six foot five and three hundred and twenty pounds. He appeared larger, even slouched down, feet stretched out in front of him, in a heavily padded thoroughly abused chair. Twelve Gauge wore his greasy red hair tied back in a pony tail. His carelessly trimmed beard was almost as greasy. Twelve Gauge was an obvious biker, even minus the black, sleeveless, tattoo revealing Harley Davidson T-shirt. Casually, in a smooth steady rhythm, he kept snapping open the breach of a sawed-off shotgun, catching the round between two fingers, reloading it with the same two fingers and a flick of his wrist, then snapping the breech shut again.

Straughton, on the opposite side of the coffee table, was bent over eyeing up close a small pile of reddish marijuana. Moving his finger through it, without looking up, he asked, "You sure you don't dye this grass?"

Twelve Gauge missed a beat, not breaking open the shotgun breach. Straughton's finger stopped moving around in the marijuana. He waited fruitlessly another beat for the breach to finally snap open, then slowly looked up. Twelve Gauge was staring at him. He kept staring at him, finally asking slowly, too slowly, "Do I look like someone that dyes things?"

A clever comeback came to mind. "Not at all. You look like someone who helps things die." Straughton quickly decided that depending upon a Hells Angels' sense of humor was a risk to be avoided. He said instead, "It's so red."

"That's why it's called Panama Red....Fuck the color! It's dynamite, the best grass there is...and we're the only suppliers."

"Here, take a drag," said Fat Rat. Fat Rat was only two hundred pounds, but all of that on a five foot seven frame. His face was so acne scarred he appeared to be wearing a mask of dog food and oatmeal. Fat Rat held out a joint to Straughton.

Straughton hesitated. He still had a buzz from the joint passed around during his last ride. This was not exactly the ideal time to be stoned. One slip of the tongue in present company could prove a capital offense. Still, gauging Fat Rat's expression, he decided to take a quick drag just to be sociable. Straughton didn't hold it down long either. He held out the joint to Fat Rat.

"Take another."

Again Straughton complied, just to be polite. His nerves were so tight, he immediately coughed it back up, exactly what he would have done intentionally if he hadn't been too nervous to think of this.

Twelve Gauge said, "Make sure you write that it's the strongest weed around."

"Certainly," said Straughton. "Any other products you care to hype?"

"Reds."

'Reds, Panama Red — red must be this month's fashion statement,' thought Straughton. "Perchance, you have a complimentary sample?"

Twelve Gauge took a pill bottle off the table. He gave it a shake by his ear for a rough count of contents before tossing it to Straughton. Twelve Gauge then turned his head to watch a woman come out of the bedroom.

A solid five foot ten, she appeared about thirty, occasionally stepped on, and an hour or two short of sleeping something off.

Straughton looked away, feeling weak. Hard women always did this to him, and a woman who could survive spreading her legs for Twelve Gauge had to be tough.

She stopped beside Twelve Gauge's chair, squinting at Straughton. "Who's this?"

Twelve Gauge grabbed a big handful of her ass. He kneaded it roughly while saying, "That's Weasel, our publicist...and star reporter for The Badger." Twelve Gauge smiled in appreciation of his own cleverness.

"Roger Basil Straughton VI, my pleasure."

"I like Weasel better," said Twelve Gauge. "Manhole, show Weasel your new tattoo."

She collapsed into a chair, shaking her head No.

"What may we say about Reds?" asked Straughton.

"That they're the best," said Fat Rat, indignantly.

"Most certainly." If they were as good as the Panama Red, they were the best. Straughton was stoned from two anemic tokes. "The best what, exactly?"

"Same as Blues,' said Twelve Gauge.

"I'll get the word out," he said, already writing.

"Shit, no!" said Twelve Gauge. "Why do you think we changed the color?"

Straughton had no idea. He wondered if this was because he was stoned. It was not Straughton's nature to say, "I don't know." He waited for Twelve Gauge to answer his own question.

"These hippy dippys gotta have whatever dope's 'in', this week's high."

Straughton was stoned enough to ask, "Why bother? I recall when you dealt only in smack and grass." A pregnant pause gave Straughton the uneasy feeling that he shouldn't be asking questions. 'This Panama Red is dynamite.'

Twelve Gauge didn't mind bitching. "Cause some clown 'ld move in and fill the gaps. Next thing you know, he's selling smack too. Then you gotta put him out of business....Fun, but a hassle. These days, to compete in the marketplace, you need a full line a product."

Straughton nodded, while the image of Twelve Gauge the biker auditing an MBA course flashed through his mind. The Panama Red had energized his imagination, his taste buds too. He had to get something to eat. "Time to take leave, Gentlemen. Perhaps you have a Baggie for my weed?"

Twelve Gauge looked at Manhole. "Get Weasel a doggy bag."

Manhole sneered, but did as she was told.

Twelve Gauge turned back to Straughton. "Make sure it's in this week's paper."

"Certainly. Sales will respond....By the way, I would appreciate you gentlemen tipping me off about any upcoming...events." Lately, the Hells Angels had been showing up at flag and draft card burnings, to beat senseless any protesters they could catch. After all, some had actually served their country. One or two even earned Honorable Discharges. "I will do my best to arrange front page headlines, large flattering photos, the complete VIP treatment."

"We'll tip you off when the cops tip us off," Twelve Gauge assured him.

'Interesting,' thought Straughton, the cops and Hells Angels working in harmony. Perhaps this really was the Age of Aquarius.

Manhole came back and handed Straughton a Baggie.

As she turned away, Twelve Gauge said, "C'mon, Momma, show Weasel that pretty tattoo." Straughton leaned forward to sweep the grass into the bag. Manhole stood a foot away, her back to him. She casually dropped her jeans and panties all the way down to her thighs. Straughton was faced, slightly above eye level, with Manhole's ample, sumptuously curved ass. The right cheek had a nicely done cartoon biker, with an exploding shotgun in place of a sex organ and the name "Twelve Gauge" tattooed beneath.

Straughton, unsure what to do, his face still a foot from Manhole's ass, waited for someone else to break the pregnant pause.

Finally, Twelve Gauge asked, "Well, what do you think?"

"A certifiable work of art," replied Straughton.

"How 'bout the ass?"

"Quite appetizing," Straughton replied.

Just then, Manhole let out a long, loud fart. There was a moment's silence until Twelve Gauge offered casually, "You wanna work your tongue up there a little, be my guest."

What Straughton wanted was not to offend. He pondered a polite refusal. Manhole still hadn't budged, and her literally breathtaking fart hung heavy in his face. Straughton felt he had to say something. The gas in his nostrils and the grass on his brain were not helping. Finally, without trying to be amusing, he took a shot. "I'll pass this time."

*****

Jake Pedersen, known locally as Screw, stood hawking The Badger on the sunny side of Bancroft Way. "Eldridge Cleaver flees to Cuba! Read all about it." This was the best job Screw had ever had. The hours could not have been more flexible — whenever he felt like it. No uniform, no dress code, no additional laundry. No one looking over his shoulder. Self-set quotas. Though it didn't pay the rent, or even cover his food bills, selling The Badger provided something more important to Screw. It transformed him from tourist, outsider, into a fully fledged participant in the coolest, craziest scene in the world. Selling The Badger gave Screw an instant and recognizable identity — "street person" — this in a town where street people were a force. In addition, selling The Badger could also pass for a job, and Screw was the type of young man who had to have a job.

Screw was a Nebraska farm boy. For the oldest son in a large family, there was always work to be done. By the time he started high school, his younger brothers had taken over a good share of his chores. This enabled Screw to work part-time jobs in town. Back in Nebraska, Screw had never had a job he liked or disliked. Those words didn't apply. A job was something you had to have. And when you had one, you had to do it right. You took pride in your work, if for no other reason than the doing. Now, for the first time in his life, Screw had a job he actually liked. This job was an introduction to anyone who cared to buy a paper from him, which, on an average day, was more strangers than he'd see in a year back home. It should also be mentioned, that selling The Badger was a convenient cover for his real source of income.

Screw had made up his mind to join the Marine Corps after high school. However, as graduation neared and Vietnam loomed, he decided to insert six short months of traveling and hell raising before his enlistment. The intended target of his travels had been a large one — the Pacific Ocean. On the way, Screw got caught within the currents of one of the strangest migrations ever to cross this country. He never lacked for company. Screw became one of the thousands of swept away, bobbing heads, buoyed by common fantasies and hyped-up on wide-eyed curiosity. The currents proved surprisingly swift, running straight towards San Francisco and Berkeley. Screw made the journey in one short month, doing far less work along the way than planned. The freedom and camaraderie of his trip had been an unexpected bonus, but the freedom he had found in Berkeley overwhelmed him. That was two months ago. His first few days in town had convinced him to spend all his remaining months here. After that, the Marine Corps could take care of his travel arrangements. At least this was his plan.

Seeing how people lived in Berkeley forced open Screw's eyes as to how regimented his life had been back in Nebraska. It took Berkeley to teach him the joys of personal freedom, a freedom that Nebraskans would have considered irresponsibility, even selfishness. Berkeley taught him the strength in numbers. If enough people were smoking marijuana, there weren't enough cops to stop them. You could smoke it right in their faces, close enough to get the cops high. Who would have thought up that one back in Nebraska? It was power — the freedom of power and the power of freedom — street people power, street people freedom. Pick the right time, and you could get away with things in Berkeley that would land you in the slammer back in Nebraska. Deeds such as the one he was contemplating right now.

Screw didn't have to put on a phony smile. He wore a genuine one, and it rarely left his face. He now aimed it in the direction of three young men carrying overnight bags. They looked to be military on leave, Marines by their skin-close haircuts. 'Soon, that'll be me,' he thought. His smile turned into a wince. 'Man, those haircuts look painful.' He felt empathy for the three servicemen.

"Berkeley Badger," he called out, then added especially for them, "Find out what's happenin' in Berkeley." Of the three servicemen, at least one had to take the bait.

One did, making a beeline for Screw. The others followed, bringing with them the usual questions — where to go, what to see, and of course, where they could get girls? Screw supplied the answers, including the painfully honest one to their last question — "Man, with those haircuts, the only women you'll get are the pros, and the amateurs put most of them out of business long ago."

Screw would have been glad to help the poor guys out with girls, and he would be even gladder to help them out with an ounce of marijuana. Screw himself was not a dealer. He was merely a facilitator. That's how he paid his rent. He'd escort them to a reputable dealer, showing them any sights along the way. Then he would take no more than fair commission for himself, in grass and money. Screw wasn't greedy. This was how he spent his days. A deal here. A deal there. Not enough to put anything in the bank, that was for sure. Still, it added up. Enough to live on. And Screw was careful. If they came out and asked him where they could score some grass, the best they would get out of him was, "Everywhere, Man, this is Berkeley." He wouldn't be lying. They'd eventually score from or get burned by someone else, while Screw wouldn't have to worry about getting busted. The only way he'd deal, was if they walked away without asking. Only then would he call them back, saying, "You dudes wanna score a little grass?" Nine out of ten times the answer would be Yes.

Those were his rules, and he had never broken them, never even wondered why he had them. Screw assumed it was fear of ending up in jail. Yet it wasn't just that. Screw thought he loved Berkeley for the freedom it allowed him, the positive freedom to do whatever he wanted. That was just part of it. Berkeley also allowed him a type of freedom of which he was not even aware — the negative freedom from responsibility. Here, Jake Pedersen did not have to be the model older brother to his younger brothers and sisters. He didn't have to be his parents' oldest, dependable son. Whatever he did here, and the impression this made, reflected only upon him. No word would get back to Nebraska. This was true only as long as he didn't get arrested. Screw knew the three Marines weren't cops, knew they meant a sure and easy few bucks. And in Berkeley, the punishment for selling an ounce of grass was just a slap on the wrist, if that. The only time they even busted you for it, was when they wanted your supplier.

Now, all the Marines had to do was walk away, so he could call them back. Two of them did, but the third one, 'Damn it!' had to ask, "You know where we can score a lid of grass?"

Screw flinched.

One of the serviceman's friends turned around, adding, "Good grass."

Screw, not fully conscious of why, flashed his winning smile and answered immediately, "Everywhere, Man. This is Berkeley. We're winning!"

*****

Straughton, thoroughly stoned and the proud new owner of a three ounce stash of Panama Red, followed his watering taste buds down the crowded Berkeley sidewalk. The aroma emanating from Rob's Cosmic Organic Fried Chicken pulled him right through the door. Rob's could have passed for your average All American lunchroom, except for two things. One, every inch of the place, floor and ceiling included, was painted in a phantasmagorical psychedelic every-day-glo-color-of-the-rainbow hyper style that must have necessitated three tabs of LSD per gallon of paint. Two, the walls were decorated with the icons of the age — large posters of radicals and rock stars. Straughton stepped inside and headed straight for the eponymous owner.

As Straughton's father would say, Rob, like Moe, "was of the Hebrew persuasion". This was a term his father used most often when complaining about the increasing difficulty in finding a competent lawyer or accountant who was not "of the Hebrew persuasion". Until college, Straughton himself had had little contact with Jews. There were always a few around, of course. Yet he hadn't really socialized with any. He, like the rest of his family, was not inclined to do much socializing with anyone outside of a tight little circle of relatives and inherited friends. This is why Straughton was quite grateful that, during his summer before college, one of his aunts had dragged him along to see Fiddler on the Roof. He credited the play for his deep understanding of this diffused Semitic tribe, whose members seemed to pop up unexpectedly in every small corner of the world.

Rob stood behind the counter slowly shaking his balding head. He was your typical Berkeley restaurant owner, except his Ph.D. was in Chemistry, instead of Philosophy or Comparative Religions. Rob wore Levis, a frilly shirt, and a single string of love beads, just enough to qualify himself as counterculture. His face exhibited that serene smile that in Berkeley indicated Oneness-With-The-Universe, and anywhere else indicated decent digestion. "Roger, you're lookin' good. Who stepped on yah?"

Straughton was anesthetized enough to painlessly reply, "Every northeastern newspaper."

"So the Prodigal Son-Of-A-Bitch returns to the scene of his many crimes."

The aroma of food teased Straughton's taste buds. "To finally write that exposé on you."

Rob laughed. "I told you a hundred times; there's no such thing as an inorganic chicken."

"Admittedly, my friend, but there are hormone free chickens."

"All animals have hormones. Some do extra."

"Like the ones you serve."

Rob held up his hands. "Hey Man, we don't drug test...the chickens or the customers."

"Exactly why I'm here."

"You're here to bum a meal, just like always."

"This too. How many complementary meals if I happen to see Jim Morrison?"

"Three, no problem."

Straughton does a double take. "For three pathetic meals, I would not waste the ink to write that Neil Young ate here."

"I wouldn't pay you one free meal to write Neil Young is a waiter here....Tell you what, five free meals if you write that Bob Dylan hangs out here."

Straughton leaned away from the counter. "I'm afraid not. The last time I wrote that, you cancelled your ad and Moe nearly fired me."

Rob held his hands up in front of him. "Okay, I'll leave the ad in."

"Ten meals," Straughton said flatly.

"Can you get it on the front page?"

"Perhaps."

Rob held out his hand. "Seven."

Straughton ruefully shook his head instead. "Ah, to waste my rare talent working for chicken dinners?"

"Practice," Rob assured him, still holding out his hand.

"Just wait, My Good Man. Soon Roger Basil Straughton VI will be muckraking in Washington, putting all those venal politicians behind bars."

"The ones who won't cut you in."

"I will still be saving the citizenry millions," Straughton pointed out.

"Seven meals," Rob repeated, still holding out his hand.

Straughton reached out to shake, agreeing, "Seven...plus one now."

Straughton congratulated himself. How easily he managed to get by in this world. No, Straughton's knack for Journalism was not his prime talent. The source of almost all of his success was his innate ability to get by, almost effortlessly. For example, school had never been a problem. All he had had to do was show up. Straughton had found that if you looked as if you knew something, and you acted as if you knew something, the hoi polloi would invariably take it for granted that you did know something. Privilege was not an inherited right, nor an advantage earned. Privilege had to be assumed. If you assumed it convincingly, the hoi polloi would not doubt that you deserved it. Straughton strolled through a world seemingly of the opinion that it owed him something. How could the man be faulted for eventually coming to the same conclusion?

*****

Rob pushed a buss tray of dirty dishes through the service window into the kitchen. The dishwasher looked up at him, his vacant eyes as bloodshot as they could be this side of a cartoon. Mike Sloan had once been Rob's best friend. They had roomed together, studied chemistry together, drank together, did dope together, and twice fell for the same woman together. Now Rob hated the sight of Mike, hated to see what dope and Vietnam had done to a friend, hated to again say to himself, "What a waste." Sloan was usually so messed up, Rob couldn't figure out how he kept himself from falling into the sink and drowning, forget about actually washing dishes. Still, Mike somehow managed to do both. And he showed up every day, the only dependable junkie Rob had ever heard of. He never even talked to Mike anymore. What was there to say — "How's the dope?"

Mike leaned unsteadily against the sink. Steam rose up from the dirty water into his nostrils, carrying with it the nauseating stench of leftover food. He lifted each soaking plate to brush off the refuse still stuck to it. Often he'd see a face in a plate. Some were hard to make out. He'd hesitate, brush in hand, until he recognized it. The best faces were the ones that meant the least, some guy from high school who did something funny. Yet the faces of those few people who had gotten close, been important, they could hurt. Sometimes the faces were from Vietnam, sometimes friends, sometimes enemies, sometimes mutilated. He'd sweep the brush across the face, leaving the porcelain a spotless, gleaming white. Mike would quickly turn away, stacking the plate by looking out of the corner of his eye, avoiding the reflection of his own face.

Mike Sloan's wary senses felt a presence. Sure enough, Pepe was standing behind him. Pepe was a small, quiet Mexican, his back still wet. He'd come to relieve Sloan and start his shift. Even if Pepe could speak English, he probably would have just stood there his entire shift, silently watching. Sloan backed up and took off his apron in a stupor. With surprising care, he reached up on to the shelf behind him and brought down his bush cover, the broad-brimmed camouflage hat he had worn in Vietnam. Before placing it on his head, he carefully dented the fabric where it was supposed to be dented, and smoothed it out where it wasn't.

Sloan's apartment was only half a mile from the restaurant. Still, this was a tiring walk, every step a fight against the drugs soaking his brain. Sloan forced himself along as quickly, as carefully as possible — a one-man patrol. There was always the chance some fool might be waiting to jump him. It had happened a month ago. He'd handled the situation no sweat. Either the muggers in Berkeley were too soft, or the pair who had tried him had been amateurs. Then again, maybe they were merely more wasted than he.

The thing Sloan really dreaded was being hassled by cops, being asked questions he loathed to answer when his mind was clouded by dope. Cops made him feel cornered, compressed like a spring, ready to explode. If the cops ever found him flat on his face on the sidewalk, they would just give him a stiff kick and be on their way. Yet all he had to do to make Public Enemy Number One was walk down the street at night. Someday the fools would push him an inch too far.

Sloan felt that faint static charge at the back of his neck. The car was still ten yards behind him. His senses sharpened as the dope cloud fogging his mind dissipated a bit. Perhaps he was wrong. Not likely. 'Keep humping. Don't mean a thing.'

Sure enough, in a flash, the beam of a spotlight skewered him. It stayed pinned to Sloan, gliding along behind at his exact pace. Sloan's anger rose⌐¬¬¬ — 'Playing games.' If they thought they had a job to do, let them do it. It was their cat and mouse theatrics, their harassment that unnerved him. 'Fuck it. Don't mean a thing.'

"Stop! Police!" said an amplified voice.

Sloan halted, gritting his teeth — 'Get it over with!'

Both cops stepped out of the patrol car. Sloan turned halfway around, just short of facing the glaring spotlight. One cop moved in front of him. He raised his flashlight.

Sloan winced as the light seared his eyes and blinded him. 'Shit, I hate this.' The way the cop held the flashlight left his throat wide open. His Adam's apple was an oh so tempting target. One quick blow would leave him sprawled out and choking on the sidewalk. He kept the flashlight's beam in Sloan's face. 'Don't these assholes know how rude this is?'

"Fuck!" said the cop, seeing Sloan's eyes. "Hands on that car! Feet apart!" Sloan did as he was told, and the cop frisked him.

"Got ID?"

"Back pocket."

"Take it out, slow....Keep the other hand on the car." Sloan drew out his wallet and placed it on the car roof.

"Take out the ID."

It surprised Sloan how much his mind had cleared with the sense of danger. The dope was a handicap, but he could now function, probably well enough to waste these assholes. He handed the ID over his shoulder.

"Marine Corps," the cop mumbled. "Okay, turn around." He was shaking his head. "You're a fucking mess, you know that?"

'I know it,' thought Sloan. The cop's gun was within easy reach. 'And I know I could still grease your empty head.'

Irritated by Sloan's silence, the cop asked, "You want to come with us?"

Sloan compromised and shook his head once, barely.

The cop accepted the compromise and handed back Sloan's ID. Turning away, he said, "Do yourself a favor, get straight."

For an instant, the cop's revolver was within reach. Sloan walked away thinking about that, feeling arrogantly superior. He could have given those cops quite a lesson. 'Yeah,' he thought sarcastically, 'I coulda been a hero...or a villain.' And then he thought about what he didn't want to think about. He could have handed over his driver's license. He'd used his Marine Corps ID instead, and not for the first time. Sure, he'd kept his mouth shut, didn't beg any favors. No, he'd done something lower, let them know he was one of the fucked-up walking wounded back from Nam. He had asked for their pity as surely as if he had dropped to his knees.

Sloan was still berating himself when he reached his apartment building. He wanted to go back to find those cops, wanted to do what he should have done. 'Yeah,' he told himself sarcastically, 'Great idea'. Sloan realized he was madder at himself than at the cops. 'Dope's wearing off.' That problem was easily solvable. Angrily, he opened the front door to his apartment building. Sloan stopped dead in the threshold, facing—

A college girl, her large eyes bright with fear, sat a few feet away on the bottom steps of the staircase. By reflex, Sloan glanced behind, searching out the source of her fear. There was no one, nothing there. Sloan felt dizzy, off balance. Her face — a rare blend of soul and innocence — recaptured his stare. Her long dark hair, though not black, brought back memories of Vietnam, powerful memories. The fear in this college girl's eyes was growing stronger. He was scaring the shit out of her. Sloan refused to just slither off. "Can I help you?" he asked, thinking immediately, 'Great question, in the shape I'm in.'

She shook her head, slightly relieved.

Sloan just stood there, trying to look as unthreatening as possible, hoping she would speak.

Marcia now regretted not waiting outside on the front steps, where she would be safe. The lights in the hall were so dim, the interior of the building so much spookier than its façade had suggested. "I'm waiting for the landlord...to see about an apartment." She glanced at her watch. "He should have been here an hour ago."

"Can't depend on that mother." There weren't many people Sloan could or would depend upon, and if you couldn't depend upon someone, best to keep your distance. Looking through squinted eyes, trying not to sway, his thoughts turned 180° — 'As if anyone could depend on me.'

The girl, still uneasy, stood. "I can't wait any longer."

Sloan moved aside to let her by. He forced himself not to look back as he headed for what he loosely termed his apartment. It was really just a storeroom under the stairs with a jerry rigged bathroom. There was space enough for a mattress, a small dresser, a clothing rack, a rusty little refrigerator, a hot plate, and barely enough room to walk in between.

The incident with the cops had cleared his mind enough for him to really see the girl on the stairs, and she had cleared his mind further, forcing him to now see the squalor in which he lived. 'What if I had gotten her in here?' This thought did not lead to any pleasant ones. 'Shit, gotta wash those fucking sheets.' Sloan reached inside the hot plate for his stash. He found more than he expected — Seconal, Valium, Dilaudid, even some acid and speed — 'Better Living Through Chemistry'.

Decisions, decisions. Those asshole cops had sure fucked his mind. Cleared it too. Maybe that was the same thing. Hell, they had cleared it enough to prevent Sloan from lying to himself. Yeah, they had only been doing their jobs, and they'd have done them better by busting him. Sloan had begged off with his Marine Corps ID. One of these days he wouldn't. He'd be stupid enough to teach them a lesson, one that could lead to his own end, where every day and everything was leading soon enough anyway. Sloan knew it. He knew something else too. That he was only thinking about the cops now because he didn't want to think about the girl. It had been a long time since he had touched, gotten anywhere near, that fine a woman. It might be a longer time before he ever did again, if ever. 'Fuck it!'

Sloan focused on the many-colored pills on his bed. He was rich. Decisions, decisions. Maybe a creative mixture. Then again, maybe he should get straight and stay that way for a few days. Sloan saw once more the fear on the girl's face. He sure hadn't turned her on. 'Wonder what she saw?' He went to the mirror — 'Cracked, of course'. Sloan didn't like what he saw. He looked fucked-up, and so much older. Yet what bothered him most was that he appeared so worn down and weak. He couldn't look himself in the eye, knowing damn well that the face in the mirror was the face he deserved. Sloan tried to brush off this admission with a little sarcasm — 'Good thing it's already cracked'.

Sloan returned to the pills on his bed. They were colorful — some pastels, some sparkling — precious little jewels. They could make him forget the face in the mirror, and about the cops, and even about the girl. They could make him feel better too. Yet not like they used to. It seemed ages since he had come down, way too long. Unless you were working up to that last O.D., you had to crash every once in a while. It had been a long time since he'd been even this straight. 'Fuckin' cops' — they had wound him up. Yet the girl had stopped him cold. He'd never get to sleep without some dope. Sloan spotted something on the floor, where the overhead stairway met it at an angle. It had to be a gin bottle. It had to be empty. 'What's to lose?' Feeling stupid, he dropped to his knees and reached for the bottle. Its weight alone told him that he would soon behold a miracle — a good five fingers of gin. That should get him to sleep without any pills. Tomorrow he'd wake up straight. He'd try to stay that way, for a few days.

*****

Marcia was late. The custodians' meeting must have already begun. Though her steps were hurried, her thoughts remained on where she had been, not where she was going. Only lately, very lately, had Marcia become conscious of her own independence. She began to think of herself as a woman of the Sixties — intelligent, resourceful, and strong. Facing that drug addict, she hadn't been. Mike Sloan had scared the hell out of her. Now, merely remembering, her heart was again pounding like a fist against the inside of her ribs. She did take some credit for not panicking, but not much. Sloan, aside from his appearance, had given her no reason to panic.

Rather than question her own nerve, Marcia chose to nurse her anger toward the landlord. She had sat waiting for over an hour in that gloomy hallway. He could have easily telephoned one of his tenants, asking them to tell her that he wasn't coming. How could people be so inconsiderate? She would never understand.

Then again, Marcia couldn't understand how blind she herself had once been to the suffering of others. Her summer job at Los Angeles County Hospital had opened her eyes. At the age of twelve, just before she lost her mother to cancer, Marcia decided to be a medical researcher. Her father was an accomplished surgeon. Yet against cancer, his successes were rare. To Marcia, cancer was treachery incarnate — a lethal enemy within, turning the body against itself. Surgeons such as her father would never eliminate it by opening up the patient and cutting out the tumor. No, cancer had to be prevented. Eventually, finally, medical research would find a way. Marcia was determined to help speed that day.

Yet it wasn't until the previous summer that she became truly conscious of some other evils just as insidious as cancer, and the obvious need to eliminate them too. Her father had arranged a job for her as a lab assistant. At first she spent her time in the same way she had spent her freshman year — huddled over her work, paying little attention to the distractions around her. Math, chemistry, physics — they seemed so neat and elegant, so self-explanatory. She could not fathom why other students found them baffling. When Marcia's studies weren't exciting her, they were, at the very least, her refuge.

Los Angeles County Hospital dragged her from this refuge. Her job did involve test tubes and Petri dishes, yet it also involved human beings. In fact, because of her lack of experience, she was a link, sometimes even a buffer, between the doctors running the studies and their subjects. And these weren't the same patients she saw sitting in the waiting room of her father's Santa Monica office. No, these people at LACH lacked their confidence, their style, and more important, their money. These people didn't go for second opinions, not when they couldn't even pay for first opinions. They never demanded the best treatment. In fact, some of them were receiving no treatment at all, this in the form of placebos that she herself handed them. Marcia thanked God that she never knew which patients were receiving these placebos. She was the one who had to look at the anxious, hopeful faces, and worse yet, receive the sincere and grateful thank yous. However important, however necessary these studies, behind them lay one incontrovertible seldom mentioned fact — the guinea pigs were human beings.

Marcia began to wonder about the lives lived by these human beings. As a medical researcher, it would be her responsibility to find preventions and cures for the diseases that afflicted them. Yet did her responsibility end there? As a fellow human being, was she not also responsible for them and their children having the chance to lead decent lives? These people seemed to be in a trap that offered slim hope of escape. Was there a way to help them? Marcia felt it a personal responsibility to find out.

The custodians demonstrating for the right to form a union, especially their stoic faces, had reminded her of the patients at LACH. That's why she had signed their petition, and also joined the campus organization that had drawn it up for them — The

Socialist Workers Union. That's why she was hurrying to this meeting.

Marcia checked her watch. She hated being late. Yet here she was, already ten minutes late to a strategy meeting called by the custodians. The Socialist Workers Union had decided to appear en masse, all two dozen members, as a show of support. When the custodians did win the right to form a union, her group would represent them in negotiations with the university.

Marcia had almost reached the small campus auditorium where the meeting was being held. In fact, she could already hear it. The turnout must be good. The closer she came, the better the turnout sounded. Marcia, smiling, entered the auditorium. Her anticipation turned into elation. The room was jammed with well over a hundred placard waving student supporters.

Marcia's elation proved short-lived. The large majority of the placards did not display the red hammer and sickle of her Socialist Workers Union. No, these were far outnumbered by ones displaying a red star emblazoned with the head of Chairman Mao. The two groups were shouting back and forth, waving placards threateningly at each other. Marcia was outraged. It was her group which had worked with the custodians from the start. In fact, her Socialist Workers Union had initiated the picketing. Now, as had been rumored, The Union of Communist Workers was trying to horn in on and push them aside. Well they wouldn't get away with it. Marcia had faith in the custodians. They would remember who had stood by them from the start. The small fact that she herself had only been involved in the struggle for two days in no way lessened her certainty.

At the moment, the custodians were looking back over their shoulders uncomfortably at the near riot taking place behind them. Even their leaders, sitting at a table up on the stage, seemed unsure what to make of this circus. Marcia, also in need of an explanation, or at least an update, scanned the room for Heather. She was nowhere to be seen.

A member of The Union of Communist Workers, waving his Little Red Book of Chairman Mao's famous and all encompassing quotations, screamed the vile epithet, "TROTSKYITES!"

"REVISIONISTS!" more than one Socialists Workers Union member shouted back.

Suddenly a white clad arm grabbed Marcia from behind. Turning, she was relieved to see Heather's smiling face, which at the moment was the only familiar thing about her. Heather wore a white peasant's outfit with a red sash for a belt. Marcia, surprised, asked, "You joined the Venceramos?"

Heather, smiling, nodded enthusiastically. They hugged as Heather begged, "Join with me."

Just then a placard bearing Mao's image on it flew by over their heads. They both ducked, and Marcia asked in a confused tone, "What did I miss."

"Just this. Lots of this."

A member of the Union of Communist Workers, swinging his placard, plowed into the Socialist Workers Union members. Immediately, some of his comrades joined the charge. Outnumbered, the Socialist Workers Union retreated, hardly fighting back. The custodians looked on in silent, puzzled amazement. Marcia and Heather looked around in fear. Their comrades were stampeding towards them and the exit. After a quick glance at each other, Marcia and Heather joined the rout. They kept running, even outside, until it became apparent that the Union of Communist Workers was satisfied with merely banishing them from the auditorium.

Marcia, catching her breath, stared back in disbelief.

Heather, little affected, pleaded, "C'mon Marcia, join the Venceramos with me."

Marcia, half paying attention and still looking back, answered distractedly, "Why now? I can wait till summer break when you go to cut sugar cane."

"No!" Heather exclaimed with a smile. "I'm going next week."

Marcia, stunned, turned her full attention back to Heather. "You're supposed to share an apartment with me!"

Heather shrugged, missing Marcia's point. "What's the big deal?"

"What's the big deal?" Marcia asked incredulously. "What am I supposed to do for a roommate?"

Heather straightened her back with indignation. "I'm going to help the Cuban revolution!"

Marcia stood speechless, her expression exhibiting more disbelief than anger.

Heather, still indignant, stared back at Marcia as if suddenly seeing her for the first time. "How can you be so selfish?"

*****

Rob could tell that Sloan was cold turkey the moment he walked through the door. Though his clothes were the same, he wore them better. His walk had lost most of its bob and weave stumble and had gained some authority. More obvious, especially up close, was the aware, calculating focus in Sloan's bloodshot eyes. Still a mess, he now looked dangerous to more than just himself. Rob had seen these same promising signs numerous times. They had always proved illusory and short-lived. Still, he hoped. "Welcome back."

Sloan just stared at him.

Rob added his usual, "You're lookin' good. Who stepped on yah?"

Sloan's serious expression broke into a wry smile. He waited a moment for Rob to grant his request without him having to ask for it.

Rob refused.

Finally, Sloan said, "You know what I want."

Rob's relief left him enough room to be peeved. "What's with you? Every other dishwasher in the world works till he has to get fucked-up, then comes back when he's straight. Mike Sloan shows like clockwork when he's fucked out of his mind, then wants off when he's straight."

Sloan, feeling drug-deprived irritable to begin with, was further irritated by Rob's remark, the same one he'd heard the last two times he had shown up straight. "It's my little way of stealing."

Rob shook his head. "Guess I'm supposed to close up whenever you go cold turkey."

Something close to a smile flickered across Sloan's face. "That'd be sweet of you."

To Rob, this hinted of Old Times. He took being the butt of Sloan's sarcasm as a good sign. "Stick around till I get somebody....Have something to eat."

Sloan's hunger was not for food. At the moment, he had more of an aversion to than an appetite for it. Still, he forced down most of a plate of scrambled eggs. Just as he was giving up on what remained, Sloan felt a hand on his shoulder and heard Screw's version of "hello".

"Hey, Man, you bring the dope?" Screw, barefoot and dressed raggedy-ass street people style, took the stool next to Sloan as if jumping on a horse. "Wow, you look different."

"I feel different," Sloan replied, and by different he did not mean good.

"Last time I saw you, you looked like complete shit."

Sloan shrugged. "It's rough at the top."

"So that's where you were....Back for good, or just visiting?"

The question slightly irritated Sloan. Screw's appearance irritated him more. This was the first time in over a month that Sloan wasn't seeing him through a drug haze. The change in Screw, though believable, was hard for Sloan to take. It seemed like yesterday, a strapping, clean-cut, corn fed Nebraska farm boy had arrived in Berkeley with the name Jake Pedersen. Now, clean but not cut, muscles wasting away, birth name replaced by "Screw", the remains of that Nebraska farm boy sat next to Sloan. The only obvious remnant of the kid was his still winning smile.

Sloan stared a Screw, wondering if he had made a mistake with the kid. Two months ago, cold turkey and literally sick of it, Sloan had gone to a dealer's apartment to score some Dilaudid. There was no Dilaudid, but there was some codeine, and also two slimy street hustlers with the just arrived Jake Pedersen in tow. Sloan had the situation down at a glance. Jake must have run into them and asked for advice on where to stay, or something similar. It had to have taken all the street hustlers' self-control to keep from drowning this Nebraska pigeon in their drool — the money in his pockets, the treasures in his backpack, the air in his head. "Man, you can crash with us," they must have told him. Of course they couldn't take the pigeon home if they were going to pluck him. No need. They'd take him to a pusher's pad, get him zonked, fleece him clean, and leave him in an alley.

The pusher gave Sloan a free sample of codeine and a predatory wink as he surreptitiously jerked his head towards Pedersen. Jake sucked on his third joint as one of the hustlers asked, "It still hasn't hit you?"

"No," Jake replied in all innocence, "What's it supposed to feel like?"

This kid, especially his smile, reminded Sloan of a friend from Nam, a close one, who went home in a box. Sloan had looked out for him, especially during those first, most dangerous weeks in country. Months later, when that kid got blown away, Sloan was left with the feeling he could have done more.

"When it hits you, you'll know," the other hustler assured Jake. He then made the mistake of saying to Mike and the pusher, "This dude's gonna join the Marines."

Sloan flashed on his friend from Vietnam again, then checked Jake for a match. It was there. So was a good natured innocence, too much of it. Could the Corps harden up this kid enough to get him through Nam?

Just then the pusher indicated Sloan with a jerk of his head, saying with a laugh, "Mike here's an ex-Marine."

Sloan mumbled, "Former Marine."

"Former Marine," the pusher corrected himself, smiling with amusement.

There were snickers from the two street hustlers, but Jake asked with interest, "You were in Nam?"

Sloan nodded.

"What was it like?" asked Jake.

'What was it like?' Sloan had repeated to himself. This was the question they always asked him, the question he never had an answer for. He could tell the truth and say it was the worst time of his life. Or he could tell the truth and say Nam was the greatest time of his life. Words were useless. To understand Vietnam, you had to experience it yourself. Otherwise, you wouldn't have a clue. That was the worst part about Berkeley, the part that drove him up the wall — the way every ignorant asshole and his brother shot their mouths off about Vietnam. None of them knew shit about Nam, about life, about anything. He himself, who knew more than any sane human being would ever want to know about Vietnam, couldn't convey the truth if he cared to, which he didn't. Sloan's lips moved slightly as he said to himself, 'Wanna know what Nam's like? Pay the price.'

"Huh?" Jake asked, bringing Sloan out of his reverie.

Sloan figured he'd tell the kid about the Marine Corps. That, at least, he could do. "You join the Marines, you'll end up in the worst places, but with the best motherfuckers in the world." Seeing the impressed expression on Jake's face, again flashing on that matching face from Nam, Sloan realized he'd made a mistake — 'Marine Corps recruiter'.

One of the street hustlers started in on a sarcastic version of the Marine Corps Hymn. "From the halls of Montezuma, to—"

A mean, threatening look from Sloan cut him short.

Fazed only for an instant, the hustler's looked Sloan over with a shit eating grin.

'Thinks I'm just some harmless junky, no danger to anyone but myself.' Sloan made up his mind to get Jake away from the two hustlers.

The grinning one asked, almost as a taunt, "Are Marines really that tough?"

"Yeah," Sloan replied, as his expression hardened. "But that ain't all of it."

"What's the rest?" asked the hustler.

Sloan skewered him with a stare. "Marines are crazy."

The hustler's shit eating grin faded from his face.

A few minutes later, Sloan walked out with the hustlers' prospective pigeon.

So far, Sloan had kept him from running off to join the Marines. Yet it was no longer Jake Pedersen now sitting next to him at the counter in Rob's Cosmic Organic Chicken. It was Screw. Looking at him, Sloan wondered if maybe he wouldn't be better off in the Marines. Screw could turn in a few different directions from here, most of them downward. With a role model such as himself, Screw could fall just as hard on drugs, harder even. And what could save him, cults? Sloan had seen smarter dudes than Screw go from drug zombies to cult zombies. The thought disgusted him. And radical politics, that was the most repulsive cult of all. Yet politics was a disease that often cured itself, though just as often led to other cults or into drugs, and on and on and on. No telling how Screw would end up. His nickname didn't help, and that was Sloan's fault. He'd taken it from that friend blown away in Nam, had passed it on to a Nebraska farm boy. In Nam you could get away with a name like that. Screw The First got it from an asshole lifer, an enemy not a friend. He had worn it like a badge of honor. So, as a matter of fact, did its present owner. Screw The First eventually fragged to death the lifer who had tagged him. By then the winning smile was long gone. Maybe Screw II would eventually frag the one who had named him. Sloan smiled at the thought. 'I deserve it.'

*****

Rob glanced around the hall, surprised to see so many people at an afternoon lecture. For him, the time could not have been more convenient — the slowest part of the day. Of course, that meant the new dishwasher had already found his way to the storeroom, was right now sucking on a warm beer and figuring out in what or under what to stash the empty can.

Dr. Paul Ehrkup, renowned professor, bestselling author, and Public Television superstar, had his audience both mesmerized and terrorized, trembling in fear of our exploding population. They stared up at him like four-year-olds on the floor in front of a TV, watching cartoons. No, Rob corrected himself, they were more like four-year-olds getting the hell scared out of them by a monster movie, one that they should not be watching. Rob wondered what percentage of these concerned citizen adults of Berkeley would be having nightmares tonight, and what percentage of those would wet their beds. Rob himself doubted that he would hear Ehrkup say anything that he hadn't heard him say in fawning interviews, taking head TV discussions, or on the evening news.

"The population bomb has already exploded," Dr Ehrkup warned. "All we can do now is contain the damage. Population growth is outstripping our resources with such phenomenal speed that between 1975 and 1985 we shall suffer the worst famine in the history of the world. Figures don't lie. Millions upon millions of people will starve no matter what we do today. The only question is what small percentage of mankind can we save.

"Economies will crumble as markets go insane. Food prices will skyrocket. A bushel of wheat will be worth a thousand barrels of oil. Don't fool yourselves into thinking that the masses will starve quietly. When the price of food explodes out of their reach, people will riot, looting whatever they can find. Warehouses will be gutted. Tractor-trailers will be hijacked and left burning on the side of the road. Trains will be robbed and tracks destroyed. The food distribution system will be obliterated. No borders will be able to contain the starving hordes. They'll cover the ground like locust, denuding everything in their paths."

Rob sat thinking that this could prove to be a problem, but a more immediate one was how to replace a sick waitress before lunchtime tomorrow. He had come to please his wife, who had come to please her best friend, who had helped bring Dr. Ehrkup to town to scare the hell out of everybody. Well, his wife, saddled with a 'six-year-old', did deserve to get out of the house. Still, Rob figured a movie might have done her more good, even one starring Godzilla. Just in time, he noticed a camera panning towards him. Rob frowned right into it. No way did he want to be one of those ever so serious, thoughtfully nodding zombies Public Television cameras were always cutting to. Rob figured the frown was enough, yet wondered if he should have played it safe by shooting a bird.

Dr. Ehrkup continued, "Even today, nothing in this world causes more widespread misery than hunger. Global Environmental Predictions, published by the UN, shows clearly that the human population is already too large for global resources. It takes twenty hectares to sustain every human being, and we are already down to fifteen each. No one, that isn't a fool, thinks that India will be able to feed its own people by 1980.

"And it's not just the food we eat. All forests will be destroyed to provide additional farm land. All trees that don't produce food will be replaced by trees that do. All insects and animals that live in and feed upon the trees we cut down will become extinct, thus further diminishing our food supply."

Rob sat thinking that Ehrkup had already pounded home his point. Continuing was sure to cost him his audience's good will. A glance at this audience disabused him of this opinion. The crowd was still mesmerized. He saw a lot of people he knew, most of them Jews. Rob wondered why his own tribe was such a sucker for this bullshit. Ehrkup himself had to be a member.

"And think about human waste. Not just the garbage that will surround us, but literal human waste. The Ganges will become so clogged with sewage it will be useless for travel, drying up hard enough to walk across. And the Mississippi, the colon of the United States, won't be far behind. I mean within a decade."

Dr. Ehrkup paused for emphasis. "Ladies and Gentlemen, I

hope I've gotten through to you. I hope you will act upon what you have learned here tonight. If you don't, by the year 2000, hundreds of millions of people will die of starvation. The next time you look into your children's eyes, remember that in a little over a decade, by 1980, human life expectancy will have declined to a mere 42 years. I hope it isn't too late. Negative population growth will not undo the terrible damage we have already done, but it is our only hope. And hope is all we have."

The audience of less than three hundred burst into a round of applause worthy of a thousand. Rob, failing to play his part, glanced over to see his wife making up for him. When finished applauding, she looked at him with a meek smile, saying, "Almost makes me feel guilty for having one kid."

Rob stared at her dumbstruck. He could not believe these words came from a woman as intelligent as Sarah. He could not remember a remark anywhere near as dumb in all the years they had been together.

She easily read his thoughts. "I wasn't serious."

Rob's tone did justice to his expression. "How could you joke about that?"

Sarah, not in the mood to argue, just shrugged. They headed outside into the sunshine, walking for a good few minutes in silence. This grated on her as much as his expression had. Finally, she could hold it in no longer. "The Population Bomb isn't a problem?"

"Sarah, it's not our problem," he said curtly.

"It certainly is. We brought a child into this world."

"And you feel guilty about it?" he asked, immediately sorry that he had.

"Don't be an idiot," she said, in a tone that told him the fight had begun.

"That kid is the best thing I ever did for this world," he said, in a tone indicating he'd drop the matter if she would.

Not ready to drop it, she said, "And I don't feel the same way?"

Rob remained silent until he noticed her staring at him, waiting for a reply. "Did you see who was at that lecture?"

This was not the reply she had been waiting for. Now she chose to remain silent.

Rob continued, "A third of the people there were Jews."

"What has that got to do with anything?"

"A third were Jews, a third were round-eyed Buddhists, and most of the rest were Unitarians, the anti-religion for people too weak to live without one....And half the Unitarians were named Cohen, Katz, Schwartz."

Sarah was losing what patience she had left. "What has that got to do with anything?"

"I mean did you see anybody there from the ghetto? Did you see any Africans, Arabs, Indians, or Pakistanis?"

Now she did know what he was getting at, and had no reply.

Rob continued, "All those self-righteous, self-important hypocrites pretending they're saving the world, while the rest of it is breeding like rats at harvest time. So instead of having 1.85 kids per couple, they're gonna have 1.26. And they're the ones who can afford to feed and educate them. How's that changing the world for the better?"

"Okay, you have a point," she admitted, "but the Population Bomb is still a problem."

"Well that's one problem they can't blame on the Jews....And if it ever is, they'll solve it....This world always finds a way to keep Jewish population down. Jews themselves do a damn good job of it. Go to any Hare Krishna, Scientology, EST meeting, and half the flakes there are self-hating Jews."

These remarks surprised her. "Boy, look who's become Defender of the Faith....When I wanted to keep a kosher home, you told me to forget it."

"I was wrong," he mumbled.

This admission really surprised her. The argument had petered out into a conversation. "It doesn't bother me that Jews are doing their share to make this world a better place."

He put his arm around her. "Sarah, I just wish we'd take a few weeks off. Especially that Bozo Ehrkup, running around trying to finish off Hitler's work for him."

This remark had her drawing back a little, staring at Rob as if gauging his sanity. She knew his anger had another angle aside from the Jewish one, and that that angle pointed directly at her. He had told her even before they were married that if he could change one thing in his life, it would be the fact that he was an only child. Her first pregnancy had been a difficult one. A year and half later,

51

she still didn't feel up to a second. Yet Rob had pressured her. This pregnancy ended in a miscarriage. He felt guilty, and she felt guilty for allowing him to feel guilty. For a few years he had hinted around about trying again. Sarah pretended she didn't catch those hints. Yet for the last two years, he hadn't mentioned it once.

Rob chose the present moment to ask somberly, "You don't want to have a brother or sister for David?"

"I do."

Shocked, Rob did a double-take. "Then why don't we?"

"I've been trying for over a year." At first Sarah had wanted to surprise him, but the last few months she just didn't want to get his hopes up.

Doubly shocked, he asked, "Why didn't you tell me?"

Sarah stopped walking and gave Rob a hard stare. "How the hell didn't you figure it out for yourself?"

He pondered hard. "I don't know....I guess I figured you were finding me irresistible."

"Rob, I don't want to hurt your feelings, but you're still every bit as resistible as on the day I met you." Sarah started walking again.

He had to laugh. "Well you should have told me anyway. I would have put my mind to it."

"Rob, your mind would not have helped."

They walked in silence a long moment, before he said in a tone that showed he meant it, "Sarah, I'm sorry. My quarrel sure isn't with you."

There was another long pause before she asked with a smile, "What happened to that idealistic Freedom Rider I fell in love with."

"I'll tell you exactly what happened to him. He came home proud that the Jews helped the blacks more than anybody, far more. And then he saw the black bigots, as vicious as any redneck bigots, explain it away by claiming the Jews were even worse than other whites....Blaming the Jews for slavery! How stupid can they get?"

"What about John Lewis?"

"Exactly, the exception that proves the rule. He had real guts, and look what those jive spouting Stokely-Come-Latelys did to him."

"And threw away some of the gains we made."

"They'd never admit it, and their hypocritical cheerleaders at The New York Times wouldn't either."

"Ah, Rob, don't be that way. I've had black friends all my life, at school and at work. They aren't any more anti-Semitic than anyone else, if anything, less....It's just the ones at the universities."

An amused smile came to Rob's face. As long as he'd known Sarah, this was the very first time she had said something that could be construed as bigoted. "Oh, you're saying, 'Sending blacks to college makes them anti-Semites, and stupider.'"

"Don't put words in my mouth."

"I thought I was just quoting you."

"Don't get cute."

"Okay. Then you're saying those black college students are always attacking Israel and putting up those lovely photos of Yasser Arafat's sweet face because of their deep affection for the 'Peace-loving Palestinian People'."

"Don't...put...words in my mouth!"

"Not just to stick it to the Jews."

"Enough!"

"Okay. Sorry." He placed his hand behind her neck.

"Rob, you'd do it all again anyway. Admit it."

"Being a Freedom Rider? No! No, I wouldn't, not if I knew other Jews were gonna pay for it."

This was not the answer she wanted, far from it.

A glance at Sarah's face told Rob so. He squeezed the back of her neck. "Well, if I knew that that was the only way I was going to meet you, then I'd do it again."

She smiled, and after a moment asked jokingly, "So you'll help us find a solution to the Population Bomb?"

"There already is a solution — the hydrogen bomb."

*****

Sloan had walked the streets for hours. Irritable and jumpy, his nose was running and he sensed a headache coming on. Going back to his apartment was not an option, no way. That's where his stash was. Flushing it down the toilet was also not an option. He'd need it soon. Sloan had made no pretense of going cold turkey for good. He was merely coming up for a little air. He had done this same thing before. He'd stick it out, go through the torture of withdrawal, just to prove that he could. Then he'd get ripped again. This painful stunt derived not from any rational decision, but from a need to prove to himself, without spelling it out, that he was not a junkie. His reason for not spelling it out was the sense that he was not proving a thing.

Telegraph Avenue was shoulder to shoulder. Unsure where he wanted to go, he knew damn well what he wanted to get away from — people. They kept crowding and jostling him. Sloan fought hard against and controlled the urge to demand some breathing space, to violently shove people away. Worse even than feeling their presence was feeling their eyes upon him. He had to flee — the crowds, the street noise, and the stink of exhaust fumes. He had to get above it all. The surrounding hills would be nice — quiet, shady, cool. Yet getting up there, that would be a hassle, too much of one. Even if he made it, he would then be looking down upon where he now was. No, he'd take a bus to the bay, feel the salt breeze against his face. Surprisingly, this idea alone soothed his mind.

The sun stayed bright all the way to the marina. A pleasant breeze met him as he got off the bus. The scent of salt in the air calmed him. Sloan was surprised to find himself actually enjoying the act of breathing it in. He inhaled more deeply, taking pleasure from each breath. Above him, the usual West Coast haze had lifted like a veil, turning the sky to an even brighter, crystalline blue. Sloan credited his luck for such a gorgeous day to go cold turkey. Then it hit him — 'If I wasn't straight, I wouldn't even notice.' He now realized that a far more malevolent veil had been lifted — the thick fog of drugs that had blanketed his mind and senses for so long.

Sloan walked the docks oblivious to the wary expressions on the few people who crossed his path, unaware of the hunger in his own eyes that was so obviously not for food. He had forgotten how much he had missed the bay.

Sloan walked down a familiar pier. He knew he'd follow it, as always, right to the end. He also knew that the sailboat he was looking for would not be there. Next, Sloan went to the pier reserved for the fishing charter boats. Almost all of them were still out. He checked the angle of the sun. Soon they'd be back, an hour at the most. He'd wait, see what they had caught. There were surprisingly few people around. All the better. He did not want to see or be seen by anyone. Sloan sat down facing out towards the bay, legs dangling off the dock. The sea gulls were wheeling and diving, screeching at the sky. They were hungry as always. He mused that if they would make half the noise, they could probably get by on half the food. Sloan smiled at the thought. Hell, he liked the noisy, gutsy little fuckers.

Without the mist, San Francisco looked even more beautiful across the water. Many times he had seen the bay like this, and many of those times he had seen it from 10,000 miles away. The picture of San Francisco Bay now before Sloan was very similar to those he had seen in Vietnam. You needed a place to escape to in Nam, during the rare moments you had the time. If you didn't have an escape, all you had was the dust, the mud, and the blood. And if that was all you had, you rarely made it home. In Vietnam, he had looked forward to returning here, to going out salmon fishing on a charter boat. Many times he'd seen them dock with loads of beautiful fish. Yeah, that was something he'd do for sure. One more reason to make it back alive. Still, these longings were not enough to keep him from wondering what home would now be like, dragging back with him the depressing truths Nam had forced him to admit.

Sloan had made it back alive. Yet he'd never made it out salmon fishing. He told himself he didn't really care, this with a vague sense of unease. He knew that he did care. One of the reasons Sloan liked fishing was because he was good at it, very good at it. Once, while fishing stoned, it occurred to him that fishing was seduction, getting fish to take the bait. This led him to the conclusion that if you are good at fishing, you would be good with women, and vice versa. He himself, in his own modest estimation, seemed to be proof positive of this. Searching for further proof, he went over the best fishermen he had ever known. Unfortunately, most of them could not get laid in a women's prison with a pint of whiskey sticking out of their back pockets. This led him to a second conclusion, one he has yet to discard — "Never trust a conclusion arrived at when stoned." Sloan now laughed to himself. It was getting chilly. He felt a slight shiver and folded his arms across his chest.

In Vietnam, he had thought a lot about sailing this bay on a beautiful sailboat with a special woman. That was something he had done, something he longed to do again. Problem was, special women with beautiful sailboats were hard to meet. And once you met them, they were hard to keep. You had to work at it, pay attention to all the subtle mood shifts, say things that were a pain to say. And if you made even a small mistake, you had to know how to defuse the situation, as carefully as you would defuse a two thousand pound bomb. Sloan had not returned to Berkeley expecting to find her again. No, she had sailed out of his life forever, leaving him behind. Still, the day after he returned from Nam, he returned to the marina, berating himself all the way there. The idea that she too had returned, and was waiting for him aboard her boat was just too ridiculous to contemplate, and pathetic to boot. Despite this, contemplate it he did. That day Sloan walked every foot of the sailboat docks, scoped out every boat. She was a hard woman to forget. 'And for good reason.'

Sloan glanced back over his shoulder. A graceful sailboat on an adjacent quay caught his eye — sparkling white fiberglass, blue trim, and a lot of rich, dark teak. 'Wouldn't mind owning her.' The boat appeared equipped with all he needed to sail singlehanded. 'Head for Baja right now....And that just for a start.' He expelled a burst of air from his nostrils in something resembling a laugh. 'Fat chance of that.'

There was still no sign of the fishing boats. Sloan fought an urge to check out the sailboats again. 'Just to kill time,' he thought, in no ways fooling himself. He fought the urge, fought it hard. He lost. Sloan rose to his feet, feeling like a fool. He felt even more pathetic a half hour later, when he returned to the charter boat dock and sat down again.

The breeze stiffened, and a chill came with it. 'Where are those fucking fishing boats?' Still no sign of them. Just to keep warm, he'd have to get up and start walking soon. His shivering increased. He was determined to stay until at least one fishing charter boat made the dock. Both baffled and embarrassed by this need, Sloan strained his eyes searching the horizon. Not a boat in sight. His shivering grew violent, too violent, obviously from more than just the chill in the air. 'Fuck it. Some other time.'

As Sloan got to his feet, a sudden wind gust sent his Vietnam bush cover into the bay. "SHIT!" With darting glances he searched for a boat hook, anything to fish the hat out of the water. The wind was carrying it away. The bay would be freezing. He was shivering already. 'Just a fucking hat,' he tried to convince himself. A few seconds and it would be gone. Sloan knew he should turn his back and say, "Fuck it!" He couldn't. With a loud tearing sound, he literally ripped off his shirt. His shoes and Levis took more precious time. The hat was going under, barely visible. In desperation, he dove off the dock. Sloan had known the water would be cold, but it was still an icy shock, so painful it was a pleasure, yet just for an instant. He felt as if huge hat pins were piercing every inch of his body. The momentum of his dive kept him gliding through the water. He opened his hands just below the surface, as if they would scoop up the hat. Miraculously, as his momentum died, his right hand felt cloth and closed on it like a mouse trap. Sloan's head came up as he treaded water, disbelieving how lucky he had been, how cold the bay. His mouth was wide open as he gasped to catch his breath. It took a second to realize that it was the very iciness of the water that had taken his breath and would never give it back. He had to get up on the dock, fast.

A man yelled, "There's someone in the water!"

A woman screamed, "He's committing suicide!"

Sloan raced back towards the dock, wanting to strangle the 'idiot' woman. Holding the hat slowed him. 'Who's the idiot?' he asked himself, now feeling every bit of one. Sloan grabbed the transom ladder of a boat and clambered out of the water. A man on the dock offered a hand. Sloan took it, and the man's strong grip pulled him up. He found himself standing on the dock in a pair of translucent briefs, facing the stares of a half dozen people, wishing the hell they would all just get lost. One of Sloan's more observant rescuers informed him, "You're soaking wet."

The breeze freeze dried his dripping wet skin. Sloan saw another rescuer rushing down the dock, life saving ring and rope in hand. Despite seeing Sloan already out of the water, he kept running, as if handing Sloan the ring in time would mean the difference between life and death.

Sloan stood shivering uncontrollably, telling himself that he had

57

a damn good excuse. Drying off was not an option. He pulled on his Levis. His shirt was nearly torn in two, but he put it on anyway. As his shivering hands struggled with his shoes, the woman who had had him committing suicide asked, "Do you want us to call an ambulance?"

Sloan refrained from answering, and also from flinging her into the frigid water. Realizing his silence made him appear crazy, he still refused to speak. Hell, if he told them the truth, that he had jumped into the ice cold bay to save his rag of a hat, he'd be giving them all they needed to call the men in white coats. Sloan disliked crowds, especially since Vietnam. Being at the center of one, even one as small as this, he disliked even more. If these people were not going to get lost, he'd have to, the faster the better.

The bus trip back to Berkeley was no pleasure. Sloan's mood was as damp and soggy as his clothes. He looked at his bush cover, still held tightly in his right hand. What was there about this weather beaten rag of a hat that he needed? Why was it so important? Now putting it on his head, he felt almost comforted. 'You're nuts,' Sloan told himself, still shivering. If this was what it was like to be straight, why the hell would he want to stay straight?

It was after dusk and a short nap when Sloan stepped down from the bus onto a crowded Berkeley sidewalk. He was dead tired, somber. His clothes were still damp. He itched from the salt. His dope free, unfiltered mind picked up more of his surroundings that he could stand. The engine exhaust nauseated, the lights blinded, the noises assaulted his ears, and the people, they'd crowd and brush up against him like perverts. Sloan didn't feel as if he were walking the streets. He felt as if he were neck deep in a river walking against the current. Sloan did not like lowering his gaze. Yet he had to, just to avoid exchanging glances. These people insulted him with their very presence. They were different. He had nothing in common with them. They were fucking androids — a thin veneer of fake skin covering transistors, circuits and indicator lights. Why did he never feel more alone than when surrounded by people?

Damp and cold, Sloan reached his building at a fast walk. He couldn't wait to rush inside his 'shithole' of an apartment and latch the door behind him.

Yet a face that he had seen only once before stopped Sloan cold.

This face, Marcia's face, was the first since he had left the marina that did not make him want to look away. Again there was fear on it. He was freaking her out. Sloan knew that he better think of something to say, fast. The best he could come up with was a deadpan, "Waiting for the landlord?"

Marcia sat on the outside steps this time, her last encounter with Sloan being the reason. Now with his shirt ripped half off of him, Sloan seemed even more frightening. Just as he was about to speak again, Marcia was relieved to hear someone exiting the building from behind her.

Straughton shot Sloan a quick, impersonal smile. Noticing Marcia looking up and back at him, his smile brightened. "Are you my neighbors?"

Sloan nodded.

Marcia, still seated, wearily shook her head. "I'm waiting for the landlord. He was supposed to be here a half hour ago."

"I'm certain he will not disappoint you," Straughton assured her.

"I wouldn't be,' said Sloan."

"I'm not," Marcia replied. "Yesterday I waited an hour and he didn't show up."

"Care to call him on my phone?"

Marcia almost jumped to her feet, glad to take advantage of Straughton's offer.

Sloan watched them head inside, wondering, 'How'd that clown get a phone so fast?' By the time he stopped wondering, Marcia was gone and he was alone on the steps. 'Sure snowed her.'

Just then Smitty, still the wide-eyed newcomer, came striding down the sidewalk. Something about the apartment building number stopped him — '2441'. It was familiar. Hadn't he heard it recently? Yeah, from that barefoot newspaper boy. Maybe this was the right street. Smitty glanced at Sloan — 'Another junkie.' Smitty had had his fill of worrying about some drug addict breaking into his car, had had enough of running back to check on it every chance he got. That 8-track tape deck he had just installed was a junkie's dream, as good as cash. He better get damn serious about finding an apartment.

Smitty asked Sloan, "Is there anything for rent here?"

Sloan nodded. He sat down on the steps, staring solemnly out at the street.

"Is the landlord here?" Smitty asked

Sloan shook his head. "On the way over…supposedly."

The junky was apparently a tenant. Not a good sign. After a moment, Smitty sat down anyway. There was another two minutes of silence before he got out the question, "What's he like?"

Sloan paused, giving some thought before answering honestly, "Like a landlord."

There was another long pause before Smitty replied, "Figures."

*****

As soon as Straughton had Marcia through his threshold, he pointed her towards the record collection. "Find something you like and put it on." He had no doubt that she could. His record collection contained over five hundred albums. He considered it a necessity, the appropriate music for every mood. Not his mood, but that of any woman he wanted to make temporarily his. Straughton had perfected a technique for building up one's record collection that rarely necessitated a trip to the store — The 2-for-1 Method. When he came upon an album he thought useful, he would borrow it, and another album along with it. Eventually he would return the other album. The owner would invariably be thrilled — "Gee, I couldn't figure out what happened to it!" With the still missing album now forgotten, he or she would practically beg Straughton to borrow two more. Time after time, it amazed him how careless people were with their records, especially when he'd show up with a few quality joints. And these same foolish dolts who squandered their money on record albums, would often sit around smoking one of Straughton's joints concocting ridiculous conspiracy theories on how the rich stay rich. To Straughton, it was no mystery at all. Obviously some people were born to throw away money, others were born to accumulate it. Some people were born to pay taxes, others to take advantage of the loopholes provided them. It was all in one's genes. Straughton was not so bold as to consider himself an expert in the sciences, but it did not take a biologist to discern that the wealthy were a species apart.

Of course when it came to social contacts, especially with women, Straughton did not discriminate as to species. Oddly enough, when once asked sarcastically if he "liked" women, Straughton had hesitated to answer. Liked did not seem the appropriate word, not at all. Certainly he had developed a need for women, you might even call it something of an addiction. Yet was this really a liking? The question in itself stretched the bounds of Straughton's urge for introspection. He was perfectly willing to leave it unanswered. Certainly the day would come when he would marry. Still, he could not actually picture himself entering into such an arrangement.

Straughton found it amazing how useful a good record collection could be for putting a strange, nervous woman at ease. She would walk through the door, eyes darting all over the place in search of torture paraphernalia, decomposing bodies, or who knows what. All he had to do was direct her towards his record collection and she would go into a relaxed trance, flipping through his albums and feeling at home. In the meantime, he would back off and give her some space while breaking out his stash and rolling a joint. By then the woman had usually chosen a few albums. As soon as he had one on the turntable, his prey would be feeling completely at home. Usually.

However, this time, Marcia hadn't taken two steps towards his expensive stereo before turning around and reminding them both, "I came to use the phone."

"Oh. Slipped my mind." Straughton smiled and pointed, saying, "It's in the bedroom."

Marcia hesitated, eyeing Straughton warily as he pulled down the hollowed-out book containing his stash. 'Don't be silly,' she told herself, and headed for the bedroom. His black satin sheets slowed her steps. The phone was next to the bed, but her eyes stayed on the sheets. To Marcia they warned of danger, and perversion to boot. She approached warily and dialed the landlord without sitting on the bed. After a dozen busy signals and two dozen quick glances at the sheets, she retreated back to the front room. There was now something disturbingly different about it — the light. Less of it. And two of Straughton's posters, the florescent ones, were glowing. Marcia quickly spied the reason. He had turned off the overhead fixture and switched on a black light. The resulting effect, though attractive, did more to put her on guard than impress her. Then Straughton's Lava Lamp caught her eye.

Though nothing new, she always found those slowly stretching and expanding globs of color mesmerizing. Marcia approached to get a better look, saying absentmindedly, "The line's busy."

'How fortunate,' thought Straughton, sitting down on the couch. He leaned over the brutally scarred coffee table to put the final touches on a joint of Panama Red. Straughton waved her towards the stereo. "Pick out a record while you wait."

"Boy, you have some collection," said Marcia, kneeling down on the rug. She flipped through the albums, recognizing many. Some brought back pleasant memories. Marcia was completely immersed in his record collection when her face lit up at the sight of a familiar Mamas & the Papas album. Out of nowhere, a lit joint appeared between her face and the album. Straughton, offering it, stood at her side. Marcia held the album out to him, at the same time shaking her head No to the joint. "Can I hear this song — Strange Young Girls....Please."

Straughton gladly complied, that being exactly what records were for. He found the song unusual, so unusual it kept his attention for all of ten seconds, a span close to his maximum. For him, music was not so much a pleasure, as a means to pleasure.

Marcia said dreamily, "I love this song, but I can't make out all the words....Can you?"

Straughton made a halfhearted attempt. He never paid much attention to lyrics, and didn't remember ever hearing this song. He must have borrowed the album along with one he really wanted, then forgotten to return either of them. Already stoned, he sat down next to Marcia and again offered her a drag.

Marcia, lost in the song, accepted the joint and took a healthier toke than she would have if she had been completely conscious of what she was doing. As always, meaning for the fifth time in her life, she coughed up most of it. Still, the last time she had smoked marijuana had been worth it. Music had never sounded so good. She heard each and every note, and heard them as if they rang out from inside her very own head. Perhaps grass would enable her to finally understand all the lyrics to Strange Young Girls. Another drag had her coughing again. As the song ended, she turned to Straughton, not even realizing she was already stoned. "Did you understand the words?"

"No," Straughton replied, thinking, 'Ah, how lovely this face would look against my black satin sheets.' Still, a face to him was merely an ephemeral treat. Eventually, all women's faces ran together in his mind. Conveniently, the girl behind this particular face had just provided him with a hook. "I know every musician in town. I'll get the lyrics from one of them."

Marcia's large eyes lit up. "Really?"

"Certainly."

"Are you a musician?"

"No," Straughton answered too soon and too truthfully, thus surprising himself. He blamed this aberration on the dope. Panama Red sure deserved the publicity he had given it in The Badger.

Marcia's stoned gaze, still directed at Straughton, got him back to business. He attempted to rectify matters. "Well, not a professional musician."

"A student?" she asked.

Straughton let out a short, condescending laugh. "I'm a journalist."

"Really? For the Tribune or the Chronicle?"

Straughton leaned back and away. "Do I impress you as someone who would hire himself out to those mediocre establishment mouthpieces?" he asked, knowing damn well that he was.

Marcia shook her head, sorry that she had insulted him. "Oh, you're a TV journalist."

Straughton's expression immediately told Marcia she had made an even graver mistake. "Hardly....I'm a reporter for the only major paper that informs the public what is really going on in this country and why, a paper that can't be bought-off by the military-industrial complex — The—"

As Straughton talked, Marcia sat wondering with her stoned brain what newspaper he could be talking about. She was quite surprised when he finally said the two words—

"—Berkeley Badger."

Now Marcia liked The Badger, found it amusing and sometimes informative. Yet she had always pictured The Badger staff as something akin to its vendors — drug crazed, rioting, extremist lunatics. Looking at Straughton, surprised by her own ignorance, she wondered how she had come by this misconception. Whatever The Badger's tone, it must require a capable staff to put it out every week. She stared impressed at Straughton, seeing an intelligent, functioning human being, certainly no drug addled—

Marcia's train of thought came to an abrupt halt when she realized that, as a matter of fact, the person now passing her the joint was drug addled, very drug addled. He had to be, if he was smoking the same marijuana she was smoking, because she was more stoned than she had ever been in her life, stoned out of her mind, thinking that one brilliantly, eloquently descriptive thought so common to marijuana smokers, thinking, 'Wow!'

Straughton misinterpreted Marcia's childlike, open mouthed stare. He mistook it as a longing for the type of cultured sexual fulfillment that was his art. 'Ye Old record collection never fails,' he thought, conveniently forgetting those numerous times it had. Straughton tended to give way too much credit for his moderately successful love life to his album collection, which did provide a clever, effective means of breaking the ice. He also overestimated his own charm. Straughton gave far too little credit to his strongest and most useful character trait — blind, dumb nerve. He now tapped this nerve, a mere fraction of proven reserves, as he leaned forward and locked lips with Marcia's already open mouth.

Marcia was so surprised, that for a moment she found herself observing Straughton's kiss more than experiencing it. Paralyzed by her first ever out-of-body experience, she peered down upon herself, defenselessly incapacitated by Killer Weed, being attacked by a stranger in a strange apartment, about to be dragged into that musty bedroom and thrown upon those repulsive black satin sheets. Picturing the sheets helped Marcia gain control, but it was actually the sensation of Straughton's huge tongue trying to strangle her from inside out, the gagging reflex against imminent asphyxiation, that enabled her to push away and free herself from his clumsy lip lock. Marcia struggled to her feet, against dizziness and nausea, as Straughton tried to keep hold of her arms, asking in bewilderment, "Where are you going?"

Marcia backed away from him towards the door. "Home," she replied, realizing immediately that home was Santa Monica. No, that wasn't where she wanted to go. Marcia, stoned as she was, realized that her immediate problem was not where she wanted to go. It was getting away, far away, from Straughton and his enormous tongue.

"But we haven't figured out the lyrics yet."

Marcia would have been far from tempted even if her confused mind understood the reference. Seeing Straughton's apartment door, she knew damn well she wanted to be on the other side of it. Marcia reached for the knob like a drowning woman reaching for a life saving ring. Straughton didn't try to stop her except with the words, "You don't care to call the landlord again?"

'What landlord?' wondered Marcia, opening the door and exiting. The sight of two people directly across the hall, help if need be, stopped her just outside the apartment — 'I'm safe.' Marcia's dry mouth had a strange taste in it. She remembered Straughton's huge tongue with disgust. Yet that was over. She was out of danger now. Her relieved yet still confused mind attempted to brush away her disgust with the thought, 'At least it was just his tongue.' It failed miserably, leaving her shocked and nauseous. 'What am I thinking?'

Smitty and a middle aged man stood looking at her.

Straughton, now standing smiling behind Marcia, broke the silence. "Mr. Heins, this young lady would like to see you."

Marcia, alarmed, thought, 'No I wouldn't! Why did he say that?'

The man looked at her. "I'm sorry, but if it's about the apartment, I just rented it to this young gentleman." He pointed to Smitty.

Marcia suddenly realized it was about the apartment. Stunned, she said, "I've been waiting an hour for you."

Heins, his tone displaying more civility than sympathy, replied, "Young Lady, I didn't see you. He was here."

Marcia added, "I was here a few days ago and you never showed up." 'A few days ago?' she wondered, 'Or was it yesterday? Or this afternoon?' It seemed like months ago.

"Miss, this young man here has already put down a deposit and signed the lease."

She turned to Smitty. "Did you have an appointment?"

Smitty had to admit to this attractive young girl that he did not, doing so by shaking his head.

Marcia, stunned by the injustice, gave Smitty a hard stare "I had one, twice. He came here to meet me."

Smitty remained silent, thinking, 'Why is this fine looking fox mad at me?'

"Do you think that's fair?"

Smitty shook his head, assuring her that he didn't. Maybe he should let her have the apartment. Then what about all his things in the car. They were sure to get stolen. Hell, they might be stolen already.

The landlord cut in, "Young lady, the lease is signed. There's nothing he can do."

Smitty felt gratitude towards the landlord for getting him off the hook. After all, how was he supposed to know she had an appointment?

Marcia, staring at defeat, thought there had to be some way to undo this injustice. 'If I just wasn't stoned.'

Smitty couldn't keep his eyes off Marcia. Yet here he was, having known her all of ten seconds, in the middle of an argument with her. 'How'd this happen?'

Marcia got a brainstorm. "Why can't you tear up the lease? It's just a piece of paper."

'She's right,' Smitty forced himself to admit. He still had no desire to give up the apartment. What he desired was to invite this girl out for a beer. No, a movie would be better. The problem was, this just didn't seem the appropriate moment. Smitty was well aware that timing could be crucial, in fact, fatal.

Straughton, however, was completely ignorant of timing. "Why don't we all go back inside and listen to some music?"

She gave Straughton an ice cold glare and turned towards the landlord.

Relieved, Smitty told himself that he still had a chance. But a chance to do what? If there was an appropriate next move, he sure couldn't think of it. Some skill and imagination were sorely needed to pull this marshmallow out of the fire. Unfortunately, it was the type of skill and imagination he had never been known for, and he knew it.

"I'm sorry," said the landlord, sounding far more impatient than sorry. "It's too late now." He walked away.

Marcia turned her resentment back towards Smitty. "Now I have to pay another week's rent at the rooming house."

"I'm real sorry....I've been sleeping in my car."

Straughton's eyes lit up. 'A car!' He held out his hand to

Smitty. "Hello, neighbor, Roger Straughton VI." They shook hands. "Allow me to turn you on to some excellent music, and some excellent herb to do with it."

The invitation sounded great to Smitty. Still, his primary interest lay in Marcia. A smile in her direction earned him a cold stare. Straughton noticed Smitty's interest, and repeated his invitation to Marcia. She answered by walking away without even looking back. Straughton shrugged and ushered a defeated Smitty into his apartment.

Marcia exited the dark, dreary building onto a brightly lit street full of smiling people, every one of them ignorant of the injustice she had just suffered. Now she'd have to start all over again. Marcia stood alone, disappointed about the apartment and confused by the marijuana. What had happened wasn't fair. Yet if the apartment she had lost was like Straughton's, it wasn't that great a loss, not at that rent. If she couldn't find a one-bedroom apartment, she would get a two-bedroom and worry about finding a roommate later. Her father wouldn't care. At the moment, she didn't really care much either. It did not occur to her that the marijuana was helping her not to care, or also that it was giving her a craving for something sweet. Marcia decided that what she really did want at the moment was a strawberry milkshake, a thick one. The thought put a smile on her face.

*****

Mike Sloan, in a cold sweat, walked through the door of Rob's Cosmic Fried Chicken. Even with his eyes squinted almost shut, the light that got through proved painful enough to have him gritting his teeth. He took a seat at the counter, directly in front of Rob.

"Mike, you're looking good. Who stepped on yah?"

Sloan said flatly, "Thanks for the encouragement....Get me some sunglasses out of the Lost And Found drawer."

Rob came back with three pairs to choose from. "How 'bout something to eat."

Sloan recoiled at the thought. "You serious?" He grabbed a pair of aviator style Ray-Bans and put them on in one motion.

"You can hold down some eggs."

Sloan shook his head, glancing around satisfied with his new eye protection. "I can't go back to my place. My stash is there."

Rob took out his key chain. He removed a key and handed it to Sloan. "No one's using the bungalow." It was behind Rob's house, and closer to a spruced-up tool shed than a bungalow. "Stay away from my kid. You'll scare the hell out of him." He then drew some bills out of his pocket. "Get some new clothes on the way."

Sloan stood immediately, wanting to flee. He drew himself up to his full height as he strode towards the door, determined to look the opposite of how he felt — formidable. Outside, Sloan forced himself to stare straight ahead, not down. If he met someone else's gaze, he would not be the one to look away. Immediately, he tripped over nothing and almost fell on his face. 'Pathetic.'

Sloan wanted to head straight for Rob's bungalow, but the thought of getting some new clothes, at least a shirt, tempted him. How long had it been since he'd done that. Seemed like years. Probably was. Some new clothes might make a difference. Sloan had had enough of the fog that was now his life. Splitting the difference between consciousness and unconsciousness was not getting it done. No future in it. Problem was, there was no future going clean either, not one he could imagine.

Nam hadn't helped. One of the reasons he'd gone there was to put off the future a while. It had done that all right. Nam was all here and now. Not even day to day. It was minute to minute, sometimes second to second. And damn if that didn't carry over some once he got back to Berkeley. He just sort of drifted and drifted, aimlessly. Maybe that was the problem. He had no goal, no target. There was nothing he really wanted. 'Which ain't as good as it sounds.'

*****

Smitty left registration feeling like a world beater. He had used The Slate to choose his instructors. Not only had he gotten every class he wanted, he had also gotten them at the times he preferred. More important, all of his classes were English courses, as opposed to accounting or economics.

At Ohio State, Smitty had intended to get an accounting degree. Cost Accounting 201 had given him second thoughts, which turned out to be relatively mild compared to the psychotic thoughts brought on by Income Tax 101. The teacher would be lisping away about the philosophy behind certain bookkeeping techniques, or about "pure accounting theory", rhapsodizing about the "exquisiteness" of this or that accounting principal, while Smitty sat there fighting the fight of his academic life against his own drooping eyelids. He'd see the teacher's beady glare dart back and forth across the room, searching out a victim. Smitty had always disliked speaking up in class, and tax accounting turned dislike to loathing. Beneath a calm, blank mask, Smitty would sit with clenched teeth, his thoughts warning that double entry Kewpie Doll, 'Don't ask me any of your dumb questions....How can you be so dead and not even know it? Arthritis, you wish. Rigor mortis, that's what it is.'

Not that Smitty had anything against accounting, or accountants either. For food, to support a family, he could surely be one, no problem. But where did accounting fit in at a university? Accounting was something that could and should be learned on the job, not discussed in a classroom like Plato's Republic.

No, Smitty would not spend his college years torturing himself with accounting theory. The books he would read would be books written to be read, for the very sake of reading, books about life. Smitty decided that if he were going to get a college degree, it would be in English. With a little luck, some time before graduation, he would figure out a use for the damn thing. In the meantime, he would go with the flow, check out what was happening in this happening decade. In fact, he asked himself, 'Hell, why not go to the place where it always happens first?'

Smitty could not think of a reason. That's why he now found himself on the campus of the University of California at Berkeley, worrying about the rental contract he had signed. His euphoria at being in Berkeley, his discomfort sleeping in his car, and most of all, his fear of leaving his possessions unattended in that car, had prodded him to give up looking for a studio apartment at a rent he could afford. Instead, he had taken a one-bedroom at far more than he could afford. Depending on whether or not he found a roommate, he would either have extra spending money or no spending money, and shortly no place to sleep. Still, he told himself things would work out. They had to. Or else he'd get drafted and sent to Vietnam.

The Off-Campus Housing Office was just up ahead. Students, a lot of them, were entering, exiting, and milling around. A good sign. Near the entrance stood something odd — a small white table, no, more like a low-sided wooden box on legs. It was full of green apples. What could this be? The answer was written across the inside back of the box — "Honor Apples 10¢". Smitty sure could use something to eat, but not sour green apples. Yet their color did not stop a girl from stepping in front of him to chomp on one before she even had her coin in hand.

'What the hell,' thought Smitty, 'Only costs a dime to find out.' He dropped one into the slot and took an apple. The first bite exploded with flavor. 'Wow, how come we don't have these back in Cleveland?' Finding a roommate could wait. Smitty finished the apple right there. He then bought another for the road.

The office was mobbed, but the mob was civilized. Smitty squeezed his way in. Students talked to clerks, filled out forms, read lists of available housing, pinned up notices, and scanned bulletin boards. Smitty needed a blue Apartments to Share card. He didn't see any around. What he did see was an attractive girl giving him a very attractive smile. He even saw his fingers combing through her bright red hair. Yet Smitty knew himself too well to think he would come up with a clever line until it was too late. Instead of trying, he merely asked, "You know where the blue cards are?"

The girl's face broke into an even broader smile. Smitty congratulated himself while she stretched across the counter to get him a card. As he filled it out, she watched. When he finished, she held out her hand for the card, read it, nodded, and ripped it in two. "I'll take it."

For what seemed like the thousandth time since he'd arrived at Berkeley, Smitty said to himself, 'Unbelievable!'

*****

Straughton sat at the counter of Rob's Cosmic Organic Fried Chicken ignoring his bartered lunch. He had just received some very bad news. To add insult to injury, he had received it from a television news bulletin. There were few things in the world he detested more than TV's blow-dried newscasters. It was not their phony cheerfulness that put him off. It was the transparency of this phoniness. They were so incredibly bad at it, rank amateurs. If, instead of being in a TV studio, these charm school honor grads were out on the street with Straughton trying to con the public, they would surely starve to death. Their only hope would be landing in jail for the prison chow. Yet this time the message bothered him even more than the messenger.

For a week now he had been writing the Eldridge Cleaver interview in his head. It was almost ready to put down on paper. He knew all the questions he would ask, and just about all the answers Cleaver would supposedly supply. Still, Straughton was no egomaniac. If Cleaver came up with better answers, he would gladly substitute them. Little chance of that, considering the previous interview. No reader would have believed that the brilliant author of Soul On Ice could have come off so completely illiterate. Straughton had had no choice but to substitute his own answers. Still, no one was more satisfied with the published interview than Cleaver himself. Straughton tried to remember where he had put Cleaver's handwritten thank you note. He hoped he hadn't lost it. Those words he could make out were very complimentary. Still, a man of Cleaver's stature should really hire someone to compose his notes, or, at the very least, to proofread them.

There were things Cleaver could do. When it came to brains, he had proven himself at least a match for the cops. Not only had he evaded them and their murder indictment, he had managed to flee the country. Eldridge Cleaver was now in Cuba seeking political asylum. Though Straughton saw nothing wrong with putting a few words in peoples' mouths, words they surely would have spoken themselves if they possessed his eloquence, he drew the line at publishing an interview that had never even taken place. If brought to light, it might be judged by some unethical. What a pity. The New York Review of Books would lick the bottom of his shoes for a Cleaver puff piece. Here he had one, already half written, but unless—'

"Whatever you're thinking, stop. Smoke's coming out of your ears." It was Rob, now standing on the other side of the counter.

"Obvious, is it?" asked Straughton.

71

Rob nodded. "My smoke alarm's battery must be dead."

"I was thinking how I might get Moe to pay for a plane ticket to Cuba."

"That explains the smoke."

"Surely there's a way."

"He wouldn't cover a bus trip to Oakland."

"I have to get to Cuba."

"You can't, not from the States…not unless you get hijacked." Rob thought this over. "Which is not a bad bet lately, no matter what your ticket says."

"I prefer a more direct route."

"Get to Miami and wait. Cuba'll come to you."

"Eldridge Cleaver won't, and I intend to interview him."

"The man's an idiot."

"The man wrote Soul On Ice," Straughton replied.

"I've talked to that moron. He couldn't spell cat."

"Cleaver is as much the author of Soul On Ice as John F. Kennedy was the author of Profiles in Courage."

"Which means they both paid somebody else to do the job."

Straughton found absolutely nothing wrong with this. "Kennedy could afford to pay, and won a Pulitzer Prize. Cleaver probably got some leftwing Jewish slut to do it for free."

The epithet irritated Rob. Still, he let it go. 'The pompous dandy,' was more of a snob than a true bigot, his remark too offhanded to be meant as an insult. Besides, Straughton was probably right. Hell, the book was probably the "Jewish slut's" idea. It was the Black Panthers, not Straughton, who were the real Jew hating bigots. "Why make heroes out of those drug dealing thugs?"

Straughton stared incredulously at Rob. "I write for The Berkeley Badger.

'Bulletproof reply,' thought Rob. "When it's Black Panthers vs. the cops, I'm with the cops every time."

"Rob, My Man, you were not with the cops when they were clubbing you in Selma, Alabama."

"And my black brothers have been making me regret that ever since."

"My Friend, you seem to be taking things a little too personally. Are you sure you're smoking enough grass?"

"Not nearly as much as I used to…with a kid around the house."

Straughton reached into his jacket pocket and offered Rob the remains of a Baggie, enough for a few joints. "Panama Red."

Rob examined the grass. "Is it good?"

"Dynamite!"

Rob slipped it into his pocket. Embarrassed about the emotion he had shown, he tried to justify it by saying, "Instead of making heroes out of thugs like Cleaver and Farrakhan, why don't you write about the anti-Israel Arabs bankrolling them?"

Straughton looked at Rob as if he were a Martian. "My Man, The New York Times and The Washington Post won't touch that. You expect The Badger to?'

*****

Smitty awoke to find himself sharing his bed with— hell, he didn't even know her name. 'Unbelievable!' Was it always this easy in Berkeley?

The closer they had gotten to his apartment, the more attractive she had seemed. With the roommate arrangement settled, it was time to work on the bedmate arrangement. He had never been much of a talker. Listening came naturally to him. He would wait, watch for a woman's eyes to light up. Then he'd start using his hands. Of course, if necessary, he was always willing to go hands first. This time the girl's eyes had been lit up from the start. She wanted him. It was obvious. Still, walking to his place, he couldn't make himself believe his search for a roommate/bedmate was to end so easily. The ice seemed broken to bits, yet he wanted a warm puddle just to be sure. "Why don't we stop for a beer?"

"Sure," she replied with a smile.

They found a rathskeller that reminded Smitty of one of the better bars at Ohio State — except that it was practically empty and dead quiet. Apparently, at Berkeley, beer was "out". Just as they sat down, Dylan's My Back Pages came on the juke box. The girl said excitedly, "Oh", and began fumbling in her purse. "I have the lyrics to that song." She pulled out a paperback on rock poetry and handed it to Smitty. He had always liked the song, but at the moment, his overwhelming interest was in the girl who had handed him the book. Smitty dutifully read the first few lines. They contained a lot of the pretentious bullshit that Dylan was so adept at getting away with, more than Smitty had ever noticed by just hearing the lyrics sung.

"Don't you love that song?" she asked.

Smitty still liked the song, especially the idea behind it. He felt no need to lie, any more than he felt a need to be completely frank. "One of his best."

Just then, to Smitty's relief, a college age waitress came over to cut the conversation short. "Would you like a menu?" she asked the girl.

"Nothing for me." She pointed to Smitty. "He wants a beer."

"You don't want anything?" Smitty asked.

"No, I've got a lid of grass in my purse for our place."

Smitty's shot a glance towards the waitress. She hadn't batted an eye. "Sorry, guess we don't want anything."

The waitress shrugged. "Hey, do your thing."

They moved their "thing" to his apartment at a fast walk. On the way, Smitty wondered if they would share the bed, or would he have to give up the bedroom and take the front room for himself. He wondered whether to ask her to sign the lease. He wondered about the light in her eyes, getting brighter with every step. Most of all, he wondered if he was really going to get laid so easily. Before he knew any of the other answers, they were comfortably stoned, in his bed, and had answered the last question.

Now, lying next to her, refreshed by more than just a night's sleep, Smitty congratulated himself on the quick seduction. She was one fine looking fox. There was something slightly askew in the way her face was put together, but her body was perfect. More important, even if she wasn't sane, she could pass. Most important, what a relief it was having someone to split the rent. Only one question bothered Smitty — what exactly did she expect of him? Sure, the sex had been fine. Still, he worried that she was more into him than he was into her. Of course that's the way it went, women taking these things more seriously. Yet here he was in Berkeley, where you could apparently get a woman any time you wanted without even trying. Smitty had no real desire to be tied down, not for a while. Then again, neither did he want to be tied down to this apartment without her. An open relationship seemed the answer. He would have to make certain there was no misunderstanding between them.

Though more than a few women had found Smitty attractive and approachable, there had sometimes been problems after the approach. Smitty had never been too talented at preventing misunderstandings with the opposite sex. Not much of a talker in general, he was even less of one with women. Still, Smitty had often been told that he was someone they could talk to, to being the appropriate word. These women hadn't seemed to notice that they were the ones doing all the talking. More observant women had told him he was a good listener. Really observant women, and they were rare, would catch him looking as if he were listening even when he wasn't, which he did more frequently than even they realized. Fortunately, some women were intrigued by his silence, even projecting an aura of mystery around it. Others however assumed he was merely slow witted. In fact, some of the slower witted ones had assumed he was retarded. Smitty was not very successful combating these false impressions. This being quite understandable, in light of the fact that the false impressions stemmed from his silence in the first place.

Smitty got along best with women who verified their assumptions. If he had an understanding with a woman, it was because she had made a suggestion and he had shrugged agreeably or said, "Okay." Now, as Smitty lay in bed thinking how to establish an understanding with his new roommate, he was naturally going over the different suggestions she might make and deciding whether or not to agree to them.

The girl lay next to him on her back, a contented smile on her face. Smitty liked the looks of it. As long as it was there, he wouldn't wake her. Her eyes cracked open a tiny bit, and she turned her head towards him. She immediately closed them again, but had seen enough to now reach out and place her hand on his stomach. Smitty said, "Can I ask you a personal question?"

Eyes still shut, she nodded Yes.

"What's your name?"

She gave out a short convulsive laugh. Her eyes opened wide. She grabbed enough of Smitty's side to tickle and cause pain at the same time. Just as he reached out to her, she bolted to a sitting position. "What time is it?"

"Eight-twenty," said Smitty, leaning away from her.

She collapsed back down. "Plenty of time."

It was a good long moment before Smitty asked, "For what?"

"What?" she asked.

"'Plenty of time' for what?"

"Oh, to meet my old man at the airport."

Smitty felt suddenly uneasy. Meeting the father was always awkward. Maybe he should try to put this off. "What's he like?"

"He's cool," she replied.

"What are you gonna tell him about us?"

"Not a damn thing."

This suited Smitty fine.

She mistook his silence for anger. "You're not pissed-off, are you?"

He certainly wasn't, but the question had him searching for a reason he might be. He found one — her "old man" just might not be her father.

She rolled over on her side to face him, wearing a mischievous grin. "C'mon, don't be mad."

Smitty didn't feel mad. How could he, at least not until he figured out what was going on?

Interpreting his silence as anger, she slithered out from the sheets and rose to her knees.

Smitty, looking up at and mesmerized by her naked body, could not have been sorry if he wanted. At the moment, all his feelings were in the vicinity of his groin.

She leaned forward and over him until her palms were massaging his chest. "C'mon, don't be angry. I needed a place to crash for the night."

It did not occur to him to say anything.

"You're not angry, are you?"

Admittedly, looking at her breasts, poised to do more than just look, Smitty certainly didn't feel angry. Surprised, confused? Yes. Angry? No. Smitty shook his head.

Her hands moved slowly down his chest, below his stomach. There was a big grin on her face. He had one to match. She straddled him, saying, "Here's goodbye."

Smitty did not get out of bed until she had gone. At a loss about how to feel, he glanced at the three joints she had left him on the night table. Next to them was her forgotten book of rock lyrics. If she returned to get it, he would have to be a good sport and invite her back into his bed for a quickie. No, Smitty did not regret the stunt she had pulled. In fact, the more he thought about it, the more satisfying the experience seemed. Yesterday he'd been a lowly, beaten down foot soldier in the sexual revolution, buried anonymously within the ranks, slogging endless distances between victories. This morning, lying in bed, he felt himself at the forefront, having singlehandedly led a charge. He'd come a long way, longer than the distance between Cleveland and Berkeley. Last night, how could that be something to regret? Hell, it wasn't so long ago that he was dry humping and grateful. Thank God the Sixties had banished that messy, sticky scourge from the face of the earth. 'So this is how it goes in Berkeley?' Smitty told himself, glad to be there. Yet — 'Wonder what her name was'.

*****

"You're lookin' good. Who stepped on yah?"

Sloan ignored Rob's greeting. His head was killing him. It felt as if someone had split his skull down the middle with a meat cleaver, graciously leaving him the embedded cleaver as a souvenir. At least he wasn't nauseous any more. No telling how long that would last. He knew he had better get some food down while he could. That was one of the reasons he had come. The other was to return the keys to Rob's bungalow or tool shack or whatever it was.

Rob fended off the keys. He knew if Sloan went back to his own place, he'd head straight for his stash. "Stay a few more days. Do you good."

"I ran out of laundry.'

Rob reached into his pocket and offered two twenties. "Buy some more clothes."

Sloan shook his head. "I'll be all right."

Rob could see that he wouldn't. "C'mon, Man. A few more days."

This was not helping Sloan's headache. His tone showed it. "Don't mother me!"

Rob took the keys and a step backwards. "Boy, you really know how to hurt a mother."

Regretting his tone, Sloan said, "Well, mother me with some scrambled eggs."

"Coming right up, My Pride and Joy." Rob was not much of a nursemaid with his own kid. He sure didn't have the patience to nursemaid a junkie, even if he thought that that would do any good. No, no matter what Rob said or did, his friend would be completely wasted the next time he saw him. If Sloan were ever going to get straight, he would do it by himself. From the look of him now, he was headed in the other direction, fast. Rob went to make the eggs.

Sloan knew he wasn't fooling Rob. He wasn't trying to. Being "all right" didn't necessarily mean staying straight, certainly not in Berkeley. He wasn't trying to fool himself either. Sloan knew he was going to his place to get wrecked. Enough of the straight life for a while, maybe a long while. If the straight life was what he had been leading the last few days, he would not miss it, not in the least.

"Are you right with Jesus, Friend?"

The question came from Sloan's left, and it wasn't just the question that bothered him. Sloan prided himself as someone who could take care of himself. To take care of yourself, you had to be aware of everything around you. That's what got him back from Nam in one piece. Being ripped could be an excuse. Yet he wasn't ripped, hadn't been for days, and here someone had sat down right next to him and he hadn't even noticed. And it wasn't only that. The question he had been asked didn't just tell him that it had come from someone recruiting for some Jesus cult. It told Sloan that he looked like a good candidate for a cult — alone, confused, weak, and susceptible to indoctrination. He had been approached by Jesus freaks before, but never when he was straight. This said it all about his appearance. No sentence spoken could have been more insulting. And he now heard that sentence being repeated.

"Are you right with Jesus, Friend?"

A very angry Sloan turned to his left to see one muscular, confident cult recruiter. His appearance made Sloan even angrier. "Are you right with a broken jaw?"

The Jesus freak said calmly, "You do not want to try that, Friend."

Sloan almost replied, "Yes I do," but he knew this was a lie.

Did he still have the strength, or more important, the toughness to handle this scavenger? One thing for sure, he didn't have the stomach to try, not right then. Sloan forced away this uncomfortable realization by asking himself if the vulture eyeing his soon to be corpse was one of the con men running the cult, or one of their drones? Leaning towards the former, he chose to believe the latter — a zombie deserving pity more than a beating. And what did he himself deserve? How pathetic he must look. Sloan tried to salvage some face. "You wouldn't turn the other cheek, Friend?"

"I'd do the Lord's work, Friend."

Sloan realized the conversation was going nowhere, but his wounded ego egged him on. "And that's not turning the other cheek?"

"Friend, that's helping you give your soul to Jesus Christ."

"I gave already…to the fucker with horns."

The Jesus freak shook his head and stood. "When the day comes, and you're ready to ask him, Jesus will be waiting to save your soul."

Rob arrived with the scrambled eggs.

The Jesus freak added before leaving, "Jesus loves you, Friend."

Rob said to Sloan, "Congratulations."

Sloan shook his head. "Do I look that pathetic?" Before the words were out of his mouth, he realized who he was asking.

"When's the last time you checked in the mirror?…Who stepped on yah?'"

"I look like cult material?"

"Hate to break it to you…but don't sweat it. You're too anti-social. You'd make history as the first man ever kicked out of a cult."

Thoughts of how he must look stayed with Sloan during the walk to his apartment. He headed straight for the mirror. What he saw stunned him. He did look pathetic, drawn out, and so much older. The sight had him glancing towards his stash, with a strong urge to get fucked up. Yet it had been a long time since drugs made him feel good. Now they did little more than fight off withdrawal. Was it just a lack of guts that kept him using?

Sloan felt his forearm. There was nothing there. He dropped to the floor, just to see how many pushups he could do — twenty, and barely that. 'Pathetic. Pathetic! Pathetic.' He turned on his back and did some sit-ups.

Sloan had felt filthy before. He now felt sweaty and slimy to boot. He could suffer this no longer. Sloan shaved and took a hot shower, then checked the mirror again. A slight improvement. Very slight. Not even thinking about his stash, still looking in the mirror, he gritted his teeth, determined to start working out. Sloan thought about what had set him off. Wouldn't it be something if Jesus had saved him? For the first time in months, a real smile came to face, and he said aloud, sincerely, "Praise the Lord!"

*****

Smitty headed for the Off-Campus Housing Office in an "Ain't it great to be alive?" mood. Before leaving his apartment, he had almost smoked one of the joints his anonymous last night one night stand had left for him. He had to laugh at that, then and now. Why waste the grass? How much higher could he get?

Despite his need for a roommate, Smitty had hesitated going to the housing office at all. Never the type to run the ladies through his bedroom one after the other, he preferred to change his sheets between women. In fact, he usually did a hell of a lot more sheet changing between women than he preferred. Still, he didn't want to make another pick-up at the housing office, not yet. Forget about changing the sheets, he hadn't even made his bed. Smitty was in luck. There were only a few people in the office, only two of them were girls. He had no trouble putting up his blue card and leaving unattached.

Still savoring the previous night, Smitty opened the front door to his apartment building only to come face to face with Screw's winning smile. "Hey man, you bring the dope?"

It took Smitty a moment to take note of the bare feet. "Oh, you're the one who told me about the apartment."

"Screw."

"Yeah, thanks."

"Congratulations, Man. You scored a ringside pad for The Revolution."

"Now I've got to score a roommate to share the rent."

80

"Hey man, we can check out People's Park. I know half the crew."

Smitty wasn't sure he wanted a member of The People's Park "crew" for a roommate. Still, Screw seemed good company, and this was too nice a day to spend holed up in his apartment. "Let's do it. You wanna take my wheels?"

"Man, it's only a few blocks. Let's walk."

It took Screw and Smitty an hour to walk the few blocks to People's Park. Screw's street tour, and it was a good one, didn't slow them down a bit. What did, was the fact that he knew every fifth or sixth person on the way. Screw would introduce everybody to Smitty, and Smitty would stand quietly while Screw traded dope of the verbal variety.

People's Park was like no park Smitty had ever seen. It was one square block in the middle of the city, containing what must have been ninety percent of the world's Frisbees and ninety-nine percent of the world's flying Frisbee dogs. There were plenty of other dogs too. After all, the park was loaded with colorfully dressed hippie couples, and wherever there are hippie couples, there are dogs and small children, usually competing to see who can get the dirtiest the fastest. The grass seemed newly sodded, and a few hippies were planting trees." Smitty asked Screw, "The city just lets you come in and plant trees in the park?"

Screw laughed, "They can't stop us." He kept laughing. "It's The Revolution....We're winning!"

Smitty gave him a skeptical look.

"I mean it," Screw replied. "We built this park, everything here, by ourselves. It was a vacant lot." He led Smitty towards a half dozen hippies sitting on the grass in an approximate circle. They had two joints circulating, both clockwise.

Smitty conceded, "Guess you saved the university some money."

"No, they hate it. They wanted to build an off-campus dorm here." A woman was holding a joint out to the oblivious bongo drummer sitting next to her. Screw, without an introduction, reached down and casually intercepted it. He took a drag.

"And they just forgot about the dorm?" Smitty accepted the joint from Screw, helping himself to a healthy toke before handing it back.

Screw laughed, releasing the smoke before he wanted to. "No! But what can they do?" He took another drag before holding the joint in front of the bongo drummer's lips so the man wouldn't have to miss a beat. When the drummer finished his toke, Screw delivered the joint to the next in line with a friendly nod of thanks, then led Smitty away.

Smitty flinched as a Frisbee bounced off the back of his head. "They can clear this place with a bulldozer and put up anything they want."

"Man, are you serious?" Screw picked up the Frisbee and tossed it back to its owner. "The People wouldn't let 'em." He led Smitty towards a hippie couple, their kids, their dog, and their joint.

"Don't tell me they're scared of you?"

Screw gave the man, about to pass the joint to his woman, a friendly nod and an empty hand. The man passed Screw the joint as if it were the natural thing to do. "Damn right they are. Try to tear down People's Park, and they'll have ten thousand angry rioters to deal with. What are they gonna do, kill us?" He passed the joint to Smitty, who took a drag and handed it back to the hippie with a nod of thanks — apparently the custom in Berkeley.

They approached two passed-out derelicts, one still clutching his empty wine bottle. Screw said, "Gotta hunch these dudes are looking for a pad. Which one should I ask first?"

*****

Unpacking a suitcase he had stored before leaving Berkeley, Straughton was pleasantly surprised to find some tablets — 'Mescaline!' Unsure that he would ever return for the suitcase, he would never have left them on purpose. Mescaline usually took you on a far milder trip than LSD. It would be the perfect pharmaceutical enhancement for a nighttime stroll. Straughton downed one of the pills, thinking, 'Just what the doctor prescribed.'

Mescaline may have been what the doctor prescribed, but these particular tablets were not the mescaline Straughton remembered, not even close. They were supercharged bootleg Dexedrine he had forgotten to flush down the toilet. Speed did not happen to be one of Straughton's chemicals of choice, unless there were no choice and he had to stay awake any way he could.

At two-thirty in the morning, Straughton was still wide, wide awake, and still wondering how a man of his experience could make such an amateurish mistake. Speed has been rumored to turn even mutes into babbling idiots, and Straughton had never been a mute. He had spent the night stalking the non-stop talker's natural quarry, the non-stop listener. Conscious trial and error and unconscious instinct led invariably towards already cornered prey — someone stuck behind a bar, a restaurant counter, or a newsstand cash register. This type of quarry had sustained him much of the night. The rest of it, he spent in deep, one-sided conversations with drunks, junkies, and schizophrenics, more than one of them prone and unconscious on the sidewalk.

A large poster drew Straughton's meandering gaze — "ZEN WORKSHOP". He sensed a conflict of terms, but didn't know enough about Zen to be sure. His ignorance disturbed him more than any conflict of terms. Here he was, living in The Round-Eyed Capital of Zen, and he had yet to write an article on the subject. Straughton read on — "Expanding the Horizons of Consciousness Without the Use of Chemicals". Well that was a different story, or, in this case, article. Straughton did not doubt that Zen could expand one's mind. Yet he was skeptical it could equal the effortlessness and effectiveness of the appropriate chemicals, colorful little pills which accomplished their magic without any boring lectures, baffling vocabulary, or airy-fairy philosophizing. Drugs being so accessible, their avoidance seemed nothing more than an artificial restraint, comparable to pleasuring oneself left-handed. His interest already dulled, Straughton then noticed that the dates for the workshop were in the previous month. This surely settled the matter.

Straughton turned away to find himself face to face with a rather ragged street person. He flinched.

The street person didn't seem to notice, giving Straughton a friendly nod before asking, "Hey Man, you know where I can get some beer or liquor…See, I swallowed this candy wrapper by accident. And when I put my hand down my throat to get it, I ripped out my tonsils by mistake." He stretched his mouth wide open so Straughton could survey the damage.

It was too dark for Straughton to see past the teeth, but the smell emanating from behind them did indicate some sort of problem, one that he in no way felt qualified to solve. Of course this did not stop him from offering the harmless suggestion, "Try washing the wrapper down with a glass of water."

The street person turned his head away to gauge Straughton out of the corner of one eye. He then turned back, leaned forward, and in a whisper asked, "You haven't heard?"

Straughton knew that chances were that he had heard. Yet he wasn't exactly pressed for time. He shook his head while taking a step back.

The street person of course took another step forward before whispering, "The fascists are diluting Berkeley's water supply."

Straughton was surprised that, No, he hadn't heard that. His source was not exactly unimpeachable, yet his best ones seldom were. He attempted another step backwards to find himself pinned to a wall.

His new source added in an even lower whisper, "Hundreds of us have already died from dehydration. The morgues are overflowing."

Straughton had no idea where this conversation was headed, and had lost all interest in finding out. "I better check on that." With some difficulty, he squeezed himself free. Already moving at a quick walk, he decided, 'Quite enough skitzos for one night.'

He decided to continue his search within the safer confines of the university's campus, and to narrow the object of this search to one very specific quarry — the freshman girl. They were known to eagerly lap up hours of ridiculous blather, especially from the mouth of someone older than a freshman boy. The plan was to bribe one with breakfast. Straughton was not the least bit hungry. He just wanted something in his stomach heavy enough to sop up half a bottle of wine. That mixture would slow him down enough to at least get into bed. And if the freshman girl proved willing to join him, all the better. At the very least, she would keep him occupied until he got to sleep. Then again, with a girl in his bed, he could forego the sleep. Straughton now found himself humming All You Need Is Love.

The beautiful thing about freshman girls was the ease with which you could satisfy them. Penetration alone was often enough. Woman with a few years of college became judgmental. Sleeping with them the first time was like undergoing a job interview. Sex shouldn't be like that. Straughton pondered this, deciding that the cause was mere jealousy. Women resented the fact that men enjoyed sex so much more than they did. And they blamed men too. Unjustly. After all, the cause must be biological and rooted in the survival of the species. How, he wondered. Suddenly, the answer struck him like a bolt of lightning right between his ears. When it came to sex, women usually held the veto power. If they enjoyed sex as much as men, women would rarely employ that veto power. Hunting would lessen, and gathering would decline precipitously. Much of the time previously devoted to child rearing would be spent child ignoring. Obviously, this could lead the decimation of the human race, even its possible extinction. The blinding brilliance of this revelation flabbergasted Straughton. Perhaps there was a book here. He really should write all this down, go over it when he was straight. In any case, he should devote more of his time to intellectual pursuits. The fact that he didn't was a sinful squandering of God's gifts. It bordered on criminal. The only thing that kept Straughton from now putting pen to paper was the more immediate task of finding a freshman girl.

Yet reality alone was proving quite enough to thwart that plan. Straughton pressed on regardless. He seemed to be the only living thing wandering around campus. Finally, just before dawn, it dawned upon him that five o'clock in the morning was not exactly the pickup hour. If he really wanted to down that wine, eating alone looked like his only option. Perhaps he could stall-off this defeat with a small snack. Straughton meandered his way to the nearest Honor Apple stand. Despite looking around and spying no one, he performed his entire Honor Apple pantomime. Straughton dug deep into his pocket as if searching for coins, withdrew his empty hand and looked at it as if to check whether the coin he did not hold was a dime. He then dropped this imaginary dime in the Honor Apple coin box. Only two apples remained — large, green Pippins. Straughton took one with a smile, and eagerly dug his teeth into it. Instead of cool, crisp Pippin, he found himself choking on soft, sour mush, yet not for long. Reflexively, he spewed this mess a surprising distance. Sure enough, a close examination of what remained, revealed the apple to be thoroughly rotten beneath its shiny peel. Straughton felt more indignant about the rip-off than nauseous from the taste. If you couldn't trust an Honor Apple, what could you trust? He placed it carefully back on the table, bite side down, then reached for its mate. This time Straughton examined the apple carefully before digging his teeth into it. His care was rewarded by a loud crunch and a delicious burst of flavor.

Hearing footsteps, he turned to see a young man headed straight for him carrying a produce crate on his shoulder. Straughton stepped back to give him room. The man greeted him with a perfunctory, "Good morning," that said, "Whatever kind of morning it is, it's not good enough to put me in a good mood." He laid the produce crate on the Honor Apple table.

Straughton, mouth full of apple, returned the greeting with a friendly nod. He marked the man for a hopelessly straight graduate student. His clothes were pure discount store, and the shirt was a bad example of even that. Straughton would have pegged him for an engineering student, but he did not sport a plastic pocket protector and there were only one pen and one pencil in his shirt pocket. He watched him unload half the crate of apples onto the stand, then unlock the coin box.

"So you, My Man, are the proprietor."

The proprietor displayed the contents in his open hand — less than two dollars in dimes, plus a few pennies. "The thieving bastards. Half the assholes didn't pay."

"How low can mankind sink?" Straughton commiserated.

Angrily pocketing the change, he said, "Lower than a snake's dick."

Straughton looked the man over with a sense of accomplishment, as if this "find" had filled in another piece in that mosaic often referred to as "Life". A heretofore faceless part of this giant university machine now finally had a face. And here Straughton was, face to face with the face of Berkeley's Johnny Honor Appleseed. His reporter's antennae began to twitch. "How exactly, my man, does the concession work?"

"Who says it works?" was the reply.

"It works for me," Straughton replied, taking another large, loud bite from his apple.

"Like any campus job. If you have the grades, you ask to be put on the waiting list. I waited a year."

"You're a grad student?"

He nodded. "Engineering."

'Ah, poor peasant,' thought Straughton, 'can't even afford a pocket protector.' The scent of a story was in the air, a human interest angle. "What exactly does this job entail?"

"Simple. They drop off five crates of apples by 4:00am. There are ten Honor Apple stands. I fill them and pick up the money every morning."

"One would think The Powers That Be could provide you a cart...so you can re-supply in one round."

"They did, but after the third one got stolen, they said it was the last."

Straughton could easily understand lifting an occasional apple, but hijacking the Honor Apple cart seemed absolutely felonious. "The depths people will sink to....Yet you can leave the money overnight, and nobody tries to steal it?"

"The junkies used to, but they learned."

"Learned what?"

"Would you waste your time breaking into one of these cash boxes for less than two dollars?"

Straughton shook his head. Nor would he cart around apples for that sum either. "You find this concession worthwhile?"

"Hell, no. I've got to pay for the apples out of this money. And I buy the best, Pippins!"

One of the characteristics that made Straughton such a successful reporter was empathy. He could turn it on in an instant. Little matter it seemed always to turn itself off before leading to any charitable or even considerate actions. Empathy imbued his stories with relevant points of view. Right now he was able to put himself in the shoes of this star crossed capitalist. "One would not think such a crime would prove so prevalent in Berkeley."

"Yeah, peace, love, and steal my apples. Apples to The People!"

Straughton's empathetic talents allowed him to just as easily place himself in the shoes of the thief. "Then again, you are a monopoly."

The vendor gave Straughton an angry stare. He sure didn't feel like a monopolist. "Yeah, stop me before I enslave the world."

Straughton slipped nimbly back into the vendor's shoes, using a more sympathetic tone. "Well, as my uncle always says, "The first million is always the most difficult. After that, things go quicker."

The vendor, suspicious that he was being toyed with, attempted to read Straughton's face. His attempt failed.

Continuing in his sympathetic tone, Straughton asked, "Why don't you quit?"

"I'm thinking about it, but I just started. If even two thirds of the people paid, it'd be worth it. Besides, there's a waiting list."

Straughton missed the logic. "My man, there's a waiting list for the gas chamber at San Quentin. Have you considered signing up for that?"

"I mean, if people are on a list waiting to do something, you'd think it would be worth doing, wouldn't you?"

Straughton shook his head. 'Obviously not.'

Though no one was within sight, the grad student whispered, "You know what I think about sometimes?" He pointed. "I think about hiding over there in the bushes with some binoculars and a baseball bat. Then, when I'd catch someone copping an apple, just as he takes a bite, I'd sneak up and coldcock him with the bat. And while he's lying unconscious on the pavement, bleeding, I'd pick up the apple, stuff it back into his mouth, then use the bat to make applesauce."

For some reason, Straughton again found himself in the shoes of the thief, lying toothless and bleeding on the pavement, his mouth stuffed with applesauce. Surely such vicious retaliation would be a disproportionate response to the liberation of one little apple. And Straughton had never been crazy about applesauce either. In a calming tone, he said, "Violence is never the answer." At the same time, Straughton assured himself that his own thoroughly professional modus operandi was beyond detection. With this realization, came another one. His eyes lit up. "I write for The Badger, and that would make a dynamite story....I'll wait in the bushes with you."

The grad student took a step backwards. "What about the cops?"

Straughton straightened with indignation. "You are not implying that I would fail to protect my sources?"

"Without pointing the finger at me, where the hell is your

story?"

The apple vending monopolist had a point, of which Straughton knew he should have been aware. Still, he was not ready to give up on this front page article. "We could wait for a cop or a university administrator to steal one. That would make you The People's Hero."

"I don't want to be a hero. I want these thieving bastards to pay for my apples."

Straughton studied the grad student. "My Good Man, I will write an article about you anyway, one that will make people think twice, even three times before stealing Honor Apples."

The graduate student's face lit up. He even smiled. "I'd appreciate that." He offered his hand. They shook and exchanged names.

Straughton watched him lift the now half-full apple crate onto his shoulder. "If you change your mind, let me know. I can probably supply the bat."

The grad student replied, less than convincingly, "I'll think it over."

Straughton watched him take off towards the next Honor Apple stand, a lone, noble silhouette striding into the rising sun. This sight gave Straughton a warm feeling, knowing that he had the power to make a difference, to do some good, to help out this deserving, hard working young man. It also gave him an appetite. This time, instead of his standard pantomime of searching in his pocket, he searched both pockets for that imaginary coin before pretending to drop it into the slot.

*****

Sloan saw a distorted reflection of himself in the puddle of sweat beneath his face. This was good, the sweat. It proved, far more than the count, that he was accomplishing something. Sloan drove himself on, wringing pushup after pushup from his aching arms. The early easy pushups meant nothing. There was no gain in them. It was the agonizing ones at the end that counted. They were the ones that rebuilt muscle. He struggled to straighten his trembling arms, to squeeze out one more. Sloan succeeded. Immediately, his arms collapsed beneath him. He jerked his head to the side, landing flat on his cheek in the puddle of sweat. The pain of exhaustion masked the agony of withdrawal.

The drudgery of washing dishes straight was debilitating. Yet thoughts of getting a decent job, and the decent apartment that would come with it, were always short-lived. No way could he stomach that human obstacle course called job hunting. The few people he was now dealing with were a few too many. Even walking down the sidewalk was an irritating hassle, keeping himself from seeing the faces a losing battle. And he hated people looking at him. It was a relief getting back to his ugly, stinking little broom closet of an apartment, especially that moment he would close, then latch the door behind him. Safe at last. Then he would glance around the room and his relief would ebb.

Sloan still hadn't thrown away his stash. Temptation that it was, he would spend more time thinking and worrying about dope if he knew it wasn't handy in case he had to have it. One thing he wanted to avoid at all costs was wandering the city strung-out and searching desperately for a score. Then the monkey wouldn't be on his back. The gorilla would be dragging him down the street by his nose. No, in Berkeley, dope was always close enough. His stash might as well be five feet away. Every time he felt driven to break into it, he would start working out, a half dozen times a day. The exhaustion, and the slight high that came with it, would save him.

Sloan pushed himself off the floor and headed for the shower. Shaving, he could see the change in his face. Yes, he was getting somewhere. After a shower, he pulled on a T-shirt. It was a little tight. Working out was showing its effects. Sloan looked in the mirror to comb his hair. Again he noticed improvement. Nothing spectacular, but surely enough to keep the cults away. He smiled at the thought, remembering that zombie herding vulture who had tried to recruit him, and also that gaunt, pathetic zombie who had attracted him, the one he had seen in the mirror when he had gotten home. 'It's true: Jesus saves.'

Sloan exited the bathroom feeling fitter and stronger than he had in months. The sight of his abode quickly deflated him. It was time to add something new to his routine. Man cannot live by washing dishes and working out alone. 'A woman would be nice.' Yet a woman could be complicated. 'Better wait.' What then could he add to his monastic routine? 'Some music would be great.' He didn't even have a radio, had hocked it. A good stereo was more money than he could scrape up. 'A book?' Sloan had become much less of a reader over the years. Writers were such jack-off artists. Decent books so few and far between. And people recommended such crap. Starting a book was a sucker's bet. Then again, the stakes were low — a few minutes time. And time was something he had plenty of, something he wanted to pass. Sloan pondered hard. Hell, he'd go upstairs and see if Screw had a book.

Sloan really didn't care to talk to anybody, not even Screw. Still, if he did have to talk to someone, Screw would be his choice. He knocked without enthusiasm. Stumbling noises came from within. Screw flung open the door — a broad smile on his face, half a joint in his hand, and a cloud of marijuana smoke behind him. "Hey Man, you bring the dope?"

Sloan tried to keep from smiling, but the sight of Screw was too much. "Never touch the stuff....You got a book I can borrow?"

"Sure, Man," Screw was pleased to reply. "There was one in the apartment when I moved in." He led Sloan inside. "Where the hell did I put it?" Screw began looking around and under things.

Sloan was less than confident Screw would find the book any time soon. "What's it about?"

"Massage. It's a do-it-yourself massage book."

To Sloan, the idea seemed more than odd. It seemed perverted. "Do-it-yourself massage?"

"I mean do-it-yourself to another person. It explains how. Photos and everything."

The book now seemed less perverted to Sloan. Still, considering the state of his love life, it could not have been more useless. "Forget it."

"It's got some bitchin' women in it...nude, full-frontal."

"Just looking don't do me any good....The opposite, in fact."

"Where the hell is it?"

Sloan headed for the door, asking, "You haven't got anything else?"

"Naw, that's my whole library so far. If you see a good bookshelf in the trash, let me know."

"Depend on me," Sloan replied, already halfway out the door.

About to take a drag from his joint, Screw stopped and asked, "Hey, you want a toke?"

Sloan did and he didn't. He wasn't afraid a few tokes would lead him back to his stash, but he didn't want to lie around his depressing apartment stoned. "Not right now."

"Hey, you been working out?"

Almost by reflex, Sloan tightened up his stomach muscles. "Some."

"It shows....Man, you weren't lookin' too good for a while."

"That's what my 'Mirror, Mirror on the wall' said." Sloan turned and was about to close the door behind him.

"Your mirror wasn't bullshitting." Screw got a brainstorm. "Hey! I know somebody with shelves of books...three or four of 'em!" Screw was already following Sloan out the door. "Smitty, you know him?"

"Not really."

"I'll get a book for you."

"Naw, forget it."

"Man, Smitty's a good guy."

Sloan was not in the mood to deal with anybody else. "Forget it."

Screw, already knocking, noticed Sloan still walking. "Hold on a minute."

Sloan felt as if he were being introduced to a blind date, and it was too late to disappear.

Smitty opened the door wearing his poker face, wondering if the guy with Screw was the junkie from downstairs. He looked halfway recovered if he was.

Screw said, "Smitty, Sloan here is a friend of mine. He lives under the stairs. You got a good book he could borrow?"

Sloan thought, 'That fits — the thing that lives under the stairs.'

Smitty nodded to Sloan, asking, "Fiction?"

Sloan, uncomfortable, gave a nod.

Smitty held up his finger and turned away. He would have asked them in, but displaying his stereo to a junkie was sort of like throwing it out the window. He didn't see much chance of ever getting his book back either, but it wasn't exactly a Gutenberg Bible. A buck or two would buy him another one. And from then on the junkie would avoid him, which would be well worth the buck or two. Smitty had learned that trick in high school, by accident. There was this handshaking epidemic. Smitty couldn't stand it. The worst offender, a guy he hardly knew, would insist on shaking hands every time they passed in the halls. Once he hit Smitty for a two dollar loan. Smitty never saw him again, except from a distance. The best two dollars he had ever spent. Now here he was bidding good riddance to this junkie for the price of a beat up paperback. The only problem was, this book would need replacing. Smitty liked to turn people on to good books and music the way others liked to turn them on to dope. He'd picked a short one, giving the junkie a fair chance at finishing it. Handing it over, he said, "A good read."

"Thanks,' said Sloan, barely glancing at the cover. He didn't read the title until he was already lying down in bed — The Loneliness of a Long Distance Runner, by Alan Sillotoe. 'The Loneliness of a Long Distance Runner? What the fuck is this?' That guy Smitty didn't seem like someone that would give him a book about loneliness or slop like that. And what the hell did loneliness have to do with running?

Sloan turned the book over and found to his further displeasure that it was set in England. He had spent two months in Europe after his sophomore year, and three weeks of that time working odd jobs in England. If there was ever a country he wanted to get out of, it was England, worse than Vietnam and this despite the fact that everyone spoke English. It wasn't just the food, which was shit even before you ate it. Or the weather, which supposedly was relatively good while he was there. In fact, the food and weather were very minor irritants compared to the people. Sloan had had no idea there were such two-faced, bellyaching phonies on the face of the earth. When Tommy was talking to you, it was behind Johnny's back. And when Johnny was talking to you, it was behind Tommy's back. And when Johnny and Tommy were talking, you could bet your ass, just like your ass, it was behind your back. And the quiet ones, they really made him nervous, looking so depressed and desperate, as if contemplating suicide, or murder, or worse yet, some perversion. The bitching and moaning about every little thing, it was enough to drive you to drink, which, as matter of fact, was what most of those sorry fuckers lived for.

Thinking about his time in Jolly Old England was not the best preparation for getting into a book about that over civilized slum. Still, Sloan was not the type to give up easily. He started leafing through the pages. To his further displeasure, which would have seemed impossible a moment earlier, Sloan noticed that The Loneliness of a Long Distance Runner was not a novel, but a long short story among other short stories. Of all the novels he had read, the ones he considered worth reading were few and far between. Yet of all the short stories he had ever been forced to read, not one, except To Build a Fire, had ever stayed with him. Novelists, though jack-off artists, sometimes tried to write novels. Short story writers were only interested in showing off their precious writing. At the moment, Sloan did not have the patience for preciousness. "Preciousness?" Sloan asked himself aloud. 'Where'd that word come from?' Was this what it was like being straight? He tried, but could not remember. Sloan felt weird, as if a stranger had snuck into his head, a stranger with plans to take over. He wanted to stop thinking, to be doing something else instead. Yet he was in no mood to read some precious short story. Again the word precious made him squirm. It was not one he would use in speech, even sarcastically. Why did it keep creeping into his thoughts? If he couldn't control his mind, he damn well better occupy it. This before it turned back to dope. Sloan was faced with a choice. Read the fucking short story, or, for the seventh time that day, work out. He mulled his choice, knowing damn well what it would be. Tired of stalling, Sloan stripped down to his underwear and took the pushup position.

*****

'This ain't gonna work,' Smitty told himself. He had been returning to the housing office two or three times a day for three days straight now. The routine had gotten to be second nature. First he would check the board to see that his blue card was visible, then he would go to the counter where he had picked up the redhead. If there was a girl there, or one came along, he'd hit her with his best line — "Do you know where the blue cards are?" Some of the girls would, some wouldn't, and he couldn't have cared less. The problem was, that despite the fact that he was in Berkeley, none of the girls dragged him home offering to be his roommate.

'This ain't gonna work,' he repeated. 'Give up.' Smitty decided to leave and not come back. Just then, a quite attractive women walked right up and looked him in the eye. Though vaguely familiar, he was positive he didn't know her. She flashed him an assured, sexy smile. Smitty caught some irony in it, but that made it all the sexier. "Do you work here?" she asked.

'Unbelievable,' thought Smitty. 'Lightening strikes twice.' A bashful smile came to his face as he shook his head.

"Really?" she replied. "I do, and you're putting in more hours here than I am." Her smile hardened as Smitty's faded. "In case you misread the sign outside, this is the Off-Campus Housing Office…not off-campus housing."

*****

Straughton arrived at the demonstration before there was a demonstration. He wanted to see who was pulling the strings. If he could get a feel for what it was really about, he'd have a good idea how far it would go and in what direction. In Berkeley, any demonstration that didn't build into a riot hadn't gone far enough, in fact, hadn't gone anywhere. This demonstration had potential. Timothy Leary, the guru poster boy and eloquent advocate of the LSD Un-Revolution — "Turn on, tune in, drop out" — had been sentenced to ten years in a federal prison for possession of two marijuana cigarettes, or as Straughton mellifluously put into prose, "five years in the joint per joint". The acid heads of the world, or at a minimum their Berkeley branch, refused to stand idly by for such blatant persecution. Who could blame them? Jesus Christ, in the form of Timothy Leary, had returned to earth to save mankind, or at the very least take mankind on a little trip. Now he was being crucified all over again.

Straughton smiled as he spotted Marco, Berkeley's number one radical rouser. Marco the Red just happened to have been Straughton's freshman roommate. He would have a good, long talk with Marco, but not right now. This particular demonstration was the freaks' show, not the radicals'. In fact, Marco was at the bottom of the stairs and off to one side, surrounded by no more than a dozen of his flunkies. He would probably be asked to speak, but only because of the symbiotic relationship between the freaks and radicals. They needed each other, and to some extent were each other. Nearly all the radicals were dopers, and nearly all the dopers were radicals. Of course, both sub-sets ran the gamut from committed to momentary. The more committed they were, the less use they had for their counterparts. The serious dopers possessed neither the inclination, focus, nor motor functions required to be effective radicals. Why bust their asses trying to change the world? It was too easy to just do some dope and change the way one experienced the world. Unfortunately for the radicals, the freaks in their numbers were essential for any successful demonstration. More unfortunately for the radicals, a hostile or bored cameraman could embarrass the cause by zooming in on the shenanigans of the more brain-fried of the freaks.

Some less than brain-fried freaks were now setting up a microphone atop the high wide steps of the university's administration building, Sproul Hall. Two huge speakers were already in place, ten yards to each side of the microphone. There was the usual confusion, people running around, barking orders to others, who in turn would run around until they had found someone else to bark at, then report back to whoever had barked at them in the first place to be barked at again. Standing apart from the barkers, and above them both in steps and in bearing, were three white robed gurus. Their long hair and equally long beards ran together in that unruly face-mop style favored by your typical Time Magazine cover Hindu Holy Man. Two of the gurus moved calmly back and forth as interlocutors between the third and the barkers. To Straughton's keen eye, it was obvious that this third guru to the gurus was the man to interview, the one running the show.

Straughton climbed the steps like a gentleman with an appointment. He headed straight for Guru #1. He almost made it too. Unfortunately, this time, blind, dumb nerve was not quite enough. One step from Guru #1, he found himself pressed up against the suddenly interceding, beatifically smiling Gurus #2 & #3. Guru #1 stared right through him.

Confidently, still chest to chest with Gurus #2 & #3, he looked straight at Guru #1, saying the magic words, "Straughton, with The Berkeley Badger....We would appreciate a few words for attribution."

Guru #1 did not blink. He could have been meditating, eyes wide open.

Guru #2 said, "Baba Rama cannot be disturbed at the moment."

In or out of the line of duty, Straughton rarely took snubs personally. There was no irritation in his tone as he looked past Guru #2 and asked Guru #1. "Baba Rama? Is that one word or two?"

Baba Rama, again, did not bat an eye.

Guru #2 batted both eyes. He also lost his beatific smile. Straughton sensed some clenched teeth in its place. Gently, without pushing him back, Guru #2 had squeezed his open hands between their chests.

Despite their loose robes, Straughton could tell that Gurus #2 & #3 were as muscular as any gurus he had ever come up against — 'No vegetarians, these two.' And there was quite a drop of steep stairs behind him. A roll to the bottom would be long, with many painful bounces along the way. Still, he decided to risk one more try, a polite one. "Gentlemen, I'm writing the article for The Badger. Perhaps there is something you would like me to say?

Baba Rama still didn't bat an eye.

Guru #2 looked back at him, and somehow seemed to pick up a sign. He reached into his robe. From an inside pocket, or something similar, he pulled out a small medicine bottle, and held it up for Straughton to see. There were a dozen purple pills inside.

Straughton was impressed. He reached for the bottle, thinking, 'Here's one guru who actually knows the score.'

Guru #2, before letting go of the bottle, said, "Drop one of these. You'll know exactly what to write."

Straughton skipped down the steps, quite satisfied. On the way, he pondered Guru #2's faint accent. 'Not Indian. Boston? Possibly. No! Brooklyn!'

*****

Smitty could not believe the desolate scene on Telegraph Avenue. All the street vendors had packed up and left, and there were hardly any pedestrians. For some reason, many of the shops were boarded up. The carnival had blown town. Worse yet, it had left behind a silence so eerie, so unnerving, as to plant doubts that it would ever return. The scene was reminiscent of those sci-fi movies in which space aliens had come and gone, leaving not a sole behind. Would the freak show return? Had he transferred universities for nothing? Warily, he scanned the street for clues as to what had happened and what would happen. There were none.

Smitty walked baffled through the ghost town formerly known as Berkeley. He thought he heard something, then was sure of it — the hum of a crowd in the very direction he was headed. The hum grew as he walked, and with it a portentous charge in the air. Something was happening on campus. His steps quickened in anticipation. He had to know what was going on, to see for himself, to be a part of it.

By the time Smitty crossed Bancroft Way, the noise emanating from the crowd was a roar. The two cops usually stationed at the campus gates were missing. Smitty then noticed, twenty yards down the sidewalk, a dozen cops huddled unobtrusively against the fence. Obviously, they did not want their presence to provoke violence.

Inside the gates, all he could see were people, thousands of them. Many were waving flags — Viet Cong, North Vietnamese, Red Chinese, Russian, PLO — none bearing the stars and stripes. Yet the flags were far outnumbered by at least a hundred different placards proclaiming, "Free Timothy Leary", "Acid Is Good", "Turn On, Tune In, Drop Out", "Drop Acid, Not Bombs", and a dozen other slogans, including the requisite, "Make Love, Not War". Smitty wove his way through the throng. The crowd completely covered Sproul Plaza, facing up towards the wide steps of Sproul Hall. A speaker, dressed in the white robe of a Hindu holy man, stood at the top of the stairs between two humongous loudspeakers. Strung above him, a huge banner proclaimed, "FREE TIMOTHY LEARY".

'My first demonstration,' thought Smitty. 'Didn't have to wait long.' Already caught up in the excitement, he scanned the scene for action, especially the kind he had seen on the cover of The Berkeley Badger — naked female action. As of yet, there was none. Still, his heart filled with hope. Smitty couldn't really get a handle on the mood of the crowd, this due to the absence of any single mood. Some of the people were angry and out for blood, shouting slogans such as, "Off the pigs." Outnumbering the shouters were their opposites, just out to have a good time, taking in, or starring in, the freak show. Others seemed zonked out of their minds on various drugs. Still others, not many, stood around awkwardly, unsure what to think or how to react. Smitty himself was a perfect example of this last category.

The present star of his local freak show was a Whirling Dervish, or at least Berkeley's version of one. Smitty couldn't be sure which, being no authority on the real item. This guy wore a turban and something resembling pajamas, both bright orange. His dirty-blond beard made him suspect, a little too Nordic, but pajama-boy could spin like a top, and he could keep spinning, doing so on a pair of bare, dirty feet. The spectators would step back to give him room as he spun around and between them. Smitty was sure he would flop on his ass any second. Yet seconds turned into minutes. The dude had talent. Perhaps not all that useful a talent, yet a talent all the same. The Dervish eventually spun into the crowd and disappeared. He was quickly replaced at the center of local attention by a not so graceful Salome, finger cymbals clicking away. She was doing a take on the Dance of the Seven Veils, already minus four or five. The crowd pretty much ignored her.

Smitty wondered why the speaker wasn't speaking, and why no one was trying to eliminate the loud hum of feedback coming from the microphone. Then it dawned on him that there was no feedback. The speaker was emitting a long, continuous "Oooooooooom". In fact, some in the crowd were "Oooooooooom"ing right back at him. Smitty felt like an idiot for not having realized immediately. 'Must be some transcendental thing.' Well he wasn't into that, nor were most of the crowd. They were doing a lot more talking than "Oooooooooom"ing.

"Free Timothy Leary." someone shouted, almost into his ear.

Scattered groups where chanting, and not in unison, "Turn on. Tune in. Drop out."

The old standby, "Power to the people!" echoed every minute or so.

The "Oooooooooom"ing came to an end. Marco walked towards the microphone, but the Ooomer began chanting in a weird language. Smitty figured Urdu, as good a guess as any. The crowd around him didn't show even that much interest. People were fighting off boredom with halfhearted chants, conversations, horseplay, and loud complaints.

Marco was as bored as anyone. He stepped forward, tapping the chanter on the shoulder to no effect. He tapped him again, and again, and again, until the chanter finally stepped back from the microphone. The crowd acknowledged this with some ambiguous cheering.

Marco took possession of the microphone. He surveyed the crowd before booming, "You know why we're here!"

"Yeah!" the awakened crowd roared back.

"You know who the enemy is!"

"Yeah!" the crowd roared even louder.

"One of us, Timothy Leary, has been railroaded to a federal prison for ten years, ten years mercifully reduced from thirty years by our benevolent slave masters. Ten years for what? For the possession of two measly joints, by this murderous fascist police state and the blood sucking capitalist pigs who own it. They claim to be protecting us, for our own good, from killer weed and LSD....Are they protecting us from atomic radiation?"

"No!" the crowd answered as one.

"The United States of America has enough coal to supply our needs for 10,000 years. Yet all over this country, the military-industrial complex is building nuclear power plants one after the other. Why? To build their bombs! To enslave us! To pollute our air and water! While they pretend to protect us from LSD. When did they start caring about what's good for The People?"

"NEVER!" some of the more experienced members of the crowd shouted.

"When did they stop caring about what's good for themselves?"

"NEVER!" hundreds of quick learners shouted.

"Timothy Leary is a political prisoner, a victim of fascism!" Marco shouted back. "Why is Timothy Leary so dangerous to them? Because we, the elite, are his followers. Because he wants us to expand our consciousness. Timothy Leary wants us to understand and to be at one with the cosmos. To see and experience the universe as it truly is — infinite. To find enlightenment through LSD. He threatens the entire system because he threatens the religions the state uses to turn us into unthinking automatons, to enslave us, to make us identical, interchangeable, disposable cogs in the capitalist-industrialist-militarist-IMPERIALIST-FASCIST-MACH INERY!...ARE WE GOING TO LET THEM?"

"NO!" and "NEVER!" the crowd roared back.

"We shall vanquish our oppressors, if by no other means than sacrificing ourselves, laying our bodies down upon the huge gears of the military-industrial complex, clogging and halting those gears with our blood, our flesh, and our bones!"

Marco paused for further affirmation from the crowd. This time, it failed to arrive. He noticed numerous people in the crowd glancing questioningly at each other. Perhaps the last sentence was a little too graphic. He would have to think about that, yet not now. "Let us not forget that while freeing Timothy Leary is our immediate cause, our ultimate goal is to bring down the fascist state that fears and imprisons him."

"Down with fascism! Down with fascism!" a few in the crowd shouted, then a few more, until, "Down with fascism!" grew into a deafening chant.

Marco, looking down upon a sea of waving placards, shouted above the roar, "Free Timothy Leary! To the Federal Building!"

Half the crowd continued to chant, "FREE TIMOTHY LEARY!" while the other half picked up the chant, "TURN ON! TUNE IN! DROP OUT!"

Smitty stood mute, his attention drawn by a dark-haired girl directly in front of him. She spent a lot of time on her tiptoes, excited by the commotion and trying to see it all. The girl seemed to be alone, and he had a hunch that she was attractive. Smitty squeezed to the side for a look at her face. He got that look, flinched, and drew back. The girl was more than attractive, but she was also the same one who had accused him of stealing her apartment. What were the odds of that?

Marcia, clapping, was too wrapped up in the demonstration to notice Smitty. She shouted back the chant, "FREE TIMOTHY LEARY!"

A few yards away, a flesh and blood fairy waving a magic wand materialized like a spirit above the crowd. Dressed in crinolines accented with a gossamer pair of wings, she sat atop the shoulders of a huge man in a Jolly Green Giant outfit. For added authenticity, his face was painted vibrant green. The giant paraded her around while the crowd called out to her. She answered by throwing them handfuls of something. To Smitty's left, the crowd roiled in excitement. The fairy girl threw another handful, this time closer to Smitty. One hit him in the face. The crowd converged upon him, knocking Smitty down, right on top of Marcia and underneath someone else. People bent over, kneeled, crawled on the ground, scrambling for the tiny objects. Everyone was either crawling over or trying to squeeze out from under somebody. People scrambled around in a frenzy, some to get away, some to pick up the little purple pills. All Smitty wanted was to get out from under the crazy freak riding him like a bronco, and to do so without squashing Marcia into the pavement. He executed something close to a wrestler's escape, flipping the freak off and onto someone else, flat on his back. Smitty found himself leaning over and face to face with this freak, who turned out to be Screw.

"Smitty!" Screw shouted with glee. "Hey man, you get the dope?" Too busy to answer, Smitty struggled to his feet and helped a frightened and disoriented Marcia to hers.

Screw jumped to his feet grinning like a jack-o-lantern. "Did you get any?" He showed Smitty his prizes, two little purple pills. "Purple Haze!"

Marcia, rubbing the arm she had fallen on, was less than awed. "Are they worth fighting over?"

Screw, astounded by her ignorance, held the pills up to her so she could see the Batman design pressed into them. "Hell, yeah! The original stuff. Made by Owesley himself."

In the background, the chant, "TO THE FEDERAL BUILDING! TO THE FEDERAL BUILDING!" battled for dominance with the other chant, "FREE TIMOTHY LEARY!".

The chants lit up Screw even brighter. "It's The Revolution. We're winning!"

Marcia backed over a freak still crawling on the ground in search of LSD. Smitty steadied her with an arm across her shoulders. Enjoying the fit, he glanced around warily to avoid another pile-up.

The chant, "TO THE FEDERAL BUILDING!" had almost drowned out, "FREE TIMOTHY LEARY!" when the demonstrators began to alternate these calls, creating one unified chant. A rumble arose as the crowd surged towards the gate.

Holding Marcia steady, Smitty asked "Are you all right?"

Still rubbing her arm, she answered, "I think so." At that instant she recognized Smitty. A hint of resentment came to her face.

Smitty caught it. "Look, I'm sorry—

The resentment left her face as she cut him off. "It's that landlord's fault, not yours." She glanced back uneasily at the crowd pushing them through the gate. "I'm just tired of paying rooming house rent."

They continued to move with the crowd, amid loud, belligerent chants of, "TO THE FEDERAL BUILDING! FREE TIMOTHY LEARY!" Smitty noticed that the few cops who had been near the gate had disappeared. He then spotted them another thirty yards down the fence, now in full riot gear. They stayed back from the demonstrators, eyeing them warily. A bottle flung from the crowd sailed straight towards them. A cop raised his shield just in time to deflect it. The cops merely stood their ground. Neither they nor the demonstrators seem to take a thrown bottle all that seriously. In fact, another bottle was quickly thrown and deflected with the same nonchalance.

Marcia, seeing this, looked at Smitty as if to ask if she was possibly more disoriented than she felt.

He just shrugged.

"Where are we going?" she asked.

Amid chants of, "TO THE FEDERAL BUILDING!" Smitty replied with another shrug, "To the Federal Building, I guess."

Suddenly remembering, she exclaimed, "I can't. I promised to help with the Honor Bikes."

*****

Straughton, experiencing an adrenalin rush, pushed towards the head of the march. This was the Berkeley he loved, the reason he'd returned. Old times. Good times. Berkeley, where it was always happening. He had to find Marco, watch him operate, see what he had learned, and how much he had changed. Marco had taken over the demonstration, given it direction — "To the Federal Building". He must be somewhere near the front of this march verging on a riot.

Straughton's freshman roommate had come a long way, much farther than Straughton would have guessed. He remembered their first meeting. A very different Marco walked through their dorm room door, dropping his suitcase in a rush to shake Straughton's hand. That was the strongest memory, this strange kid running around trying to shake the hands of everybody on campus. The young fellow had an uncanny knack for making people uncomfortable. They would back away, as if asking themselves, "What's he selling?" The answer was himself — a twenty-four hour politician on the make.

Marco had not been on the make for long, not even a year. His high school civics teacher had him nominated for Senior Class President, thus transforming a cocooned bookworm into a left-winged butterfly. Marco had no desire for the job itself, not to mention the socializing necessary to attain it. Politics was not something you could learn from a book, or so the bookworm thought. His teacher proved him wrong. She found one — How to Win Friends and Influence People. He studied it as he would a text, analytically and competitively. The most important lesson he learned from it, one that would become his mantra, was to never forget a person's name. Whenever Marco learned a new name, he spent the next few seconds matching it to the face before him, imprinting both upon his memory. This book inspired him to read others, on self-help, making friends, salesmanship, statesmanship. He kept reading, even after he won the election, read every book from cover to cover, including many worthless ones, in hopes of mining even a single useful sentence to underline, to copy, to memorize.

Straughton never guessed this. All he knew at the time was that Marco, this underdog, would-be world beater, so anxious to shake his and everybody else's hand, needed some friendly advice. First there was that waxed crew cut that should have been in an anthropology exhibit. And his meticulously worn clothes were all wrong, discount store copies of what a forty year old accountant would wear. Unfortunately for Marco, friendly advice was not something his new roommate offered to anyone. The Straughton's were not bred to make friends. No, the Straughton's were bred to keep distances. And some of Marco's characteristics inclined Straughton to keep him at slightly more of a distance. His skin, it was a touch too dark, his unibrow more than a touch too thick. Wherever the young man called home, it was surely not a Wasp nest. All this did not mean that Straughton experienced any repulsion. In fact, he quickly came to respect Marco for what he was — a fast learner.

That first year, the fraternities still wielded power, a power that to most freshmen seemed awesome. Piece by piece, Marco's geek wardrobe disappeared, replaced by discount Ivy League. When Straughton would take up invitations from the rich-boy fraternities, Marco proved ingenious at attaching himself for the ride. This often proved awkward for Straughton, when he was invited back and Marco wasn't. The only thing he could say was, "Take it as a compliment from those classless snobs." This would save Marco some face, about a pimple's worth, at least until Straughton eventually became a fraternity brother of "those classless snobs".

Receiving a call from one of the more desperate fraternities, Marco managed to convince himself of the advantages of being a big fish in a little pond. Later, comparing notes with Straughton about the hassles of being a pledge, Marco decided he had made a smart choice. His fraternity brothers hardly ever bothered him and his fellow pledges, this aside from their constant pleas to set them up with freshman girls. He saw no significance in this until his first fraternity party. It resembled an Irish wake, minus the corpse in the parlor and with a paucity of female mourners. The fast learner found one month of fraternity life enough. A big fish had no future in a mud puddle.

Well, Straughton now had to admit, it had taken a big left-finned fish to transform today's demonstration into a march. He finally found that fish about twenty yards back from its front. As Straughton approached, he could see a dozen of Marco's flunkies taking turns running instructions forward to other flunkies who were leading the march. Marco's expression was as serious as a general's, and it didn't get any lighter when Straughton stepped alongside, exclaiming, "Marco!"

Marco would have had to ponder a long time to think of someone he cared less to see than Straughton. This despite all the helpful publicity Straughton was always ready to provide. To Marco, it was a matter of principle. Straughton had absolutely no convictions or morals, not to mention what he did have, the nerve to be born very, very rich. Marco had many other reasons for disliking Straughton. Yet the main reason was one he never admitted even to himself — Straughton had witnessed and surely remembered Marco's first few weeks at Berkeley, and the missteps he had taken. The man knew too much.

"Straughton," Straughton said with a grin, as if there were a need to jog Marco's memory.

Marco forced a smile. "You came back."

"To where it's always happening."

In a flat tone, Marco said to his henchman beside him, "Stop the war now."

The henchman began to shout, "Stop the war now! Stop the war now!"

Marco smiled with satisfaction as the marchers picked up the chant. He turned back to Straughton, saying innocently, thus all the more wittily, "I imagined you already working for The New York Times."

Straughton felt the needle bend and break against his pachyderm hide. "You call that rag a newspaper?'

Marco was about to innocently admit that he always had, when up ahead the crash of a large storefront window sent shivers through him. He turned to the attractive girl now at his side, "No violence!" Marco caught himself getting too shrill. He switched to a more measured screech. "Tell them, 'No violence.'"

She rushed forward with his order.

Marco watched her, feeling frustrated. He could not adjust to using messengers. They left him once removed from his minions. Yet carrying around a megaphone had often left him once removed from his senses, and with large lumps adorning his skull. Nothing attracted swinging nightsticks like a megaphone.

'No violence?' thought Straughton. 'No violence, no story.' He had to ask Marco, "You're into Gandhi, or Martin Luther King?"

The irritation on Marco's face was now directed at Straughton. "I'm trying to get this march to the Federal Building. There, they can break all the windows they want. They can burn it to the ground." Again he turned to a henchman. "To the Federal Building! Stop the war!"

His henchman dutifully got the chant going again.

Straughton asked, "What's a little broken glass along the way?"

Marco shot Straughton the look that was his trademark, the look that asked, "How can you be so stupid?"

For Straughton, it was more of a nostalgia trip than a put-down. 'Ah, same old Marco.'

As if fighting to control his anger, Marco finally replied, "The pigs can move faster than we can. They have barricades, horses, dogs…tear gas. If we get violent, they'll stop us before the Federal Building."

Straughton figured the cops would find an excuse in any case. The Federal Building had a lot of windows. When it came to getting a story, Straughton had learned that arrogance was best met with clueless admiration. "Wait a minute! You turned the acid heads' demonstration into your march."

Marco was too flattered to reply. Who else in Berkeley was capable of such organization?

Seeing the pride in Marco's expression, Straughton judged the time right for sticking in the needle. "How far you've come. Remember when you quit your fraternity, and almost volunteered for Vietnam?"

Straughton's needle hit a nerve, angering Marco far more than the shattered storefront. It brought back a memory he had almost managed to erase. Teeth gritted, he replied, "That was just—"

Another shattering storefront cut Marco short. With an exasperated jerk of his head, he sent one of his acolytes running.

Straughton longed to see those gritted teeth again. "With your leadership ability, you surely would have made president of your fraternity…or found glory in Vietnam."

Marco stifled a scream, replacing it with something between a whisper and a hiss. "I was never in a fraternity. Pledged a few weeks, that was it.…And I sure as hell don't remember anything about volunteering for Vietnam."

Straughton did. Marco had worried that the absence of Vietnam service would leave a hole in his résumé, thus dooming his political future. Straughton was about to assist Marco's memory, when another shattered storefront had the man flinching as if the shards were falling on his head. He whined, "It's like trying to re-take Stalingrad with an army of half-trained monkeys."

Straughton glanced around at Marco's troops. He doubted if many of them possessed the attention span of your average chimpanzee, or smelled better. Marco's army chose that moment to smash the front window of a liquor store. Some marchers turned into looters, and the rest halted to watch. Marco and his lieutenants rushed to stop the looting, at the same time shoving the marchers forward.

Freaks looting whiskey bottles surprised Straughton, but soon many of the unopened bottles were flying through other plate glass storefronts. A few of these businesses also proved lootable. Marco's lieutenants quickly pleaded themselves out. Those possessing the strength turned to shouting. Marco himself stood mute and helpless as the forward momentum of his march dissipated into anarchy.

Straughton, on the other hand, felt a sense of relief, especially in his feet. The Federal Building was still a long, long walk away. Up ahead, he heard a familiar sound from the past — the pop of a tear gas canister. Sure enough, this march was over. His eyes darted around looking for a safe haven. Screams came from the crowd. Marchers rushed by as a phalanx of billy club swinging cops ran towards him. He spied the entrance to an apartment building a few yards away. It could be unlocked. A quick dash told him that it was. He kept running, straight up the stairs to the roof, which provided a first rate view of the riot below.

Straughton, having escaped the low creep of tear gas, felt quite clever. Below, a baton wielding cop rushed right by some other demonstrators to bash Marco from behind. Three sharp blows had Marco off and running, doing so with surprising speed. From Straughton's God-like perch, the tableau below seemed to unfold at a more gradual, comprehensible pace. He was a lord, gazing down upon his subjects, in at least two senses of that word. Straughton felt a kinship with and sympathy for those struggling below, felt it far stronger than he ever had at eye level. Why shouldn't he? Their purpose was to amuse and inspire him. Straughton took out his notebook and pen, gazing down as tear gas crept slowly along the street — 'on little cat feet'. Ah, another perfect Berkeley afternoon.

*****

Marco sat alone in the dark, and not by choice. Yet if he had had a choice, he might very well have chosen, at this moment, to be alone and in the dark. Of course he would not have chosen to be alone and in the dark sitting upon the damp floor of a janitor's closet, nor inhaling the scent of soapy water, and not the pine-scent-fresh variety either. No, this was the sour smell of old soap on carelessly rinsed mops. Despite it, for the moment, Marco was content to stay right where the cops had chased him, janitor's closet or not.

He felt beaten, and for good reason. Both his shoulder and shin ached from nightstick blows. The pain would be even worse if the cop had not anesthetized him first with a blow to back of the head. The sound in his ears was calming rather than bothersome, more of a humming than a ringing, like vibrations from a distant gong. Marco felt stoned, better in fact. The few times he had smoked marijuana, years ago, had not been pleasant experiences. And the one time he had dropped acid had been a paranoid, cowering nightmare. Yet his antipathy to dope was not strictly personal. Drugs and cults, not the establishment, were his immediate competition. He had not only lost numerous acolytes to them, he had also lost a few mentors.

Marco found it hard to understand the attraction of drugs. Why would anyone want to give up control of themselves — their perceptions, their thoughts, their actions, and most of all, their words? Drugs sliced open your skull, letting your innermost thoughts stream out. Even worse, allowing total strangers to peer right into your mind. Worse yet still, drugs made you do things you ordinarily would not do, and nearly all of those things were embarrassing mistakes. Marco had no desire to lose control of himself, even for an instant.

Losing control was what had happened today. Maybe he would go back to using a megaphone. Unconsciously, he reached up and touched the large, tender lump on his skull. 'Maybe not.' Not yet, anyway. For sure he had controlled himself. It was the march that got out of hand. The most unnerving aspect of this was that even now he could not think of a way to have retained control. The demonstrators he had gathered, the ones he was always doomed to depend upon, did not know the meaning of discipline. How could he organize the undisciplined? The thought itself was a conflict of terms. Then again, if discipline was what these freaks wanted, they would have joined the army and ended up in Vietnam. What a paradox. It took respect for authority to fight authority. This was one horse size pill to swallow.

Marco judged today's march a failure. Sure, it would get some lines in the newspaper, and probably some photos too, but what did it accomplish? Just one more demonstration turned into a march turned into a riot. These days, that was nothing new, nothing out of the ordinary. It certainly hadn't added any momentum to the radical movement. Merely this week's riot. Americans had become inured to these demonstrations, immune even, the same way they eventually gained immunity to a new strain of mosquitoes. Today's demonstration was merely a slight itch they would not even bother to scratch.

Yet Marco could feel that the United States, the entire world even, was on the cusp of extraordinary, revolutionary change. He sensed it almost every morning. The both exhilarating and frightening aspect of this crucial moment in history was the uncertainty of the direction it would take. It could just as well end in fascism as in socialism. Marco saw Berkeley as that spot on the once still, mirror-like pond where the first stone had landed. It was from Berkeley that a concentric series of waves spread out over our globe. Berkeley would be where the next stone would land, and the next stone after that, until, finally, change would come. And to think, it was he who had been anointed to throw that first stone. Aside from himself, there was no one truly capable of aiming the next stone. A tremendous responsibility weighed down upon him. Now, in the darkness, on the cold, damp floor of this janitor's closet, Marco sat determined to shoulder that responsibility, no matter what dangers and difficulties lay ahead.

*****

Marcia closed the Crescent wrench around the nut, then turned it clockwise to tighten the front wheel. Again the wrench slipped. She hesitated calling Smitty away from the back wheel. He had put on the front one for her, plus the washers and nuts. All she had to do was tighten these silly things. Again she tried and failed. Having talked Smitty into coming here instead of marching to the Federal Building, she was determined to do her share. Again the wrench slipped.

Smitty was now standing over her. He held out his hand for the wrench. Reluctantly, Marcia gave it to him. He shook his head. "This wrench is worthless." He showed her how loosely it fit together. "Take mine. I'll get another one."

Marcia, with little confidence, tried Smitty's Crescent wrench. It held its grip. So she had not been at fault. Relieved, with a real sense of accomplishment, Marcia tightened the nut. If only the people back in Santa Monica could see her now. She probably knew more about bicycles than any of the boys in her neighborhood. Marcia took pride in this thought, and even more pride in being part of the Honor Bike Project.

Five hundred bikes had been rusting away over at the campus police station — some stolen, most abandoned. The university wanted badly to get rid of them, and at no cost. Only at Berkeley would someone come up with the idea for Honor Bikes. All workers would be volunteers. All supplies, such as grease and paint, would be donated. All tools would be lent. Thirty volunteers were now making three hundred good bicycles out of five hundred abandoned wrecks. Trash that would have clogged the city dump was instead being put to useful purpose. Over fifty bikes were already finished, painted the university's colors, blue and gold.

Marcia marveled at the simplicity of the plan. No student would own any of these bikes. They would all be owned by the student body in common. If someone wanted to ride across campus, all she had to do was spot a blue and gold Honor Bike and get on. When she arrived where she wanted to go, she could just leave the bike for someone else to take. There would be enough Honor Bikes circulating around campus for everybody, whenever needed. 'Only in Berkeley,' thought Marcia, proud to be there, and to be a part of what made this place special.

Smitty approached with a set of box end wrenches. "Now we're in business." Marcia was tightening the front wheel. The streak of grease on her cheek added to the earnestness of her expression. She was more than attractive and he was more than attracted. 'Too good looking?' he wondered. 'One way to find out.' Smitty dropped to his knees. Checking the tightness of the front wheel, he said as casually as he could, "Look, if you don't find a place tomorrow, you can stay at my apartment until you do."

Silence.

Smitty waited for some sort of reply. He couldn't keep fooling with that nut forever. He'd have to look at her sooner or later...sooner more than later...in fact, right now. Smitty nodded, "Good," referring to her job on the wheel.

Marcia stared at him with her head tilted to one side, sizing up Smitty the way little children do grownups.

Still kneeling, he leaned back a bit, at the same time holding up his hands chest high. "No strings of course."

A smile came to Marcia's lips.

Smitty turned away to hide his own.

Marcia stood to help him with the handle bars. "I'll see what happens tomorrow." There was something about Smitty. He had a nice complexion, darker than hers, which wasn't saying much. 'Probably tans easy.' She didn't. His jet black hair was straight enough to be oriental. 'Cute yet strong at the same time.' She liked that. He had this bashful smile too, and a childlike tendency to hide it by lowering his head or looking away. Why would anyone be embarrassed to smile? Thinking about this, she herself smiled. Smitty looked up at her, and Marcia realized what was really different about him. He didn't merely look at you. More often than not, he gazed right into your eyes, as if stoned. This was odd, yet somehow appealing. It did not occur to Marcia that her father often looked at her this same way.

As Smitty put the last turn on the handlebar nut, an irresistible urge came over him, one he knew could end in embarrassing disaster. He hopped on the bike and peddled hard, intent on recreating a stunt he hadn't done since childhood. Turning the bike, he put on some speed and headed straight back towards Marcia. At the last instant, he turned the handle bar and hit the brakes. The bike skidded sideways and slid out from under him fast enough to allow Smitty to keep his balance. It stopped inches short of Marcia, much closer than he had intended.

Startled, she jumped back anyway, and did not appear the least bit impressed.

Smitty pretended that he didn't notice, trying to squirm out of the situation by grading the job they had done. "Pass."

Marcia shook her head at him.

Realizing he had made a mistake, Smitty still couldn't keep a smile from his face.

Marcia finally smiled back. They were both still smiling when a thick joint came into his field of vision, right in front of his face. 'What timing,' he thought, inhaling the welcome aroma. Smitty looked to his side in search of his benefactor. Screw appeared very, very stoned. 'Must be killer weed.'

Screw read his thought and grinned. "Dy-namite....Here Man, put on an edge."

Smitty glanced at Marcia.

She shrugged nonchalantly. This was Berkeley.

Smitty took the reefer and a long smooth toke, first asking, "How come you're not marching?"

"Things got mean. Trashing Stores. Throwing bricks at cops. I went home to stash my acid, then figured I'd come here."

Smitty was stoned by the time he exhaled. Marcia looked really nice. Yes, this one he wanted to take home. He passed her the joint.

She smiled, then took a delicate toke.

He liked the way she did that. The scent of grass seemed unbelievably strong, that is, until Smitty noticed that practically all the volunteers were taking marijuana breaks. The idea of this, aided by the grass itself, again made him laugh.

Screw laughed too, taking the joint and pointing to the adjoining building. "Man, you know what that is."

Smitty shook his head, not really caring.

Screw's grin widened even more, turning his eyes into slits. A jerk of his head again indicated the building. "Headquarters, campus cops....It's The Revolution, Man. We're winning!"

*****

As Marco neared home, he fought to eliminate his newly acquired limp. Someone in his position must exhibit as much gravity in his walk as he did in his countenance and speech. The hum in his ears had gratefully faded to insignificance. Yet his shoulder and shin still ached from the nightstick blows, and his fingers told him that he now had a lump on his head the size of half a walnut shell. Marco, in his pain, wondered exactly when in his past he had been 'anointed' dangerous enough for such a beating. The memory that came to him seemed ages ago.

It was just after he had quit pledging his fraternity. Returning to his dorm room, he had found a note on the door asking him to please telephone Geoffrey Blair. Now Marco did not know Blair personally, but he had certainly seen his photo and read about him in The Daily Californian, the appropriately named campus paper. Blair was a big shot upperclassman who was leading many of the civil rights battles on campus. Marco was flattered and telephoned immediately. Blair wanted to meet him, also immediately, at the Student Union. He claimed Marco had been recommended to him. Recommended for what, Blair didn't say. Marco wondered about this as he searched for him in the Student Union.

Where Blair was supposed to waiting, Marco didn't find anyone except a good looking light complexioned Negro. From the photos Marco had seen in The Californian, he knew that Geoffrey Blair was white, of course. Now, after circling the Student Union for the third time, Marco again found himself in the supposed meeting place, facing the lone seated Negro. Perhaps someone was playing a joke on him. Just then the question, "Are you Marco," brought him out of his reverie. It had been asked by the Negro.

Marco, still wondering what was going on, nodded.

The Negro, studying Marco, stood and offered his hand. "I'm Geoffrey Blair."

Marco was so surprised, his jaw dropped and, completely out of character, he forgot to extend his own hand. "Oh, I thought you were white."

Blair did a very obvious double take as his arm fell back to his side.

Marco realized he had made a mistake. "I mean from the photos." Those in The Californian were usually grainy, but not that grainy. Marco pondered why he had assumed from them that Blair was white.

Blair's eyes now showed suspicion. He motioned and said, "Please, sit down."

Marco attempted to put Blair at ease with some small talk. He noticed that they were wearing similar shirts, and mentioned it to him.

"Mine's bleeding madras." Blair replied.

'Bleeding madras?' Marco wondered. That didn't sound like anything anyone would want a shirt to do. They looked almost the same to him.

Blair chose to get right to the point. He wanted to demonstrate against the fraternities. Give them a choice. Either integrate or be banished from campus.

Marco listened in wonder. Lately, his fantasies of revenge against fraternities had been giving his sexual fantasies a run for the money. Blair had struck a chord worthy of a pipe organ.

Marco's enthusiastic expression had Blair wondering, 'Is this guy acting?' If he was, he sure had the knack. Blair feared he was making a mistake. 'Could be just a nut job.' Blair tried to remember who it was who had recommended Marco — 'Straughton!…That could explain it.'

When Marco left Blair, he shook his hand so energetically and for so long, it was as if he were trying to make up for his failure when they first met. This Negro was exceptionally refined and well spoken. Athletic looking too. He had materialized out of nowhere to help make Marco's fantasies come true. Marco felt the need to compliment Blair. Effortlessly, the words came to him. "You know, you look a lot like Harry Belafonte." When Blair did not seem overly flattered, Marco figured, 'Maybe he doesn't like calypso.' Perhaps a jazz reference might have gone over better. Unfortunately, he knew next to nothing about jazz, and nothing at all about jazz musicians. Little matter. He had no doubt that Blair too had sensed what a momentous meeting of minds had just occurred.

Marco launched himself into the preparations like a Labrador Retriever with a running start leaping off a dock into a lake. His job, and that of a dozen other organizers, was to scour their dormitories and departments, scraping up all the demonstrators they could. He succeeded in gathering over fifty enthusiastic students.

Marco and his energized band waited outside their dorm for Geoffrey Blair to arrive. They were chomping at the bit to join the march. Pulling back the reins on them, Marco experienced a surprising sense of power. He doubted that any of Blair's other organizers had done as well, and longed to see the impressed look on the man's face. Fifteen minutes later and still waiting, the need to reign in his band had long passed. After another restless fifteen minutes, what remained of their energy was directed at Marco. Many threatened to leave. Marco dreaded facing Blair alone. What would he think? Where the hell was he? Marco begged his demonstrators to stay. They agreed to give him five more minutes, but only if he would telephone Blair to find out what was going on.

Marco went back into the dorm. Yet he was in no hurry to phone. What good would that do? Blair wouldn't be in his room. He'd be on his way. Marco peeked out the window to see if he'd finally arrived. Not yet. Still, if all Marco's marchers left, that would be Blair's fault. He would tell him so. Marco could not go back out without word from Blair. No choice but to hole up by the phone. Restless, just to pass the time, he decided to telephone anyway. To his surprise, Blair answered.

"This is Marco."

"Marco, who?"

Marco explained who, and Blair explained why. It seemed all Blair's "Negro" friends, who had originally greeted his idea so enthusiastically, had decided they would be hurting their own cause by demonstrating with white students, who were lately acquiring reputations as free love advocates, drug addicts, and worst of all, dyed-in-the-wool communists.

Marco could understand Blair's reasoning, could see his point. Yet there was one thing he refused to accept. "Well, why didn't you let me know the demonstration was called off?"

"I'm sorry." He sounded it, sincerely. Yet his next words did not help. "You have to understand, Mark, I deal with a lot of people. I can't remember all of them."

'Mark?' thought Marco. If Blair had wanted to intentionally insult him, he could not have found a better way. Marco's anger increased as he thought about all the time and effort he had wasted, and increased even more when he realized that he'd been cheated out of his revenge against the button-down world of fraternities. Yet the thing that really wounded Marco was that he would never receive the approval from Geoffrey Blair that he had so conscientiously earned.

"I have fifty marchers waiting."

"Sorry, Man."

Marco dreaded returning to his band of would-be demonstrators. He saw no way of doing so without losing face. His fears proved justified. Followers no longer, they assaulted him with far more anger than he had shown Blair, doing nothing for his mood or self-esteem.

One of the girls shouted, "Are we gonna give up so easily?"

A few Yeah's seconded her.

"But who's going to lead us?" asked Marco, assuming that a protest for Negro rights should be led by a Negro.

"You started this," the girl shouted back.

More than a few Yeah's seconded her.

Marco scanned the angry faces. Seeing little choice, he decided to at least go through the motions. "All right. Follow me." Marco led them single file towards Fraternity Row. Immediately, the mood of the students behind him improved. He could hear excitement in their voices, and glanced back with satisfaction to see them pumping their placards as they chanted, "Two, four, six, eight, fraternities must integrate." He joined them, excitement now in his own voice. A surprising, exhilarating sense of power and purpose infused him. Marco relished the feeling.

A reporter and photographer from The Daily Californian were waiting for them. Geoffrey Blair had also failed to notify them. The next morning's paper had a large front page photo of Marco leading the demonstration. The article beneath it was four columns wide. It compared Marco and his band to Martin Luther King and the Mississippi Freedom Riders. It was especially effusive about them all being white, and rightly taking the lead in this matter. During the next few days, out of the corner of his eye, he'd catch people pointing at him. Students he didn't even know approached with offers to help.

Only now, as he limped home, did Marco fully appreciate the fact that that very first protest march was the fulcrum that changed the direction of his life. Never again would he be the outsider struggling to get inside, struggling merely to be accepted. No, he would be the outsider pushing all the insiders aside. A line ran directly from that day to the moment he forced the resignation of the high and mighty chancellor of California's university system. And that line has continued and would continue, just as straight, right into the future. Now, remembering that first demonstration, he wondered, 'What ever happened to Blair?…He sure looked like Harry Belafonte.'

Marco trudged up the front porch steps of his rented single story frame house. A neatly lettered sign next to the front door read:

"The People Welcome. No Pigs Allowed." The door was ajar, meaning his wife Susan was at home — 'Damn it.' He reached for the handle of the screen door, but stopped short of grabbing it. Instead, he turned towards the bench swing. It was the old, heavy, wooden slat type, appropriately painted white. He collapsed onto it, still feeling beat.

The thing Marco was dying for at the moment was a hot shower, better yet, a long bath for a change, and afterwards a bed to dive into. The problem was, to get to them he would have to get past his wife. Right now, she was the last person he cared to see.

Marco sat gently swinging, trying to regain some strength before facing Susan. Their relationship sure had deteriorated over the last few months. He had no clue as to why, and a strong aversion to even wondering. There was a part of him that did not want to know, a part with little confidence he could make things right. There was also another part of him, a part he tried to shut up, that told him that Susan would soon find someone else. So far, fortunately, he had seen no evidence of this.

Still, Marco rationalized his marital troubles with one single word — "women". And he would readily admit that "women" was not a subject he knew a lot about. Truth be told, Susan was the first and only woman he had actually been "serious" with. He could not believe her interest in him. Susan caught this, and with it the need to make the marriage proposal herself. As far as looks went, and looks usually seemed to be the determining factor, she was way out of his class. Until Susan, he had never realized how descriptive the term "trophy wife". And he had won his trophy on the first try. He could not stand next to her without feeling as if he were being envied by everyone. She was the ultimate radical leader's wife — intelligent, serious, committed, fearless, and beautiful. Marco would be the first to admit that he still had trouble telling the difference between a beautiful woman and one with long hair and pleasant smile. Yet Susan had neither, and no woman had ever mesmerized him as she had. The best description of her he had ever heard, he had heard recently from an acquaintance, one who hadn't known she was his wife. Marco was talking to him when he spied Susan nearby. The guy's eyes widened, and even his jaw dropped. He stared entranced while saying, "That is one seriously good looking bitch." As Marco recalled this incident, again without amusement, his wife chose to walk out their front door. She showed no surprise at finding him home. Her face rarely showed any emotion, unless calculation could be considered one.

Susan held her Siamese cat comfortably on one arm, while abstractedly scratching the back of its head with her opposite hand. She had named the cat Killer despite the fact that it was female, or perhaps because of that fact. In any case, no cat had ever done a better job of living up to its name. At least once a week, Killer would exhibit her latest kill by placing it in the center of the kitchen floor or hall. The carcass of that uneaten rodent or large insect would always be whole, showing little sign of struggle. No, these cold kills were proof of her lethal prowess. Marco often got the feeling that every new corpse was another warning, directed at him. Each morning, on his staggering trek to the bathroom, he would force open his half-shut eyes, so as not to hear underfoot the sickening squish of Killer's latest victim. He had learned this lesson the hard way, once even falling on his ass. That had been the last time he ever attempted the journey in bare feet.

Marco hated Killer. Yet he never got the feeling that this hatred was mutual. No, worse still, the cat seemed to hold Marco in too little regard to inspire hatred. If Killer accepted Marco at all, it was as one of Susan's very distant, uncultured, and of course illegitimate relatives — unworthy of notice. The animal displayed arrogance to a degree extraordinary, not only for cats in general, but even for the Siamese variety.

The affection Susan showed towards Killer was not the baby talk kind. There was a distance to their relationship, shared equally, yet a far smaller distance than the one now between herself and Marco. She would often pet or scratch Killer. Yet the only time the cat would return that affection was when Marco put his arm around or touched Susan, which he hardly ever did anymore. Susan had practically cured him of the habit, if not the urge. When he had done it, the cat would force her way between them, purring and meowing loudly all the while. Yet the most damage the cat had done to their relationship, Killer had not actually done at all. Twice Marco had dreamt that Killer was ripping flesh from his bloody face in long, ragged strips. One of those times he actually screamed out in pain, waking Susan. From her expression, it was clear that she did not find this type of bedroom behavior a turn-on. Marco lay awake the rest of the night, hoping Susan would have forgotten the incident by morning. She hadn't.

At the moment, Susan stood above and looking down upon the gently swinging Marco. Her black hair was parted on the left and cut almost as short as an early Sixties boy's cut. These days, there was hardly a man or woman on campus who didn't wear their hair longer, much longer. Despite this, with her soft perfect complexion and fine, elegant features, she could not have looked more feminine. Her lips were unusually thin, yet unusually red. Even the darkest lipstick would have made very little difference.

Marco was transfixed by the remote way she petted that damn cat. There was something diabolical and familiar about it, the way her hand moved above that spoiled self-satisfied beast. Marco was sure he had seen someone else do the exact same thing, perhaps some evil genius in a mostly forgotten B-movie.

In a flat, even tone, she asked, "What are you doing?"

"Thinking," Marco replied, in no mood for her sarcasm.

In the same flat tone, Susan said, "And the establishment trembles."

*****

Sloan was reading like a maniac, as fast as he had ever read in his life. He had to leave for work in a few minutes. No way did he want to spend his dishwashing shift wondering if the main character had the backbone to actually do what he seemed intent upon doing. The fucker may be a Brit, but he had no shortage of integrity, not so far anyway.

Sloan had started the short story almost by accident. He had had trouble getting to sleep, slept lousy when he did, and had woken a few hours early wanting nothing more than to get back to sleep. If only he still had his copy of Narciss and Goldmund. It had disappeared when he was heavy into drugs, when he had no use for it. Months earlier, his hippie chick bedmate couldn't stop raving about the book, she and half the people in Berkeley. Finally, to shut her up, he agreed to read it too. Sloan hadn't finished three pages before he was out like a blackened, blown light bulb. He tried to finish the book, God knows he tried. Yet he couldn't read more than three, or on rare occasions four pages without conking out. Finishing the damn thing would have taken him years. To get the chick off his back, he even attempted reading it in the daytime. He could stay awake then, but after a page or two he'd have no idea what he was reading. He would end up reading the same sentence over and over again like a mantra, in too much of a trance to turn the page. This could go on indefinitely, or until he was shocked back to consciousness by something such as his chick asking hopefully, "Is it getting any better?" It wasn't. Sloan was still on page 23 when his flaky bedmate read a book on Zen and got off drugs. The fact that they had turned into a mixed couple, junkie and former-junkie, took too high a toll on their relationship. She tried to get him off drugs and into Zen. Once she tried to save his life by asking, "What is the sound of one hand clapping?"

"Zen," Sloan replied, and she didn't talk to him for two days. The end came when he refused to join her on something called The Zen Diet. Sloan was left alone, yet with no regrets that dope couldn't anesthetize. He eventually received word that she had had the willpower to stay on The Zen Diet and off drugs for six months, which unfortunately proved long enough to starve herself to death. This did not seem possible, but he later learnt that she had not been the first victim of the Zen Diet, at least not according to the newspapers. To Sloan, starving oneself to death made OD'ing look comparatively attractive.

Sloan had lain in bed for a half hour groggily pining for his long lost knockout drop of a book. He would have even settled for a copy of Sidhartha. Out of curiosity, Sloan had experimented with that other piece of Hesse's excrement. Sidhartha proved nowhere near as dependable as Narciss. Even when it did work, it took at least ten or twelve pages to put him to sleep. Still, right then it would have been worth a try. That's when Sloan's imagination and resourcefulness kicked in. He could read that shitty short story about those worthless Brits. If he could just find the damned book. How the fuck could he have lost it in an apartment so small that a single fart could prove fatal? Turned out he couldn't, just then spotting it less than an arm's length away.

Sloan grabbed the paperback and read the title — 'The Loneliness of a Long Distance Runner'. The title alone almost put him to sleep. He opened the book, hoping soon to be in La-La

Land. He never got near there. Within a few pages, he was wide awake, sorry he hadn't read this short story before going to England. It explained a lot about the guys he had worked with there. Knowing where they were coming from would have made him more tolerant. Halfway through the story, Sloan was even wider awake, extra-wide. Sometimes he even found himself identifying with the main character — 'This fucking Brit ain't so bad.' The "fucking Brit" who did the writing wasn't bad either. He closed the book to look at the cover — 'Alan Sillotoe, never heard of him.' Sloan recalled an author he'd heard way too much of, Herman Hesse — 'Guess you gotta be a pretentious phony.'

The more Sloan read, the more he not just identified with, but also respected the main character. 'This fucker could be a Marine.' He finished the short story with the sense that he had actually met someone worth a shit. It then occurred to him that the reason this was so satisfying was the paucity of people he did respect.

Sloan checked his watch. There was barely enough time to return the book. He'd have to hurry if he didn't want to keep his sink full of dirty dishes waiting. For the first time in a long time, he bounded up the stairs. Sloan knocked on Smitty's door. He heard nothing. He knocked again as the building's front door opened. Maybe that was Smitty. It wasn't.

Screw, climbing the stairs, spotted him. "Did you bring the dope?"

"I'm clean," Sloan replied.

"Fine with me." Screw noticed the book. "Hey, was it any good?"

"Best short story I ever read."

"Serious?"

"Dead."

Screw held out his hand. "Let me read it."

This was not the way Sloan did things. He was the one who had borrowed the book. "You can get it from him."

"C'mon, Smitty won't mind."

Sloan felt uncomfortable. After all, it was Screw who had gotten him the book. He could always buy Smitty another copy. "Don't fucking lose it."

"Don't worry. I'll give it to him as soon as I finish it."

"No," Sloan said, as if he were talking to a child. "I borrowed it.

You give it to me. I give it to him." He handed over the book.

"Sure, whatever you say."

Sloan had wasted too much time. He bounded down the stairs and out into the street, feeling good. The best he had felt in a very long time.

*****

Smitty headed for campus to pick up his student ID. Afterwards, he'd have to make sure his card was still up on the "Apartment to Share" bulletin board. He didn't have a phone or phone number yet, wouldn't have one for a few more days. So far, no one had come around to enquire about the apartment. If he didn't find a roommate soon, he'd have to start looking for a part-time job. No money meant no college meant no draft deferment meant Vietnam. Having already lost two friends there, that was a possibility he did not care to contemplate at the moment.

The food vendors' carts in front of the campus entrance reminded him of another thing he had to do, get something inside his empty stomach. As usual, the line for quiche was the longest. What were these people trying to prove? Hell, maybe he just got a bad quiche and lived to tell. Another try wouldn't kill him. 'No, some other time,' he told himself, 'when I'm hungrier, much hungrier…and had smoked a joint.'

The next most popular cart was selling knishes. He had tried one of those too. It had tasted like a stick of yesterday's mashed potatoes wrapped in soggy, flaky pastry. Now Smitty had nothing against mashed potatoes, in their mashed as opposed to stick form, especially when drowned in butter. He just preferred a little more flavor. The pizza cart had a few customers, but he had given that two chances. Smitty liked his pizza crispy enough to hold in one hand. Try that with the mushy slices from the pizza cart, and the crust ends up pointing down at the sidewalk, directly at the red and yellow puddle that used to be its topping. Crispy pizza didn't just taste better to Smitty. There was something downright sad, pathetic even, about a slice of pizza that couldn't hold an erection.

The one remaining cart sold donuts, and from the looks of things, it did not sell many of them. Lately, except when he was really stoned, Smitty's sweet tooth had been laying off him. Right now, he had no desire for a mouthful of doughy sugar, even if it was called a donut. Still, the absence of a line proved too tempting. Smitty stepped up and pointed at a large, crenellated donut.

"French cruller?" the guy behind the counter asked.

The donut Smitty wanted did not look particularly French, and he wasn't sure they were talking about the same one. Still, he doubted the filled donuts to each side of his choice would be fatal. Then again, he was the only customer in sight. Smitty took a chance. He nodded and laid down his quarter. Sure enough, his fearlessness was justly rewarded with the donut he had wanted. 'Pays to take a chance,' he told himself. The large donut seemed unusually light in his hand. He hadn't taken two steps before his mouth was open and the donut was right under his nose. Smitty stopped dead and closed his mouth. The donut had a really pleasant aroma. He sniffed again, unable to guess the magic ingredient. Smitty took a healthy bite. The taste was even better than the aroma. The cruller had a rich sweetness, yet without a hint of sugar. He couldn't ever remember tasting anything so pleasantly sweet. Before he knew it, the once healthy bite of donut had melted away in his mouth. Smitty took another quick bite to see if he were imagining things about the first. He wasn't. This was by far the most delicious donut he'd ever tasted. Smitty scarfed down the rest of it in a few quick bites. He was still chewing when he turned and headed back to the donut cart. Smitty ate the second cruller more slowly, savoring its flavor and lightness. What an extraordinary discovery!

Smitty headed back towards the gate. Just outside it, in the same threadbare black suit, that preacher, or evangelist, or whatever he was, fulminated away predicting Hell and damnation to a measly three students. One of them was the same wise guy who was harassing the last time. Looking at them, Smitty almost tripped over a large, vase shaped basket set in front of a turbaned sidewalk flutist. Still walking, he suddenly realized that the flutist was wearing Gunga Din shorts. Smitty stopped dead and looked back. That basket just might contain a cobra. 'Possible? This is Berkeley.' He pictured a pissed-off cobra dangling between his legs. 'Ouch, that could smart.' He turned away, pain still on his face, immediately seeing something else that stopped him — a picket line parading across the entrance to the university. 'What is this, an obstacle course?' His summer job on the loading dock had reinforced his sympathy for labor. Still, his student ID was not going to come to him. Most people were crossing the picket line, pretending not to notice it. As he debated what to do, Smitty saw something that put a smile on his face. Marcia, mistress of half his waking thoughts, was one of the picketers. 'Could've blown that fantasy.' She appeared every bit as lovely as he remembered. Here the kid was, mixed up in a labor dispute. Things could get rough. The girl might need some protection. For that job, Smitty was willing to fight.

Marcia carried a picket sign that read, "BACK THE CUSTODIANS". Other signs read: "UC ANTI-LABOR", "ALL WORKERS DESERVE A UNION", "CUSTODIANS MUST ORGANIZE", "UC TOOL OF CAPITALISTS", "WORKERS OF THE WORLD UNITE". Those refusing to cross, milled around, asking newcomers to do the same.

Marcia tried not to be bitter towards all those breaking the picket line. Still, this was difficult when they crossed right in front of her. She took comfort in the small crowd honoring the line. A surprised smile came to her face when she spotted Smitty in it.

Smitty smiled back, pleased by her reaction. She motioned for him to join the picket line. This honor he would just as soon pass up. Smitty did not see himself as the picketing type. Marcia motioned again. Hell, for her, he'd prostitute himself. Smitty held up his finger, indicating, "Just a moment." He went to buy two more French crullers before joining the picket line at her side. One he offered to Marcia.

"What am I supposed to do with that?" she asked with a smile.

"I'll show you," he said, taking a huge bite out of his. To further illustrate, he chewed it down as if it were trying to choke him. "Think you can handle it?"

She laughed, saying, "No, and I'm not hungry."

Again he offered the cruller, saying, "An army marches on its stomachs," immediately thinking, 'Or something like that'. His words had not made much sense, even to him. He tried to remember who it had been who probably hadn't said anything close to that.

"No thanks," she said.

"These are great."

"No," she laughed.

"For The Revolution."

Marcia took the donut and a tiny reluctant bite. Her eyes lit up. She took a larger bite to make sure. "It's delicious!" After swallowing, she said, "You can taste the eggs."

'Eggs?' he wondered, taking a bite of his own cruller. It did have the taste of eggs, a large part of the taste he had liked. And that was the aroma too. "Speaking of eggs, you find a nest yet?"

While answering, Marcia pondered why such a seemingly clever remark was not the least bit funny. "No, I'm checking two places this afternoon."

Smitty flashed on offering to go with her, and flashed again on the realization that he was in no way interested in helping her find some other apartment. "You know if they kick you out of that boarding house, I wouldn't let you sleep in the street."

"That's nice to know."

As the picket line curled back again, Smitty felt his small talk falling flat. He gave up on it. This made him more conscious of and self-conscious about what he was doing. He started checking out the pickets, seeing if they looked as stupid as he felt. They didn't, not particularly. Yet none of them looked like custodians either. "Hey, where are the janitors?"

"They're working."

*****

"Definitely homo sapien," was all Sloan could say about his reflection. Then, deciding not to stick his neck out so far, he qualified that conclusion. "Or close enough to pass." He had just shaved, showered, and combed his hair. Looking in the mirror was nowhere near as painful as it used to be. Exiting the bathroom, the sight of his apartment was just as painful. Sloan figured he better find something else to look at. A TV might do the job. Musing about where he could get a used one, an unexpected sound brought him out of his reverie. It was a knock on his door.

When Sloan opened it, Screw said, "Hey Man, here's the book."

"Good.... You know where I can get a used TV?"

"Naw, get a new one."

Sloan shook his head. "No coins."

"What about that $90 check you got?"

Again Sloan shook his head. "Dope."

Screw shrugged. "Least you didn't waste it."

This brought a smile to Sloan's face, wishing he himself could look at it that way. "C'mon. Let's take the book back to Smitty." As they climbed the stairs, Sloan asked, "What'd you think?"

Screw studied him. "Were you serious when you said it was the best short story you ever read?"

"Yeah. You didn't dig it?"

"No Man, it was weird."

Sloan chuckled as he gave Screw the once-over, thinking, 'Maybe he's too young.'

Screw knocked on Smitty's door. Through it, Sloan could hear Jimmy Reed on the stereo — "You got me runnin', You got me hidin'". This brought back memories. You heard blues in Berkeley, but not much Reed. Not enough.

Smitty opened the door, beer in hand. Sloan appeared surprisingly civilized. Maybe he wasn't a junkie.

Sloan offered the book. "Thanks for turning me on to this. Best short story I ever read."

Smitty smiled. "One of my favorites."

Sloan pointed inside, to where the music was coming from. "Reed, one of my favorites."

Smitty's smile widened. Sloan was the first person he had met in Berkeley who had even heard of Jimmy Reed.

Sloan pointed at Smitty's beer and added, "Best beer drinking music in the world."

Smitty nodded, surprised and impressed by Sloan's refined tastes. "You know it.…Come in for a cold one."

Sloan had not been angling for an invitation, but the idea was too appealing. "Sounds good."

Smitty turned to Screw. "Ever hear of Jimmy Reed?"

"Nope."

"We'll turn you on."

Smitty headed for the refrigerator and pulled out two more beers.

"Not for me," said Screw. "You got a soda?"

"This is beer drinking music," Sloan protested.

Screw said, "Beer is counter-revolutionary. I'll stick to weed."

Sloan laughed, wondering if the kid had ever liked beer. "It ain't a question of one or the other."

"I'll take a soda."

Smitty found him one, and turned to Sloan. "What did you think of that guy in the story?"

"The fucker had backbone," Sloan replied.

Screw could not believe what he was hearing. "He was a scumbag!"

"They breed 'em like that in England — with a bad attitude and a chip on their shoulder. Those fuckers are handed a stacked deck on the day they're born....Be grateful you're an American."

"I am....So he should purposely lose a race he can win?"

"There it is," said Sloan.

"Right on," Smitty agreed.

"You guys are crazy," said Screw, looking at them as if he believed it. "What's the point?"

Sloan replied, "To fuck over the reform school and the shits running it."

"Is that worth losing the race?"

"Fuckin' A right it is," said Sloan.

Screw looked towards Smitty, hoping for help.

Smitty was nodding agreement with Sloan.

Screw shook his head. "I don't understand."

Smitty said, "Screw, put yourself in his place. You're in reform school. The guys running it, are they your friends?"

Screw remained silent.

Sloan cut-in, "They're your enemies."

Smitty phrased it in the language of the time. "They're running the system that's oppressing you."

Screw asked, "That makes losing better than winning?"

Smitty asked, "You wanna make the bastards look good?"

"Well how do I look, losing a race I can win?" Screw protested.

Sloan cut-in, "That's just it — you shouldn't give a shit what you look like. You yourself know you can win. You are winning till the last, when you let that sucker pass you."

Smitty asked, "What are you going to get if you win?"

"If you let them use you?" Sloan interjected. "A pat on the back? Some smiles?"

Smitty added, "It's all ego. You have to control your ego." He glanced over to see Sloan holding up his beer in agreement. Smitty returned the compliment.

"I don't know," said Screw, cowed but not convinced.

'Someday you will,' thought Sloan, 'If you join the Marines and get your ego stripped away.'

"You want another beer?" asked Smitty.

Sloan did. He was not only feeling good, he was feeling good in a particular way that he had not realized he had missed so much, and for so long. This Smitty, he may be all right. He could talk for two minutes without reciting some Berkeley bullshit and pissing you off. Beer, how long had it been since he'd really enjoyed a beer. And topping it all off, Jimmy Reed, on an album he had never heard before. There was this guy interviewing him, as a short intro to each song. How could anyone listen to Reed's easy drawl without smiling? This was the way it should be. "Bright lights, big city, gone to my baby's head—"

Smitty gauged Sloan, deciding that even if he were, had been a junkie, his brain remained largely undamaged. He had some taste too, enough to appreciate Sillotoe's book. Smitty began to doubt that his stereo and lesser valuables were in any immediate danger. As the album side came to an end, he broke out another round of beers. Smitty got the urge to further test Sloan's taste in music. "You into folk blues?"

"Like what?" Sloan asked.

Smitty was already on his feet. "I'll show you." He dug out an album and cued it up. "This is Wanderin' by Dave Van Ronk, one of the greatest cuts ever recorded."

Sloan was always skeptical of big buildups. Yet Smitty had been right about The Loneliness of a Long Distance Runner. Sure enough, the harsh sounds issuing from the stereo blew away all of Sloan's skepticism with the first few verses. Van Ronk sang with the rawest, most visceral voice he had ever heard, and the lyrics spoke to him too. The song actually left Sloan drained. "Man, no white dude can sing like that."

"This one can," Smitty assured him.

"He's white? You shittin' me?"

Smitty shook his head, liking Sloan's reaction.

Screw cut in, "He's not white!"

Smitty flipped Screw the album cover.

It now struck Sloan how much he had missed the pleasure of some decent music in his drug fogged state. "Hey, play it again...louder." As Smitty cued the song, Sloan added something he had not said or felt in a very long time. "Man, I'm glad I met you."

*****

Marco surveyed his crowded living room with pride. All the chairs and the sofa were occupied. People sitting on the floor were squeezed so close together there was barely room for anyone else. Another dozen or so attendees stood against the back wall. Still, the new faces, as usual, had brought on his paranoia, which only slowly subsided as the meeting wore on. Things were going smoothly. If his audience proved as committed as they appeared, he would have more than enough picketers for every supermarket in the city still selling grapes.

"I got a question," a man standing at the back wall called out in a tone more suitable for a complaint. He was one of only two black men in the room, and the one that Marco did not know. This was enough to ramp back up his paranoia. Until arriving at Berkeley, Marco had had little contact with black men, and none at all with the angry variety so prevalent here. All but the most cultured of black men made Marco uneasy. It wasn't just that he didn't know how to talk to them. He didn't know how to listen to them either, or more specifically, to distinguish the bluster from the serious threats. In simple terms, most black men scared the crap out of Marco, including the man now wanting to ask a question.

Fortunately for Marco, few of Berkeley's black men attempted to enter his circle. Black women were always among the faithful, and he valued them. However, black men would drift away after only a meeting or two, leaving Marco with a strange sense of relief. Chandler, the other black man in the room, was an exception. Chandler's genteel, southern accented words had never seemed threatening. No, Chandler's words issued forth as if they were the essence of thought and reason. Marco valued the counsel of very few people, Chandler among them. In part, for this reason, Marco glanced at him now. The other part was that Chandler too was black. It was as if, by reflex, Marco had turned to Chandler to

130

say, "One of yours. How should I handle him?" Marco caught himself almost immediately, though too late to escape Chandler's notice. He turned back to the questioner. After all, what was there to worry about? The man might prove quite pleasant, Marco told himself, though to little effect, "Please, tell us your name and go right ahead."

"Genghis Khan," he said, in a tone worthy of his namesake. "I been standing here for an hour listenin' to you rap 'bout picketing supermarkets and how the white man is using urban renewal to steal the black man's property. Hell, there ain't gonna be no property in Oakland. That jungle's 'bout to explode in a race riot that'll make the LA Watts riot look like a love-in. What's your plan of action to join the brothers, fight alongside 'em? Hell, you should be in the ghetto now, helping to start that riot....Is this all you honkies do — rap, rap, and rap about picketing supermarkets?"

"No—" Marco started to reply before being cut off. He had no desire to set foot in the Oakland ghetto again. He organized and carried out Oakland's first successful rent strike. The black radicals didn't show up until the victory press conference. Then it was all brotherhood and solidarity. Yet within days, the blacks had run all the white radicals out of town.

"You think The Man gives a shit what goes on in front of supermarkets?"

"Well—" Marco started to reply before again being interrupted.

"What are you doing about the one million political prisoners in US jails? Every black man incarcerated in this fascist country is a political prisoner. What you doing to break them out? The only thing The Man understands is guns and bombs. You can't reason with the beast. You gotta kill the beast!"

"I beg to differ."

"Honky, differ all you want, beg all you want. Differin' an' beggin' ain't gonna get no one nowhere." Genghis Khan, his expression now exhibiting more disgust than anger, headed out the door, followed by a five-man horde.

Now Marco was not accustomed to being addressed in this manner — except by his wife, and even then not in front of his minions. If there were a trick he could now use to re-establish his leadership, he was ignorant of it. He handled the challenge the only way he knew, by ignoring it. Marco spent the next fifteen minutes summarizing what he had already said about the coming week's picketing, and hammering home the importance of it. When done, he was confident that he had succeeded. He was not wrong.

As the meeting broke up, Marco scanned the room and caught Chandler staring at him. He walked over to him. "Well?"

"Well what?" Chandler said coyly, knowing that he wasn't fooling anyone. Still, he wanted Marco to spell out his question.

"That. That's what." Marco replied, refusing to spell it out.

"You mean him?" Chandler asked, meaning, "You mean my fellow Negro?"

"Yes, him," Marco admitted.

"An angry young man...probably with valid cause....A young man sure to have spent a good deal of time behind bars...which does not tend to lessen ones anger."

"Is that all you can tell me?" Marco asked.

"Genghis Ex-Con is the type of young man who rarely lives to be an old man...and rarely fails to take a few others with him."

"Well, then we can count ourselves lucky to have seen the last of him."

"I would not bet on that," said Chandler.

*****

Smitty climbed the front steps of his apartment house with his arms around a big cardboard box. It contained the last of Marcia's belongings. She held the door open for him. Tonight he would have her in his apartment — 'So far, so great'. The trick would be getting her to stay. He warned himself not to think about sex, not to get horny. Women somehow sensed that. It turned them off.

Just as he reached the threshold, someone behind him called out, "Excuse me, do you mind holding the door?" Smitty, box and all, turned to see Straughton dragging an Honor Bike up the front steps. Marcia, still holding open the door, stared on incredulously as Straughton walked the Honor Bike through the threshold. He had a friendly smile for both of them, yet didn't seem to notice that Smitty could use some help with the box. Peering around it, Smitty watched Straughton lug the bike up the stairs.

Marcia looked to Smitty for an explanation.

He just shrugged.

She called after Straughton, "That's an Honor Bike."

Straughton looked back, replying happily, "I know."

Marcia again looked to Smitty for an explanation.

He had none.

She turned back to the disappearing Straughton. "You're not supposed to take them off campus."

At the top of the stairs, without looking back, Straughton replied, "I'm writing an article on them."

Again Marcia looked to Smitty for an explanation.

Straining under the weight of the box, Smitty asked, "Literally?"

Marcia missed the joke, but caught the strain in his voice. She quickly led him up the stairs, still thinking about Straughton. It wasn't until she reached his door that Smitty's question intruded upon her thoughts. She pictured Straughton writing the article while literally sitting on an Honor Bike. 'Oh, it was a joke,' she thought without amusement. His sense of humor was a little weird. She'd have to pay closer attention.

Marcia had Smitty place all her suitcases and boxes between the front door and the couch. She didn't want to give him any ideas. This was just a temporary arrangement, and she was quite wary of it. If Smitty thought he was going to get her into his bed, he better think again. Marcia eyed the couch. It looked kind of ratty. In fact, plain ratty. She would cover it with a sheet, and it would have to do. Heather sure had left her adrift. Considering the short time she had known him, Marcia found it hard to believe that Smitty was now the closest friend she had on campus. This bothered her. Sure, he was cute. Sure, she would go out with him. After she had found her own apartment.

"What do you want to drink?" Smitty asked her.

The thought of some wine seemed nice, but she said instead, "Whatever you're drinking."

Smitty headed for the kitchen, while Marcia decided to check out his taste. She sat down on the floor to flip through his albums. Smitty returned and sat down next to her, holding out a beer. She disliked beer. She disliked the fact that teenagers and college students were supposed to like it. She disliked it straight from the bottle, and even more straight from the can, which of course was exactly how Smitty served it. He had been gallant enough to pop the top for her. Marcia felt no need to be like other people, or to like the same things other people liked. Still, she decided to give beer another try. Marcia took a cautious swallow. This time it wasn't that bad. Nothing anyone would really want to drink, yet no worse than most medicines. Besides, She was thirsty. She took another dainty swallow, feeling like a pro.

Marcia came to Jerry Jeff Walker's Mr. Bojangles album. "I've heard someone else sing this. It's nice."

Smitty set her straight. "Walker wrote it. He's the only one who sings it right." Smitty took the album from her to place it on the turntable.

'Awfully sure of himself,' thought Marcia, taken aback by his matter-of-fact, bordering on arrogant tone.

After putting on the record, he turned back towards her for affirmation, again looking right into her eyes with that naively serious expression of his.

As the music started, she noticed a self-assured smile forcing its way onto his face. Marcia couldn't help but smile back. Perhaps he made up for in honesty what he lacked in tact. The song was nicer than she had remembered. She listened as if to a short story, picturing the lyrics as they were sung. Walker did sing it better, far better. She studied the album cover. 'He has good taste…at least in music.'

Smitty could see by her expression that she liked the song. Grinning, he asked, "What do you think?"

She nodded, smiling.

"The next song's even better," he said. "It's called Little Bird.…Listen to the words."

She always did. Words were important. She couldn't listen to the radio without being baffled by the popularity of so many songs with such asinine lyrics. She listened carefully to the words of "Little Bird" as Smitty stood up and headed for the bedroom. It only took a few lines before the song's imagery had floored her.

Smitty felt like smoking. Actually he felt like talking. Well, he didn't really feel like talking. It was just that, from his vast experience with women, he had learned that when you were alone with one of them, they appreciated a little more conversation than the occasional yes or no. And from his occasional experimentations with marijuana, he had discovered that it loosened his tongue and heightened his sense of humor, or seemed to. He really couldn't be sure. It may have just lowered his threshold for humor, which was not a problem if it also lowered that of the woman with whom he was smoking.

Smitty returned with one of the joints left him by his last, short lived roommate. Marcia had accepted a few tokes when they worked on the Honor Bikes. At the very least, she shouldn't mind him 'putting a little edge on'. Smitty examined the joint in front of her with a puzzled "what have we here" expression.

Marcia didn't jump out the window.

He lit the joint, took a toke, and offered it to Marcia.

As she reached for it, Marcia flashed on her experience with Straughton. She froze, then drew back suspiciously.

Smitty, surprised by her reaction, mimicked it by drawing back himself. This got an amused rise out of her. He again offered the joint, this time along with an evil grin. "Try it, My Lovely."

She didn't even smile.

Smitty changed tack, saying as seriously as he could, "Live fast, die young."

This time she did smile, almost laughed. Smitty could be awful cute. He was nothing like the boys she had known in Santa Monica, especially the ones at her private school. Smitty reminded her of the gang members in West Side Story — dangerous yet not really bad. There was something exciting about him. The word sexy did not occur to her.

He sensed her caving in. "For The Revolution."

Smiling, Marcia finally took the joint.

In the middle of what was for her a long drag, Smitty said, "Easy now. Don't OD on me."

Marcia lost the smoke in a short spasm of laughter that turned into a long spasm of coughing.

Smitty gritted his teeth — 'Shoulda kept my mouth shut.' Yet he was too stoned to keep from laughing. "Sorry."

Marcia's coughing, slowly, erratically, turned back to laughter. "You think that was funny?" she asked.

"No," Smitty assured her, still laughing. "But you did....This must be laughing grass."

"I hardly got any."

The evil grin returned as he again held out the joint. "Killer Weed, just what you need."

Marcia took a healthy toke. Attempting to keep the smoke in her lungs, she forced herself to be serious, starting with her expression.

He mocked that expression, trying to look overly serious. Finally, he broke out laughing.

She did the same, only harder.

Smitty reached out, placing one hand on her shoulder and the other on her face.

Marcia drew back, yet kept her smile.

"I like your face," he said, nodding.

"Why shouldn't you," she shrugged with a smile.

He held out the joint. "Another toke, My Pretty."

Marcia leaned forward and took a long drag, allowing Smitty to hold the joint. When she blew out the smoke, she nodded her head to tell him that she was stoned.

Smitty nodded back.

She said, "Play Little Bird again. I want to hear it on grass."

Smiling, he shook his head No.

"Why not?"

"So you'll have to come back again to hear it."

"I can buy the album."

"Tonight," Smitty assured her, "you'll hear a lot of songs you'll want to hear again. You can't buy all the albums."

"Put on Little Bird, and I promise I'll come back."

"Deal." He reset the needle and lay back on the rug, placing both throw pillows beneath his head.

Marcia, stoned, wanted to lie back too. "Hey, let me have a pillow."

Smitty shook his head.

"You're selfish."

Again Smitty shook his head. "I've got a nicer pillow for you."

Marcia glanced around without seeing one. "Where?"

Smitty pointed to his stomach.

Marcia leaned away suspiciously, shaking her head No.

Smitty said, "Try it. You'll like it."

She again shook her head.

Smitty made a face that said, "C'mon, take a chance."

Marcia lay back purposely hard on Smitty's stomach, perpendicular to him.

He didn't flinch.

She did, complaining, "It's hard as a rock."

"You want me to blow it up a little?" he asked.

"Yeah," she replied.

He did.

"More," she requested.

He blew up his stomach further, asking hoarsely, "Is that enough?

"No," she replied.

Smitty deflated his stomach.

Marcia swung her arm back as if to hit him.

He caught it and held her hand.

Marcia did not try to pull it away.

Smitty lay back listening to the end of the song, feeling very, very satisfied. Things were going all right. She had on a loose sweat shirt that would practically slip off by itself if their scene got hot and heavy. Her skin-tight Levis were a problem though. You could lose a finger just trying to get them unsnapped. He'd need some cooperation. Smitty wondered why the sweatshirt couldn't be a little tighter, and the Levis a little looser. Skintight Levis — the Sixties' chastity belt.

"Oh," said Marcia, "I wasn't paying attention. Play it again."

Smitty was too comfortable to move. "Naw, listen to the rest of the album. It's all good."

This boy was obviously no gallant knight waiting to do her bidding. "Please, I'd like to hear the words."

Smitty asked lazily. "You'll be here when I get back?"

Marcia answered him by squeezing his hand.

Smitty liked her reply. He took back his stomach, replacing it with his throw pillows. After cueing the cut, he lay back down again, reclaiming her hand in the process.

They listened stoned and contented until the song ended and Marcia said, "You've got good taste in music."

"Aw shucks, go on now" he replied bashfully. "I bet you say that to all the boys."

Marcia laughed to herself. He did have a sense of humor — an odd one, but definitely a sense of humor. She squeezed his hand again. "Do you like the "Mommas and the Pappas?" she asked.

"They're all right."

Marcia now had sudden doubts about his taste in music. "All right?"

Smitty could tell he had thoughtlessly broken her heart. Still, he wasn't going to lie. "They're okay. They're not the Doors or the Stones."

"Some of their songs are really good."

"Yeah," Smitty agreed, after too long a pause. "I have two albums Momma Cass did years ago with a commercial folk group. Some of the cuts are better than anything she's done with the Mommas and the Poppas."

"Really?" Marcia asked. "What were they called?"

"The Big 3."

"Were they all fat?" Marcia asked.

Smitty burst out laughing. "No, she was bigger than the two guys put together."

Smitty's laughter was contagious. Marcia, relaxed and happy, was enjoying the nicest high she had ever experienced. "I'd like to hear them."

"When you come back."

"You know there's a song by the Mamas & the Papas I want you to hear, Strange Young Girls."

Smitty remained silent, thinking, '"Strange young girls", had more than my share.'

"To help me figure out the words."

"Bring it over some time," Smitty replied, knowing damn well that her record collection was a few feet away.

Marcia was getting to like his sense of humor. It was different. "You carried it up the stairs in one of those boxes."

Smitty remained silent, pleasantly stoned. He could live without the Mommas and the Pappas, especially right now. More important, he liked the feel of Marcia's head upon his stomach, and her hand in his.

"Would you like to hear it?" she asked.

'Yeah, next Tuesday,' thought Smitty, and thought about it enough to keep from saying it. Yet this seemed awfully important to Marcia. Well, she had simply asked the wrong question, and he wasn't going to lie. Then again, he wasn't going to answer at all unless she made him. Here they were, listening to a great album, and she wanted to get up and start unpacking. 'Unpacking! Hell! Sounds great!' In fact, that was this evening's project — getting her unpacked and moved in. One measly album wouldn't settle the matter, but it was a start. "Sure," he answered belatedly, "dig it out."

Smitty watched with a sense of accomplishment as she opened the box and pulled out the album. He put the record on and had Marcia using his stomach for a pillow again without any problem. Surprisingly, the song was very different from anything else he had heard by them, haunting. Still, Smitty had never gone overboard for "haunting". Despite this, wanting to please Marcia, he strained to decipher the lyrics.

"Can you make out the words," she asked.

Most were easy, yet some were indecipherable. "This LP may be a bad pressing."

She said, "Let's listen to it one more time."

Smitty had no desire to. At the moment, he was into Marcia, not the Mamas & the Papas. Besides, deciphering lyrics was a hassle, a hassle he wasn't up for just then. And just then, he remembered the book of rock lyrics his last, short lived roommate had left behind. No chance it contained the words to this song, not enough to get him on his feet.

Marcia herself cued the cut again. "You try too."

"Okay," he replied without enthusiasm.

"I have to know all the words," Marcia said with determination.

'This is getting weird,' thought Smitty. The mood sure wasn't what it had been moments earlier. Not that he wouldn't like to solve her problem for her. Smitty laughed to himself — 'That problem too.' What were the chances these all important lyrics were in the book his first Berkeley Babe had left behind — 'Close to zero.' Yet if they were, 'I'll be a hero. What the hell?'

Smitty slid out from under Marcia, again swapping out his stomach for the throw pillows. "Be right back." Smitty felt stupid wasting his time. He entered the bedroom and picked up the book, repeating to himself, "Strange Young Girls". He checked the table of contents. There it was, right in front of him, the first thing he saw — "Strange Young Girls". 'Impossible!' He found the page. Sure enough, the lyrics were credited to John Phillips. In a moment he was going to blow Marcia's mind. 'Unbelievable!' In fact, the coincidence was too unbelievable. The planets were aligned. Lady Luck on his side. For the first time, Smitty really believed that tonight Marcia would end up in his bed.

He put on his blankest expression, which wasn't really necessary in that Marcia was still gazing up at the ceiling. A confident smile forced its way onto his face — 'When you're hot, you're hot.' He smoothly switched out the pillows for his stomach. In a moment he was going to make this girl very happy, perhaps happy enough to help him help her out of her skin-tight Levis. Then they'd both be happy — very, very happy.

Lost in concentration, Marcia said, "This song will drive me nuts."

"No it won't," he assured her.

"What makes you so sure?"

"I'll see that it doesn't."

"How?"

"Have confidence in me."

Marcia hesitated. "I don't know you."

"I'll give you the chance." He stood the book, open to the right page, on top of her stomach.

"What's this?" Marcia shot to a sitting position. Stoned as she was, Smitty's producing the lyrics seemed an amazing magic trick. "I don't believe it!"

"You don't know me, remember?" Smitty replied in a bored tone.

Marcia read a few lines to make sure. She turned and leaned over Smitty, asking with glee, "Where did you get this?…How did you do it?"

"You wanted it. I got it."

"You're amazing!"

"That's what all the women say," Smitty assured her.

Marcia gave him a quick peck before turning her attention back to the lyrics. Halfway through them, she stopped just long enough to say, "They are beautiful! I knew it," and then gave Smitty another quick kiss.

He lay still, looking up at her excited expression, taking full credit for it. He had really floored her. What luck. 'If only it holds,' Smitty told himself, now really confident that it would hold. Some things were meant to be. Smitty remembered his last roommate asking if he were angry. 'That woman don't owe me a thing.' This woman, the one he was now looking at, was the one he wanted. For more than just tonight. 'This could end nice.'

When Marcia finished reading, the dreamy look was still on her face. "These lyrics are poetry. Can I read them to you?"

Still looking up at her, Smitty asked innocently, "You're not trying to seduce me, are you?"

Marcia, fighting a smile, shook her head. "What if I am?"

"I hate to tell you, believe me, I hate to tell you, but poetry don't work."

"No?" she asked.

"Uh-uh. I've tried it.…Poetry is the key to celibacy."

Marcia remembered the time some hapless jerk had tried it on her. She began to laugh, hard.

Smitty started grabbing and squeezing her in various places, all of them respectable.

"Stop it!" Marcia demanded, finally able to control her laughter. "Let me read this to you."

Smitty gave her an overly serious, attentive look. As she recited the lyrics, he actually did get into them. "Nice, very nice," he said, meaning what he said, but at the same time thinking, 'Enough with lyrics'. He stretched his arms up reaching for her head. They fell short. He raised up just enough to place his hands on her cheeks, then drew her back down a little. "Do I get a reward?"

Marcia lowered her head until their lips met.

Smitty put just enough pressure on her back to lay her on top of him. A minute of kissing led to enough rolling around on the rug to get most of the wrinkles out. Smitty's hands quickly found their way inside the back of her sweatshirt. They passed over the clasp of her bra, hesitating there again, and again, and again. The one time he put his hands on her ass, she helped him remove them, undamaged at least. A few more tries, and she would get used to them there. He felt amazingly confident, confident enough to be in no hurry.

For a moment, Marcia saw herself as if from a distance. She gazed surprised and somewhat uneasy at what was happening. Was it the marijuana? He seemed nice. She liked him. And he wasn't a grabber. He moved his hands slowly, predictably. Anything sudden would have put her on the defensive. There was something different about Smitty. Still, things were happening too fast. More than once, she made up her mind to call a halt. Marcia waited for an excuse. Eventually he would try to unhook her bra, or get too insistent with his hands. Then she'd put an end to it.

To Smitty, she seemed relaxed, content, willing to continue. Yet he sensed no hint of passion, no encouragement to go farther. He wished he could really turn her on, but hell, things were now way better than he had expected. Why push? He soon found himself with his back on the cold floor. 'Uh oh.' Rolling around was for rugs, not ice cold floors. He rolled Marcia right back onto rug, and himself gently on to her.

She kissed him and said, "I think it's bedtime."

Smitty saw no reason to argue. "Outa sight."

"We're not thinking the same thing."

Pleasantly stoned, he found himself making those little comments he would normally keep to himself. "We'll work it out."

Marcia laughed. "I already have it worked out. I'll sleep on the couch....By myself."

"Why would you want to do that?"

"That's the way we planned it."

"Those were rough plans."

"They'll do fine."

"That's ridiculous. Why should you sleep on that bug infested couch when there's such a big, comfortable bed available?"

'Bug infested?' Marcia could believe that, but he was probably just trying to scare her. "Because I'd have to share it," she replied, thinking that two bottom sheets would be a good idea.

"C'mon, that bed is so big, it'd take a semester to find you in it...unless you snore."

Laughing, and with some resistance from Smitty, she pushed herself to her feet. "I'm sleeping on the couch."

Smitty stood, putting his arms around her and drawing her close. "Wait a minute. You don't think I'm the cave man type, do you?"

Amused, Marcia leaned back to get a better look at him. To her, he looked overpowering. She hoped he wasn't the cave man type. "Are you?"

Smitty thought this over a moment. "No, but I do requests." He grabbed a hunk of her hair.

Marcia pushed him away. "I have a request. Let me sleep on the couch."

"I know. You're afraid you wouldn't be able to resist me."

"Exactly," she admitted.

"Don't sweat it. I can defend myself."

"You've never seen me aroused," she assured him.

"I'm working on that."

Marcia pulled herself away and towards the couch. "Good night."

Trying to sound serious, Smitty said, "I'd feel like a heel if I let you sleep on that raunchy couch."

"Keeping me up doesn't make you feel like a heel?

Smitty forced a serious expression on his face. "You're right. We'll get this over with right now, by flipping a coin. Let chance decide."

"Great," Marcia agreed. She was really tired now. "And that'll be it?"

Smitty already had a quarter out. He tossed it in his hand. "Okay. Now if it's heads, we take the bed. If it's tails, we take the couch. And if it stands on edge, you take the bed and I'll take the couch."

Marcia, too tired to really laugh, collapsed onto the couch. "What happened to you?...You've talked more in the last five minutes than in all the time I've known you."

'Good dope helps,' thought Smitty, answering instead, "Beats me, but I like the way I'm feeling." He took Marcia's tired face in his hands. His words were as serious as his expression. "Tomorrow morning, when I wake up, you have to be there."

Marcia stared up at him, right into his eyes. Her face still in his hands, she shook her head No.

Smitty nodded her head up and down.

Marcia felt herself wavering. This night was something different, special. Smitty was different too. The way he looked right into your eyes, so innocent. 'Different?' Who was he, the boy who wouldn't open his mouth or the one who wouldn't shut up? Yet she liked one as much as the other. Still, she really didn't know either of them, certainly not well enough to jump into bed. Though that was the way it seemed to be done in Berkeley.

Smitty sensed she was about to give in. He leaned closer, playing his thumb gently along the side of her face. "C'mon, I have faith in you. You can resist me."

"You think that's possible?"

"Believe me, it's been done...too many times."

Marcia gave out a weary sigh. The couch was looking even skuzzier up close. She forced a serious expression on her face before demanding, "No wrestling."

"Promise," he replied, despite the fact that wrestling was one of his more refined skills.

"Okay," she said, getting to her feet. "I'll get my pajamas."

"Why not," he agreed. Then, knowing he was risking it all, Smitty couldn't help but add, "You can keep them under your pillow in case of fire."

Marcia again collapsed wearily on the couch, shaking her head No in tired laughter.

Smitty gently pulled her to her feet, then to the suitcases for her pajamas. He even got her halfway to the bathroom before she shoved him away. Standing alone in the living room with a huge grin on his face, he stretched his arms to the ceiling in a victory yawn. Yet he reminded himself, 'Nothing's settled.' Still — 'No mistakes so far'. He didn't want to make one either. No, he'd take things slow. See what happened. More of the same would not be bad. Hell, pajamas were sexy, almost as sexy as no pajamas. Not really, but pajamas offered a hell of a lot more hope than skintight Levis. He had never wanted a woman so much.

Marcia came out of the bathroom wearing her pajamas. They were not the sexy shorty-type he had expected. They looked like the ones he wore years ago, when he still wore them. On her, they did look sexier. Marcia gave him that serious, no nonsense expression favored by rookie high school teachers on the first day of class.

Smitty felt his blood rushing south. Pajamas were sexier than he had realized. She looked great. He opened his mouth to say something, but no words came. Closing his mouth, he nodded to himself a few times before managing an innocent, "You know, you're not a bad looking woman?"

Marcia, amused, remaining silent, fought to keep the serious expression on her face.

Smitty nodded to himself again before asking innocently, as if he had a hunch, "You've been told that before?"

Marcia, to keep from breaking out into a smile, answered, "Not in those exact words."

Smitty shook his head in disappointment. "You gotta be fast."

Marcia took a step forward, losing her serious expression and placing a hand on his shoulder. "I'm tired."

"Oh," he said, "Go on in. The bed's the big square thing....Can't miss it."

Marcia shook her head and started for the bedroom.

Smitty headed to the bathroom and brushed his teeth. Then he brushed them again to make sure. A shower would be nice. 'Too dangerous.' Marcia might fall asleep, or even escape the apartment. He sniffed his left armpit. 'Pass.' He sniffed his right armpit. 'Pass.' Still, Smitty did not want to take a chance. He gave himself a "dry cleaning" — a quick spray of aerosol deodorant under each armpit. That should do the job. Hell, in funky Berkeley, this was enough to get him branded a hygiene fanatic.

The moment of truth had arrived. He headed for the bedroom. The pinkish glow from the street lamp made turning on the light unnecessary, which Smitty wouldn't have done even if it were necessary. Marcia was under the covers lying on her back. Her eyes were closed or close to it. Smitty stripped down to his undershorts. He thought of apologizing for his lack of pajamas, asking if she preferred lending him a pair of hers. He immediately thought better of it.

Smitty doubted she was asleep, just pretending to be. He suddenly got the urge, as a joke, to kneel down at the side of the bed to say his prayers. '...And if I die before I wake, I pray the Lord this girl to make—' No, that would be too much. Way too much. God, was he stoned. Was it just the grass?

Smitty compromised with himself, whispering, "It's just me," as he slipped beneath the covers. There was a lot of space between him and Marcia, miles. Smitty stared up at the ceiling. He was not the least bit tired. It could be years before he got to sleep. There was no other place in the world he'd rather be. It was just that he'd rather be doing something else there besides staring at the ceiling. Still, Smitty, at that moment, was very, very happy. Frustrated, yet happy. He glanced over at Marcia. Her cheek glowed in the pinkish light. Her eyes were still closed and she hadn't moved an inch. Yet he was certain she was wide awake. He even thought he could see a faint smile on her lips.

Marcia lay motionless, ready to jump out of bed. She was sure Smitty would try something. She wouldn't get angry. She wouldn't say anything. She'd just head for the couch. Determined, that's what she would do. Marcia lay still, for what seemed like a very long time, long enough to give her doubts that he would try something.

Smitty, remaining on his part of the bed, turned on his side to face Marcia. He propped up his head with one arm. Sure that she would finally open her eyes, he just waited, and waited. In the light of the street lamp he couldn't be sure, but it seemed that she was definitely smiling. Finally, she opened her eyes wide and turned her head slightly towards him. They stared at each other a long, long moment, their smiles widening. In one surprisingly smooth motion, without touching her, Smitty slid over right next to Marcia.

The smile immediately left her face. She stared solemnly up at the ceiling.

Smitty, still on his side, head propped up on his arm, asked softly, like a defeated husband, "You're not gonna pull that headache business again, are you, Dear?"

Marcia focused all her strength to keep from laughing. It wasn't enough.

Smitty knew it was now or never. He made his move, and Marcia didn't flinch. Soon they were in the middle of a kiss, one far too long for the good night kind. This was just as well. It was quite a while before they did get to sleep, well after dawn.

*****

Marcia awoke to the sound of a shower. She sighed contentedly. Despite only a few hours of sleep, she felt surprisingly refreshed. Things had not gone as planned, far from it. Yet she had no regrets. Smitty baffled her. How could he seem so strong and yet be so gentle? His hands never seemed to touch her except where and when she wanted to be touched. How did he know? If he came out of the shower and over to the bed, she would open her arms for him, hug him tighter than she had ever hugged anyone.

Boy, things had happened fast, fast enough to make her feel dizzy. Well, she had a place to live now, and a roommate. It just then sunk in that this roommate was a boy. She had not planned on that. Oh God, what would her father think? Well he hadn't been too crazy about Heather either. More than once, she had caught him giving Heather a sideways glance. Still, Marcia did not try to kid herself. Her father would have preferred Heather to any boy. God, how could she break the news to him. Marcia had not a clue. If only she had a mother to tell him. Well, she wouldn't have to say anything until she and Smitty got a telephone. Maybe they wouldn't get a phone. Of course they would. Somehow, she would just have to find the right words.

'What's done is done,' Marcia told herself. These were her mother's words, one of the few strong memories she had of her. There had been a beautiful lead crystal ashtray in their home. If Marcia moved it in her hand, the glass would be full of flickering little rainbows. Her mother, worried she would break the ashtray, had told Marcia never to pick it up. Yet when her mother wasn't watching her, Marcia was often drawn to it. She would lift it carefully, move it slowly to make the tiny rainbows, then gently, silently put it back down. She had done this dozens of times. It was her secret. One day, when she was seven years old, she got careless and dropped the ashtray. It broke into a dozen pieces, some of them still containing rainbows. Marcia remembered letting out a wail that she had never heard before or since. Her mother came running, a distraught look on her face. She saw the pieces of ashtray on the floor. Her mother kneeled down, hugging Marcia and telling her not to cry, saying, "There's nothing we can do now. What's done is done." These words comforted Marcia, then and now. Yet the memory that came with them saddened her.

Marcia asked herself how things had changed so fast. The answer came to her immediately — Smitty had tricked, seduced her. And he had seemed so honest, naive even. Marcia knew from past experiences that she was not the best judge of character, not even a good one. Here she was, about to move in with someone, unsure she could trust him, not after what he did to her last night, which in fact was wonderful, which made things all the more confusing. Making matters even worse, Smitty, had gotten to her.

She had fallen for him, hard.

Still, then and there, Marcia decided not to take the chance. No, she would move back to the rooming house for another week, try to find an apartment for herself. If Smitty wanted, she would go out with him, learn what he was really like, and how much he liked her. Would he help her move back to the rooming house? That would be a test. Marcia was determined to give him that test.

The bathroom door squeaked open. She closed her eyes, feigning sleep. Marcia could not talk to Smitty, not right now. She listened to him get dressed, open the apartment door, and then lock it. A moment later she heard him unlock it and walk back into the bedroom. Marcia knew he was standing over her. Still she refused to open her eyes. He continued to stand over her, finally asking, "You'll be here when I get back?"

Marcia opened her lips to say No. She couldn't, not without an explanation. At that moment, she did not have the words to offer him one. Besides, his tone had been so innocent, almost plaintive. Marcia found herself mumbling the single word, "Yes."

She listened to him leaving the apartment, surprised at what she had done, yet thinking, 'What's done is done.'

*****

Smitty walked towards campus with a huge smile on his face and an expansive feeling in his chest. If he could have seen himself walking towards himself he would have asked himself, "What's with that idiot?" Not one thing that had happened to him since his arrival at Berkeley could hold a candle to the previous night. Despite her innocence, there was nothing weak or helpless about Marcia. She radiated a quiet, level headed intelligence. Every time he had first slept with a woman, no matter how much of a surprise it might have been, no matter how long the previous drought, no matter how much pleasure she had given him, the next day or soon thereafter, he had always taken a step backwards, asked himself, "What exactly have I gotten myself into?" Now, walking towards campus to his first day of classes at Berkeley, without being completely conscious of it, he knew that this time he would not ask himself that question. Whatever he had gotten himself into, he was damn glad to be into it. Marcia had something he had never come across before, something he hadn't even known he was looking for, and it did not bother him a bit that he had not a clue as to what this something was. Just as long as she had it, and he had her.

Smitty reached campus at a fast walk. He was going to be late for his first class. Rushing through the gate, he noticed a dozen Honor Bikes parked right inside it. 'Outa sight!' He turned back and literally jumped on one. Smitty was on his way in an instant. He felt again the same sense of freedom that riding bikes had given him when he was a kid. What a fantastic idea these Honor Bikes had been. If only the whole world worked like this. Some day it might. He smiled at the sight of other students riding Honor Bikes, felt a kinship with them. He also took pride in knowing that he had been among the few who had brought the Honor Bike idea to fruition.

Smitty arrived at his class early, yet he still had to squeeze through a knot of people at the door. He was surprised to see that he had entered a small auditorium of about a hundred seats. He was more surprised to see every seat taken, and close to half a hundred more people lined up against the walls. He made his way to the least crowded spot, the far back corner. Even here he found no room against the wall, and had to block the view of an attractive blond girl. He shifted around, looking for a solution.

The blond girl turned sideways to make room for him against the wall.

"Thanks," he said.

She gave him a bright, fresh smile, one that hinted at country, perhaps even farm. Her straight blond hair was down to her shoulders.

Smitty asked, "What's going on?"

"You're not taking this course?" she asked. "I'm taking it. Looks like half the campus is too."

"Most of them are just sitting in today, to see what happens.…You know who he is, don't you?"

"According to The Slate, the easiest grader in the English Department. I needed at least one crip course."

Her smile broadened. "You got more than that. He's the most popular instructor in the department." The crush of students pushed Smitty and the blond girl together. "Too popular.…That's why the faculty won't give him tenure."

A tapping on a microphone drew their attention to the front of the auditorium. "Hello," said a friendly voice. It belonged to a man of average height and slight build. He looked over the class from behind a pair of old fashioned wire-rimmed spectacles, the only style of glasses a self-respecting Berkeley hippie would wear. Despite the glasses, this man was not dressed anything like a freak. He wore a dark, stylish suit, and a tie to match. It was not until he took the microphone in hand and stepped out from behind the podium, that Smitty noticed the speaker's conservative suit was accented by a pair of white, high-top sneakers.

"Welcome....Unless you care to irritate me, you will not call me 'Professor', 'Sir', 'Mr. Bunker', or even 'Prof'. I request you call me by my given name, 'Peter'. If for some reason you can't bring yourself to do this, then 'Hey, You' will do fine." The class greeted these remarks with sprinkled chuckles and a substantial, if slightly forced, laugh at the end.

"I certainly hope most of you are just sitting in, because I have no intention of grading so many papers." This brought a hardier, unforced laugh from the room. "We might as well get started. As an introduction, I have arranged for a talk by Professor Hans Strumpmeyer. His subject will be the subject of this course — Reality as Literature.

Bunker held his arm out in the direction of a bearded man in a black ill-fitting suit who was climbing the steps at the side of the stage. Bunker began to applaud, and so did the entire room. Professor Strumpmeyer, carrying an ugly black briefcase, looked like some slapstick actor's idea of a feckless college professor. In fact, Strumpmeyer stumbled both on his way up the stairs and again just before reaching the podium. A quick, awkward grab for it was the only thing that kept him from falling on his face.

Strumpmeyer placed his briefcase on the podium, and immediately began searching in it. While doing so, he mumbled in some unintelligible foreign language, just loud enough for the microphone to pick up. His searching increased in ferocity and his mumbling increased in volume. Soon he was cursing loudly in English, made almost unintelligible by an over-the-top German accent. Finally, he glared at the audience, shouting the question, "You want reality? You want reality? YOU WANT REALITY?...I'LL SHOW YOU REALITY!" With this he pulled a minimum three pound raw steak from his briefcase. He held it up high for the audience. "THIS IS REALITY!" Strumpmeyer then swung the steak sideways at his own briefcase, sending it and all the papers in it across the stage. His next swing was at the microphone, which hit the floor with almost enough force to blow out the speakers. He then began banging the raw steak down upon the podium. Strumpmeyer soon tired and had to be content to leave the steak on the podium and pound it with his fist, all the while continuing to shout, "This is reality!" When he finally collapsed to his knees, taking the steak with him, his shouts were now closer to wails. Strumpmeyer was soon laid out on his stomach, still pounding the steak with his fist, whimpering, "Take this. This is reality."

Nearly everyone in the room greeted this performance with hysterical laughter, too hysterical. Embarrassed by all this forced laughter, Smitty noticed that the blond girl wasn't laughing either. If there were some hidden hilarious joke in all this, he must be missing it. Smitty doubted he was missing anything. He guessed that, among other things, this clown must be "beating his meat", but the idea did not seem all that humorous, or deep either. He shrugged at the blonde as if the joke had eluded him. She shrugged back. Still, Smitty had to admit that this lecture was far different from any he had attended at Ohio State.

It was then that he heard his very own thoughts shouted from the stage — "THIS ISN'T REALITY! IT'S BULLSHIT!"

Their shared opinion had been offered by a coed who now stood above Professor Strumpmeyer, kicking him. As she continued to do so, he struggled to his hands and knees, at the same time trying to get off the stage. Cheers of joy came from the class when he finally fell headfirst down the steps.

The coed, striding triumphantly back to the center of the stage, shouted, "YOU WANT REALITY?"

"YES!" half the class shouted back.

She thereupon ripped open the front of her dress, slipped out of it in an instant, held her arms out to her sides, and, buck naked, shouted, "THIS IS REALITY!"

An instant of complete silence ended in a few gasps, which were quickly drowned out by raucous cheers, soon mixed with laughter and applause. Still without a stitch on, the coed leaped from the stage swinging her dress over her head like a lariat. Continuing to swing it, she ran up the center aisle and out the door. The knot of people clogging it made way, but she had to do some squeezing to get through and outside, still naked as a jaybird.

Smitty's eyes were as big as saucers. His grin was far larger. He would gladly come to class for this. Every day. Especially for a different coed each time. Smitty suddenly realized that he, like half the class, was still applauding. He stopped, saying to the blond girl, "You were right. This class ain't boring."

Professor Bunker announced, "I think we have covered, or uncovered, enough for one day. Class dismissed."

His words were met with cheers. Instead of leaving, at least a fourth of the audience moved forward to surround Professor Bunker in a tight ring of students. The blond girl jerked her head towards these worshipers, asking Smitty, "You don't have any questions?"

"I think I got it all," he assured her.

The knot of students at the door had thinned. As they headed towards it, she asked, "Are you sure?"

"When I get home, I'll go over my notes."

"I didn't take any. Can I borrow yours?" Her smile broke into a laugh, one so wholesome Smitty found it a pleasure. Her shoulders hardly shook. They had strength in them, bred for the farm. Smitty pictured her hair in two long braids, not realizing he was imagining Hollywood's cliché fresh faced milk maid. Who was she? Accents always intrigued him. He was good at placing them, yet the milk maid's was faint enough to be a mystery. Did he detect a hint of Pennsylvania Dutch, perhaps a generation or two off the farm? "Pennsylvania?" he asked.

The question was so out of the blue, she found it surprising. Even more surprising was the fact that he had guessed right. She stared at him with obvious admiration. "How did you know?"

Smitty shrugged. He stood silent a moment, thinking, 'When you're hot, you're hot.' And being hot, he noticed his Honor Bike waiting where he had left it. Ever the gentleman, he offered it to her.

"Is it yours?" she asked.

"Ours," he replied, explaining to her the Code of the Honor Bike.

"Don't you want it?"

"I'll get another one." He glanced around to see none in sight.

She caught this, saying, "I'll ride the crossbar."

This was an offer Smitty could not resist. Soon they were on their way. The breeze he made felt great against his face. Her long, blond hair was flying back an inch or two away from him. He got the urge to speed up until he could feel it against his face. This took some hard pedaling. Her hair brushed his face in an irritating yet pleasurable tease. He felt like a kid again, realizing that he was acting like one too, going much too fast for the crowded square. Yet the thrill in the girl's smile kept Smitty from slowing down until they reached the campus entrance.

As they split up at the gate, Smitty said, "Can I ask you a personal question?"

She moved her head back a little, suspicion replacing most of her smile. "You can ask."

"What's your name?"

Her smile returned. "Rachel."

*****

Susan stared at Marco's boxer shorts. White with dozens of red hearts printed on them, they lay in the middle of the bathroom floor. How could she be married to a man who would wear such ridiculous underwear? It was not just a question of bad taste. How could he not know that his underwear was a comedy cliché? Though Marco did have exceedingly poor taste in clothes, his boxer shorts were not an example of it. Taste had nothing to do with his choice of underwear. If he hadn't found them in his drawer, she doubted he could have even recognized them as his own. Marco didn't choose or pick out underwear. He just found the cheapest in his size and bought them, underwear the store probably would have paid him to dispose of. Marco, the husband who could spend a half hour deciding between the two ugliest shirts in a store, couldn't care less about his underwear. Underwear? Who would see them besides his wife? Well his wife was looking at them right now, and she did not like what she was seeing. Susan could leave them right where they were for Marco to pick up. Yet if she waited for Marco to come home, she would have to look at them every time she entered the bathroom. No, that would be too much. Susan bent down and picked up Marco's underwear with two fingers and dropped them into the hamper. She made no conscious decision that Marco would pay for this. The decision was completely subconscious.

Susan had thought she was marrying another Lenin. The way he could rally the masses, get them to do his will. What skill he had. She could not imagine ever losing her awe of his gifts. Her imagination had proved far too limited. Any trick gets old if you see it enough. So now she found herself married to a one trick pony. Sure he could get up a riot in no time, but to little effect except enriching the local glaziers. He should have married one of their daughters. With Marco, it was the same thing again and again, obviously leading nowhere. Change? Where was it?

Susan had read a lot, especially about the masses, been inspired by and believed in them. Now she had seen them up close, many, many times. Sure, they could break windows, overturn police cars and set them on fire. And what had that proved? Just that glass and police cars were easily replaceable.

Change was coming. Susan could feel it. Still, the masses would never bring it about, at least not with Marco leading them. No, Marco's trick had gotten old even for them. When change did come, he would be lucky to survive the first act. Marco was the no-name band that opened for the superstars. He was the small time comedian who warmed up the audience. Someone else would have to take it from here, and Susan doubted the masses would play more than a secondary role. She had lost her respect for them. The main reason why was the way the masses let themselves be manipulated by people such as Marco, her husband, a man who had never had even one original idea.

*****

Smitty rushed up the stairs to his apartment. A gnawing fear had hung over him the entire way home — Marcia would be gone, for good. Earlier that morning, as he had hesitated outside of his locked apartment, his pride told him not to go back in. He ignored it. Smitty did not want any misunderstandings. Women were prone to them, at least with him. He reentered the apartment to ask her,

"You'll be here when I get back?"

"Yes," she had murmured.

About to ask her, "Promise?" he had caught himself. This was getting embarrassing.

Her one word reply had been enough to send him bounding confidently out the door to his first day of classes. And what a day it had been. He couldn't wait to tell her about it. For that, she had to be there when he opened the door. He'd been lucky so far. Too lucky. And luck evened out. He deserved some bad luck after those lecherous thoughts about Rachel during the bike ride. Well lecherous was way too strong a word. Still, here it was, the day after the sweetest— the sweetest— the sweetest night, yeah that was a better word, the sweetest night he'd ever had, and already he was going through the preliminaries with some new chick. The least he could have done was hold out for a decent interval — a week or so. Well Rachel had given him that interested look. Still, for all he knew, she gave that look to everyone. Yet she was not just any chick. She was a fox, quite a fox. Who could blame him? He then answered his own question. 'Marcia, for one.'

Smitty opened the apartment door with the old situation comedy standby, "Honey, I'm home." The smile on his face grew larger when he saw Marcia's boxes still clogging up the living room. A quick check of the bedroom told him that he was home alone. The bed was made, making his shabby surroundings less shabby. 'Ah, the feminine touch.' He'd use his situation comedy entrance another time. At least he wasn't worried now. Even if Marcia were splitting, she'd have to come back to get her things, and to get by him on the way out. He headed for the refrigerator, looking for a note from Marcia on the door. Nope. He took a long drink straight from the water jug. Still swallowing, he reminded himself that he now had a roommate. Better start using a glass. Smitty shook his head, remembering how some casual lay of his had once caught him sucking on the water jug. She'd gone rogue, called him a disgusting slob, and not five minutes after having given him the most accomplished blow job he had ever received.

Marcia still wasn't home. It had been…two minutes, at least. 'Relax!' She wasn't going anywhere. How the hell did Marcia become so important to him in such a short time? By being the girl he wanted more than he had ever wanted any other girl, that's how.

155

"Enough!" Smitty berated himself aloud. He needed to get his mind off Marcia for a few minutes. Fortunately, he knew just the subject that could get his mind off anything for a while — food. Smitty was hungry. First he needed a plate, and not one from the cupboard. Those had to be washed afterwards. He had been no more than a first semester sophomore when, in a flash of insight, Smitty's Theory of Dirty Dishes had come to him: Washing less than a full sink of dishes was a waste of time, effort, soap, and water. Along with this theory, in the same flash of insight, came its four corollaries. 1) You always run out of at least one dish you need before the pile in the sink surpasses countertop level. 2) The dish you need is always near the bottom of the pile. 3) Between you and the needed dish, there is sure to be at least one cockroach. 4) Washing that dish singly, or less than a full sink, violates Smitty's Theory of Dirty Dishes.

As far as Smitty was concerned, your traditional plate would do in a pinch, but it was no substitute for the perfect plate — your good old American newspaper. Spread enough of it on the table. Pig out to both your heart and stomach's content and gluttonous desire. Afterwards, gather all battlefield debris in center of newspaper. Roll paper around it. Knead into a tight, round ball. From a sitting position, applying just enough backspin, arch the ball into the garbage can. Two points for Smitty's Theory of Dirty Dishes.

A quick search of the apartment yielded enough newspaper for an entire set of dinnerware. Smitty gathered his ingredients and dumped them on his "plate". The sourdough roll made his mouth water. Now Smitty didn't claim to know anything about bread that you couldn't read off the wrapper, but he'd claim to have learned something about sourdough bread in the short time he'd been out West. San Francisco sourdough bread was a completely different animal from whatever the hell it was that they sold as sourdough back in Cleveland. How had he lived so long without the real thing? It did the seemingly impossible, it made mayonnaise taste even better.

Smitty cut his sourdough roll sandwich-wise. He covered the bottom with a quarter inch of sliced turkey, then a doubled over lettuce leaf. It was now time for the most important ingredient — mayonnaise. He put on a heaping tablespoon. For Smitty, a heaping tablespoon was as much as you could load and balance on a tablespoon. He had found that the turkey and lettuce lent the mayonnaise just the right flavor, and chewy sourdough bread made that flavor last. Smitty knew he had applied a sufficient amount if, after his first bite, the mayonnaise was visible on all sides of the sandwich. After a second bite, at least one of his hands should be sticky with it. The third bite should be impossible to take without some of the mayonnaise dripping onto the newspaper. And the extra mayonnaise sure did grease the way down for those tastier King Kong sized bites. Long ago he'd discovered that the best method for keeping the maximum amount of mayonnaise inside the sandwich, was to always rotate his bites to the edge oozing the most mayonnaise. Taste depended upon more than just the ingredients and how you combined them. Taste also depended upon your eating style. He remembered some lines from a Henry Miller novel. That you could buy the best wine in France, bring it back across the ocean to America, and it wouldn't taste near as good. Smitty had no doubt this was true. Well the French had their wine, but we had Hellmann's mayonnaise, and he doubted it would taste as good in France.

Smitty had just finished the last bite, sitting there with a satisfied, mayonnaise encrusted smile on his face, when Marcia walked in. "Hi."

"Hi," Smitty replied, making a dash for the sink. He gave his face and hands a quick rinse, then came back to clear the table. She was already sitting. He came up behind her and put his hands on her shoulders. "Missed you."

She bent her head back as far as she could to get a look at him. "I've got some exciting news."

Smitty put on the goofiest gleeful grin he could muster. "We're going to have a baby!" He had used the line before, never failing to get a laugh.

It didn't fail this time either. "No, not that I know of....The University gave in. The custodians can form a union!"

Now Smitty had not been losing much sleep over this issue, so he found it easy to control his own excitement. In fact, he had to ramp it up a bit with his choice of words. "That's great."

The smile left her face. "It's going to mean a lot of work for me."

"How do you figure?" Smitty asked, rolling his "plate" into a ball.

"I'm on the contract negotiating committee. When they choose our union to represent them, we'll have to bargain with the University."

"Why are you so sure they'll choose you?" he asked, flipping his plate from hand to hand.

Marcia gave Smitty an indignant look. "The Socialist Workers Union, that's us, was the first union to fight for them. The Union of Communist Workers didn't help out until the end, and they rioted at the last meeting. I'm sure the custodians didn't appreciate that."

"You're the only two unions they have to choose from?"

"No, there's the State Employees Union, but they refused to help until now. And then there's the Teamsters. But everyone knows they're the most crooked union in the country."

Everyone included Smitty, who had learned from personal experience on the loading dock. "Yeah," he agreed. "Their president is in the slammer." He stared sadly at Marcia. "Don't you want to know what I did today?"

"Of course. How was your day, Dear?"

"Oh, I don't know," he said, in intended understatement. Smitty followed with a detailed recap of his Reality as Literature class while putting back into the refrigerator whatever was supposed to go there.

To Smitty's surprise, Marcia showed no surprise, or even amusement. He figured she must be used to such shenanigans from her freshman year, until finally—

She asked, "Why would anybody want to do that?"

"Do what?"

"Run around naked in front of a class."

Now Smitty was not one to look a gift horse in the mouth, so this question had not occurred to him.

Marcia, fortunately, moved on immediately to her next question. "Was she pretty?"

"No, not really, he answered, then added with a smile, "Not compared to you." Smitty was already congratulating himself on his cleverly inserted compliment when he noticed it had failed to register.

Marcia was still seriously pondering the motivation behind

Bunker's presentation, and more important, the students' reactions to it, especially that of Smitty. Such seemingly purposeless acts were not a part of Berkeley that held any interest for her. In fact, they separated her from the large majority of students. Marcia would have preferred not to be separated. "It just seems childish to me."

Smitty, after a moment's thought, could not argue otherwise. His fantastic adventure had shrunk even in his own eyes.

Marcia glanced at a small grocery bag she had laid on the table, before saying with disappointment, "You couldn't wait ten minutes?"

"I didn't know when you were coming home."

"My note said 5:00, and that I would make a spaghetti dinner for us."

"What note?" asked Smitty.

His eyes followed hers, only now noticing that the typing paper at the center of the table was not blank. Upon it, inside a large mayonnaise stain, was a short, single line of small, neat script. By not looking at Marcia, Smitty was able to keep a straight face while saying, "Well, you should have put it some place where I'd see it."

"On the refrigerator?"

"Exactly!…Hey, it was just a little hors d'oeuvre. I got room for more."

Marcia stared at the stain obscuring her note. "Did you get any mayonnaise on your hors d'oeuvre?"

"A dab," he assured her.

Smitty decided to get rid of the evidence. He reached for the note and wrapped it around the "plate" he had been tossing between his hands. "You look tired."

"I am."

"You have a right to be."

They laughed as she said, "Both of us have."

Smitty jerked his head towards the bedroom. "Want to lie down before supper?"

Marcia nodded.

"Here, let me get the dishes." He squeezed the paper ball tight, and without getting up, tossed it into the garbage.

Again Marcia nodded, saying, "Two points."

Straughton lay on his black satin sheets staring up at the ceiling. It was stained and peeling, with spider webs in three of the four corners. He hardly gave a thought to the three occupied corners or the even large spider hanging from the light fixture, halfway between it and his feet. The fourth corner was the one which attracted the attention of his perpetually inquiring mind. Why was it vacant? Was something wrong with it?

As Straughton pondered the behavior of spiders, an older, recurring conundrum came to mind. Albert Einstein earned a Nobel Prize for calculating the speed of light. Yet, as far as Straughton knew, no one had yet figured out the speed of dark. Straughton's intuition told him that it was equal to the speed of light. Logically, if the speed of light were faster than the speed of dark, it would overtake it. The speed of dark would never be able to catch up. This meant it would be light all the time. And if the speed of dark were faster than the speed of light, it would be dark all the time. However faultless his logic, Straughton knew that he would have to find a physical way to prove this. Perhaps he should sit in on some Physics courses. This would be just the type of groundbreaking article the Pulitzer Prize Committee drools over.

Yet the back of Straughton's mind was occupied with a more immediate problem demanding a more immediate solution — reporter's block. Though serious, this problem was not nearly as serious as writer's block. Eventually something would happen, an event that would practically write itself. In Berkeley, even a blind reporter with a cane would eventually trip over a good story. A veteran reporter such as himself, if necessary, could instigate or completely manufacture one. Tonight Straughton needed to. Tomorrow was payday. Trying to pry money out of Moe, unless you first greased his palm with an article, was time consuming and no fun. Straughton was confident he would think of something. He always had. Still, the process could be a pain, in some ways similar to and almost as degrading as actual work.

Straughton had recently read somewhere that lipstick contains lead, and that the average woman ingests about 5 pounds of it from just licking her lips. Now lead has been proven to lower one's IQ.

This would help explain the difference in intelligence between men and woman. Yet it may explain much more. Five pounds of lead would have to make a woman's lips sag. He pictured women tripping over their lower lips. No, even five pounds would not make their lips sag anywhere near that much. Still, it could explain the sour expressions on most of their faces. Furthermore—

A loud knock on the door caused Straughton to flinch. 'What now?' he thought, getting to his feet. The knock came again, this time louder. "Who is it?"

"Screw. Open up. I got the dope."

Thinking, 'I have all the dope I need,' Straughton opened the door anyway.

Screw, even more excited than usual, came flying into the room. "I got a great story for you, Man. A scoop!"

Straughton had heard similar claims before. However, at the moment he was more inclined to waste the time. "A scoop is something I would greatly appreciate."

Screw looked Straughton straight in the eye. "What would the world be like if everybody could get stoned for nothing?"

"Completely stoned."

"Right-on!" said Screw. "And here's the scoop; you can get stoned from bananas."

"From bananas?" Straughton asked matter-of-factly. He eyed Screw with the indulgent expression of a nut house intern. "From slipping on them and banging your head?"

"No! From smoking them."

Straughton tried to picture someone smoking a banana. He succeeded, but found the results suspicious. Aside from appearing ridiculous, how would you light a banana in the first place, with a blow torch? Would you peel it first? Or just one end of it? If so, which end? The one in your mouth? The one you lit? How would you keep it lit? And how, pray tell, would you squeeze out a drag by sucking on the end of a banana? Surely you would get a hernia first. Straughton felt ridiculous for even contemplating the possibility of smoking a banana. He studied Screw like never before. "Per chance, was the gentleman who provided you this scoop quite short and unusually hairy?"

"No!" Screw protested, "And I didn't meet him at the zoo either."

"How exactly would one smoke a banana."

"You don't smoke the whole banana, only the peel!" Screw gave Straughton a satisfied smile, as if he had just explained everything.

To Straughton, Screw had explained nothing. For every way he pictured smoking a banana peel, there was obviously something very wrong with the picture. First of all, the peel always flopped down the smokers chin like a skinny yellow goatee. Even the suave Cary Grant would look absurd trying to light Ingrid Bergman's banana peel. And Bogart himself couldn't Bogart one. Straughton gave Screw a look questioning his sanity.

Screw took the look personally. There was some anger in his tone as he said, "You dry it out first, bake it in the oven." Straughton did not change his expression, further offending Screw. "You're so sure it won't work, let's try it."

'And waste the time,' thought Straughton. Yet it would be a hell of a scoop if it did work. 'Unfortunately, it won't.' Still, besides time, what was there to lose? "My Friend, you happened to catch me in an indulgent mood."

"You got a banana?"

"Certainly." Straughton walked over to the refrigerator and brought a full bunch of bananas down from on top. He and Screw stared at them. The bananas had been slightly green when he had put them up there. They must have turned yellow unnoticed, because now they were black with green blotches of mold. This was not the first time bananas had gone bad on Straughton. More than once he had told himself that the top of the refrigerator was a dangerous place for them. The kitchen table would be a better spot, make it easier to keep tabs on them. Bananas were a relatively difficult fruit. They demanded a more watchful eye and more responsibility than apples or pears, and only slightly less than Cocker Spaniels. Straughton looked up at Screw. "Maybe they'll still work....Maybe even better."

Screw gave a slight shake of his head. "Smoking those 'may be hazardous to your health'."

"They are what I have."

"I'll knock on some doors. Warm up the oven."

"What temperature may I ask?"

Screw pondered. "Two hundred degrees, I think he said."

As soon as Straughton had the oven going, Screw was back with two bananas. While he peeled them, Straughton came over with a piece of tin foil for the skins and a plate for each naked banana. "Who said?" asked Straughton.

"'Who said,' what?" asked Screw, as he placed the peels in the oven.

"Who said, 'Two hundred degrees'?"

"The guy who told me about smoking them."

"Obviously," said Straughton. "May I ask why, My Good Man, you chose to believe him?" Straughton pulled out some silverware and headed for the table, motioning Screw to follow.

"You would have believed him too if you had seen him."

Straughton set down one of the plates with a banana on it, then set a knife and fork next to it. He motioned for Screw to sit down. "Because he was stoned?"

"No!" Screw protested. "This guy is a genuine graduate student in Physics, and wow does he look it — port hole eye glasses, one shoe untied, different color socks. If this dude wasn't a sure bet to be the next Einstein, the world would have let him starve to death years ago." Screw couldn't take his eyes off Straughton, who was now eating his banana with a knife and fork. 'Is he putting me on?' Screw doubted it. Straughton could not be that good an actor.

Slicing off another piece of banana and impaling it gingerly on his fork, Straughton thought to himself, 'What a scoop. Front Page.' He could even picture the headline — "BERKELEY GOES BANANAS". And International headlines! — "THE WORLD GOES BANANAS".

Screw picked up the knife and fork. About to use them, he glanced suspiciously at Straughton. This was ridiculous. He immediately put them down. How dirty could his hands be? Checking, they were dirtier than he had expected. Despite this, Screw picked up the naked banana between two fingers, trying not to leave prints. Five quick bites and all questions of etiquette were outdated.

Straughton lowered his fork onto his plate. "How long must one cook these peels?"

"Beats me. I'll check." Screw stood and opened the oven. "They got a way to go."

Straughton was not in the mood for waiting. "How much longer will this take?" There was skepticism in his tone.

Screw said, "You don't understand what this means."

"That you can get stoned from smoking bananas."

"A hell of lot more than that."

"Perhaps I am missing something. Would you care to go over the implications?"

"The Man can't outlaw bananas. No more banana pie, banana custard, banana splits, banana bread, banana in your corn flakes. No way! The People would revolt."

Straughton had to admit to himself that the kid was right. Bananas could change the world. "Well, how much longer do I have to bake them?

"I don't know. Relax, will yah....Hey, while we're waiting, let's do a number?"

"Excellent idea," said Straughton. Soon they were passing a joint and listening to some good music to boot. Their moods continued to improve as they raided the freezer for some ice cream. Before eating it, Screw said, "Hey, we should have saved some banana for banana splits."

"Pity," Straughton agreed. "Yet one must not dwell upon the past."

"There's still the future. I could borrow two more," Screw mused, knowing damn well that the inertial effects of the marijuana they had smoked would keep him anchored to his chair. It took him a good while and a Herculean effort just to traverse the few feet back to the stove. Only then did it occur to him that the instructions he had received did not cover the actual smoking. Chopping up the peels like grass seemed his best bet. Screw rounded up all the necessary equipment and placed it on the table. He turned up the stereo to improve working conditions. Thanks to the marijuana he and Straughton had just smoked, Screw rather enjoyed the chopping. However, rolling the result into a joint proved far less enjoyable, at least for Screw. Straughton watched with amusement as Screw went through half a pack of papers, trying the one-paper style, the two-paper style, and even the classic Jefferson Airplane style. The shredded banana peels ended up everywhere except inside the papers. Finally, Straughton stopped laughing long enough to suggest, "Perhaps you are supposed to roll the dried banana peels into a cigar."

Though scant in humor, this remark, amplified exponentially by marijuana, had them both in hysterics. It was a good while before Screw gained enough control to ask, "You don't have a pipe or anything?"

"Certainly, My Man," replied Straughton, again losing control.

Screw's laughter kept him from putting as much anger in his words as he felt. "You let me waste half my life trying to roll a banana peel joint when you had a pipe all the time?"

Screw was even angrier when he saw the pipe. It was a hookah, one of those three foot high Middle Eastern water pipes, with four separate hoses and mouthpieces. Straughton had found it a useful tool for debauching ingénues too innocent and inexperienced to draw sufficient smoke from a rolled joint. Screw watched entranced as Straughton set up the exotic contraption. A mere few minutes of sucking on it had them both quite mellow.

Screw asked, "How do you feel?"

Straughton smiled back at him. "Stoned."

"So do I."

*****

Smitty was deep in thought as he and Marcia walked to the custodian's meeting. Marcia had never said or done one little thing to irritate him, or even put him on his guard. Last night, effortlessly, she had managed to do both. 'Could the honeymoon be over before the marriage?' he wondered.

What baffled Smitty about women was their seeming immunity to the laws of cause and effect, or more correctly, their unfathomable reactions to seemingly innocuous events. To complicate matters, though he was always willing to ask himself, "What did I do now?", he found it almost impossible to ask others. And these "others" were almost always women. It occurred to him that if there were no women, the question, "What did I do now?", would probably disappear from English usage.

But there were women, millions and millions of them. A fine example walked right next to him, not two feet away. Now what the hell did he do wrong, if he had done anything wrong, which a half hour of searching his memory made him doubt very much. You could never tell with women. They could appear flawless

165

from the outside, yet inside, they were sure to have at least a few wires crossed.

Things were fine until he and Marcia had gotten into bed last night. As usual, Smitty initiated some good old fashioned sex, the basic type they had stuck to so far. Halfway there, he thought about checking her pulse. Instead, Smitty just gave up and retired to his side of the bed. He lay awake a good hour trying to figure out what the hell had happened. Could she be worried about the next day's meeting? The custodians were going to choose the union to represent them. No chance. How could something so unimportant have any effect on something as important as their sex life?

Perhaps Marcia had tired of him already. Thoughts such as this could chip away at the old ego. Perhaps it was time, past time, to get more imaginative. Smitty doubted that this was the problem. He had certainly kept her attention until last night. He was even more certain it wasn't something he had said. After all, he hadn't smoked yesterday, which meant he had hardly spoken to her at all. Marcia had seemed all right during dinner. She should have, the way he wolfed down her watery spaghetti again. Thank God he was hungry enough. That spaghetti could eventually prove a problem. Still, it was one hell of an improvement over the canned Chef-Boy-R-Mush. Still, he had to figure out a diplomatic way to tell her to drain it better. Hell, from her, watery spaghetti was a problem he could live with, for a very, very long time. If things got desperate, he could always tell her he didn't like spaghetti. Yet that would be lying. No, eventually he'd figure out a way to get the point across without actually lying. And just then, that's exactly what he did. He would buy her a present — one of those aluminum bowls with all the holes in it — and pick up some thoughtfulness bonus points to boot.

Smitty heard a commotion up ahead. Marcia had told him about the riot at the previous janitors meeting. Wary of a repeat, Smitty had figured he better come along. Protectively, he now stepped slightly ahead of her as they approached. Instead of a riot, he found two dozen people standing in a circle, as if watching a fight, which turned out to be Berkeley's version of that. A huge Hare Krishna — shaved head, saffron robes and all — sat atop a tiny almost obscured pipsqueak. The Hare Krishna straddled the protesting pipsqueak's waist and held his arms down and out to his sides. The pipsqueak's face was red with anger as he struggled to free himself. Smitty gave him little chance of succeeding. It would take a crane to lift a Hare Krishna that size.

Marcia peered around Smitty to see that the two combatants were fighting it out next to a bike rack, with an Honor Bike lying on its side next to them.

"You're not a student!" yelled the pipsqueak.

"Yes I am," was the calm reply from the Hare Krishna.

It occurred to Smitty that if the Hare Krishna had an ID to prove that, then there must be pockets in his robe. Or else in his underwear. Or he had a wallet or purse stuck somewhere. Smitty had never wondered about that before, and wouldn't be wondering about it now if all the action weren't verbal.

Marsha asked him, "Are Hare Krishnas allowed to ride bicycles?"

Smitty shrugged. "It's all right with me." He then pictured a saffron robe getting caught in the bicycle chain. 'That could be life threatening.'

"That was my Honor Bike," protested the pipsqueak.

"They're for all of us," the Hare Krishna said beatifically. He could afford to, being in the more comfortable position of the two.

"I rode it here," groaned the pipsqueak. He sounded as if his diaphragm was being crushed, which was close to the case.

"You weren't on it when I got on," the Hare Krishna pointed out. "That's the way they're supposed to work."

Marcia, whose sympathy had been with the undersqueak, now realized that the Hare Krishna had The Law of Honor Bikes on his side. Still, the idea of fighting over one seemed to be disturbingly counter to their purpose. "Can you believe this?" she asked Smitty.

Paying more attention to the rather static fight than Marcia's question, he replied, "No, never seen one that big."

"What are you talking about?" she asked.

'What could I be talking about?' thought Smitty before informing her, "Hare Krishnas."

Thinking, 'Could he be serious?' Marcia attempted to read his face. Hard as it was to believe, she decided that he could be serious. Wondering why she wasted her words with him, Marcia decided not to waste any more. Yet being a facilitator of the Honor Bike system, she felt an obligation to see this matter settled without further violence. Marcia stepped forward and yanked shoulder-high on the Hare Krishna's robe. "Excuse me."

The only reaction she received was from the pipsqueak. He began twisting this way and that, like an earthworm in a bird's beak, at the same time doing some cursing worthy of a far larger man. Marcia feared that if the pipsqueak ever did get out from under the Hare Krishna, he would be in two pieces, separated at the waist.

Smitty pulled Marcia away. Even if the fight had been interesting before they'd arrived, and he doubted it had, the interesting part was over.

Marcia said, "I didn't know Hare Krishna's were allowed to fight."

"Bet the little guy didn't either."

Smitty's attention was already on the demonstrators up ahead. He stared contemptuously at the sign carrying members of the Union of Communist Workers. They marched belligerently in front of the small auditorium. Inside, the school's custodians must already be voting to choose who would represent them. Though Smitty had volunteered to come along tonight because he feared another riot, Marcia had mistaken his protective instincts for social commitment. Smitty caught this misunderstanding, yet gladly let it ride.

He now scanned the possible attackers. There weren't more than a few members of the Union of Communist Workers seemingly capable of throwing a decent punch, and, with a single exception, they were all female. The other males, at their fiercest, appeared to be no more than scratchers and biters. Some of them were trying to look tough, but they reminded him of yapping lapdogs. Sure, they'd snap at the back of your heels, but all you had to do was turn around and stomp your foot to put their tails between their legs. The scene before him brought back a memory from high school. He had once dragged a date to the movie West Side Story, anxious to see how the big city gangs rumbled. What he ended up seeing was two packs of greaseball pansies prancing and dancing around with switchblades in their hands. His date, though, had found it all "enthralling".

Just then a decent looking guy walked up to them. "Marcia, will you to be my assistant in the negotiations?"

"Sure," she said with a lovely smile.

Matching her smile, the guy warned, "It'll mean a lot of work."

Smitty did not care for either smile. The guy's good looks did not make him any the more endearing, not to Smitty.

"Let's hope they choose us," Marcia said, looking right into his eyes.

The word "us" grated on Smitty. He stood ignored off to the side. Apparently Marcia had no intention of introducing him.

"They will," the guy assured her. They know it was the Union of Communist Workers who started the brawl at the last meeting."

"What about the State Employees Union?" Marcia asked.

The guy's smile widened. He leaned closer, conspiratorially, taking Marcia's hands in his. "They didn't even send anyone. The custodians aren't good enough for them....And today, two more Teamster officials got indicted. Everyone knows they're Mafia."

Smitty could not take his eyes off the guy's hands holding Marcia's. They were not the hands of someone who had spent the summer working on a loading dock. Still, the guy had a decent build and two inches on Smitty, who was thinking, 'Hell, I could break him in half.'

The auditorium doors swung open. Two custodians began setting up a microphone. Smileyface took off in their direction. Marcia turned to Smitty, glee in her eyes. "He wants me to be his assistant. Isn't that wonderful?"

It did not occur to Smitty to fake joyfulness.

"Oh, I'm sorry I couldn't introduce you. I forgot his name."

'His name?' thought Smitty, before banishing this thought and giving Marcia the benefit of the doubt.

There was a tapping on the microphone. The leader of custodians began to speak in Spanish accented English. "Thank you for coming tonight. It was you wonderful students who gave us the idea to form a union, and then you helped us fight for the right to organize. We will never forget our debt to you. I know you will all be glad to hear that our unanimous choice, the Teamsters Union, has agreed to represent us."

*****

Marco stalled starting the meeting. Embarrassingly few people had shown up. He wanted to believe more were on their way. Yet what he wanted to believe and what he could believe were two different things. The boredom of picketing had again depleted his forces. Every day, fewer of his acolytes had shown up. The last two days he had had to cancel the picketing altogether. If he had had his minions breaking windows all week, his living room would now be standing room only. An overturned police car would have had people outside hanging on the window sills.

About to give up and start the meeting, Marco heard the screen door slam, and slam again. This buoyed his spirits, that is until he saw who had entered. It was the belligerent black from the last meeting — 'All I need'. A dozen people straggled in after him. Marco was relieved to see that half of them were his own regulars. Still, the presence of this black man unnerved him. He scanned the room for Chandler, spotting him talking to Susan. 'Good,' thought Marco. This way he did not have to be so obvious in putting Chandler on the case. Walking over to both of them, he said, "Genghis Ex-Con just showed up. I would appreciate it if you two would find out what the hell he wants."

Susan and Chandler exchanged glances, reading each other's minds. Marco, unnerved by this, felt as if they were talking behind his back right in front of him, which by definition should be impossible. Marco had always felt envious of Susan's ability to read people. For some unfathomable reason, he had never mastered the skill himself. Mind reading? It seemed like hocus pocus. He'd find himself standing next to her, faced with the dilemma of either pretending he also understood what was going on, or of appearing to be an idiot by coming out and asking. Susan would sense his ignorance and discomfort, and do her best to increase it. Sure enough, right now he had that recurrent idiot feeling. She headed for Genghis. Chandler gave Marco a cold eye before following behind.

Genghis met Susan with an out of character smile. He recovered in time to acknowledge Chandler with his characteristic glare. As Marco started the meeting, Susan engaged Genghis in conversation. Chandler, listening in, stood ignored, suiting him fine. All three of them paid scant attention to Marco's presentation until he opened the floor for questions.

Marco called on a lady in her late thirties. "Yes, Barbara, go ahead."

"I just wanted—"

Genghis loudly cut her off with, "I didn't come here to rap about rapping and rap some more. I heard enough rapping tonight to give me a headache." He was looking at Marco, and his look was not friendly.

Marco was very tempted to suggest that it was Genghis' own mouth giving him the headache, and to further suggest that he take both mouth and headache somewhere else. In fact, he would have surely done so if Genghis were any color other than black. He was still pondering a reply, when Genghis interrupted his thoughts.

"When we gonna do something to get The Man's attention?"

Marco saw an opening, and both his look and tone were stern as he said, "Excuse me, Friend, where were you when we forced the resignation of the President of the Board of Regents of California's entire university system? When we threw The Man out of City Hall? Where were you when we stood up to The Man and claimed People's Park for The People?"

"What's changed at City Hall 'sides the people? What did it get us? The Man don't give a damn 'bout no piss poor People's Park! The Man's got the whole U. S. of A. under his greasy white thumb, including three million incarcerated black political prisoners. The only thing The Man understands, the only thing that will bring down the system is violence!" With these words, Genghis again marched out of the meeting, taking his dozen followers with him.

Marco, relieved to see him go, would have been even more relieved to be certain that Genghis would not show up again. What did this maniac want from him? Anxious to know, Marco adjourned the meeting early and headed for his ambassador to angry blacks, Chandler. "What did you find out?"

"That Genghis Khan was a black man."

"What?"

"The original Genghis Khan was black," Chandler repeated in a self-satisfied tone.

Marco was willing to compromise, using the terms of the day. "He was a man of color."

"No, black."

"And what did you say?"

"Nothing. Why should I? You white folks never said anything

when you found out Jesus was black, and Cleopatra, and then the Pharaohs. Genghis Khan was as black as any of them. Soon Leif Erickson will be too."

Marco found Chandler's tendency to toy with him less than endearing. "Knock it off. What the hell does Genghis Ex-Con want from me?"

Chandler paused to study him, "You didn't see?"

"Hell, no, I didn't see. What the hell does he want from me?"

"Recruits. He walked out with a half dozen of your followers."

*****

The last few minutes of dusk found Smitty and Marcia walking down the crowded sidewalk. Smitty held three heavy plastic bags of groceries in his left hand. His right arm was across Marcia's shoulders. She had one arm around his waist while carrying another bag of groceries in her opposite hand.

"It didn't bother you, the custodians choosing the Teamsters?"

"I don't know anything about negotiating union contracts."

"That's the easy part," Smitty assured her. "Catching university administrators in a dark alley and breaking their legs, that's where it gets complicated."

"I'd just as soon leave that to the Teamsters."

"They are the experts."

Marcia was smiling as she said, "I thought the unions sold out their own members by taking bribes from the employers."

"That too."

"And eventually they all end up in jail together."

Smitty looked over at Marcia with an amused smile. The surprising hint of cynicism in her expression became her. One arm across her shoulders was not enough. He stepped in front of Marcia and faced her, placing the arm holding the three grocery bags over her shoulder, doing so carelessly enough to bang her in the back. They both started laughing. This led to a brief make-out session right in the middle of the sidewalk.

Smitty had lived with one other girl, for less than a summer month. That had been an adventure, an experiment in cohabitation. Now, walking home with Marcia, he experienced something entirely different. The words "domestic bliss" wouldn't have occurred to him, would have made him squirm. Still, he would not have been able to come up with a better description of what he was now experiencing.

Marcia, also contented, looking straight ahead, asked Smitty, "What did you say to the girl in the market?"

"What?"

"That made her give you that dirty look."

"Oh, 'Plastic'."

Baffled, Marcia asked, "'Oh plastic'?"

"No," he laughed. "She asked, 'Paper or plastic?' I answered, 'Plastic.'"

"And she got angry?"

"Homicidal. You saw her."

Marcia said, "Well, paper is better for the environment. Next time we'll get paper."

Smitty squeezed her closer. "And walk home with both arms wrapped around paper bags?"

She smiled, half laughed. "Guess it's plastic for us."

Smitty did not remember seeing any bananas bagged. "Hey, did you get the bananas?"

"No, there weren't any."

"How could a supermarket be out of bananas?"

"They were," she replied.

Smitty pointed across the street. "There's a market."

They crossed over only to come up empty again. As they left, Marcia said, "There's one more little market before we get home."

Smitty asked seriously, "Is Berkeley boycotting bananas or something?"

"Just grapes, as far as I know."

"This is weird."

Marcia tried to read Smitty's face, figuring that she was missing something. "Weird?"

"Yeah. Screw came over the other day desperate for bananas. I gave him two."

"And you're looking for a complicated reason?"

"No," Smitty replied, not sure what he had been looking for, and perfectly willing to give up the search.

Marcia, the scientist, had been trained to accept the simplest explanation. "Maybe he just wanted a banana."

Smitty thought over this explanation and decided he could live with it. Talking about bananas gave him an immediate urge for one. At Ohio State he had worked himself up to a dollar a day banana habit — the ultimate "peel and eat" addiction. You don't even have to rinse them off, unless you're a raccoon. Banana, the fillingest fruit.

At the last market on their way, the clerk pointed to where all the bananas should have been. Only a half bunch of extremely over ripe ones remained.

Smitty asked, "You want to get them?"

"Look at the price!" They were marked $4.95 a pound.

Smitty shrugged. When it came to food, he'd never been much at "shop and compare".

Marcia turned to the clerk. "Is that a mistake?"

"No mistake," the clerk assured them. "There's an article in The Badger. You can get high smoking them."

Holding up the bananas, Smitty asked, "You want to try smoking these?"

She looked towards the clerk. "Do they really work?"

"Lady, I don't smoke the cigarettes I sell. You think I smoke the bananas?"

Smitty asked Marcia. "What do you think?"

"Five dollars a pound?"

"Yeah," Smitty agreed. "Compared to grass. That's no bargain."

They exited the market to the roar of revving motorcycles. Twenty Hells Angels were parked right in front of their apartment. Marcia turned to Smitty in disbelief, "New neighbors?"

Smitty shrugged.

They climbed the front steps of their apartment house to the accompaniment of revving motorcycles, a god-awful roar which easily destroyed the pleasant, relaxed mood that had stayed with them all the way home. Marcia and Smitty hurried upstairs, anxious to get their apartment door closed behind them.

*****

When Straughton looked out the window at the revving motorcycles, he made the connection immediately. Twelve Gauge had never before paid him a social visit. Straughton, if he'd been offered the choice, certainly would have passed up the honor this time. Now with Twelve Gauge in his face, Fat Rat directly behind him, three more Hells Angels behind Twelve Gauge, and three Honor Bikes behind them, his apartment had never seemed so small. Sweating like a strung-out junkie, he struggled in vain to look cool. Twelve Gauge's expression made one thing evident — putting on a record would not improve the mood. Besides, if there were appropriate music for this occasion, he was ignorant of it.

The three Hells Angels in back of Twelve Gauge were examining Straughton's fleet of Honor Bikes. "Schwinn." said one of them.

"No, Huffy," said the other.

"Asshole," said the first, "Mine's a Schwinn. Yours is a Huffy."

"What's mine?" asked the third.

"Piece a shit," answered the first.

It was taking Twelve Gauge a while to come up with his first question. Luckily for Straughton, it turned out to be an easy one. "Fucker, are you trying to put us out of business?"

"No," Straughton nervously assured him. "Did you try smoking banana peels?"

"When we're sitting on a trailer truck of Panama Red?…And every toker between Frisco and LA is buying bananas instead?"

Straughton tried to smile, in the sense of friendly not amused. "Gentlemen, banana peels will not get you high, even if you drag on them until you get a hernia."

"No shit! But everyone in California thinks they can. Orange County wants stickers on bananas saying, "Caution, smoking banana peels can be hazardous to your health." The Oakland City Council is passing a law that you can't have bananas in a moving car."

Straughton's face lit up. "All the better for you. As soon as the car starts moving, they'll have to smoke dope instead."

Twelve Gauge took one step forward, forcing Straughton to take one step back. This was all he could take. The three bike enthusiasts were now racing around him and Twelve Gauge in a circle, supplementing sound effects. Twelve Gauge and Straughton were chest to chest, or rather chest to face.

Twelve Gauge spit both his words and saliva down into Straughton's face. "Then why the hell did you write that dumb fucking article?"

Straughton fell back upon Berkeley's all purpose alibi. "I was stoned."

Twelve Gauge's look got even meaner. "Not from bananas?"

"No, but I thought I was."

"You thought you were?"

"It's all quite simple. While we were baking the banana peels, we smoked a joint. And afterwards too, when I wrote the article."

"WHY?" Twelve Gauge shouted, taking another step forward. "Why shouldn't I break your skinny neck? Give me a reason!"

Straughton cringed at the question. He attempted to take another step back, flinching as a circling Honor Bike clipped his ass. All Straughton's self-assurance had deserted him. "Deadlines" he said meekly, then, straightening up a little, added, "Deadlines are the bane of a reporter."

"Is that right?" Twelve Gauge asked, displaying absolutely no sympathy.

Straughton tried to assure Twelve Gauge with words he was more likely to understand. "As they say, 'Deadlines are a motherfucker'."

"Well I got a friend downstairs that's not only a motherfucker, he's also a reporter fucker. How'd you like to meet him?"

Straughton's anus tightened by reflex. So did his larynx. All he could do was shake his head No.

"Weasel, you cost us money. How the hell do you plan on squaring things?"

"Rest assured, Panama Red will be the best known dope in the Bay Area....I guarantee it." Straughton got a brainstorm. "We'll have a strength test between Panama Red, Acapulco Gold, and banana peels. Red will win hands down." Straughton got another brainstorm. "One of the testers will OD on Red!"

Twelve Gauge's hand shot forward. Grabbing the front of Straughton's neck between thumb and forefinger, he squeezed and lifted at the same time, until Straughton was eye-level. "What?"

Straughton's reply was too choked to be intelligible, followed by just plain choking sounds.

Fat Rat stepped forward. "Twelve Gauge, an OD or two always gooses up smack sales."

Twelve Gauge thought this over, at the same time lowering his publicity agent to the ground and loosening his choke hold. "Okay," he agreed, trying to calm himself. "Our clientele's always looking for the most asskicking dope." He then added, almost to himself, "Grass so strong you can OD on it. Sounds good." His voice became sterner as he turned his attention back to Straughton. "Another thing. After Scarecrow's funeral, we're having a keg party to push some dope retail. Get that in the paper too."

"Impossible. You'll have to buy an ad."

"Hells Angels buy an ad, are you out of your ass?"

"Moe will sniff that out a mile away."

"How much is an ad?"

"Two hundred will get you something nice."

Twelve Gauge gave Straughton a look that bored right into him.

Straughton said, "One hundred. Give me one hundred, and I'll take care of it."

Twelve Gauge pulled out a hundred dollar bill and handed it to Straughton.

As Straughton stuffed it into his pocket, he felt Twelve Gauge's cold eyes upon him. They stayed there until Straughton guessed nervously, "You want a receipt?"

Twelve Gauge replied calmly, "Do I look like someone that needs a receipt?"

Straughton had no idea what Twelve Gauge had meant, and his expression showed it.

As one of the racers goosed Straughton with a bike's front wheel, Twelve Gauge shook his head as if he were trying to explain the Big Bad World to a little kid. "Hells Angels don't pay twice."

*****

For a change, it was Marcia reading The Berkeley Badger as she and Smitty lay in bed. She seemed so deeply into it, he had to ask, "Whatcha reading?"

It was a long moment before she finished reading. "Some Berkeley students are volunteering at San Quentin, tutoring prisoners. They're helping them earn their GED's….They're really making a difference."

Alarm bells went off inside Smitty's head, bells loud enough to

177

have his brain scrambling for an exit. Two of his former acquaintances were now in prison, one serving a well deserved life sentence. Visions of Marcia tutoring that thug scared the shit out of him. "They're in jail for a reason."

Marcia replied quite logically, "That doesn't mean they can't turn over a new leaf."

Smitty realized that he couldn't fault her logic. His mind raced for a reply. All it could come up with was a temporary solution. "If we do it, we'll do it together?" — 'Trap baited.'

"OK."

"I want to concentrate on my grades this semester. Let's put it off until next semester." — 'Trap set.'

"OK."

'Trap sprung!' — Smitty congratulated himself. At the very least, he had kept Marcia alive for the rest of the semester. By then, he'd think of a better excuse. Yet just to make sure, he asked, "You won't do it without me?"

"No, I said I wouldn't....Do you want to read the article?"

"Sure," Smitty replied, wanting nothing more than getting it out of Marcia's hands. He took The Badger and actually read the first paragraph before his eyes wandered over to the Personals. After an appropriate amount of time, he said, "Here's something you might be interested in for this semester: "Full professor, studiously handsome, 30, W, Libra, with non-swinging mate, seeks discrete lady in same fix."

Marcia shot him a disapproving look.

Smitty feigned innocence. "You don't like Libras?"

Marcia grabbed The Badger back. She herself began to read the Personals. "What's a 'golden shower'?"

Feeling some embarrassment, he told Marcia to, "Guess."

"Well, it's probably wet, right?"

"Right."

"Do you do it in the shower?"

"Not necessarily."

"Does it have anything to do with rain?"

"No."

Marcia pondered a few seconds before saying, "Give me a hint."

Now it was Smitty's turn to ponder a few seconds.

Unfortunately, he could only come up with, "It has nothing to do with chicken soup."

Stunned by a flash of intuition, Marcia exclaimed, "No!"

"Yes," he assured her.

"Are you serious?…Why would you want someone to do that to you?"

Smitty resented the accusation. "I wouldn't."

Marcia seemed somewhat relieved. "I mean men."

"Why just men?" he asked.

Marcia had the proof. "It says right here. 'Single black female gives golden showers. Call 669-1342'."

Smitty reached for The Badger. "Let me see that." His search was distracted by an ad for a "full body orgasm". Now that sounded interesting, certainly worth a try. He couldn't really picture it though, and not for lack of effort. All he could picture was an abundance, a flood, of bodily fluids. They soaked his imaginary bed, poured down upon the floor, even leaked under his apartment door and out into the hall. As this flood made it to the stairs, Smitty was able to cut the vision short. He got back to his search, immediately finding what he was looking for. "Here! Here's a single hetero white male that gives golden showers, and here's an Asian."

"God, that's sickening," Marcia said to herself as much as to Smitty.

'How the hell did we get on this subject?' Smitty asked himself. He wanted to inch over to Marcia's side of the bed but realized this conversation wasn't exactly putting her in the mood. He decided to wait things out, feeling lucky that at least she hadn't asked him about a related service offered ubiquitously in The Barb — "hot lunches".

*****

Straughton walked towards The Badger office with deep trepidation. Moe had phoned. He had asked politely, thus completely out of character, if Straughton could drop by. Surprised enough by Moe's tone to think he had changed his mind about that ticket to Cuba, Straughton agreed. Yet when had Moe ever asked anyone to "drop by"? Never. Moe told people to, "Get your ass over here, fast." He told them, "I want to see your ugly face right now." He told them, "Get your slimy butt up to the office." Moe never requested anything from his reporters, certainly not to "drop by". Straughton now realized he should have stalled for a day or two. Moe must be coiled like a snake, ready to strike, and pissed-off enough to be venomous.

Straughton pondered the possible reason. The only thing he could come up with was the banana peel article. Yet Straughton had his doubts. Luckily, he had an ace in the hole — the Hells Angels' $50 for the ad. Straughton had broken the $100 bill on the way over, cutting himself in for a reasonable commission. Moe would be glad enough to see a fifty. If need be, Straughton could hand over two of them. Just then his limitless imagination came through with an idea for a follow-up article that might please both Moe and Twelve Gauge — Can You Become Addicted to Drugs That Don't Effect You? He'd call Synanon to see if they had a treatment for banana peels.

Straughton reached the landing to see Moe at the top of the stairs. Sensing danger, he was not usually the type to run. No, he was the type to freeze, freeze everything but his lips. Straughton's confidence in his ability to talk his way out of tight spots was usually enough to compensate for any deficit of courage. Yet when he saw Moe's smile, he came within an instant of bolting. He'd seen that smile twice before, both times while Moe was throwing someone down the stairs. Like an answered prayer, Straughton heard the phone ring. Moe disappeared. The coast now being clear, Straughton rushed up the stairs in time to see Moe toss the receiver aside. Straughton slid sideways into the room, trying to place Moe between himself and the stairs. He succeeded. Still, he couldn't relax, not as long as Moe wore that smile. Should he cough up the $50 now, or save it for the right moment?

Moe spoke in an alarmingly quiet and civilized tone. "Come here a minute, Roger."

Never before had Moe used his first name. Straughton felt himself drawn closer, but managed to remain out of range of Moe's right fist, which he noticed was clenched.

Moe's left fist held a copy of The Badger, which he thrust in Straughton's face. "What the hell is this all about?"

Straughton leaned back, so his eyes could focus on the print. "I trust you are referring to the article on smoking banana peels."

"You trust fucking right. What is this bullshit?"

"A carefully researched article."

"Scumbag, I ain't no born yesterday hippie. You can't get high smoking banana peels."

Straughton, if he hadn't been fearing for his life, would have blurted out a bewildered, "So what?" Since when was The Badger's staff restricted to writing the truth? Reporters can't run around with one hand tied behind their backs. Like Moe himself used to say, "When the government and every newspaper in the country is lying, The People are depending upon us to stand up for them and do the same." Instead, Straughton asked as calmly as he could, "Moe, why take this one article so seriously?"

"Schmuck, the subject dearest to the hearts of our readership is not politics, not music, not even sex. It's dope! If they can't trust what we write about dope, we lose all credibility."

Admitting to himself that Moe had a point, Straughton judged it a minor one. After all, any serious toker would relieve his disappointment with some real weed. Yet pointing this out to Moe would be a tacit admission of guilt, a step he hoped to avoid. Instead he would survive this mess the same way he had survived his run-in with Twelve Gauge, by talking his way out of it. "Where exactly did we lose our credibility?"

"How the fuck are you supposed to smoke banana peels?"

In a flash of insight, Straughton realized that Moe himself must have wasted a few hours trying to get stoned. About to make the possibly fatal mistake of suggesting to Moe that perhaps he had gotten a bad banana, Straughton caught himself and simply answered the question. "The most convenient method involves the use of a water pipe."

"And that'll get you stoned."

"That's what they say."

"That's what you say."

"Not exactly....I state that people are smoking banana peels to get stoned."

Moe pounced on him. "Name one!"

"I myself, as a matter of fact."

"And you got stoned?"

"After a few drags, I was stoned out of my mind."

Moe never trusted any answer that could have been a simple Yes or No and wasn't. "Stoned from banana peels?"

Straughton mused, 'Moe would make a good lawyer....Or is that a conflict of terms?' Moe took a step forward, and Straughton realized immediately that this was not the appropriate time for musing. Nor was it the appropriate place — a mere few feet from the head of the stairs. Straughton preferred descending them in the least painful manner — one at a time.

"Stoned from banana peels?" Moe repeated in a harsher tone.

"Well, you might say the experiment was conducted under less than laboratory conditions."

"How much less."

"It took time to bake the banana peels. While we waited, we ran a joint."

"Questionable science, or piss poor science?"

"Well, considering half this town is smoking banana peels—"

"The half that can find them," Moe interjected.

"—I trust some more experienced scientists will redo the experiment under stricter laboratory conditions." Straughton got an idea. "I'll write a follow-up article when they do."

"That'd be peachy," Moe assured him. "But not today. Today the phone is off the hook because your public, which is every idiot pothead in Berkeley, is calling up to find out how to get high on banana peels. Today, tomorrow, maybe for the rest of your life, you're gonna sit here answering their calls."

Straughton felt more than relieved. He felt needed. Moe had never had any intention of breaking his neck. Moe needed him, to answer the phone. Straughton walked over to it and replaced the receiver. Instantly the phone rang. Someone on the other end was asking, "Hey Dude, you know that article on banana peels?"

"Yes," answered Straughton, now admitting to himself that some articles are best left unwritten.

*****

Smitty looked at the stain on the shoulder of his favorite shirt. An off-white denim, its cowboy cut was hardly noticeable because of the solid color. The shirt was his favorite because its perfectly shaped collar somehow stayed in just the right place. Irritated, he went to the sink to remove the stain with soap and a brush. Smitty was rinsing off the soap when he heard the apartment door unlock. Marcia was soon behind and up against him with both her hands on his shoulders and her head peering around his side. "What you doing?"

"I'm trying to get a stain out."

"Here, let me."

Smitty was glad to. They traded places, his arms around her waist, holding her tight.

"What is it?"

"Beats me." He watched her work, his chin resting on her shoulder.

"If you'd tell me what it is, I'd have a better chance of getting it out."

"Okay, I admit it. It's lipstick."

She smiled as he squeezed her tighter. "Black or grey?"

He gave her a gentle bite on the neck. "Blackish-grey."

Watching this striking woman work on his very own shirt, Smitty's thoughts reduced to three words — 'She's so fine.' He flashed on the mysterious affection his parents showed one another. 'So this is what it feels like.' He liked the feeling, a lot. "You do nice work."

"Do I get the job?"

Smitty moved his hands along her waist. "For as long as you want it."

Marcia couldn't help but smile. She felt a faint, erotic cramp in her stomach. Words could be a pleasure. From Smitty, they were few and far between.

He took a harder bite out of her neck.

"Ouch," she flinched, now laughing.

Suddenly remembering, he asked, "Hey, am I gonna be able to wear that shirt to class?"

"When's your class?

He removed his left arm from around her and checked his watch, saying deadpan, "Five minutes ago." Smitty gave her a squeeze, then grabbed another shirt and rushed out of the apartment.

Marcia was left in a very pleasant mood. She wanted to please Smitty by removing the stain. Brush and soap were getting her nowhere. A better idea came to her. She would do something special for him. She remembered how happy she had been, long ago, when her grandmother had taken one of her favorite blouses, one Marcia hadn't worn for months because of a stain, and how she had watched her grandmother embroider a beautiful butterfly over the stain. Marcia asked her how she had learned such a clever thing. Her grandmother replied that her own grandmother had taught her, and that if Marcia wanted, she would teach her. Then, someday, Marcia could teach her own granddaughter. This memory, precious as it was, had been lost to her for years. With its return came a calming pleasance. Marcia was grateful for the feeling. She would surprise Smitty by embroidering over the stain.

*****

Marco had been thinking about the custodians the entire walk home. The university exploited them merely because they were "people of color". Their cause had become a popular one. He now regretted ignoring it. Yet the revolution simply had too many fronts — police brutality in the ghetto, the illegal war in Vietnam, urban renewal used to confiscate valuable black property, rent strikes against blood sucking landlords, fighting the draft, sexual freedom, homosexual rights, support for Fidel Castro and the Cuban Revolution, bringing down the Shah of Iran, friendship with the Soviet Union and Red China.

Marco had left a vacuum and the Teamsters had filled it. He felt as if the Mafia had muscled into his territory. Yet, the Feds were incarcerating Teamsters one after the other. This just might provide his opening. Perhaps he could convince the Teamsters to put themselves under his protection. Then, at the right time, in say a year or two, he could take over the Teamsters Union, throw out the Mafia, revolutionize it, turn it into a force for change.

Upon reaching his own front door, Marco's thoughts switched to exactly what he would say to Susan. He found her in the bedroom, reading Marcuse's One Dimensional Man. Marco opened his mouth, but nothing came out. The sight of Killer, curled up on his pillow, right next to Susan, threw off his train of thought. This pillow business was getting to be a habit. More than once he'd awakened in the middle of the night spitting out cat hairs.

More than once he had chased Killer off the bed. Marco had the urge to do so now, but this was no time to antagonize Susan. Well aware of his presence, she didn't bother to acknowledge it, keeping her nose in her book.

"Susan," Marco said, to get her attention.

She gave no indication that he had.

Marco decided to assume he had anyway. "Susan, have you been keeping up with the custodian issue?"

"More or less," she replied distractedly, still reading her book.

"I think it's time I got involved. I'd appreciate it if you went to their next meeting, to feel them out."

"Not interested," she said, nose still in her book.

"But I'm interested."

"You shouldn't have blown them off when they came for help."

"I was busy…and half of them couldn't even speak English."

"Nine-tenths, and they still can't."

Marco's tone began to show exasperation. "They were just interested in higher wages, not in changing the system."

Still with her nose in her book, Susan replied with exaggerated glee, "There's your in! The Teamsters can get them higher wages, and you can help them not change the system."

"What the hell do you mean by that?"

"Exactly what I said — that nothing you do is ever going to change anything….Sit-ins are just sitting on your ass!"

Marco was astounded by the ignorance in this remark, especially coming from Susan. "I've exposed our government for the fascist plutocracy that it is."

"Without changing it."

"I've shaken the entire system of higher education."

"Without changing it."

"May I remind you just who I brought down!"

Susan finally took her nose out of the book. She sat up, dropped her feet to the floor, and stood facing Marco. "And what changed? Berkeley got a new chancellor."

"He wasn't chancellor. He was President of the Board of Regents of the entire California university system."

"Oh, excuse me."

"I destroyed him."

"They destroyed him…because he didn't have the balls to

185

destroy you....And they replaced him with a bigger balled fascist. And they'll get rid of him if he doesn't shut you up....or until those morons realize how harmless you are....You're no threat to them. You're just an embarrassment."

Marco opened his mouth to reply, but he could not think of anything to say.

"I'll tell you what you've accomplished," Susan continued. "You've gotten Ronald Reagan elected governor, just to shut you up. And they say Richard Nixon is going to run for president, to shut up all the Marco's in all fifty states. You'll help get him elected too."

Angry as Marco was, the absurdity of this thought amused him. "That loser! He'll never get elected."

"Of course not, but some fascist just like him will....The masses hate your guts!"

"The masses will come around."

Susan felt exasperated by Marco's blindness. "No...they...won't!...The masses are asses....And so are your college students. If they ever eliminate the draft, you'll be able to hold your demonstrations in a phone booth."

"You should be working for Reagan!"

"You are working for Reagan! You might even get him elected president."

Again Marco was amused. "Don't be ridiculous! That B-movie actor?"

"Ridiculous? You want to see something ridiculous?...Go look in the mirror." Susan slowly shook her head at him, as if she couldn't believe what she herself was seeing. "You are so bourgeois."

Marco loathed when Susan used epithets. Not only were these deflating to his ego, but against them, logic, his most effective weapon, proved ineffective. 'Bourgeois?' he thought, no one had ever slandered him with that charge. 'Bourgeois,' his mind repeated, as the vile epithet burned forever into his memory. At a loss for any other reply, barely holding back the tears, Marco asked petulantly, "Then just what should I be doing?"

"Whatever it takes!"

"What does it take?" he asked, trying to disguise his petulance with sarcasm.

"More than name calling, more than sticks and stones, more than broken storefront windows. It will take people with guts, real guts, willing to stick their necks out, way out, people ready to sacrifice....To bomb! To kill!"

Marco questioned his own hearing for a second. No, she had said it. "That would be the fastest way to get some fascist elected president."

"Fascist are already running this country. It's time to rip off their masks!...If people like you had the guts, there wouldn't be elections."

"No?" Marco asked skeptically.

"No! We could make this country ungovernable, bring down the establishment. Enough bombs and enough bodies, and the masses would turn to us on their knees to run this country, a cadre of intellectuals ready to do whatever it takes."

Marco could not believe the stupidity of what he was hearing, and from his own wife. "You sound like that idiot that came to our meeting — Genghis Ex-Con."

Susan smiled in satisfaction. "Thanks for the compliment.

*****

Dusk was coming on. Marcia walked at a brisk pace. She was still ten minutes from Sather Gate, where Smitty better be waiting for her. She had left her Women's History 101 class in a very serious mood. The fact that women were second class citizens was of course old news to her. Yet the lecture had opened her eyes to the actual weight of the oppression borne by her and every other woman, an oppression every bit as evil as slavery. Yet the slaves were now free. Well, women will be too, and a lot sooner than men thought.

Yet some things covered in the day's lecture left Marcia uneasy. She empathized with her instructor's suffering at the hands of her husband — the beatings and verbal abuse. She was outraged by the incompetence of the police and the lack of protection offered by our legal system, forcing her instructor to leave everything, including her daughter, and run away. Yet the woman seemed to be bragging about supporting herself through prostitution — "They rented me, but never owned me." That was one fact she could have kept to herself. Even more disturbing, and downright impractical, was her idea that women needed a homeland where men would not be allowed. This would necessitate women seizing the means of reproduction, using scientific research to find a way to eliminate birth by pregnancy, which her teacher described as, "Primitive and barbaric, like shitting a watermelon". Again, Marcia flinched from merely recalling this extremely painful simile.

Her teacher's claim that no one was a hundred percent male or one hundred percent female seemed creditable to Marcia. And it may follow that the pressure to be strictly male or female is a form of oppression. Still, Marcia was not convinced that true female sexuality could only be fully expressed through bisexual or lesbian relationships, or that male/female sex, by its very nature, requires sadistic dominance on the part of the male and masochistic submission on the part of the female. Smitty had never exhibited even a hint of sadism. Or had he? Perhaps she should pay closer attention. Still, she had faith in Smitty, that he could change. All that was necessary was to make him aware of the little ways in which he oppressed her. She would have to have a serious talk with him. Yet that was a problem too. Unless he was stoned, she could hardly get a word out of him. He would just look in her eyes, seeming to agree with everything she said. It suddenly occurred to Marcia that Smitty appeared more stoned when he wasn't stoned. She laughed to herself.

A blue and gold Honor Bike came out of the dusk heading straight towards her. The cyclist's only reaction was to open his mouth in wide surprise. Marcia jumped out of the way without an instant to spare. Feeling the adrenaline rush of a narrow escape, she took confident pride in her reflexes. She also took pride in the fact that she had worked on the Honor Bike project, perhaps even worked on that particular bike. Marcia was so satisfied with herself, it didn't occur to her to be angry with the reckless cyclist, who hadn't even glanced back. In fact, she was grateful to him for reminding her about Honor Bikes. There were a couple of them in a rack just up ahead. For the very first time, she would take advantage of one.

Marcia pulled a bike from the rack only to have the front wheel roll away into the bushes. She again took pride, this time in knowing exactly how to fix that. All it would take was a Crescent wrench, which unfortunately, she didn't carry around in her purse. No matter, there was another Honor Bike in the rack. She pulled it out, but only halfway. It was stuck somehow. She pulled harder and got nowhere. In the dim light of dusk, she searched for the problem. It turned out to be a lock and chain attaching the bike to the rack. Marcia couldn't believe this. Didn't the selfish person responsible realize he was defeating the entire purpose of Honor Bikes? Apparently not everyone understood how things were supposed to work. Perhaps there should have been an educational campaign. Perhaps she would see about starting one.

Approaching Sather Gate, she spotted Smitty waiting for her. He stood out barely enough to be noticed. For some reason he looked out of place, a little awkward, yet in an incongruously nonchalant way. Marcia smiled. She noticed that he was wearing that nice shirt she had embroidered to cover a stain. The sight of it made her feel good, as if by wearing it he had again given her a compliment. The first time was when she had shown the shirt to him. There was actually a light in his eyes as he thanked her, saying she must have her father's hands. Marcia hadn't a clue as to what he had meant, until Smitty explained that he had noticed how "deftly" she used her hands. Her father being a surgeon, he'd assumed she had acquired this trait from him. Smitty said maybe she should switch from medical research to being a surgeon too. Until then, Marcia had never realized that yes, she did seem able to use her hands more skillfully and quickly than those around her. And the word deftly made Smitty's remark even more of a compliment. It was such a nice word, one people did not use enough. From Smitty, English major or not, it seemed out of character. She even laughed to herself at the thought of this, and then at the thought that the only compliment she could remember receiving from him was such a nice one. 'Thank God,' she laughed, his first compliment could turn out to be his last.

It was Friday evening. They had plans — straight to dinner at a little Chinese restaurant, a movie afterwards, and then a trip into the center of Berkeley, in search of a nice place to have a drink. This would be their first real date. Marcia felt somewhat uncomfortable about that. Seems that she and Smitty had put the cart before the horse. Well, this evening would set things right, at least to an extent. Exactly how, she wasn't quite sure. In any case,

Marcia looked forward with real anticipation.

The restaurant had been Smitty's choice. Chinese food was great with a bunch of people, everyone passing around and sharing this and that. However, tonight, with just the two of them, she would have preferred a more romantic Italian restaurant. Well, Smitty was certainly no Cary Grant. She better get used to that. Then again, maybe at home Cary Grant also strolled around his apartment in his T-¬shirt and underwear, with a can of beer in his hand. In any case, she liked Smitty the way he was. She liked the comfortable way she felt when she was with him, and when she thought about him, like right now.

The feeling stayed with her throughout the meal and halfway through the movie. Then the picture got a little too serious and ended sadly. It was no date movie, that was for sure. She wondered if Smitty knew the difference. Beneath his quiet, low-key sense of humor that she had started to appreciate, she detected a surprising honesty, or perhaps just an innocence he now allowed her to see. As they exited the theater, she was glad to get out into the bright lights, to leave the darkness of the movie behind.

Just then a voice brought her out of her reverie, asking plaintively, "Can you spare some change. I haven't eaten all day."

Marcia looked over to see a beautiful young girl, sixteen at the most, holding out her palm. A dirty knapsack lay at her feet. With her blond hair and child's complexion, she appeared one bath shy of transforming into an angel. Marcia hadn't brought her purse. She turned to Smitty. "Do you have a dollar for her?"

Smitty took out his wallet, at the same time using the corner of his eye to observe the pronounced profile of the girl's rear end. If there was such a thing as a perfect curve, Smitty was sure he had found it. He handed the young girl a dollar.

Marcia, now doubting she was even sixteen, asked sympathetically, "How old are you?"

"Eighteen," the girl replied.

'Just right,' thought Smitty.

Marcia said, "Are you sure you're telling me the truth?"

Losing her smile, the girl replied, "Hey, believe what you want."

Marcia, mothering instinct taking over, was not offended. "How long have you been in Berkeley?"

"Two days," was the sullen reply.

'Can't believe she's alone,' thought Smitty.

Marcia was bombarded by thoughts about what the typical Berkeley predator could do to a child like this. "Are you on the street?"

The girl was losing patience. "Looks that way."

Marcia said in a motherly tone, "I really don't think you're old enough to be out on the street."

"I'm seventeen, and nobody's gonna give me an apartment until I get a job and get some money."

"Are you really seventeen?"

Smitty guessed sixteen. 'Too young.…Too bad.'

"I said I was."

"A minute ago you said you were eighteen."

The girl refused to answer.

"I'll tell you what," Marcia indicated Smitty. "My friend will give you five dollars if you can show me two ID's that say you're seventeen."

'Nice of me to offer,' thought Smitty, anxious to move on.

Marcia said, "Tell me how old you are, and we'll take you to eat."

The girl hesitated before saying, "I'm fourteen."

'Ouch,' thought Smitty. A deer in the headlights mug shot of him flashed through his mind, stamped diagonally in bold red letters — "PERVERT". 'Your Honor, I honestly didn't—' He started to check out her rear end one more time, but quickly forced himself to look away.

She said her name was Donna. She wanted to eat at McDonalds. The city of Berkeley had successfully fought off McDonalds as if it were a chain of whore houses. Donna had to settle for pizza. She headed for the restroom and left them to order. "What should we do?" Marcia asked.

Smitty shrugged. "Get her the Kiddie Meal."

Marcia flashed him a look he hadn't seen since the time he "stole" her apartment. "This is serious. What are we going to do with her?"

"I thought we were going to buy her supper."

Marcia was losing patience. "I mean afterwards."

Smitty said logically, "We can't adopt her. We're not married."

Marcia wasn't sure if Smitty was being serious or sarcastic. More important things on her mind, she gave him the benefit of the doubt. "We can't leave her out on the street."

Smitty thought to himself, 'If we really made up our minds to, we could.' Yet the idea of leaving a fourteen year old girl with Donna's looks out in the street did make him uneasy. He imagined how she would look even in a week or two. "What about turning her over to the cops?" Smitty felt guilty as soon as he said it.

Marcia shook her head. Still, she felt uneasy about taking a stranger to their apartment, even one so young. And there was the responsibility involved, a lot of it, responsibility that Smitty would have to share. Marcia knew what had to be done. Yet she wanted desperately for Smitty to suggest it. Obviously, he was not about to. "We'll let her sleep at our place tonight. Then we'll figure out what to do tomorrow."

Smitty bit his tongue. It seemed like yesterday he was praying for a roommate. Tonight, he'd somehow acquired a complete family. Talk about commitment, responsibility.

By the time they got Donna back to their apartment building, they had a rough outline of her life story, or at least her latest version of it. Donna's mother was a divorced waitress. 'The runaway's mother of choice,' thought Smitty. He immediately felt guilty for thinking this. Whoever Donna had for a mother, he was sure it wasn't by choice. After Donna had had enough of Marcia's attempt to convince her to go back home, she added another detail. Her mother's boyfriend was always trying to get her into bed. Smitty found this easier to believe than Marcia, who preferred to assume that Donna's imagination was at work. Smitty even had the feeling that mom's boyfriend had done more than try. In any case, both Marcia and Smitty believed enough of Donna's story to make sending her home a betrayal.

As they opened the front door of the apartment building, a bicycle tire nosed its way out. "Thanks," said Straughton with a big smile, assuming correctly that Smitty would hold open the door for him until he got the Honor Bike outside. While Straughton walked the blue and gold bike down the stoop, Marcia stared angrily at him, finally asking, "You know Honor Bikes are supposed to stay on campus?"

"Exactly where I'm headed," Straughton assured her with a

smile. Marcia was still mulling over Straughton's wholly inadequate reply as she entered the apartment.

Donna bee-lined for the record collection as soon as she was through the door. "You got any Beatles?"

As if talking to a child, which she was, Marcia replied, "Why don't we take a bath first?"

Donna already had an album in her hand. "Let's hear this first."

"We can do both," Marcia pointed out. "I'll turn it up so we can hear it in the bathroom." She pulled Donna reluctantly to her feet.

'Lovely,' thought Smitty, as the album started. It was early Beatles, what he considered "bubble gum" music. He headed towards the fridge for a brewski. The beer felt good going down, but would feel even better accompanied by some Jimmy Reed beer drinking music. He turned to see Marcia heading for Donna's pack, an outstretched arm holding dirty clothes. She dropped them beside the pack and rummaged inside. Smitty strolled over to check out what the kid was carrying.

Marcia did not seem pleased with what she was finding. "They're all dirty."

Smitty found this news less than astonishing. He downed a healthy slug, and, out of common courtesy, asked Marcia, "You want a beer?"

Marcia stared up at him. If Smitty had scored any thoughtfulness bonus points, this was not apparent in her expression or her tone. "Do I look as if I want a beer right now?"

If there were any particular way a woman looked when she wanted a beer, Smitty, in his short life, had yet to pick up on it. One thing he had picked up on, not only from his own vast experience with women, but also from witnessing the experiences of other men, including his own father, was one very simple rule for survival — Any Question From Any Woman That Could Be Interpreted Or Misinterpreted As Rhetorical SHOULD BE! He was sure that obeying this rule had saved him an extraordinary amount of trouble. What did most to convince him were the regrettable few times he had broken it. Besides, he believed strongly that when a woman really wanted an answer, she never much minded repeating the damn question.

Marcia's reply had given Smitty pause for another reason. He had caught the fact she used as if instead of like, something he himself rarely remembered to do. 'Maybe she should be the English major.' He found this endearing despite the uncharacteristically stern look remaining on Marcia's face? Smitty accepted the blame for this look, and decided to remove it with an apology. Problem was, he could not think of anything to apologize for — offering her a beer? Perhaps an explanation would do instead. Hesitantly, calmly, reasonably, he said, "I was going to get myself a beer, and I thought I would ask if you wanted one too."

Marcia replied in a slightly, very slightly less irritated tone, "Why always beer? You know I prefer wine."

"Okay...would you like a glass of wine?"

"Are you having wine?"

'Wasn't planning to,' thought Smitty. He glanced at the empty beer bottle in his fist. "I'm easy".

Marcia had no desire to drink or talk, just to end the matter. "Okay, let's have some wine....But remember, the bottle of French wine is a present for my father."

Smitty had remembered. He pulled down a bottle of the cheap stuff and twisted off the cap.

Marcia said distractedly, "You know I really don't feel like a drink. You have one by yourself."

Smitty stared at the cap in his palm. He twisted it back onto the bottle, placed the now opened bottle into the refrigerator, and pulled out a can of beer, now more than willing to drink alone. In fact, he was more than willing to drink something stronger than beer. He replaced the can in the refrigerator and reached up into the cupboard for the fifth of Bacardi. About to take a healthy slug right from the bottle, he spied a clean enough glass in the vicinity. The dark rum looked so enticing that he held it up to the light. It appeared even more enticing. A toast, though silent, seemed obligatory. 'To women, and all the pleasure they give us.' The rum went down more smoothly than usual. Sated, contented, and in suddenly expansive mood, Smitty thought, 'Just what I needed.'

Marcia interrupted his reverie. "You're going to have to take her clothes to the Laundromat."

'Huh?' thought Smitty, having somehow missed the premises that would have made this conclusion logical. Yet he did see logic in getting out of his suddenly crowded apartment for a while. In fact, it was a perfect excuse, one he should have been looking for.

Smitty walked to the Laundromat with an uneasy feeling about his here-to-fore ideal arrangement expanding into a threesome. It just seemed there should be a longer interval between shacking up and family life — nine months minimum. All at once, the logic behind gestation periods became apparent to him — 'Mother Nature knows her shit. Shouldn't mess with her.' And it wasn't just losing the convenience of strolling the apartment in his underwear that was bothering him. He wouldn't have minded, in fact he would have appreciated the concern and patience Marcia was showing towards Donna, except for the lessening concern and patience she was showing towards him. Marcia must be seeing this on his face. He had never made much of an effort to mask his feelings, and this had gotten him into trouble before. Maybe he should start practicing.

As he walked, Smitty recalled a conversation he had had with some stoned, freaked-out flake the last time he had been to the Laundromat. The flake was complaining about how boring the place was in the daytime. At night, he claimed, there was often a nude woman or two doing their only set of clothes. Smitty did not find this hard to believe. He had immediately decided to start taking care of his dirty laundry after dark. Of course he had immediately forgotten this decision until now. In his mind, he thanked Marcia for more or less reminding him. His steps quickened unconsciously, in anticipation of what he would find.

The Laundromat proved to be a fluorescent-bright nighttime oasis. Over a dozen people were inside, all of them clothed, and most of them actually doing laundry. Yet what they lacked in numbers they made up for in strangeness. How they were dressed was the least of it. Every face told a story, and Smitty was not anxious to hear any of them. These were some moody, lonely looking people. Not only weren't they talking to each other, they were even avoiding eye contact.

The scene and its lighting reminded Smitty of Edward Hopper's painting, "Nighthawks at the Diner". He saw all as if it were a painting, removed and from a distance, that is until he caught himself throwing little girls' underwear into the washing machine. 'God, I'm one of them.' Smitty glanced furtively to both sides to check if someone had noticed. No, he seemed to have gotten away with it. Back to business. Smitty reached way into the bag in search of any outlaw laundry that had eluded him. Instead, he found the can of beer he had slipped in before leaving. The thought had been that at least he would have something to do during the boring wait. He now hesitated pulling it out. His fellow Nighthawks might judge it a breach of Laundromat etiquette. More serious yet, he might get arrested for drinking in a public place, which this probably was, though that didn't seem to faze the couple sucking on a joint three seats down. Legal implications tended to make Smitty dizzy. He laid his laundry bag on the floor, accompanied by the embarrassingly loud clang of his already forgotten can of beer.

Smitty stepped outside only to find that a few of his fellow Nighthawks had had the same idea. It would not be smart to stray too far from Donna's clothes. He went back inside, doing a fairly adept job of avoiding eye contact. The washing machine part proved no problem, but sitting in front of the dryer window made him very self-conscious. The dryer was practically empty, and Donna's panties kept flying by the window. He sat waiting, sneaking the occasional furtive glance at his brother and sister Nighthawks. Remembering his unopened beer, Smitty decided not to lug it all the way home, the liquid part anyway. Hell, to arrest him, the fuzz would have to practically trip over the couple to his left, now working on their second joint. He pulled out the beer and went on a crime spree, watching contentedly as Donna's clothes tumbled across the dryer window.

Smitty made it home to find his stereo amplifier and turntable still on, but the lights out and Donna asleep on the couch. He placed her laundry next to her by the light of the street lamp, which also allowed him to see her face clearly. Scrubbed and clean, fast asleep, she did have the face of an angel. Smitty suddenly noticed that Donna's arms were wrapped around a tiny teddy bear. That explained why there had been so few clothes in her pack. He felt a tinge of guilt as he pictured her out on the street. Smitty was glad Marcia had brought Donna home with them, very glad.

The bedroom was also bathed in the light of the street lamp. Marcia lay above the sheets, fully dressed except for her shoes. Eyes wide open and directed at the ceiling, she was obviously doing some heavy thinking. Smitty did something to Marcia he had never done before, gave her a gentle kiss before starting take off his clothes. She remained deep in thought. Smitty kept looking at her face, now realizing that she was a woman, the first actual woman younger than himself who he had ever slept with. He wasn't sure what this meant. Still, the thought pleased him.

Marcia appeared as if she were going to lie there all night, fully dressed and staring up at the ceiling. Instead of getting into bed, Smitty walked over to her feet and gave the bottoms of her Levis a little tug. Marcia didn't respond. He kept at it, each subsequent tug just a little harder. Finally, he broke Marcia's concentration enough to get her to undo the button and zipper to her jeans. This did not help. Marcia, still not looking at him, finally broke into a smile. To help out the poor guy, she started bouncing her butt off the bed. The Levis began inching towards that critical point — halfway down her ass. Smitty persevered. Suddenly the Levis broke free. Smitty fell backward, adding some extra momentum for effect. Even as he crashed into the wall, with far more of a bang than intended, Marcia failed to look at him. Though her smile did get larger, she warned, "Quiet! You'll wake Donna."

Project complete, Smitty got into bed. He wondered if, because of Donna's presence in the next room, this would be one of those long nights without sex. Smitty, the family man, was experiencing some very different feelings for Marcia. Yet they made him want her as much as he ever had. He looked to his right. As usual, Marcia's profile stood out clearly in the soft, pink light from the street lamp. He raised himself on one elbow to better see her face. Marcia's eyes were wide open, still staring vacantly at the ceiling. Her expression was very serious, very sexy. Marcia had seemed to get prettier every day. Tonight she was gorgeous. Just seeing her profile aroused him. He felt the blood rushing to his groin. This night was going to be long on passion and short on sleep. He could feel it.

Smitty slid his hand gently between her hair and cheek. He played his thumb over a thick lock of her hair, at the same time moving the back of his hand gently against her cheek.

Marcia's distant expression became even more serious, more intense, as she tried to concentrate, tried to block Smitty from her thoughts.

This made her look even sexier. His prick ached as he lowered his head to brush his lips against her face. They were almost touching when she asked matter-of-factly, "You know what I'm thinking?"

Smitty stopped dead. By her tone, he knew damn well she wasn't thinking what he had been thinking before she banished that enjoyable thought. "Beats me," he replied, flopping back on his pillow. Now they were both looking up at the ceiling.

There was an edge of irritation in her voice as she asked, "You don't even want to know, do you?"

'Well,' thought Smitty, 'to tell the truth—' Still, he knew that he should want to know. He also knew that he should tell the truth. However, this was definitely one of those situations where the truth could cause more trouble than it was worth. Luckily, a lie was unnecessary. "Why do you say that?" he asked, summoning all the bewilderment he could muster. And before she could answer, he added, "Tell me. What are you thinking?"

Marcia, mollified and not the least bit suspicious of his interest, was quick to answer, "I think there should be a place for kids like Donna."

There already seemed to be, thought Smitty, 'On our couch.'

Marcia continued, "This summer, there's going to be thousands of kids just like her, pouring into Berkeley from all over the country."

Smitty cringed. "Shit, we better get a few more couches."

Marcia gave him a long, dirty look before asking, "Well?"

"Well, what?"

"You weren't listening!"

Smitty blew off the steam in a burst through his clenched teeth, then spoke with as little irritation in his tone as he could manage. "'Course I was. About all the kids needing a place to stay this summer."

"Well?"

"Well, what?" he asked in exasperation.

"Well, what are we going to do about it?"

"We?"

"Yes!"

"Are you sure this is our problem?"

Marcia gave out one of her rare "you're so impossible I could tear my hair out" sighs before wiggling away to the far edge of the bed. Smitty stared up at the ceiling, trying to figure out exactly how and what had happened. The blood that had made it to his groin had long since made it back to wherever it had come from. In fact, he had already forgotten it had been there.

"It's everybody's problem," she said with determination. "This summer, Berkeley is going to be filled with runaways, fourteen year olds just like Donna...younger even, coming here to be a part of what's happening. What if they run into somebody besides us?"

'Guess we'll just have to live with it,' thought Smitty.

Marcia didn't wait for a reply. "They'll need a safe place to stay, people to watch out for them."

Smitty, unsure where this conversation was headed, was wary of the possibilities. "Where do we come in?"

"We can't do it alone."

'Thank God she realizes that.'

"We'll need money to rent a place, and for food."

"I can hardly afford this place," Smitty pointed out.

"People will contribute. They'll volunteer to collect food and supplies...and to fix up the place, and to look after the kids." She sat up in bed, raising her fist in the air. "This is Berkeley. Power to the people!"

Smitty couldn't believe Marcia's sudden transformation into an all too local activist. Without thinking, he verbalized the sarcastic type of thought he would normally have kept to himself. "What are you going to call it, 'The People's Crash Pad'?"

Marcia's face lit up so brightly it shone in the darkness. She leaned over, grabbing and kissing him with glee. "That's it! That's what we'll call it, 'The People's Crash Pad'."

Astonished, Smitty again did some uncharacteristic verbalizing. "Are you serious?"

Marcia looked at him with equal astonishment. "Why not? It's just as good an idea as Honor Bikes."

Again Smitty was so astonished, he did some ill advised verbalizing. "Honor Bikes? They're turning into the biggest fiasco since Mao's Cultural Revolution."

Marcia's tone was angry. "You wouldn't have laughed at Mao, because he's a man....Just because I'm a woman, my ideas are no good."

Smitty lay thinking, 'I wouldn't have laughed at Mao because I like living.' He regretted not keeping silent. 'It's that Women's Lib course she's taking.'

Marcia got out of the bed in a huff?

"Where you going?"

"To the living room." She turned to face him, saying determinedly, "I'm going to write down some plans. You'll see!"

Smitty lay in bed, silent, alone. What the hell had happened? How had it happened? The thought came to him, 'Maybe bed isn't such a good place to talk.' Upon further thought, this idea didn't seem too brilliant. 'Maybe bed ain't such a good place to think either.' Dismissing this thought, he kept thinking. 'How did she get so pissed-off, and over nothing?' If Marcia ever became really serious about saving the world, his life could get unbelievably complicated. Still, her heart was one of her main attractions, right up there with her face. No way did he want to lose her. Smitty made himself admit that he liked the idea, as opposed to the reality, of her bringing Donna home with them. He'd help Marcia as much as he could with her People's Crash Pad. Just then the door opened.

Marcia stood in silence.

As Smitty was about to apologize and offer to help her, she spoke. "Donna's gone."

"Why?" Smitty asked in surprise.

"I'm not sure," Marcia said haltingly, then added, "but she took some of my records…and your stereo amplifier too."

*****

Rob came out of the kitchen to find less than a dozen customers left over from the lunch hour rush. It had been one of the busiest since he'd opened. Now it looked as if the afternoon would be dead. He didn't care, thankful for a chance to catch his breath. Rob poured himself a coffee and sat down next to Straughton at the end of the counter.

Straughton, lost in thought, did not even acknowledge him. He had just heard that Eldridge Cleaver had left Cuba for Algeria, to set up a Black Panther Government in Exile. Cleaver in Cuba had been bad enough. Now he was just about as far away as he could be, making an interview both more desirable and less likely. Straughton saw his chances for syndication fading.

Rob stared amused at the rare, contemplative side of Straughton. "What's with you?"

"I have to get to Algeria," he said distractedly.

"Not enough rag heads in Berkeley?"

Still distracted, Straughton acknowledged to himself that there were plenty of Arabs in Berkeley. It took a moment for him to also realize that this fact had nothing to do with the problem at hand. He didn't want to get to Algeria to see Arabs. He wanted to see Eldridge Cleaver, badly. Still only half aware of his surroundings, he heard Rob speak, as if from a distance.

"Hit up your old man for the ticket?"

Straughton was way too distracted to laugh. He'd have a better chance with Moe, which was close to no chance at all. As Straughton stood, he struggled to put on his confident front. "I'll talk to Moe again."

"Yeah, that'll do it," said Rob, his words of encouragement spoken in a far from encouraging tone. Turning back to his coffee, he received a friendly nod from the customer who had been sitting next to Straughton. Rob returned the nod, and started again on his coffee. Almost by reflex, he glanced back at the customer. There was something familiar about him.

The customer reminded him of Craig Neiman, a geek from two doors down in his freshman dorm. But this guy couldn't be him. Neiman was a mousy, pasty-faced kid from New York City. This customer had some muscle to him, along with an outdoorsy pallor.

The customer turned his head back towards him with a questioning expression. "Rob?"

Could it be him? "Neiman?"

Neiman nodded, wearing a self-assured smile. "Yeah, how's things?"

"You're lookin' good." Rob was too surprised to add his usual, "Who stepped on yah?"

"You look the same, minus some hair."

'Thanks for reminding me,' thought Rob. "A wife, a kid, and the restaurant business — don't help the old hairline."

Neiman's smile brightened. "I've got three kids."

'Could it have been that long ago?' Rob asked himself. "Looks like they keep you in shape."

"Farm work keeps me in shape."

'Only in the Sixties,' thought Rob. He had to smile. A New York City bookworm comes to Berkeley and ends up a farmer.

"You ought to bring your wife and kid up some weekend. Get away from the city."

"Sounds nice." The invitation was tempting. Rob wouldn't mind getting away from the bustle and noise. Even more tempting, he'd like to see his kid running around barefoot in the country. Yet the invitation was also surprising. Neiman and he had never been friends, hardly even acquaintances — a nod and a hello here and there. As far as Rob knew, Neiman hadn't had any friends. He'd always seemed so fidgety and insecure, unable to look anyone in the eye. Apparently, something had changed him for the better, given him confidence. It was nice to see. "Where's your farm at?"

"Not a farm, a commune."

The idea of a visit lost its appeal. Almost all the communes Rob had visited were rural slums. Even the idyllic looking ones had been far less than idyllic beneath the surface. Rob's expression gave away his loss of interest.

"You really should come. Your kid would love it."

"Maybe," said Rob, with no enthusiasm.

"It'll change your life."

That was a weird thing to say. "Huh?"

Neiman focused on Rob with a look of calm certainty. "Rob, I found Jesus....You can find him too."

Rob got a queasy feeling. Things were becoming clearer. That wasn't self-assurance in Neiman's expression. It was the certainty of a brainwashed zombie. "You're in a cult?"

This accusation appalled Neiman. "No, I joined The Children of God."

Rob knew enough about The Children of God to know that if it was not a cult, there was no such thing. He looked at Neiman with disgust. 'Another Jew bites the dust.' If it wasn't the cults doing them in, it was radical politics, the same horseshit. If religion was the opiate of the masses, then communism was the opiate of the intellectual, especially the self-proclaimed type. Rob understood the attraction. The end of religion meant the end of being a Jew, an outsider, an object of abuse. Fantasies for the gutless. As if the nonsense they were born into wasn't at least as good as anyone else's nonsense. As if Buddhism had done such great things for the

Red Chinese.

Rob actually felt too nauseous to finish his coffee. He stood up without even looking at Neiman. As he passed in front of him on the other side of the counter, Neiman said, "Remember, Rob, Jesus loves you."

Without even looking back, Rob knew that Neiman had a beatific smile on his face.

*****

Marcia slept little the night of Donna's disappearance. It wasn't the loss of her precious record albums that kept her awake. No, Donna's disappearance made her more determined to prove to Smitty that a People's Crash Pad was a good idea, even if she, a woman, had thought of it. Marcia mulled over their argument, the one Smitty had no idea he'd participated in. It wasn't what he had said. After all, he hadn't really said anything, even about his stolen amplifier. It was what he had not said that hurt her. Here they were, living together in Berkeley, witnessing the dawning of a new age, The Age Of Aquarius. Marcia had found her own way to hasten this dawn. Did he encourage her? Did he offer to help? No, he sure didn't.

Marcia was up at seven o'clock the next morning. All her classes were in the afternoon. This left plenty of time to spend at City Hall, which since the last election, thank God, was radical-captured-territory. Those new city officials would see the need for a People's Crash Pad. She was even more convinced of this after her arrival at City Hall. The place was a first-run freak show. Long hair, afros, and beards prevailed, and the dress code had gone radical. All over the walls, signs proclaimed, "Power To The People", "Stop The War", "Free The Presidio Six", and "Fight Fascism". 'It's happening,' thought Marcia, 'just as Screw says — The Revolution.'

She soon found out that if it was happening, it wasn't happening until well after lunch. The Supervisor of Housing, whom she had been advised to see, didn't show up until two in the afternoon. Instead of "hello", he greeted her with the phrase, "Power To The People", and offered her a toke from his joint. Before she had exhaled, he had bounced her to the Supervisor for Tourism, who didn't show up until three and quickly sent Marcia to the Youth Programs Coordinator, who directed her to the Supervisor of Hotels and Motels, whom she suspected did not exist. It took Marcia four days and a dozen skipped classes to get bounced back to the Supervisor of Housing, who didn't have time to see her again, not to mention offer her a toke from his joint, which she could very well do without because half the other city bureaucrats had offered her, as a public service, the cannabis they supplied their supplicants in place of the public services these supplicants had come to request. Marcia of course was too serious about her People's Crash Pad project to really take advantage of all this mind zonking courtesy, that is, until her last day of fighting city hall, when failure seemed imminent. She sucked down and coughed up enough smoke to cause a smog alert.

*****

Sarah sat next to David at the counter of Rob's Cosmic. He was drawing with Crayons. Rob was a waitress short. She was there to help out with that and the cash register. The place was practically empty, no help needed, not yet, anyway. Sarah rarely helped out anymore. She didn't much like being there. Nor did she like seeing Rob there. Here he was, with a PhD in Chemistry, running a restaurant. This seemed like a ridiculous waste of a degree. Even more irritating, it seemed like a criminal waste of intelligence. Though she had made her feelings known long ago, Sarah had never stood in his way. At least he was making a go of it, "being a good provider", as they said in the Midwest. If owning a restaurant was what he wanted to do, she could live with that, and live with him too. Sarah felt she had a lot to be thankful for.

Just then, David, the son she was most thankful for, said, "Mommy, I don't want to draw anymore."

"What do you want to do, Dear?"

"I want to go home."

There was some crankiness in his tone. Sarah regretted not taking more of an interest in his drawing, just to keep him interested. "Do you want me to teach you a poem?"

"What's a poem?"

"It's like a song without music."

David pondered what this could be before saying, "Okay."

Sarah worked with David on the poem, surprised to see how quickly he was picking it up. Her exceptional child had an exceptional memory.

Rob walked over to hear what was going on. He was wearing his single string of love beads. More than once Sarah had been tempted to surreptitiously break that string. Well, one of these days, he himself would throw the silly thing in the trash. She couldn't wait to compliment him on that act.

"What's going on here?"

"David is learning a poem."

"Can I hear it?"

Before Sarah could say, "Not yet."

David said,

> "He who knows not, and knows not he knows not,
> He is a fool, shun him.—"

Rob said, "Very good."

"—Wait! I'm not finished....Do you know what 'shun him' means?"

"What does it mean?"

"It means don't play with him."

"Very good."

Sarah asked, "Do you remember any more?"

"Yes.

> He who knows not, and knows he knows not,
> He is simple, teach him.
>
> He who knows not—"

Sarah interjected,

> "He who knows, and knows not he knows,—"

Sarah waited for David to continue. He didn't, so she did.

> "He is asleep—

"WAKE HIM!" David cut in, before she could finish.

"Do you know the last line?" Sarah asked.

David shook his head.

Sarah said,

> "He who knows, and knows he knows,

He is wise, follow him."

Rob said, "David, you did wonderful. I want you to learn that poem and never forget it. Do you know why."

David shook his head.

"Because we live in Berkeley, California, and there are more people in Berkeley 'who know not, and know not they know not' than in any other place in the world."

*****

"No!" Moe repeated for the third time. Of course Straughton did not know what the word meant. Even if Moe could have explained it to him, he wouldn't have. Reporters who didn't know what the word no meant were few, far between, and damn valuable.

"Moe, the money you're making from all those new ads for massage parlors and nude model storefronts could pay for a hundred tickets."

Moe gave Straughton a look withering enough to make it clear he had crossed a line. "What I make is none of your fucking business." Adding to his anger, was the knowledge of Straughton's own little advertising racket. Moe couldn't let on that he was wise to it. For the principle of the thing, he would then have to fire him, and kick him down the stairs to boot. Moe figured the scam was no real skin off his nose, certainly not enough to cost him his best reporter.

Straughton surmised that an antagonistic line would get him nowhere. He had to be on Moe's side. "Think how much money you could have saved by buying me a ticket to Cuba. One to Algeria is five times as much."

The ticket I ain't buying you to Algeria is costing me exactly the same as the one I didn't buy you to Cuba."

Straughton realized that he should be encouraging Moe's greed instead of criticizing it. "This interview could put The Badger on the map."

Schwartzman still hadn't removed the cigar from between his teeth. "I get here every day without a map."

Straughton was distracted by the fact that not only was Moe

speaking with his teeth clenched, his lips were not moving — 'The man could be a first-class ventriloquist'. Yet now he was being a first-class tightwad, a trait Straughton secretly admired. The tightest wad in existence happened to be his own father, who, thankfully, had passed the gene on to Straughton himself. "Moe, syndication rights will pay for the ticket ten times over. Playboy! We could sell the interview to Playboy for a fortune."

The word "fortune" irritated Moe. Straughton already had his fortune, or would have it when his old man kicked the bucket. This unnerved him every time Straughton asked for money. As little as Moe paid him, it was still another perfect example of the rich sucking the blood of the poor, in this case Moe himself facilitated by Moe himself. He felt as if the capitalist system had somehow co-opted him. Every cent he paid Straughton was robbed from the working class. Of course Straughton was worth a hell of a lot more than he was being paid. Still, a raise would be out of the question, counterproductive. Moe had given out three or four during The Badger's first years. Every time he had, the employee soon quit or got lazy. For some reason, giving newspaper people a raise seemed to ridiculously inflate their sense of self-worth. No, a raise was out of the question.

Yet Moe was a man who trusted his senses, and he sensed that Straughton would not remain at The Badger for long without further incentives. The slimeball had one of Eldridge Cleaver's hairs way up his ass. It then occurred to Moe that Straughton might want more than Cleaver's hair up his ass. Though Little Lord Fauntleroy was certainly no man's man, Moe had never suspected him of wearing silk underwear. The possible ambiguities of the phrase "man's man" suddenly occurred to Moe. Still, that was neither here nor there, and neither were Straughton's sexual inclinations. And thinking about sexual inclinations led Moe to a brainstorm. "You want more money, Straughton?"

Straughton had been waiting patiently, assuming that Moe was pondering a decision about that airline ticket to Algeria. This question, that he couldn't believe had come out of Moe's mouth, shocked him to his core. "Yes, yes," he stammered, unsure he had heard correctly.

"The New York Review of Books copped our book and movie reviewer. Take over, and I'll double your salary."

Now Straughton was certainly interested in doubling his salary, but he was far more interested in how The Badger's reviewers got jobs at The New York Review of Books. Of course The Review's staffers were not exactly Straughton's type of people, at least according to his uncle — "Over privileged Stalinist aesthetes, guardians of the proletariat who would run straight to the oncologist if they ever got a callous, which, fortunately for them, was not a serious possibility." Straughton had found this rant so impressive, he had not only committed it to memory for future use, he had actually gone straight to the dictionary to look up aesthete and oncologist. Still, Straughton had no qualms about suffering such hypocrites and nincompoops, not when they were some of the highest profiled hypocrites and nincompoops in all of New York. Their politics certainly weren't contagious. His interest was more than whetted. "Both Sexton and Philby were hired?"

Moe was disappointed in Straughton. "There are no Sexton and Philby. Both columns are written by Sinclair, Chelsea Sinclair."

'Chelsea Sinclair?' Straughton had never heard of him. He knew Sexton and Philby only by their bylines. Straughton would sometimes finish reading a movie review, but he rarely got past the first paragraph of a book review. He could not imagine himself writing either. Both activities carried with them the stigma of actual work. Still, Straughton disliked using the word no as much as he disliked hearing it. His favorite tactic to avoid either was to change the subject, this time back to what it had been. "I thought we were talking about my going to Algeria?"

"I sure as hell wasn't," Moe assured him. He was less than devastated by Straughton's seeming disinterest in reviewing books and movies. Getting someone to work much cheaper shouldn't be a problem. Changing the subject was also one of Moe's favorite tactics, this time back again. "When do you want to talk to Chelsea about taking over?" Moe noticed a young woman standing at the top of the stairs. He had no more desire to talk to her than he did to Straughton. Still, talking to her would be a good way to get rid of Straughton.

Marcia scanned the room, sure she had made a mistake. The office was such a dusty, unorganized, trash strewn mess. Could this really be the source of The Berkeley Badger? Then she spotted Straughton and a fat, bearded man standing at the far end of the room. Marcia again experienced the gagging sensation of Straughton's tongue down her throat. Could a tongue really be that long? It certainly had felt that long. Marcia fought off her disgust and walked towards him.

"He wrote Soul On Ice," Straughton insisted.

Marcia could now make out Moe's disheveled, dirty appearance. He was obviously homeless. She wondered why Straughton was arguing with him.

"If Cleaver wrote Soul On Ice, I wrote Pride and Prejudice," Moe insisted.

Marcia could easily tell that this slob with half his lunch in his beard was not Jane Austen. Obviously he was not homeless either. No homeless person would be that fat.

"Eldridge Cleaver is not only an icon of the Sixties, now he is a fugitive too."

"This town is asshole to belly button with Sixties icons and fugitives. When you finish interviewing all of them, then talk to me about a plane ticket to Algeria!"

It was now apparent to Marcia that this formerly "homeless" man now ignoring her was probably Straughton's boss. Straughton, with his back to Marcia, wasn't even aware of her presence.

"Moe, you are being penny-wise and pound-foolish."

Fazed by the priggishness of Straughton's words, Moe caught a glimpse of Marcia out of the corner of his eye. He then did something completely out of character — a double-take. Embarrassed, he quickly turned back to Straughton. "Tell your buddy Ben Franklin The Berkeley Badger never had a foreign correspondent on the payroll and never will." Then, with the unlit cigar still clamped between his teeth, without looking directly at her, he said to Marcia, "We already bought our Girl Scout Cookies."

Marcia stared mute at Moe, his rudeness leaving her at a loss for words.

Moe caught the hurt in her eyes. "Sorry Sweetheart, how can I help you?"

Marcia told him.

Moe listened with more patience than he had shown anyone in years, all the while thinking, 'What is this little doll doing out in the world all by herself?'

Straughton listened too, with the same lust that had consumed him the first time he had seen Marcia. Now that she lived down the hall from him, it was merely a question of catching her at the right moment, or in the right condition.

Moe waited for Marcia to finish. For him, a surprisingly long while. "You want us to write a story about this Peoples' Crash Pad to be?"

Marcia nodded.

"Sorry Sweetheart, I'm not Santa Claus. I'm the editor of a newspaper. When you want something, ask him. When you have news, come to me."

"A Peoples' Crash Pad isn't news?"

"No," Moe assured her. "A demonstration about a Peoples' Crash Pad, that can be news, especially if it's violent. Someone getting beat up or arrested by the cops, that's news, especially if we've got pictures."

"You want me to get beat up or arrested?"

"Wouldn't dream of it, Sweetheart," Moe assured her. "But you're a pretty girl, and smart too. If you put your mind to it, you could get someone else beat up or arrested."

Before Moe turned and walked away, Marcia saw something close to a smile appear around his cigar. Otherwise she would have taken this last remark as serious advice. Now she wasn't sure how to take it.

Straughton, seeing an opening for a clean start with Marcia, interrupted her thoughts. "City Hall is captured radical territory now. Have you tried there?"

Marcia just nodded.

"Have you ever heard of Sylvia O'Reilly?"

Marcia had no desire to talk to Straughton, or even look at him. Still, for The Peoples' Crash Pad, she was ready to make the sacrifice. "That lawyer who's always in the news?"

"Yes. A People's Crash Pad might help her stay in the news....Look her up."

*****

Sloan glanced out from the service window towards the buss tray station. There were not enough dirty dishes to retrieve, and this irritated him. His desire was not to wash more dishes, but to get a better look at the woman sitting next to the buss trays. She had this shade of hair he had never seen before, somewhere between blond and red. It was different, and attractive. Still, that was not the source of his interest. The source was her seeming interest in him. The day before, when he was picking up a buss tray, she had given him a look he had not seen in a while. It wasn't close to that wide-eyed worshiping "You're my God" look he'd seen on all of his dogs and a few of his women. It wasn't even the "You turn me on" look the girls sometimes give you when the party is coming to an end or when the bar is about to close. It was more of a "You know, we might be good together" look, which was as good a look as he'd received from a woman in a long time. Now here she was, sitting in the same chair as yesterday. Sloan wondered if she would give him that look again, knowing that if she did, this time he would find out exactly what it meant.

Sloan had not touched a woman since he'd gone cold turkey, and he hadn't touched a woman who wasn't heavy into drugs for a lot longer. Lately, he had tried to keep from thinking about women, which was impossible. Hell, they were everywhere. The problem was the problem he'd had the last time he'd gone off drugs — an embarrassing equipment malfunction with a woman attractive enough not to have witnessed many. No way did he want to go through that again. Yet this woman by the buss trays seemed just what he needed. Her features were nice, if plain. Her complexion was not bad either, light with a rosy outdoor hue. Sloan found her figure a turn on, slender yet with some well defined curves. Even more enticing, she had a few years on him. Sloan had a hunch she would be the patient, passive type, exactly what he needed to get back into action.

There were now enough dishes to retrieve. 'Moment of truth,' he thought. Sloan started towards the buss trays, wondering if he had imagined her interest the previous day. A second before he entered her field of vision, she looked away. "Shit," Sloan mumbled.

Just then she looked back. The smile that came to her face was even more enticing than yesterday's. Sloan gave her a friendly nod as he knelt to replace the fuller buss tray with an empty one. She kept on looking at him, even as he switched some dishes from the second buss tray to the one he was holding. This was all the encouragement Sloan needed. "Seeing a lot of you lately."

She kept smiling.

He kept talking. "What are the chances of seeing you when I'm not working?"

"Good," she said right away, then added, "When are you off?"

Sloan told her, then headed to the kitchen wearing a huge grin. 'That was easy.' He got to the dishes immediately, and was halfway through them before he noticed Rob standing a few feet away, staring amused at him. Sloan, still smiling, just shrugged.

Rob said, "You're lookin' good. Who stepped on yah?"

"Lately, no one."

Satisfied, Rob left Sloan to his fantasies.

Sloan figured that if she did show up, the deed would get done. It had been suspiciously easy. Yet sometimes that's the way the deal went down. One thing for sure, if she didn't show, or he didn't score, he would not turn back to dope, not right away anyway.

She did show up, and early enough to keep him from wondering if she would. Sloan walked her out the front door. Through the glass he noticed Rob watching, wondering exactly how and when he had pulled it off. Sloan enjoyed the look on Rob's face.

"My name's Kathleen," she said.

"Mine's Mike."

Kathleen smiled. "My father's name is Michael."

'Hope she likes her father,' thought Sloan. "What do you say we catch a flick?"

"Fine."

A shift of washing dishes never left anyone smelling like a rose. Sloan caught his own scent, and a mild scent from Kathleen too. Neither scent was deodorant. Hers wasn't anything that would put the brakes on a night of fun. The woman just didn't happen to be any cleanliness freak. Still, he better get some of the stickiness off his own self. "I need a shower first."

Sloan waited a good, long moment for Kathleen to say, "Come over to my place."

She didn't. He'd have to take a chance on his dump. Luckily, he had changed the sheets this week, or was it last week? In any case, the sheets were passable, that in contrast to the rest of his broom closet. Sloan had never had much talent or need for small talk, so they got to his apartment on the bare minimum. Now, with a woman at his side, the place looked even worse than he remembered. Sloan waited for Kathleen to bolt. She didn't. He searched her face for panic or disgust, seeing no hint of either. 'Crunch time approaches,' he thought before saying, "You don't mind my taking a shower?"

Kathleen looked at him questioningly. "Should I?"

Sloan shook his head. "Can't think of a reason."

Kathleen shrugged in a joking sort of way.

Sloan entered the bathroom wondering whether she would be there when he came out. He stripped and entered the shower. Just as he reached for the water knobs, Sloan changed his mind. He opened the door, exposing little more than his head and chest.

Kathleen was now sitting on the bed facing him, a calm expression on her face.

He held up the bar of soap. "We're in luck. There's enough for two."

Kathleen kept her calm expression. She stood and walked toward him. Turning her back, she offered Sloan the buttons to her blouse.

*****

There had to be some mistake, thought Marcia. She took out the piece of paper with the address. The number on it matched the number on the building. No mistake. Sylvia O'Reilly, the famous lawyer, worked out of a surprisingly rundown office building in a rundown section of Oakland. The cage elevator was right out of a 1930's black and white movie. Marcia would have headed for the stairs, except six flights were just a little too much of a climb. Instead, she pushed the collapsible metal grate to the side and entered. That was all the door there was. This proved just as well. The stench of urine would have been even worse. Taking off with a jerk, the metal cage shook and rattled all the way up, as if it were as frightened as Marcia. She tried to turn her discomfort into an educational experience. So this was what the inside of an elevator shaft looked like — fifty years of grime. She filed this epiphany way back in her mind, under the heading, "Once is Enough".

The dark sixth floor corridor was no improvement on the rest of the building. She was anxious to get out of it and into Sylvia O'Reilly's office, which of course was situated at the far end. The hall was so eerily quiet, Marcia was hesitant to break the silence. She gave the door a barely audible knock. No reply. Marcia knocked again, this time with some added muscle. No sign of life. Marcia glanced back down the eerie corridor. She tried the door knob. To her relief, it worked.

Marcia entered Sylvia O'Reilly's waiting room. Not much larger than a Santa Monica walk-in closet, it too could have been right out of a 1930's movie. The light was so dim, everything in the room was in shades of grey. Marcia walked towards what she assumed to be the office door. Just as she gave it a gentle knock, the loud ring of a telephone from within startled her. A booming voice came from the other side of the door. "One moment." The voice continued to boom, now obviously involved in a phone conversation.

Marcia backed away from the door and glanced around the room. Though her eyes had adjusted to the lack of light, the room remained in shades of grey. There was a picture frame containing some strange printing hanging on the near wall. Marcia approached and saw that it was the front page of a Russian newspaper. She guessed the picture near the center was the reason it was on display. A little man stood in something close to a military uniform. Another man and a woman in civilian clothes stood at his sides. Any clues to what was happening in the picture were in Russian, thus no help to Marcia. She backed away and noticed another framed newspaper on the opposite wall. This one was printed in English. She was startled to find herself looking at the front page of The Daily Worker, the official organ of the Communist Party of the United States. She had heard of this paper many times, yet had never seen a copy. Just looking at it made her feel subversive. And here were the same three people again, this time smiling and raising their glasses in a toast. The caption read, Comrades Sylvia Cohen and Jack O'Reilly toast Stalin's health. It was obvious to Marcia that Sylvia Cohen must now be Sylvia O'Reilly. Less obvious to Marcia was the fact that the funny little man in the picture was Joseph Stalin himself. This came to her in a flash that left her jaw dropped. Marcia drew as close to the picture as she could. Yes, definitely Stalin. Soon she would be talking to a woman who actually toasted Stalin, a giant out of the history books. Another thought occurred to her. The O'Reilly's must be card carrying communists. But that was illegal. Or was it? Maybe it is now, and wasn't then. Or maybe it never was. Why would she have incriminating evidence framed and hanging on her wall?

The phone conversation on the other side of the door seemed increasingly heated. Sylvia O'Reilly would not be in a very good mood by the time she was done. Still, Marcia was curious to meet her. What would she be like? By the sound of her voice, she was certainly no shrinking violet. There was the bang of a slammed down receiver, then a loud voice, more impatient than welcoming. "Come in. Come in."

Marcia entered to find the office not much larger than the waiting room, and a good bit more crowded. There were the obligatory shelves of law books, with the optional coat of dust. A rather thick one at that. Manila folders were everywhere, stacks of them — on the filing cabinets, on the floor, and on O'Reilly's desk.

"Sit down," came the raspy order from somewhere behind these folders. Her tone also could have been out of a 1930's movie, where the warden calls the convict to his office and orders him to sit down.

Marcia followed the order and finally got a look at Sylvia O'Reilly. Though manila folders were stacked over two feet high from both front corners of the desk to both rear corners, there was a clear corridor from Marcia's chair to O'Reilly's, right down the middle. This corridor, though free of folders, was thick with smoke. Marcia found it hard to believe one cigarette could be the source of it all. It wasn't. In addition to the cigarette in O'Reilly's hand, another one almost as long burned away in the ashtray.

Sylvia O'Reilly was a small woman, in her fifties or sixties, with unruly and untended frizzy grey hair. Her bright red lipstick was applied only approximately, without a mirror or with an unsteady hand, possibly both. The rouge on her powder caked cheeks was almost as red as her lipstick. O'Reilly did not look to Marcia like any lawyer, real or depicted, that she had ever seen. And she had appeared much taller in the newspaper pictures. It occurred to Marcia that Stalin must be even shorter. Or rather he had been shorter, now being dead of course.

O'Reilly stared Marcia straight in the eye, as she asked, again in the tone of a warden, "You know what's worse than capitalism?"

Marcia could think of a lot of things worse than capitalism. Communism, for one. Still, she decided upon the safest answer she could think of. "No."

"Family, that's what's worse than capitalism."

Marcia never would have guessed that. In fact, if she were the arguing type, she would not have let this opinion go unchallenged. Her father was practically the only family she had, on the West Coast at least. She had always envied people with large families. Marcia surmised that the phone call must have been personal, not business. O'Reilly still sat staring at her, as if waiting for an answer. Marcia nodded, as if giving one.

This seemed to satisfy O'Reilly. "Well, what can I do for you, Honey?"

Marcia started telling her, and O'Reilly started shaking her head. She kept shaking it until after Marcia had finished. This had not made the telling any the easier.

Finally, O'Reilly asked in a sympathetic tone, "Who sent you to me, Honey?"

"A reporter for The Badger."

O'Reilly convulsed in laughter for a few seconds, then coughed her lungs out for a long minute. This spell was prolonged by numerous impatient attempts to speak. All O'Reilly could get out were the words, "I knew—".

At one point the coughing got so violent Marcia feared she was witnessing O'Reilly's death throes.

Finally, the coughing subsided. "I knew it had to be some idiot that sent you."

Marcia pondered whether to take these words as a personal insult. She certainly had no desire to defend Straughton. In fact, thinking back, she wondered why it never occurred to her that he just might be an idiot. One thing for certain — this was the second time she had been embarrassed by him.

There was sincere sympathy in O'Reilly's tone as she continued. "You seem like a sweet girl, not like my own rotten daughter. But I'm a criminal attorney...and I've just about had it with even that."

O'Reilly mistook Marcia's silence for confusion, explaining,

"It's just not worth the trouble, Honey. My clients come to me because they're guilty and everyone knows they're guilty. I don't even attempt to defend them. I transform them into radical martyrs. My shtick is to put the white power structure on trial instead — the cops, the legal system, capitalism. We seat as many flakes or nincompoops on the jury as we can. After a week or two of my spiel, we can always get to one of them, and half the rest of the jurors don't know where the hell they are either. I get the killers off scot-free. We have press conferences. I make radical heroes out of them. I'm a hero too. Then, a few weeks later, they murder someone else and here we go again. Believe me, I'm not easily embarrassed—"

Marcia did believe her.

"—but how many times can I stand in court or at a press conference and give the same speech, sometimes for the same murderer....Honey, it's diminishing returns."

With little hope, Marcia asked, "Maybe you can talk to city hall for me."

Again O'Reilly began to laugh, this time with very little coughing. "Waste my time talking to those pot heads? If they were any more stoned, we'd have to put diapers on them."

So Marcia had again wasted her time. She now wanted nothing more than to get away. Standing, she said, "Thank you. Do I owe you anything."

O'Reilly shook her head. "Good luck." Marcia already had her hand on the door knob when O'Reilly called to her, "Wait! Sit down a minute." Marcia did so, as O'Reilly disappeared behind her desk. By the noise she made, she was obviously searching the drawers for something.

Marcia waited patiently with a smile on her face. It hadn't been a waste of time after all. This woman was going to help her.

O'Reilly finally surfaced, handing Marcia two framed, desktop sized portrait photos, one of a boy and one of a girl. "These are my rotten kids."

Marcia took the photos, fixated on the nicotine stains on O'Reilly's fingers. How many cigarettes did it take to get them that brown? Could tobacco alone have really done that? How long would it take to get her hands clean? Marcia was stumped. She turned her attention to the photos. Neither of O'Reilly's kids had

had much luck as to appearance. Worse yet, they were full grown, with no hope of a change for the better. Marcia guessed that lack of space was not the reason the photos were now hidden away in a drawer. Then why was O'Reilly showing them to her?

"I gave those ingrates everything I could. Raised them as good socialists. I even sent them to Young Pioneers summer camp in Russia. You think that didn't cost a pretty penny?"

Marcia shook her head, wondering where this was going? She had no idea Americans could, or would, send their kids behind the iron curtain to summer camp. Did the kids go canoeing, or did they work in steel mills, or something?

"So how did they thank me? They joined a Doomsday cult. Sylvia Cohen O'Reilly's kids fell prey to a pack of wackos. Can you believe it?"

Marcia could.

"What did I do to deserve that?"

Though Marcia had not a clue as to exactly what O'Reilly had done to deserve it, she had suspicions that O'Reilly had done more than enough. The question that was really stumping her at the moment was what did all this have to do with her, and where was this conversation leading. Still, Marcia couldn't but sympathize with O'Reilly. "It must have been very hard on you and your husband."

"My husband?" O'Reilly repeated derisively, "I got rid of that drunk when they were still in diapers....Sent him to jail for a few years too."

Marcia tried again. "It must have been hard losing both children."

"The loonies got their claws into my daughter first. I sent my son to get her back, and the cult got him too."

"Where are they now?"

"Who the hell knows? In a cave somewhere, waiting for the end of the world. Probably for the tenth time already....That's why I'm showing you the pictures. In case they ever show up at your crash pad...if you ever get that crash pad."

The thought did not fill Marcia with anticipation. Among other things, O'Reilly's kids looked way too old. "How old are they?"

"About thirty."

"My crash pad will be for kids."

"They may show up anyway…recruiting. Who knows?…Don't call the cops. Call me."

"I will. What are their names?"

"Christopher and Christina, both Chris for short."

*****

The front door was locked of course, meaning Susan wasn't home. Today Marco had forgotten to take his keys. He knocked anyway. For the last week or so, she had been disappearing somewhere. There wasn't a chance the back door would be unlocked, not when Susan was the last to leave the house. Marco dragged himself over to and collapsed upon the porch swing. No telling how long he would have to wait for her.

Feeling like an idiot for forgetting his keys, Marco swung in the porch swing. He felt like even more of an idiot for not knowing where the hell Susan was. Despite his best efforts, he could not keep from thinking that she might be having an affair. He attempted to brush this thought aside with the fact that Susan always returned in the same sour mood as when she left. What kind of an affair could she be having? Marco had even stopped asking her where she was going. It made him feel like his own mother. He'd ask Susan the same question his mother had always asked him. "Where you going?"

And Susan would answer in the exact same words, or rather word, as he had. "Out."

Despite himself, he'd repeat his mother's next question. "To do what?"

And damn if Susan didn't give his exact same answer. "Nothing."

It was uncanny. How did Susan know? Marco was able, barely able, to force himself to believe that this was merely a coincidence. Coincidence or not, it gave him added sympathy for his long suffering mother. Susan's replies seemed like divine retribution. And Marco had no trouble believing in both the divine and retribution. Though he never told anyone, especially Susan, the "Fear of the Lord" was in him.

Swinging comfortably, Marco felt himself dozing off, a feeling he welcomed. That's when a single fly showed up. Though flying

219

solo, it sounded like a swarm. The pest had a built-in amplifier. Marco forced himself to ignore it, edging closer and closer to sleep. Then the damn thing landed right on his nose. Eyes closed, conscious of the danger, feeling he had no choice, Marco took a swipe. The fly escaped. Marco's nose stayed right where it was. The pain wasn't anything near enough to make a grown man cry, but it was more than enough to banish all hope of sleep.

What had gone wrong between him and Susan? What did he do? What did he say? Marco didn't have a clue. An old and bitter grudge returned to his thoughts. Surely things would be different if not for those incompetent fascists on the House Un-American Activities Committee. Marco had literally drooled while watching their hearings on TV. He had been so ready for them. Marco had toiled day after day on his speeches — one for his opening statement and one for the press conference afterwards. He even stayed at home for two straight weeks, making sure to be around when they came with their subpoena. Yet what did those grandstanding, pontificating fascists do? They subpoenaed that hag lawyer, Sylvia Cohen O'Reilly, Moe from The Badger, and a collection of washed-up, irrelevant Old Left has-beens. And what the hell did those fossilized troglodytes do? They all took the Fifth Amendment. Marco knew damn well that he would never have stooped to hiding behind the Fifth. His speeches were masterpieces. If only he had been able to give them. He would have put the House Un-American Activities Committee in its place, exposed it to the world. How many times, just thinking about this, had he heard the cheers from the gallery, been blinded by flashbulbs as the masses carried him triumphantly down the Capitol steps on their shoulders? He would have become a national hero, his picture in every newspaper and his speeches on all the network news programs. Things could now be so different. Susan couldn't have helped but glory in the fact that she was his wife.

Suddenly, for the first time, Marco realized that he had underestimated the House Un-American Activities Committee. They had not overlooked him. They had avoided him; somehow knowing they were no match for him. Feeling triumphant and energized, he rose to his feet.

Now already standing, Marco decided, for the hell of it, to check the back door. Surprisingly, it was not only unlocked, but ajar. His relief was short-lived. Did an intruder leave it open? He could not imagine Susan forgetting to lock it. A sense of danger, and a shiver that accompanied it came over him. Could Susan be inside, dead, lying in a pool of blood, killed by an assassin sent to murder him? The thought made him queasy. He and Susan were having their troubles, but he did not wish that on her...not yet, anyway.

Marco tiptoed silently up the back steps, which fortunately led right into the kitchen. He picked up a knife similar to the last one seen by Janet Leigh's character in Psycho. Still, Marco hesitated. Should he call the police instead? That would get quite a laugh down at the station. "Ha! Ha! Marco the Red calling the pigs for help." And first he'd have to rip off the "No Pigs Allowed" sign beside his front doorbell. And who knows, the pigs might plant some dope in the house? No, this job he must handle alone.

Silently, Marco took a step, silently except for the squeak of his sneaker. Removing his shoes would be a good idea. He did, leaving his socks on. Marco entered the hall. The guest bedroom was to his left. Knife in the On Guard position, he entered and checked out every inch it, even the closet. The next room was his and Susan's bedroom. He got another chill when he saw the door, a way he rarely saw it, closed, not completely closed but not even cracked open a little. That was really strange. Marco's hand almost touched that door, with the intent of slowly pushing it open. Visions of Susan's body on the floor, in the requisite pool of blood, gave him pause. Then came a vision of Susan's murderer, standing just behind that door, bloody knife raised and ready, a blade that made Marco's look like a letter opener. Marco then pictured a machinegun in his other hand. This vision convinced him that he should check out the rest of the house first. This he did, and it took him a lot less time than he would have preferred. Now, all too soon, he found himself standing back at his bedroom door. There was nothing else left to do. Marco screwed up his courage. With the tips of his fingers, he placed delicate, constant pressure on the door to open it as silently as possible. The hinges squealed like a stuck pig. Marco, cringing, couldn't believe how loud. Yet now the door was open. There was nothing unusual in what he could see. Still, from where he stood, there was plenty he could not see. Knife at the ready, Marco entered the room, giving it a scan. The first thing he noticed was Susan's cat Killer raising her head off his pillow. He saw no other living thing, and no corpses or pools of blood on the floor. Marco relaxed and let out a breath. Only the closet remained to be checked. Confidently, he walked right over to it, finding nothing unusual.

When Marco turned around again, the sight of Killer, now back to sleep right in the middle of his pillow, infuriated him. He could taste imaginary cat hair in his mouth, and actually tried to spit it out. Marco, who had just stood up to his wife's possible killers, his own bloodthirsty assassins, and with no more than a kitchen knife in his hand, was now in no mood to take any crap from this arrogant little fur ball. "Get the hell off my pillow!" he demanded.

Killer calmly raised her head, stared Marco in the eye, yawned at him, and lay her head back down again.

Marco, further incensed, taking Killer's yawn as a personal insult, yelled in an even angrier tone, "I said get the hell off my pillow!"

Killer, eyes upon Marco, didn't even raise her head.

Marco, who had just searched his entire house, armed with nothing more than a kitchen knife, walked straight towards the arrogant ball of fur.

Killer shot to her paws, arching her back menacingly. Her malevolent eyes gave no quarter as she spit saliva through her teeth.

Marco, incensed, thought, 'Who the hell does this cat think she is?' His hand shot forward to grab the scruff of Killer's neck. Yet before he could get any kind of grip—

The cat sunk her needle-sharp fangs into his wrist, deep enough to hit bone. Marco screamed in pain. The forgotten knife fell from his other hand, right through his sock, also finding bone. Marco screamed even louder as—

Killer let out something between a squeal and a growl as—

Marco hopped away into the bathroom for some do-it-yourself medical attention. He ran the water in the sink and placed his hand under it. With his other hand, while standing on one leg and nearly losing his balance, he removed the bloody sock from his injured foot. Though he was feeling far more pain in his hand, his foot was bleeding worse. The bathroom tiles were a mess. Marco removed his hand from under the water. He lifted his foot up into the sink, again almost losing his balance. Steadying himself, he replaced his hand under the water too. The wounds would not stop bleeding, yet the pain from them was nothing compared to the discomfort from keeping one hand and one foot in the sink. Marco, pondering this challenge in triage, was just about to relocate operations to the shower when, thankfully, his hand stopped bleeding. Not only was he now able to add another hand to his grip on the sink, he was also able to remove the mercurochrome from the medicine cabinet.

When Marco finally made it out of the bathroom, he was dead tired and dying to lie down. That's when he was reminded of the source of his injuries. Killer lay as before, sleeping contentedly on his pillow. Marco's anger returned. He was certain that Killer was only faking sleep. He took a few steps towards the kitchen to get the broom, to teach her who was boss once and for all. The pain in his foot slowed him, but it was the memory of a nightmare he'd recently had that actually stopped him. He now saw it even more vividly than when he had dreamed it. Marco lay helplessly paralyzed in his bed, head resting upon the pillow he shared with Killer. He relived the excruciating pain as the cat, now as large as a lion, ripped, by jerking her head from side to side, long, ragged, and bloody strips of flesh from his face. Marco felt dizzy as he stared at Killer. He was tired. And the cat, by way of Susan, did have her rights. They would simply have to make peace somehow. He certainly could not stay awake all night every night just to keep Killer from eating his face. Marco headed for Susan's side of the bed, comforting himself with the thought that, at the very least, he'd live to fight another day.

*****

Straughton was getting restless. He had been standing for a good half hour at the entrance to the zoo, waiting for Chelsea Sinclair. He still had no great desire to take over as The Badger's next critic. At first, he also had no desire to talk to Sinclair. Yet the more he thought about it, the more reasons to do so occurred to him. Moe kept using his failure to even meet with Sinclair as a way to change the subject every time Straughton requested airfare for the Cleaver interview. And there was no logical reason not to take over the columns. He could easily write a movie review when he felt like it. And when he didn't, he could pocket Moe's money and get someone else to do it for the free tickets. The book reviews he could farm out for half the fee to some English major. That lug down the hall, Smitty, would do quite well. And most important, Straughton was dying to know how exactly Sinclair got his job at The New York Review of Books. Finally, decisively, it occurred to him that the NYRB editors would drool at the thought of an Eldridge Cleaver interview. They worshipped all the cant spouting thugs of the underclass.

As Straughton waited for Sinclair, he decided to definitely have a talk with Smitty. Straughton himself had nothing against reading a book every once in a while. In fact, he quite enjoyed doing so. The problem was, that if he did enjoy a book, he could not read it critically. And if he was not enjoying a book, he could not make himself keep reading. Doing so for a reviewer's pittance would, at the very least, be pure masochism and border on outright prostitution. Besides, Straughton was certain that literary criticism was just not in his genes, literally. The craft seemed to require both anal and effeminate qualities. Now Straughton had nothing against homosexuals. How could he? Half the males in his family seemed so inclined, all three of his mother's brothers. The twins in fact made a quite agreeable couple. Still, Straughton was proud of his own heterosexuality, an only child who would pass on the Straughton name. He again wondered why, since he had proved such a splendid specimen, that his parents had not added to their brood. This time, while wondering, memories of some childish taunts about his father intruded upon his thoughts. Ridiculous taunts. People could be so jealous of a Straughton. No, his father was not the least bit effeminate. In fact, he was quite the hunter and fisherman. Straughton had always been grateful that his father had never tried to drag him along on these so-called "manly pursuits". It now occurred to Straughton that his father's hunting and fishing companion was his mother's older brother, far from the manliest of men. This line of thought was proving somewhat discomfiting. Straughton would have banished it immediately if the mesmerizing sight of Chelsea Sinclair had not done the job for him.

Straughton had no idea what Chelsea Sinclair looked like. Sinclair, being about to leave town and pressed for time, had asked to meet while taking his nephew on a long-promised tour of the zoo. Now walking straight towards Straughton were a man and a preteen boy. Straughton had seen a dozen such pairs in the last half hour. Yet there was no doubt in his mind that this had to be the pair for whom he had been waiting. Chelsea Sinclair was clearly an original in a town with no shortage of them. To qualify as an original in Berkeley or San Francisco, one must be one without trying to be one, by being one's self, and having one outrageous self to be. Yet prime examples sometimes get lost and submerged within a sea of phony emulators striving to appear as such. Straughton could tell the difference at a glance.

Chelsea Sinclair strolled towards him this sunny day wearing the immaculate bright-white uniform of southern aristocracy, accented by a ruffled white shirt, a red carnation, and a red string tie. His shoes were also an un-smudged white. In his right hand, instead of a mint julep, he held a red umbrella. This young cross between Tom Wolfe and Colonel Sanders had the rosy complexion of an infant. There was an oddly juvenile skip to his slightly mincing gait. Straughton, smiling as if he had just discovered gold, now regretted not having met the man sooner.

Sinclair immediately proved himself worth the wait. He had been kind enough to prepare for Straughton a two page list of contacts plus some helpful hints on criticism. Straughton had little interest in the latter, but contacts were any reporter's life's blood. Sinclair spoke with a gravity that seemed to infer that he was passing on to Straughton the sacred torch of literary criticism. Straughton gained the uneasy feeling that Sinclair was purposely talking over his head, this despite the fact that Straughton was by far the taller of the two. The fellow had a way of lecturing people instead of conversing with them. Still, Straughton was not one to take such manners personally. He almost always thought of the people he met as performing for his sole benefit upon life's stage. Little matter if the actors sometimes took themselves too seriously.

They walked casually towards the first exhibit, Sinclair lecturing, "I have found that my criticism improves immeasurably if, instead of writing for my actual readers, I write for the most intelligent readers I can imagine."

Straughton was certain this would be detrimental to his reporting, but he could see where it might improve his criticism, if he ever did attempt any. Still, he had to let Sinclair know how much he valued his advice, even taking it up a notch. "Imagine your reader to be even more intelligent than yourself."

On Straughton's suggestion, Sinclair tried to imagine just that. He failed. "One should never overtax one's imagination."

Straughton had no reply to that, but he didn't need one. They were already at the first exhibit.

Sinclair turned to his nephew, a sturdy lad of eight. "Tommy, you notice the difference?" he asked, pointing towards the camels.

The boy replied immediately, "Some have two humps and some have one."

"Exactly," Sinclair said with a smile. "Which do you find aesthetically superior?"

The boy looked up at him questioningly.

"What do you think looks better, two humps or one?"

Accustomed to being quizzed by his uncle, the boy replied without hesitation, "Two."

Again Sinclair smiled. "Exactly. The single hump is too large, completely out of proportion with the rest of the camel." Sinclair realized the word "proportion" probably meant nothing to the child. "The hump is so large that the camel looks silly, as if it will lose its balance and fall over."

The child nodded his understanding, but his expression said otherwise. The camel approached within ten feet. Tommy's eyes widened in fear.

"Don't be afraid," said Sinclair. "What do you think of the camel's head?"

The child had no idea how to reply.

"Is it pretty?"

Tommy shook his own head.

"Does a horse have a pretty head?"

The child nodded.

"Can you see the difference, why a horse has a pretty head and a camel doesn't?"

Again Tommy shook his own head.

"There are a lot of reasons. A horse has shiny hair, not wooly like that. It's eyes are nice and big, not dumb and squinty like a camel's. And the camel has big ugly lips and silly ears....Do you see?"

The kid nodded, but not very convincingly.

"Tommy, there is never an excuse for ugliness, even in nature."

Now Straughton had only been half paying attention. In fact, less than half. He doubted Sinclair could teach him anything useful about camels. What Sinclair could do was be his connection at The New York Review of Books. Walking to the next exhibit, he asked, "Who did you know at the NYRB?"

"No one," Sinclair replied.

Straughton found this answer baffling. You did not just get a job at The New York Review of Books unless you knew someone, or unless they suspected you of being a fiery bona fide communist. He eyed Sinclair suspiciously. His white outfit did not exactly scream, 'To the barricades!' "Then how, may I ask, did you acquire the position?"

"An editor came across a review I wrote....He judged the defense of Socialist Realism it contained as the most brilliant he had ever read."

This reply Straughton found quite believable, and quite useless. Perhaps submitting an article on explosives would do the trick. Their best selling issue ever had front cover instructions for assembling Molotov Cocktails.

Tommy pointed and called out, "Zebras!" They walked over.

Sinclair asked, "Can you see the difference between zebras and horses?"

"Yes," Tommy replied with confidence.

"What is it?"

"Zebras are fat."

"Yes," Sinclair agreed. "But what else."

"Stripes!"

Exactly. Which are prettier, zebras or horses?"

"Horses," Tommy replied without hesitation.

"Exactly! You are a very smart boy. Can you see why zebras are not as pretty?"

Tommy studied the zebras, trying to see. Finally, he shook his head.

"Look at the stripes," said Sinclair. "They are in the wrong direction. They should be lengthwise instead of every which way. Wouldn't that be more pleasing to the eye?"

"It'll blow your mind," Screw assured Marcia. "You'll really dig it." They were walking down a street of small frame houses not far from their apartment building. Marcia was quite hopeful she would "dig it". Screw's confidence buoyed her interest. The neighborhood was a little rundown, but any of the houses would be perfect, that is, except for the next one. All its windows were boarded up, and by the looks of the boards, had been for a long time. The house's wood siding wasn't in much better shape. The little front yard was a trash pile. Screw held out his arms like a proud real estate agent, his hand almost touching the weather beaten "CONDEMNED" sign. "Here it is — The People's Crash Pad!"

Marcia was speechless. Obviously there was some sort of misunderstanding.

Screw mistook her silence for overwhelming gratitude. "Outa sight, ain't it?"

"It should be," Marcia said, more to herself than to Screw.

Screw, blind to Marcia's doubts, replied, "It will be! A little cleaning and some paint."

Marcia had recovered from her disappointment just enough to restrain herself from rejecting Screw's suggestion out of hand. "Have you been inside?"

"Sure, almost slept here my first night in town."

"How'd you get in?"

"From around back. Come, I'll show you." Screw climbed happily over and through the trash — in his bare feet.

Marcia hesitated, looking for a way out yet not wanting to appear the ingrate. "Are you sure we're not trespassing?"

Screw turned back towards her, amazed. "Trespassing? How can The People trespass on The People's own property? We're liberating The People's Crash Pad!"

Marcia reluctantly followed Screw. The trash grew denser along the side of the house, in some places two feet high. Her legs sank into the garbage as if into quicksand. Marcia fought to keep her balance. She tried to comfort herself with the thought, "Thank God I'm wearing jeans and sneakers." A skirt would have had her headed home already.

Screw, after nearly falling himself, came back to take her hand. Marcia did not appear as thrilled as he had anticipated. "You have to picture how it's gonna look."

The only thing Marcia was picturing was the next place to put her foot. The stink of garbage had her breathing through her mouth, and the stench only increased. Apparently the freshest garbage was piled in the backyard. Flies buzzed so loudly they were making her dizzy. She inhaled one. In a paroxysm of coughing, Marcia leaned against the house. She struggled to expel the fly while it danced up-side-down on the rear of her palate. The stench of garbage now had her nauseous and on the verge of vomiting. She held back, not realizing a good retch would probably rid her of the fly.

Screw kept asking, "What's wrong?"

Marcia finally got it out — an explanation, not the fly itself.

Screw, wanting to help, couldn't figure out how except by holding her up. Then came a brainstorm. He gave her a slap on the back almost hard enough to burp an infant.

Marcia was too busy gagging and coughing to notice.

For his next slap, Screw erred on the forceful side.

Marcia recoiled in shock, from the sound more than the pain.

Screw guiltily pointed out the upside. "You stopped coughing."

Marcia, realizing he was right, straightened up in relief.

Screw asked, "Did you get the fly out?"

She had no idea, losing her sense of relief. Retreat on her mind, Marcia glanced backwards. Had she really managed to slog through that much garbage? Well, she had come too far to turn around. Then, looking forward, she realized she had not come near far enough. Still, the worst was over, maybe. At worst, the worst wasn't likely to get much worse. "Let's finish this and go home." Marcia headed for the side door, ignoring the fact that it was boarded up.

"Over here," said Screw, pointing to a broken out, half boarded up window. He made a stirrup with his hands. "Put your hand on my shoulder.

Marcia stared at the darkened window. "I'm not going in there."

Helping her up from inside would be close to impossible. "There's nothing to be afraid of."

Marcia was less than convinced. "When was the last time you

were in there?"

Screw admitted to himself she had a point. Who knows what could have happened since? "I'll check it out first."

He took out his lighter and placed it up on the sill. Screw then pulled himself up and halfway through the window. The sill cutting into his abdomen made this one painful perch. He lit his lighter. Screw couldn't see more than a few feet, but those feet contained nothing but floor, more than enough to stand on. He jumped down from the window. "Nothing. I'll help you up, and I'll be standing right next to you before you turn around."

Screw was true to his word, but this didn't make Marcia any the more comfortable. Lighter in hand, he led her out of the empty bedroom into a hall. There, among the trash, Screw found a candle stub. He lit it. The stink inside the house was different from the stink outside — no improvement, but different. Screw led her into the living room, where some of the refuse turned out to be the human variety. Marcia was petrified, squeezing Screw's arm as she pressed against him. One of the bodies stirred and moaned. The candle illuminated a hypodermic needle nearby. "They're alive?" Marcia asked.

"Yeah,' Screw assured her, "Dead bodies don't stink this bad."

*****

The sky was a pure, bright blue, without a hint of the usual west coast haze. Sloan had to squint. A crisp breeze carried the fresh scent of salt. Kathleen's smiling face took on a very attractive glow in the late morning light. She strolled the marina looking like an enticing magazine advertisement for flower power.

Sloan walked beside her, sorry he had come. His expression showed it. He had blown his day off, and when you weren't on dope, you needed some relief every once in a while. Sloan had just wasted a long, frustrating hour trying to get Kathleen out on a sailboat. Someone from his sailing days, by chance bumped into on the street, had invited him out. Sloan, dying to get offshore himself, thought he would surprise Kathleen. He couldn't even get her to step aboard. To make things worse, she wouldn't give him a reason. Her face gave no clue. If she were scared of drowning or just the water, that he could understand. Yet she denied being scared of either. A beautiful day wasted. The very least she could do would be to come up with an explanation.

Kathleen was definitely a little squirrelly. Sloan could accept that in a woman. He'd learned to. Most of his women had been to some extent squirrelly, at least in his opinion. Compared to a few of them, Kathleen was a paradigm of sanity, so far. Yet that really wasn't saying much. Kathleen was squirrelly in a way he had yet to come across, and Sloan had a hunch that he still didn't know the half of it. The tip-off was when they were in bed making it. If he really got her going, which, fortunately, he often managed to do, she'd start calling out to Jesus. Now this was something Sloan had experienced with other women, many times. Except there was a difference with Kathleen. When she called out to Jesus, she seemed to believe that Jesus was actually listening, maybe even watching. This tended to unnerve him just when he should be most enjoying himself. Sloan did not like to be thrown off his game. Lately, for this reason, he'd been skewing their sex more to the oral side. Kathleen knew enough not to talk to Jesus with her mouth full, so far anyway. If she ever forgot — Sloan winced at the thought, though he found it more amusing than frightening. Since Nam, there weren't many things that scared him. Sloan was half conscious that he was amusing himself with this line of thought merely to keep his mind off their aborted sailboat ride. He had expected a lot from it, too much, not just the sense of freedom, of flight, as salt air rushed against his face, not just the calming lap of waves against the hull, but also the aphrodisiacal effect of salt air and water upon him and Kathleen. Now the blown opportunity was having the opposite effect. Still, he knew, all in all, he had nothing to complain about. The sex with her was first rate. Kathleen, squirrelly or not, had enabled him to prove that he hadn't lost a thing. Besides, most of his female friends had thought he was crazy. Who knows, maybe all of them. Maybe they were right too. And maybe, when it came to women, he had gotten what he was looking for. Perhaps what he deserved.

They came to the end of the same pier where Sloan had retrieved his hat. Kathleen said, "This is nice, but your next day off, I want you to come up to the commune with me."

Sloan thought to himself, 'Just when I was counting my blessings.'

"Will you?" she asked.

Sloan said, "Let's sit for a while." Before doing so, he pulled his bush hat down tight. No way did he care to go swimming again.

"Why don't you want to?" she asked, sitting down beside him. Their legs dangled from the edge of the dock.

Sloan had the same opinion of communes as he had of communism. Neither worked unless some very ruthless son-of-a-bitch was running the show and some scared shitless underlings were doing the work. "I've been to communes. I don't like them."

"You'd love ours," she said in a sing-song tone.

"Look, Kathleen, it's not just the hippie communes. That's amateur stuff. In Nam, I saw the real thing. I saw what it does to people, and it ain't pretty."

Kathleen's reply was in her same sing-song tone, showing Sloan she hadn't understood a word he'd said. "At our commune, you'll see more love than you've ever seen any place else."

Sloan remained silent. He thought about his hunch that, concerning Kathleen, he did not know the half of it. Now he had a new hunch — he did know the half of it, and the other half too.

*****

Marcia found herself alone, standing outside, well outside, Screw's suggestion for The People's Crash Pad. So it had come down to this or nothing. She stared at the condemned sign, squinting at the small faded print.

An elderly female's voice came from behind her. "Disgraceful, isn't it?"

Marcia turned to see a woman in her seventies walking a small scraggly dog. Her wrinkled face suddenly broke out into a sweet smile, as if her previous expression had been a forced mask. Marcia asked her, "Who owns this house?"

"By now, the lawyers, I don't doubt....A mortgage company and the city have been fighting over it for years. They keep promising to raze it."

"It can't be fixed up?"

"Not if they wait much longer, Dearie....They could have done it long ago for practically nothing, but they never had any intention."

"Why not?" asked Marcia.

"Because of those real estate lawyers, Dearie. They want the whole neighborhood to look like this."

"Why?"

"So they can tear down all the houses and build themselves big apartment buildings."

*****

Straughton had been trying to thumb a ride for one of the longest hours he had ever experienced. The drivers flashing by deserved Academy Awards for acting, acting as if they didn't see him. Squinting right into the sun did not make thumbing any the pleasanter. His jaw ached from holding the mandatory, teeth flashing, hitchhiker's grin. It seemed sadistically unjust that the harder to catch a ride the harder you had to smile, and to do so for so much longer. Yet Straughton had no choice.

The Black Students Union at San Francisco State University was striking. That gang meant business. He had better make it there before the action started. Besides, and just as important, the Black Panthers would probably be there. Some of them had to be able to put Straughton in touch with Cleaver. Not only was the interview practically written, he now had a connection at The New York Review of Books, the Radical Chic¬-y-est rag in the world. All that remained was for Straughton to get within shouting distance of Eldridge Cleaver. First, however, he had to hitch a ride to San Francisco State. Yet the big smile on his face continued to fail him. At least his teeth were getting bleached white…or could the sun be tanning them? He doubted that. He also began to doubt that he would ever catch a ride.

Straughton was distracted by a dog walking hesitantly towards him. It was an obvious stray, ribs sticking through its mangy coat. No authority on dogs, even he could tell it was a puppy. The puppy stopped three feet from Straughton, waiting for permission to advance and lick his shoes. Straughton did not give it. His heart held no soft spot for dogs. Mother couldn't live without hers — pampered, spoiled, ill tempered little bitches. Oh, they were real nice to her, but they would snap like mouse traps whenever he got near. Straughton glanced at his hand, searching for scars from past encounters.

The puppy got down on its belly to inch closer.

"Get lost," said Straughton, stopping it in its tracks. The little dog's big eyes grew larger and sadder. No matter. Straughton had seen this act before, was on to their racket. The phony way they looked up at and worshiped you, their superhero, and the way they just had to play with you, had to be your best friend. The little brownnosers were born and bred to kiss your ass, or, at the very least, nuzzle it. Disgusting habit. No, Straughton would not allow himself be used by any four-footed flea hive. Still, he did not enjoy being looked at by those pleading eyes.

Straughton glanced over at his Honor Bike. There was little chance he'd get a ride back to this exact spot. That meant retrieving the bike could be troublesome. It was a good thing he had two others. Straughton congratulated himself on his foresight. Maybe he should pick up one more. They were getting scarcer lately. He had better act fast.

He had better get a ride fast too. Straughton put the wide, winning smile back on his face. It did not help. The drivers continued to pass by as if he were the un-bandaged Invisible Man. Again he checked his watch — 'Cutting it close.' Why hadn't he ingratiated himself to that English major down the hall yet? He knew why. Whenever he saw him, he was with his girlfriend. When she would look at Straughton, the look was a cold one. She obviously didn't want her boyfriend to know that she and Straughton had a past. He'd solve that problem somehow. He had to. Hitchhiking was such a pain.

Straughton checked his watch again. He would never make the demonstration in time. That settled it. He unlocked his Honor Bike and hopped on. A few minutes later he was standing at Smitty's door. This was no time to be shy. He knocked, hoping that Smitty, not Marcia, would answer.

Smitty did.

Straughton said with a smile, "I'm your neighbor from down the hall. Have you ever been to San Francisco State?"

*****

234

Screw got off on walking beside Marcia. He had never met anyone like her. She was obviously a "brain", but she was "neat" too. This had been a great day from the start. The Weather Underground had broken Timothy Leary out of federal prison. Who would have thought they were capable of anything more complicated than blowing up buildings. They really poked the Feds in the eye this time, and nothing could have been better for business. The Badger's headline had been "The Great Jailbreak". Screw had never sold out faster. In fact, he sold a second load of papers just as fast. And he could have sold a third if there were any left at the office. Just about everyone in Berkeley wore a victory grin. They had won a great battle in their war against the federal government.

Screw, time on his hands, decided to help Marcia along with The People's Crash Pad. "Wait till you meet this dude," he said. "There's a lot of smart people in Berkeley, but Marco beats 'em all." The door was wide open, so Screw did not knock. He led Marcia into the living room where about thirty mostly college age people sat around on the couch, chairs, and floor. One of them, a paradigm of the Wire Rimmed Earnest Looking Freak, was asking, "When are we going to develop a detailed platform to offer as an alternative to this fascist police state oppressing us?"

Screw and Marcia sat down cross-legged on the bare floor as all eyes turned towards Marco for a reply. Screw jerked his head towards him, as if to say, "Wait'll you hear this."

Marco, sitting regally straight in a high backed wicker chair, replied derisively, "Platform? Let the Peace and Freedom Party worry about platforms. We're not running for office. This would merely lend legitimacy to the illegitimate, corrupt process enabling the tyranny that refers to itself as the United States government. Fortunately, there are not enough real fascists in this country to form a pure dictatorship. Unfortunately, there are enough liberal do-gooders willing to work within and be co-opted by the fascist power structure, thus enabling it to accomplish its aims. These liberal do-gooders are just as responsible for Vietnam and the other atrocities as the fascists themselves. Our intention is not to challenge, not to change, but to destroy."

"Right-on!" someone called out, followed by a few more

right-on's and some applause.

The earnest freak, too earnest to accept defeat, asked in all earnestness, "But what about Marx's dialectic? We must provide an antithesis to challenge the existing thesis if we want to bring about a synthesis."

There was no doubt in Marco's mind or his answer. "I assure you, we don't. Is anyone in this room willing to settle for a combination of the fascist oligarchy we now live under and the government we strive for? No! We want a pure people's democracy, uncorrupted by the regime preceding it. A democracy, but not of the ballot box, but of the streets, of The People. Our mission, our duty, is to first destroy the existing order. Then we'll worry about replacing it."

The Wire Rimmed Freak seemed less than convinced, but took his seat.

A girl right behind him raised her hand and stood at the same time. Her face was sad, seemingly on the verge of tears, and her tone was plaintive enough to match it. "Marco, why are we spending so much time demonstrating in support of the grape workers, the Cuban revolution, civil rights, and homosexual rights, when we should be spending more time demonstrating against the atrocities being committed daily, in our name, in Vietnam? Stopping the war should be our overriding cause."

Marco answered calmly, "Because the Vietnam War is not a cause. It's an effect."

The girl rose to her feet again, interjecting in anguish, "But we could stop it. We could go to North Vietnam, place ourselves at every target as volunteer hostages. Don't you see, when the bombs start killing us, it would bring the war home. Think how huge the demonstrations back here would be. They'd force our government to stop the senseless bombing, stop napalming little babies."

Marco found the logic in the girl's argument impressive, especially because it had issued forth from the mouth of an obvious nut job. Crazy people frightened him. Fortunately, there were no shouts of "Right on", no enthusiasm to become "volunteer hostages" on the other faces before him. Marco kept his calm. "More babies are dying of hunger in our ghettos. The Vietnam War is a symptom, not the disease. So are the tyrannies against blacks, and gays, and grape workers. The disease is the fascist military-industrial complex that sucks our blood. The Vietnam War had to happen, if not in Vietnam, then somewhere else. As long as this fascist, capitalist system remains in place to oppress us, there will always be Vietnams somewhere. The real war is being waged here, not in Vietnam.

"What we are fighting for is what Thomas Jefferson wanted — a continuous revolution. The Second American revolution is long, long overdue, a hundred years overdue. Chairman Mao is right. The United States Government is a paper tiger. It is our duty to confront it. Our politics are the politics of confrontation. And we must fight this tyranny on all fronts, all fronts at the same time."

Calls of "Right On!" and "Power to The People!" came from the audience.

Marcia had not realized that things were so bad. In fact, she wasn't quite sure they were. Yet Marco seemed very intelligent and sure of himself.

A studious looking young man, who had been sitting cross legged on the floor, rose to his feet. "Marco, maybe we can do it all, the North Vietnam hostage thing too. We could demand the university make it a part of the Junior Year Abroad Program." Now Marco figured it would take one hell of a lot of demonstrating to force the university to add the option of getting blown to bits in North Vietnam to the Junior Year Abroad Program, more demonstrating than even he had patience for. Nor did he have the patience to discuss the matter further.

Luckily, a regular who had never spoken-up before rose to his feet. Today, as always, he looked as if his Home Sweet Home was a dumpster. In surprisingly flowing English, he suggested, "Perhaps, in protest to the war and military spending in general, each and every one of us should deduct 20% from the income tax we pay."

Marco found this idea as elegant as the speaker's language skills. There was promise in it. Then the fact occurred to Marco that he himself had never in his life made enough money to pay taxes. He scanned the room without finding anyone else who appeared above the zero tax bracket. He scanned again, this time relieved to spot Chandler — 'He must pay taxes.' Still, Marco doubted that this would bring The Gears Of Oppression to a screeching halt. He then realized that his thinking was too local.

While the idea was practically worthless within activist Berkeley, nationally it might be dynamite. He then became aware that all eyes were upon him, waiting for his verdict. "Excellent idea! All in favor, say, 'Aye'."

The room roared, "Aye".

"Then it's unanimous!" Marco replied, failing to notice that Chandler was not among the Ayes.

Marco stood. "We've gone about as far as we can go today. I want all of you here by ten o'clock next Wednesday for the demonstration."

Sounds of surprise and moans of irritation came from his audience. Someone asked, "Why so early?"

Marco didn't miss a beat. "It has yet to be decided what we're demonstrating against — police brutality in the ghetto, the draft, who knows? We'll have to make up the placards just before the demo."

Everyone stood, but no one headed for the door. The crowd divided up into shifting clumps of conversation. The largest clump gathered around Marco.

Screw pulled Marcia to her feet. "C'mon."

"I don't know." Her People's Crash Pad did not seem all that important compared to Marco's lofty concerns. Perhaps she shouldn't bother him.

"C'mon, what have we got to lose?" He led her to Marco. "Marcia here wants to set up a crash pad for the young kids coming to Berkeley this summer, the ones too broke to pay for a bed."

Marco replied flatly, "Youth hostels don't interest me."

He had already turned towards Chandler, who was standing at his side, when Screw added, "We found a house that's been condemned for years, but the bureaucracy won't let us use it."

Marco had opened his mouth to say something to Chandler. Though his mouth stayed open, no words came out of it. He turned back towards Screw and Marcia, mouth still open. He studied them a long, silent moment. "That we can discuss."

*****

"Berkeley Badger," Straughton protested, as two very

intimidating Black Panthers strong armed him back out the glass double doors. "I'm covering this strike for The Badger."

One of the strong armers said, "Cover it from outside."

Straughton had plenty of company outside, on the steps of San Francisco State University's administration building. Nearly everyone was shouting the endless chant, "Strike! Strike! Strike!" Few if any in the crowd appeared to be administrators. After being thrown out of their own building, they had quickly deserted the area. Straughton mused that the administration, wherever it was hiding at the moment, might be regretting its refusal to allow cops to interfere in university matters. Police were only invited on campus to handle crimes such as mass murder. Student expression, apparently up to and including the physical assault of administrators, was protected. Thus, a hundred members and supporters of the Black Students Union were able to chase, push, or carry out of the administration building everyone who was supposed to be in there.

Unfortunately for Straughton, he had arrived post action. Fortunately for him, he had gleaned enough to fake an eyewitness account. Straughton scanned the crowd for Smitty, hoping he hadn't been left stranded. Smitty had appeared somewhat moody after Straughton had asked him to turn on the car's air conditioner. How was he supposed to know that the dilapidated wreck didn't have one? He certainly never claimed to be an auto mechanic. And then Smitty had asked why the hell anyone would need an air conditioner in the Bay Area. That's when Straughton had made his second mistake, admitting that he had merely wanted Smitty to roll up his window. The young brute simply could not fathom that there was something common about riding around in a sedan with your windows down. For that, one required a convertible. Mulling this over, Straughton finally spotted Smitty. He was talking to some hippy girl. Then again, she seemed to be doing all the talking. Straughton relaxed. He still had his ride home.

The strike organizers, one carrying a bullhorn, milled around the steps in preparation for a speech or statement. Six Black Panthers — aviator sunglasses, black berets, black leather jackets over tight black T-shirts, black combat pants — were banishing anyone except themselves and the organizers to the plaza below. None of the Panthers appeared much like students to Straughton, but who could tell these days. The few dozen blacks who did appear to be students were greatly outnumbered by their white classmates. Four young gentlemen in Arab headdress stood alongside Straughton. One of them waved a familiar flag he couldn't identify. Considering Yasser Arafat's puss on the placard waved next to it, Straughton figured the flag must be Palestinian. Three of the four gentlemen looked anything but — more Scandinavian than Semitic. The flag holder was a mystery, wearing his keffiyah mask-style. Straughton assumed the completely keffiyahed one was also an Arab wannabe. A few seconds later he was able to reclassify him as a her.

An angry group of shouters stood under an SDS placard. One of Straughton's most quoted articles had contained some interviews with members of the Students for a Democratic Society Underground. In it, they had taken credit for a number of bombings, some with fatalities, and even one the FBI hadn't yet tried to pin on them. That article alone should have gotten him a job on any paper in the country, or so Straughton thought. He also thought that one of these SDS demonstrators now before him, the angriest of them, looked familiar. No, he finally decided, Mr. Ready To Explode And Take A Building With Him was not a wanted-for-more-than-questioning underground acquaintance. Still, a few of their faces looked insane enough to have surreptitiously surfaced for an old-time's-sake demonstration. Most of the other placards merely said "Strike!" Of course the requisite number of Viet Cong flags were being waved by some very un-Vietnamese looking freaks, whatever that had to do with the Black Students Union.

"Off the steps! Move it!" ordered a Panther standing above Straughton. The tone was familiar to him — 'Excellent cop impression.' He credited this to an overlooked advantage of living in the ghetto.

Straughton had allowed himself to be banished from the building. Now he found himself banished even from its very public steps. There seemed little point in arguing legalities. The more serious affront to his stature in the media was his being forced to stand shoulder to shoulder with the hoi polloi. He needed a face-to-face provocative, better yet incendiary, headline quote. And he knew exactly where he could get it. The Black Panther in charge strolled around above and aloof from his men. This was no lackey. He could be a direct link to Eldridge Cleaver. Straughton still hadn't decided upon a title for the interview — Cleaver on the Lam wouldn't do. Cleaver Underground might. Perhaps Eldridge Cleaver, Notes From Underground. What play it would get. How envious The New York Times and The Washington Post. How rewarding to have them come calling.

Yet what good was any title if he couldn't get hold of Cleaver? Straughton, re-charged by thoughts of syndication, wearing a determined stare, took off confidently back up the steps, straight towards the Black Panther leader. He raised his fist in a black power salute. "Straughton, Berkeley Badger. I did the Eldridge Cleaver interview."

"Honky, I don't give a shit if you did Eldridge Cleaver."

Disdain appeared on Straughton's face in the form of a pleasing smile. "I'd like—"

"I don't give a fuck what you'd like." calmly spoke the head Black Panther, all the while staring at Straughton as if he were a turd floating on the surface of a punchbowl. "Stick that lily-white fist of yours up your honky ass, and get 'em both off these steps 'fore I make you my bitch!"

This was definitely not the quote Straughton was looking for. Yet, at the moment, he did not feel up to defending the freedom of public places, nor even of the press. Though his profession often entailed chronicling battles fought upon principle, Straughton never had much taste for waging them himself. These angry black radicals had no appreciation for what brilliant reporting could do for them, not the way their white counterparts did. They looked down their noses at the press — deigning to give interviews yet treating questions with silence and disdain. And it worked. More than once, the press had helped them get away with murder, literally. He attributed his lack of rapport with these primitive ingrates to the absence of two traits he neither possessed nor coveted — masochism and guilt. Fortunately for the Black Panthers, there were more than enough reporters who did possess these traits.

One of the strike leaders raised his megaphone. 'The speech,' thought Straughton, reluctantly pulling out his hated notebook and pen. For God's sake, he was a reporter, not a stenographer. In addition, Straughton found that he often took his own notes too seriously. They stifled his imagination.

By now everyone on the steps was black, except for a few Oriental chicks. Straughton had just picked up on this trend. At first the black radicals' tastes had tended towards Jewish sluts, then blond ones. Now their tastes, or lusts, had shifted to Orientals. Where would they go from here? Straughton found this question intriguing. He pondered hard for an answer. 'Eskimos?' No, he couldn't picture this. Straughton then realized that his failure at picturing this was because he was picturing Eskimos wearing fur lined parkas and riding on dog sleds — something, one of the few things, you never came across in Berkeley. Still, this was Berkeley, home to everything else. There had to be a few leisurely dressed Eskimos wandering around, most likely on scholarship. It then occurred to him that if he could locate one or two, he could surely work up an interesting article. He himself was curious to know if it were true that they liked to swap wives. Perhaps he could spice up the article by pulling off a trade himself. Yes, an article on Eskimos would certainly be a fine addition to his portfolio. Why hadn't he thought it before?

Straughton tried to remember what had set off such an interesting and fruitful train of thought. 'Oh, yes — Oriental sluts.' Straughton was not one to attribute black success with women to any sexual superiority. No, he assumed that they were merely better able to supply their women with a degradation that the masochistic harlots craved. It never occurred to Straughton that his views, the pure result of his detached powers of observation, might be racist. After all, introspection had never been his forte. None of the Straughtons had much talent for it. And this Straughton, this reporter, was a hard news hound, no aesthete op-ed columnist. Though words were his forte, he made headlines out of them. Little matter that Moe usually made completely different headlines out of them. As Straughton looked at the Oriental girls on the steps, he wondered about the word "slut". What did it mean in the Sixties? He himself certainly had nothing against easy women. Personally, he had often found them a godsend. 'Godsend?' If he ever saw fit to put these thoughts down on paper, he would need a synonym for that word. 'Where was I?' Yes, what would qualify a woman as a slut these days? Was the term merely relative, or did it denote a status now suddenly unattainable? Would the word soon be followed in the dictionary with the notation "archaic", or perhaps even left out completely? Was all this the final result of the sexual revolution, or was this merely its start? Would blind dates eventually be replaced by gang bangs? Would he someday interview a husband who tells him, "Yes, I was almost at the end of the line, but I'm grateful I waited those two long hours. We've been happily married twenty years now." Straughton suddenly realized with astonishment how deep and how far into the future his fertile mind could lead him. Such a rare gift, such a pleasantly unfair advantage over those common dolts who were his competition. And another thing, he had accomplished this fantastic mental journey without the aid of marijuana. Being straight was not the handicap some made it out to be.

Just then a strong, loud, self-assured voice came through a megaphone. "We, the Black Students Union, in the name of all peoples of color, demand changes in this racist, oppressive, Jew-infested, honky institution sometimes referred to as San Francisco State University!" The ninety percent white crowd went wild with chants of, "Black Power!"

"The days of appeasement, nonviolence, and Candy-Ass Martin Luther Coon are over!" The crowd went wilder.

"DEMAND NUMBER ONE!: A completely autonomous Ethnic Studies Department, in no way under the thumb of university administration with their slave-owner mentality." The crowd went wilder still.

"DEMAND NUMBER TWO!: Open admission to all peoples of color, regardless of academic or criminal records, who by their personal histories, know more about ethnicity, and life in general, than any honky Ph.D., not to mention high school graduates." The crowd went even wilder, especially its bona fide honky segment.

"DEMAND NUMBER THREE!: At no time, will the ethnic studies teaching faculty have less than two members of the Black Panther Party." The plaza, as Straughton's article would later describe with only a touch of artistic license, "erupted into a vast sea of waving Viet Cong and Palestinian flags, accompanied by shouts of, "Free Huey! Off the pigs!"

*****

Marcia did not want to be late for her own demonstration. She hurried down the sidewalk, with Smitty a few steps behind. Marcia had felt some placards would add a nice touch, some authenticity. She and Smitty had barely enough time to finish six of them. Marcia glanced back at him, checking to see how he was handling this load. He did not look pleased. "Do you need some help?"

The question displeased Smitty all the more. "No." Though he had the placards arranged so nobody could see the writing, he still felt like an idiot. Just carrying the damn things was bad enough. Soon, to his dread, he would have to walk around holding one up. Smitty sure hoped there wouldn't be any news cameras there, though this would surely disappoint Marcia.

Something even more serious was bothering Smitty. The Cleveland Browns football team was playing on television. Even back in Ohio, where all the games were televised, Smitty would have arranged his schedule around the game. Out here on the West Coast, where he might not get to see another Browns game until the playoffs, this single televised game was way more important. He'd like nothing better right now than to be sitting in a bar, even a lousy Berkeley bar, cold beer in hand, watching his team. Smitty winced when he thought about Marcia's reaction to his very diplomatic suggestion that she get Marco to postpone the demonstration a day — "For a silly football game?" Now carrying his unwieldy load of picket signs, Smitty realized his father had been right. Women just don't appreciate the sacrifices men make for them.

A sudden thought did put a smile on Smitty's face. Maybe the demonstration would quickly turn into a riot. He might catch the end, maybe even the whole second half. And a good riot, that was a rush hard to beat. He had been involved in some great ones, football riots at Ohio State. Raising hell with impunity, right in front of the outnumbered cops. What a power trip. The poor bastards didn't dare arrest anyone. When the crowd caught onto this, mayhem and destruction ensued. Merely recalling these riots supplied Smitty a jolt of adrenaline.

Yet the placards, more awkward than heavy, were still slowing him down — 'Gotta get some exercise.' Smitty was now anxious to reach the protest merely to drop his load. Then another reason came into his head — naked female demonstrators. Could Marcia's very own demonstration be the one he was waiting for? 'Naw, too much to ask.' He'd settle for just enough freaks to take the placards off him. Smitty couldn't picture anyone getting riled up over a People's Crash Pad. Face it, the Donna's of this world were better off back at home anyway. Too bad Marcia hadn't figured that out. Well, he sure wasn't going to waste time or risk an argument trying to wise her up. Yet wasn't he wasting even more time right now. 'No!' This was part of his education, the part he had transferred to Berkeley to get.

Marcia was expecting a big turnout, the people who had been at Marco's place, plus fifty, maybe a hundred more. She couldn't imagine any decent person not being enthusiastic about a People's Crash Pad. The very first one would be right here in Berkeley. The idea was sure to spread. Soon there would be hundreds of them, all over the world. Every major city would have at least one. And the original idea had been hers and hers alone.

In excited anticipation, Marcia turned the corner to Tentative People's Crash Pad #1. What she saw stunned her — cops, a lot of them. Four squad cars and a barred-windowed paddy wagon were parked across the street directly opposite the house. Fronting it, a dozen cops in riot gear lined the inside edge of the sidewalk. Marcia had sudden, unexpected visions of violence. Things could go wrong, terribly wrong. The sense of adventure deserted her. She actually flinched at visions of cops wildly swinging their nightsticks, smashing them down on the bloody skulls of her fellow demonstrators, even on Smitty's head. A dead serious expression on her face, she warned him, "I don't want you fighting back against the cops. Just go limp and let them carry you off."

Smitty restrained himself from making light of her expert advice, almost immediately thinking that he wouldn't mind getting dragged to jail if they had the Browns game on TV there.

The sight of a calm Marco tempered Marcia's alarm. He would know what to do. His followers, a mere dozen of them, were already parading up and down the sidewalk in front of the cops. Their placards read "People's Crash Pad Now," "Power To The People", "Down With Fascism", and "Crash Pad For The People". That was a lesson Marcia absorbed. Her placards were a little wordier, such as, "Establish A Crash Pad For Runaways".

Marcia headed for Marco. He, Straughton, and Straughton's cameraman stood in the street only ten feet from the protestors. Yet they watched from an emotional distance, as if grading the demonstration. The cameraman shook his head, saying, "This ain't getting it."

Straughton nodded, turning to Marco. "Rather tame, you must admit."

Marcia reached them, giving Straughton a quick, nervous, "Hi," and saying to Marco, "You said 12:00."

The cameraman leaned around Straughton to check out Marcia's body. It checked out fine, and he gave Straughton an impressed nod.

Marco, ever the field general, kept his eyes on his troops while replying to Marcia, "I like to set things up myself."

Marcia pondered the implication, fairly certain she didn't care for it.

Smitty, standing back holding the placards, still feeling like an idiot, watched with irritation as the cameraman re-checked Marcia's ass.

Marcia, brushing aside Marco's implication, felt obligated to say something. "Everything seems to be going okay."

Marco turned away from his troops to look incredulously at Marcia. "It sure isn't okay.'

The cameraman gave Straughton an elbow in the ribs, shaking his head derisively, as if to ask, "Is she blind?"

Smitty caught this. He checked out the cameraman's ass, tempted to run the pointed end of one of the placards right up it.

"What do you mean?" asked Marcia.

"Not enough protestors, and the pigs are showing restraint."

The cameraman cut in, "Been to porker obedience school."

Marco added, "Graduated with honors."

Smitty, dying to drop his embarrassing load, asked, "What do you want to do with these?'

Marco shot a glance at the placards, not Smitty, dismissing them with the words, "That's not what we need."

The cameraman said to Marco, "Hey, there's nobody watching this but us. That means no undercover cops."

Straughton, as if to sympathize, said, "Marco, My Man, you are not receiving the respect that is your due."

Just then, the cop in charge said something to two of his subordinates. They headed for their squad car, removing their riot gear on the way."

Straughton leaned over and said to Marco, "My Man, I would take that as a further insult."

Marco did. He stepped up to one of his demonstrators and whispered, "Piss off the pigs. Now!"

Meanwhile, the cameraman had turned to Smitty, eyeing his placards and saying, "Those handles aren't thick enough. Hit somebody with 'em, and they'd snap like match sticks."

Smitty was very tempted to verify this on the cameraman's noggin. He looked around for a place to ditch the placards. There was none. Smitty felt like just dropping them down in the street. A glance at the cops dissuaded him. If he was going to get arrested today, no way would it be for littering. Pondering if this were likely, he watched the demonstrators bait the cops with pig grunts.

Despite their riot gear, Smitty could see the cops exchanging amused glances at each other, as if to say, "Oh yeah, they really know how to hurt a guy."

Marco griped, "It's the camera. If that wasn't here, they'd be banging heads already."

"Without a photo, what good would that do?" Straughton pointed out.

The cameraman threatened, "If I don't get a photo soon, the camera won't be here."

Straughton, as if to mediate, said to Marco, "Have one of your young ladies strip? That's always an excellent bet for page one."

Marcia not only disliked what she was hearing, she was uncomfortable listening to it.

Marco answered irritably, "The free-love crowd is still in bed doing it."

The cameraman pointed out, "I got a good shot of that big blonde last month."

"Today you won't," Marco replied. "She has to be zonked."

The cameraman turned to Marcia with a yellow tinted smile and all the charm he could muster. "What about you, Babe? It's your demonstration."

Marcia couldn't believe her demonstration had come to this.

Smitty couldn't believe he was just standing there, and that the cameraman was still on his feet.

The cameraman reached around and slapped Marcia on the ass, saying, "You got nothin' to be ashamed of."

Smitty's sweet swing of the placards left him nothing to be ashamed of either.

The cameraman did okay too, keeping his balance as most of the placard handles shattered around him like match sticks. A Berkeley pro, he also kept his focus well enough to snap a picture of a cop, nightstick raised, deflecting an out of frame placard. In the foreground, two demonstrators ducked to avoid another out of frame picket sign. Later, even the cameraman would be surprised by the brilliant tableau he had captured. With the addition of Moe's caption, "Police Brutality vs. Peoples' Crash Pad", it made front page top.

*****

Rob stood at his favorite post, behind the counter looking over the dining room. His feet weren't bothering him, so he drank his coffee standing up. Lunch hour had been slow. Through the plate glass windows, he saw why. Street traffic was far less than usual. Could there be some demonstration that he hadn't heard about?

Looking out the window, he noticed Neiman peering in. Rob put down his coffee cup. The sight of Neiman irritated him. The weak creep had been using Rob's counter for cult recruiting. Every time Rob turned around, Neiman would be sitting next to another mixed-up looking kid, trying to turn him or her into a zombie. This morning, Rob met him before he got halfway to the counter. All he said to him were two short sentences. "Get out. Don't come back." Neiman had gotten at least the first part of the message. He left without a word. Now Rob stood waiting to see if he had gotten the second part, ready to move as soon as Neiman touched the door.

Neiman didn't touch the door. Instead, he tapped the plate glass window with a coin. A few customers looked, but only Kathleen got up and went outside. Rob watched, baffled, as Neiman and Kathleen exchanged a few words as if they knew each other. They walked out of view.

Rob, unsure what he had seen, was sure he didn't like it. A steady girlfriend was just what Sloan needed to keep him off dope, and Kathleen seemed to be doing a good job of that. If Neiman turned Kathleen into a cult zombie, she'd leave, and leave Sloan with a great excuse to relapse, 'Thanks to fucking Neiman.'

Here Neiman was, trying to turn Sloan's woman into a zombie, and his friend Sloan back into a junkie. Yet here he was, standing behind the counter doing nothing. Kathleen and Neiman had been gone a while. Maybe they were gone for good. He could at least go outside to see.

Rob walked out the front door having no idea what he would do. This proved just as well. He was not prepared for what he now saw. Kathleen and Neiman were a few yards down the sidewalk. If Neiman was trying to turn her into a Jesus freak, he was going about it in a very strange way. He held Kathleen by the shoulders, and was kissing her. Though not the most passionate kiss, it was intimate in a very familiar way.

Rob walked up to them, now more confused than angry. Neiman dropped his hands from her shoulders, and she looked back to see Rob.

Rob calmly pointed at Neiman but spoke to Kathleen. "You know he has a wife and three kids?"

Kathleen nodded, and Neiman started to speak.

Rob, with a pointed finger, cut him off. "Shut up!" He turned back to Kathleen. "You'd cheat on Mike with this?"

Again Neiman tried to speak, and again Rob cut him off with, "Shut up!" Yet Neiman refused to shut up.

When Rob turned, ready to slug him, Kathleen blurted out, "He's my husband! Leave him alone!"

More puzzled than shocked, Rob looked them both over before turning to Kathleen. "Where's Mike fit in?"

It was Neiman who spoke up. "We're taking him back to the commune with us."

The word we're explained a lot to Rob. "Like hell you are."

Kathleen cut in, "What does he have here?"

Neiman answered for Rob. "A dishwasher's job, a drug habit?"

*****

Marcia was cutting up a tray of brownies. They came out crumbly again, like cake. What could she be doing wrong? One of her strongest childhood memories was watching her mother make brownies. The wonderful aroma that filled the kitchen. That long wait for the brownies to cool enough to be cut, it had seemed like an eternity. And they were so much fun to eat, moist and chewy. If she could only figure out how to make them like that, it would be as if her mother had taught her. Marcia could not understand why cooking was so difficult for her, yet chemistry so easy. After all, cooking was the same thing, plus a sense of taste. And her sense of taste was pretty good.

Marcia carried the brownies out to the living room. She had been worried that again there would not be enough people at tomorrow's crash pad demonstration. That's why she had Smitty invite everyone in the building they knew, to remind them, even the drug addict from under the stairs and Straughton. With the addition of Screw, that made all of three people. The addict seemed to be off drugs lately, but Straughton still gave her the creeps. Still, he did get that phony riot picture from the last demonstration placed on the front page of The Badger. Smitty claimed that that would bring out at least twenty more people. She wondered if he was just trying to keep her from worrying.

Marcia found Smitty and their guests as expected — sitting contentedly while a joint circled among them. As soon as she lay down the plate, Straughton exhaled his toke and exclaimed, "Ah, hashish brownies!"

Marcia took the remark as criticism. "What's the big deal about hashish brownies?"

Screw said, "There the only kind in Berkeley…except in the bakery."

Marcia asked, "Why does the hashish have to be in the brownies? They'd taste better if you'd smoke it before."

Straughton explained, "If one ingests it, the high lasts longer….Did you ever see 2001 stoned?"

"The flick?" Smitty asked. "Yeah, I saw it stoned."

"Not the star gate scene," said Straughton. "by then you had come down."

Smitty looked at him questioningly.

Straughton explained, "Where all the lights come at you, as if you're flying through them."

Smitty realized Straughton was right. The scene came late in the movie. And that would have been the best scene to see stoned.

Straughton continued, "If you had eaten brownies instead of smoked, you would have been stoned for the entire movie....2001 did for hashish brownies what marijuana did for Twinkies."

'What are Twinkies?' Marcia wondered, yet not enough to ask.

Screw's mouth began to water. 'Could use a Twinkie right now.' Then again, what was wrong with the brownies in front of him. He reached for one.

Sloan sat silently, regretting he had come. Smitty had insisted, even after hearing that Sloan had to work during the demonstration. Sloan felt uncomfortable and out of place. The four people around him were at least three too many. He had begun to feel this way shortly after returning from Vietnam. There had to be a connection, but for the life of him, he could not figure out what it was. The feeling itself was bad enough, but not knowing the reason for it was unnerving. This discomfort brought on an urge to get away, maybe north somewhere, to live like a hermit. These thoughts made no logical sense to him. It was as if there were a stranger in his head, maneuvering for control, wanting to lead him off into the woods. Sure, making it on his own in the north woods, that would be a challenge. Yet what was the real attraction? The gnawing urge made him question his own hold on reality. Though the very questioning of this urge seemed somehow, however tenuously, to affirm it. In the back of his mind he had heard someone asking him a question. Sloan retrieved the words so as to reply.

Marcia had asked, "Wouldn't you like a brownie?"

This proved an easy enough question to answer. "Sure." He looked at Marcia's face, another reason for coming and not coming, finding it every bit as interesting and attractive as he first had, thinking, 'What a doll.' Kathleen had been steadily wearing out her welcome. Maybe Smitty didn't know what he had. Maybe he would make a mistake.

Yes, he would like a brownie. Ridiculous as it seemed, if Smitty hadn't mentioned brownies during the invite, Sloan probably wouldn't have come. The word brought back memories. He now decided to do his piss poor impersonation of a normal human being with some small talk. "In Nam, we used to ask our folks to send frozen Sara Lee brownies. It was a high anytime we got them."

"By mail?" Screw asked.

"Yeah, cakes would be a mess, but Sara Lee brownies came perfect....If we thought we were going to get a chance to smoke in a day or two, we'd save them, carry them around in the bush."

Marcia heard these words as if spoken somewhere in the background. She was staring at Straughton, again remembering his tongue plunging quickly and forcefully down her throat, like that of a huge chameleon. By reflex, she actually gagged a little. Though Straughton was in no ways ugly, there was definitely something repulsively reptilian about him.

Straughton caught Marcia staring at him, and she guiltily looked away. A self-assured expression came to his own face, realizing she must be thinking about their exciting little hors d'oeuvre of a tryst. Smitty was surely boring the poor child stiff by now. This realization had first occurred to him when she sent that mute of an English major over with her invitation. What could she possibly have seen in him? There was no point in waiting for Marcia to make the first move. He'd have to invite her over to his apartment at the very first opportunity.

Once again Straughton caught Marcia copping a glance at him. He fought to keep a triumphant expression from his face, only succeeding by joining the conversation, saying to Sloan, "It's my understanding that the marijuana over there was of premium quality, opium cured."

"It was overrated," Sloan answered, uncomfortable at being the center of attention. "Can't compare with Panama Red or Acapulco Gold."

"It was garbage?" Screw asked.

"Naw, it got the job done. And came pre-rolled, in cellophane packs." Sloan felt as if he'd been droning on and on for hours. He attempted to bail out of the conversation by taking a bite of the brownie. 'Sara Lee, this ain't.' He smiled and nodded to Marcia anyway.

"How 'bout some sounds," Screw suggested.

Marcia, the only un-stoned member of the crew, got up to put on a record.

Smitty watched her, sorry that his zonked-out reflexes had slowed him. Sure enough, she picked out an early Beatles album. "Not that one," he said.

Marcia wasn't ready to surrender. She held up the album. "Does anyone else want to hear this?"

If they did, no one admitted it.

Sloan could not think of a better way to ruin his high than having to listen to the Beatles whine, "I wanna hold your hand". His expression must have been transparent, because Marcia stared right at him.

"What's wrong with it?" she demanded to know.

Smitty saved Sloan a reply. "It's bubble gum music."

"What's 'bubble gum music'?"

Only the dread of sitting through, "She loves me, yeah, yeah, yeah," gave Smitty the courage to reply. "Teeny bopper music."

Marcia, no masochist, knew an insult when she heard one. "Well I'm tired of Sgt. Peppers."

So was Smitty. He wondered why she kept playing it. He also wondered why he had been careless enough to use the phrase "bubble gum music". Wincing at the expression now on Marcia's face, Smitty attempted a repair job, a compromise. "How 'bout Rubber Soul?"

Marcia really didn't care. Still, she was tempted to stand her ground until Screw said, "Yeah, I like that album."

The brownies, crumbly as they were, only lasted a few songs. When the cut I'm Looking Through You came on, Screw said, "This song's groovy."

Straughton flinched. "My Good Man, I would appreciate it greatly if you would avoid the expression, 'groovy'. Say, 'It's a groove'."

'What's the difference?' thought Smitty.

"Why," asked Screw.

"'It's a groove' is far more evocative than groovy."

"'Evocative'?" asked Screw.

"More descriptive," explained Straughton.

Screw replied testily, "I know what evocative means. Believe it or not, we got evocative back in Nebraska."

"Then you will have to admit that 'in a groove' is more evocative than 'groovy', especially when one is describing an activity."

"Have to?" Marcia cut in.

"Well, he does not have to admit anything, but the difference is obvious."

"To you," said Screw.

"My Man, the difference should be obvious to anyone....When you say you are 'in a groove', you are saying that you feel like a record needle, in the groove of a big LP. You do not have to worry about turning left, or turning right, or making decisions. All that's left for you to do is enjoy the world as it slides by."

"And 'groovy' doesn't say the same thing?" Screw argued.

"Not even close, My Man. It's an expression too far removed from its source, evoking nothing. It even sounds childish, as if it should be spelled G R O O V I E."

"I don't see the difference," Marcia insisted.

'I do,' thought Smitty, and thought about it long enough to keep his mouth shut. Straughton had made his point, an interesting if useless one.

Right on cue, Straughton asked, "And what does our English major think?"

No way was Smitty going to side against Marcia. That "bubble gum music" remark of his was more than enough for one day. After all, he would not be sharing his bed with Straughton tonight. Picturing this repulsive thought further reinforced Smitty's decision. "Why argue? Say, 'Outa sight!' instead."

Screw was too stoned to object. "Yeah, I guess that sounds more Sixties anyway."

"Sixties?" asked Marcia. "They were saying that back in the 1890's...at least."

Everyone turned towards her as Screw asked, "Huh?"

"It was in Maggie, Girl of the Streets, by Steven Crane," Marcia added. "We read it in high school."

Straughton attempted to clarify things. "'Out of sight'."

"No!" Marcia insisted. "'Outa sight'— O-U-T-A S-I-G-H-T."

Screw felt oddly conned.

Smitty was impressed. His very own woman could make it as an English major.

Straughton tried to salvage some respect by displaying his erudition. "Crane, he wrote The Red Badge of Courage." No one seemed awed, so he turned to Sloan. "Did you earn your red badge of courage in Vietnam?"

"Yup," Sloan replied grudgingly. He hated all the idiots asking him if he'd been wounded, second only to asking him if he killed anyone. Sloan pondered the word courage, adding, "My Red Badge of Zigging When I Shoulda Zagged."

Screw, feeling the grass, tried to regain his bearings. "Hey, what were we arguing about a minute ago?"

Sloan said, "Whatever it was, forget it."

Straughton asked disparagingly, "What then should we argue about, football?"

"At Ohio State, pre-grass," said Smitty, "We talked football. When we argued, it was about segregation or eating pussy." Smitty regretted the remark as soon as it was out of his mouth, and regretted it more when he felt Marcia's sharp elbow jab him in the rib cage. 'Fucking grass. Gotta keep my mouth shut.'

Sloan, amused by Smitty's pain, said, "Believe it or not, when I got to Berkeley, that's what we argued about…more about eating out than segregation." He noticed Marcia giving him a hard stare. 'What the hell? Never get her to the north woods.'

"Which side were the women on?" asked Screw.

Smitty and Sloan went into laughing fits, and Straughton joined them. Marcia stood up in disgust, much of it real. She headed for the bedroom.

Screw, irritated, asked, "What's so funny?"

When Sloan managed to stifle his laughter enough, he said, "Screw, we didn't argue the pros and cons of eating pussy with the women."

Smitty added, "No. There was no argument there."

"They were pro," Sloan assured him.

*****

Straughton set off for the demonstration an hour early. Before he had taken two steps down the sidewalk, someone stepped in front of him with a smile on his face and shoulders wide enough to block his way. "Roger, I was just coming to see you."

This was far from the first time that Straughton had been approached by someone he seemingly should recognize but didn't. In fact, this had happened often enough to allow Straughton to perfect the appearance of knowing who people were until he could

255

actually figure it out. "Been quite a while, hasn't it?"

"It sure has," the smiling face agreed.

"I'm a little late?" Do you mind walking along with me?" Straughton replied, hoping this mystery face would mind.

"No problem," said the face. They began walking towards the proposed People's Crash Pad. "I want to talk to you about what's going on at The Badger."

"Feel free," Straughton replied in an accommodating tone, thinking, 'As if it's any of your business.'

"The Badger has abandoned its mission."

'Its mission?' Straughton had never thought about The Badger's mission, or even assumed it had one. Whether it did or not, The Badger seemed to be doing fine. 'Who is this beefy peasant?'

"We're supposed to be the voice of the counterculture. We're supposed to be bringing the war home."

This last cliché had never made any sense to Straughton. Wasn't the war doing enough damage over in Vietnam? It seemed best to just leave it over there. What was the point of blowing up buildings and sending letter bombs here in the States? My God, the postal service was unreliable enough as is? Straughton felt it would make much more sense to take all these idiots who wanted to bring the war home, and ship them over to the war instead.

The still nameless face continued, "All Moe is interested in is more massage parlor and nude model ads."

Straughton had to admit that this advocate for the counterculture, whoever he was, had a point, an exaggerated one, but a point just the same. Every vacant storefront seemed to be turning into a whore house disguised as a massage parlor or a nude model studio where they handed you a cheap camera to hide the drool on your chin. The Badger's sex ads had gone from a few at the bottom of a page to two full pages.

"And we're helping him exploit these women."

Now this did seem unfair to Straughton. Women being exploited right under his nose. Where was his cut?

The face added, "Moe's making a fortune."

This point, intended to enrage Straughton, instead placed Moe in a more favorable light. Straughton had always seen Moe as ne'er-do-well socialist rabble rouser. Here, right before Straughton's eyes, Moe had transformed himself into a fellow capitalist. What could be more admirable than striving to improve one's financial position? After all, that's what makes the world go round.

"And doing it on the backs of his workers, paying us starvation wages."

Now this fact, and fact it was, did strike a nerve with Straughton, in fact, more than one. Though duly sensitive about being exploited by Moe, Straughton was even more sensitive about being reminded that he was being exploited. Would not this imply membership, forced or not, in the proletariat? The very idea repulsed him. He thought of himself as an independent contractor. Moe really wasn't his employer. Moe was his publisher. Subconsciously, this arrangement allowed Straughton to do something that made The Game of Life exceedingly more enjoyable. It allowed him to keep his own score. At least that was the way Straughton chose to look at their relationship. Thankfully, at the moment, he had reason not to dwell upon this. The nameless face had used the words, "paying us starvation wages." This meant he worked for The Badger. 'Now we are getting somewhere.' Straughton's mind did a quick shuffle of the paid, to use the term loosely, positions at The Badger. Only one fit the nameless person walking next to him. The self-assurance, the manipulative skill, the passable vocabulary — he had to be dealing with a fellow writer, and that could mean just one person, his only real rival at The Badger, that son-of-a-bitch Brad Cavanaugh.

Cavanaugh was The Badger's exponent of the new, artsy-fartsy stream-of-consciousness hold your hat breathless Gonzo prose that put the writer at the center of, not only every paragraph, not only every sentence, but almost every adverb and adjective. Straughton could not fathom the appeal of this loose vowel syndrome. It was a sure sign of the nouveau literate — ostentation. Though Straughton did have his professional fantasies, none of them encompassed writing for Rolling Stone. Yet all this contributed only slightly to Straughton's disdain for Cavanaugh. Straughton's dislike for him stemmed from a more personal source. Cavanaugh seemed to have wangled a partnership in Straughton's Hells Angels franchise, and a major partnership at that. They seemed to be his favorite topic. He had managed to turn these greedy, sadistic thugs into Gonzo Super Heroes of the counterculture. Straughton had noticed that

Twelve Gauge and his men were depending upon him less. He felt expendable around them, and expendable was the last way you wanted to feel around Hells Angels. In fact, it was probably the last way many people had felt around them. And here Straughton was, walking next to, he guessed, the man who had made him expendable. And that man was now staring at him, as if waiting for the answer to a question that he had not even asked. Straughton decided to ask his own question, and find out the answer to another one at the same time.

"Brad, what exactly do you want from me?"

"We're going to strike The Badger, and we all want you with us."

Straughton's first reaction was pride that he had guessed right when Cavanaugh did not flinch at the use of his name. Straughton's second reaction was disgust at Cavanaugh's invitation. To think that he would taint his heritage with membership in the proletariat, to become a turncoat to his own class, one on par with some of the most notorious bomb throwers of the Thirties and Sixties. No Straughton had ever supported any strike, never mind taken part in one. By birth, breeding, and taste, the Straughtons took pride in being the targets of strikes, not their perpetrators. It was the civic duty of the Straughton's to hire those who crossed the picket lines. And to hire the Pinkerton's, and if need be, even more thuggish louts, to protect these strike breakers.

"Well," said Cavanaugh, "Can we depend on you?"

Straughton looked him straight in the eye, saying with determination, "Did you doubt it for an instant?"

*****

Smitty and Marcia, determined to be prepared, set off for the demonstration a half hour early. This made the scene that greeted them there all the more "Unbelievable", as Smitty mumbled. The street in front of the house was packed with over three hundred festive demonstrators, most of them street people. The "police brutality" photo in The Badger had worked a miracle, except in the eyes of the dozen outnumbered cops trying to keep control.

Smitty felt energized. 'This is more like it.' The aroma of marijuana was overpowering. A smoky haze was actually visible

258

above the crowd. 'This could be the day.' Naked demonstrators, topless at the very least, were a real possibility. He looked towards Marcia, his fantasy woman, with wide-eyed admiration.

Marcia, standing in place, searching out Marco, felt as overwhelmed as the cops. A large, happily stoned freak cut off her view as he held a generous joint to her lips. She stepped aside, shaking her head No.

Screw appeared out of nowhere to take a quick hit from the joint.

The freak kept his eyes on Marcia. When Screw returned the joint, he again stepped in front of her. Marcia glanced absentmindedly at the joint before again stepping aside. 'Where's Marco?'

The freak turned towards Screw with an expression that asked, "What did I do wrong?"

Screw shrugged and smiled. He again relieved the freak of his joint, taking an even longer toke before passing it over his shoulder to Smitty.

Smitty always felt more comfortable with Screw around, and not just from the joints he scrounged. Screw himself was a contact high. Of course this didn't stop Smitty from adding to that high. After a quick drag, he proffered the joint to the freak, as if asking, "Did you lose this?"

Screw exhaled in time to say, "It's The Revolution. We're winning!"

Just then Marcia spotted Marco. She squeezed her way towards him. Smitty and Screw followed casually behind. Marco was talking to a group of reporters as they set up their video equipment. Marcia was right next to him before he noticed her. In a no nonsense tone, he whispered, "You ready?"

Marcia nodded.

"Say exactly what I told you, no more, no less....And let me handle the questions."

Marcia again nodded.

Marco placed her before the microphones, then circled in front of them to personally explain to the reporters that Marcia was the prime mover behind the crash pad.

Smitty looked on with grudging respect. She had gotten a hell of a lot further than he had expected. She was sure to make the local news, maybe even Walter Cronkite. Try as he might, he couldn't actually picture her giving a statement to reporters. Yet the act itself seemed imminent. She was doing great.

For Screw, this was just another entertaining Berkeley day. Back in Nebraska, you waited all year for the circus to come to town. In Berkeley, the circus refused to leave. Good company, a potent joint, and a worthwhile cause — what more could your recent high school grad ask for? Well, a bitchin' woman wouldn't hurt. Still, who could complain? Especially, as stoned as he was. Screw took another drag as Straughton's cameraman strolled up to him, whispering, "I wouldn't pass that joint to your left." Screw glanced over to see a familiar looking freak, scruffy yet well built. Screw turned back to the cameraman, who whispered, "Oink."

Screw, trying to remember where he had seen the supposed cop, slipped the cameraman his reward — the joint. The memory suddenly came back to him, with a jolt strong enough to make Screw wince. "Muscles" had once tried to score some grass off of him. The slimy bastard had come very close to succeeding. Stoned as he now was, Screw still warned himself to be even more careful.

Marco concluded his circle around the media with a few words to Straughton, who stopped him with, "My Man, the young lady resides down the hall from me." Marco started to move off, but Straughton smoothly grasped his shirt. "If you care for another page one photo, see that my cameraman is properly placed."

Marco suppressed his irritation. People such as Straughton had no understanding of the organizational complexities involved. Not every demonstration could be turned into a riot, or even an orgy.

A few voices began to chant, "The Crash Pad belongs to The People." Marco leaned nearer the microphone and joined in, bringing along many of his supporters. His crew chanted louder. Yet most of the crowd failed to respond. They were too caught up in the carnival atmosphere to get enthusiastic about anything besides the numerous joints being passed around. Any complaints they might have had before the demonstration were forgotten by now. The chanting soon petered out. Marco moved quickly to disguise this little defeat by tapping on the microphone.

Marcia swallowed deeply. Most of the reporters' eyes were already upon her. Some of their cameras had distracting red lights on. It suddenly occurred to her what this meant — 'They're running!' Momentarily she would have to start her statement. Uneasy as she was, Marcia yearned to begin. Anything would be better than the nervous anticipation she was now experiencing. Marcia felt relief as Marco turned back towards her and nodded. She swallowed, swallowed again, then began her statement.

"As we look around here today, the questions we all should be asking ourselves are: Why did the people of Berkeley again find it necessary to demonstrate? In whose interest is it to see this abandoned, decaying house continue to be a blight upon this neighborhood? Why is the establishment again working against us? What possible harm could there be in creating a People's Crash Pad, a place of shelter for those too defenseless to survive upon the streets?"

This time Smitty's respect wasn't the least bit grudging. There was strength and control in Marcia's voice, without a hint of whining or histrionics. How capable she was proving herself. He was proud of her. Despite his pride, when he heard a completely anomalous sound from behind, Smitty could not help but turn around. It was a sound out of his childhood — the bell of an ice cream truck. Of course that couldn't be the case this time. Yet it was — 'Only in Berkeley.'

A battered white ice cream truck waded slowly and surely into the crowd, like a car easing through a puddle deep enough to stall it. Freaks, not water, finally did stall it. They encircled the ice cream truck, refusing to let it pass, chanting, "I scream. You scream. We all scream for ice cream!" This chant captured the mood of the crowd far more successfully than, "The Crash Pad belongs to The People." Some freaks and street people began dancing around the truck in a circle. Of course they met some other freaks dancing around the truck in the opposite direction. After some major confusion and minor collisions, the clockwise dancing freaks enlarged their circle to enclose the counterclockwise dancing freaks.

The ice cream truck driver eventually came to the realization that he wasn't going anywhere. Deciding to take the freaks' chant literally, he stepped down in his bright white uniform and opened for business. He had the bushy mustache and dark complexion of an immigrant, plus the smile of someone about to make his fortune in the Land of Opportunity. No sooner did he have the freezer door open than people began weaving their way through the two concentric circles of dancers to buy ice cream. He worked the shiny coin dispenser attached to his belt faster than the eye could follow. Still, he couldn't serve his stoned clientele fast enough. An impatient freak opened a second freezer door and started tossing out large cups of ice cream. The vendor panicked, slamming his freezer door shut and running for the open one. He angrily shoved the impatient freak into the circling ones, sending a few of those to the pavement.

A peacemaker, dressed naturally as a court jester, shoes as pointed as his hat, tried to calm the ice cream man with a few dollar bills. He accepted them grudgingly. A few more freaks stepped forward with money. A girl wearing a dozen strings of love beads took one off and tried to place around his neck. He stepped back suspiciously, but then let her have her way. Soon he had the freezer door open again for business. Another hippie girl took a flower from her own hair and placed it in his. All the while the chant grew louder and more raucous — "Ice cream. You scream. We all scream for ice cream!"

Marcia increased her volume to fight for the crowd's attention. She was losing badly and she knew it. Glancing towards Marco for a cue, she caught instead his furious expression. Was he mad at her? Why? No, he must just be mad. Marcia saw that even Smitty was looking towards the ice cream truck. Half the cameras were now pointed at it too.

Smitty watched as a freak in baggy white pantaloons and a flimsy purple vest danced around like a Whirling Dervish, at the same time spooning out ice cream to the girls. This was not easy, and he wasn't very good at it, usually missing their mouths. He missed one face completely, accidentally dropping a large spoonful between two globular breasts. Their owner, shocked by the cold, nearly jumped out of her flimsy halter. Nearly not being nearly enough, she lowered it herself to flick away the ice cream. As heads turned her way, she stood with one hell of a smile and two fully exposed breasts, making no effort to pull up her halter. Instead she merely scraped off the ice cream with her finger. In a flash, her whirling benefactor skidded to a stop, his head landing neatly between her breasts. Tongue flicking in and out of his mouth, he cleaned up the last of his own mess. Her widening smile indicated that she found his tongue one hell of an improvement over her own finger. The Stopped-Whirling Dervish took his time, doing an extremely conscientious job, while the hippie girl patiently sucked the remaining ice cream off her fingers.

Smitty, torn in two directions, looked back at Marcia. Deaf to what she was saying, his heart was still with her. He wanted to put his arms around her. His eyes were another story, continually copping glances in the direction of the ice cream truck.

Marco, with both anger and urgency, shouted into Screw's ear, "Do something!"

Screw was too mesmerized by this inventively appetizing way of eating ice cream to reply.

Marco insisted, "If we don't piss off these cops fast, this demonstration is just going to turn into another freak show."

As far as Screw was concerned, it already had, an excellent one with infinite possibilities. Marco's shouted words, though right in his ear, were just background static. Screw's attention lay elsewhere.

Marco tried again. "I can't go around throwing bottles myself! They know me."

Still not looking at Marco, Screw replied distractedly, "You're right." He then headed straight for the ice cream truck.

Marco, ready to explode, looked around for another acolyte. Instead he saw Smitty, also mesmerized by the festivities.

Smitty turned back towards Marcia in time to see the last microphone disappear from in front of her and head towards the ice cream truck. Marcia stood audienceless, though not yet speechless, facing a furious looking Marco. Smitty walked towards them with the urge to slug Marco. Marcia had done fine. What the hell did he want from her?

Marco saw Smitty coming and read his expression. Removing the anger from his own face, he said to Marcia without enthusiasm, "You did okay. This is how it goes sometimes." He then turned and left her standing there.

Smitty put his arm around Marcia. "He's an asshole. Don't worry about it."

Marcia was worrying about it. "I did my best."

"You did damn good," Smitty assured her, at the same time gently steering Marcia towards the ice cream truck.

Marcia, more hurt than angry, watched the circus before her in a daze. Though the original girl with the ice cream topping on her breasts had disappeared, two others hippie girls, one of them also whirling like a Dervish, had taken the first's place. Of course there was no shortage of eager volunteers to lick their breasts clean. In fact, way more volunteers than breasts. Marcia saw no humor in the scene. It was disgusting. If they weren't interested in The People's Crash Pad, why were they here? Someday, they themselves might need a place to sleep. She hoped that then they'd remember what had happened today. "Is this why they came?" she asked Smitty.

'Probably,' thought Smitty, managing to keep the thought to himself. Though it wasn't why he came today, it was why he had transferred to Berkeley. This and exactly this. What a show! Just then another girl ripped open her top to expose a remarkable set of gravity defying breasts, perfectly round globes, without a hint of droop. Smitty could not recall ever seeing a pair like them, even in Playboy. 'Wow!' How were they possible? 'Helium?' he mused, half seriously. These were a pair for the record books. The cameramen all agreed, their lenses zeroing in like compass needles finding North. And sure enough, here came an eager volunteer with ice cream to spare. He used his spoon like a tongue to gently apply it. The girl responded with ecstatic flinches and erect nipples. The crowd responded with "Oooohs" and "Ahhhhs". The ice cream vender too stood mesmerized, postponing a sale or three. Even after returning to the making of his fortune, he continued to cop glances. Another volunteer arrived without ice cream but with a tongue eager to remove it. Smitty couldn't believe who — his boy Screw. What guts! Smitty knew he could never pull a stunt like that. Screw was doing a hell of a job, doing so well that his competition retreated.

The girl smiled down on him as Screw managed to find ice cream where there appeared to be only naked nipple. He then took an instant's break to scream for, "More ice cream! More ice cream!" Two volunteers, spoons in hand, were there in a second. The girl stepped back and waved them off. Alas, too late. One spoonful of ice cream still found its mark. Screw took a quick step forward to remove it. No sooner had he finished the job than the original Whirling Dervish reappeared, spoon digging into his ice cream. Screw stepped back, allowing him room to do his magic. To everyone's surprise, this time he seemed to be aiming for her belly button. To everyone's greater surprise, he instead slipped a finger between the girl's belly button and waist band, gaining just enough separation to drop the ice cream down the crotch of her panties. She swung her head back in a moan of glee. The Dervish was already on his knees in front of her, fingers hooked in the sides of her pants, wiggling them slowly down, striptease fashion.

'Naw, she'll never let him,' thought Smitty. Yet she sure wasn't stopping him. In fact a thick band of ice cream smeared pubic hair was already visible. The chick sure had a sense of humor, squirming around laughing while being de-pantied in public. 'Yeah, she is gonna let him,' Smitty decided. People were crowding closer, squeezing in front of him and blocking his view. To get a better angle, he dragged a reluctant Marcia a few feet to the side.

It was then that Smitty heard some commotion coming from the other end of the street. No way was he going to turn around. This was sexier than any strip show he'd ever seen. The commotion from behind grew louder, interspersed with distant sounds of panic. Smitty felt Marcia yanking on his arm. "Wait a second!" he groused, wishing she'd relax. Some shrill screams finally got his attention, and got it fast. Smitty felt the crowd pressing towards him in fear. People to the rear, hidden from view, were screaming in panic or pain. Whatever was happening, he sure didn't want it happening to him.

He grabbed Marcia's arm and started running down the street. The crowd in front of him had already taken off. Those to his rear were overtaking him.

"What's happening," Marcia asked in fear.

Without slowing down, Smitty glanced back to find out. Off to the side, he saw a cop tearing after some stragglers, swinging for the fences with his nightstick. And another cop doing the same.

He knew there must be others too, many others, behind these. Marcia wasn't running fast enough. The screams from behind got louder and closer. "Run!" he yelled, pulling on her arm. "FASTER!" She did run, but not fast enough. An instant's glance backwards revealed a riot geared cop swinging his nightstick like a maniac. A freak went sprawling, hair glistening with blood.

Looking forward again, Smitty felt the imminence of nightsticks beating on Marcia's head. He could picture her going down, to be beaten, to be trampled. She wasn't running fast enough. This was not good!

Smitty jerked Marcia off the street and across a lawn. They headed between two houses. The screams grew more frightening. They crossed into the next backyard. Neither one of them looked back until they had broken through to the street. No one had followed them. Yet they could still hear shouts and screams. Marcia had slowed to a walk. Smitty put his arm across her back, forcing her to speed up a little, saying, "Let's go one more street."

*****

Rob pondered what to do. Sloan would be leaving in a few minutes, and Rob hadn't said a word to him about Kathleen. Should he? Sloan was no kid, no weak sister. He must have seen things in Vietnam that Rob didn't even want to contemplate. He doubted Kathleen could turn him into a zombie, but this was possible. The cults had their ways. If she ever got him up to the commune, there would be a whole team there ready to break him. And the alternative, if she couldn't recruit him, was just as bad. Losing his woman, realizing he'd been played for a sucker, these are not things that tend to boost one's self-esteem. Hell, Rob remembered the time one of Sloan's girlfriends had sailed off on him. Within days, he had recklessly dropped out of college and joined the Marines. Yet Sloan was not the type that went around asking for advice, even before Nam, before he really got into drugs. And Rob wasn't the type that went around giving advice. He usually had plenty of his own problems to work out first. Rob knew at heart that it all came down to a single thing — friendship. He also knew there wasn't a faster way to lose a friend than to come between him and his woman. Still, friends watch out for, take chances for friends. There were things Sloan had to hear. If he chose to shoot the messenger, so be it.

"I'm going," Sloan called through the service window.

"Wait. I need to talk to you."

"About what?" asked Sloan, anxious to get out of and away from the kitchen.

"Come here and I'll tell you," Rob said irritably.

Taken aback, Sloan came through the kitchen door.

Rob pointed to a seat at the counter.

Sloan gave him a funny look before taking it.

Rob walked over and stood in front of him, on the other side of the counter. And that was all he did. A serious expression on his face, he could not get the first word out.

Amused, Sloan took on an overly sympathetic tone and played the wise guy. "Rob, we can't help you unless you let us help you. You have to trust us....We're your friends. We want you to get well....You want to get well, don't you? Now tell us your problem?"

Rob came close to laughing. This was the first halfway humorous remark Sloan had made to him in a while. If that wasn't a good sign, there was no such thing. Now more confident that Sloan could weather the blow, he said, "The problem is yours, Pal. Kathleen is playing games with you."

Sloan shrugged. "Fun games, at least."

Rob was losing his patience. "She's married! She has a husband and three kids."

"Really?" asked Sloan with a surprised smile, then added, "She's got one hell of a lover too."

Rob felt foolish, thinking about all the hesitating and procrastinating he'd done. "It ain't love?"

"If it is, love's overrated."

"This is serious. She's recruiting you for a cult."

"I know."

Rob felt like a sucker, the joke now being on him. "You know?"

"Yeah, she's flirty fishing."

"Flirty fishing?"

"Never heard of it?"

"No, sounds perverted."

"It should. That's what The Children of God call it."

Rob was more irritated than amused. "You knew it from the start?"

Sloan shook his head. "Naw, took me longer than it should have."

"And you still haven't thrown her out?"

Sloan looked at Rob sideways. "Hey Man, she ain't exactly

torturing me."

"She's playing you for a sucker?"

"I'd like to think she wouldn't try so hard for just anybody."

"How do you stomach the preaching?"

"There wasn't any at first. Now it's about 70% sex and 30% proselytizing. When it gets to 50/50, I'll dump her."

Rob asked, "Who clued you in about this flirty fishing?"

"This guy I met when I first got back from Nam. He warned me there were now so many cults around Berkeley, they were having a recruiting war."

Amused, Rob repeated, "Recruiting war?"

"Yeah, using pussy as bait."

"How did this guy know?"

"The lucky bastard had a close call. Threw the hook at the last minute."

"How?"

"This guy and his fantasy woman made it all the way to the gate of her commune. He had to stop there to take a piss."

Rob was waiting for Sloan to finish when he realized Sloan was waiting for him to end the story. He thought a moment. "The clap?"

Sloan nodded. "The clap."

*****

Marcia wore a self-assured expression as she knocked on Marco's door. Getting possession of the house and permission for The People's Crash Pad had been the difficult part, and no sure thing. The rest was now just a matter of hard work, and hard work was always rewarded.

The front door swung open and Marcia found herself facing a strikingly pretty woman she assumed to be Marco's girlfriend or wife. Marcia found herself shifting glances between Susan's arrogant expression and the equally arrogant expression on the face of the Siamese cat she held on one arm. Susan's cold demeanor made her uncomfortable, exactly as intended, she guessed. Marcia avoided rude people if possible. Not only didn't she understand them, she didn't know how to handle them. Knocking chips off people's shoulders, even with a choice word or two, was not her nature.

All Marcia wanted was to give Marco the good news, and to thank him. Making no effort to remove what remained of her smile, she asked, "Is Marco here?"

Susan, keeping her deadpan expression, said, "Come in." She led Marcia to the dining room.

Marco sat at the table, absorbed in editing a hand written speech. Without looking up, he said, "This coffee's cold."

Susan stuck her finger in it. "Right again."

Marco caught this, but kept himself from looking up.

Satisfied anyway, Susan left the room.

Marcia stood quietly, wondering if Marco was unaware of her presence or purposely ignoring her. Seeing that he treated his wife with no more respect than he treated her, Marcia's first reaction was a sense of relief. Seeing that Susan gave as good as she got made Marcia question her own submissiveness. Still, brushing off slights and avoiding arguments was her nature, and Marcia saw no need to change. It was just a pity she had to deal with someone such as Marco. Then came the realization that she no longer had to. A confident expression came to her face. Marco, continuing to edit, did not see it. Marcia wondered again if he was even conscious of her presence, then wondered why she cared. He had surely heard her knock on the door. His rudeness irritated her even more than his arrogance. Marcia had difficulty keeping her feelings out of her tone. "I have good news."

Still immersed in his editing, Marco said distractedly, "I told you, I'll handle the demonstration. All you need to do is show up."

"We won't need another demonstration," Marcia said with pride.

Marco looked up at her in disbelief. "What?"

Marcia was bursting to tell him. "I got the permit."

Marco stood, eyes on fire. "You what?"

Marcia was sure Marco had misunderstood her. There was even a smile on her face as she said, "I received permission for The People's Crash Pad."

Marco stood staring at her, about to explode.

Susan entered the room with a cup of coffee in her hand. Instead of giving it to Marco, she sipped it herself while listening in. Between satisfying tastes, something between a smile and a sneer would appear on her face.

Marco ignored her, asking Marcia angrily, "Who gave you permission to ask?"

Marcia couldn't believe the question. "Who gave me permission?" She not only stood her ground, she attempted to take some back. "The People's Crash Pad was my idea!"

Astounded, Marco asked, "Do you actually think this was about a ridiculous crash pad?"

Marcia was thrown off balance. That was exactly what she had thought.

Marco leaned forward and got in her face. "You idiot."

Marcia moved back. Only now, too late, coming up with a reply to his question — 'For me, it was about a crash pad!'

Marco, staying in her face, followed her. "Do you realize how many people I could have had at next week's demonstration?"

Marcia kept moving backwards, feeling used and abused.

Marco kept moving forward. "A thousand, at the least…maybe two thousand!"

Marcia, though still moving backwards, had had enough. "We don't need another demonstration!"

Marco kept coming. "You idiot. Do you realize how much time I've wasted on this?"

Marcia was already half way through the door, and saw no need to answer.

Marco slammed the door behind her. "Idiots! I'm surrounded by idiots."

Susan stood watching him from a few feet away. No hint of sympathy in her expression, she held out the almost empty cup. "Your coffee's getting cold."

*****

Marcia couldn't believe how many eager, energetic volunteers kept arriving at the crash pad to help clean it up. Over a hundred people eventually showed, many not even stoned. All the broken furniture and garbage had already been hauled outside, enough to overflow and bury the huge dumpster at the front curb. Upstairs, people were scrubbing the walls and floors. Marcia directed the work with a minimum of interference. At first the volunteers had been equally divided between college students and street people. Now that half of them had wandered off, most of the remaining workers were college students, and most of the remaining street people were too wasted to keep out of the way. Still, Marcia was thrilled that so much had been accomplished in just one day, and without electricity. They would easily finish the cleaning today. Tomorrow they would paint.

A full hour before dark, Marcia was able to turn over The People's Crash Pad to a few trusted watchmen. Dead tired, she still felt like a world beater. During the walk home, when Smitty put his arm around her, she asked, "What do you think now?"

Smitty gave a nod of admiration. She had a right to be proud of herself.

And Marcia was proud of Smitty too. He had stood by all day, doing anything she asked and ready to straighten out the numerous difficulties that arose. The last few hours, his main job had been herding the zonked-out street people towards the door so the college students wouldn't have to scrub and mop around them. Most important, he had supervised the difficult installation of the bathroom fixtures. A "new" bathtub and sink had miraculously appeared — perfect colors too. The bathtub was a bright reddish-orange, and the sink was a shiny purple. Smitty had also converted an adjoining closet into a second toilet, code-correct vent and all. Marcia was confident that with a little luck, the next day's painting would go just as smoothly.

It didn't. Things looked good at first, two dozen Berkeley art students having arrived to do the painting. Their enthusiasm was not only evident on their faces, it was palpable in the atmosphere around them. Marcia decided not to get in their way, to merely stand back and wait for them to finish. By twelve noon, she was still waiting for them to start. As was often the case in Berkeley, the problem proved ideological.

The majority of the art students wanted to paint The People's Crash Pad en vogue day-glo bright colors of the rainbow psychedelic slash of this phantasmagorical splash of that. However, the two black students wanted the front of the house for a black power mural, with raised fists, black berets, fascist cops, and all the violence and gore that their supply of red paint would allow. The single Chicano student then suggested a compromise mural of Mexican peasants, a la Diego Rivera. No one seconded her. An Anglo student suggested a mural honoring Mao and his communist revolutionaries. He received some strong support, none of it from the three Asian art students whose parents had escaped the honor of living under these revolutionaries. The argument narrowed to psychedelic versus black power. It probably could have been settled quickly and quietly if the three loudest of the white students hadn't decided to sever their connections to their race and take up the cause of black power. "You lily white honkies," shouted the waspiest of the lot, "is slitting your throats the only way to stop you from oppressing peoples of color?" Of course this didn't settle the issue. As soon as the painting got started, for some reason no one could explain to Marcia, the Black Power faction walked off the job, leaving the Psychedelic faction in charge.

*****

It occurred to Sloan that, 'Maybe I was born to be a chemist....Just like Salome was born to be a witch.' He hadn't seen the woman in years, since long before Vietnam. There had always been something "witchy" about Salome, though until now he had never thought of her in that light. She was a good ten, maybe fifteen years older than Sloan. She, the older woman, had seduced him — directly, openly, quickly. He had liked the idea of that when it was happening. He had liked the results even more. She had taught him things, added to his confidence. In fact, some of her own self-confidence may have rubbed off on him. That was the most alluring thing about Salome. Her looks were nothing special, but she acted as if she could have anyone she wanted, and her acting was so convincing she probably could.

There was more to Salome than her self-confidence. There was a sense of mystery and danger. Twice widowed, she seemed too young to be widowed even once. Sloan often wondered if this widow might be self-made. A not unpleasant chill usually accompanied this thought. Three was Sloan's favorite number. Of course, if he didn't marry her, and he had no intention of doing so, he couldn't widow her, and she couldn't widow herself. Though this realization did lessen the sense of danger about her, it did not eliminate it.

Sloan had run into Salome that afternoon on the street. He had been pondering how to wrap things up with Kathleen. The sex was still good, but the rest, especially her commune pitch, was increasingly irritating. She had to know she wasn't getting anywhere, yet she kept trying. Sloan still took this as a compliment, but the compliment was getting old. Worse still, maybe she was getting to like his bed so much that one day he'd come home to find Kathleen and her three kids in his broom closet of an apartment? Sloan had to laugh. He couldn't be that good — 'Maybe she's just stubborn.'

"What's so funny?" Kathleen asked. They were walking down an unlit side street, yet the full moon was so bright she could easily make out his expression.

"Nothing," Sloan answered truthfully, and there wasn't, not about her having three kids. What a world. The surprising thing was how unsurprising it all was. Like running into Salome that afternoon. Here he was thinking about how to break off with Kathleen, and Salome practically jumps back into his life. She smiles warmly, says a few words, then just like an old friend that was now a cosmetics saleswoman, she hands him her card. Only her card doesn't say cosmetics. And it doesn't say butcher, baker, or candlestick maker. No, this is Berkeley. Her card says, "Priestess". And it doesn't just say "Priestess". It says "Priestess of the Berkeley Coven".

Sloan realized immediately that his old lover was telling him that she was a witch. Even in Berkeley, finding out you had slept with a witch comes as something of a jolt. Sloan would never have guessed. If Salome was a witch, witches were getting a bad rap. One thing for sure, her tits were no colder than those of any other woman he had known.

So he had slept with a witch. The idea of it really began to appeal to Sloan. It added exotic value to their long ago affair. As he basked in the memories of it, an extraordinary idea popped into his head. The chemist, the catalyst in him, immediately suggested an experiment — mix one Jesus freak cult recruiter with one witch coven recruiter, and observe the results. Sloan sensed a volatile reaction, perhaps even an explosion, one that would blow Kathleen cleanly out of his life. At the very moment this thought was running through his head, Salome had invited him over for some sort of twelve midnight ceremony. Fortune had given Sloan a shove. Yet Fortune cannot be trusted. For the first time in weeks, Kathleen didn't come home until just before midnight. Salome's place was already in view, but they would be a good twenty minutes late.

It was a modest frame house, little more than a bungalow, left to Salome by her second husband. Not a single light shone from within or without. Sloan knocked. No answer. He knocked harder. Still no answer. Sloan tried the door knob. Locked. "Got a credit card?" he asked Kathleen.

"Me?" she asked incredulously.

'That was a stupid question,' Sloan admitted to himself. Well, not that stupid. He himself had just received one in the mail. Some pusher must have recommended him. Too bad he hadn't brought it.

Sloan searched his own wallet and came up with his laminated Marine Corps ID. Salome had to be somewhere in the house. Damn if he was going to call off this experiment now. He slid the card into the crack between the door and threshold.

"What are you doing?" she asked nervously.

Sloan was already holding open the door for her.

"I'm not going in there."

"C'mon, she's a friend." That's what Sloan had originally told Kathleen, and that they and some other friends were invited over. He took Kathleen's hand and led her inside. It was then that Sloan remembered that Salome had a revolver in her night table drawer, and he wasn't sure it was her only one. He glanced around with the help of moonlight. The place looked the same. It could have been some little old lady's house. Certainly didn't look like any witch's den, whatever one of those looked like. Not until they reached the kitchen did he hear the ethereal chanting. It was coming from the backyard.

Sloan and Kathleen stood looking out the back door. He noticed that the fence was new, higher and affording more privacy. But that wasn't what held his attention. About a dozen naked people stood in a circle holding hands. Salome, also naked, stood in the center, upon a small two-foot platform. She held her arms high and slightly outward, so that her body formed a Y. Her hands were open, palms up. She must have been looking directly at the moon because it shone on her face like a spotlight. Her figure had never been her main attraction, but it hadn't lost a thing. This sight brought back some very pleasant memories. In the glow of moonlight, she looked damn sexy.

Sloan, amused, thought, 'This witch trip'll give you a hard-on.' Then he remembered that he was holding Kathleen's hand and that she was standing next to him. He looked over to see her completely mesmerized. "Let's go outside?" he said.

Kathleen did not even blink. She was in a trance.

He squeezed her hand. "C'mon, let's go outside."

She shook her head nervously without taking her eyes off Salome.

'This could get interesting,' thought Sloan. He gently pulled Kathleen closer.

She resisted, taking baby steps backward, eyes still fixed upon Salome. Kathleen pulled Sloan with her until they could no longer see out the back door. Then she turned and dragged him out of the house.

*****

The thick fog of marijuana smoke made movement hazardous. Combined with diminished motor skills, this kept most people stationary. Marcia stood with her back to a wall, watching Smitty approach through the haze with two paper cups of wine. She took hers as he put his arm around her. Marcia was exhausted, stoned from lack of rest alone. Smitty leaned against her, at the same time putting his weight on her shoulders. Laughing, they slid down the wall until they were sitting on the floor, like most of the volunteers at The People's Crash Pad. Smitty accepted one of the numerous joints being passed around. After a casual drag, he held it to Marcia's lips.

All the hardest workers, the surviving two dozen, were scattered around the living room. The mood was a mellow mix of exhaustion and pride. Almost every face had a tired, satisfied smile on it. The music reflected that mood, an early Joan Baez album — "Little did my mother think, when first she cradled me. The lands I was to travel in, and the death I was to dee." Barely conscious of the words, Marcia experienced sad comfort from them. Somehow they seemed connected to the long ago loss of her mother.

C.C. and Bonnie were sitting directly across from Marcia. C.C. had her arm across Bonnie's shoulders the same way Smitty's was over hers. Apparently, Smitty was right. These two late arrivals were lesbians. Well, as Smitty had said, "That's their affair." She smiled, now as then, at his double entendre. If you paid attention, Smitty could be amusing. He sure could be helpful too, boosting her confidence merely by being around. She would have to tell him how much she appreciated his help. Then she got a better idea. One of today's volunteers had been wearing a pair of Levis turned into bellbottoms by splitting a foot of the outside seam and inserting a bright colored triangle of paisley scarf. She had thought how nice they would have looked on Smitty. Well, she would fix a pair of his jeans just like that.

Of all the other volunteers, none had been as helpful as C.C. and Bonnie, especially C.C. That's why Marcia had offered them their own room upstairs to run the crash pad. They were older, in their mid-thirties probably, and more mature than everybody else. Bonnie even claimed to have managed a motel in Louisiana. She sure didn't seem like a lesbian, or Marcia's idea of one. The same could not be said of C.C. In any case, Marcia liked both of them, and she needed someone to run the crash pad. After all, she was going to college.

And there was Screw sitting in the corner. A long legged girl, a good few years his senior, was crawling all over him. Screw was clowning around, allowing himself to be seduced. Just looking at Screw usually made her smile. People such as him were a gift, a pleasure to have around.

Marcia felt as fulfilled as she could remember, and she would have felt that way even without the marijuana. Her vague vision of a People's Crash Pad had taken form so quickly, so colorfully, and so successfully. The entire adventure seemed like a magical dream. She remembered her skepticism when Screw had shown her the boarded-up, refuse strewn house. Now she sat in that house, that house cleared, cleaned, and transformed. It wasn't just painted every color of the rainbow. No, the pastels of the rainbow were not gaudy enough for Berkeley. The house now seemed to be painted every bright color ever splattered on a circus wagon. The People's Crash Pad was ready for occupancy.

Marcia felt a bite on her neck. What was it with Smitty? Part terrier? She turned to see that look in his eye. He wanted to take her home. He wanted to take her to bed. Nice idea. A jerk of his head, and they were struggling to their feet. From the door of the crash pad to the door of their apartment, he never took his arm off her shoulder. They dragged each other along with tired, stoned smiles and steps more staggered than need be. It wasn't until the next morning that Smitty remembered that he had driven to the crash pad, that he had left his car there.

*****

Moe felt like Captain Bligh, and the feeling wasn't bad. Though he had never admitted it, even to himself, Moe had always had a soft spot for the sadistic martinet, the way he kept his dignity when Fletcher Christian and the rest of his mutinous crew threw him off his own ship and set him adrift in a dinghy. Well the tough son-of-a-bitch sailed that dinghy back to England. Bligh showed what he was made of. Without knowing exactly why, Moe had always looked with a jaundiced eye at pretty boy Fletcher Christian. How the hell was Bligh going to keep his motley crew in line without applying the whip to a back or two every once in a while? Rewarding that mangy lot with extra desserts surely wouldn't get the job done. And even those seadogs were pedigrees compared to the flea infested strays now facing Moe — almost the entire staff of The Berkeley Badger. Two dozen of his employees stood staring at him, and their faces did not look friendly. He hadn't seen so many people in the office at one time since the days it had also served as the staff crash pad.

It occurred to Moe that the people facing him were one of the reasons The Badger office was no longer a staff crash pad. He couldn't stomach any of them for more than a few minutes. It wasn't like that when he was their age. He had admired, trusted his fellow leftists. Sure, a few of them turned out to be rats. But some of them were the best people he had ever known. They'd split their last dime with you. You could depend upon them not to run out on you when the goons showed. Again he scanned the faces before him. There wasn't one he would trust to cover his back in a fight, not one — 'The New Left'.

Moe noticed, not surprisingly, that Straughton hadn't joined this lynch mob. He doubted that Straughton knew more than two or three of those present, and probably avoided even them. If these were his coworkers, what must that say about him. Straughton's disdain for them was more than matched by their distrust of him. In fact, thanks to Straughton, Moe had not been blindsided by this strike.

The insurrection was being led by Brad Cavanaugh, Moe's second best reporter after Straughton. Coincidentally, Cavanaugh had always reminded Moe of Marlon Brando, Hollywood's most famous Fletcher Christian. As physically imposing as Brando, Cavanaugh was nowhere near as handsome. Once or twice, Moe had actually wondered why. He could have been early Brando's ten pounds overweight fraternal twin. The features were similar, yet carelessly put together. Facing Moe, his fellow mutineers standing behind him, Cavanaugh did display the determination of a Hollywood Fletcher Christian.

"We refuse to contribute our labor to a newspaper that has been co-opted by the lowest elements of the capitalist establishment. We have watched you, out of pure greed, turn the proudest voice of Berkeley's counterculture into an advertising rag for scams and rackets that objectify, abuse, and denigrate women."

This charge did broadside Moe. He had not expected a carefully crafted speech attacking his radical credibility. He had expected a simple demand for higher wages, which he would have met with a simple No. Admittedly, for the first time since he established The Badger, he was making a decent living. Yet once you've been broke, penny pinching was a hard habit to break. Besides, paying subsistence wages had proved no impediment to putting out a newspaper. In fact, it proved the opposite. Raises and bonuses merely fed their greed. Breaking in a new staff would be a pain in the ass, but every one of his employees was easily replaceable. This thought caused him to scan the mutineers, contemplating the ones he'd most enjoy getting rid of. Cavanaugh, of course was at the top of the list, as if he gave a shit about the defense of women. Hell, in Cavanaugh's time, Moe had known him to denigrate far more than his share. The more Moe looked at him, the more Moe looked forward to getting rid of him. How hard could it be to find another passable reporter? There's never a shortage of shit eating worms dying to crawl up everyone's ass. Yet Moe found it hard to believe that the mutiny had been Cavanaugh's idea. Who had put him up to it?

Moe didn't have to look far. Standing right in back of Cavanaugh was Molly, his latest denigree. As if to confirm Moe's suspicion, she dropped her gaze as soon as his eyes landed upon her. Being Moe's bookkeeper, she would know exactly how much he was taking in from those new sex ads. Could she be stupid enough to think that he would give up all that gelt? Moe had no intention of spending his old age sleeping in a cardboard box on some Berkeley sidewalk. The fascists in Washington sure weren't going to keep him from starving or freezing to death. Those massage parlors and nude model storefronts that had sprung up in Berkeley were a retirement plan windfall, and in fact, a just reward for thirty years service to The Cause.

He stared back angrily at Cavanaugh. Who was this loudmouthed pisher to tell him how to run his newspaper? "Those sex adds pay for putting out The Badger. You think our readers give a shit? They don't want to read 'em, all they have to do is turn the page." Moe's anger turned to self-righteous indignation. "If those perverts with the cameras didn't have naked models available, they'd be peeking in your window. And if there weren't massage parlors for creeps who can't get a free hand job, who knows how many more rapes we'd have? And what do you think those denigrated women would be doing for food, or dope, or whatever they're buying, teaching at Berkeley?" Moe realized he had gone too far, remembering that Cavanaugh had written about two who had. Cavanaugh didn't call him on it, having forgotten himself. Moe did notice him flinch as—

Molly poked him in the back, demanding that he stand up for all those denigrated women. "Moe, it's us or the ads. Take your choice."

Moe was pleased to be faced with such a simple, clear cut choice. He would certainly choose the ads over this worthless crew. Still, his decision left him uneasy. Moe cherished his stature on the Left. The only thing in the world worse than scabs were the bloodsucking capitalists who hired them. The ignominy of having his very own workers call a strike weighed heavy upon him.

Cavanaugh felt he had waited long enough for a reply. "Moe,

it's us or the ads. If you don't stop running them, we are prepared to start our own newspaper, which will be a true sentinel of the Left. We'll rent a house, to be our office and our home. We'll call our paper The Clan, because we'll live together as a family, making decisions by consensus, and share equally all profits. We will put The Badger out of business!"

Moe, surprised and elated, could not believe his good fortune. A weight had been lifted off his chest. There would be no embarrassing strike, no pickets, and most of all, no need for scabs. With a few bums off the street, he could put out the paper no sweat. Well, there would be some sweat. He had not worked that hard in years.

Cavanaugh repeated, "Us or the ads?"

Moe's smile was too broad for his beard to hide. Not only would there be no strike, in a month or two, there would be no Clan. He'd weather both the loss of staff and the competition these fools would attempt to provide. The clowns thought they would put him out of business. No, instead, he would watch them feed on each other until The Clan was not even a memory. He knew his mutineers too well to fear them or anything they could do. For sure, at the root of this mutiny was Cavanaugh's ego. He wanted to run his own paper. Moe looked forward to watching Cavanaugh's ego trip end shipwrecked and smashed upon the rocks.

Again Cavanaugh asked, "Which is it Moe, us or the ads?"

Moe said calmly, "You have two minutes to get down those stairs. Don't ever come up them again." He saw no fear or regret in their faces as they turned to leave, just confidence and defiance. Moe, the Old Left, watched the New Left file down the steps. Once, in one of his darker moments, he had divided it into three types. The rarest was the true leftist. Next came the over privileged brats merely assuaging their guilt and masochism by banging their heads against the Establishment. Far more common were the phony self-righteous hypocrites pretending they gave a shit about anyone besides themselves.

Cavanaugh himself was as pure a fascist as ever walked the earth. That's why they chose him as their leader. Every terrorist bombing filled him with glee, no matter how many innocent schmucks got blown to shit. Every dead cop was a victory to him. Lyndon Johnson and Ronald Reagan were fascists, while pure fascists such as the Hells Angels, Black Panthers, and Black Muslims were his and the New Left's heroes. Moe comforted himself with the thought that at least he wouldn't have to publish any more of Cavanaugh's gonzo puff pieces on those lying, racist scumbags. The thought that he never had to in the first place did not enter Moe's head.

Moe felt surprisingly satisfied, with the outcome and with himself. He'd survive this mutiny just fine. Who were these ignorant fucks to tell him how to run a newspaper? What God damn difference in the world did a few ads make? After all, today's newspaper is tomorrow's shit paper. That's a fact.

*****

Smitty watched C.C. do her thing. The woman could handle a wrench. They stood in the street right in front of The People's Crash Pad, both of them leaning under the hood of his car. To his own ear, C.C. had it humming like new. Yet she claimed to hear a faint knock. Smitty asked, "Where'd you learn this?"

"My old man," she replied. "Stepfather. Never knew my real father."

"He was a mechanic?"

"He owned a gas station in Islamorada...Florida Keys....That's the place I'd like to spend the rest of my life."

"Why you here?"

"Bonnie got some idea we'd be freaks there."

"Huh?"

"Here, the freaks are the ones who aren't freaks."

Smitty started wondering if that was what was bothering him about Berkeley. Did he feel like a freak? 'Sometimes.' It depended upon the people around him. If you felt like a freak in Berkeley, did that mean you weren't a freak? He remembered the definition of sanity from his high school psychology course — the ability to adjust to your environment. If you didn't feel like a freak in Berkeley, did that mean you were? Could you be a freak in Berkeley and not a freak in Cleveland, or vice versa? Was it impossible for the same person to be a freak in both Berkeley and Cleveland? Or normal in both Berkeley and Cleveland? Was location, location, location the determining factor of freakcosis?

281

Could it be cured by a plane ticket? If you felt like a freak in Berkeley— 'Enough!' he told himself. Smitty felt stoned. 'Haven't smoked for days.' If you smoked enough marijuana, could you get flashbacks, like with LSD? Could marijuana be eating away at his brain?

"There," said C.C., before slamming the hood shut. "Enough gas fumes for one day."

'Gas fumes?' thought Smitty, 'Coulda been gas fumes.' He preferred this explanation to his previous one.

"Friends of yours?" asked C.C., a wariness in her tone. She was looking right past him.

Smitty turned to see three young black men crossing the street, walking straight and deliberately towards him. The one in the middle, a step ahead of the other two, had a red paisley bandanna covering his short hair. The two young men following him both had Afros, one huge, almost shoulder width. None of them looked the least bit friendly. Smitty was inspired to gather up C.C.'s tools and place them in their box, everything except a large torque wrench. He held it as nonchalantly as he could manage.

"That The People's Crash Pad?" the one in the middle asked, his tone no friendlier than his expression.

"That's right," said C.C. "How can I help?"

"We need a place to crash."

"I'm sorry," said C.C. "It's for kids from out of town this summer."

His tone took on added belligerence. "Kids? How old?"

"Youngest kids first, seventeen year olds maximum."

He indicated the two men to his sides. "Kedrick and Lashon are both seventeen."

C.C. doubted this. Kedrick could have been seventeen, but he looked about twenty. Lashon had to be twenty-five. Their spokesman was surely older. C.C. forced herself to smile. "Fine, if they come back in the summertime with picture ID's, we'll be glad to put them up for a week or so."

"I ain't talkin' 'bout no summertime. I'm talkin' 'bout right now."

"I'm sorry—"

He cut her off, "'Sorry' don't do shit for us. Is this The People's Crash Pad, or is it The White People's Crash Pad?"

Smitty waited for a sign from C.C. to back her up. The trouble he had sensed coming now seemed imminent. Pondering ways to avoid it, he failed to come up with any.

C.C. purposely kept her eyes off Smitty. Getting him involved would only make matters worse. "This is everybody's crash pad."

"Everybody with white skin!" His voice had gained in volume as well as belligerence.

Smitty saw no chance civility or reason would solve this problem. Just walking away seemed their only option.

C.C. seemed to read his thoughts. She took the tool box and headed for the door.

So did the three young black men, their spokesman continuing the argument, turning it into a speech. "The days are past when the white man can walk all over the black man. The black man is through taking it. The oppression of peoples of color this country is built on is gonna stop, starting now, today! We'll burn this racist fascist country to the ground."

They were almost at the front porch. Smitty pondered how he could get the door shut and locked before his three new acquaintances knew what had happened. They were right on his ass. He may have to slam the door in their faces. Discomfiting as he found this thought, he preferred it to fighting these three thugs by himself. The two sidekicks didn't appear much of a problem, but the loudmouth in the middle could do some damage. Hell, with his mouth, if he couldn't fight, somebody sure as hell would have killed him a long time ago.

Smitty was one step away from the door, still unsure what to do, with Big Mouth right on his ass. Smitty crossed the threshold intending to slam the door. Instead, he spun around, grabbing the door jamb with his left hand and the door with his right. The torque wrench, also in his right, hit the door with a sharp crack. Big Mouth already had his foot through the threshold. Slamming the door wouldn't have worked, and Smitty was glad he hadn't tried it. They were now eye to eye, and Smitty figured he had no more than ten, maybe fifteen pounds on the guy. Glancing down at Big Mouth's foot, he said in a tone less polite than his words, "Excuse me."

Big Mouth left his foot right where it was. His silent stare told Smitty that he wasn't moving it. "Honky, you better get outa my way."

Smitty did not share the average white college kid's fear of blacks. He'd grown up with them, had friendships and fights with them going back to grade school. It was the crazies, white or black, who made him wary, the don't give a shit types capable of losing it in an instant and getting themselves and anybody close by killed. Big Mouth did not seem that type. The belligerent fuck probably thought too much of himself to put his ass on the line.

While Smitty's hands were high on the jamb and the door, Big Mouth's were free. They were low, almost at his sides, both of them in loose fists. Smitty figured he could charge forward, take Big Mouth down, and break one or both of his legs. But could he do it fast enough, before Big Mouth's two sidekicks got involved? One of them had to have a shiv. The vision of it sticking out of his back was less than pleasant. Plan B — smash his heel down on the foot, jerk the door open, out of Big Mouth's grasp, knock him off the porch with a kick to the chest, then slam the door shut. Yeah, that'd work better. If it didn't, torque wrench time. One way or the other, he'd handle it, he hoped.

"Cracka, get your ass outa my way."

The epithet "Cracka" incensed Smitty. The stupidity of it! He was from Cleveland. Then his own stupidity hit him. What the hell was he thinking about? The first move better be his. The shorter afroed one looked the weakest, and mentally out-of-it. He could be saved for last. Adrenaline was coursing through Smitty in a torrent. Ready to stomp, watching Big Mouth's eyes, he waited only for him to glance to either side.

"Cracka, I ain't got all day."

Marcia's voice came from behind them. "What's the problem?"

'Fuck!' thought Smitty.

In a no-nonsense tone, C.C. said, "I told them the crash pad is for kids."

"White kids," said Big Mouth. "Me and the brothers are claimin' The People's Crash Pad for The People."

"Thank you, but we've already done that," said C.C.

Marcia cut in, using the instructive tone of a third grade teacher. "I'm sure we can settle this civilly?"

Smitty thought, 'You're sure.'

Then he noticed that the face in his face did not have even the tiniest little scar. Big Mouth was either one hell of a boxer or one hell of a coward. Smitty, gaining confidence, was ready to bet his ass on the latter.

Marcia asked, "What's your name."

"Muhammad Abdul Muhammad," he replied, accent on the "Mo".

"Well, Muhammad," Marcia said patiently, accent on the "Mu", "the crash pad is for the young children that will be coming to Berkeley this summer."

"All we see is a sign that says, 'People's Crash Pad'. Black men are people too."

Smitty started to boil. He'd seen this act before and loathed it. Muhammad kept switching roles, from badass thug to poor oppressed black, playing on white guilt. An instant away from making his move, Smitty thought, 'One or the other, Cocksucker. Pick a hustle and stick with it.' He could actually feel his face turning red, and struggled to contain his anger.

In the same sweet tone, Marcia said, "I don't know what I can tell you."

Smitty thought he knew exactly what she could tell this phony.

Muhammad said, "I know what you can tell this cracka here — to get out of the way before I use him as a doormat."

Smitty, despite Plan B, yearned to hear the sharp, crisp crack of Muhammad's breaking legs. And his un-afroed head was proving a too tempting target for the torque wrench. Better yet, he hoped Mo would be stupid enough to start things off with a kick. That would be a gift. Smitty could see himself bouncing Mo-the-People's head right down the steps. Unfortunately, there were Mo's sidekicks — 'Better stick to Plan B'. And he was raring to implement it.

Marcia decided to save Smitty's life. "How long would you need to stay?"

'Fuck!' thought Smitty.

"Wait a minute," said C.C.

"Three days," said Muhammad.

"Well, I guess that will be all right."

C.C. leaned close to Marcia's ear, and whispered through gritted teeth, "These guys are trouble."

Marcia turned to her. "Just for three days."

C.C.'s words were spoken slowly, and her expression was stone cold. "I thought you asked me to run this crash pad."

"I did, but we have room, and it's only for three days."

C.C. turned and headed upstairs.

Muhammad said, "You heard the lady, Cracka."

Smitty was still barring the door, hoping Marcia would come to her senses.

Instead, she said, "Let them in."

Without stepping backwards, still staring at Muhammad, Smitty swung open the door.

Muhammad, Kedrick, and Lashon walked in and past Smitty and Marcia. They did not wait to be shown the house. Though Kendrick and Lashon glanced around warily, as if they expected to be banished from The People's Crash Pad any second, Muhammad strolled confidently through the house. With his eyes, he probed each room, nook, and cranny, like a prospective buyer ready to slap down a deposit.

Marcia caught Smitty's cold stare — a side of him she had never before seen. It stunned her. She felt pinned to the wall. "I did it for you."

He spoke in a tone that matched his expression. "Next time you do something for me, make sure it's something I want you to do."

*****

Marco had rushed to the library. One of his followers had mentioned that a large selection of new books had been put on display. Unread books gave Marco a sense of possibility and power. They were a source of words and ideas, his weapons. He panned them for gold, willing to sift through hundreds of pages for the excitement of finally finding a tiny fleck of bright, shiny ore. The new selection did not disappoint him. There were at least three books he wanted to read. Little matter that he would have to wait until they were available for checkout. He'd return just before the library opened Monday morning. All three books would be his, and he would be the first to read them.

Marco was in a good mood, the best mood he had been in in weeks, no months. New books were not the only reason, not even the main reason. No, Susan was the main reason. Yesterday she had been gone the entire day and most of the night. Marco couldn't get her off his mind. He stewed about where the hell she could be, even decided to hire a private detective to find out. The idea of this truly bothered him, yet not as much as his ignorance. After all, Susan was his wife. He had a right to know where the hell she was spending so much time. The previous night, Marco was already half asleep when she came home. He was doubly glad, that she had come home and that in the dark he would not have to suffer the denigrating looks she had been giving him.

The change came about just this morning. Marco awoke to the smell of pancakes. Susan hated cooking, found it degrading, knew all the reasons and excuses to avoid it. Making salads, cold dishes, and sandwiches she did not mind at all. In fact, she was good at that. Yet actual cooking, putting heat to food, she rarely did. And when she did, it put her in a bad enough mood to make anyone around her sorry that she had. Pancakes were the exception. She hadn't made them in a long time. Marco had never tasted pancakes so delicious, none even close. They were so light, fluffy, and clean tasting, he could finish a stack of four and still have half his glass of buttermilk left. She knew just when to turn them. They were never soggy or dry inside.

So Marco awoke with the aroma of pancakes in his nostrils and the imagined taste of them on his tongue. What a pleasant way to start the day, that is, until he awoke fully to the realization that, 'The bitch isn't making them for me.' No, Susan was playing one of her games, torturing him with the aroma of her delicious pancakes. Food had never been that important to Marco, which, being married to Susan, was of course quite fortunate. Still, memories of the taste of her pancakes were almost enough to make him get out of bed and ask to join her, almost. Marco was brooding about this when Susan called to him, "C'mon, I made you breakfast."

Marco lay in bed, surprised by her invitation, and even more surprised by the tone of it, a sweetness he hadn't heard in a very long time. "Let me brush my teeth," he said, his own tone as suspicious as his thoughts.

Marco still wore a wary expression when he entered the kitchen. Susan's smile was bright enough to banish all suspicions. He returned her smile with one of awe. Marco sat down and Susan sat down opposite him. He couldn't believe what was happening, couldn't believe the beatific expression on her face.

Susan slid a little bottle towards him. "Here, I bought some maple syrup."

He studied the bottle, asking, "Is it better than Log Cabin?"

Susan laughed.

Marco found this a forgotten pleasure, this despite the fact that she was laughing at him.

Susan asked in disbelief, "Are you serious?"

"What do you mean?"

"You've never tasted real maple syrup?"

Marco shook his head.

"Try it."

He did, seeing the difference immediately. "Wow!"

Susan's smile widened. Wow was not a word she had ever heard him use before.

The pancakes were every bit as good as Marco had remembered, and with the maple syrup, even better, a hell of a lot better. He would have gobbled them up in a minute, but he couldn't keep his eyes off Susan's contented, confident face. It told him that all was forgotten or forgiven, that everything would be better, starting now. He had no idea what caused the change and was too happy to care.

As Susan picked up the plates and turned to place them in the sink, a jolting thought flashed through Marco's mind — Susan had poisoned him. He felt paralyzed, desperate for breath yet unable to breathe. Marco told himself he was imagining things, that no one hated him that much.

Yet it took Susan's concerned expression to convince him. "What's wrong?"

"Nothing," Marco replied, a little tight in the throat.

Susan even kissed Marco goodbye when he left for the library. Though nothing passionate, this was still a pleasant surprise. As Marco walked down his front steps, he berated himself for not trying to get Susan into bed. Quickly, he came to his own defense, pleading shellshock. Marco decided to go back and give it a try right then and there. Two steps back towards the house and he changed his mind again. No, that would make him look silly. He would only be at the library an hour or two anyway.

When Marco did walk back from the library, thoughts of getting

Susan into bed quickened his pace. He wanted to see her smile again too, especially the gorgeous contented one she wore as she kissed him goodbye at the door. It was as if Susan, his beautiful wife, seemed to have made peace, not just with him, but with the world. The thought of her smile quickened his pace even more.

Marco reached his front door to find it locked. He felt a twinge of disappointment. Could Susan have gone out? He'd only been away an hour. A quick check of the house confirmed this. Well, maybe that was just as well. He hadn't shaved this morning, and could do that now. More than once his beard had rubbed Susan's face raw. She had not appreciated that. He could take a shower too. But the first thing he would do was take a damn piss, and fast. Marco was doing just that when he got the odd feeling that something was different in the bathroom. Susan's hair brush wasn't in its usual place. And a few other things, he wasn't sure what, were missing too. Then he noticed something that really stunned him. Her toothbrush was gone. He now realized that the cat's water dish had also been missing, and the cat too. Marco felt weak in the knees as he mumbled aloud, "She left me." Dazed, confused, his mind meandered back to what he was doing, which at the moment, was pissing all over the bathroom floor.

*****

Smitty followed Sloan through the door. Sloan seemed markedly different, and not merely less wary. There was a cold confidence in his look, and in his walk. Smitty's own steps slowed to a stop. Something else was different. The room itself radiated an unfamiliar, puzzling ambience. Smitty, now the warier of the two, glanced around uneasily. This different feel in the air, he wondered what it could mean. Over two hundred metal chairs had been set out in even rows for the meeting. There were barely enough people to fill a third of them. Everyone now stood at the back of the hall, around a table of wine filled paper cups. That was the difference — the people. It wasn't just those few in wheelchairs or on crutches. The clothes were Berkeley enough. So were the hair and beards. It was something in their eyes, the way they looked at each other and glanced at him, something formidable.

"What you looking for, booby traps?" Sloan stood in front of him, holding out a cup of wine. Smitty surfaced from his thoughts and took the cup. Sloan jerked his head towards the table. "C'mon, I'll show you why we're here." After hearing so much about Vietnam Veterans Opposing the War, Sloan was surprised and disappointed by the small turnout. Still, he felt good among his own.

Smitty followed Sloan around the table, nodding to people and picking up snippets of conversation. Sloan kept grinning at him, as if to say, "Real human beings for a change." Smitty began to relax. A few of the women were nice to look at. Maybe this had something to do with Sloan's desire to come here. He had mentioned that Kathleen had moved out on him, giving no details. The last few days Sloan had obviously been on the prowl. Now one particular woman seemed to have caught his eye, and he hers. Sloan walked right up to her. A few words from him and she was smiling, a very attractive smile at that. Smitty noticed in Sloan a relaxed, worldly confidence he had never seen before. Smitty was impressed. He himself was feeling relaxed, relieved to get away from the college brats and freaks for a while, though half the people surrounding him could be either.

Now Sloan was really glad he had come. Hadn't been there two minutes, and already he was talking to an interesting, fine looking chick. Then a loud voice came from behind. "If LBJ ever shows up in Berkeley, I'll blow his fucking head off." Both Smitty and Sloan turned to see a long, tall hippie cowboy wearing an Airborne patch. His one-woman audience looked up at him in awe. Sloan looked at him with something far less.

There was a hum from the loudspeakers, then a tapping on the microphone. "When everyone's seated, we'll get started."

Sloan turned back towards the woman only to see her being led away by two friends. He stood irritated with himself. Her name was Diane. She had been a nurse in Nam. Sloan was interested. There were already a half dozen people between him and her. He gave Smitty a jerk of the head, and they followed behind. Diane sat down between two other girls, one of them a knockout. The good news was that Diane probably didn't come with a guy. The bad news was that now he could not sit next to her. She had seemed so level headed. Sloan laughed to himself. This was not a quality he remembered valuing much in women. 'Maybe I'm growing up.'

Sloan sat one row back from the last occupied seat. He'd catch Diane at the end of the meeting. Definitely. Smitty sat down next to him.

Tom Hillebrand, president of Vietnam Veterans Opposing the War, Berkeley Chapter, stood behind the microphone. He was tall, slender, and clean-cut except for a droopy mustache. Though his words were calm, his tone possessed a peevish edge. "Glad you could make it tonight. Too bad more of us couldn't....If no one objects—"

"I object!" a joker called out.

"If no one important objects," came Hillebrand's good natured reply, "we'll dispense with the minutes and get down to business. Our business of course, is getting our friends and fellow veterans, The Presidio Six, acquitted.

The audience broke into applause, eventually drowned out by the chant, "Free the Presidio Six". The chant continued until The Presidio Six, apparently already free and seated in the front row, were forced to stand and take some clownish bows.

Now everyone seemed in a good mood, including Hillebrand. "Thanks, heroes. You may remain seated for the rest of your lives."

"Jealous?" asked one of The Presidio Six.

"Out of order!" Hillebrand proclaimed. "Let's get right to the progress report from our lawyer, Mr. William Pussler.

Pussler's name was met with a long round of applause, sincere for a change. He made his way towards the podium, arms raised and pumping like a victorious boxer. His age was late fifties, but his thinning hair was late Sixties — long, stringy, and unruly. He grinned broadly while surveying his type of crowd.

"Thank you, thank you," Pussler repeated until the applause died down. "We're gonna win!" The applause started anew. Pussler's smile broadened. Applause was not something that embarrassed him. As it faded, Pussler raised his hands to stop it. "We're gonna teach the establishment a lesson!" The applause was sparse. "We're gonna free The Presidio Six!" The audience reaction wasn't much louder.

Pussler decided to end the pep rally and start his speech. He pointed to The Presidio Six. "Our brave brothers put it all on the line to stop this genocidal imperialist war. We won't abandon them. We'll fight the system until they're acquitted. And they will be acquitted, despite having a fascist kangaroo court run by Her Dishonor Frau O'Conner....Before we can win in the courtroom, we have to win in the media. We have to prove the innocence of our comrades to The People. We have to show The People that the real crime is the criminal genocidal war the fascists in Washington are waging on our brave brothers, the people of Southeast Asia. We have to stop the ruthless murder of peaceful South Vietnamese civilians, the napalming of little babies. We need to bring the war home!

"Saturday, at our next rally, we want twice as many people as at our last one, enough to overflow the streets. All of us, working together, doing what needs to be done. We'll fight this oppression, and continue to fight it until we win. And we won't stop there. We'll keep fighting until we've brought the war home to America, brought down the fascist-imperialist system responsible. Power to The People!" The audience gave Pussler a big hand as he backed away from the podium, again pumping his fists victoriously.

Hillebrand stepped forward, still applauding. He turned back towards Pussler, "Thank you." Hillebrand faced the audience. "You heard Mr. Pussler. If we want our friends acquitted, Saturday's rally has to be a success. We have to make it a success by mobilizing everyone willing to help bring out a crowd. At the end of this meeting, we'll break up into our various committees to plan just that. Now, are there any comments or questions from the floor?" The woman who had caught Sloan's eye raised her hand. "Diane."

"I notice some new faces. Would any of these people like to join?"

Sloan felt encouraged. She had to be referring to him.

Hillebrand scanned the room. His eyes came to rest upon Smitty.

Smitty pretended not to notice. Soon the eyes of everyone in the room were upon him.

Hillebrand finally asked, "Would you like to introduce yourself."

Without standing up, Smitty indicated Sloan as he replied, "I'm with him."

Sloan didn't look at Smitty, but his subtle expression in profile said, "Thanks, Pal." All eyes were now upon Sloan. They stayed upon him. He stood. "My name's Mike Sloan. I was with the Second Battalion, Ninth Marine Regiment." Sloan sat.

Someone in the audience called out, "Are you with us?"

Sloan made no reply, so Hillebrand asked, "Would you like to join Vietnam Veterans Opposing the War?"

Without standing, Sloan replied, "Maybe."

There was a rumble from the audience, but Hillebrand smiled and asked, "Why don't you get up and tell us what you're thinking."

Sloan slowly got to his feet. "I'm kinda wondering what you're trying to do." He noticed Diane looking back at him with interest.

"Stop the war," someone called out.

There were sounds of agreement from the audience.

Hesitantly, Sloan said, "I'd go along with that. We ain't gonna win it doing what we're doing...but what's this about bringing down the 'fascist-imperialist system'? What's this about the 'ruthless murder of peaceful civilians'? Am I the only one here that actually was in Vietnam?"

"Hell, no," was the angry reply of someone in the audience, followed by hostile murmurs.

"Why the hell are you here?" someone demanded to know.

Sloan paused, asking himself the same question. A quick glance at Diane caught a hint of agreement on her face, or was he imagining that. Sloan answered calmly, "To find out what you stand for. Is it just stopping the war you want? Then count me in. If you're trying to make heroes out of communist fanatics, count me out." There were some unfriendly rumblings from the audience. Sloan felt his anger rising. "If you think you're gonna overthrow the US government, you're idiots."

The rumblings of disapproval grew louder. The Airborne cowboy rose to his feet, turned and faced Sloan. "You sound like some FBI plant to me."

"You sound dumb enough to believe that," Sloan replied.

The Airborne cowboy wasn't cowed. He stared at Sloan with determination, proving him right with, "I sure as hell am."

There was some muffled laughter as Sloan mumbled, "I'll take your word for it."

"What?" the cowboy demanded.

Sloan replied loudly, "You better hope I'm no FBI informant. If I am, you'll be in jail tomorrow. Threatening the life of the president of the United States is a federal crime….Hell, if you ain't sitting in jail tomorrow, you gotta be a plant." Sloan glanced around. "I'll bet my ass half the people here are informants, informants informing on informants."

The audience's rumblings took on a meaner edge. Hillebrand interjected, "Let's keep things calm."

But someone yelled to Sloan, "Why don't you get the hell out?" Others voiced agreement.

Smitty, sitting next to the center of attention, did not like the hostile expressions on many of the faces. 'May have to fight our way out of here.'

Hillebrand tried to calm things down. "Hold on a minute."

"Maybe I should go," Sloan replied to the hecklers. "That phony lawyer of yours turned my stomach. Are any of you really dumb enough to believe he gives a damn about any Presidio Six…or any Vietnamese civilians?"

Sloan waited for someone to agree with him.

Instead, the heckling continued, got even angrier.

So did Sloan. "Napalmed babies? Hell, there's only two things he gives a damn about — himself and his communist bullshit." Sloan scanned the faces. "You got used in Nam. Now you're letting left wing hypocrites like him use you. Maybe you like being used. Maybe you deserve to be used."

Smitty now regretted that he and Sloan hadn't taken the first invitation to get the hell out of there. 'The guy's about as subtle as a cold chisel.'

"Bullshit." someone yelled.

There were numerous Yeah's and hard stares in Sloan's direction.

Again Sloan glanced at Diane. She was biting her lip. Whatever that meant, Sloan doubted it meant anything good.

Hillebrand said calmly, "Friend, maybe you better leave."

"Maybe," Sloan calmly replied. He looked over the room. "You mean there ain't one person in here who agrees with what I said?" Again Sloan scanned the faces, Diane's being the last. Now she was really biting her lip. If there was one person there who agreed with Sloan, that person refused to admit it. He gave Smitty the sign. They both headed for the exit. On the way out, Sloan grabbed a half-full wine bottle off the table.

*****

Marcia walked in the dark towards The People's Crash Pad. Having sat through a long day of classes, she wished she were home studying for her biology test. At this thought, she quickened her pace. Still, Marcia dreaded arriving. Muhammad and his friends hadn't moved out as promised, and she had little hope she would now find them gone. Smitty had been right. So had C.C. Though Smitty seemed to have forgotten about her interference, C.C. hadn't. Marcia didn't blame her. 'Live and learn,' she told herself. Next time she would know.

Marcia arrived at The People's Crash Pad to find music blaring from within, and the house lit up as if the electric company paid the user. With hardly any money left in the kitty, Marcia did not relish the thought of making the rounds for contributions again, not so soon. She would have to say something to C.C. Entering, she pondered how to do so diplomatically. These thoughts were banished from her head as she passed the living room. Muhammad, his friends, and a half dozen teenagers were listening to music. Most of them lay on their backs, looking up at the ceiling. Plates and soda cans were strewn all over. No one noticed Marcia, and this was just as well. She was too stunned to speak.

Marcia retreated up the stairs to find C.C. and Bonnie. They were in their room, behind a closed door. Bonnie answered her knock, staring at Marcia deadpan a long moment before moving aside to let her in. Now C.C. was staring at her too, and Marcia could not think of a thing to say.

C.C. could. "I told you."

"You were right," Marcia admitted. "What are those kids doing here?"

"Muhammad and his thugs rounded them up."

"But we're not ready."

"You are talking to the wrong person," replied C.C.

"Okay, I'll talk to Muhammad," Marcia said with resignation.

"Don't...waste...your time."

Marcia was glad for an excuse not to.

C.C. added, "Get rid of them…fast!"

"How?" Marcia asked helplessly, but then got hold of herself and quickly added, "What do you suggest?"

"Smitty and a few friends could handle it."

Marcia did not appear enthused by the idea.

C.C. added, "They're all mouth, pushing white people around. Spades would tear them apart."

Marcia remained silent, worried that Smitty might get hurt. Asking him would be too embarrassing anyway.

C.C. said, "It's Smitty or the cops."

Even Marcia knew that in Berkeley the cops were the enemy, a last resort if that. "Give me a few days?"

"A week," said C.C. "If they're not gone, then we are."

*****

Screw stood restlessly on the front steps of his apartment building. A half hour ago, hungry as hell, he had smoked a joint and taken off in search of food, especially something for his sweet tooth. He hadn't gotten ten yards before cutting one of his bare feet on a pop-top. The bandage now adorning his right foot looked as if he had applied it using only his left foot. Little chance it would stay on for the half block hop to the market. And if, by some miracle it did, it would be a bloody mess by the time he got home. Of course, if and when starvation became an issue, he'd have no choice. In the meantime, he waited for the first two-footed friend or acquaintance to pass by.

Sure enough, Sloan and Smitty came meandering down the sidewalk. Sloan held an all but empty wine bottle. Neither he nor Smitty looked too happy. Sloan drained the last few drops as he walked, just in time to toss the bottle into a garbage can.

Screw called out, "Hey, you bring the dope?"

It was Smitty who replied. "I brought him."

Sloan laughed despite his mood.

As if praying, Screw held his hands together in front of his chest. "Please, munchies, anyone?"

Smitty said, "I've got some Clark Bars upstairs."

Screw dropped to his knees and wrapped his arms around Smitty's legs. "How can I ever repay you?"

"By letting go." As Smitty pulled open the outside door, he noticed Sloan sitting down on the front steps. "You're not coming in?"

Sloan, still depressed about the Vietnam Veterans Opposing the War meeting, had little desire to go up to Smitty's apartment, and none at all to enter his own. "I'll sit out here a while."

Marcia wouldn't be home yet, so Smitty saw no reason to go inside either. A pleasantly mild breeze was blowing. It was nice out. He handed Screw his keys. "The Clark Bars are in the top cupboard on the left." Smitty felt thirsty. He turned to Sloan. "You want a beer?"

"Yeah," Sloan answered, then asked, "Got any wine?"

"Yeah," Smitty replied. "That stuff on the way home wasn't bad." He turned to Screw. "Bring down a bottle. From the next cupboard over."

Sloan, out of the corner of his eye, caught Screw hopping through the door. "He playing hopscotch?"

"Got his laundry wrapped around his foot." Smitty and Sloan sat down on the landing, feet on the second step. "Almost got us in a fight tonight."

"Wouldn't a been much of a fight....Those losers weren't the guys I was with in Nam...office pogues, I bet." Sloan felt dishonest, knowing that a lot of those at that meeting had to have been out in the bush. "Maybe it's just the Berkeley Chapter. This town attracts jerks like that."

Smitty, the residents of Berkeley parading before him, saw some truth in Sloan's words. This was the first time he had sat on the outside steps since he had moved in. Front stoop people watching didn't seem to be a West Coast thing. The weather was perfect for it, and the wine he had drunk didn't hurt either. Still, after a few minutes, he was bored. "What's taking Screw so long?"

Sloan said, "Probably making a cheese plate and hors d'oeuvres to go with the wine."

Smitty actually pictured Screw doing this, and the picture made him smile. "He's a good kid."

"Too good."

"How's that?"

"If you wanna get back from Nam alive, don't hurt to have a little meanness in you."

Smitty asked, "You really think he'll join the Marines."

"That's what he says."

"Hate to see that."

Sloan was not anxious to see this himself, but he kept from saying so.

"Where the hell is he?" Smitty asked, just as Screw stepped outside. "What took you so long?"

"Had trouble getting the cork out."

As soon as Smitty heard the word cork, dread crept into his thoughts. He looked up at the bottle Screw was holding. "Aw, shit."

Screw asked, "What's the problem, Man?"

"Marcia bought that. There were two bottles of California screw-top right next to it."

"What's the difference?" Screw asked.

"About twenty bucks," Smitty informed him. "She was saving it. Something to do with her father. Wouldn't tell me what."

Sloan said, "Probably for when the rabbit dies."

Screw sounded relieved as he said, "No problem then! Just don't knock her up."

Smitty did not sound relieved as he said, "She sees that bottle gone, I'll never get the chance."

Sloan suggested, "Put the cork back in and put it in the refrigerator."

Screw said, "The cork's inside the bottle."

"Great," said Smitty.

"Here, let me see that." Sloan examined the bottle with an expert's eye. "Yeah, it's in there all right….Outstanding job, Screw." He checked the label. "Hey, this is French."

"Good to know," said Smitty, in a tone indicating otherwise. He was still thinking with dread about Marcia's reaction. He'd just explain how it happened. And he'd wear those bellbottoms she made for him by splitting the seam of his Levis and inserting a red paisley triangle. He hated them. Too flashy, and the red triangle was real shiny, from a silk scarf or something. If it were blue, it wouldn't be so noticeable. They'd still be bellbottoms though. Well, he had to make it up to her somehow. Unless he could think of a better way, it was wearing those bellbottoms.

Sloan took a swallow. His face lit up. It tasted nothing like the wine he had swiped from the VVOW meeting. "Hey, this stuff is good." Sloan took another, healthier swallow. "Smitty, you tell your woman that this is the best wine I have ever tasted."

Reaching for the bottle, Smitty said, "She'll be thrilled." He took a half-hearted swallow. The wine was good, better than he too had ever tasted. Smitty took a longer swallow, proving to himself that he was not mistaken. "The French ain't completely worthless." Again he remembered Henry Miller's quote about buying the best French wine, taking it to America to drink, and how it wouldn't taste as good. Smitty tried to imagine how good this wine would taste back in France. He couldn't. Sticking to what he could do, Smitty took another swallow. He was not disappointed.

"Leave some for me," said Screw. Smitty handed him the bottle. He took a sip. "Hey, this stuff is different." He took another swallow before adding, in a perfect imitation of Straughton, "I find its robust expressiveness more than compensates for its lack of complexity."

Screw's wine review left Smitty with no regrets about keeping his own to himself — 'It does something funny to the back of your throat.'

Sloan gave Screw a double take. He had underestimated the urbanity of this farm boy from Nebraska. Checking out the floating cork again, he began to smile. Something funny was going on, but he wasn't sure what. Then he realized. "What's wrong with this picture?"

"Huh?"

"What?"

Sloan repeated, "What's wrong with this picture?"

"I don't know."

"Beats me."

"I'll give you a hint: What's the word?"

"Thunderbird," Smitty replied immediately. They both started laughing.

Screw asked, "What's so funny."

Still laughing, Sloan explained, "Here we are on the front stoop drinking twenty dollar French wine with the cork floating in it, when we should be passing around a paper bag covering up a two dollar bottle of Thunderbird wine.... That's what's wrong with this picture."

Screw watched Sloan and Smitty break up in laughter again. "I don't get it."

"You had to be there," Smitty explained.

Screw didn't get this either, but he did not waste any time worrying about it. "Hey, you guys hear what they did today?"

Smitty shook his head.

"They off'd the County Superintendent of Public Schools."

Sloan said, "That ought to bring the military/industrial complex to its knees."

"Why'd they kill him," asked Smitty.

"Cause he's black," Screw replied. "They think it was the Ku Klux Klan."

Smitty wondered who "They" were.

Sloan found it hard to believe that Berkeley had its very own chapter of the Ku Klux Klan. Then again, in this town, even in sheets, the Klan was relatively pedestrian enough to go unnoticed. 'Hell,' he thought, 'it's a miracle if we don't have the Klan in Berkeley.' He'd seen, by their outrageous actions, how the left and right recruited for each other. 'Can't have one without the other....But the Klan in Berkeley?' Despite the wine, Sloan was still skeptical.

Smitty was more so. "You mean to say the Klan sent an assassin from Mississippi to Berkeley to do a job on the Superintendent of Public Schools?"

Put that way, Screw began to have his doubts.

Smitty thought about the Klansmen he'd seen on television. "Screw, do you have any idea how much organization it would take to send some Good Ole' Boy and his weapon all the way across this country?"

Sloan added, "By pickup truck?"

Smitty tried to top him. "With a shotgun rack and a Wallace bumper sticker."

Sloan countered with, "And a big, bare foot out the passenger side window."

Smitty refused to give up. "And a month's supply of Red Man Chawing Tobacco on the seat between them."

Sloan won with, "Leaving a 2000 mile trail of tobacco juice down the interstate."

Screw's doubts had strengthened, but he was distracted from

them by Straughton, pulling up on one of his Honor Bikes.

"Gentlemen, we seem to be having a jolly good time."

"Jolly good," Sloan assured him.

"They are," said Screw.

Smitty held up the empty wine bottle. "And you missed it."

Sloan dug in his pocket and came up with a five dollar bill which he held out to Straughton. "Tell you what, Sonny, we'll keep the party going and you're invited. Peddle on over to the market down the street and get us a bottle of Thunderbird wine."

"Make sure it's the real thing," Smitty cautioned.

Sloan chimed in, "Accept no substitutes."

"And make sure they put it in a brown paper bag," Smitty added.

Straughton asked, "And why exactly am I assigned this quest?"

Sloan indicated the Honor Bike. "Because you're already saddled up."

Straughton had no desire to play the errand boy, but the market was only a half block away, and it all seemed in good fun. He took off, sitting completely erect, as if he had a stick up his ass instead of a bicycle seat.

Screw called after him, "And get a dozen Twinkies."

Turning back to Smitty and Sloan, he found them grinning, as if they had again gotten a joke that he had missed.

Sloan said, "You know this ain't bad."

"We gotta do it more often," Smitty suggested.

"You know what we need?" Sloan asked.

"Whatever it is, we're doing fine without it."

"Tell me this wouldn't add to the atmosphere. Right here," Sloan indicated just to the side of the steps, within reaching distance, "One of those stands they have in the restaurants, that they bring over when you order Champagne."

Smitty nodded, smiling, "With the bucket of ice on top."

"Exactly!"

"To keep our Thunderbird cold," Smitty added.

They both started laughing again as Sloan agreed, "There it is."

Screw said, "Tell you what's funnier, Straughton going into that dump of a market, with his big words and snooty accent, and asking for Thunderbird wine and a dozen Twinkies." This picture set off a new round of snickers.

Smitty asked, "Is that accent real or phony?"

"Both," replied Sloan.

Smitty said, "It's a good thing we're not smoking dope."

Sloan agreed, "We'd of rolled down these steps long ago."

Screw added, "Right into the gutter."

They were still doing their laughing on the steps when Straughton returned. He had two bottles of Thunderbird, explaining, "It was so reasonable, I purchased one for myself."

Smitty took a bottle, and held it in front of Screw's face while he twisted off the cap. "See, American ingenuity, for people like you." He held the bottle out to Straughton. "Here, the honor is yours."

Straughton took that honor and a genteel sip. His face screwed up in distaste. "They market this effluvium as wine?"

Sloan held his hand out for the bottle. "Here, let me see that." He took a cautious swig, nodded, and took a healthier one. "Good as ever."

Smitty took the bottle and a decent swallow. He shook his head. "Definitely ain't French....And probably ain't grapes....Hey Sloan, you were a chemistry major. What do you think they make this out of?"

"Gimme another sample." Sloan sloshed some Thunderbird on his palate. "It's not fruity. It's not smoky." He had to give his palate another shot. Finally, a smile of satisfaction came to his face. "Ah hah." He congratulated himself with another swallow.

"Clue us in," said Screw.

"Thunderbird has an unmistakable earthy quality. This can only mean one thing."

"What thing?" asked Smitty, feeling a distinct buzz and absolutely no pain.

Sloan, who hadn't felt any pain for quite a while, announced his results. "The earthy taste is a dead giveaway. Thunderbird wine is definitely a petroleum byproduct."

"Ain't everything?" asked Smitty, taking the bottle and another swallow.

Straughton said, "That would explain the taste."

Smitty offered the bottle to Screw.

Screw, eating a Twinkie, refused it.

Smitty asked, "How can you eat a Twinkie without some

Thunderbird to wash it down."

"Just watch me," said Screw.

Straughton said, "I must back up the young gentleman on that. In our region of Connecticut, Twinkies with Thunderbird would be considered a faux pas....As would either one of them alone."

Noticing again the crude bandage on Screw's foot, Smitty asked, "What happened to your paw?"

"Stepped on a pop-top."

Sloan, who was way passed the buzz stage, laughed to himself as he said, "Domestic punji stick." Again he wondered if this kid would be lucky enough to get back from Nam in one piece.

Just then, Smitty asked Screw, "You still gonna join the Marines?"

"That's the plan. If I don't do it soon, I'll just get drafted into the army."

Smitty asked, "How close are you to getting drafted?"

"Haven't a clue."

"Ask your draft board," Smitty suggested.

"I almost did, but I'm scared they'd tell me, 'Oh, Jake Pedersen, we forgot all about you.'"

Smitty said, "I would not worry about that."

Screw said, "I been thinking—"

"Thinking," Sloan repeated. He went on with a slight slurring of his words. "Less of that, the world would be a better place."

"—when I get back, I can go to Berkeley on the GI Bill."

"If you get back," Sloan pointed out.

"I've been thinking about that too," said Screw. "Maybe I should start Berkeley, get a draft deferment. I can always deal some grass on the side."

Sloan asked himself what would be worse for the kid, Nam or Berkeley? VC or dope?

Smitty asked Screw, "You sure you can get in?"

"I had a B average, almost a B-plus."

"That could do it. What are your College Boards?"

"1230/1290."

Smitty was surprised. "That'll do it....What would you major in?"

This question, one he had never thought about, caught Screw off guard. He pondered hard a moment, until a smile came to his

303

face and he raised his fist in the air. "Revolution!"

Smitty wondered how it was possible that you could not get a degree in Revolution at Berkeley. Surely an oversight soon to be corrected. Berkeley, where it always happens first, will be the first university in the country to have a Department of Rioting and Revolution.

Straughton cut-in, "I must say, My Man, that makes more sense than joining the Marines. Only a complete fool would do that."

Sloan sat thinking, 'This "complete fool" ain't too drunk to knock you off your Honor Bike.' He glanced around for the wine bottle. "Where's the Thunderbird?"

Smitty held up the empty bottle as he said to Screw, "You're a California resident already. You don't have to pay out-of-state tuition."

Straughton held out his unopened bottle to Sloan. "My Man, you are welcome to it."

"Thanks," Sloan said gruffly. He grabbed the Thunderbird and ripped off the cap.

Straughton added, "I doubt quite seriously I will ever be that desperate."

As Sloan swallowed, he thought, 'Desperate, am I? Don't doubt "quite seriously" that I might knock you into the gutter.' Yet his thoughts were still centered on Screw. Though it had been the kid's idea to join the Marines, Sloan had encouraged him. He felt a sense of responsibility. Would the Corps harden him up enough? Tipsy as he was, an idea came to Sloan. He remembered the shit that the drill instructors threw at American Indians in boot camp. The "drunken Ira Hayes" slurs were the least of it. Yet anyone better than half blind could see their respect for Indians, even while beating the crap out of them. The ethos that these drill instructors were trying to inculcate in all the recruits was that of the ultimate warrior — the Indian brave. Sloan sensed even more than that. The drill instructors themselves wished they were Indians.

Sloan decided to find out then and there if he should discourage Screw from joining the Marines. "Screw," he said with a slight slur, "When you were a kid, and you used to play cowboys and Indians, did you want to be a cowboy or an Indian?"

The question that took over Screw's mind was not the one Sloan had asked. 'Where, out of nowhere, did that dumb question come from?' A moment's reflection gave him the answer, 'From the wine.'

The question also puzzled Smitty and Straughton, enough to draw their full attention. They both stared at Sloan.

Sloan did his staring at Screw, waiting for a simple answer to a simple question that just might decide the kid's fate. Finally, he had to repeat it. "Cowboy or Indian?"

Screw glanced at Smitty and Straughton for clues, but they appeared just as baffled as he himself. Sloan was leaning forward, intent on receiving a reply. Screw shrugged, saying, "Cowboy."

Sloan leaned back and relaxed. He took a long, comforting swallow of Thunderbird. It was settled. He'd see that whatever the kid did, it wouldn't be joining the Marines.

Screw, starting on another Twinkie, sat wondering what was happening. Apparently Sloan had no intention of explaining. Again Screw looked towards Smitty and Straughton, and again found them equally baffled. He shrugged, saying, "A cowboy, just like everyone else."

Thinking, "'Everyone else'?' Smitty asked in disbelief, "You never wanted to be an Indian?"

"No, they always lost."

"Not always," Smitty insisted.

"Most of the time."

"But Indians were cooler."

"How do you figure?" asked Screw.

"They rode bareback. Shirtless. They wore war paint, feather headdresses."

"But they lost," Screw insisted.

"Who cares? They were cooler."

"Who cares?" happened to be just the question that Straughton was asking himself. Still sitting upon his Honor Bike, he wondered if he could actually be hearing two college students, or one college student and a would-be student with higher College Board scores than he had received — this despite much tutoring and cheating — argue about who was cooler, cowboys or Indians?

Sloan found nothing wrong with the argument. In fact, Smitty was impressing him. Maybe he should join the Marines. Yet the job before him was talking Screw out of doing so. Before he could speak—

Screw, desperate for allies, turned to Straughton. "What were you when you played cowboys and Indians?"

Straughton's nose shot up an inch or two, saying disparagingly, "We never played cowboys and Indians....We played Pilgrims and Indians."

Sloan said, "And you were a fucking pilgrim."

"Most certainly."

A picture came into Smitty's head of an eight year old Straughton playing a short pants, stick up his ass pilgrim. This was enough to get him laughing. Sloan and Screw quickly joined him. It was Straughton's turn to not get the joke.

Sloan's mood had improved. Though drunk, he decided to take care of business, right then and there. "Screw, how many people you know done the Marines and Berkeley?"

Screw pondered long and hard, finally remembering, "Just you."

"That's right, fucker. Yet you fail to ask my advice."

"Okay, let's hear it."

"If you go to Berkeley, you can always join the Marines. If you join the Marines, that may be the last thing you ever do."

Screw said, "So I should go to Berkeley?"

Sloan nodded slowly. "Or somewhere else."

"I might," said Screw.

Smitty looked at Sloan with new respect. The wine had loosened his tongue. "For an ex-junkie, you're not a bad guidance counselor."

Sloan did not laugh — "'Ex-junkie'?' He did not like that label, no matter how well it fit.

Smitty caught a look from Sloan that told him to watch his words, or better yet, keep his mouth shut.

Straughton was saying to Screw, "My Man, you would have to be a complete idiot to join the Marine Corps."

'Is that right?' thought Sloan. Was the "ex-junkie" invisible, or were these fuckers purposely insulting him?

Smitty said to Screw, "Don't do it. I'll find out how you qualify for in-state tuition."

Screw said, "Yeah, why desert The Revolution to join a civil war?"

"What revolution?" Sloan mumbled, to himself more than

anyone else.

Screw couldn't believe Sloan could be so blind. He held his arms wide. "This revolution!"

Smitty glanced along the sidewalk, as Berkeley's shaggy army of irregulars paraded haphazardly before him. There was certainly no shortage of revolting people, but not in the sense meant by Screw.

Sloan warned himself, 'You better split before you lose it.' Instead, he said, "If this is a revolution, we're lookin' at the losing side."

Screw doubted what he was hearing. Again he spread his arms out wide. "C'mon, Man, it's obvious. We're winning."

Sloan asked flatly, "How did the Peace and Freedom Party do in the last election...the one where Reagan got elected governor?"

Screw couldn't believe Sloan was being such a down. "Man, talk to people. The world is changing. We're winning."

Sloan had no desire to argue. Nor did he have the sober control to sit and listen. "When was the last time you talked to a cop, or a construction worker, or a Mexican immigrant, or to your old man?"

Screw remained silent. It had been a while.

Sloan continued, "You think everyone thinks like you because people like you are the only ones you talk to."

Screw studied Sloan a few good seconds before asking, "Hey, whose side are you on?"

Sloan felt a drunken anger rising within him. 'If you can't tell who your friends are, you don't deserve any!' He pushed his anger back down, and, against his better judgment, tried once more to explain. "When I got to Berkeley, everyone wore Gant shirts, Bass Weejuns, Canterbury belts, and the fraternities ran the campus. I figured there couldn't be anything phonier. Now everyone has long hair, dresses like freaks, smokes dope, talks revolution, and the radicals run the campus. They put about as much thought into it as students used to put into their clothes. And now the place is even phonier."

"How do you figure?" asked Screw.

"At least the fraternities admitted being elitist snobs. All this peace and love and Age of Aquarius bullshit. Go hitchhiking dressed like a freak, and you're more likely to get picked up by a traveling salesman. Put on a shirt and tie, and you better pray for a traveling salesman."

Straughton had to admit, "Unfortunately, I've noticed that."

Smitty cut in, "I'd still rather have the freaks running things."

Sloan stared him in the eye. "Freaks run nothing but their mouths. If Marco and his sick crew ever got hold of this country, they'd turn it into North Slobovia."

Screw looked at Sloan as if seeing him for the first time. "You've been co-opted by the establishment."

Sloan made no reply, sorry he had bothered in the first place. He scanned those around him. How could they be so fucking ignorant? He thought about the guys he had known in Nam, who didn't claim to know shit, except maybe how to survive. Sloan felt old. He took another slug of Thunderbird, trying to tune out the conversation. For a relaxing few minutes, he succeeded. Sloan stewed in silence until the conversation turned to Vietnam.

"They do not want us there," said Straughton.

Smitty asked, "If they want to be communists, what right do we have to stop them?"

Sloan was pained to admit that he had overestimated Smitty. 'As ignorant as the rest of them. Fucker's just better at keeping his mouth shut.' Sloan thought of all the Vietnamese he had met who hated the communists, many of whom had fled from North to South Vietnam for that very reason. What did these ignorant fucks know about Nam? What some left-wing college professor told them? What some phony reporter said on TV? Sloan simmered, seeing no point in saying anything? Sometimes it seemed as if there were only two types of people in the world, those who had been to Nam and didn't want to talk about it, and those who hadn't and couldn't shut up about it. Nothing drove him up the wall like hearing people who didn't know shit about Nam shooting off their mouths.

Straughton said, "When all those black Vietnam vets get back to the States, we are in for a civil war."

This was too much for Sloan. "Horseshit!" he practically spit at Straughton. "What the fuck do you know about black Vietnam vets? What the fuck do you know about blacks?" The wine was handicapping him — slowing his thoughts, slurring his words, adding to his anger. "When they come home, they'll thank God they were born in a country like this. They'll get jobs and they'll work their asses off, and they'll hate the guts of all you college campus philosophers. Because you don't know shit! They learned more in Nam, the dumbest of 'em, than you'll ever learn."

Straughton could not believe Sloan's reaction to a remark that passed for common knowledge in Berkeley, one that he had never heard challenged.

Smitty sat stunned. He sure hadn't seen this coming. Hesitantly, he tried to make things right. "Man, take it easy. He didn't mean anything."

"If you don't mean anything, then don't fucking say anything. Keep your fucking mouths shut." Sloan pulled himself up by the railing. "Why the fuck am I wasting my time?"

Screw felt it was now up to him to play the peacemaker. "Take it easy, Man. Don't go rogue on us."

Sloan already had the front door open. He turned his head back to give Screw one hard, mean stare. "Kid, you don't know what rogue is.…You got no fucking idea."

Sloan burst into his tiny apartment and slammed the door shut behind him. He leaned hard against in the darkness, as if some thundering horde would attempt to break through. Shitty as his apartment was, it afforded him refuge, held the world outside at bay. What a relief this was. Even a dead man needed one last hole.

He flicked on the light switch. An instant's blinding flash was followed by the bulb's loud pop, then darkness. Sloan froze, trembling. Even after Nam, loud noises didn't faze him. Darkness never had. Yet an innocuous flash and pop had. As Sloan gained control over his breathing, fright turned to embarrassment, and finally to anger. A table lamp was within reach. He turned it on. Its light seemed to focus on and illuminate the hotplate where he kept his stash.

His apartment appeared to claustrophobically shrink around him. Sweating, he felt as if he were about to suffocate. He paced the few desperate steps available here and there, feeling like a caged, nervous animal. His excuse for an apartment had now turned into the second to last place he wanted to be. The first being outside it. No way did he want to see those ignorant faces he had left on the front stoop, or any other faces either.

Sloan knew he had overreacted, knew the wine had played a

part. What had happened at the Vietnam Veterans Opposing the War meeting had played a larger one. And the chance he blew with that nurse, that too. His thoughts turned to Kathleen. His days with her hadn't been bad. Sure, her leaving had been a relief. Yet the way she split was weird, without a word, which seemed preferable at the time. Still, if he had her there now, he'd sure fuck the shit out of her, fuck her harder than he ever had. And she'd dig it better than ever. He was sure of that. Why the fuck was he even thinking about Kathleen? Why had he blown up so easily on the front stoop? From the same horseshit he had been hearing again and again since coming home? Yet this time he had finally opened his mouth. It was useless, he knew that. Still, Sloan was too angry to be sorry. Listening to ignorant assholes talk about Nam was worse than being there. Again it occurred to him that being there wasn't all bad, far from it. That's something these know-it-alls could never comprehend. He didn't even understand it himself. Sloan's right hand was closed tight into a fist. About to smash it into the plaster of the wall, he caught himself. No, that would be too soft, too easy. Instead, he slammed his fist into the wooden dresser. It didn't give at all, and this felt good.

He scanned the room. What next? His eyes again found the hotplate where he kept his stash. He felt no need for dope, no real desire either. Yet he walked over to the hotplate and removed his stash. He spread the pills on his bed. Sloan pictured himself stuffing them all into his mouth — one last hell of a high. Would it be torture? Would it be ecstasy? Immediately, instead, he pictured himself flushing them all down the toilet. No, no way would he do that. Because growing stronger deep inside him was an insurgent compulsion to do something mean and violent, even if it was only to himself. No time to waste crushing pills. His hands moved swiftly, opening a number of the capsules into his palm. Sloan snorted them — fast, hard, and deep — like a ravenous beast.

*****

"We quit," said C.C., her tone angrier than her words.

Marcia felt her strength draining out of her. Not that she was surprised. Bonnie had phoned, telling her to get over to The People's Crash Pad right away. Marcia had been too afraid to ask why. Silently holding the receiver, she had sorted through the possibilities. All of them involved Muhammad. Marcia assumed the worst, and wanted some time to think. The walk over there provided that. Yet it did not provide a solution to the problem now facing her, the one she had dreaded most.

All Marcia could say was, "Please. I—"

Bonnie cut her off with, "We've had enough."

"You said you'd give me a week."

"That was before the cops showed up," Bonnie answered.

"The cops?" asked Marcia. "Why?"

C.C. answered, "Muhammad & Company are dealing, and I doubt grass is the worst of it."

Marcia found this easy to believe. Yet it occurred to her that if Muhammad and his friends were arrested, that would solve the problem. "What did they find?"

"Nothing. I didn't let them in."

"Why?"

C.C. stared at Marcia as if she had been born yesterday. "You know I just might have a joint or two around myself.…And Bonnie could stock a pharmacy with what she's got under her mattress."

Bonnie gave C.C. a dirty look before turning to Marcia. "When the pigs come back with a warrant, we don't want to be here."

Marcia's face lit up with an idea that could save the day. "I can keep all that at my place."

C.C. just stared at her, wondering, 'Where's this kid's head at?' Finally, she asked, "Don't you think I can find a place to stash it?…I just don't want to deal with cops."

"Please," Marcia begged, "Just four more days…to get Muhammad out or to get someone to replace you."

Again C.C. stared at her. The kid was in way over her head. She would never get Muhammad & Crew out by herself. Yet she just might get someone to replace her and Bonnie.

Bonnie saw C.C. wavering. She cut in with a determined, "No!"

Marcia concentrated on C.C. "I have a big chemistry test the day after tomorrow."

C.C. shook her head. The poor kid was absolutely hopeless — Rich Miss. College Coed crying about a chemistry test on Miss. Hardscrabble's ragged blue collar. Still, she found the idea of leaving Marcia alone to deal with Muhammad discomfiting. This thought alone would have been enough. Yet that something in Marcia's look which had always turned her on did not hurt one bit. C.C. stared at Bonnie with an expression that said, "Let's give the kid a few more days."

Bonnie walked away in defeat.

C.C. turned to Marcia. "Okay."

*****

It was 11:00 AM and Rob was in the worst mood he'd been in for months. Sloan had shown up fucked-up. Rob had just started believing that he had put drugs behind him. He felt like a fool. He also felt as if he had lost his best friend, this time for good. Something told Rob that he would never again see Sloan straight. Then a former dishwasher of his had wandered in, a drunk. He was looking for work. Rob had told Sloan to get out, that he didn't want to see his face.

And that was just the start. Lunch hour was a half hour away, and he was minus a short order cook and a waitress. Worse yet, the ladies room toilet, which as far back as he could recall had never caused him any grief, chose today to get stopped up and overflow. This meant he was also minus the dishwasher, now trying to unstop it. Which of course also meant there was not a single clean sauce pot, so he himself was scrubbing one. It was then that he heard a familiar and very unexpected voice.

"Daddy."

It was his five-year-old son, and he was crying his eyes out. "Davy, what's the matter?" he asked, not really wanting to know. What he wanted to know was why the hell his wife wasn't handling this.

The child mumbled something between sobs that Rob could not make out. He bent down and held the kid's face in his hands. "You'll be okay. Don't cry." Rob took his son's hand. He walked him into the dining room so his wife could take over. But his wife was nowhere to be seen. Turning to the kid, he asked, "Where's mommy?"

The child shook his head, to say he didn't know.

Baffled, Rob asked, "How did you get here?"

"Walked."

"By yourself?" Rob asked, knowing this could not be the case. The child nodded.

Stunned, Rob couldn't believe it. The school was only a few blocks from the restaurant, but Rob had no idea the kid knew the way. Just then a waitress passed by them. He told her, "Call my wife. Tell her Davy's here, and to pick him up right away." He turned back to his son. The kid's nose was running. "C'mon, let's go into the kitchen."

Rob got a clean towel and wet it, thinking, 'God, I don't have time for this.' He dropped to his knees and wiped off the kid's face. "Now tell Daddy what happened."

"Damian hit me."

Rob could believe this. Name a kid Damian, and what choice did he have? He could be a bully or a pansy. Rob actually felt some sympathy for poor Damian. "Why did he hit you?"

"I said he was a liar."

"Well you shouldn't call someone a liar unless they really are liar."

"Damian's a liar."

"Why, what did he say?"

"He said I was a Jew. Daddy, I'm not a Jew, am I?"

Rob could not believe what he was hearing. How did some other 'six-year-old' know that his kid was a Jew, when his kid didn't even know. It seemed astonishing. There had to be an adult mixed up in this. Rob wanted to wring his neck. And then he realized that the neck most in need of wringing was his own. How was it possible that his son did not know that he was a Jew? This was more than negligence? Rob felt a sense of guilt so strong it actually turned his stomach.

It was at that moment that the dishwasher chose to appear behind his son, pushing along a wheeled bucket with the mop and a plunger in it. He reached into the bucket and pulled out a dripping menstrual rag for Rob's inspection. At first speechless, wondering what the hell he was supposed to say, Rob finally said the only thing he could think of, "Good....Throw it away....Outside....And wash your hands." That was one problem solved. At least he wouldn't have to call a plumber.

"What was that, Daddy?" his son asked, meaning the menstrual rag.

Reminded he had a more difficult problem to solve, Rob refused to get sidetracked. "I'll tell you later," he said, meaning years later.

The mystery of the menstrual rag shoved aside, his son returned to his need for assurance. "I'm not a Jew, am I Daddy?"

'Wow,' thought Rob, 'Hate to break the kid's heart.' This was a problem far more complicated than a stopped-up toilet. If there were a simple, easy solution, or some magic words, he sure couldn't think of them. "Of course you're a Jew. So is Mommy, and so is Daddy. Being a Jew is a good thing. You should be very proud."

The child looked puzzled. "Damian says Jews are bad. They steal peoples' land, and peoples' money."

Rob lost all sympathy for little Damian. "Damian's a liar. Jews don't owe this world a thing. If anything, it's the other way around." Rob paused, knowing he was not doing a very good job of explaining. Despite this, he asked, "Do you understand me?"

The child nodded Yes.

Doubting this, Rob asked, "You do?"

"Yes, people owe Jews money."

Rob forced himself to be patient. "No, that's not what I meant." Here he was, for the first time trying to explain something very important to his son, and he had no idea how to put it into words. Until today, the only words he had had for the kid, aside from the occasional admonition, were unthinking compliments — what a good baseball player he was, or what a good student, or what a talented artist. When the kid prattled on and on, Rob would half listen, just enough to stick in the occasional, "That's nice." If he had ever really communicated with the kid, he might not be so clueless now.

"Look, Davy, you should be very proud you are a Jew. A lot of famous people were Jews"

A little light appeared in the kid's eyes. "George Washington?"

"No, not George Washington." Rob opened his mouth to list some famous Jews, but no sound came out. Einstein and Freud would not mean a whole hell of a lot to a 'six-year-old'. Salk neither. At the moment, using Jesus as an example did not seem all that appropriate either. Marx, he was no one to brag about. There was Moses. Not exactly the type of example Rob had been looking for, but he would have to do. "Moses, do you know about Moses?"

The child nodded.

"Well Moses was Jewish. See, you can be very proud, because you're Jewish too, just like Moses….If anybody says anything about you being Jewish, you just tell them you're proud of it. Okay?"

The child nodded. "What if they hit me?"

"Then you'll hit them back, and they won't hit you again. I'll teach you how to fight," Rob assured him, thinking, 'The way I should have already. The way my father taught me.' He smiled. In Berkeley, teaching a kid how to fight was probably child abuse. This thought made him even more determined. Placing his hand on his son's cheek, he asked, "Now is everything okay?"

The child nodded.

"Mommy will be here soon. Daddy's very busy. I'll find you a pencil and you can sit and draw till she gets here." As they exited the kitchen, Rob asked, "You're sure everything is okay now?"

"Yes Daddy, but I don't want to be a Jew anymore."

Rob felt the words deep in his chest, where his heart was, or where he thought it was.

Just then, a waitress complained, "The salad isn't made yet."

The patience he had been showing the child did not carry over to the waitress. "Five minutes!" he said irritably. "Gimme five minutes."

Rob, at a complete loss, steered his kid back into the kitchen. He got down on one knee right in front of him. "Davy, I'm going to explain something to you now that you won't understand right away. But I promise that soon you will."

The child looked at him questioningly.

"Like when Mommy was teaching you how to add and subtract numbers. Remember how hard it was at first. Then all of a sudden you understood, and it was easy, so easy. Well that's how it is going to be with what I tell you. You won't understand right now. But any time you want, we'll talk about it. And soon you'll understand it perfectly. Okay?"

"Okay, Daddy."

"You're a Jew. So is Mommy, and so is Daddy. There are many, many reasons we should be proud of this. Now every Jew, when they're your age, or a little younger, or a little older, meets a bad person or a stupid person that tries to make fun of them, or

315

pick on them, just because they are a Jew. Now some Jews fight back — with words against words, or fists against fists. And the bad or stupid people never bother them again. But some Jews, because they don't know how to fight, run home to tell their mommy or daddy that they don't want to be Jews anymore. That's what you did. And you know something amazing? That's just what I did when I was a little boy."

Rob looked into his son's eyes. It hurt to see the pain in them. Yet he forced himself to ignore it. Rob knew that what he was saying right now might affect the kid for the rest of his life. His thoughts were not about what he wanted this little boy to become. They were about what he feared the boy might become. Rob thought about all the self-hating Jews. The ones who never had the guts to fight back. The ones who spent their lives trying to hide the fact that they were Jewish. The so-called intellectuals, who convinced themselves that they were above religion, or above any religion except perhaps Unitarianism, as if being a Jew was only about how you looked at the world, and not just as much about how the world looked at you. He thought about the Yiddisher captains of industry, paying lip service to their religion, yet, by neglect or design, steering their children into Wasp weddings. None of them had the backbone to be different, which unfortunately was all their religion meant to them. No matter how rich or powerful they were, Rob saw only their pathetic weakness, their repulsive cowardice. And he'd seen so many of them, ready to fight for any cause except their own, ready to fight against their own, prostrate themselves before the goyim just to prove they weren't really Jews. No, he had never met, never even heard of, a self-hating Jew who wasn't at heart, at the core, a gutless, worthless, masochistic piece of shit.

As Rob looked into his little son's eyes, he knew that he would see that this child, his child, would not spend the rest of his life ashamed and running away. His son would not yearn to be just like everyone else. His son would grow a backbone. He'd see to it. Yet the right words continued to evade and frustrate him. Rob realized that this little child before him was far too young to understand them anyway. He would keep explaining as best he could, year after year, until the child grew into a man who did understand.

Right now, all he could say was, "My father taught me how to fight back, and then nobody bothered me. I'm going to teach you how to fight back, and nobody is going to bother you. I promise."

*****

Marco had not gotten out of the house much since Susan had walked out. Still hoping she would return, he wanted to be home if and when she did. Also, lately, he felt uncomfortable around people, friends as well as strangers. Susan's leaving him seemed to point to a weakness in himself, one obvious for all to see. He felt this way despite the fact that, as far as he knew, no one was aware that Susan was gone. Yet the main reason he rarely got out of the house was a complete lack of energy and motivation.

For the first time since high school, Marco began watching a lot of television. Before, aside from a sneering interest in all the news and public affairs programs, he had shied away from this obvious, insidious establishment tool for the preservation of the status quo. Yet he now found himself mesmerized by situation comedies, especially the daytime reruns of those he had seen as a kid. Oddly enough, he would also get a craving for the snack he had munched when first watching these programs — popcorn. Marco had a few minutes before his favorite show came on, so he decided to make some. He reached up into the cupboard and pulled down some Jiffy Pop. It came in an aluminum pie pan with a wire handle. The instructions were printed on the label, a round piece of cardboard that fit neatly on top of the pan. Though he knew them by heart and had made so much Jiffy Pop he could do it in his sleep, Marco always removed the cardboard and read the instructions again. It was part of the ritual. He lit the gas burner, catching a whiff of propane. What was there about this purposely unpleasant smell he found so pleasant? When Marco made popcorn, he entered a relaxed trance. Each necessary step was a logical extensions of preceding one. He'd place the aluminum pie plate on the fire. A flattened, wrinkled layer of tinfoil remained where he had removed the cardboard label. The popcorn kernels were still hidden within the plate and foil cover. Marco took the wire handle and shuffled the plate back and forth across the fire so the kernels would heat evenly without burning. One of them popped, then another, and a few more. Then the exciting part. As the kernels popped, you could see the top layer of tinfoil expanding. It would get bigger and bigger until the flat foil cover magically transformed into a beautifully symmetrical dome. Not half a sphere, but an elevated dome, like a rotunda. Was that the right word, he wondered. Was the rotunda the dome itself, or the dome and its sides, or maybe just the room under the dome? He would have to look up rotunda. It was a nice word. As the last kernels popped, Marco smiled upon the filled-out dome that meant a successful experiment. It reminded him of those he had done in his high school science class, or better yet, the ones he had seen as a child on the Mr. Wizard TV program. That had been a fantasy of his, to be the good looking kid — Bobby, or Johnny, or something like that — who came over to Mr. Wizard's house to watch him do experiments, standing there all wide-eyed, asking the questions that Marco wanted to ask. Mr. Wizard seemed like a really nice guy. Mr. Smith, his high school science teacher was a nice guy too. Except that when he and Marco were alone, or when no one was looking, Mr. Smith was always putting his hand on Marco's shoulder, or the back of his neck. He never really did anything bad. It was just that he never touched Marco unless no one was looking. That's what made it creepy. Marco wondered if Mr. Wizard was the same way, but only for a second. He stopped himself, not wanting to think about things like that. Besides, the aluminum foil dome was perfectly formed and the popping had stopped, which meant the popcorn was done.

The aroma of popcorn filled the entire house. That was another thing he liked. Marco knew that aroma improves taste. He wondered if he would like liver and onions if it smelled the same as popcorn. He did not wonder long. If he didn't turn on the TV fast, he would miss the start of his program. Marco sliced open the top of the tinfoil dome, receiving a slight steam burn. After dumping half the popcorn into a large bowl, he headed for the living room.

Marco switched on the television, moved his favorite chair a little closer, and sat down. The familiar theme song of the Dick Van Dyke show put a smile on his face. Only a few minutes into the program, he could tell that it was an episode he had seen, the one about walnuts. He had probably watched both the original showing and the following summer's rerun. Marco enjoyed remembered episodes far more than the ones that seemed new to him. Munching on popcorn, he was really into the program when jarring music came on, along with the flashing word, "BULLETIN!"

"Awww," said Marco aloud. He could tell from the look of it that the local station, not the national network, was interrupting one his favorite episodes of his favorite program. This made it more likely that they were breaking in for some inane, ridiculous reason — an old lady passed wind in church, or something like that.

An unseen announcer, in his gravest tone, said, "We now send you to a suddenly called press conference at the county sheriff's headquarters."

This announcement was followed by a solid minute of adjusting and fumbling with microphones before a police officer finally took the podium. "We have some new information for the public concerning the murder of County School Superintendent Julius Johnson. I have here a letter, supposedly from a group calling itself the Siamese Liberation Army. In it, the group claims credit, I mean takes responsibility, for Mr. Johnson's murder. They also provide, in that letter, information that only the killers would know....Now I'll open the floor for your questions." The police officer pointed to one of the off-screen reporters in the audience. "Yes."

Marco pulled his chair closer to the TV set. Dick Van Dyke was completely forgotten. The dirty fascists had assassinated a school superintendent. Marco himself was a far more prestigious target. The thought gave him chills.

While the camera remained on the police officer, the off-screen reporter said, "Jack Reilly, with the Chronicle....Did the letter reveal any connections to other rightwing extremists groups?"

"No," the officer replied. "No connections to any groups were revealed. The letter does make clear that we were mistaken in our assumption that this is a rightwing group. These people are on the other end of the political spectrum." He pointed out into the audience again. "Yes."

Marco sat shaking his head. 'Sure, blame it on us.' The fascists must think The People are as stupid as they are.

"Bart Hannum, with the Mercury....Why would a leftwing group assassinate the county's first black school superintendent?"

"In their words, he had been co-opted by the establishment."

"How?" Hannum called out.

"By taking the job."

Another reporter called out, "Can you read us the full statement?"

There was an edge in the police officer's tone as he said, "I'm not here to spout radical propaganda. We will distribute copies of their statement after the press conference....Then you guys can do that." He pointed to the audience again. "Yes."

"Stan McClosky, the Tribune....What part of the statement confirms their involvement?"

"The Siamese Liberation Army claims to have used cyanide tipped bullets. Tests just completed at our lab confirm this." He searched the audience. "Yes."

"Roger Straughton, The Badger—"

Even on the TV, Marco could make out the police officer rolling his eyes, as if to say, "How'd I make that mistake." He stared straight at Straughton, memorizing his face for the next press conference.

Straughton continued, "Considering the assassin walked up behind Mr. Johnson and fired two bullets into the back of his skull, should not the placement of cyanide on those bullets be considered overkill?"

The police officer was at a loss how to answer this question. In any case, something told him that he shouldn't. "You might take that up with your friends in the Siamese Liberation Army. That'll be all the questions, Gentlemen."

Marco sat pondering the type of idiots who would assassinate the county's first black Superintendent of Public Schools for merely accepting the job, the type of idiots now charged with arresting them, and the type of idiots covering the story. A picture of three blind mice came to mind, each biting on the tail of the mouse in front of it, and all running around as fast as they could in the circle thus created. Could it be that he was the only sane, intelligent person in the world?

*****

For the first time in weeks, Marcia walked to The People's

Crash Pad with a smile on her face. The reason walked beside her. Delores, a friend of a friend of an acquaintance, had recently returned from Africa after finishing two fulfilling years in the Peace Corps. A Berkeley graduate with a degree in elementary education, Delores had nothing except the occasional substitute teacher assignment to occupy her time until the start of the new school year. She was looking for a challenge.

"Marcia, I've admired what you're doing ever since I read about you in The Badger."

Marcia had never learned how to acknowledge a compliment except by blushing, which she was doing right now. Out of the corner of her eye, she glanced up at Delores, who was quite tall. Delores stared straight ahead, chin up and radiating confidence. Marcia envied her self-assurance. "Your teaching experience should come in handy."

"Oh, I don't believe in teaching," Delores replied.

Marcia found the remark puzzling, especially coming from a teacher.

"I believe in empowering," Delores continued. "I don't think you can teach anyone anything. You can only empower people to learn for themselves — instill a thirst for learning, provide a conducive environment, acquaint them with available sources of knowledge, and then stand ready to encourage and guide them."

This made sense to Marcia. Delores seemed to be just the understanding adult she needed to handle the runaways. With Delores around to help, C.C. and Bonnie would be more likely to stay. This thought reminded Marcia that she only had two more days to get rid of Muhammad and his friends. Two more days and not a clue how to go about it. Marcia hoped she would find them gone when she arrived. What a relief that would be. A miracle, rather. Well, miracles happen.

Marcia did not find any miracles when she arrived at The People's Crash Pad. What she did find was her greatest fear realized — C.C. and Bonnie stuffing their belongings into the trunk of their car. Marcia's mind jumped from thought to thought until an object sticking out of C.C.'s waistband mesmerized her — a small pistol. 'Where did that come from?'

C.C.'s face was literally red with rage while violently forcing a stubborn cardboard box into the trunk. She wouldn't even look at

Marcia.

It was left to Bonnie to say the obvious, "We're outa here."

"Why?" asked, Marcia, despite having a damn good idea.

C.C., still livid, glanced over as she took a breather from rearranging the trunk to get the box in. "We left for a half hour, and those thugs broke into our room."

"Stole C.C.'s revolver and a radio."

As if losing C.C. and Bonnie were not bad enough in itself, the thought of a revolver in The People's Crash Pad, and in the hands of Muhammad, gave Marcia the shivers. She pointed at the pistol in C.C.'s waistband. "She has a revolver?"

"Had," Bonnie corrected her. "She still has her automatic. They didn't find that."

Marcia's first thought was to go upstairs to get the revolver back. Her second thought was that attempting that would surely prove fruitless, possibly deadly. Her third thought was that she had just lost Delores too. A quick glance up at her seemed to indicate no such thing. Delores' expression, if anything, appeared even more confident.

C.C. had finally managed to squeeze the carton into the trunk. She headed towards the house, saying, "I'll get the last of it."

"No!" Bonnie commanded, grabbing her arm and holding tight.

C.C. struggled to free herself.

Marcia again stood transfixed at the sight of the pistol handle sticking out of the back of C.C.'s waistband. For Marcia, guns were something you saw on TV, or safely in the possession of policemen. Seeing should have been believing, but the sight seemed unreal.

Surprisingly, Bonnie had the strength to keep hold, asking, "You want to go to jail for killing some worthless niggers?"

"Damn straight!" C.C. replied, jerking her arm free.

Bonnie grabbed it again. "Some other niggers'll kill 'em soon enough."

Nigger was not a word Marcia was used to hearing. It made her cringe, and stopped her from pleading with C.C. and Bonnie. She glanced up at Delores to check her reaction to this unreal scene.

Delores' confident expression had been replaced by a stern one.

C.C. stopped trying to get away.

Bonnie, still holding fast, turned to Marcia. "They locked

themselves in their room. I had to drag C.C. away before she blew the door open and killed them."

Marcia felt dizzy. She could not believe what was happening. What did all this have to do with a People's Crash Pad? Never had she imagined the complications now swirling around her. Not only was she losing C.C. and Bonnie. Surely Delores would now want no part of the crash pad either.

C.C. said to Bonnie, "Okay, you get the rest." She reached back and pulled the automatic from her waistband. "Here, take this."

Bonnie shook her head No and headed for the house.

C.C. turned to Marcia. "Kid, those niggers are poison. Get rid of them any way you can…fast!"

Delores said sternly to C.C., "I don't like that word."7

"Well I don't like thievin' niggers," C.C. replied.

In an even sterner tone, Delores said, "I don't care to hear that word again."

C.C., a head and a half shorter than Delores, did not look up at her. Instead, she raised the pistol until she was holding it in front of her face pointing straight up, not at Delores. She twisted the pistol in her hand, examining it from different angles while saying through gritted teeth, "You can't always get what you want."

As Marcia watched the situation escalate, she actually wondered if she were experiencing a nightmare.

Delores said calmly, "You won't shoot them, but you'll shoot me?"

Still without looking up at Delores, C.C. gave a little laugh and replaced the pistol in her waistband.

Marcia, despite the unreality of all that was happening, realized that Delores had shown her something, revealed an enviable calmness and capability.

Bonnie came down with an armful of clothes on hangers. C.C. helped her place them on the rear seat. When she turned back toward Marcia, the rage had faded from her face. C.C. hugged Marcia tight, saying before she let go, "Honey, you be careful."

Marcia, surprised by this show of affection, stammered, "Good luck. Thanks for everything."

Bonnie was already in the passenger seat.

Marcia watched as C.C. got in, and kept watching as they drove away.

Delores said, "Well, give me a tour of the place."

Marcia heard these words with disbelief and relief. Her strength returned in a rush. She led Delores towards The People's Crash Pad, very grateful she did not have to take this walk alone. Marcia looked up at Delores with reinforced respect. "You were so calm."

"In Africa, more than once, I had to face down Ak-47's."

"You weren't scared?"

"Yes, but I knew things would turn out all right."

"How did you know that?"

"I'll tell you a secret I learned. The crime depends just as much upon the victim as the perpetrator."

Marcia was not sure she had heard right. "You don't mean that the victim is just as guilty?"

Delores replied, "In a way, yes. The person being attacked sends signals to the attacker."

Marcia found this idea disturbing. There was suspicion in her expression as she looked up at Delores. "Why do you say that?" she asked, and the reply she received disturbed her even more.

"I used to volunteer at a rape crisis center. It takes a certain type of woman to get raped."

*****

Things had not been going well for Straughton, yet there remained hope in his heart. There was always hope in Straughton's heart. Whenever reality became too oppressive, his mind had a knack for filtering it out. He had just tried getting his father to pay for his trip to Algeria. There had been no chance of success. Yet while dialing the number, he had managed to convince himself otherwise. Instead of a bank draft, Straughton had received a lecture on financial responsibility, a reminder that he would now be working for the New York Times or The Washington Post if he had allowed his father to use his influence, and also an admonishment for not earning a useful degree, such as Finance. The conversation, though negative in outcome, had left Straughton with renewed respect for his father. After all, some day the entire family fortune would go to him. It was his father's responsibility to steward it in the meantime. Straughton was comforted to know that his father was taking the job seriously. A few minutes later he was further comforted by some interesting news that Moe should find even more interesting.

Straughton was now on his way to The Badger's office. Once more he would try to wheedle a plane ticket to Algeria. All his past attempts must surely be wearing Moe down. It had to be just a matter of time. Soon Straughton would be winging his way to Algeria for the Cleaver interview, and that would surely set him on the solid path to his destiny — fame and fortune in the East. The key was merely to catch Moe in a good mood. Deep down, Straughton knew this was an all but impossible task. No worry. He himself would put Moe in a good mood. He had news of Brad Cavanaugh and his new rag, The Clan, that would do the job nicely.

Straughton was so sure of success he was already planning his victory celebration. A trip to Sausalito would be perfect. He had not been there since the previous school year. The picturesque little town had a number of excellent restaurants that would be most happy to exchange a tasty meal and some fine wine for a complimentary mention in The Badger. Perhaps he would even meet an older woman up there. Straughton had had enough of silly college girls, this despite the fact that he hadn't, not even close.

Straughton climbed the stairs to The Badger's office only to be immediately skewered by Moe's lead penetrating Stink Eye. Immobilized, he forgot everything — why he'd come, the news he'd brought, even how to speak. Only when Moe turned his back and walked away did Straughton's memory return. He followed Moe, deciding to break out the good news sooner than he had planned. "Moe, you'll be interested to know that our former colleague, Brad Cavanaugh, is having his troubles at The Clan — a rebellion. Half his staff quit to form their own, more radical paper, appropriately titled The Struggle."

"You think that surprises me?" Moe asked, appearing neither surprised nor pleased.

If Straughton had put Moe into a good mood, Moe was doing an excellent job of concealing it. Luckily, Straughton had another trick up his sleeve, or up an even darker place. "I'm thinking about an article on the split, one with some well camouflaged gloating."

Moe's voice took on an added edge. "No! I told you, as far as we're concerned, they don't exist. I guarantee you, in a few months, they won't."

So much for the great news that was going to put Moe into a good mood. Well, Straughton was here already. He might as well further piss off Moe. Straughton opened his mouth to speak when—

Moe focused his glare like a laser. There was something so frighteningly emphatic in his expression and tone, Straughton would never have the nerve to broach the matter again. "Ask me one more time about a trip to anywhere, I'll give you a headfirst trip down the stairs."

*****

Rob was in a good mood. It was 4:00 pm and the restaurant was still almost full. This was something new. For the first few years, the place would fill up for lunch and dinner. Lately, the in between hours had been steadily busier. This increase had come at a good time too. Rob had been losing interest. New problems, however aggravating, were a challenge. But he'd now been in business long enough to experience about everything that could happen. Old problems repeating themselves were not a challenge. They were a pain in the neck, among other places.

Yet it was more than just running the business that bothered him. Rob had always gotten off on meeting new people, hearing their stories. Lately, the people he met rarely interested him. And many of those who had once interested him, didn't anymore. Take Straughton, for instance. There was a character. No one you'd trust, but an amusing guy to watch in action. He could play more angles than a pool shark. You had to admire the slimeball's style. Yet even Straughton had begun to tire him.

Rob thought to himself, 'Maybe it's the place.' Berkeley itself had been getting on his nerves, especially the people. He scanned the room. No one offensive caught his eye. He did notice how familiar everyone seemed. You could sort all of them into a few categories. Maybe restaurant customers eventually repeated themselves in the same way as restaurant problems. Could be true. Yet he felt there had to be more to it. 'Probably the town.'

A kid entered, sporting the official Black Muslim uniform — black suit, white shirt, black bowtie. Rob shook his head in disgust.

'One of Farrakhan's idiots.' Yet the kid didn't look like your typical Black Muslim ex-con — 'Too soft'. Rob's teeth clenched anyway, thinking about how Farrakhan's morons were explaining away all the Jewish help during the Civil Rights Movement by making the Jews out to be the worst of the whites. They were all over the streets now, selling their illiterate newspaper. This was the first time one had come into the restaurant. 'Kosher enough for them?' He laughed, but without a smile, telling himself that if the kid were in here selling papers, he'd throw him out. Just then, Rob saw that he was holding newspapers, and that he was hustling them to a table of customers. They ignored him.

The Black Muslim went to the next table. 'Can't allow that.' But he was allowing it. Confrontation was something Rob avoided. He was good at that, having the patience to wait things out. This usually made confrontation unnecessary. Rob had always been big for his age. Bullies had rarely bothered him. Even now, though barely over six feet and with a paunch, the right expression was enough to make him look intimidating. He'd honed that expression as a Freedom Rider. That was the main job of the bigger white guys. They were spread around, to give the rednecks second thoughts about getting physical. There had been a real need for this. Freedom Riders had a knack for attracting the meanest variety of redneck. Rob discovered his own knack for repelling them, to an extent he himself found surprising.

The Black Muslim was now at the table directly across from him. He was no kid after all, probably thirty. Rob knew that he should throw him out. He didn't actually decide to wait. He merely slipped into his procrastinating mode.

The black held out the newspapers. "Here, read the truth."

A college kid, about twenty, was sitting alone at the table. He ignored the outstretched paper.

"C'mon, Man. What's twenty-five cents?"

The college kid again ignored him.

"You're a Jew, ain't you?"

The college kid showed no emotion, but Rob did. 'Where the hell did that come from?' It hadn't occurred to him before, but the college kid did look Jewish. 'Not for certain,' Rob mused.

The Black Muslim repeated, "You're a Jew, ain't you?" this time more as a taunt than a question.

The kid still showed no emotion as he nodded Yes.

Rob, standing behind the counter, was boiling. If The Nation of Islam was a religion, then so was the Ku Klux Klan.

The black continued in a taunting tone, "Soon it's gonna be the blacks against the Jews." He leaned his face closer, smiling, "And we're gonna win....Us blacks are gonna beat the Jews!"

'Where do they get this crap?' Rob asked himself. Yet he knew, not just from Malcolm X, Elijah Muhammad, and Louis Farrakhan. From half their black "intellectuals", half of them owing their jobs to Jewish liberals, and many of them teaching college. Assholes who believed the best way to get up in the world was to find someone to step on, hypocrites crying racism while proving blacks could be as bigoted as the lowest redneck. Rob regretted not throwing the idiot out when he had first noticed him. Yet it wasn't the Black Muslim who was really angering Rob. No, it was the Jew who was sitting there taking it. Though slender, he was about the same height as Rob, and half a head taller than the black. 'Tell the little piss ant to get lost, why don't you?' Rob made up his mind to toss out the paper vendor. Again there seemed to be an expanding delay between making up his mind and moving his ass.

The Black Muslim's voice took on a meaner edge. "C'mon, Jew! Hand over some bread."

The kid reached into his pocket to do exactly that.

Rob couldn't believe it. He was out from behind the counter and headed towards the vendor in an instant. Coins and newspapers went flying as Rob grabbed his shirt and jacket collar with one hand and his belt and waistband with the other. The panhandler seemed light as a feather as Rob carried him prone, kicking and yelling, all the way to door.

"Let me down! Let me down!"

Conveniently, someone was just then coming in. Mouth agape, he held the door open for Rob as he tossed the panhandler outside with enough force to slide him on his stomach halfway across the sidewalk.

'Strike!' thought Rob, turning back into his restaurant. He felt good, in a way he could not remember feeling for a long time. His expression showed it. Then he saw the Jew and lost his smile. The gutless shit was staring him down. Rob stared back. Still, he would have walked right past him.

Then the kid said, "You didn't have to do that."

With twice the force he'd used on the Black Muslim, Rob yanked the kid, by the hair, right out of his chair. Arm straight behind him, Rob pulled the kid, doubled over, toward the entrance. Once there, he yanked him, still by the hair, straight up and against the door. Rob's other hand shot forward, getting hold on the kid's throat. He released the hunk of hair in his other hand, much of it coming away stuck to his palm. Rob moved his face within an inch of the kid's, whispering, almost hissing, "To a Jew, you'll stand up." With his free hand he shoved the door open, at the same time lifting, by the neck, the kid off the ground. He had the Black Muslim outweighed by at least twenty pounds. This incensed Rob all the more. He straightened his arm and the kid flew backwards, landing flat on the sidewalk. Rob, from where he stood, heard the kid's head bounce off the pavement. It made an unusual sound, hollower than expected. Interesting. Rob noticed that some of the kid's hair was still stuck to the palm of his hand. He stared at it as if it were excrement, then quickly brushed it off with his other palm.

Experiencing an exhilarating rush, Rob strode back inside. He felt like a world beater. The stares of his customers almost stopped him dead. Their looks screamed, "Psychopath!", "Serial Killer!", and that old Berkeley standby, "Fascist!" He had an urge to drag out every customer, one by one. It then occurred to him that for what he had just done, he could get arrested, or worse yet, sued. That's all he needed, with a wife and kid to support. 'You're losing it. Calm down,' he warned himself. 'You want to kill somebody?' Then came a more realistic thought, 'Or get yourself killed?'

*****

Muhammad stood with a no-nonsense attitude over Kedrick and Lashon, who were both sitting on their beds. "Just keep your dumb mouths shut," he said to them.

Lashon did the opposite. "That white bitch came in here and told us to straighten-up our room and the rec room."

"And that's what you'll do," Muhammad assured them. He glanced around the messy room, sniffing as he did so. "This place stinks."

Kedrick, the older of the two, cut in, "That bitch talks down to us, like we're ten years old."

"Motherfucker, what you care how she talks? We got one sweet setup here."

"You do!...Me and Lashon ain't seen no profits."

Muhammad took a step forward. "What you mean by that?"

Kedrick lowered his head, showing Muhammad the top of his almost shoulder width afro. He remained silent.

Muhammad took another step forward, repeating, "What you mean by that, nigga?"

Kedrick's reply was soft yet grudging. "Nuttin'."

"You think we been makin' serious bread. Shiiiit. Chicken feed. This ain't no town for dealin'....Too much competition."

Lashon cut in, "So why we wastin' our time?"

Muhammad was losing what little patience he had. "You don't like the way I run things, leave, both a yous."

Kedrick and Lashon remained silent.

"This man's got plans, for makin' serious bread. That means stayin' right here."

No belligerence in his tone, Kedrick asked, "How's that?"

"We gonna be the colonizers. 'Bout time the black man did some colonization."

There was sarcasm in Lashon's tone as he asked, "They gonna be our slaves?"

Muhammad smiled. "Exactly...if you motherfuckers keep your mouths shut and do what I tell you."

"Do what?" asked Kedrick.

"Let me handle that. Long as she thinks she's running things, we do as we please."

Lashon said, "But that bitch is calling us in to throw us out."

"Probably," Muhammad agreed. "Them two dykes wanted to throw us out too. Got rid of them, didn't I?"

Lashon and Kedrick remained silent.

"Let's go see what she wants." As Lashon and Kedrick got to their feet, Muhammad added, "And keep your mouths shut."

Delores welcomed them into her room with a businesslike yet accommodating demeanor. "We've had our disagreements, quite a few considering the short time I've been here. It's best for all of us to forget and start anew. We can't have the pigs banging on the door every time they feel like it. That means all drug activity must stop immediately. We will police ourselves. You three gentlemen will be The People's Crash Pad's Police Force."

*****

Straughton was in a strange mood as he strolled down Telegraph Avenue. All day he had had the feeling that something was missing. For him, this was the rarest of feelings. Rare and gone in an instant at the sight of a face. It took a moment to dawn upon Straughton that this face from the seemingly distant past was actually from less than a year ago. It was the face itself, aged at least ten years, that had played havoc with Straughton's sense of time. Little matter. This was a face he was glad to see.

Surfer was the first street dealer Straughton had tried to locate when he got back to Berkeley. He didn't just look like a surfer. He looked like the good looking lead in a surfing movie — sun bleached hair, tan, and that cocky grin. Surfer's grin had always been a con, one that he was proud of and often let you in on. Now that same grin was just about all that was left. Upon Surfer's gaunt, drug ravaged face, this grin looked bizarre and insane, a joke fallen flat.

The sight of Surfer standing on the corner doing the St. Vitus Dance with all the nervous tics of a long gone, gone for good junkie was not the source of Straughton smile. No, it was the memories of the mescaline Surfer had once sold him. Pure magic in the form of a pastel pill that had sent Straughton on a relaxed, mellow trip the likes of which he had never experienced before or after. He had spent the entire day, a sunny one like today, strolling the streets of Berkeley. The bougainvillea was in bloom. The bushes were often a block apart, but he could spot their purplish light from even farther away. Straughton meandered from living torch to living torch, iridescent waypoints that led him on and on in a trek all over the city. He'd stand in front of each bush, mesmerized by the glowing fluorescence of the flowers. That was the first time Straughton had realized that bougainvillea was not always the same color. The flowers ran from soft pink to dark purple, and all the shades in between. Never had Berkeley seemed so beautiful.

As soon as the mescaline wore off, Straughton began a search for Surfer, more like a treasure hunt, that lasted half the night. It ended in success, and Straughton bought all of Surfer's remaining stock to take back to Connecticut. He did not regret it either. Two of those pills enabled Straughton to bed his best friend's woman. Friends were important, no doubt about it. He spent much of his vacation tripping on that mescaline, the greatest summer he ever had. This wasn't industrial strength LSD that had you walking around with your jaw dropped seeing the world through flying saucer eyes. You could function on this stuff, meet and greet all the relatives. You still thought, 'Wow!' but you didn't say it every ten seconds.

'Wow,' was what Straughton was thinking right now, staring at the living remains of Surfer, wondering if it were possible Surfer could again turn him on to the mellowest dope he'd ever done. That would be too much to ask, a very minor consideration that never had and never would keep Straughton from going ahead and asking anyway.

"Surfer, My Man, how's life?"

"Cowabunga, Dude," exclaimed Surfer, in a game but weak attempt to fake recognizing Straughton. "I'm hangin' ten."

'That's life,' mused Straughton. The "Dude" has wiped out so spectacularly hard he doesn't even know it. There was little if anything left behind Surfer's blank, bloodshot eyes. If he was hanging ten, it was upside down by his toes. "Excellent to hear, My Good Man. I would be very appreciative if you could provide me with some of the mescaline you were distributing last year."

"Last year?" Surfer couldn't believe the request. It'd be a groove if he could only remember last week. 'A fucking miracle!'

"They were baby-blue," Straughton added.

"Oh!" Surfer's eyes came as close as they now could to lighting up. "Those were great — horse tranquilizers!"

Straughton shook his head No.

Surfer held his fingers apart, indicating a pill large enough to choke a horse, a large horse. "This size? Baby-blue?"

"No." Straughton held his fingers apart, indicating a pill twice the size of an aspirin. "Baby-blue. The mellowest mescaline I ever did."

Surfer shook his head. "Dude, half the mescaline sold in this town is horse tranquilizers.

"These pills were surely representative of the other half."

"Connoisseurs prefer horse tranquilizers."

"I don't."

Surfer again shook his head. "Not much call for anything mellow anymore." His brain started to throb from all the thinking. Surfer suddenly realized he had been distracted off his spiel. "This stuff I got now is dynamite!"

Straughton was disappointed, but he had nothing better to do. "What is it?"

Surfer's mind took off for another galaxy, leaving a large black hole in their conversation.

Straughton repeated, "What exactly is it?"

"Can't remember, Man?"

"Well then, you might take it out to jog your memory."

Surfer was already checking his pockets. He checked them all. He checked again.

This raised Straughton's curiosity about the drug he had missed. "Well then, what effect do they have upon one?"

Surfer grinned large enough to show he had lost a few teeth since last they met. "Fucks you up, Man. You'll like it."

"How, precisely, does this wonder chemical go about fucking you up?"

Again searching his pockets, thinking hard. "Well it — I can't remember."

"My Man, there is no chance these pills fuck up your memory?"

"Naw, naw. It don't do that." He smiled. "Makes you feel good."

"The way you feel right now."

Surfer forced a grin. "For sure."

"Is that what you're on?"

"Yeaaah." Frustrated, running his fingers through his hair, he said, "Must have lost my whole inventory. What a fucking bummer." He immediately tried to convince himself otherwise. "Maybe I sold it all."

"Undoubtedly," Straughton replied, feeling that he'd wasted enough time. Disdain appeared on his face in the form of an ingratiating grin. He backed away.

Just then Surfer scratched behind his ear. A cardboard tube the size of a pencil nub fell towards the ground. In a graceful instant, Surfer bent his knees, and with a smooth, effortless swipe of his hand caught the tube before it hit the sidewalk.

Straughton stood amazed. Dead brain cells apparently had no effect upon one's reflexes. Or if they did, Surfer's reflexes must once have been beyond belief.

He said with embarrassment, "Shit, Man, had it behind my ear all the time....Best place, you know. Cops never frisk behind the ears?" He opened one end of the tube. "Never happen, Man. Best place to hide your stash."

Surfer turned the tube over. Ignoring the fact that all the pills had already spilled out into the palm of his hand, he opened the other end. "If your stash is small enough."

"And your ears are large enough," Straughton pointed out. The pills looked homemade, pink and half the size of aspirins....What price are you asking, My Man?"

"....Lemme see. Damn if I can remember. Five dollars a tab?"

"What exactly are they?"

"Dude, quit hassling me. I told you I don't remember."

"I do recall you mentioning that. Pray tell, then, exactly what species of dealer are you?...You don't even seem to know what you're dealing."

"Dude, I told you to quit hasslin' me. You think this job is easy? You try dealing for a while, see how long you last."

"Sir, you are conversing with someone who possesses an abiding belief in the division of labor."

"Hey, Dude, you gotta understand, dealing ain't the profession it used to be."

"A complete lack of ethics."

"For sure....And not just that. Once, all there was was grass, speed, mescaline, and acid...and smack and blow which I stayed away from. Now it's a new damn pill every fucking week — different shape, different color, different trip. It's enough to make you dizzy. And all they want is this week's hit pill, like last week's dope ain't cool enough anymore. It don't pay to memorize what you're dealing. Next week you're dealing something else."

Straughton commiserated, "In the old days, all you needed was some healthy paranoia."

"Right again, Dude! Now you need a college degree in running a drug store."

"Pharmacology."

"Naw, no farming. Other dudes handle that....Just plain dealin'll fuck your mind these days."

"My Man, scoring these days will fuck up your mind." Straughton gave his own words some thought. "Yet I suppose that's the point."

Surfer stared straight at Straughton with two bloodshot squinting almost focused eyes. "You know something, Dude, if I didn't feel I was providing a groundbreaking service, I'd just walk away."

'Stagger,' would be the more appropriate verb,' thought Straughton. Yet the words that really caught his attention were "groundbreaking service". Essential, risky, Yes. "Groundbreaking?" he had to ask.

Still trying his best to look Straughton in the eye, Surfer took a small, staggering step closer. "Dude, do you know who you, me, and my customers are?"

Straughton could not claim that he did, and he wasn't completely comfortable being among this select company.

Surfer took another step forward, coming face to face with Straughton. "Dude, we are The Astronauts of Inner Space."

Straughton pictured himself as an Astronaut of Inner Space. The picture was flattering, heroic even. In fact, he felt a little weightless, perhaps, more correctly, dizzy. Never before had he experienced Surfer's philosophical side, and experiencing it face to face was a little too crowding. Straughton took a step backwards, then another one.

"Hey Dude, don't you want 'em?"

Reminded of the purpose of their conversation, Straughton stopped backing away. "At five dollars a tab?...For potluck?"

"Okay, okay. I gotta get rid of these before they fuck up my mind. Three dollars a tab."

Straughton took a step forward, willing to take a chance. "I will tell you what I am prepared to do, just to save you some trouble. I am willing to take all these pills off your hands for one dollar a tab."

Surfer could not believe what he had heard. "One dollar, Man?" He stared at Straughton as if he were missing something, and trying to figure out what. Then a strong hint of his old con you right out of your jock strap grin appeared. "Hey, Dude, I'm the dealer. I'm supposed to be ripping you off."

Straughton smiled back. "My Friend, I was merely trying to help you out….You are never going to remember what those pills are. You are never going to remember what you paid for them. Most important, you are never going to remember what you are selling them for. I'll be glad to take them off your hands, and you will no longer need to remember a thing."

Surfer started to think so hard he began to sway. Getting rid of his entire inventory could really simplify his life. He began chasing the pills around the palm of his hand with the end of the little cardboard tube. Of course, with the other end still open, every time he righted the tube to let a just scooped pill fall to the bottom, it slid right out of the other end. There seemed to be quite a few more pills than there seemed to be. He squinted to count them. "Twenty."

"Twelve," Straughton corrected him.

"There's a dozen in the tube already."

"None in the tube," Straughton said with confidence.

Surfer flipped over the tube to prove Straughton wrong. Nothing came out. He looked down the tube seeing only daylight. A nervous glance at the sidewalk around his feet turned up nothing. Dealing was getting way too complicated.

"Okay, I'll sell you six for ten dollars."

Straughton felt he had wasted too much time already. Still, the pills could be mescaline. He'd take one to the Free Clinic to have it analyzed. The rest he could do or resell, depending upon what he found out. Straughton handed over a ten and took the tabs.

Surfer was left swaying on the sidewalk. Again he started scooping the remaining pills into the tube. It only took him two pills to remember that both ends of the tube were open. A quick look down it again showed daylight. Surfer threw away the tube, glanced at the six pills in his palm, then tossed them all down his throat. A smile of relief come to his face, one that said, "Life simplified."

*****

336

"You did what?" Marcia asked in disbelief.

Delores said calmly, matter-of-factly, "I made Muhammad, Kedrick, and Lashon our People's Crash Pad Police."

Marcia had now heard Delores say it twice, yet she still didn't believe it. Feeling dizzy, she sat down, almost collapsed, upon Delores' bed. At a loss for words, Marcia just wanted to be somewhere else, anywhere else.

Delores continued in a confident tone. She was in no ways making an excuse, not even a case, just stating facts that should be obvious to anyone. "Changing people is hard, sometimes impossible. Redirecting them is much easier. Let them do their own thing, but to accomplish your ends instead of theirs. Muhammad's thing is intimidation. Intimidation in itself is neither good nor bad. It's neutral, and present in all social structures. We cannot run The People's Crash Pad without some degree of intimidation, not without inviting chaos....You understand?"

Marcia, dizzy as she was, did understand the words. She just failed to find them convincing. She also understood that Delores was waiting for a reply. All Marcia could come up with was, "You made Muhammad our policeman?"

"Of course! He'll be a natural. Intimidation is a policeman's first recourse. Before, Muhammad was using that intimidation against us. By making him our policeman, I've co-opted him to our side."

"We can trust Muhammad?" Marcia asked.

"The old Muhammad, no. The new Muhammad, yes."

Marcia just shook her head.

Delores said, "Believe me, now that we've given him some responsibility, you're going to see a changed Muhammad."

Marcia mumbled, "I don't know."

"Trust me, Dear."

Marcia had no choice. It was either Delores' way, or showing her the highway. Without Delores, Marcia would have to move in with Muhammad and his friends. Marcia was distracted from this dilemma by a polite knock on Delores' half open door. Muhammad was visible in the opening.

"Come in," said Delores.

Muhammad took only a single step into the room.

To Marcia's surprise, there was not even a hint of belligerence on his face.

He said, "Delores, we have someone that wants to crash here awhile."

"Bring them in."

Marcia, still recovering from her shock at The People's Crash Pad's new police force, was now shocked even more. Muhammad politely ushered a young girl into the room, a girl Marcia recognized immediately as Donna. A confusion of various thoughts assaulted her. This was the ingrate who had returned her kindness by stealing Smitty's amplifier. Yet, this ingrate was also a child, the innocent inspiration for The People's Crash Pad. Her return to make use of it, somehow seemed to justify all Marcia's efforts and aggravation. She would have greeted Donna with a hug if not for the memory of how she left.

Delores greeted Donna with a warm smile, motioning to a chair facing Marcia. "Come, sit down."

Donna did so, returning Delores' smile with a grudging one of her own.

Marcia wondered how Donna could fail to recognized her. Her time on the street had added some hardness to her expression.

Delores asked sympathetically, "Dear, what's your name?"

"Samantha," Donna replied.

Reflexively, Marcia said, "I thought your name was Donna."

Donna did not flinch, making obvious to Marcia that she had recognized her all along.

Delores held up the palm of her hand to Marcia, as if to say hold off just a moment. Whatever this child's real name, there was little chance it was either Samantha or Donna.

Donna, looking at Marcia, said nonchalantly, "Nothing personal about liberating your stereo. On the street, you do what you gotta do."

Marcia felt a flash of anger, but it was quickly smothered by the realization that this child probably knew more about the harsh side of life than she did, hopefully more than Marcia ever would. If there were an appropriate reply, it did not come to her.

Donna asked reasonably, "You can't blame me, can you?"

Marcia was not so sure about that, but she was sure there would be no point in doing so.

Donna, as if to prove that the money she had received for the amplifier had not gone to waste, stretched out her leg to show Marcia her ankle. "With the bread left over, I got this tattoo." It was one of those all the rage little butterflies.

*****

Smitty lay in bed fully dressed, except for his shoes. He had finished the entire week's reading assignments an hour ago, right before dusk. Now he just lay in the dark, thinking. Things with Marcia, who had just left, weren't what they used to be. He wouldn't say they were worse. If anything, she meant more to him. He'd gotten accustomed to her. Well if things weren't worse, what were they? 'Harder!' he decided. That was it. It used to be so easy to light her up. A few words. A touch. It was a high, not just pleasurable, but rewarding.

Lately, Marcia had been too serious, moody even. He checked the calendar. She wouldn't be on the rag for another week. Yet with her that never had been a problem, not like it was supposed to be. Maybe her moods had something to do with the crash pad. Smitty wondered what was going on there. Was it open? Too bad she didn't want to talk about it. When he asked her, a few weeks ago, if Muhammad and his thugs had moved out, she wouldn't even answer him. Marcia must have thought that he was rubbing it in. Well, if she didn't want to talk about the crash pad, that was her business. By now, those thugs had to be gone. He did not care to imagine them still there.

Smitty told himself he had nothing to complain about. Marcia was never on his ass, bitching about anything he did. It was just that living together meant being together sometimes when you'd rather be alone. Things would go a hell of a lot smoother if he were more adept at reading her moods. If he were psychic.

Psychic, Smitty wasn't. Yet at the sound of a knock on his door, he guessed correctly that Straughton was on the other side of it. Momentarily, he would be trying to wangle a ride somewhere. Sure enough—

"My Man, have you ever been to Sausalito?" Straughton asked.

"No," Smitty replied. He had heard about Sausalito, that it was a nice place to take a woman.

To Straughton, Sausalito was a nice place to scrounge a free meal. He looked upon such opportunities as one would look upon some tempting fruit hanging from a tree. Not to pick it, letting it fall to the ground and rot, seemed such a waste. "My Friend, the drive would be scenic, and the food and drink on me."

Smitty knew that the food and drink would be in exchange for a few complimentary words in The Berkeley Badger. This in no way bothered him. Yet the ride was an awfully long one for just a meal. Still, Smitty was tempted by the thought of getting Marcia out of Berkeley and to a nice place for a few hours. That might cheer her up. "Can my woman come?"

"Certainly. My pleasure."

*****

Marcia was again making the dreaded walk from her apartment to The People's Crash Pad. She had stopped asking Smitty for a lift. The short ride there did not allow her time to think. The longer walk did. Still, thinking had yet to give her any answers. She would arrive just as confused, and far more depressed than when she had started out. Delores was proving impossibly stubborn, already insisting on doing everything her own way. To make matters worse, she was way too skillful at justifying her ways. Worse still, some of Delores' ways were quite weird, weird enough to make Marcia nervous. Of one thing Marcia was certain, the way the crash pad was being run was no way to run a crash pad. She would have to spend more time there herself, and the time she was already devoting to it was hurting her grades. The crash pad shouldn't even be open until the summertime influx of kids. Closing it completely till then would be the best solution. First she had to get rid of Muhammad and his friends. And it was her fault they were there. Smitty had warned her, C.C. too. Why hadn't she stayed out of it and let them deal with him?

As Marcia stepped off the sidewalk toward the front door of the crash pad, two men came out of it. She froze in fear. Something told Marcia they were cops, real cops, not the crash pad variety. Marcia glanced back towards the street, looking for a police car. There was none. By now the two men were right in front of her. Both had big smiles for Marcia, the one on the better looking man was downright salacious. They split apart to let her pass between

340

them. Marcia glanced back for clues as to what was going on. Both men were also glancing backwards, checking out her figure. Being caught at this did not seem to bother them a bit. In fact, they were still leering when Marcia looked away. Embarrassed, uneasy, asking herself, 'Who are they?' she quickened her steps towards the door.

What Marcia saw when she got inside made her forget about the two men. The People's Crash Pad had not been this neat and clean since the day it had opened. Two young boys were placing brooms back in a closet. Delores might be exactly the person Marcia had needed. The anxiety that had accompanied her on the way over had evaporated. Things just might work out after all.

The house was quiet, no loud music. Marcia did hear the sound of what she thought was a radio coming from the rec room. Sticking her head in, she found a few young girls watching a soap opera on a television. Somebody must have donated it. This thought gave Marcia a good feeling, wondering whether she could thank Delores for the TV too. As she passed the living room, Marcia was again surprised, this time to see a middle aged man sitting on the couch as if waiting for someone. He was very distinguished looking, and gave her a nice smile as she passed. Marcia returned it.

By the time she reached Delores' room, Marcia was ready to kneel at her feet.

Delores put down the book she was reading to give Marcia one of her calm, self-assured smiles.

Marcia gushed, "I can't believe what a wonderful job you're doing."

Delores came close to laughing. "I'm not sure that's a compliment."

Marcia laughed. "You know what I mean."

Delores nodded, smiling warmly.

"Who donated the television?"

"No one. We bought it."

Marcia lost her smile. "We've barely enough money for food till the end of the month."

Delores' smile broadened. "Don't you worry. We've enough now for three months."

Marcia felt a weight lifted off of her. Few things made her more uncomfortable than begging for donations. She stood and gave the still sitting Delores a joyful hug. "Thank you! Thank you!"

"You can thank Muhammad."

This took Marcia aback. "How?"

"It was his idea."

A slight unease tempered Marcia's happiness. "How?"

"Well, what have you noticed about runaways, especially the girls?"

Marcia shook her head.

"Almost all of them suffer from low self-esteem."

"Muhammad said that?"

"No. No, but he must have sensed it, because he came up with the solution."

"What solution."

"Well, how can you raise self-esteem?"

Marcia did not feel like guessing.

"You prove to these girls that they are worth something."

Marcia began to feel uneasy, with no real clue as to why.

"You give them a way to measure their self-worth, a way they'll easily understand."

"How?"

"Well even the youngest, the simplest of them understand that money is a measure of things."

It hit Marcia in an instant. It hit her like a hammer. So that explained the two men who passed her on the way in, and the middle-aged man waiting downstairs on the couch. A feeling of nausea that started in her stomach rose slowly towards her throat.

Delores could see from Marcia's expression that her explanation had been less than convincing. "Morals and mores are completely relative in this world. What is frowned upon in one society is exalted in another."

Marcia lowered her head, fought for breath, not wanting to even look at Delores, as if not looking would block out another of her twisted, dizzying arguments.

"Child, c'mon now. What's marriage, after all?"

It was then that Donna stuck her head into the room. "Delores, a client's waiting for you in the corner bedroom."

*****

342

Marco had chosen a beautiful day to finally force himself out of the house for a while. He had not been to Golden Gate Park for a long time. It was one of his favorite places. He figured seeing it again would do his head good. The weather was so pleasant, Marco felt like walking there. Of course this was out of the question. Even by bus it was a long trip. He then got another idea. Why not go to his own park, a place within walking distance.

Marco arrived at People's Park, immediately grateful that he had come. The colorfully dressed hippy families, the flying Frisbees, the leaping dogs proved a soothingly idyllic sight, one surely deserving of immortalization on film, or even on canvas. This same scene he had viewed so many times before, had finally gotten to him. He felt at home. Marco took pride, experienced a sense of accomplishment, in the knowledge that he had played a vital part in the creation of this People's oasis. And the park had turned out far better than he or anyone had ever imagined. Its self-justified existence said, "We were right, and we did it right." Of course, originally, People's Park had made a more defiant statement — "We took it to the Man and won!"

A family of hippies a few yards away was getting up to leave. The father had an abused newspaper in his hand. He glanced around looking for a waste basket. Not seeing one, he did see and recognize a solution. "Marco," he called, "It's today's. Want it?"

Marco didn't know the man, and was flattered to be recognized. He didn't really want the paper. Since Susan had abandoned him, he had lost his craving for the latest news. It always seemed more of the same. Nor could he concentrate on it, no matter how hard he tried. This realization both surprised and bothered him. He felt like a quitter.

"Sure," Marco said, walking over for the newspaper. It would keep him from getting restless, give him something to do.

Handing it to him, the man said, "Word is they'll try to take back the park."

Marco waved his arm around with pride. "Look at it. They wouldn't dare." He watched the hippie family depart, smiling and feeling more contented than he had at any time since Susan had left him. In one smooth, childlike motion, Marco opened the front page of the newspaper, dropped to his knees, and practically dived on his stomach into the grass. He read the headline — "COP KILLED BY SNIPER". The four words left him neither sorry nor glad. A small drawing caught his eye — the face of a Siamese cat. Marco smiled at the thought that at least Susan had the decency to take her miserable cat with her. He returned to the article, reading that the previous night a cop had been shot in the head and killed by a sniper. He had been a rookie, on the force for less than two months. An only child, his name was Johnny Wong, the first Asian ever hired by the Berkeley police. To diversify the force, they had lowered their height requirement two inches.

Marco's eyes returned to the little drawing of the Siamese cat. It was at the center-top of a photocopied letter that had been dropped off at the newspaper during the night. Above the cat's face were the words, "THE SIAMESE LIBERATION ARMY". Under the drawing, centered, was, "People's Justice — Whatever Needs To Be Done".

As he read the letter itself, the contented smile on Marco's face faded to a solemn mask. He read it a second time, almost in a trance, overcome by the sense that his life had changed, drastically and forever. The letter stated, among much rhetoric, that, "In the name of The People and The Revolution, The Siamese Liberation Army had struck a blow against the fascist establishment by offing a pig." His eyes were drawn back to the drawing of the Siamese cat. Marco feared that he had seen that cat before, many times. He told himself that all Siamese cats looked alike, otherwise they would not be Siamese cats. Though his logic was flawless, the feeling remained. It was not a pleasant one.

*****

Smitty lay in bed reading The Daily Californian, UC Berkeley's student newspaper. The front page held some very good news. The university had suspended permission for students to tutor San Quentin inmates. Some of the students had been caught smuggling contraband to the prisoners. 'One less thing to worry about.' He had an urge to go into "told you so" mode and mention this news to Marcia. He also had the self-control not to.

Marcia lay next to him, deep in thought. Tonight would be one of those nights their bed would be strictly for sleeping. Even if he did get Marcia going, he probably couldn't get her into it enough to justify the effort. Maybe she had problems at The People's Crash Pad. Could Muhammad and his crew still be there? Smitty did not care to think about that, but damn if he didn't want to know. Yet how can he ask her without seeming to rub it in. He better wait to catch Marcia in a really good mood. Lately, Smitty had been congratulating himself on his ability to pick up her vibes. This newly acquired skill was making their life together easier.

Smitty threw aside The Daily Californian for The Badger. It contained another article on a Sexual Liberation Front party, this one with Straughton's byline. Though curious about the subject matter, Smitty was even more curious about how Straughton and his date had gotten there. Could the leach have found a new sucker to chauffer him around? Nice thought, but not likely. They probably took Honor Bikes. Smitty skimmed the article. Enticing, but nothing new. Still, visions of what these parties must be like flashed through his mind — naked women rubbing up against him, grabbing him, yanking him. Would they be feeding him grapes? Probably not. 'Oh, the boycott. Definitely not.' Well who gives a shit about grapes, as long as all the women were bare-assed? Then came the realization that since only couples were admitted, there would be an equal number of hairy asses and swinging dicks in the mix. This vision Smitty found much less arousing. Still, he should get at least one orgy under his belt, sort of like losing his virginity.

Smitty wondered whether Marcia would be up for an orgy. He'd doubted it very much, and would like to think she wouldn't. Well, that meant he'd stay a virgin as far as orgies go, as if there were such a thing, which luckily there wasn't. If Marcia would go along, would he be jealous? Damn straight! Should he be?

Marcia, at the moment, had Smitty on her mind too. How selfish could he be? How disinterested in her interests? He knew what The People's Crash Pad meant to her. Yet he never even asked about it, never offered to help, except to give her a lift there, which lately she hadn't wanted. And even when she did, he never came inside. Was he really that self-centered? Or was he just holding a grudge because she let Muhammad and his friends stay, which was worse?

Marcia had committed an act that morning that deeply shamed her, an act as treacherous as one could commit in Berkeley. She had turned to the police for help in evicting Muhammad and his friends. The act itself was not the sole source of her shame. Its results had added to her humiliation. "Well, Little Lady, it's not so simple. You talk to a lawyer first, get all your papers in order, go before a judge, then come back to us with an eviction notice. We'll take it from there...unless, of course, we can find an excuse not to....You did refuse us entry...twice." They told her that if it were up to them, they'd close the place down, riot or no riot. Of course, criminal activity would be another matter. She could make out a report and they would have to act on it. Marcia pondered her choices. To turn in people for smoking marijuana would be hypocritical. As for possible child prostitution, Marcia found this too disgraceful to disclose. She knew she should, but she just couldn't, not to this cop, not right then.

Marcia had no idea what to do next. If there was child prostitution at the crash pad, her inaction made her complicit in it. She could not live with that. Marcia knew only one person she could turn to. He was lying on the bed right next to her. Again her resentment rose at Smitty's lack of interest in the crash pad. She'd have to ask him right out of the blue. And how would he react? This would be a real test, one she feared he would fail. And there was something else that frightened her even more. If he didn't fail the test, was willing to help, how much danger would she be placing him in? After all, Muhammad had a gun and two friends to help him. Could Smitty get rid of them without endangering himself? She didn't see how. And that's why she lay next to him, not saying a word, thinking, and thinking, and thinking.

Smitty lay thinking too, still about the next Sexual Liberation Front orgy. He had pretty much decided that no orgy, no matter how great, was worth involving Marcia. He glanced over at her. She looked so serious, and at the same time so innocent. It was a turn-on. He thought about getting something going despite the vibes, then thought again. Well, at the least, he wanted to talk to her, which in his case meant mostly listening to her. Smitty decided to start a conversation. "The Sexual Liberation Front is having another orgy."

It took a good fifteen seconds for Smitty's words to sink in. Even then, Marcia doubted she had heard them correctly. She turned her head and just stared at him.

One thing Smitty had learned about women, no reaction was usually preferable to a delayed reaction. As he watched Marcia's expression harden, he realized that the present case was no exception to this rule.

Marcia now had no doubt she had heard correctly. She spoke in a serious, neutral tone, looking at Smitty as if she had just realized something about him. "You said the same thing the last time they had an orgy."

Smitty had no memory of this. It was possible, but he did not remember. The look on Marcia's face told him to accept her word for it, no ifs, ands, or buts.

"You want to take me to an orgy," she said in disbelief.

"No," Smitty replied in all honesty. "What makes you think that?"

There was anger in her voice as she asked, "Then why are you always telling me about orgies?"

'Always?' Smitty thought to himself. Twice, if that, was far from "always". Still, he wasn't looking for debating points. He was looking for a way out. A minute ago, when he had wanted to hear Marcia's voice, her present tone was not the one he had had in mind. If only he could go back and start over, or not start at all.

Marcia's anger and disbelief reached a peak as she asked, "Is that what you think of me?"

"No. No," Smitty assured her as he slid closer on his side.

Marcia tried to escape him by jumping out of the bed. Smitty was quick enough to catch her around the waist first.

"Let go," she demanded, surprising him with an elbow sharp enough to make him flinch.

Smitty held fast, saying, "Wait. Wait."

Marcia lay still, staring straight up instead of at Smitty. "You want to take me to an orgy."

"No, I swear I don't." For some reason, fortuitous as it was, his conversation with Straughton popped into his head. He had forgotten to tell Marcia about it. "I want to take you to Sausalito."

The mention of Sausalito out of nowhere stopped Marcia cold. She had never been there, wanted to go. It was supposed to be beautiful, romantic, so romantic that Smitty's coming up with the idea seemed completely out of character. Her tone was neutral as she asked, "When did you decide that?"

"A day or two ago." He wasn't even sure when he had talked to Straughton. It seemed like years ago. "We'll find some restaurant with a really great view, and food to match, and we'll order the best wine they have."

Marcia wondered if she had underestimated Smitty, asking with a smile, "You sure you can afford it?"

Smitty smiled back at her. "Straughton gets it all for free."

Marcia felt as if she were missing something. "Straughton? What does he have to do with this?"

"It was his idea."

'Boy!' Marcia realized, she had been missing something. Straughton, Straughton of the boa constrictor tongue. He still gave her the creeps. Smitty's romantic plan for an evening had suddenly lost ninety percent of its romance. "It was his idea for the three of us to go to Sausalito?"

"No, he wanted me to drive him up there, but I wouldn't go without you."

"Oh, thanks for including me." Still, this was something. Not all that much, but something. Marcia found herself stifling a laugh, she wasn't sure why. What a blockhead Smitty was. A loveable blockhead, but a blockhead just the same. She pictured their romantic meal, wine glasses raised, looking out over the water — her, Smitty, and of course Straughton.

Marcia suddenly shot to a sitting position, asking in a panic, "What day is today?"

"The twenty-second."

She wilted in relief. "Thank God you reminded me."

"Reminded you of what?"

"My father's birthday."

Smitty did not see how he had reminded her, but tonight he was perfectly willing to take any credit she would grant him.

"You've got to mail his present for me tomorrow. I won't have the time."

Smitty was more than glad, he was thankful to be of help. "No problem."

Marcia smiled as she thought about her father receiving the present. "It's his favorite wine, the right year and everything." She did not mention that the wine's being her father's favorite had something to do with her late mother, she wasn't sure exactly what. Marcia's eyes lit up as she told Smitty, "He hasn't found it in years. I check every wine shop I pass. I never expect to find it. This time I did, right down the street, the last bottle. It was covered with dust."

Seeing the happiness in Marcia's eyes, only now did Smitty realize how depressed she had been for the last few weeks. Her face was one he would never tire of. Smitty was sure of it, admitting to himself, 'I love her.' When she turned away and got out of bed, he did not want her to leave. "Where you going?"

"To wrap up the bottle."

There was a smile on his face as he watched her exit the bedroom. Then a thought came into his head. His smile drained away. His stomach tightened. He mumbled aloud, "Oh, shit." Smitty waited in dread, hearing the clinking of bottles in the cupboard, thinking, 'God, is she gonna freak out.' Finally, Marcia called his name, asking him to come. There was no anger in her voice. There couldn't have been. It was pure fear.

Marcia waited silently for him. The bottle of wine had to be somewhere in the apartment. She had told him distinctly not to drink it. He couldn't be that irresponsible, that selfish.

Smitty walked into the kitchen experiencing a sense of dread he had not felt since childhood. The deed had been done. The damage irreparable. There was no way out.

Marcia stared calmly at him, wanting to believe in him. Fear in her voice, she asked softly, "Where is the wine?"

Smitty had to force himself not to lower his head as he mumbled, "We drank it."

She just stared at him in disbelief.

Smitty found the hurt in her eyes excruciating. Tears began to roll down her face, faster and faster. He had never seen her cry before. He hated to see women cry. He hated to see anyone cry. Ordinarily he would have looked away. Not this time. He forced himself not to. Some women looked so pathetic when they cried, ugly even. Not Marcia. She looked just as beautiful. Smitty wanted with all his heart to stop her tears, knowing there was no way. Finally, Marcia collapsed into a chair, looked down at her own lap. Smitty did not have to see her cry anymore. Still, he had to listen to her sobs, standing there silently for a good long time.

Finally, Marcia asked, with such obvious deep down

disappointment, "How could you do it?"

Smitty felt like a rat, but said anyway, "Screw did it. He opened the bottle."

Still looking down at her lap, Marcia, for the first time, spoke in anger. "Screw broke down the door, tied you up, and opened my father's wine!"

With little confidence it would make a difference, Smitty said, "We were out on the front steps. I sent Screw up for a bottle of the cheap piss I bought. He came down with that, opened already....With the cork floating inside."

Marcia, still with her head down, refusing to look at Smitty, thought about how the bottle got opened, pictured it.

Smitty added demurely, "It was delicious."

These words stunned her. Was Smitty trying to compliment her, comfort her? Was he that big an idiot? This was a question she did not care to think about, not right then anyway. Her thoughts returned to Smitty's explanation of how the bottle got opened. It had nothing to do with selfishness. Could she have expected him to remember that her bottle was with the cheap ones? Maybe not. Then sending Screw up to get the wine wasn't that irresponsible. It was all just an accident. She could accept that. Yet there was one very important thing she could not accept, and she made that very clear with the tone of her next question. "Why...didn't...you tell me?"

For Smitty, there was nothing to say but the truth. "I forgot."

The tears that had slowed started coming faster than ever. Of course he couldn't see them, with Marcia looking down. But he could hear her sobs. Smitty then did something he had never done for any woman. He dropped to his knees, placing his hands on her knees. "I'll make it up to you, I promise. Tell me how."

"You can't," she sobbed.

Smitty couldn't imagine how he could either. Something inside of him said, "Well, if you can't make it up to her, get off your fucking knees." Yet something far stronger was saying, "You did her damage, damage she never deserved....If it'll make things right, lay on your back and piss all over yourself." Smitty decided he had to try again, but he didn't know what to try, didn't have a clue, finally pleading, "Is there anything I can do? I'll do anything you say."

Marcia slowly got control of her tears. Still not looking at him, she began to nod.

Grabbing the chance, Smitty asked, "What? What can I do?"

Marcia's answer was, "Don't talk to me."

*****

'The hell with Susan!' thought Marco, walking home from the library. There was determination on his face and in his step. 'The hell with that bitch!' He had been sitting all by himself, doing research. This cute little freshman from France walked by and immediately turned around. "Are you Monsieur Marco?" she asked.

The "Monsieur" business and the star struck look on her face threw him off. He almost answered No. When he did answer in the affirmative, star struck turned to awe-struck. Looking at her adorable French face, Marco felt like a rock star, a Beatle even. She began to tell him how much she admired all he was doing, which lately was nothing at all. His mind searched fruitlessly for something to say that would keep her from walking off.

In the middle of listing all the wonderful things she had heard and read about him, she interrupted herself to ask breathlessly, in a sexy French accent, "May I sit down?"

"Of course," Marco replied, now realizing that asking her to sit down was exactly what he should have done in the first place. 'Must remember that next time.' What a wonderful change it was, hearing compliments from a woman, being built up instead of being torn down. The cute little thing was coming on to him. It was obvious. Marco stared entranced, so content to just look at and listen to her, that he had no desire to speak. The French girl finally talked herself out. There was an awkward silence before she stood to leave.

Marco pondered how to get her phone number, as if this involved some complicated process instead of just asking for it.

She interrupted his pondering to say, "I would like to help sometime. I will leave you my number." She wrote it down and handed Marco the paper. "Or if you want to talk some time."

Marco interpreted her last sentence as, "If you want to take me to bed sometime." Watching her walk away, he thought,

351

'"Sometime"? What's wrong with right now.' Of course he thought it too late to say it. But he had her phone number. Marco looked at the paper. Above the number was the name "Michelle". 'Pretty name,' he thought, the Beatles' song echoing in his mind.

Marco was humming Michelle as he unlocked his front door. The house was a mess. He'd have to straighten it up a little before inviting Michelle over. Marco switched on the TV and turned it up loud to catch the news. He then headed for the bedroom to dump his shirt and pants. What he saw there was so unexpected as to stop him cold. Susan's cat, Killer, was napping comfortably on his pillow, as comfortably as if she had never left. Susan had come back to him. Marco's sense of relief was so great, it surprised even him. He had forgotten how much he wanted her.

Marco quickly checked the house, every room, every closet, and even the back yard. No Susan. The house was exactly as he had left it except that the cat's dish and water bowl had returned to their place, and half a bag of Killer's food was atop the kitchen counter. To Marco, every act contained intent and meaning. He always had some inner need to know this meaning. The closer an act infringed upon his existence, the more important to know. No one had ever possessed Susan's sadistic knack for confounding him, no one had ever come close. Pondering the meaning of this latest act, while the news blared from the television, Marco got an idea. He practically ran to the bedroom closet. Sure enough, his fear materialized. More of Susan's clothes were missing, and there was a new pile of dirty laundry on the floor. Okay, this explained why she had come back, but why would she leave her damn cat? Just to irritate him? No, there had to be a better reason.

Marco stared at Killer. The cat sensed this. Its eyes opened to shoot Marco a condescending glance before slowly closing again. Marco's anger towards Susan amplified his hatred for Killer. "Now it's just you and me, bitch. We are going to come to an accommodation!' This accommodation was delayed by Marco's train of thought turning off onto a sidetrack. Technically, the word bitch applies to female dogs, not cats. Yet when it came to being a bitch, no female dog could compare with cats, male or female. Susan could, but no dog. This seemed an injustice to female dogs. A failing of language. Marco suddenly realized his train of thought was a failing of concentration. Or was he just stalling, putting off his showdown with Killer? No, Marco decided, stepping up to the bed.

Killer did not raise her head from her paws, but she did open her eyes and keep them open, staring up at Marco.

Marco did not flinch, demanding, "Bitch, get off my pillow!"

Killer didn't budge.

Marco raised his hand.

Killer sprang to her feet, hunching her back and spitting.

Marco faked an open-handed slap.

Killer held her ground, hissing even louder.

Marco was pondering his next move, perhaps yanking the pillow out from under Killer, when the blaring television captured his attention. The repeated word "bulletin" drew him back into the living room like a magnet. The announcer said, with all the import he could intone, "Pamela Kane, Berkeley student and newspaper heiress, has been kidnapped from her apartment. Reliable sources say the police believe this is the work of the Siamese Liberation Army."

*****

Smitty had completely forgotten about the trip to Sausalito until he heard Straughton's knock. Marcia had slept on the couch the previous night, stayed away all day, and refused to talk to Smitty when she returned, refused to even look at him. No way was he up for a drive to Sausalito. 'Don't owe him shit.' Reluctantly, he opened the door. "Sorry, Man, can't do it."

Seeing Smitty's frown, Straughton put on a grin from the opposite end of the spectrum. "My Man, certainly you can. Just put your mind to it."

Smitty jerked his head back towards the bedroom. "Got a little problem. She won't go."

Straughton kept his smile. "Then it's just you and me!"

Smitty shook his head. "Can't leave her."

Straughton took a step to get around Smitty, saying, "I'll talk to her."

Smitty held up his open palm in front of Straughton's face. His expression made words unnecessary.

Surprised, yet far from nonplused, Straughton said, "Then you ask her...one more time."

Smitty had no desire to go to Sausalito, no desire to ask Marcia to go. Yet he had no respect for people you could not depend upon. And here he was, punking out on Straughton, leach that Straughton was. 'Hell,' he told himself, 'Maybe she'll go,' damn certain that she wouldn't.

Smitty went into the bedroom to find Marcia lying on the bed fully dressed except for her shoes. It hurt to see her so sad, so damaged. And he had done that damage. She had never appeared more beautiful, so full of soul. He ached to lie down next to Marcia and put his arms around her. Yet he was too numb to move, almost too numb to speak. 'This ain't gonna work.' Finally, he said, "Marcia, you know how sorry I am....I told Straughton I'd drive him to Sausalito. Come with me so I don't have to back out."

Marcia turned on her side, away from him, drawing up her knees.

Smitty stood there a moment before walking towards the bed. When he was just a step away—

Marcia said softly, evenly, "Don't touch me."

Smitty admitted to himself right then that there was only one way to end this, with him on his back pissing all over himself. But he'd have to wait a day or two — for her to calm down and for him to store up enough piss. Smitty left the bedroom.

"No dice," he said to Straughton.

"Then you and I will go."

Smitty applied the salve of irony. 'Hard to say No to someone who knows the difference between "I" and "me"?' Yet he did, shaking his head.

"My Man, leaving her alone for a few hours might be just the thing."

'Possibly,' thought Smitty. Of course the opposite might also be true. Still, for him, getting away for a while sure would be a relief. Smitty had never realized you could feel so in-the-way in your own apartment.

Where words were the weapons, Straughton was loath to admit defeat. Searching for the right ones, he happened to slip a hand into his pocket. There he came upon an unknown object, paper wrapped around something. Removing and opening it, Straughton saw the pills he had purchased from Surfer.

"What are those?" asked Smitty.

Straughton saw his opening. He had a hunch the pills were Quaaludes. "Just what you need. Something to relax you."

"They're good?" Smitty asked, not really interested.

"The best," Straughton replied, popping one into his mouth. He held another out to Smitty in his open palm.

Smitty shook his head No.

Straughton continued to offer the pill. "You need to get out for a while."

Smitty felt trapped — by his claustrophobic apartment and his depressed mind. The pill in Straughton's open palm offered a temporary refuge from both. 'What the fuck.' In one motion, he took the pill and tossed it down his throat.

"Come on," said Straughton.

"Wait a minute." By the time Smitty got into the bedroom, he had himself convinced that Marcia was as uncomfortable with him around the apartment as he was being there. Marcia was lying the same way he had left her. "I have to drive Straughton up to Sausalito. May be back late." He almost added, "I love you," but something stopped him.

*****

When Marcia heard Smitty lock the door on his way out, she wasn't sure how she felt. She did experience a slight sense of relief about having the apartment to herself for a few hours. Still, Smitty had disappointed her again. Now it was as if he were running away from his punishment. Not that she really wanted to punish him. She wasn't sure what she wanted, maybe to move out and get away from him, for a while anyway. She would probably stay, but she wasn't sure. Even if they weren't living together, they could still see each other. Yet the truth was she didn't feel like seeing anyone. Maybe men just weren't worth the trouble, at least not right now.

Smitty wasn't the only thing on her mind, certainly not the most disturbing thing. What was she going to do about The People's Crash Pad? Her idea had not merely failed, it had transformed into a nightmare. The People's Crash Pad, meant to protect young children, was turning them into prostitutes. Yet what could she do?

Delores would have to go. Muhammad and his friends too, of

course. But how would she get rid of them? There had to be a solution. Every problem had one, including this one. Even if she walked away from the crash pad — she'd thought about that too — she would have to stop what was going on there first. It was evil. And she was responsible. No one in the world was more responsible.

'What else could go wrong?' she wondered, getting out of the bed. The kitchen was a surprise — neat and fairly clean, Smitty's idea of spotless, which she would settle for right now. There wasn't even a dirty spoon in the sink, not to mention a plate. A faint smile came to her lips as she thought, 'Poor Smitty, the blockhead'. Then she remembered what "Poor Smitty, the blockhead" had done. The smile faded from her lips.

Marcia hadn't even tried to find another bottle of wine. She was too disappointed to look for any present. Even if she found one tomorrow, it would not reach home in time. More than once since she had purchased the wine, Marcia had fantasized about the phone call with her father when he opened her present. Now she would just telephone to wish him a happy birthday. It would be hard making that call, thinking about the call she had wanted to make.

These thoughts reminded Marcia of another call she hated to make. She hated it enough to again think about walking away from The People's Crash Pad, just quitting. Marcia did not like the sound of that word. She wasn't a child anymore. She was a woman. And women weren't quitting. They were standing up for their rights. She saw it all around her. As much as she hated to hear the oh so logical nonsense that poured forth from Delores' mouth, she would force herself to phone, to see if Delores needed any supplies. It was either work with Delores for now, or quit and walk away. That was the choice, and Marcia refused to quit.

She dialed The People's Crash Pad. One of the kids answered. "May I speak to Delores please?"

"She doesn't live here anymore," said the girl.

A debilitating tremor shot through Marcia as she gasped, "What?" Her knees weakened and she wilted into a nearby chair.

"Delores moved out."

She had to say something, anything. "What happened?" Marcia asked, as if it made a difference.

"She came back from the hospital with a cast on her arm. Just packed her things and left."

Marcia hung up the phone, too stunned to talk. What would she do now? She looked around for Smitty, who of course wasn't there. She would have talked to him then, said what's past is past, said they'd start off new. But where was Smitty when she needed him? On his way to Sausalito, having a good time. Slowly, surely, a determined expression came to her face. "Well, what's done is done."

*****

The headlights bore an eerie, endless tunnel of light into the darkest of darkness, illuminating nothing but two-lane blacktop. Above, an infinity of sharply sparkling stars spread throughout the heavens. Smitty stared wide-eyed through the windshield. The blacktop led him towards these stars, as if, in the distance, the road somehow split off at a tangent from the curved surface of Earth, projecting straight out into space. Awed yet relaxed, he enjoyed the wonder of it all, the pleasure of driving through the cosmos.

Smitty gazed at the dotted white lane markings. They reminded him of the dotted line along the edge of a big cracker box. He saw a huge thumb, nail pointed down, dig into the dotted line, slicing the blacktop in two, just the way he used to slice open the outside wrapper on a box of Saltines. Never, in the countless times he had seen dotted lines, had he ever seen one so distinctly. How reassuring it was in its endless certainty, forever slipping behind yet dependably appearing up ahead. And our gently spinning planet was covered with them, wherever there were roads. Perhaps they even crisscrossed other planets. Or perhaps our earth was unique, known throughout the universe as the pinstriped planet. Smitty pictured himself in some intergalactic bar, buying drinks for the house — Cyclops's, Triclops's, and other acne differentiated alien life forms. "This round's on me," he calls out, "Space traveler from the pinstriped planet." The idea brought a grin to his face. Suddenly aware of it, he felt silly, and the need to be serious.

Still, there was no law against driving in space. And it was so effortless compared to driving on earth. The beautiful dotted line stayed the exact same distance to his left. He wasn't even steering. Just then he caught the wheel moving. His hands must be steering by themselves.

Out of nowhere came something that made Smitty's jaw drop. Mouth agape, he stared ahead in wonder. A ball of the whitest, brightest light he had ever seen came hurtling towards him from outer space — a gigantic shooting star. Could this be a message from another world? Perhaps one just being born? Never had a shooting star come so close, so directly at him. Long rays of rainbow hued light burst away from it in pulsating flashes. The star kept hurtling towards him, yet Smitty felt no fear, knowing without thought that it would pass just to his side, knowing also that it was merely the headlights of an oncoming car. Slowly and surely, the light divided into two, like some crazy psychedelic amoeba.

"Wow!" He asked Straughton, "Did. You. See. That?"

"Did I!" Straughton replied in disbelief, "A double comet."

"Exactly," Smitty agreed. He liked the idea of a comet even better than that of a shooting star. "Hey, what is this stuff were on?"

After a pause, Straughton replied, "I am not quite sure yet."

Smitty wondered if he had heard correctly. It seemed that at least one of them should know what drug they were doing. "Now I'm not complaining," Smitty assured him, "But why didn't you take it to the Free Clinic?"

Straughton's eyes lit up. He spoke with rare gratitude in his tone. "I knew there was something I forgot to do today!"

Smitty was glad to have been of help, but there was still something vaguely disturbing about their current situation.

"Another comet," Straughton said in awe.

"Where?"

"From behind.…It's red."

'Outa sight!' thought Smitty. He fought the urge to turn around. That would be dangerous. He was driving. He had to keep watching the dotted line.

Straughton said, "It's blinking." After a moment, he corrected himself with the more descriptive term, "Flashing."

Between the for some reason disturbing word blinking and the for some reason even more disturbing word flashing, Smitty got a brainstorm. He would be able to safely see the red comet by merely looking into the rear view mirror. He did. The flashing light was the brightest ruby ¬red he had ever seen. Though unbelievably gorgeous, there was definitely something ominous about it. The realization why slowly and surely dawned upon him. Smitty now knew exactly what the gorgeous light was — a pretty red bubble gum machine on the dashboard of a cop car. Seeing one in your rear view mirror was not generally considered good fortune. He knew that.

His stomach contracted to the size and hardness of a walnut as—

Straughton said, "I'm afraid it's an officer of the law."

Smitty lost hope. They both couldn't be wrong. What they both could be, was in very serious trouble, especially the one driving, which happened to be him. Smitty felt a need for advice. "What should I do?" He waited endlessly for an answer, staring mesmerized into the rear view mirror at the gorgeously flashing red light. Flashing sure was the right word.

Straughton's answer was a good two and a half light years in coming. Still, his thoughtful, logical tone seemed to justify the wait. "This wonder drug we're on...whatever it is...is not meant for car chases."

'This is true,' thought Smitty. But the dope they were on, whatever it was, sure wasn't meant for conversations with cops either. "Uh, what should I do?"

"I suggest we pull over."

Smitty asked dejectedly, "Do I have to?"

Straughton, as if to take himself off the hook, added, "I do not claim this is a great suggestion. Just the best I can come up with at the moment."

Smitty was far from floored by the brilliance of Straughton's advice. Still, he could not come up with an alternative. Smitty then experienced a minor epiphany — 'This dope, whatever it is, sure ain't meant for thinking either.' Yet it didn't seem to hinder the imagination. Smitty pictured the silhouette of his head through the car's rear window. Instantaneously, he pictured that window disintegrating in a fusillade of bullets. That settled it. Smitty slowly pulled over to the shoulder of the freeway. The car seemed to stop. Smitty checked the speedometer to make sure. The needle was on zero all right. So far, so good. "Hey, what's the speed limit?"

Straughton answered immediately. "Seventy."

Smitty was surprised and impressed that Straughton had known.

He then realized that he too had known, and had asked the wrong question. 'No harm done.' All he had to do was ask the question he had meant to ask. He did. "How fast was I going?"

Straughton shrugged. "I assure you, I have not a clue....Never did I receive the impression that you were speeding."

"And I was driving okay, right?"

"Quite skillfully," Straughton assured him.

"Then what should I say?"

"That of course depends upon what the officer asks." Straughton realized his answer had not been very helpful. He sincerely wanted to be helpful, for his own sake as well Smitty's. Suddenly, his blank mind exploded in a flash of intellect. Yes, there was a way out. Saved! Straughton had remembered something he'd learned long ago from television, from all the cop shows. Or was it the lawyer shows? "You do not have to incriminate yourself."

"Huh?" Smitty asked, not in the least relieved.

"The cardinal rule in this type of situation is not to incriminate yourself."

Smitty couldn't argue with that. In fact, this seemed very good advice, until it occurred to him, 'Good advice for a Mafia boss.' Smitty decided to discuss the matter further. "Take the Fifth Amendment with the Highway Patrol?"

"No, no need for the Fifth. Just choose to remain silent until you talk to your lawyer."

"Lawyer? I don't have a lawyer. I don't want a lawyer."

Straughton heard footsteps. "There is a strong possibility you will change your mind....Remember, do not incriminate yourself...or me."

Smitty straightened his back. 'Act normal,' he warned himself, just as another set of headlights did their twin comet light show straight at him. 'Wow!' he thought, but immediately, 'No time for that.' And there wasn't. He sensed the highway patrolman's presence. Smitty slowly turned his head towards the window. Yep, there he was, his stomach just outside the driver's door, his slight paunch bulging over his belt, his too tight shirt tugging on its row of buttons, his chest with a badge on it, and then, looking way up, Smitty saw his chin, and above that the silhouette of his hat. This was one very big cop. This was one very serious situation. 'I'm fucked,' he thought, more resigned than frightened.

Smitty straightened his back further, again telling himself, 'Act normal,' and then, 'Don't incriminate yourself.' The cop didn't move, didn't say a word. 'Doing okay so far.' Despite his dread, Smitty wanted very much to see the expression on the cop's face, to know exactly where he stood with this very big cop. The cop began to bend slowly at the waist. Soon he would know. The cop's face descended down from the heavens, towards Smitty, who cringed in fear, the words, "Don't incriminate yourself," repeating themselves in his mind like a mantra. The cop's face stopped two feet from his own. Surprisingly, it was a very calm face, without a hint of anger. The expression was serious in a studied sort of way. There was no meanness in it.

Finally, thankfully, the cop broke the silence, asking calmly and slowly, "Son...do you know how fast you were going?"

Smitty relaxed a little. There was fatherly understanding in the cop's tone. Perhaps he had a son just like Smitty...also a college student...maybe just as zonked. Well, that was pushing it. Still, maybe the cop wouldn't arrest him, just give him a ticket. Smitty started to relax when a warning ricocheted through his soft fuzzy brain, jolting him like an electric shock — 'Don't incriminate myself.' His dope addled mind searched for the politest way to say, "I'll have to confer with my lawyer before answering that."

'What lawyer?' he suddenly asked himself. He didn't have a lawyer. The cop's voice had been surprisingly calming. Yet how could Smitty answer his question without incriminating himself. He suddenly realized how. His mind was working fine, sharp as a razor despite the dope. Smitty would merely tell the truth. He looked the cop straight in the eye, his forthright honesty obvious to the world, answering, "I don't know."

The cop's calm, serious expression remained unchanged. He stared deep into Smitty's eyes, as if gauging the depths of his soul. Smitty stared back in all sincerity. Zonked-out or not, he had told the truth. Still, he would feel more comfortable if the cop would go ahead and say something instead of just staring at him.

Finally, the cop spoke, again softly and with a fatherly patience. "Take a guess, son. How fast do you think you were going?"

'Uh-oh.' As patient and understanding as this cop seemed, he just wasn't going to take, "I don't know," for an answer. 'The important thing is not to incriminate myself.' But taking the Fifth Amendment just didn't seem like that good an idea. Smitty looked into the cop's eyes. They were very calm and gentle. Smitty could see tiny sparkling stars in them. Shit, he had to say something. Maybe if he incriminated himself just a little. A speeding ticket would be very nice, considering. Smitty wanted to please this cop. He spoke calmly, sincerely, asking a question more than answering one. "Seventy-one…miles per hour?"

The cop appeared hurt as he slowly shook his head.

Smitty realized his failure to know how fast he had been driving had deeply disappointed the cop. Guilt took hold. Smitty was determined to be straight with this understanding police officer, who was waiting so patiently at such a confusing time. Well, he supposed he could incriminate himself just little more. "Seventy-two?"

Again the cop slowly shook his head. "Son…would you like to take one more guess."

Smitty had absolutely no desire to take one more guess. Still, he had no desire to offend this nice, huge cop, who by his mere presence was scaring the shit out of him. Smitty hesitated, building up his courage, struggling to ignore the consequences, forcing himself to make a serious attempt at a guess, finally, saying meekly, "Seventy-five."

Again the cop slowly shook his head, but he did something more. He moved his huge face closer until it was just inches away. He stared patiently at Smitty, again peering into the depths of his soul, trying to understand him.

Smitty waited for the cop to speak. He kept waiting, for light years, eons. During the endless silence, entire galaxies progressed from birth to extinction. Smitty felt the weight of this silence upon him. He could endure it no longer, and only he could end it. He'd do so with a question, a question whose answer was completely irrelevant to him, whose only purpose was to end the interminable silence. Meekly he asked, "Officer, how fast was I going?"

There was no change in the cop's expression, except for the slow opening of his huge cavernous mouth. First his lips spread exposing a set of enormous white teeth. And as the lips spread further and further, the teeth grew larger and larger, until they weren't even human teeth, they were those of a horse. And then the teeth slid slowly apart, the upper ones rising like a huge white garage door. Behind this door there was nothing, nothing but the endless blankness of space. Smitty felt himself floating upward, being drawn slowly and relentlessly into this huge black hole. He held on to the steering wheel like a lifesaving ring. And then something rose up out of the darkness of that black hole. Smitty recognized it. It looked just like one of those huge disgusting cow tongues in delicatessen display cases, yet infinitely larger. It was the cop's tongue. Smitty knew that, and also that the cop was going to speak, going to answer his question.

And the cop did speak, still calmly and slowly, but this time with a tone indicating he was telling Smitty something that he should already know. He spoke distinctly so Smitty would be sure to understand him, so even a three year old child would have been sure to understand him. He spoke as if each letter in each word were a syllable in itself, and each of these syllables were so slowly drawn out that Smitty actually saw them issue forth, spelled letter by letter, as in a cartoon, from the cops huge black hole of a mouth. And the four words the cop so patiently and unequivocally conveyed to Smitty were, "T.W.E.L.V.E. M.I.L.E.S. A.N. H.O.U.R."

Smitty was very surprised. By himself, he never would have guessed, or even come close. Could there be a mistake, perhaps a radar malfunction? The cop's mouth was now closed. He was waiting for a reply, or some sort of reaction. Smitty pondered the situation, trying to delve to the bottom of it. He knew he should say something. Thoughts about not incriminating himself had been swept from his mind. He was about to say the most sensible thing he could think of, something relevant, something to indicate to the cop that his mind was working flawlessly, unimpaired by any chemical substance. He was about to say something that would show he had been paying perfect attention. He was about to say, "Then I wasn't speeding."

Yet just before he could, a shout came from the patrol car behind them. "Harry, bad wreck, ten miles south. Let's go!"

The cop glanced back at Smitty. "Stay here," he ordered, then ran back to his patrol car.

Smitty and Straughton watched over their shoulders as the cop car scratched out across the blacktop and median strip in a U-turn.

Smitty looked to Straughton. "What do you think?"

Straughton said exactly what Smitty wanted to hear. "Floor it!" Gravel was already flying when Straughton added, "Take the first off ramp…and keep it over twelve miles an hour."

*****

The bang was deafening. Marco, awaking in fright, shot to a sitting position. Susan and the Siamese Liberation Army had broken down the front door. They were here to kidnap him, the way they had kidnapped Pamela Kane. 'Wait! Is this just a nightmare?' These thoughts and others raced through his mind in the seconds between the sound of his front door bursting open and the shout, "Don't move! FBI!"

'What should I do?' Marco asked himself. Well, he shouldn't move, not if he didn't want to get shot. And if he didn't move, he couldn't very well do anything, even turn on the light. Trembling in fear, he listened to people running through his house, more shouts of, "Don't move! FBI!" Marco sat frozen in his bed — waiting. For what? A bullet in the head? Every second seemed an eternity. A beam of light hit the wall. The flashlight quickly swept the room before coming to rest upon him.

An FBI agent, armed with a rifle, shouted, "Got one, white male!" In a quieter, disbelieving tone, he asked, "You sleep with a cat?…What kind of man are you?"

Behind Marco, Killer was sitting up on his old pillow. Marco had surrendered it and taken over Susan's side of the bed. At the time, this had seemed the intelligent, civilized thing to do, as opposed to starting up the old feud again. Now Marco began to question his decision.

Other agents continued the search for a few minutes. One by one, they ended up in Marco's bedroom. He sat silently in his pajamas, blinded by the flashlight. An agent finally asked, "All right, Marco, where is she?"

Another agent cut in, "Wait a minute. Marco, you have the right to remain silent. Anything you say can be used against you."

Marco replied logically, "In that case, I'll remain silent." Still trembling in fear, Marco surprised even himself with the calm, confident tone of his words. He had no clue that this tone did not

364

match the frightened expression on his face. The first agent to have spoken spoke again, trying a different tack to put him at ease. "We don't want you, Marco. We want your wife. Play ball with us, and you've got nothing to worry about."

Far from putting him at ease, Marco found these words dismissively insulting. Here he was, the man who had brought down the head of the California university system, the man who, with the snap of his fingers, could send thousands of protesters into the streets, who could turn any protest into a riot, and yet the FBI had no interest in him. No, they were chasing Susan, Genghis Con, and their band of idiots, a pack of incompetents who killed the county's first black Superintendent of Schools and the city's first oriental cop. Yeah, they kidnapped Pamela Kane, but so what? And so what that they got her father to print their childish manifesto in all his newspapers? Feeling slighted, a petulant expression on his face, Marco tried futilely to come up with just the right words to inform these ignorant federal agents with whom exactly they were dealing.

The agent misinterpreted Marco's lose for words as stubbornness. "In that case, Marco, we'll tear this house apart. It will take you weeks to put it back together again."

Marco was still searching for the right words. His failure to find them angered him more than the threat.

"Where is she?"

"Where's who?" Marco asked, playing dumb.

"Don't play dumb with us," warned the same agent. "Where's your wife?"

"I don't know." Deeply embarrassed by this fact, Marco hoped they thought he was lying,.

Another agent cut in, "Marco, murder and kidnapping are both capital offenses. Lie to us and you're on your way to the gas chamber as an accessory after the fact....Now where is she?"

Marco, stunned by the thought that he could spend the rest of his life in jail, mumbled, "I wish I knew." Sitting up in bed, in his pajamas, blinded by a flashlight, a circle of literally dressed to kill FBI agents staring down at him, Marco had already felt like a helpless fool. Admitting that he did not know where his wife was made him feel even more insignificant.

"Do you expect us to believe that?" asked the agent.

"Yes," Marco answered, part of him hoping that they wouldn't.

"Wanna play hardball, Marco? We'll play with you. Stand up."

Marco did.

"Put your hands behind your back."

Being handcuffed was not the pleasantest experience Marco had ever had, but at least the flashlight was not in his eyes. He glanced down to see if anything was peeking out of his pajama bottom. Not at the moment. All the agents except for the one asking the questions left the room. They began turning on lights and searching the house again. The remaining agent gave Marco the silent treatment, which had its effect almost immediately. Marco asked over his shoulder, "What do you want my wife for?"

The agent had had enough of Marco's playing dumb. He shoved him forward.

Marco landed face down on the mattress. He lay there plotting revenge in the form of a brutality complaint, when another agent called out, "Bring Pinky in here."

The agent grabbed Marco's arm, jerking him to his feet and into the bathroom. The agent that had called for him was wearing rubber gloves. In one hand he held a waste basket, in the other a tampon. "This your wife's?"

Marco, feeling violated, replied testily, "No, it's mine."

The agent, still holding up the tampon, stepped closer, "Comrade, you are aware that lying to a federal agent is a felony?"

Marco straightened his back. "Then I'll remain silent." He heard Killer meow, and looked down to see her rubbing up against the agents leg. He bent down and scratched his new friend's neck, whereupon Killer began to purr like a Harley Davidson. Marco congratulated himself on never having trusted that damn cat. No one could claim he wasn't a good judge of character.

The agent straightened up and called out the door, "Okay, Men, we're not getting any cooperation here. Let's take this place apart."

'What do I care?' thought Marco. It took only a few minutes of watching the agents do their work to show Marco how much he did care. They filled a cardboard box with every bit of writing they could find. Would he ever get it back? Much was personal, some very personal, musings he now regretted putting on paper. These thoughts would give them good laugh or two, or ten, or twenty. And there were also words they would find personally offensive.

'Good!' Marco then realized they could make him pay for everything he had written. From what he saw and the sounds from the other rooms, they were literally tearing his house apart. A feeling of nausea overcame him as he thought about the cost in time and trouble of putting it back together. Marco had never felt so brutally violated. He was seething when a grinning agent came over to him with an object he had found under some clothes in Susan's drawer. At first he thought it was a flashlight, but the end where the light should have been was oddly shaped and opaque. "Men, get a load a this," the agent called to his buddies.

Marco had never seen anything like it. 'What the hell is it?' He searched the agents' faces for clues. He found one — their obscene smiles. That had to be a damn good clue. Yet to Marco it provided no answer. His own ignorance was irritating enough, but being laughed at for who knows what was humiliating. 'What can it be?' he thought to himself.

Finally, the agent holding the object turned it on and it began to vibrate. "Guess this is yours too, Tampon Boy."

As the other agents laughed out loud, Marco finally figured out why. For a fraction of a second, he felt some satisfaction in this feat of intellect. The loud laughter cut that short. Marco wanted to jump into his bed and crawl under the covers. Before he had felt violated. Now he felt gang raped. And it was all Susan's fault.

*****

Smitty awoke to have his fears realized. What he had hoped was a chemically induced hallucination or a plain nightmare had been neither. He had returned from his and Straughton's aborted, drug-fueled drive to Sausalito still significantly under the influence. This was no condition to receive the kick in the head that awaited him. Marcia was gone. Her records and most of her stuff remained, but her books and at least a suitcase full of clothes didn't. Somewhere, deep in the back of his drug addled mind, he knew that finding and confronting Marcia in his present state would only make matters worse. There was nothing to do but crawl into bed and hope morning would prove it ain't so, Joe.

Morning proved the opposite. It was so. Marcia was gone. He had to figure out how to get her back. Using the telephone was not the way. Smitty dragged himself to the mirror for a reading on his condition. His reflection proved less than impressive. A shave and a shower would help, but would that be enough? Only one way to find out. He did, feeling somewhat better afterwards. Still, the bloodshot eyes were a disaster. For the immediate future, sunglasses would be a necessity. This would not be the optimum look for conversing with Marcia, but holding fire until he could see the whites of his own eyes was not an option. He'd wear his favorite shirt, the one she had embroidered for him. He'd wear the flashy Levi's she bellbottomed too. No way did they fit his mood, but he'd wear them anyway.

As Smitty approached his car, he strained his eyes checking for damage. He had no memory of any vehicular faux pas, but he had the feeling a lot must have happened on that drive that he didn't and never would remember. The feeling was strong enough to get him to circle the car twice before getting in. The front grill drew special attention. Fortunately, the only remains stuck to it were those of insects.

Smitty reached The People's Crash Pad with a good idea of how he would conduct himself and what he would say. Failure was not an option. He'd get Marcia back. He'd make things up to her. And he would be damn careful in the future. He'd do whatever he had to do. The first thing he had to do was open the front door. It was locked. He knocked. Whoever was answering the door slipped on the chain. What Smitty saw when that door cracked open made him forget all his plans, made him lose his cool. Muhammad's face brought back all the old animosity. The dirty thug was still there, had been all along. There was no quarter in Smitty's tone as he said, "Let me in. I want to talk to Marcia."

Without a word, before Smitty could react, Muhammad slammed the door in his face and locked it.

Smitty banged his shoulder into it twice, then thought better of the idea. He could hear Muhammad climbing the stairs. Maybe he was getting Marcia. Smitty decided to wait a few minutes. He tried to calm himself down. This was no time to start acting like a maniac. Yet that's exactly how he felt. The idea of Marcia living in the same place as Muhammad and his thugs enraged Smitty. He heard someone coming down the stairs. It didn't sound like a woman.

'Be cool,' Smitty told himself. He waited.

From the other side of the locked door came Muhammad's words, spoken in a told-you-so taunt. "She don't want to talk to you."

Smitty lost it. "Well, I wanna talk to her!"

"I told you, Cracka, she ain't gonna talk to you."

The indignity of speaking through a locked door, to someone he considered an ignorant thug, about a person who meant as much to him as Marcia, enraged Smitty. "She can damn well tell me herself!" Smitty heard Muhammad's footsteps going up the stairs. They seemed louder this time, Smitty assumed for his benefit. He hit the door with his shoulder. It didn't give. He hit it again. It still didn't give. Once again, and it gave a little. Encouraged he could break it down, Smitty really put his shoulder into the door, and it gave even more.

Marcia could hear what Smitty was doing even through her own closed door. She then heard steps going fast down the stairs, a lot of them. Marcia rushed to the top of the stairs to see Muhammad, Kedrick, Lashon, and some redheaded kid waiting near the door for Smitty to break in. The faces she could see had grins on them.

Muhammad taunted, "You makin' a mistake, Cracka!"

Smitty answered with another shoulder to the door.

Marcia still didn't want to face him, but fear of what might happen had her running down the stairs. "Smitty! Wait! Wait!"

He did wait, but no more words came from the other side of the door. "Marcia?"

"Smitty, I don't want to talk to you."

He said calmly, "Marcia, I'm not leaving till you do....Please, come outside."

"No, Smitty."

"Then I'm coming inside," he said calmly. Again Smitty put his shoulder to the door, and there was the sound of ripping wood.

"Smitty, please," she begged.

"Come out....Please," he said calmly.

Marcia noticed Muhammad smirking at her. Embarrassed, and ashamed for caring, she said flatly, "Smitty, go home and I'll telephone you."

"No."

"Then I won't talk to you at all, never."

Smitty thought hard about what to do. "When will you call?"

"In a half hour."

Again he thought hard and long. "Okay."

The drive back to his apartment was as frustrating as it was angry. He berated himself for failing her. He berated himself for leaving her at the crash pad, especially with Muhammad. And he berated himself, in a voice that did not even sound like his, for being "pussy whipped". It was an epithet he had used on a few of his friends, a way to make fun of their pathetic states. Until today, it had never been an appropriate description of him. Now it was, to a T. Well, so what? Marcia had gotten to him like no woman ever had. "Pussy whipped' he would be, just as long as he got her back.

Thinking about Marcia made him feel weak, pathetically so. Smitty forced himself to think about Muhammad instead. Feelings of anger replaced those of weakness. That was better, much better. He pictured himself breaking Muhammad's legs, imagined the sound of them cracking. Smitty smiled. He could take that phony punk, no sweat. He would take him. Smitty kept thinking about Muhammad all the way home.

Marcia telephoned as she said she would. Smitty picked up the receiver on the first ring. "Hello."

There was silence on the other end.

"Marcia, I'm sorry....I love you....I want you back."

"...Smitty, I just can't talk to you now. I need time to think."

"...How much time."

"I don't know."

"You'll meet me?"

"I don't know?"

"Will you call me?"

Marcia didn't reply.

"Will you call me?"

"Yes."

"When?"

"...I just don't know....In two weeks."

Smitty said evenly, "That would be torture?"

"Okay," she said quickly, "a week," and placed down the receiver.

*****

370

'Just what the doctor ordered,' thought Marco. He felt better than he had at any time since Susan had deserted him, better in fact than he had since a long time before. Sitting next to Marco on his living room couch was Michelle, his little French fantasy come true. He loved the way she looked into his eyes with that worshipping innocence. All it had taken was a short phone call and she had come running. Why had he procrastinated for so long? He certainly didn't owe Susan anything. She had abandoned him. And who knows what was going on now between her and Genghis Con? Marco did not want to think about that. And why hadn't she saved him the embarrassment and taken her vibrator with her? Marco didn't want to think about that either. He'd never caught her with it. Maybe she never used the damn thing. Maybe it was a gift. Maybe she was just keeping it for a friend. 'Thinks she's a big shot now, FBI's Most Wanted.' The hell with Susan.

Marco was now going to catch up on something that had eluded him when he was a freshman, freshman pussy. The question was, how to go about it. Should he just grab Michelle's hand and lead her into the bedroom. Or should he start with a sudden, passionate kiss. Perhaps he should take her face between his hands, and draw it closer until he was gazing right into her eyes. Subtlety might be more effective. He could place his hand upon her shoulder, playing the mentor she craved.

"All I wanted," he was telling Michelle, "was to make a small difference. The next thing I knew, I had started a revolution."

Michelle grabbed his forearm with both hands. She began running one hand up and down the inside of it. "I want to help."

'You're helping already,' thought Marco. Her hands might as well have been between his legs. There was something about French women, and it wasn't just the accent.

Her hands abandoned his forearm, and reached out to grab Marco behind his neck.

He found himself being pulled closer, until their faces were inches apart. 'Boy, this is going to be easy.'

"Please, let me help," Michelle begged. She pulled him closer, embracing Marco in a passionate kiss.

Marco found his hands on her shoulders, alongside her neck. He had placed them there reflexively, more in self-defense than lust.

Marco had never been raped before, not even close. Talking was out. She had him lip-locked. He decided to see what would happen if he tried to undo the top button of her blouse. Michelle did not seem to notice, not until he had her blouse completely off. That's when she started on his shirt, almost ripping it away. The next thing Marco knew, he was leaning back awkwardly over the arm of the couch, with Michelle kissing and biting him while practically perched upon his chest. His back was killing him, but pleasure in other places far outweighed the pain. Suddenly most of the pain was gone, as Michelle backed off far enough to start undoing his pants. Marco didn't like the feeling of the couch's rough upholstery. He had to get Michelle into the bedroom. But how? By dragging her there, that was how.

Marco worked his way out from under Michelle. With one hand holding his up pants, and his opposite arm across her shoulders, Marco led Michelle quite willingly into the bedroom. Of course they would have to share the bed with Killer, who was lying across the pillow he had abandoned to her. Marco debated whether having the entire bed to themselves was worth a fight with Killer. A glance towards Michelle cut the debate short. She had discarded her panties and hopped onto his side of the bed. She pulled him forcefully down on top of her. Marco skillfully dropped his pants on the way down, but they got caught around his ankles. It took some awkward kicking to rid himself of them. He had been optimistic enough to wear his favorite pair of boxer shorts, the ones with the hearts on them. Well, he sure didn't need them anymore. Marco awkwardly worked his way out of them.

Here he was, already lying in bed with this cute French girl, both of them naked. How easy it had been. And to think of all the time he had wasted being married to Susan. Let her be the FBI's Public Enemy #1. Marco thought about those arrogant FBI agents. The way they had laughed at him, especially about that vibrator. If only they could see him now. Marco was relishing that thought when another thought barged into his head. Maybe they could see him now. Of course they could. He had always assumed they were bugging his phone. That's why he disconnected it. He now realized that the FBI would not give up so easily. They must be bugging his house with microphones and cameras. 'The bastards!'

Michelle started to say something, but Marco placed his finger over her lips. He strained to hear the listening devices and the whirring of the cameras, quickly realizing that he probably wouldn't be able to.

"What's wrong?" Michelle asked.

Marco certainly wasn't going to tell her that the house was bugged, and that there were probably cameras too. Yet that was not the subject of her question. No, her question was more specific. His appendage of the moment had shriveled back to its normal size. Michelle was shaking it between two fingers, trying to bring the poor thing back to life. She was not succeeding. His meat was as dead as ground beef. Marco again scanned his bedroom, searching for the hidden cameras that were saving his present humiliation for posterity.

"I know what to do," Michelle said confidently. She worked her way down on him until his limp dick was in her cute little mouth.

Marco liked the idea, but its execution seemed to be doing little good. Still, at least she wasn't talking, being recorded. Maybe he should get out Susan's vibrator. But what if Michelle didn't know how to work the thing any better than he did? And maybe the batteries were dead. Did he have any spares in the house? Gee, if the French were all they were supposed to be, they probably never needed vibrators. Breaking one out would make him look inexperienced, even impotent. But that's exactly how he was looking. Inexperienced was better than impotent. But what if the FBI caught him on film using a vibrator? Anger consumed him, against the FBI agents who were now taking it all in and laughing at him, against Susan who had betrayed him by not just abandoning him, but by abandoning him to the FBI and their microphones and their cameras. He existed in a world of betrayal. Even his own penis was betraying him.

*****

Smitty finished off his sliced turkey, lettuce, and mayonnaise, on a sourdough roll. He then drained what remained of his large glass of ice water, which he had substituted at the last second for an about to be opened beer. Since Marcia had walked out on him, he had treated himself to a few too many midday beers. He did not want to make this a habit. All things in moderation, including booze, dope, and sex. Well, maybe not the last, but booze and dope for sure. Too much sex had never been his problem. Little chance it would prove so in the immediate future.

Smitty scanned the sad remains of his culinary orgy. He patted the old stomach in satisfaction. Well, it was time to clean up and do the dishes, in this case only one, made out of newspaper. He rolled his "plate" into a ball and squeezed it tight, all the while admiring the spotlessly clean table beneath. 'That's housekeeping,' he said to himself. An involuntary glance at the sink revealed it overflowing with dishes. He rationalized this sight with the thought, 'Keep the place too clean, everyone'll think I turned queer.' Only one final act remained, the failure of which could prevent his meal from going down as a 100% complete success. Smitty leaned back in his chair, carefully aimed his newspaper plate, and took a smooth, one-handed set shot at the garbage pail. Dead center. Swish.

Smitty's fist shot skyward as he gave out a loud, celebratory belch. Living alone had its advantages. A man could belch and fart whenever and as loud as he wanted. 'Who am I kidding?' he then asked himself. To get Marcia back, he'd cork both ends. 'Fucking A right, I would.' What he wouldn't give now to have her in front of him, squeezing into a pair of skintight Levis. Other women had done it before, thousands of them, but Marcia had turned it into her signature move, made all the rest look like amateurs. He could see her in his mind as clearly as if she were in front of him. Left foot forward, right foot back, hands at her sides gripping the waistband. She'd give that cute little hop into the air, just high enough to scissor her feet into opposite positions. With a tug on her waistband, her Levis would be another inch or two up her ass. A graceful toss of her head would fling the hair now in front of her face back over her shoulder. For the first time Smitty realized that the act involved some precise coordination. Hell, it should be an Olympic event, far more watchable than most of that gymnastic prancing. Marcia would be a shoo-in for a gold medal — tens across the board. Any fool suicidal enough to give her a 9.9 would have to deal with him.

And another thing, Marcia's little two-step was a hell of lot better than the dances those American Bandstand greasers came up with — The Mashed Potatoes, The Fly, and a dozen other ridiculous perversions he could not and did not want to remember. "'I'll give it an eighty-five. I liked the beat.'" It's a miracle the Republic survived them. Wonder what those greasers are putting their talents to these days? That's a question they should ask Dick Clark next time he's on TV. "Dick, I'm sure our audience would be curious to know, out of all those kids who used to dance on your program, how many of them went on to win Nobel Prizes?"

Smitty started laughing to himself, and then out loud, very loud, until he asked himself, 'Hell, am I going nuts?' Knowing damn well he was all alone, Smitty still glanced around his apartment to see if anyone was looking at him. 'Shit, better get out of here.' Yet he found himself immobilized by an inertia far stronger than his will to fight it off. Besides, there was no place he cared to go. Lately, Straughton had been treating him like his personal chauffer. This had begun to rub Smitty raw. Though at the moment, despite the rawness, Smitty would have appreciated one of Straughton's Off To See The Wizard field trips. This time minus the chemical additives. 'Where is that leach when you need him?'

As if in answer to Smitty's question, came a recognizable knock on the door. Smitty slapped his back pocket checking for his car keys. An hour later, Straughton's little field trip had turned into Straughton's epic scavenger hunt. The idea had been to meet with some chemist turned dealer, or vice versa, who had come up a new and improved mind altering drug. Straughton would get a story, and both he and Smitty would get some free samples. This seemingly fantastic idea, as most of them do in Berkeley, turned out to be a bad one. The chemist/pusher, not surprisingly, considering his mind altered state, was not where he said he would be. Unfortunately, he had left a follow-able trail. Smitty again found himself double-parked and waiting for Straughton, outside the fifth place that trail led them. The car was hot and Smitty was steaming. They were supposed to have given up if the fourth place hadn't panned out. Smitty, sitting with his teeth gritted, wondered again if Straughton was 'shitting' him about not being able to drive. From now on the leach could hire a cab.

And here he came, wearing that phony smile that gave no indication whether he had found the chemist/pusher/turd or not. Straughton slid into to passenger seat with a cheerful, "No luck."

Smitty took the news stoically, relieved that Straughton wasn't giving him directions for an additional leg to this scavenger hunt. He would have ignored them anyway. Smitty pulled out, heading back to his apartment, which, at least, he now found far more attractive than two hours previously when he desperately wanted to get out of it.

Straughton glanced over at Smitty to see a surly look on his face. You would think he understood that not every tip led to an article, or in Smitty's case, free dope. Still, Straughton perceived an immediate need to mollify his sole means of transportation aside from Honor Bikes. Smitty would surely value some words of wisdom as compensation enough for this mildly misguided adventure. "My Man, let this be a lesson to you. While pushers are an essential element of our society, one can never depend upon them."

Smitty found Straughton's words of wisdom more irritating than enlightening. His expression showed it. About to say, "Remind when we get home so I can write that down," Smitty caught himself, realizing that Strauton would.

Straughton, in serious fear of losing his chauffeur's good will, came up with another ploy to mitigate his anger. Smitty was an English major. He should be interested in an article Straughton had just read. Well not in its entirety, just the first one and half paragraphs. "I recently read about the novel being dead. How could something like the novel be dead? Was the novel ever alive?"

Smitty sat dumbstruck, thinking, 'Where the hell did that come from?'

To Straughton's surprise, his keen sense of observation detected even more anger in Smitty's demeanor. He took this as a further challenge. A first class journalist such as himself should be able to get anyone to open up. All now necessary was a direct question necessitating and unequivocal answer to pull him out of his shell. "You're well read. You read novels. Do you think the novel is dead?"

Smitty was inclined to remain silent, stewing slowly in his own juices. He couldn't. "I think anyone who thinks about horse shit like that is dead."

'Victory!' thought Straughton, this despite Smitty's tone, still pissed-off expression, and obvious insult. He sensed real progress and decided to press onward, abruptly switching to an alternate tack. "My Friend, you often state that the few remaining bars in Berkeley are always empty and depressing. I happen to be familiar with an establishment not two blocks from here, sure to be more to your liking."

Smitty had the urge to reply to this invitation with a curt, "Be glad to drop you there." However, waiting in the car had given him quite a thirst. And another thing, a short layover for a couple of beers would enable him to avoid the five o'clock traffic.

Straughton then sealed the deal with two words that seemed completely out of character — "I'm buying."

They had to park a block away from the bar. On the short walk over, Smitty actually found Oakland's gritty, gloomy sidewalks a relief from the Technicolor, kaleidoscopic riot that was Berkeley. The bar was the neighborhood type, barely noticeable from outside. Its spacious, timeworn interior was further dulled by a light haze of cigarette smoke. A full complement of neon beer signs along the walls and windows fought back valiantly against the afternoon gloom. Despite his appreciation for neon and its comforting buzz, Smitty was most pleased to see his favorite beer sign of all time, one that had gotten rarer and rarer over just the few years since he had acquired a false ID. It hung from its deserved place of honor, the center of the ceiling, lighted from within — a revolving Schlitz globe of the world. The sight of it alone would have made him forget the frustration of Straughton's scavenger hunt. Smitty now felt securely within his comfort zone, having entered an almost forgotten world, one he had missed without realizing it.

Then a familiar song came on the juke box, familiar despite the fact that he hadn't heard it since he was ten or twelve years old — "If I could have a mountain made of gold, and diamonds like the stars above…" There was something about the singer's voice he had always liked, that he still liked. What was her name? 'Rodgers…Eileen Rodgers!' Smitty was proud of himself for remembering. He remembered the song's title too — 'Treasure Of Your Love'. Now, listening to it, he experienced a calming forgotten pleasure, one from very long ago.

He and Straughton approached the bar, ordering and drinking on their feet. Even the beer itself tasted better than any he'd drunk in Berkeley. Yet the most appealing aspect of his surroundings were the patrons themselves. Smitty glanced around. The man sitting to his left had calloused hands the likes of which he hadn't seen since Cleveland. And the hands on the guy to his right were almost as calloused. These were serious working class people, only a few of them female. The few that were, were not the type you would look at as such, at least Smitty wouldn't. He did notice one man in a suit. "Hey, isn't that the crazy preacher, the one who stands by the university gate?"

Straughton glanced over, saying without surprise, "Holy Joe."

"What's he doing drinking a beer?"

Straughton shrugged. "Perhaps he's not Baptist....Papists drink like fish."

Smitty found something in Straughton's words amusing, but before he knew exactly what it was, a realization cut his amusement short. "Hey, that guy he's with, that's the one usually harassing him." Smitty's face lit up with amusement. "You think Holy Joe saved his soul?"

Again Straughton glanced over. "Hardly. That's his son, his permanent antagonist."

Confused, Smitty took another look. There was a strong resemblance. "They seem to be getting along now."

Straughton found himself surprised by Smitty's innocence. "My Dear Friend, it's all an act....If you were to come upon Holy Joe preaching, you would walk right by. Holy Joe arguing, being insulted, that's a matter of interest. For that you stop."

In the back of his mind, Smitty wanted to protest that he had never stopped. Yet he had, and had been completely conned. There was real hurt in his expression as he said, "Gee, in Berkeley, even the preachers are frauds."

Again Straughton was surprised by Smitty's innocence. "My Man, religion has never been without components of theater and artifice."

Smitty said exactly what he was thinking, "Where the hell are you coming from?"

Straughton had no idea what he meant. "Come again."

"Man, are you making excuses for them?"

"Is that necessary?"

The weirdness of their conversation was getting to Smitty. How could two people speaking simple words in the same language find it so difficult to understand each other. "They're fucking con men!"

Straughton thought hard, trying to understand Smitty's point of view. Again he glanced at Holy Joe and Son. "My Friend, look at the clothes they are wearing. And have you ever seen the car they drive?"

Smitty did and he had. If these two clowns were con men, you would think they could come up with a more profitable con.

Straughton continued, "They are trying to save souls."

Smitty searched his mind for a better explanation. His search failed. Staring hard at Straughton, he told himself that the man must be more complex than he had assumed, then realized that 'more complex than an amoeba' was not very complex at all. "Are you religious?"

Straughton thought this over. "I choose to believe there is an order to things."

Just as interesting as Straughton's answer, was the way he raised his chin high as he gave it. To Smitty, this seemed to indicate that this order Straughton believed in had himself placed very near the top.

"And you, My Friend, are you religious?"

Smitty shook his head.

"I should introduce you to Holy Joe. Perhaps the man can save your soul."

Smitty stifled a chuckle. "You know him?"

"Of course. I've written two articles about him.…Come, I'll introduce you."

Smitty shook his head No.

The bartender turned up the television behind the bar as an anchorman talked excitedly about a bank robbery. A number of the patrons got up to move closer to the screen.

"What is going on?" Straughton asked.

"The Siamese Liberation Army held up a bank in Los Angeles. I heard it on the car radio while I was waiting for you. The cops claim Pamela Kane was a willing participant."

Straughton stood. "I must see this." He picked up his beer and walked towards the TV.

Smitty did the same. "How do you like the way she made her

old man print her letter in his newspaper, calling him a fascist and explaining why she'd joined the Siamese Liberation Army?"

"Ah, only in Berkeley," said Straughton. He watched the security tape of the bank robbery. Sure enough Pamela Kane was holding a rifle, covering the rest of the gang. "I had assumed they made her write that letter." With the hand holding his beer, Straughton indicated the television. "Now I doubt it." For the first time, the TV showed pictures of the suspected members of the gang. A few people in the photos looked familiar. The last woman didn't, but her name certainly did. "That's Marco's wife."

Smitty was just as surprised as Straughton. "Bad picture of her."

They ordered two more beers and Straughton said, "Come, My Man, I will introduce you to Holy Joe."

Smitty, beer mug in hand, could not think of a reason to object. He followed Straughton over to Holy Joe, who greeted them with a smile and an out held hand to shake. "Roger Basil Straughton VI, praise the Lord."

Smitty stood impressed by Holy Joe's memory. He had forgotten Straughton's full name months ago. Smitty took a seat, leaned back, and let the others do the talking. After a minute or two, he found himself surprisingly interested.

Straughton said, "My Friends, apparently saving souls is a hard day's work."

Smitty saw the truth in this. Despite his amiable smile, Holy Joe looked tired, and his son more so. They fit in well among the working class patrons.

Holy Joe replied, "The Lord's work is never easy."

His son cut in, "And not always successful."

Holy Joe said, "Junior questions our methods."

"They're failing us," said Junior, "The cults recruit armies, enticing the weak with sex, false promises, and damnable lies — brainwashing them into zombies. Engaging in all the perversions of Sodom and Gomorrah, doing the Devil's work in the name of our Lord. They seek them out, reach them first, in every dark corner. And of the few we get to, fewer we save. Failure is painful. Our failures become their slaves."

Smitty craved to feed his own skepticism. So far he had failed to.

Straughton, trying to lighten the mood, said, "My Friends, you must have saved a few souls lately."

"Yes," replied Holy Joe, smiling, "One you know well."

"Who, may I ask?"

"Eldridge Cleaver."

Straughton could not believe what he was hearing. This chance meeting, preceded by a chain of spur of the moment decisions, was apparently leading him straight to an interview with Eldridge Cleaver. 'Goes to show, ninety percent of reporting is just keeping moving.' — "Cleaver is in Berkeley?"

"No, he's in Algiers," said Holy Joe with a smile.

Stunned, Straughton asked, "Then how did you save his soul?"

"By telephone."

'Back to square one,' thought Straughton. Cleaver's proximity had been too good to believe. Deflated, he still had to know more. "How did this come about?"

A beatific smile came to Holy Joe's face. "Through you, Roger. You were as much an instrument of the Lord as I myself."

Straughton would have been glad to share the credit, but he was still too deflated to appreciate this news, or even ask exactly how he too had come to be an instrument of the Lord.

Holy Joe wanted him to know. "Remember your interview with Eldridge. Since the day I read it, I knew that if I could just talk to that poor lost man, I could save his soul."

To Straughton, this explanation explained nothing. There was hardly a word in that interview that did not come straight out of Straughton's own imagination. Could Holy Joe's reaction be saying something enlightening about he himself as opposed to Cleaver. Quickly deciding he preferred not to go down that path, Straughton asked, "And you succeeded."

"Completely. Eldridge Cleaver has been born again as a Christian."

Straughton was entranced by the idea of this. "That vicious murderer of blacks and whites? How did you do it?"

"With the Lord's help. I caught Eldridge in a time of need."

"How so?"

"Let us just say that the law was catching up to him."

"But Algeria refuses to extradite him back here."

"That's a separate matter....To keep afloat the Black Panther Government in Exile, Eldridge was forced to organize a car theft

381

ring. They steal the cars in France, smuggle them to Algeria, and sell them there."

"The Algerians caught him?" asked Straughton.

"No, the Algerians were quite appreciative. After all, the cars were stolen in France, and Eldridge was quite generous when it came to graft."

"So what was the problem?" asked Straughton.

"The French caught on. But those cream puffs are too scared they'll antagonize their own Leftists. They're quietly pressuring the Algerians."

"To put Cleaver out of business?" asked Straughton.

"Yes," answered Holy Joe, "But the Algerians are just demanding more graft from Eldridge instead. The corruption is driving the poor man nuts."

Smitty sat wondering if he were the only person at the table who found it odd that a car thief would be complaining about corruption.

As if in answer to his thoughts, Holy Joe Jr. went on to explain, "Eldridge claims that when you're living with Arabs, you have pay people off for permission to wipe your own rear end. He says, with them, you can actually lose money stealing."

Straughton reflected, "One more way black people are driven to crime."

Smitty sat wondering if Straughton had any idea what he had said, deciding correctly in the negative.

Straughton's thoughts happened to be centered upon 'The Amazing Eldridge Cleaver' — street thug turned rapist turned murderer turned convict turned Black Muslim turned ex-con turned revolutionary turned Black Panther turned award winning best selling author turned intellectual icon of the New Left turned presidential candidate turned indicted felon turned fugitive turned Head of the Black Panther Government in Exile. Once again Cleaver had spiced up his résumé, turning into a car thief and smuggler and finally turning to Christ to be born again. Was there a turn upon life's path this man would fail to take? Could his turn into the arms of our Lord possibly be his last turn? Not if his past was any indication of his future. Straughton thought back to when he first met Cleaver. Who would have guessed that the personable thug and coldblooded killer would go on to positively redefine The

Renaissance Man? Or would negatively redefine be more correct? Both, probably.

Dizzy from trying so hard to get his head around all this, Straughton distracted himself with the mechanics, asking, "How did you get his phone number?"

Holy Joe's eyes lit up. "The Lord works in mysterious ways.…Junior and I were building this huge cross when my hand drill burned out. I was searching the Oakland Telephone Directory for the nearest Black and Decker repair shop. Instead I came across the listing for the Black Panther Government in Exile, Algeria. A clearer sign the Lord could not have granted me."

*****

Marcia moved into The People's Crash Pad intending to tread lightly the first few days. Muhammad had greeted her with a smile. It was not the most comforting or pleasant smile she had ever seen, but it enabled her to delay any confrontation until a time of her choosing. He even had two of the kids help clean up the mess Delores had left in her room. Marcia closed the door and immediately started rearranging the furniture more to her liking. She realized quite well that she did so to keep her mind off the imminent rearranging she would have to do outside her room.

The next morning, Marcia made a thorough check of the entire crash pad. She found no serious problems. There were only eight teenagers living there, six of them girls. They all seemed surprisingly well behaved, a little too well behaved. They also seemed wary of her, too wary. Of greater import, and to Marcia's relief, there were no Johns hanging around. Perhaps the prostitution had been Delores' idea, not Muhammad's. Marcia wanted very much to believe that.

Muhammad seemed to be taking the responsibility of running the crash pad quite seriously. There were some minor changes Marcia thought necessary. Despite the fact that two rooms remained empty, all eight teenagers were sleeping in the same room on four sets of bunk beds. Marcia wanted the boys and girls sleeping in separate rooms. Also, she found some of them still watching television at two in the morning. The TV set should be turned off at eleven, twelve at the latest. She could easily take care of both matters herself. Yet it seemed a good idea to see how Muhammad would handle them.

Muhammad took Marcia's instructions silently but with a nod. 'Well that was easy,' she thought. Marcia waited all day for Muhammad to move the boys to their own room. He didn't. At two in the morning she found half the kids still watching television. Marcia turned off the TV and quickly cleared the room. Both boys were up, so she moved them to their own rooms then and there. Muhammad had better learn who was running the crash pad, and he better learn fast.

Marcia spent the entire next day in her room. The need to catch up on her school work and study for a test was excuse enough. At one in the morning, getting ready for bed, the sound of the television finally drew her out. Half the teenagers were watching it. Placing herself between them and the screen, she said sternly, "I thought I told you no more TV after eleven o'clock."

The teenagers remained silent, glancing at each other, until Donna spoke out in a belligerent tone. "Muhammad said we could. He says he's running things."

Marcia felt it was time to put her foot down. As calmly as she could, she said, "The People's Crash Pad was my idea, and I'll decide how it will be run." She switched off the television and pulled out the cord. "If you want to stay here, you'll do exactly as I say. Now off to bed, every one of you." To Marcia's relief, the kids stood and headed for their rooms. Marcia followed behind to make sure they got there. That's how she found out that Muhammad had moved the boys back into the girl's room. She immediately moved them out again.

As tired as she was, Marcia was too upset to fall asleep. She lay in the dark trying to figure out to what purpose Muhammad had contradicted her. In any case, she had to find a way to get rid of him. She couldn't turn to Smitty, knowing that Muhammad probably still had C.C.'s gun. The police wouldn't get involved. Marcia thought about getting her own gun, forcing Muhammad out at gunpoint. And as she thought, Marcia heard the sound of someone sliding a key into her door lock.

Marcia froze in fear. Someone was walking towards her bed in the dark. She knew this had to be Muhammad. How she wished she had her own gun now. Muhammad walked slowly yet surely right up to her bed. He looked down upon Marcia and began to speak. Marcia's frightened, confused mind tried to figure out how he knew she was awake. Was there enough light to see that her eyes were open, wide open? Muhammad's words were not in the blustery, belligerent tone Marcia had come to expect. No, this Muhammad spoke confidently, calmly, coldly, and he was far more frightening.

"Get this straight. The People have liberated The People's Crash Pad. If you can't handle that, get out…get out before you wish you had."

*****

Smitty found himself alongside Rachel as they exited Instructor Bunker's class, "Literature as Reality". Smitty, almost against his will, copped another glance at her. She was more attractive just about every time he saw her. Her milkmaid looks were a turn-on. Yet it wasn't just her looks. Rachel radiated a uniquely good natured self-assurance, without a hint of arrogance. Aside from Marcia, she was the only girl in Berkeley who held any lasting interest for him. It now occurred to Smitty that in many ways Rachel was almost the exact opposite of Marcia. Could that be the added attraction? Whereas Marcia always seemed so serious, Rachel usually wore this amused, mischievous smile. The girl knew how to have a good time. Smitty wondered if she had a boyfriend. He had wondered before, yet had never asked her the right questions to find out. That would have been like cheating on Marcia. Not exactly cheating, but a step in that direction.

"What do you think he'll ask on the test?"

Rachel shook her head. "Beats me."

"It's half our final grade."

Rachel shrugged. "How about a ride to the gate?" She had somehow given so simple a request an erotic aura.

Smitty actually blushed. So she remembered that ride the first day he had met her. Well, so had he. Smitty sure wouldn't mind doing that again. Still, lately, Honor Bikes were hard to come by. He jerked his head towards the bike rack. "Let's track down some wheels."

Surprisingly, there were five Honor Bikes in the rack. Not

surprisingly, two were wrecks and three were chained to the rack. Smitty was shaking his head to Rachel when two ten-year-old black kids came walking up with a bolt cutter almost as tall as they were. They went to work, each holding a handle of the bolt cutter, then both holding both handles as they squeezed it shut and sliced a chain in two.

"What you guys doing?" Smitty asked.

Without looking up, already cutting loose another bike, one of them answered, "Liberatin' Honor Bikes."

As soon as the second chain fell, the kids mounted the bikes.

Smitty said, "Hey, how 'bout liberating this one?"

"Cost you a buck," said the same kid who had spoken before.

Taken aback and amused, Smitty said, "Hey, I built those bikes."

The kid looked him square in the eye. "A buck."

Smitty felt as if he were being mugged by a ten year old. A buck was a decent lunch.

Rachel, who was standing behind Smitty, said, "I'll pay."

Smitty, feeling cheap, pulled out his wallet and beat her to it. A minute later they were flying across Sproul Plaza towards the front gate of the university. Rachel sat far enough back on the crossbar for her hair to whip across Smitty's face. He loved it, thinking, 'Worth a buck, easy.' In too short a time, as far as Smitty was concerned, they reached the front gate. He came to a gradual, gentlemanly stop. To balance the bike, he had to hop off the seat still straddling the crossbar. This left him pressed right up against Rachel. She smelled nice. Hating to let her go, he let loose of the handlebar so she could hop off.

She did, but stepped back towards Smitty, standing quite close to him. "You want to study for the test together?"

The idea seemed brilliant, until thoughts of Marcia came into his head. No telling what would happen between him and Rachel. Still, he'd been waiting over a week for Marcia to phone as promised. He stood mute, staring at Rachel, thinking.

Rachel had waited long enough. She slapped Smitty on the ass, and the slap ended in a grab. "C'mon."

Smitty shot to attention, except for the grin on his face. "Okay," he blurted out, thinking, 'Who could say No to that?' The pressure was rising on the front of his pants. He copped a glance down to see how evident. Only an expert could tell. 'Thank God for Levis.'

"Want to go to your place?" Rachel asked.

For in instant, Smitty thought, 'Great,' then thought better of it. Rachel in Marcia's bed? No, he couldn't have that. "It's a mess," he lied, before remembering that he had spoken the truth.

"My place is small," she said.

"How many people are going to be there?" Smitty asked in all innocence.

Rachel stifled a laugh. She spun Smitty in the right direction. Her apartment was in back of and on the second floor of a private house, with its own stairs and entrance. Climbing those stairs, Smitty did have thoughts of Marcia and the guilt that came with them. Maybe nothing would come of this, he told himself. The memory of Rachel's grabbing his ass did not help to convince him. How long had it been since a girl had done that? Not since way before Marcia, and never one who was sober, that was for sure. He felt another stab of guilt for accusing Marcia of who knows what.

Rachel's pad did turn out to be small, barely twice as large as Sloan's broom closet. It was surprisingly neat and clean, with everything in its place, as if Rachel had gotten up a half hour before classes, just to leave her apartment perfect. She sure had Marcia beat when it came to housekeeping. Smitty felt another stab of guilt. Marcia would probably keep their place like this if he wasn't around to mess it up.

There were two chairs, both under a card-kitchen-diningroom table that was the only one in the room. Smitty plopped himself down on the couch bed. Rachel went to the little refrigerator and pulled out an ice tray. Smitty felt as if she had read his mind, watching her fill two tall glasses with ice. "Water or Coke," she asked.

"Water."

"My favorite drink," she said, handing him a glass.

"What do you think he'll test us on?" Smitty asked.

Rachel sat down next to him, closer than necessary. "I told you, beats me."

"Well, what do you think Bunker is trying to get across to us?"

Rachel answered immediately, "That he's a cool guy."

The truth in her answer staggered Smitty. He saw now that the entire course, every lecture, was Bunker trying to show how cool he was. The way he pandered to his students, kissed their asses even. Why hadn't Smitty seen that for himself? "You're right, but that won't help….What type of a test is it anyway?"

"They say he always gives a one question essay test."

"That's not fair."

"Well, the worst you can get is a B."

"Huh? How do you know?" asked Smitty.

"I heard from people who've had him….He gives half A's and Half B's. You didn't think I took his course for the strip show?" Rachel laughed at her own remark.

Smitty joined her. He put his hand on her shoulder, alongside her neck. "No, I kinda hoped you liked men."

"I do," said Rachel, still laughing. She gently banged foreheads with him, then their lips met.

Smitty pulled Rachel down on top of himself, which had both of them dangerously near the edge of the couch. He grabbed the foam backrest and tossed it away, turning the couch back into a bed and giving them more room. Yet only for a moment. The other side of the room was so close, that the backrest bounced off the wall and back on top of them. Already being in a good mood, Smitty and Rachel found this hilarious. He got rid of the backrest again, this time for good.

They traded a few kisses, more playful than passionate. Then Rachel started a game of Paddy Cake on Smitty's chest.

"Do me a favor," he asked.

Still playing Paddy cake, Rachel replied, "What?"

"Take my shirt off."

She laughed, asking, "Why?"

"Because I want to feel you up against me."

Rachel nodded. "I can understand that." She unbuttoned his shirt without a problem. Getting it off Smitty was another matter, with him on his back and her on his chest. Though Rachel's method was not the gentlest, it proved good for laughs. When done, she collapsed for a rest, her head on his chest.

The buttons to her blouse were along the back. Smitty tugged gently on the bottom one, asking, "Should I return the favor?"

Rachel shook her head No.

Smitty undid the button anyway. He played his hand on the exposed part of her back, and a little further up than that. This got the next button undone, and the one after that, all the way up to bra. When he went for the next button, Rachel dug her chin into his chest.

What the move lacked in subtlety, it made up for in clarity. Surprised, Smitty returned his hand to the lower part of her back. Had he hit a speed bump or come to a dead end?

Rachel inched up his chest and started kissing him again.

'Speed bump,' Smitty decided.

His hand made a slow, steady trip up Rachel's back to her bra. When he started to unhook it, she rose up a little and shook her head.

Smitty wondered whether he were being teased or just made to work. 'Let her make the next move.' He removed his hand from Rachel's back and allowed it to fall alongside the bed. This was almost a serious mistake. His hand brushed the water glass he had placed on the floor, nearly tipping it over. The glass was cold, still full of ice. Now there was an idea. Maybe Rachel had never experienced the old ice cube massage. Even if she had, maybe it was one of her favorites. Smitty placed his left hand on her back to keep her from getting restless. With his right, he silently removed an ice cube from the glass. He held it as long as he could to let the water drip off, even shook it once. 'It's now or frostbite.' Smitty ran the ice cube down her spine, from the bottom of her bra to her waist.

Rachel flinched, gasped, and pressed herself against his chest to get away from the cold. She raised her head, demanding to know, "What are you doing?" Yet her face was flushed with excitement.

Smitty played dumb. "You want me to stop?"

Rachel laughed, saying, "I didn't say that."

Smitty went back to work with the ice cube, changing hands more than once.

Rachel pressed against him, issuing purring sounds and the occasional gasp.

Smitty said, "I still can't feel you up against me." He undid the remaining buttons to her blouse.

Rachel raised herself up to work herself out of it.

Smitty was glad to help, finally tossing the blouse as far away as he could. "That better?"

Cheek on his chest, she nodded.

Smitty said, "You know, we can make things better yet."

Rachel laughed, raised herself up, and had her bra unhooked before Smitty could help.

He took it from her, and tossed it in the same direction he had tossed her blouse. Smitty had his confidence back and then some. He rolled Rachel over and played the ice cube on her stomach.

Rachel grabbed it away and pressed it against his chest.

Smitty flinched and grabbed her wrist, reminded, 'That's why they like it.' The ice cube fell between them. Rachel searched for it while Smitty reached for a new one. He lay on his side while she lay on her back. He played his ice cube along her stomach and breasts, while she kept pleasantly surprising him with the places her cube would show up. If Rachel's expression had not been enough to convey her excitement, her erect nipples would have been. Smitty's tight pants had been getting progressively tighter. They were now killing him. He undid his fly and started to wiggle out of them.

"What are you doing?" Rachel asked with surprising surprise.

Smitty stopped dead, playing dumb again. "You didn't know these things came off?"

"I'd heard rumors," Rachel informed him.

Smitty got his Levis down low enough to kick them away. "Free, free, free at last." And he felt free. He felt great. He lay atop Rachel, then quickly rolled her onto himself. "Now I feel you up against me." He kissed her. Rachel was wearing a knee-length skirt. He put his hand under the skirt and lay it on her panties. If she minded, she failed to let him know. Smitty lifted her skirt in the air and gave it a little tug. "Expecting company?"

Rachel just laughed.

Smitty slipped his hand inside the back of her panties. He then lifted her skirt straight up again, giving it another tug.

Rachel raised her head and shook it.

Smitty chose to take this as permission. He had the skirt undone and was pulling it towards himself.

Rachel said, "Blouses and bras come off this end. Skirts come off the other end."

"I'm on this end. You want me to get down there on the other end?"

"That's all right," she said, raising herself up so he could pull the skirt over her head.

"You know I never claimed to be any expert at this," he said, slipping both hands inside the back of her panties.

"You're getting the knack," she informed him.

"Aw, shucks, go on now. I bet you say that to all the boys." Smitty felt her flinch slightly.

The smile left Rachel's face. She pushed herself up and off of him. "No. No, I don't."

Smitty wished he had kept that last little joke to himself. He slipped his hands out of her panties and held both arms straight up along her cheeks, saying seriously, "Then it's even more of a compliment." He crossed his wrists behind her head, easing her down to give her a kiss. Rachel seemed to welcome this. No damage done, maybe. He played his finger across her lips, and received a love bite for his effort. Smitty put his arms around her and stretched his head to the side, so he could see her face when he squeezed her. She smiled, and he felt better. He worked his hands down her back and inside her panties again without a problem. When he tried to lower them, she again pressed her chin into his chest.

Smitty stopped dead, fearing a cracked rib. 'Can't she just say No?'

After a long moment, he gave it another try. Same results. Progress seemed to have stalled. Smitty figured if he got another ice cube and tossed it down the back of her panties, then held her arms so she couldn't get it out, that might do the trick. It might leave bruises on her arms too. The girl was no weakling. Instead, he took his hands out of her panties and played them up and down her sides. She seemed to like this better.

"You know," she said, "We're not getting much studying done."

Smitty smiled. "I'd take you over an A any day." He flipped her beneath himself and started kissing her all over her face and neck. The pleasure in her expression told him not to stop. He felt her panties slide lower, realized that she was trying to get rid of them herself. He reached a hand down to help her, got them a little farther down her thighs. His foot took them the rest of the way. She laughed at this. So did he. Her expression said to him what his words had said to her when he rid himself of those tight Levis,

"Free, free, free at last."

*****

Rob fumbled in the dark with his keys, trying to find the right one. The front porch light had burned out two weeks ago. Numerous times he had reminded himself to replace it, but never when he had the opportunity. His wife, without a word, reached around him and tapped on the door. She had not spoken to him since they had left the coffee shop.

The babysitter opened the door and went with his wife to check on the kid. He wanted to get a look himself, but figured he better keep his distance. Rob had the urge for a shot of something strong. It was a rare urge, so rare that they had no liquor in the house. There was some wine, but tonight that would not get the job done. He went to the refrigerator and found half a chicken. Rob twisted off the drumstick and was working on that in the standing position when he heard Sarah walk the babysitter to the door. She then walked herself into the bedroom, without stopping by the kitchen. He told himself this was probably for the best. The woman was seriously pissed-off at him.

Rob was tired, dying to hit the sack. Still, he was not going into that bedroom until the light went off. It seemed like an unusually long time before it did. He spent that time eating more chicken than he had an appetite for. Rob entered his kid's bedroom on the way. He stood watching him sleep, feeling a vague sense of guilt. The connection was there, if tenuous. By angering his boy's mother, he had somehow failed the child.

Rob entered his own bedroom and got undressed as quietly as he could, which necessitated stifling one hell of a belch. All that chicken could prove a serious mistake. He lay down hoping for a decent night's sleep and a fast, argument free escape in the morning. It was too much to hope for.

"Proud of yourself?" Sarah asked, calmly and coldly.

"No," he answered truthfully, hoping beyond hope that his honest answer would end the conversation.

"Rob, what's gonna be?"

Hopes dashed, Rob knew those words meant she wanted a serious discussion, one that could end in a serious argument. All he could do was tell the truth. "I don't know."

"You do know that Mildred is my best friend, that every once in a while I'd like for us to go out to a movie with her and her husband."

Rob realized he was leaving himself open, but he tried to get away with it. "If we had left it at just a movie, things would have been alright."

There was irritation in her tone as she said, "Two couples don't go out for just a movie. Afterwards, they stop for something to eat, or something to drink."

"I just didn't feel like talking." This seemed like the truth when Rob started to say it, but before he had finished he knew that it was only half.

There was anger in her tone as she said, "Don't give me that! You made it perfectly obvious to everybody that you wanted nothing to do with Carl."

Rob matched her anger, saying, "You want me to put on some phony act, as if I like Carl?"

Her tone was even angrier as she said, "No! I want you to be polite! That's not being phony. It's being civil."

Rob knew that she was right, but being civil was not always easy, especially lately. He managed to lower his voice a notch. "But I can't stand Carl. I can't stand his bullshit."

She went a notch in the other direction. "You can't stand any of my friends' husbands.

'That's a fact,' Rob admitted this to himself, but saw real danger in admitting it to Sarah. This argument had the potential for a knock-down drag-out affair. Afraid she'd wake the kid, he decided to just keep his mouth shut.

"The only friend you have is a junky."

'Ouch,' thought Rob, before also thinking, 'Well he'll be dead soon enough.'

"Madge's boyfriend seemed perfectly alright, and you were the same way with him."

Again she was right, but he had his reasons. "A lot of people in this town seem okay. Then you talk to them for five minutes, and you find out they're all off the deep end about something — politics, oriental bullshit, EST, hugging trees, organic tomatoes."

"Why do you have to prejudge everyone?"

"It saves time," he could not stop himself from saying, knowing damn well he should just keep his mouth shut.

Sarah's tone, in addition to anger, now exhibited a loss of patience. "The word prejudge is the root of the word prejudice. You're proud to be prejudiced?"

'Lot of things I'm not proud of.' Unnecessarily pissing off his wife was one of them. More to the point, by accusing him of prejudging people, 'She really hit the nail with my head, that time.' Though he sometimes felt guilty doing it, Rob couldn't stop himself, at least not in Berkeley. The word prejudge did more than hit a nerve. It brought back a memory.

"Answer me!" Sarah demanded

"Give me a minute," he said, deep in thought. So it wasn't just in Berkeley that he did it. That was one thing he couldn't blame on America's capital of self-delusion and mass hysteria.

Surprised by his tone, she wondered what he was thinking.

It was a good while before he finally spoke. "You just reminded me about something, something I never told you."

His wife had no idea where Rob was coming from or where he was going, but his unusually thoughtful tone got her interested enough to hold fire a moment.

"It happened when we were Freedom Riders," he continued. "Remember when I had to get back home?"

"Of course," she answered.

"Remember how I shaved off that ridiculous goatee?"

"Yep."

"You know why?"

"No."

"Because I was scared."

"Because you were sane!"

"Scared," he repeated.

"That was right after the lynching," she insisted.

"They hadn't found the bodies yet," Rob pointed out.

"Everybody knew what must have happened."

"I guess," he said, "but I was scared, so I shaved off the goatee....When I got to Montgomery, I still felt as if every redneck could tell I was a Freedom Rider. Nervous as I was, they probably could....I was starved for something to eat and I went into this diner. There were two empty stools, together. The guys sitting to each side glanced back at me, two of the meanest redneck faces you'd ever want to see. One of them was huge. The other was even taller, but skinny as a rail. So naturally, coward that I am, I take the seat next to the skinny one."

Rob's wife listened intrigued, never having heard him go into such detail. As much to herself as to him, she said, "You really remember it all."

He said slowly, "I'll never forget it….Anyway, the waitress comes right over for my order, and just as I'm about to say, 'Burger, French fries, and a coke,' I realized that as soon as I open my mouth, everyone in the place will know I'm a Freedom Rider."

She interrupted, "You don't have a northern accent."

"I don't have an Alabama one either. You have to understand, I'm not just scared, I'm paranoid….Anyway, to hide my accent, or lack of one, I mumble my order." Rob gave out a short, choked laugh at the memory, then added, "Not fooling anyone."

Sarah lay in the dark with an amused smile on her face, picturing perfectly the scene.

"Well the waitress walked away without jumping up and down and pointing at me, screaming, 'He's a Freedom Rider! He's a Freedom Rider! Let's String him up!' Rob laughed.

So did his wife.

"I sensed something behind me. It was not a good feeling. I glance back out of the corner of my eye to see a tall black man standing there. Slender, probably eighty years old, seventy at the least. And he was wearing this black suit, maybe half as old as him. Back when he bought it, I'll bet he paid five dollars new." Rob could not believe how clearly he was seeing it all again. "And hot as it was that summer, he was wearing a tie, and the whitest, cleanest shirt you'd ever want to see. All frayed on the top of the collar, but so white….There was this unexplainable dignity about him.

"He had a few coins in his hand and he was counting them, and studying them, and recounting them. That's when I noticed something that really got to me — the only thing holding his glasses together, you know those thick black plastic frame type, was some Scotch tape around one hinge. And it wasn't holding them very well. The tape was loose, and they were a little crooked on his face.

"He shuffled on up against the stool between me and the big redneck. The waitress walked over and asked, "What would you like?" not mean, not friendly, businesslike, matter-of-factly. That poor old black man looks down as if to count his money again, looks up, and says, 'Toast and jelly.'

"Without thinking, I slide over on my stool to give him enough room to sit down. Then it hits me where I am, and I'm surprised they're serving him inside, even if they won't let him sit down. And I glance back again and I see something else I'll never forget, something I hadn't seen in so many years I had forgotten they ever existed — a cardboard suitcase. It was green plaid, with all the edges taped, and it was still falling apart. This poor eighty year old black man was on the road, leaving behind who knows what troubles heading for who knows what pain, and they wouldn't even let him sit down to eat the toast and jelly he could barely afford.

"I wanted to slip him a few bucks, but I was afraid of insulting him, and anyway, all I had on me was my ticket, an unbroken twenty, and a few coins."

She cut in, "I lent you that twenty."

Rob remembered now. "And paid for part of my ticket too.…All these thoughts started running through my mind, making my head spin, making me dizzy. As much as I wanted to help that poor man, I didn't want to give away to the rednecks that I was a Freedom Rider. At the same time, the injustice, the meanness, the inhumanity of it all made me proud I was a Freedom Rider. It justified everything we were doing. I never felt so righteous, and at the same time I never felt so guilty. Here I was, in my twenties, sitting on my fat ass while an eighty year old man, with the dignity of saint, stood waiting patiently, like a slave. He had his handkerchief out by then, mopping the sweat off his face. I wanted to tell him to take that empty seat, rest a while, that whatever happened, I'd handle it."

She cut in, "You would have gotten lynched. Both of you."

"Beat up, maybe. Arrested for sure."

"And he wouldn't have sat down anyway."

"Of course not," Rob agreed. "He didn't survive eighty years in the South by being a fool."

"So why did you feel guilty?"

"'Cause I sat there just like every segregationist redneck in the place and did nothing. I watched that eighty year old man take that white paper bag with his toast in it outside to eat, dragging that pathetic cardboard suitcase with him. You know how many times I've wondered how far he got, how long he survived? How much of a difference it would have made if I had slipped him my twenty? Or even my hamburger, which I was now too sick to the stomach to touch?"

She felt as if she should say something, but had no idea what. Finally, a question came to her, one that seemed too unimportant to ask. Yet ask it she did. "How come you never told me about this before?"

"I don't know....I never told anybody." To himself, he now wondered, 'Was it shame?'

There was a long silence before another question came to her. It seemed even more irrelevant, but again she asked it anyway, feeling a little guilty doing so. "What exactly does all this have to do with what we were talking about?"

"I haven't told you the most important part yet."

"There's something more important?"

"Well, it's all important. But this is the part that says the most about me....Without getting off my fat ass, I watched that man go out the door. And when I turned back towards the counter, I saw that that huge, mean redneck had watched him leave too. And what that redneck said just burned a scar right into me."

She waited to hear these words, and kept waiting, finally asking, "What did he say?"

"That mean vicious looking redneck stared me square in the eye, shook his head, and in the deepest, softest southern drawl, said, 'It's a pity. It's a pity.'"

*****

Straughton stared at the number in the Oakland Telephone Directory. Sure enough, there it was — "Black Panther Govt. in Exile, Algeria". He had searched numerous frustrating times over the last few days, reluctantly concluding that Holy Joe was either lying or delusional. Then one morning, exiting his apartment, he tripped over the new phone book. Now staring at the number, he mentally apologized to Holy Joe for his lack of faith.

Straughton debated dialing station-to-station instead of person-to-person. He had quite often used this method within the States, but never before to call outside the country. Being a man who appreciated a bargain, Straughton took satisfaction in the money station-to-station had saved him over the years. Yet the process itself often left him with a vague feeling of being conned. The phone company was encouraging gambling, not only an illegal act, but more important, in the long run, a mathematically proven money losing proposition. There were just so many ways to lose. You could be given an incorrect number, even by a phonebook. You could misdial the correct number. Just as frustrating, the person you called might not be home, and someone else could answer. Even if you hung up immediately, you would be charged for a full three minutes of conversation, and with absolutely no legal recourse. Straughton stared at the number printed in the phonebook. It was surprisingly long. He doubted there were that many phones in the entire world. If only one little digit of it were wrong, his attempt to reach Cleaver would fail. Straughton found it hard to believe, in any case, that these simple, seemingly random digits would be able to connect him to the elusive fugitive, thus enabling him to conduct his interview. Still, the three minute charge would not be much more than a minute at the person-to-person rate. And any possible charges seemed insignificant against all possible gains. Skeptic that he was, Straughton decided to roll the dice anyway.

The phone rang, and rang again. Doubting anyone would answer it, Straughton mused that it did sound far enough away to be ringing in Algiers, far enough away to be ringing on the moon.

A female voice startled him, a young voice, distinct enough to be speaking from Oakland. "Yeah, Black Panthers Government in Exile."

Straughton's skepticism took over again. This female had an accent that must have originated in deepest, darkest Brooklyn, one so thick, so local that you would think it had to lose something by just crossing the Canadian border, not to mention trekking all the way to Algiers. Also, now, in the absence of her voice, Straughton could hear the distinct sound of her carefree chomping on a wad of gum, one that had to be big enough to choke a hippo, never mind a horse. Still, there seemed no cogent reason not to place himself in the hands of The Fates and continue. "Eldridge Cleaver, please."

There was a pause at the other end of the line, and when she ended it, her tone was no friendlier than her words. "Who the hell are you?"

Straughton considered himself an expert at controlling this type of situation. He had to get the upper hand immediately or he would never get by so uncultured a delinquent. The conversation would end with one of those dreaded little clicks. Straughton's time honored and almost always successful strategy was to put the enemy on the defensive. "Young Lady, may I remind you, that when you answer this telephone, you are representing to the world the Black Panthers Government in Exile."

Still on the offensive, she answered, "You sure as hell may not! And if you want to do any remindin', remind the Black Panther Government in Exile us slaves ain't been paid for months."

So much for putting the young lady on the defensive. Now, finding his own self on the defensive, Straughton pleaded, "May I please speak with Mr. Cleaver?"

"Probably not," she replied. "Definitely not, unless I find out who the hell you are."

Straughton could still hear her chomping loudly on her gum. He felt as if he were stuck somewhere in the center of that sticky wad, and that any second she would spit it out and him with it. "Would you be so kind as to convey to Mr. Cleaver that Roger Basil Straughton VI would very much like to speak to him."

Again there was a pause before she asked in a non-combative, neutral tone, "The Sixth? You a king or somethin'?"

"No," Straughton replied, before realizing he should have lied. He heard the sound of her carelessly dropping the receiver on a desk or table or toilet seat or whatever it was. Only then did it occur to him that Cleaver probably wouldn't remember his name, and that he should have mentioned The Badger and his previous interview. Straughton checked his watch, wondering how much money he had wasted so far on this call, and how much more he would waste waiting for that ignorant peasant of a receptionist, or cabinet member, or whatever she was, to give him the brush-off. To his relief, she started fumbling with the receiver in a clumsy attempt to pick it up.

"Straughton!" It wasn't her. It was an excited Eldridge Cleaver.

"Man, it's great to hear from you. What's hap'nin'?"

Straughton could not believe his success. "I want to do an interview with you."

"No problem, Brother."

Straughton went into silent, euphoric shock. 'Technology! What a boon to mankind!'

"Fire away."

Straughton struggled to regain his bearings. This cold blooded murderer of blacks and whites seemed to have discarded his intimidating arrogance. So unaccustomed to being at a loss for words, Straughton tried to remember if he had done some dope since rising. No, not even pot.

"Roger, you still there?" asked a worried Cleaver.

"I'm trying to think of some questions."

"Man, don't sweat the small stuff. Make it all up, like you did the last time.... That was the best interview I ever gave."

Straughton suddenly remembered that he already had the interview ninety percent written. A few minutes talking to Cleaver would provide the other ten percent, and perhaps some spice for the rest of it.

Cleaver continued, "Man, you gotta get me out of here."

Straughton was ready to help. "To where?"

"Home!" Cleaver said, as if Straughton should have known.

This came as a surprise. "And jail?"

"I'll take ten years with a shot at parole, take it in a second."

This came as a bigger surprise. Straughton asked, as much to himself as to Cleaver, "How bad can Algeria be?"

"Man, you wouldn't believe it. Just passing through don't do this place justice. You gotta live here to know just how fucked up these Arabs are.... I never been so proud to be black."

Straughton had to ask, "Is it true you've been reborn?"

"The Lord's truth — I'm saved! Hallelujah! My calling, for the rest of my stay on God's earth, is to spread the Gospel of Our Lord Jesus Christ."

"If I remember correctly, you were a Muslim.

"Islam afflicted me, and Muslims cured me.... You should see what goes on in this dump of a country. Islam don't work for shit."

Holy Joe had spoken the truth. Startling and newsworthy as this was, there was no way to include it. Printing interviews with New

Left turncoats was not a habit of The New York Review of Books nor The New York Times. Straughton, with his innate cynicism, wanted badly to take Cleaver's words as a con and plain lie. Yet his reporter's acumen told him otherwise. What he was hearing was way too weird not to be true. Fiction never attained such heights of imagination. It then occurred to Straughton that Cleaver's born again conversion would not have to go to waste. He would write a second interview later, peddling that one to The Christian Science Monitor or such.

Cleaver continued, "You know Holy Joe, that preaches by the entrance to the university?"

"Yes."

"Next time you see him, ask if he got me a new lawyer. The one the Panthers got me ain't doing shit....Hey, maybe you can get me a good lawyer."

Straughton let his father handle all legal matters. "Maybe." He checked his watch. This call would not be cheap, quite worthwhile, but not cheap. "Well, I have got to go. It—"

"Wait! Wait! What's the hurry, Brother? In that interview, you gotta mention my book, Soul And Ice."

"Soul On Ice," Straughton corrected him.

"Yeah, mention it three or four times, tellin' what all those critics said, like that I'm 'The eloquent voice of the New Left' and all that."

"Certainly, My Man."

"Don't forget. I need the commissions."

"The royalties," Straughton corrected him.

"The bread! Who gives a shit what it's called?"

"Rest assured. Well, good—"

"Wait, wait! One more thing. My momma lost her copy of that interview you did with me. You got another one to send her?"

"I can acquire one."

"Well send it to her. And if you have a copy typed out, send that too. Momma, poor thing, can't see the way she used to. That newspaper print is hard on her eyes."

Straughton checked his watch again. "My Man, you can depend on me. Goodbye—"

"Wait! I'll give you her address."

"No. I will call you back when I get everything together."

"You swear?" Cleaver asked suspiciously.

Straughton tone displayed both hurt and indignation. "My word is my bond."

"Then keep the faith, Brother."

*****

The day after Muhammad had threatened Marcia, the Johns started showing up again. She was a prisoner in her own room. A self-imposed one, but a prisoner all the same. Marcia had found herself faced again with the same simple choice — leave the crash pad or get Muhammad and his friends to leave. The latter would be difficult and dangerous, but the former meant quitting. Marcia still refused to quit, especially after all she had been through. Anonymously, pretending to be a neighbor, she would report that The People's Crash Pad was being used for prostitution, that children were being coerced into it. No matter how much the police hated the idea of a crash pad, they would be forced to act. There was a danger they'd close it. Then Marcia would have to fight to get it open again. If she failed, no crash pad was preferable to the evil now taking place.

Marcia, enclosed in her room, could hear what sounded like a scuffle. She went to the door and put her ear up against it. Silence. Well at least it was over. Then there was the sound of Muhammad's door opening, followed by someone running down the stairs. Again there was silence. Marcia wanted a peek into the hall. She waited a few minutes to make sure the silence continued. It did. Marcia told herself not to open the door. What would she be able to see? Nothing. Whatever had happened was over. She almost convinced herself. Not quite. Marcia cracked open the door. Saw nothing. Cracked it a little more. There was a wet stain on the hall floor. It could have been anything. Yet she had to know what. Marcia stuck her head out the door. No one was in the hall. She walked silently towards the stain, noticed another one just like it. A trail of them led towards the stairs. It had to be blood. If it was, someone was bleeding badly. She rubbed her finger across it. Blood. Muhammad had C.C.'s pistol. Maybe he shot someone. No, she would have heard the shot. Well, someone could have been stabbed. Marcia felt like returning to her room and locking the door. She couldn't. One of the kids could be bleeding to death.

Marcia silently followed the stains down the stairs, careful not to step on the blood. They led her into the kitchen. One of the boys was leaning over the sink. She inched closer, relieved to see that his wound was no more than a bloody nose. "Are you all right?" she asked.

Startled, he turned his face towards her. Still bleeding, eyes red with tears, he glared at her, as if to say, "Great. I'm doing just great."

Marcia winced at the sight of his nose, obviously broken. "You'll have to go to a doctor."

Washing away the blood again, he said coldly, "Just leave me alone."

Marcia's first thought was to wonder why he blamed her. Her second thought was to wonder at the stupidity of her first thought. Of course he blamed her. As far as he knew, she was just as responsible for what went on here as Muhammad, maybe more so. In fact, she had seen bruises on two of the girls, yet had managed to push thoughts of abuse from her mind. Now Marcia had to admit to herself why the kids were so docile and obedient, even to her. She hadn't seen because she had not wanted to see, had told herself that the kids would certainly leave rather than be abused. Now it was clear to her that they wouldn't. Far from it. The abuse they were suffering from Muhammad must be a relief compared to the abuse they suffered on the street. That she could not even imagine.

Anger propelled Marcia upstairs. She asked herself, 'How did I get into this mess?' An answer occurred to her, one that gave her strength. 'For the right reasons!' Yet The People's Crash Pad had turned into a disaster. 'Why did this happen to me?' It seemed so unfair. Suddenly, Marcia felt repulsion for the question itself. She identified it for what it was — weak self-pity. That would not help. She raised her head, and her expression took on a determined cast. Still frightened, knowing it all could end badly, her guilt outweighed her fear. Her anger fortified her determination. There was justice in this world. The fact that it was on her side gave her strength.

Muhammad's door was slightly ajar. She knew that if she stopped to knock she would lose her nerve. Marcia pushed the door

403

out of the way and took a step into his room. What she saw made her freeze. Muhammad, his two friends, and two of the girls sat on the floor in a circle. Between them burned a candle with a spoon lying next to it. One of the girls, who could not have been more that fourteen, had a surgical tubing tourniquet on her upper arm and a hypodermic needle stuck in the inside of her elbow. She stared determinedly at Marcia a long beat, then pressed the hypodermic's plunger.

Marcia watched mesmerized as the evil liquid disappeared into the child's vein. The scene hit her like a blow to the head. So fear of the streets wasn't enough to keep these kids at the crash pad, nor their cut from the prostitution either, if they were receiving any. No. The idea of Muhammad addicting children to control them had been beyond her imagination. Even seeing for herself, she still had a hard time believing. Marcia stepped forward, right up to the circle of people sitting on the floor.

Muhammad calmly watched her.

Marcia said to him, "Get out. You and your friends. Or I'll call the cops."

*****

"You're nervous," Rachel said to Smitty.

"Naw," Smitty replied, now even more nervous. Could it be that obvious? Obviously, it could. Smitty felt more nervous than he had on his first date. Hell, if only he could be as nervous as he had been then. Rachel seemed unbelievably calm. Well, it was her idea. Smitty had found that hard to believe. Out of nowhere, she had asked if he wanted to go. The Sexual Liberation Front was having its monthly party. His wildest secret, sexual fantasy, and she was offering to make it come true. Thinking 'Do I!', he mumbled, "If you want to," as if agreeing to go to a chick flick.

Rachel took the initiative to knock on the door. From the other side of it, came the laughter and voices of people having a blast. As the seconds passed, Smitty began to hope that no one would answer. They were late, and could always go home and try again some other time. Rachel looked over at him with a big, innocent grin. How could she be so calm? Her nonchalance increased his nervousness.

The door swung wide open. In the bright light of the entryway stood a naked, potbellied, hairy from head to toe hippy. This stranger looked at Smitty and Rachel as if he had been expecting them. "Welcome." He turned and led them inside.

Smitty and Rachel followed his disproportionately small, hairy ass. Smitty, looking past their guide, could see nude partiers of both sexes, obviously enjoying themselves. No Adonis came into view. Smitty felt slightly more relaxed. 'Hung as good as any of 'em.'

The naked doorman turned and handed them two grocery bags. "Here, put your things in these." Smitty stood holding the bags as Rachel immediately started to take off her top. Ever the gentleman, he stepped behind to help with her bra. This proved unnecessary. She hadn't worn one. He held out a bag to her. Still smiling, she tossed in her top, then looked at him questioningly, as if to ask, "Well?"

'Oh,' thought Smitty. He put down both bags and tossed his shirt into one. Hesitating, he glanced over at Rachel. 'She's got balls,' he thought, just as she proved him wrong. Rachel was bending over bare assed to place her shoes in the bag. He felt a stab of possessiveness and jealousy, then resignation. 'Well, better get going.' Smitty felt blood heading towards his cock. He didn't want that, not just yet anyway. He got out of his shoes and socks, then quickly lowered his Levis and underwear at the same time. No embarrassing hard-on stuck its head out. Will he get one if he needs one? Sexual freedom? Is that what this was? He felt more forced than free, and like an idiot to boot. 'Quit being so uptight,' he cautioned himself

The naked doorman handed him a marking pen. "Write your names on the bags." They did so. "No drugs," he warned. "Don't wanna to give the pigs any excuse for a raid."

Smitty stood thinking, 'Yeah, buck naked, where the hell would I be stashing any drugs?' He then realized there was a place, though a not very appealing one. The guy probably meant no drugs in the bags anyway. This brilliant inference brought a grin to Smitty's face.

The doorman misinterpreted it. "What we're doing here is as important as anything going on in Berkeley. By eliminating the guilt and taboo inculcated by a false, neurotic, hypocritical morality, we're leading the way to a healthier society, one that will be much more reluctant to go marching off to war. If everybody were naked, there wouldn't be any more wars."

Smitty doubted this, but felt no urge to argue. Then again, he had to admit to himself that his lack of feistiness might have at least something to do with the fact that he was naked as a jaybird. Fighting a war that way would, at the very least, prove something of a handicap.

The doorman locked the bags in a closet off the foyer before disappearing.

Smitty and Rachel glanced at each other. She broke into a smile, almost a laugh. He shrugged and jerked his head towards the living room. They paused a moment at the entrance. Everyone sure seemed to be relaxed and having a pleasant time. People were standing or lounging around conversing as if at your typical soiree. A few were dancing. Others were making out, most to the opposite sex. There were some possible instances of intercourse going on. Make one of those a definite. The sofa, the chairs, and every rug were in use. The overflow was making do with the bare wooden floor. Splinters did not seem an impediment. He heard the old standby repeating itself dully in his brain — 'Unbelievable.'

Still, Smitty was not sure what part to play in all this. He had read that at the last meeting they were finger painting each other's naked bods. There was no shortage of naked bods, but he didn't see any paint. It seemed to him this orgy could use some structure. Or was that a conflict of terms? What the hell did he expect anyway, to come in a find a writhing mountain of naked flesh in the middle of the floor? To take a running jump and pile on? Now feeling like a wallflower, and a wilted one at that, Smitty pondered his next move, his first move as a matter of fact.

At that moment, he was blinded by a flash bulb. A naked photographer had just taken a full frontal of him and Rachel. Smitty's first thought was, 'I'm fucked.' Without a doubt, his life was now ruined. No telling where that photograph would turn up, but it was sure to do so at the very worst time and place. How would he ever get a job now. A hopeful thought flashed through his mind, 'Maybe it's a Polaroid, like in a nightclub. He's selling the guests souvenir pictures.' Smitty was just about to try buying the picture when he realized that his wallet was not stuck to his naked ass. No, those pictures were taken strictly for blackmailing purposes. He turned to Rachel to comfort her.

Rachel looked back at Smitty like a grinning idiot. "Groovy, a real orgy."

Smitty nodded tight lipped agreement. He looked around. The photographer was snapping away. Nobody else seemed concerned about blackmail. No, the thing on their minds seemed to be sex. After all, this was an orgy. 'And I'm standing here like a eunuch.'

Just then, from out of nowhere, a petite, long haired blonde was standing inches in front of him. She looked up at Smitty, right into his eyes. He realized that if he now had an erection he would be touching her. No problem so far. That was a relief. She placed her hands on his sides. Problem or not, within seconds he was touching her. 'Look Ma, no hands!' She smiled up at him. He wasn't just touching her now, he was punching her a new belly button, or was that already her belly button. What exactly did this very cute and very naked girl want from him? By the look on her face, considering their surroundings, it could only be one thing — sex. Smitty certainly had no objections to that. But Rachel was right next to him. He glanced over to apologize, for what, he wasn't sure.

Rachel gave him a big grin and a "knock yourself out" shrug. Smitty was ready to. He looked back at the blonde. She slowly nodded her very cute head. Though his own head wasn't quite ready, his prick was raring to go. He followed its lead, placing his hands on her small delicate waist. She stretched up towards him, and he met her halfway in a kiss. She kissed nice, no phony passion. Her tongue was soon in his mouth. It was a nice tongue, the feel of it, the way it moved around. An exceptional tongue. Talented. She had her hands on his back. They too knew what to do, finding their way to his chest. She pulled away from his lips and kissed his cheek, the side of his neck, his Adams apple, moved her lips down the center of his chest. This tickled. He lowered his head to get another lip lock. But she lowered hers, and her hands too. The woman was actually going down on him. Her course was meandering, but she kept sliding slowly, relentlessly lower. He was thrilled. The worry left him quickly as her hands and lips drove him wild. When her tongue would get to where it was going, and it was almost there, his prick would be waiting for her as hard as a rock, igneous.

Yep, she found what she was looking for, swallowed it whole, or at least it felt as if she had. Smitty, for the life of him, could not figure out what exactly she was doing with her tongue, but it was driving him wild. Here came that word again — 'Unbelievable'.

From behind, a couple brushed by Smitty and his new friend, something he would not have been so conscious of if they all weren't bare-assed. Smitty realized then that he and Rachel had been standing in the entrance to the living room. Not very considerate of them. A glance towards Rachel revealed that she had shown more consideration for others. She had disappeared. Where the hell was she? 'What the fuck,' he thought. 'Let her have a blast.' Blast? Smitty felt one coming on, an imminent, explosive blast of a climax. Wow! But shouldn't he hold it off for a while. In a flash of concerned consciousness, he realized that everybody at the party must be looking at him. A quick glance around showed no one was. Still, Smitty did not want to seem like an amateur to his new and talented acquaintance. He tried to stall by getting his mind off sex. This may have been the proper time, but it sure wasn't the appropriate place. Another couple brushed by, so Smitty sidled out of the entrance, taking itty bitty steps, and with a hand on the back of the blonde's head. No way did he want to leave her behind.

Just as she got her rhythm back, there was another guy kneeling behind her behind. Was he going to do her from there? Smitty was not in a sharing mood. He gave the guy one dirty look. Of course this went unnoticed in that the guy wasn't looking at Smitty's face. Again Smitty relaxed with the thought, 'What the fuck.' It was up to the girl to complain. This was turning out to be a pleasantly "what the fuck" evening.

Smitty's next thought was, 'WHAT THE FUCK!' The guy had slid the blonde out of the way and had taken her place, trying to swallow Smitty whole, dick first. What had happened? How had it happened so fast? The blonde was working her way back up to his lips again. Smitty didn't like this, the guy part of it anyway. Yet he really couldn't tell the difference without looking. And Smitty did not in fact care to look, except at the blonde. The guy had a tongue technique similar to the girl's. 'Fuck that!' Smitty wanted out, but by now the blonde had made it to his lips, keeping him occupied.

Her kissing was as accomplished as her sucking. Her lips felt nice. Yet Smitty felt nauseous, his confused mind unable to keep up with whose mouth was where doing what. He berated himself for not shooting his wad when she was working single-handed. 'Or single lipped? No, double lipped.…Oh, hell.' Belatedly, the thought came to him, 'No such thing as premature ejaculation with oral sex.…Or is there?' Smitty wasn't sure. Yet he was damn sure he didn't like what was going on. That's when he saw the naked photographer coming around again.

Smitty gently pushed the girl away from him and, despite the increasing suction, backed right out of the guy's vacuum cleaner of a mouth. He turned to the side and glanced down at his wet hard-on. Now what the hell was he going to do with that? 'Walk it off? Keep moving,' thought Smitty, turning away without looking back. He couldn't believe what he had just let happen, and how long he had let it continue. Suddenly, he was in a very bad mood. His expression showed it. Smitty didn't know where he was going, but he knew damn well that he wanted to get away from the scene of the crime, thinking, 'That was a homosexual act.' For the rest of his life, every time he got a questionnaire that asked, "Have you ever been involved in a homosexual act?" Smitty would have to check the "yes" box. How would he ever get a job? Hell, he'd lie. Smitty did not like to lie, and rarely, very rarely had to. He found it degrading, even when the purpose was to protect another's feelings. Still, homosexual acts were damn well nobody's business but his own. Smitty didn't like the sound of this thought either. Shit, an orgy was supposed to be fun. Here he was, five minutes into one, and he already had a new deepest, darkest secret, by a mile — a homosexual past. Shit! But wait, maybe he never would be asked. Yet if he were, from now on, for the rest of his life, the answer would be Yes.

'Where the hell is Rachel,' he wondered. Yet he didn't want to see her just then either. Smitty found himself in a hall. He passed a bedroom with the door wide open and a couple, or at the very least a couple, going at it on the bed. He wondered if one of them was Rachel. No reason to think so. Hell, for all he knew, it could have been two guys. Just then a woman slinked halfway out of another bedroom. She had to be in her thirties, a nice age but a below average specimen of it. She shook her head admonishingly in reaction to Smitty's dour expression.

He stopped, chastised in his tracks.

The woman gave him a come hither finger.

Smitty began to nod. She was far from attractive. Still, who knows, her technique might be tens across the board. Besides, Smitty now had something to prove — his heterosexuality. He followed her into the bedroom. It was dark. He liked that, and would have liked it even better if there hadn't been another very active couple on the other side of the conveniently wide mattress. Smitty was mentally worn out. His thoughts slowed. The woman took over. She seemed to be playing the courtesan and getting off on it. She played it well. The lady's technique was accomplished — 'A nine, minimum.' Smitty was getting off on her, both figuratively and literally. He stopped thinking period, except about what he was doing. The fact that he was at an orgy faded into the background. They took their time. The time proved worthwhile, leaving Smitty spent and relaxed.

The room was too dark to really see the woman's face now. Curious about his latest "conquest", though the word did not seem all that appropriate, Smitty pictured her from memory. It occurred to him that she could very well be an instructor at Berkeley, maybe even a full professor. He imagined her standing at the front of a lecture room as he walked in for the first day of classes. 'Wow!' That could be embarrassing. Or would it? Who would be more embarrassed, her or him? Or would either of them? The lay he'd just given her was nothing to be embarrassed about. Hell, he might have even improved his grade. She was either completely satisfied, or one hell of an actress, maybe a drama instructor. Naw, she could be teaching anything. Probably not religion. English, she could teach that for sure. But that was ridiculous. What were the odds she was a college instructor? Times the odds that he would find himself in one of her classes? Very long. And she didn't even look like a college instructor — a little too spacey. Now that didn't sound right. Could anyone look too spacey to be a college instructor? At Berkeley, especially? Well, she did, Smitty assured himself. She looked more like one of those chain smoking, on the verge of going batshit, high school guidance counselors. Smitty had kept his distance from those crazies. Just a glance from one of them would make him nervous.

Smitty wanted to get out of the bed, but he did not want to be rude and just leave this guidance counselor, or whatever the woman was, lying there alone. That might hurt her feelings. On the other hand, they weren't exactly going steady. Surprisingly, orgies involved some difficult questions of etiquette. As he pondered a polite solution, the woman solved Smitty's problem for him, leaving with a playful pinch to his side. Smitty took this as a compliment. It put a smile on his face.

Finding himself alone, sharing the bed with a very active couple gave him the creeps. He quickly got up and headed for the door. Just before he was through it, Smitty had second thoughts, thoughts that included cutting in — 'Excuse me, can I have this fuck?' A threesome might be interesting. Smitty suddenly realized that a threesome, that type of one, was what he had walked away from a few minutes earlier. No, he wasn't up for another of those. He took his leave unannounced.

Smitty, more or less at peace with the world, entered the living room looking for Rachel. It wasn't so much that he had had enough, more that this was still the scene of a crime he'd rather forget. There was Rachel's naked ass in profile. She was talking, probably Seventeenth Century literature, to some geeky looking guy. Then, just to her side, he noticed a party of three going at it. His little blond friend stood right in the middle with her tongue down a guy's mouth, while at the same time her partner or employer or permanent relief man was honking the guy's horn. 'Sonofabitch!…Suckered again.'

*****

Sloan moved along the sidewalk with slow, uneven steps. His drug fogged mind provided no refuge, allowed no respite. He did not see any humor in the thought, 'Dope ain't what it used to be, if it ever was.' Sloan tripped over thin air and staggered a few feet. 'This ain't getting it.' He meant his whole life. Where the hell was he headed? 'Who knows?' he answered himself. Yet he did know. Sloan stepped off the curb just as he thought it. 'Straight for the gutter.' There was a grate beneath his feet. 'And down the sewer.' Is that where he wanted to end up? 'No.' Yet that's where he was headed, 'Sure as shit.' This unintended joke he did catch. Sloan grunted out a short laugh. 'Clever sonofabitch, ain't I?...Who looks like shit...like shit headed for the sewer....Sure as shit.' But he wasn't headed straight for the sewer, just staggering around in the gutter, headed for a slip or shove. The problem— and he had known the problem for a long time — was that he saw no alternative direction. 'Gimme a place to go, I'll fucking get there,' he told himself. 'Gimme something worth doing, I'll fucking do it.' Because for sure, he had no desire to end up in the sewer. Sloan had seen plenty of people get washed down it, and had little sympathy for them, little sympathy for most anyone since Nam.

The problem was, to escape, you needed a place to escape to. How the hell do you get away when what you want to get away from is people? That, he now guessed, was behind the weird appeal of the north woods. The more eyes upon him, boring into him, the more estranged and isolated he felt. Did Nam do that to him? Did Berkeley? Or did Nam and Berkeley together? Whatever the cause, Sloan knew that the condition was not normal, far from it. Humans were not born to be loners. They yearned to be members of the tribe. It was deep in their genes. Were the north woods just a way to die, away from all eyes, alone.

'Alone,' he thought. Yeah, was that the appeal? Being able to lay down and die without all these assholes tripping over your stinking corpse? A smile came to his lips. If a man drops dead in the woods, but there is no one to smell his corpse, does his corpse stink? If his corpse doesn't stink, is he really dead? The smile left his face, his own sense of humor disappointing him. 'Cut the shit. You ain't as clever as you think you are.' Nam had taught him that.

Sloan had learned a lot in Vietnam, yet one thing above all others. He went there assuming he knew everything there was about loyalty, courage, self-sacrifice. 'Didn't know crap.' No, in the mud of Vietnam he saw them for real, in all their awesome wonder. He saw and learned other things too. Yet the one most unforgettable, overriding thing that he saw, that he learned, was that human beings died just like bugs. They got blown to a bloody stinking mist before they knew what the hell had hit them. They got their arms and legs and balls blown off, and lay there knowing it before they died. In agony, they squirmed around in the mud like squashed cockroaches, leaving their guts behind them in trails of obscenely ugly iridescence. One thing Sloan never saw in Nam —

the human soul rise heavenward from the dead. What were loyalty, courage, and self-sacrifice, in all their sad stubborn humbling magnificence, up against the fact that human beings lived and died just like bugs? Loyalty, courage, self-sacrifice — nobility among cockroaches.

No, Sloan did not come back from Vietnam with any desire to sip tea, take tiny bites of dainty little pastries, and discuss, "What is art?" He did not come back with a burning desire to build highways and bridges so people could get into their cars and really look like the little bugs they are. He did not come back to either save the world or give it what it deserved. Chemistry, he did like chemistry. It was a language he spoke and understood, a neat and intricate three-dimensional puzzle, so gratifying to put together. Nature's elegant, mind blowing version of Tinker Toys. But to what purpose? To make better tires? Fabrics? Drugs? The thought of making better drugs, that had intrigued him once. No more. Sloan had even lost his faith in drugs, especially for recreational use. 'Medicines, maybe' — a bug making bug medicine for a giant pharmaceutical company run by bugs that treated its workers like bugs and its customers worse than bugs. Getting up for that would not be easy. Still, it would be possible, if he ever earned his degree, which basting his brain with dope did not make likely. No, more likely he'd end up in the sewer.

Sloan, walking along the sidewalk, asked himself, 'What do I want?…To think straight, that'd be nice for a change.' Despite his drug fogged state, Sloan knew the reason he could not think straight was because of the dope he had taken to prevent himself from thinking at all. 'Sure ain't working.' Still, he knew one thing he did not want — 'No more dope.' It just wasn't getting the job done anymore. Here he was, thinking. Proof enough. Being a junkie gave life a single overriding purpose — getting your next fix. So if he didn't want a fix, then his life had no purpose. Sloan found some humor in that thought, unsure exactly why. But the question was, 'What the hell do I want?…To get home, for one.…Home?' Sloan smiled at the idea that he could consider his broom closet with a toilet home. He'd have to get one of those "Home Sweet Home" signs to put up. His sense of humor surprised him and he laughed to himself. 'Dope's really wearing off.'

Sloan decided to ask himself a simpler question. 'What do I

like?' He immediately answered, 'Women,' though admittedly there hadn't been much evidence of this for a while. A little dope helped with the women, but not the over-generous quantities he consumed, unless you were looking for junkie companionship, which he wasn't, in part to avoid being reminded that he himself was one.

Would he ever get near a decent woman again? Not around here, he decided. Memories returned of his last Berkeley Babe before Kathleen. She had claimed to have been drawn to him by his wounded aura. Sloan now smiled at that, and at how he had briefly considered applying to the Marine Corps for another Purple Heart, and to the Veterans Administration for disability payments for his wounded aura. The freaky little whack job would have him lay face down on their bed so the healing energy of the earth would rise up from its center and enter his naval. Then she would move her hands a few inches above his body without ever touching it. He now laughed to himself, thinking how irate she'd get when he'd inevitably start snoring. She'd slap him awake, saying, "You're not working with me." She was one sweet lay, but not much else. Funny, how getting it free often feels more like paying for it than paying for it.

Thinking led him back to memories about the best woman he'd ever had, the one who sailed right out of his life. Sloan knew he damn well better change the subject. He forced these memories aside, going back to his original question — 'What the fuck do I want?' So far it was getting him nowhere, but he forced himself to continue anyway. 'Got nothin' else to do....Think! What do you like?' An answer came to him immediately — 'The ocean....And the boats that sailed it.' A sailboat would solve the women problem too. The only way to get women off one was to sink it. He could sail all over the world, maybe find something worth looking for, not even knowing what that was until he found it. He could even live on his sailboat and go to college. Hell, what a waste. Sailboats cost money. Well if he wanted one badly enough, and he did, he could get the damn money. All it would take was a good job. He'd fucking have to get straight, and stay that way.

Sloan found it hard to believe that he was thinking so clearly. His mind was doing all he asked of it. The drugs he was on, he couldn't remember which, were failing him, thankfully. 'Bad dope?' he wondered. Sloan could not remember the last time he had tried to figure a way out of the hole he was in. 'The First Rule for getting out of a hole — STOP DIGGING!' In this case, digging into his stash.

Sloan now had his way out, or at least a direction that did not lead down the sewer. Suspicious of his own mind, he wondered if the dope was fooling him. Was a sailboat really goal enough to keep him on course? And hell, if he got one, could he still keep a sailboat on course? Couldn't be sure till he got straight again, stayed straight a while. He'd do that. And just as he thought this, a shiver went down his back.

The car headlights behind him mocked his pace. In a minute, a cop's spotlight might be on him. Sloan gritted his teeth. 'Ain't in the mood for this.' Maybe the pigs would pass him by. And at just that instant, a spotlight skewered the back of his head. 'Fuck!'

"Police! Hold it right there."

Sloan froze in anger. Hell, he was practically straight. For him, anyway. The red light on the squad car's roof swept across his back in flashes, stigmatizing him as the center of police attention. "Bad time,' he thought, realizing he was neither straight enough nor anesthetized enough to handle this drill well. But he had to. Maybe for the last time. 'Just one more time,' he thought.

A cop circled around in front of him, while his partner held back a few feet to cover them. The cop facing Sloan gave him a hard, arrogant look. This time Sloan saw something different, not just the badge and uniform. He saw the person wearing that badge and uniform. The cop appeared so damn young, a kid, barely old enough to shave. His cocky expression was that of a schoolyard bully. Sloan's eyes were drawn to the way he was already tapping his big flashlight into the palm of his hand. 'Bad sign.' The kid was dying to use that flashlight — 'On my head'. Then came the light beam searing Sloan's retinas. This did more than blind him. It tortured him. And for spite, the cop kept the light beam in Sloan's eyes. He felt toyed with, humiliated. Worse yet, he felt impotent.

The cop called to his partner, "Check out this red-eyed rat we got."

Sloan experienced a forgotten feeling, a savage animal urge to strike. The feeling itself felt good, yet its results would be suicidal. Still, the feeling grew inside him. Sloan's instincts for survival forced it back down, replaced it with a calm and cunning animal viciousness. 'Keep cool.' His ability to think clearly continued to surprise him.

"Seen one, seen 'em all," said his partner, coming no closer.

Sloan noticed that the second cop, a good ten pounds overweight, looked younger than him too. 'Kids with badges.'

The first cop got back to business. "Over to the squad car. Move it!"

Sloan turned and did as he was told. The cop followed behind, now slapping the flashlight into his palm even harder than before. His partner placed himself off to the side, waiting for them.

"C'mon, you know the drill!"

'Better than you,' thought Sloan. The idea that he was being ordered around by a rookie cop years younger than himself gnawed at Sloan.

The cop was strutting around with his big bad flashlight, trying to play tough guy. He didn't look the part, and he couldn't act it either.

Sloan spread his legs, then leaned forward, falling until his palms landed on the hood of the car. He was now too off-balance to make a move. That was the idea. 'Just as well,' thought Sloan. He decided to show his driver's license when asked for identification. No way would he beg these punks for sympathy with his Marine Corps ID.

"C'mon! Spread your legs!"

They were spread. This cop was trying to provoke him. Sloan got his legs a few inches farther apart, as much as his Levis would allow. 'Anything to please.' Sloan would not be provoked. No, he'd play their game.

Just then the game took an unexpected turn. "Spread 'em!" shouted the cop, at the same time backhanding his flashlight into Sloan's kidney.

The pain was excruciating, the shock debilitating. Sloan's elbows unlocked. He was barely able to keep himself from collapsing onto the car hood, from falling to his knees. The pain proved mental too. 'Figure the junkie is harmless...Probably right.'

"Excuse me," said the cop, as if he had accidentally brushed by Sloan in the supermarket.

Trying to hide his pain, attempting to save some face, Sloan countered with casual bravado. "Don't mention it." Merely speaking hurt. Dreading another blow, he quickly pushed off from the car, locking his elbows and spreading his legs again. Pain, real physical pain, was something he had not experienced in a long time, that thanks to dope. It was worse than he had remembered, much worse. 'Punk lost his manhood somewhere,' Sloan explained to himself. 'Wants mine.' Still, he warned himself, 'Stay cool. They got the guns.'

Sloan congratulated himself on his self-restraint. 'Survive these clowns....No matter what.' And just as he thought this, the cop slammed the flashlight into his other kidney, even harder than the first time. Sloan caved onto the squad car's hood, hugging the warm steel with his cheek. Mouth wide open and drooling, he slid across the metal as his legs buckled. Sloan did not even attempt to lock his knees, thinking, 'I'll kill him. I'll kill the punk,' knowing that he wouldn't, because the cop's partner would kill him first.

It was then that this partner said, "Take it easy on him."

The cop with the flashlight said calmly, cruelly, "Sure, I'll take it easy on him."

Sloan, still collapsed with his cheek upon the very front of the hood, his knees bent behind him, sensed what was about to happen, knew that he would let it happen. The cop stomped on the back of his leg. His knee hit the pavement with a sharp crack. Sloan slid off the hood, face against the grill, into a kneeling position. He struggled to regain his feet. The cop tried stomping his leg again. Sloan, in pain, struggling to his feet, moved it. The cop missed, losing his balance, tumbling on top of Sloan. Somehow, Sloan ended up with the cop's arm in his grasp. He saw the hand of this arm holding the flashlight. That was it. Sloan jerked the arm sideways, then straight up. The cop released the flashlight. It bounced off Sloan's skull, telling him that he had gone too far, that he was committing suicide. 'Too late.' Still struggling to his feet, bending the cop's arm, Sloan saw his Adam's apple — naked, unprotected — saw his hand, by reflex, slice into it. The cop staggered backward. Sloan grabbed him, kept him upright, as a shield against his partner. Yet Sloan knew for certain that he was taking too long, moving too slowly, that in an instant he would see the flash, hear the report of the round that would kill him, thinking, 'So this is how I die. Fuck!'

Yet thinking itself did not slow him. He knew enough not to let it. The other cop, his gun out, stepping to the side for a clean shot, tripped over his own feet and was already on his way down. Sloan, disbelieving his luck, flung the first cop on top of the second. He stomped on the second cop's hand, the one holding the pistol, then kicked him in the groin hard enough to lift him off the ground.

The revolver lay free. Sloan grabbed it, spun towards the first cop, who had rolled off of the second and onto his back. This one wasn't thinking about his gun. He was holding his crushed windpipe, trying to suck enough air through it. Sloan, on him in a instant, delivered another swift kick to the groin. He grabbed this cop's revolver too. "Did it!" Sloan exclaimed in disbelief. He tore off into the night like a madman, which at the moment he was.

Sloan dashed down the sidewalk, a gun in each hand, loving the adrenaline rush. He had cheated death. Running joyously, like a kid, Sloan thought, 'Fucking amateurs. Lost their guns.' They were fucked. 'Deserved it'. Their incompetence had saved his life. 'Send the fuck-ups a thank you card.' He was actually smiling as he ran. It was then that Sloan realized that he had fucked up too. His fingerprints were all over the hood of the squad car. 'Fuck!' What would he get, ten years? Twenty? He was screwed. What could he do? 'Nothing.' Yes, there was something. It would take guts, maybe cost him his life. He turned and ran back in the opposite direction, at the same time stuffing the revolvers into his jacket pockets.

The cop with the crushed windpipe and broken nose was gagging on blood, still trying to catch his breath. His partner had the front passenger door open. He was half inside, lying across the seat, reaching for the radio. Sloan spotted targets of opportunity, too exposed to ignore. Again he kicked for the groin. The cop dropped the radio microphone. He slithered back out of the car, ended up writhing on the pavement, next to his partner. Sloan grabbed one of their hats to wipe down the hood. He gave the front grill a once-over too. His sense of humor kicked in. A memory flashed through his mind — a week spent working at a car wash. 'Never did a squad car....Check the ashtray for change?' Was this the dope taking over again? Gallows humor? Insanity? A desire to get caught? This last thought alarmed him, took the smile from his lips. 'Get fucking serious. Get out of here!' Just as he started to run, one of the cops tripped him. He fell to the pavement, banging his knee. A revolver, with his finger prints all over it, fell out of his pocket and slid under a parked car. He crawled under after it. Both cops, still on their backs, were kicking him as he backed out. 'Serves me right,' he thought before turning around and pointing one of the revolvers, saying, "Who wants it first?" Neither cop answered. Both stopped kicking him. "Punks with badges," he cursed them, staggering to his feet and taking off again.

Sloan ran unwinded, like he hadn't run in years. The cold air against his face and in his lungs exhilarated him. He spotted a sewer grate. 'Ditch the pistols.' Yet he didn't want to stop running. After two more blocks, now wheezing like an old man, he had to stop. Sloan pledged to himself to get in shape. Hands in his pockets, he felt both pistols. Where's a sewer when you need one? At that very corner, in fact. Sloan tossed in the guns. The sound of their splash made him smile. He knew he should ditch his jacket too, but decided ditching it with the guns was not a good idea. One more block and there would be another sewer. Yet that wasn't a good idea either. And he hated to give up the jacket. Berkeley was awash in military field jackets just like it. He had gotten his the hard way, in the Marine Corps. It didn't mean anywhere near as much to him as his bush cover—

An ice cold shiver ran through Sloan as he reached up to make sure he was still wearing his broad brimmed camouflage hat. He felt nothing but sweat soaked hair. All sense of exhilaration drained from him in an instant. He'd fucked up bad. Sloan wasn't worried about the cops finding his hat. It was not as if his name or address were in it. He had paid dearly for that hat. More important, he felt embarrassingly vulnerable without it. Perhaps its loss was the price to be paid for the crazy, self-destructive stunt he'd just pulled. For such an embarrassing loss of cool, the price should have been much higher — his life. One thing for sure, if he didn't get off the streets fast, the hat would not be the only price he would pay.

*****

Straughton strolled the dark sidewalk with a smile on his face and a bottle of Champagne in his hand. The New York Review of

Books had telephoned, not written a letter, telephoned. They were so excited about his Eldridge Cleaver interview that they were trying to rush it into the very next issue. Still, a letter instead of a phone call would have been a nice addition to his portfolio. Then again, once the interview was published, Roger Basil Straughton VI will have no further need for a portfolio. And he will probably get even more money for his next Cleaver interview, the one with the born again bombshell the NYRB would not have appreciated. Yes, tonight was a night to celebrate.

Straughton entered his building and stopped across from Sloan's door. He would have liked to invite Sloan to celebrate with him. He wanted to invite the world to celebrate with him. Yet Sloan seemed to have something against him. What could it possibly be, jealousy? Well, tonight was not the night to worry about that. Besides, the last time he had seen Sloan, the psychopath was obviously back on the hard stuff. Let Smitty or Screw drag him upstairs if they cared to.

Straughton climbed the steps and knocked at Smitty's apartment. He waited, then knocked again. Jimmy Reed was playing on Smitty's stereo. He had to be home. Asleep maybe. Maybe even dead drunk on the floor. Smitty could use some cheering up since Marcia had walked out on him. Straughton knocked one last time, harder than before. Waiting for Smitty to answer, the thought of celebrating with Marcia alone brought a smile to his face. He had come ever so close to seducing her, alas, only to set the table for Smitty. Ah, some things were just not meant to be. Thinking of Marcia, he knocked again.

Smitty opened the door with a beer in his hand and a less than friendly look on his face. He had recognized Straughton's knock, wondered where the hell the 'leach' wanted a ride to now.

Straughton ignored Smitty's expression. It would never occur to him that anyone could answer his knock and not be thrilled to see him. He held up the Champagne bottle. "You are cordially invited to join me in a celebration. My Eldridge Cleaver interview is to be published in The New York Review of Books."

'Whoopee,' thought Smitty, 'now I don't have to drive him to Algeria.' Yet the only change in his dour expression was a slight hint of surprise. Not at Straughton's news, but at the fact that he wasn't trying to bum a ride. Smitty searched his memory. Had this ever happened before? He could not think of an instance. The bottle Straughton held did not look the least bit tempting. It was not exactly The Beverage of Choice when shit on by one's girlfriend. Marcia should have called more than a week ago. He found it almost impossible to believe that she hadn't, not after telling him that she would. Smitty just shook his head.

"My Good Man, a little Champagne is exactly what you need."

Again Smitty shook his head. "Not in the mood."

"If you change your mind, come over to my place. Perhaps we can lighten your mood."

"Thanks....Congratulations on the interview."

"Thank you, My Man." Straughton refused to let Smitty's loss in love dampen his celebration. There was always Screw, the cheeriest of the lot. 'Hope the young man is home.'

Screw was home, answering Straughton's knock with his usual, "Did you bring the dope?" Down as he was on booze, Screw decided to make an exception for Champagne on this particularly special occasion. Soon they were at Straughton's place, toasting Chelsea Sinclair. What a useful contact he had proved. Straughton savored the Champagne, recalling the pleasant day he had spent with Sinclair at the zoo. Screw savored his drink, memorizing the brand, which he assumed was "Chelsea Sinclair". A short time later, he was holding the upside down Champagne bottle above his open mouth, waiting for the last drop to hit his tongue.

Straughton had just finished rolling their third joint. He felt abnormally horny. For too long now, he had been embarrassingly celibate. In his mind, paying for sex was just about the only thing concerning sex that could qualify as a sin. Yet tonight, considering the occasion, and considering it under the influence of Champagne and marijuana, the sin of paying for sex seemed an easily forgivable one. "What a pity," he mused. "All Berkeley's finest whores, run out of business by mere amateurs."

Screw pondered this problem a good two seconds before replying, "What about all those massage parlors?"

It struck Straughton as odd that he never considered these massage parlors the whorehouses they actually were. Thinking about their ads, he wondered if they ran all the legitimate massage parlors out of business. For instance, these days, how would an actual massage parlor distinguish itself, let you know that it actually gave massages. This could prove a problem. As he pondered that problem, Straughton suddenly realized that the problem wasn't his. His curiosity and horniness combined to form a restlessness. "Let us visit one of these establishments. I'm buying."

Screw sat astonished that the words "I'm buying" had somehow issued from Straughton's mouth. Here was a genuine occasion to celebrate. "Outa sight!"

Straughton was already working on the spiel he'd use to trade a mention in The Badger for services to be rendered. And he would surely get an article out of the experience. Who knows, he might even get a massage to boot.

*****

Smitty, beer in hand, sat somberly listening to Jim Morrison and The Doors sing about The End. This was far from his favorite cut on the album. Too pretentious, even for The Doors. They had balls though. The Doors took chances. If he were stoned, the music would send him drifting off to a place where the lyrics were more than words. But he wasn't stoned. Wasn't drunk either. The beer — three down and the fourth on its way — wasn't working its magic, if magic it could be called. He was still pissed-off, at himself more than anyone else. His mood and the music were a perfect match.

What made his mood even worse was the knowledge that he should be happy. He was living out his most imaginative fantasies. He'd never wanted a woman more than he had wanted Marcia, and damn if he hadn't gotten her, shacked up with her even. So Marcia splits, and Rachel dives right into his bed. The only other fantasy woman he had had while living with Marcia, and he gets her too. Hell, she practically rapes him. Only now that he's got her, it's like he's going through the motions. He should be ten feet off the ground. Of course with Marcia, it wasn't just looks, or sex, or fucking around. He wondered how he would feel if he had been living with Rachel first, and then Marcia jumped into his bed. Would he now be going through the motions with Marcia? He doubted it.

One thing Smitty didn't doubt, he wanted Marcia back. What he wouldn't give to see her right now, doing that adorable two-step jump into a pair of tight Levi's. There was no doubt in his mind that he would do whatever necessary. The question was exactly what should he do. 'Whatever it takes,' he told himself, but exactly what would it take? In the last few days, thoughts about Marcia had metastasized and taken over his mind. Studying was impossible. He'd given up any attempt at it. 'Pussy whipped,' he berated himself. Yet Smitty knew it was more than that. He was worried about Marcia. That fucking People's Crash Pad meant too much to her. When it went down, and it would, she just might refuse to step back. Smitty avoided thinking about the real source of his worries — Muhammad and his thugs.

Though the beer hadn't gotten to Smitty's head, it sure had reached his kidneys. He took a long satisfying piss, relieving himself in more ways than one. On his way out of the bathroom, he caught his own reflection in the mirror and wished he hadn't. Sure, he looked the same. He wasn't. Old Smitty had a reputation for coming through in the clutch. New Smitty replayed the scene in which he left Marcia alone to go to Sausalito. That was the clutch. He'd choked. New Smitty thought about the things he could have, should have said to her, the words that might have convinced her to stay, to be there when he got back. What use is it being good in the clutch, if you don't have enough sense to know when the hell you are in the clutch?

There was a soft knock on the door, then a hesitant repeat. He couldn't believe it yet believed it anyway. This had to be Marcia. Smitty headed for the door with a thankful sense of relief. He waited a moment before opening it, wishing, 'Let it be her.'

It wasn't her. It was Sloan. Smitty felt as if he'd been punched in the gut. Not seeing Marcia before him was enough in itself. Seeing instead the wreck that was Sloan, that was something he did not have the patience to handle, especially right now. Apparently, unfortunately, Sloan wasn't still pissed-off at him. Everything about him appeared strung-out, everything except, surprisingly, his eyes. They focused upon Smitty with purpose, bored right into him. Sloan had never appeared so dangerous. Had he flipped out?

Sloan, entering the building, had heard The Doors — 'Marine Corps music'. Maybe Smitty would do it. He had come down on him awfully hard on the front steps. Hadn't said a word to him since. Yet Sloan's only other choice was Screw, a kid likely to make a mistake. Hell, Smitty had never impressed him as petty enough to hold a grudge over a few harsh words. Now, faced with Smitty's less than friendly expression, Sloan contemplated aborting.

Smitty interrupted his thoughts. "Want a beer?"

"Heard The Doors." Sloan entered, thinking, 'He can handle this.' Would he though? That was the question. And why would he, that was another question?

Disappointed as Smitty had been not to see Marcia, Sloan was at least a distraction. At the moment, he would have settled for any distraction other than Straughton.

Sloan was still riding the adrenaline rush, the best rush of any kind he had experienced in a long while. Restless, still sweating, he was in no mood to beat around the bush. A healthy gulp from his beer and it was out. "I could use a favor."

Smitty nodded, thinking, 'Couldn't we all.'

"You can get your ass in trouble, but not if you're cool."

Smitty replied deadpan, "I'm cool."

The smile that came to Sloan's face showed an appreciation for Smitty's sense of humor. "I lost my hat."

Smitty had noticed. "Didn't even recognize you."

"I can't go back for it."

'Strange,' thought Smitty. His mind searched for possible explanations. 'He left it in Hell?' This thought was more amusing than convincing — 'Too literary'. Thankfully, his long awaited buzz had finally arrived. In fear of losing it, he took another healthy slug of beer.

"I know about where I lost it."

"Then what's the problem?"

"There'll be cops there....They don't like me."

Smitty sat thinking, 'Maybe they won't like me either.'

"If you can't pick up the hat without the cops seeing you, just walk by. They can't bust you for that."

Smitty was damn curious why cops would be around. Still, if Sloan had wanted to tell him, he would have. This added an aura of mystery, a sense of danger. Smitty found both attractive, especially the latter. Intrigued, he felt himself being drawn in. A voice in his head warned that he would be crazy to get involved. Another voice told him that Sloan was a decent guy who needed a favor. Yet another voice reminded him that Sloan was a junkie, destined to wreck more lives than just his own. Smitty, unaccustomed to and uneasy about hearing voices in his head, decided to end the background noise, to tell the voices, 'Fuck it. I'll take a chance.' It had been a while since he had to. Too long. A little hairy excitement might be exactly what he needed. It did not occur to him that danger seemed appealing because it would get and keep his mind off Marcia for a while.

As soon as Sloan had explained where to go, Smitty was ready to leave the apartment. Sloan stopped him. "Put on a jacket. So you can stash the hat in your waistband."

Smitty grabbed a light jacket.

"You got anything hard to drink?"

Smitty pointed to a cupboard. "There's some Bacardi in there....If you want, wait for me here."

"Put on that Van Ronk album?"

Halfway out the door, Smitty said, "Knock yourself out."

Sloan cautioned, "Don't take any chances."

Smitty thought immediately, 'That's exactly what I am doing.' Just how dangerous a chance he wasn't sure. The air outside was colder than he had expected. It felt good. Though damn curious why Sloan couldn't retrieve the hat himself, Smitty took pride in not having asked. Thinking about this, he realized that if he got caught, no one would believe he was sucker enough to do what he was doing without knowing exactly why he was doing it, and the "why" involved not only Sloan's motives for asking, but also his own motives for agreeing. And all for that rag of a hat. It had to have something to do with dope. Smitty smiled. In Berkeley, that was one safe bet. What here did not have something to do with dope? Sloan might have ripped-off a pusher, maybe even mugged him. Yet this didn't seem to fit Sloan's style. Then again, when Sloan was wasted, he didn't have much style. And a junkie is capable of anything, especially something stupid. On the other hand, Sloan could have acted in self-defense. And that would mean Smitty was just helping out a friend, his best friend in Berkeley. Who just happened to be a junkie. Smitty thought good and hard about that. His best friend in Berkeley was a junkie. That didn't say much about Berkeley. More to the point, it didn't say much about himself.

It was then that Smitty noticed the flashing lights up ahead. He was still two blocks away from the Point A of his search. There seemed to be more than one squad car. What could Sloan have done? Whatever he did, the hat was evidence. Smitty realized that he would be tampering with evidence. That was probably a felony. Nothing could fuck up your résumé like a felony or two. Well, he hadn't done anything yet. If there were a chance of getting caught, he wouldn't take it. Sloan himself had told him not to.

The flashing lights were getting brighter, and there seemed to be more of them too. What the hell could Sloan have done? Anxious to know just that, Smitty picked up his pace. The closer he got to all the commotion, the greater the commotion seemed. By the time he reached the barricade, Smitty could not believe the sight before him. At least an entire block of road was cordoned off. Inside were four squad cars and some other police vehicles, all with their flashers going berserk. This was by far the best light show he had seen in Berkeley. A joint would be nice, but Smitty was glad he had stuck to beer. Functioning would be easier.

A good sixty or seventy people were enjoying the show from his end of the street. The scene seemed out of some Fifties science fiction movie, where the cops had a flying saucer roped off to keep the gawkers back. But those movies were in black and white. The present scene was in flashing splashing Technicolor. The red, blue and yellow lights played eerily across the faces in the crowd. Most of the people looked fairly compos mentis, for Berkeley anyway. Still, it was a thin majority. There were of course the requisite wide-eyed tokers grooving on the light show. Some had even brought their munchies along, the most prevalent being boxes of Screaming Yellow Zonkers. Outnumbered and out of their minds were the handful of acid heads — slack jawed, open-mouthed, and mesmerized by the lights.

It occurred to Smitty that if the Berkeley cops ever wanted to round up all the dopers in town, they could merely go from intersection to intersection, parking their squad cars with the flashers on. The dopers would be drawn in like moths to a flame. Except, of course, for the speed freaks. The cops would have to flush those paranoids out of the bushes. Yet what would the cops do with all of them? There were not enough jails in the entire state to hold half of Berkeley's pot heads.

Smitty stood wondering what had gone down to cause this scene. He would have asked around but that was what everyone else was doing. It seemed to be the question of the moment.

"Hey Man, what's happening?"

"Beats me, Man, but it's a trip."

"I'm digging it too. How 'bout some munchies?"

"Sure, Man, grab some."

"Hey, Guys, what's happening?"

"No clue."

"Those flashers are outa sight."

"Like to take one home."

"Can you buy 'em?"

"Beats me. I'd sure trade my lava lamp for one of those."

"You think they make them with black lights?"

"Never seen one….Ask the cops."

"Man, they wouldn't know."

"Hey, Dudes, what went down?"

Being in the middle of a freak show did not keep Smitty from some serious speculation. There were enough cops around to fill two donut shops. In a flash of insight, it occurred to him that that was a thing both stoners and cops had in common — a love of donuts. This didn't make Smitty feel any the more comfortable being around so many cops. One thing for sure, whatever the hell Sloan did, it was worse than jaywalking. He might have actually killed someone, a cop even. This was a chilling thought, literally. Touching that hat could mean real trouble. Well that was one thing he didn't have to worry about. If Sloan was expecting him to cross those barricades, he was expecting too much. Then Smitty noticed people walking along the front lawns. Only the street and sidewalks were closed off. The front lawns would give him a pretty good view of where Sloan had asked him to search. He could get closer to the cops too, maybe get an idea about what had happened.

Smitty started walking. Where there was crime scene tape between trees and bushes, it was as close to the sidewalk as possible. A cop was watching some workers lift the grate from a storm drain. Smitty figured it took a damn serious reason to get cops to search the sewers. He kept walking, scanning the area around the sidewalk for Sloan's hat, hoping he wouldn't see it. A cop was shining a flashlight under a car, and another was doing the same a little further down on the opposite side of the street. Smitty reached the first squad car. The others were within twenty yards of it, and there were cops all over the place, some of them detectives in suits. What the hell did Sloan do? Mass murder? Was he a serial killer? Could he be the Zebra Killer or the Zodiac Killer? The thought gave Smitty a chill, but only for an instant. The Zebra Killers happened to be blacks who killed whites, and the Zodiac Killer wasn't making his rounds on a bus pass. In any case, Sloan was no serial killer. Even if he aspired to be one, being zonked out so much of the time would have held down his body count well below Zodiac Killer level? Smitty pondered the outsized and anomalous role serial killers were playing in the Age of Aquarius. They seemed oblivious to the rules, or the zeitgeist. Zeitgeist, Smitty thought to himself with pride. He could definitely make it as an English major. Just then a connection occurred to him. Aquarius was a sign of the Zodiac! Asking, "What's your Sign?" as a pick-up line was already a cliché. Yet still damn popular. Smitty wondered if the Zodiac Killer asked, "What's your sign?" before he blew someone away.

"'Hey, what's your sign?"

"Libra."

BAM!'

Smitty decided, 'Not likely.' Far more likely that the Zodiac Killer blew away people who asked him his sign.

Smitty felt slightly stoned, letting his thoughts run away with him. Better get back to business. "Business," whatever it was, now seemed far more serious than he had anticipated. Up ahead, at the apparent scene of the crime, a dozen people stood bellied up to a hedge. Smitty joined them. He watched the lethargic cops going through the motions. One of them seemed to have nothing better to do than lean over the hood of a squad car and watch the crowd. Smitty looked back a good few minutes before asking the guy next to him, without even glancing over, "What went down?"

The guy didn't glance over at Smitty either. "Some bikers jumped some cops."

Well that made no sense. Neither did standing around watching a cop watching you. Heading home made sense. Still, another block or two of searching wouldn't exactly be heavy lifting, even if he found the hat, which he wouldn't. That's when someone asked, "You put it on your head?"

Smitty glanced over to see the guy standing right next to him wearing Sloan's hat, or some rag that resembled it. Naw, it was Sloan's all right, just worn with less style. 'Unbelievable!'

The guy explained to the questioner next to him, "To see if it fits."

"That skuzzy rag?"

Smitty wondered, 'Should I tell him it's mine?'

"I'll wash it."

"In boiling water to kill the lice….Might shrink it down to your size too."

Smitty assured himself that he was not going swipe the hat. He could not see himself running home for Sloan's help either. What could he do — 'Follow them?'

Just then the guy took off the hat. "It's too big. You want it?"

"Get serious," was the reply.

'I'll take it,' thought Smitty.

The guy, turning to go, Frisbee'd it high up onto a bush in the center of the yard.

'What fucking luck!' thought Smitty, Sloan's, not his. Still, it would take a good vertical jump, maybe two or three, to get it down. If that didn't work, he could easily retrieve it with a stick.

Waiting for them to get a reasonable distance away, Smitty glanced back at the scene of whatever crime had gone down. The cop was still leaning over the squad car. He seemed barely able to keep his eyes open. Or was he tricking someone along the hedge into making a move, a dumb one like pulling that hat off the bush. Smitty figured he'd simply out-wait the cop before retrieving it. The cop out-waited him. Smitty decided to take a walk and pick up the hat after the cops left.

A girl was walking a few yards ahead of him. Dark hair, fine figure, she could be Marcia. Of course she wouldn't be. Of course Smitty had to make sure anyway. He picked up his pace. The girl glanced back, saving Smitty further effort. Well, he could return to his apartment, do some studying. No, that wouldn't work, not with Marcia on his mind. Why not go over to The People's Crash Pad now? Because how he handled that situation would be critical, and he still didn't have a clue. 'Fuck it.' Smitty turned in the direction of The People's Crash Pad. It was a ten minute walk. He'd figure out something by the time he got there.

Smitty reached the front door, still without a clue. Turning around would be the smart thing to do. 'Fuck the smart thing!' He would do whatever he had to do to see Marcia, and whatever he had to do to bring her home. Determined, angry with himself for having waited this long, Smitty pressed hard on the doorbell. The place was dead quiet, not a voice, not a radio or TV. There should be some sign of life from inside. This worried him. He'd just ask Marcia if he could talk to her, get her to come for a walk, get her away from this dump.

A less than welcoming voice came from the other side of the door. "Who's there?"

"Where's Marcia?" he asked.

Someone attached the latch chain before unlocking and opening the door, just a crack.

Behind the chain, Smitty could barely make out an afro. 'One of Muhammad's thugs,' he thought, and the thought was enough to both anger and worry him — 'Gonna be trouble, bad trouble.' Smitty got the urge to slam his body into the door. The chain would pop open, no problem. Still, he forced himself to stay calm until he had no choice. "Tell Marcia I want to talk to her."

The door closed in his face, and the owner of the afro re-locked it. Again there was dead quiet, until the sound of someone quickly descending the steps. The door opened just far enough for Smitty to recognize a smiling Muhammad.

Smitty fought the urge to crash through it.

In the time it took Muhammad to say, "She don't wanna talk to you," he slammed the door shut.

Smitty cursed the fact he hadn't crashed his way inside, ready to do just that now. "Hey!" he shouted, hearing nothing in return except footsteps up the stairs. He slammed his forearm against the door, shouting, "Hey, get back here!" Smitty was livid. He banged his shoulder into the door. It gave a little. Now nothing was going to stop him. One, maybe two tries more and he would have it flying open.

That's when Muhammad said calmly, "Try again, Cracka."

Enraged, Smitty did just that. The sound of cracking wood told him that one more try would do the job.

"C'mon, Cracka."

Muhammad's calm tone gave Smitty pause. He had to be waiting on the other side of that door with a surprise — a knife, a meat cleaver, who knows what? Breaking inside could prove fatal. With the law on their side, those thugs could do anything they wanted to him. 'Fuck it!' Smitty told himself. Yet he waited, fearing what was on the other side of that door. If only Marcia would come down. She had to have heard the noise. Smitty had the urge to cry out to her. Too proud, he fought back that urge. Smitty waited, hoping she would come down anyway.

"I hear you breathin', Cracka. One more try 'ill do it."

Smitty, dying to squeeze his hands around Muhammad's neck, almost gave it that try. Instead, reluctantly, he backed away. 'What should I do?' He was too pissed-off to think. He'd come back, only with a plan. Defeated and humiliated, Smitty headed for his apartment. Never had had felt so gutless.

In his anger, Smitty walked two blocks before remembering that he had intended to pick up Sloan's hat on the way back. "Fuck the hat," he told himself. He couldn't care less. Yet, for some reason, he did not want to return without it. "Fuck, I'll get the fucking thing," he said to himself with determination. He changed direction.

Smitty returned to find the same scene he had left. If anything, there were even more gawkers. This did not help his mood. Well, there was little chance that same cop would be leaning on the squad car, looking right where Smitty needed to grab the hat. Slim chance or not, he was there, looking as if he hadn't moved a muscle. 'The worthless fuck,' thought Smitty. He was getting more pissed-off by the second. 'Fuck it!' He headed straight for the hat. It would take quite a leap to reach it, and he damn well wanted to do that on the first try. Without even looking at the cop, Smitty jumped up and grabbed Sloan's hat with the very tips of his fingers. He kept walking, now feeling cocky enough to put the hat on instead of stashing it in his jacket. He adjusted it, just like Sloan wore it, thinking, 'Fuck the world!'

*****

Sloan was still experiencing an adrenaline rush as he watched

431

Smitty leave the apartment. He felt confident, as indestructible as tempered steel. How long had it been since he had felt so alive? Not since Nam. Yet tonight there had been a difference, an important one. In Nam there were times he thought he could die. Tonight, for a heart stopping moment that seemed like an eternity, he was sure that he would die. Only the cops' incompetence had saved him. With this sobering thought, Sloan felt the adrenaline bleeding out of him. Reality would soon force itself in. He was soft, way out of shape. And his mind was fucked. Depression lurked within him, ready to take over.

Sloan reached up into Smitty's cupboard for the Bacardi. The dull ache in his side exploded into raw pain, as powerful as the kick of a horse. He froze, mouth agape. Still, Sloan wanted that rum, now even more. He paused, breathing heavily, waiting for the pain to fade back to a dull ache. He could bring over a chair, but climbing on chairs in his condition could be hazardous to his health. He reached up again, this time more slowly. The pain increased yet proved bearable. He came down with the Bacardi. Sloan rejected the urge to take a long swig right from the bottle. This would be bad form. The bottle was not his. He searched around for a clean glass, finding nothing close. No choice but to wash one. The overflowing sink offered him plenty of dirty glasses to choose from.

Sloan sat down and poured himself three thick fingers of rum. He took a slow, steady swallow, enjoying the way it burned its way down. A sleek sailboat came to mind, gliding through a light chop. Just picturing it settled his nerves, made him feel at peace. Then another sailboat came to mind, a wreck of one — its journey over. He saw himself jumping off it onto a dock, then glancing back at a bird perched upon the cabin railing, thinking, 'We made it.' This scene, a few years in the past, seemed lifetimes ago.

That was the day he let her sail away. Sloan realized immediately he might have made one hell of a mistake. She had not given him, or anyone else he knew, a forwarding address. What kind of a person, what kind of woman did something like that? She had never talked about her past, only her plans. Almost all of them centered upon a cruise around the world. How she had acquired the sailboat was a mystery to him. She could have inherited it, or the money to purchase it. Then again, she could have earned the money by doing who knows what, by teaching kindergarten or by robbing banks. The woman had nerve, and she was sharp. He had never met anyone, male or female, more capable. He would have had no qualms about sailing around the world with her. Yet he chose not to. Then again, she had never come right out and asked him, given him that choice. Still, he was certain she had wanted him to sign on. They talked about it enough, even made some hypothetical plans. In the end, he had come up with excuses — get his degree, put some money in the bank. The real reason, he decided later, much later, was to put some distance between himself and the woman he might end up marrying. The idea of settling down, whenever it seeped into his thoughts, had made him feel old. Yet this was not a woman you marry to "settle down" with. No, it must have been the idea of divorce that really gave him cold feet. No way did he want to go through one of those. Divorce, the word alone made him cringe as if from nails on a blackboard. His own father had recently completed his third marriage. Not until he watched her sail away, did it occur to Sloan that refusing to leave him a forwarding address might have been her way of saying, "Come with me now, or I cut you out of my life." The realization stunned him.

An hour later, Sloan found himself on an old, beat up wooden sailboat. Rob had bought it for peanuts, and Sloan was helping him refit her. He had some tools out, but was making pathetic use of them. Sloan just wasn't in the mood. A short sail might improve his mood, just as far as the Golden Gate Bridge. Sloan would not have admitted, even to himself, that he was hoping to find his woman there.

The wind was enough for a very pleasant sail. The rickety boat handled effortlessly. Sloan felt in control. His thoughts were relaxing ones. He reached the Golden Gate Bridge in what seemed like no time. The gentle seas outside it beckoned him onward. 'What the hell!' He sailed under the bridge and out into the ocean. Sloan followed the course that she must have, not realizing that the calm he was experiencing was that clichéd one before the storm. The winds picked up, refreshingly brisk. They and an ebb tide had the little boat cruising along faster than he had ever sailed her. He scanned the horizon for a sign of his woman. There was none.

He sailed on contentedly, though a melancholy cloud hung over him, figuratively and literally. Yet how could one not feel thankful for being alive on such a beautiful day? Just then, Sloan was surprised by a series of drenching waves. The salt spray burned his eyes and changed his attitude. 'Better get the hell home.' He scanned the horizon for her boat one last time, then reversed course. Sloan was well aware that this beautiful ocean that he loved so much couldn't care less about him. 'Just as soon drown me as keep me afloat.' The waves now pushed him against the tide, back towards the bay. The little sailboat cut through the slop surprisingly well. Sloan loved the feeling, was glad he had ventured out, and even gladder that he had done so alone. The wind increased and so did the speed of the sailboat.

Exhilarated, Sloan stood at the wheel like an old salt, glad that he had a wheel instead of a tiller. They were rare on boats this small. Just as Sloan thought this, he heard a snap and the wheel spun uselessly. Sloan dived below decks for the emergency tiller. As soon as he had it in hand, he felt the boat turn and heel way over. Sloan lost his balance and his grip on the wooden tiller. It fell hard on the arch of one foot. Ignoring the pain, he bent down to grab it and was immediately drenched by a wave crashing through the cabin hatch. As the boat violently rolled and pitched, he fought his way up the stairs. The rudder was only a few feet away, but halfway there he slipped, banging his knee on the deck and his forearm on the cockpit side. Again ignoring the pain, he crawled along the violently heaving deck, toward the rudder. Of course it was way to one side, snapping back and forth, making attaching the tiller even more difficult. Sloan wasn't wearing a life jacket. The boat rocked all over the place in ways he could not anticipate. He stayed as low as he could, pressing himself against the wire of the safety lines. It would take some real luck to get the emergency tiller on the rudder before he was thrown overboard. That much luck he had. Placing the tiller went way faster and easier than expected. Relieved, starting to turn the boat, Sloan admitted out loud, "Pure luck." Just as he said this, his luck changed with the god-awful sound of splintering wood. The boom had snapped right before his eyes, leaving the mainsail flogging out of control. His first thought was, 'I'm fucked.' His second thought was that he better put on a life jacket. His third thought was that the only good that would do him was a slow death in the fifty something degree water. He hadn't told anyone he was going out, not to mention where. No one would be searching for him until morning, if then. He was not the type who looked first to others for help, and the stupidity of going out with the VHF radio on the blink had not yet occurred to him.

Sloan found he could use the rudder to control where the waves were pushing him much better than he had expected, yet not always. Some of the waves were breaking over the stern. It seemed a mere matter of time before the little boat went under. Sloan now decided he would prefer a slow, cold death to a quick drowning. That would mean reaching the life jackets. And that would mean lashing the tiller and hoping the boat would hold course for a few seconds while he made the dash. This plan proved victorious. Back at the tiller, now wearing the life vest, he thought triumphantly, 'Slow death it is!'

His victory encouraged him to try to do something about the sail. Again he lashed the tiller and staggered forward. Despite the flogging part of the sail slapping his face and beating the hell out of him, he was able to lash part of it to the remains of the boom. The results of his own imagination and jury rigging truly amazed him. So did his luck, until a rogue wave rolled the little boat and sent it heeling over.

Sloan lost his footing. He slid like a shot, feet first over the side, until his ass was halfway off the boat. Only his locked arms catching the lowest wire of the safety lines kept him from disappearing into the sea. And only the boat righting itself, along with a desperate push from his arms, gave him the leverage to get his legs back on deck. In a panic, he dived and crawled his way to the stern.

Sloan untied the tiller, asking himself, 'Did that really happen?…God, that was close.' He then asked himself, 'Is any of this really happening?' He decided that it was, all of it. And if it wasn't, he better act as if it was anyway. The boat seemed easier to steer. Yet every few minutes a wave would hit it in a way that made the rudder useless, that rolled the little craft so far over it seemed about to capsize.

Then the rain started, blindingly hard. Sloan had never experienced such a freak squall in the Bay Area. If it didn't let up, he did not see how he could survive. 'Matter of time.' Squinting through that rain, he noticed a quite small bird with its claws clutched tight around the cabin roof railing. It did not look like any sea bird he'd ever seen. Spray from a wave jarred it, but the stubborn little fucker held fast. Sloan wondered if it would manage to fly away when the boat capsized. Or would they both drown together? He'd soon find out. No, he probably wouldn't.

The sight of this bird brought back the memory of another, one out of his childhood. While walking with his mother, he had thrown a rock at it with no expectation of hitting anything but the ground. He had certainly never hit a bird before. He'd rarely come close enough to make one take flight. To his own great surprise, this time the rock found its mark. The bird fluttered out of the tree and fell stone cold dead in a twisted, awkward heap. He remembered the hurt in his mother's eyes as she admonished him, "That bird had a right to live too."

Now, seeing this other bird clutching onto the cabin roof for dear life, he thought 'So do you, little bird....So do I.'

Oddly enough, Sloan felt a sense of responsibility to get the bird and himself through the squall. He would not give up. He'd fucking fight till the end. Squinting into the blinding rain, Sloan felt inadequate and helpless against the storm's awesome power. Yet a realization came to him. He did not have to beat this force of nature any more than he had to submit to it. The storm, as fierce as it was, would pass. All storms pass. He merely had to outlast it. Nothing more. And this meant concentrating on what he was doing instead of some dumb bird. 'Get serious!'

So many things had gone wrong, Sloan waited apprehensively for the next emergency, the next trial. He squinted into the rain, trying to make out the Golden Gate Bridge. He couldn't, not for a long time, and even then he was not sure it was the bridge that he was seeing. How could it have been so close and so invisible. As he sailed under it, the wind and rain were as vicious as ever. Still, being in the bay gave Sloan confidence he would survive.

The storm did not seem to let up, not until it was obvious to Sloan that it had. Then it died surprisingly fast with the marina barely in sight. The seas abated too, more quickly than they seemingly should have. He checked his watch and figured that he could get back before dark. This too surprised him, in that the squall he had weathered must have lasted much less than an hour.

It had seemed to go on forever. He took pride in outlasting it. Too much pride. The wind quieted to whisper, barely loud enough to keep him going.

Sloan tied up at the marina, feeling pleasantly stoned, and both grateful and lucky to be alive. The wind had died completely, yet his ears continued to ring from it. He was still wearing the life jacket when he jumped onto the dock. There he received another surprise. Both his legs turned to jelly and bent at the knees. They almost gave out on him. He straightened them, stood there a minute, then stomped his feet alternately on the wooden planks. Never had they felt so solid, so good. And he too felt good, in a state of exhausted euphoria.

Sloan glanced back at the boat. The bird still held fast to the cabin railing. 'You owe me, little fucker....Saved both our asses.' The bird ignored him. Sloan smiled anyway. He sensed a connection between this bird and the one that stayed in his memories all these years, the one he had needlessly killed in front of his mother, the one she said had a right to live too. Sloan gave a gentle whistle to get its attention. The bird turned its head towards him and seemed to give a barely perceptible nod before spreading its little wings and darting away into the dusk. Anchored on the dock, he watched it turn into a speck and then disappear. For reasons he didn't understand, Sloan too felt free as a bird.

On the bus ride home, the feeling of euphoria stayed with Sloan while his feeling of exhaustion dissipated. He entered his apartment thinking, "'The sailor is home from the sea.'" A twinge of loneliness hit him. He brushed it aside with no concern as to its source — the lack of someone to meet him, to share his euphoria. Sloan headed straight for the refrigerator, his mouth already watering. He withdrew a beer, held it tightly, taking pleasure from the coldness of the can in his hand. He headed for his best chair, propped up his feet, and took a long, relaxed swallow. No beer had ever tasted so refreshing. He savored it, slowly, along with the memory of the frightening test he had just passed. Sloan took pride in beating that storm, forgetting that he had merely outlasted it. In the back of his mind, he had always considered himself a survivor. Now he had proof. Feeling had become fact. He felt changed, in some important ways a different person. He had a final the next day. Sure, he could pass it with what he already knew. Still, he should do some studying, get as good a grade as he could. Yet Sloan knew that he wouldn't. He'd have another beer, maybe two, then get some sleep. He might even sleep right through the final. Surprisingly, it did not seem so important. Now, compared to what he'd just been through, neither did college. He'd had enough of Berkeley, at least for a while. Sloan wanted a break, a real break. An idea that had been way in the back of his mind loomed larger, now that he had proved that he was a survivor. He took another swig of beer.

Sloan's feeling of confidence stayed with him the next day, during and after the final. It triggered an act both surprising and crazy, seemingly out of the blue. Ignoring every reason he had given his woman for not sailing away with her, he enlisted in the Marines

Not until a year later, in Vietnam, did Sloan think about why. It was during a calm quiet evening in the bush which followed and contrasted with a frightening, exhausting day. He lay looking up at the stars, wondering exactly how the Hell the Chemistry major had ended up in Vietnam. Sure, he had been pissed-off about losing his woman. And tired of college. Yet the main reason had to be making it through that storm. Not many people would have, not in such a wreck of a boat. He had proved himself a survivor. Joining the Marines hadn't scared him. Ending up in Vietnam didn't either. Just two more tests. He would survive both, the way he had survived that storm.

'So far, so good,' he thought, laying on his back looking up at the stars. So far he had survived. Ironically, he did not feel anything like a survivor, not after what he had seen a few hours earlier. He felt more like that little bird clutching the cabin roof railing for dear life. He was a Marine Corps rifleman in Nam — his fate still up in the air.

The vision of that little bird brought with it that of the other bird, the one that failed to survive a carelessly thrown rock. Again he heard his mother's words, "It had a right to live too." Sloan had never thought to doubt them. Now, lying on his back in Vietnam, he saw himself earlier that day, standing on the edge of an arc light crater, the work of a huge B-52 bomb. His whole platoon, even his company could be buried within it without a trace. Thinking about the force that bomb had unleashed, the way people die in war, the unrecognizable mess it can make of them, led him back to a supposedly more peaceful time, getting knocked around by a vicious storm, fighting a tiller for his life, waiting for that final freak wave which would wash him away, a little man on a tiny boat on a vast ocean. Now, gazing up at thousands of sparkling stars, Sloan realized that neither he himself nor any living thing on this earth had any damn right to live, not against the awesome, arbitrary powers of nature and man, powers that make us so relatively and infinitely small and helpless in the sum of things.

Recalling these thoughts as he waited for Smitty to return, with or without his hat, again Sloan did not feel like a survivor. Still, he was one. Getting back from Nam proved that, yet not just that. Surviving Nam had taught him that being a survivor had its price, sometimes a very steep one. Would he survive Berkeley? And was survival worth the effort just to live in a drug induced fog? No, not even close. He'd kick drugs, get out of that fog for good. There was no doubt in Sloan's mind. 'I'll survive Berkeley too....Even if being a survivor ain't all it's made out to be.'

The Doors record was coming to an end. As much as Sloan wanted, needed a drink, he decided to put on the Van Ronk album first. For smoking weed, you couldn't beat The Doors. Beer was brewed for the woozy blues of Jimmy Reed, or maybe vice-versa. Now, for liquor, he'd try a little Dave Van Ronk. If it worked, and he had little doubt it would, he'd have to thank Smitty for turning him on to Van Ronk. Still, out of respect for The Doors, he'd wait for their song to end.

Sloan thought about the job he had done on those cops. A smile came to his face. 'Survived them too.' He could still handle himself, even doped up. 'But they were amateurs, fuckups who got what they deserved.' He pictured them searching the sewers for their pistols, if they had the sense. He lost his smile with a related thought. The sewers are where he should be right now. Every day, people died for losing their cool the way he had. Tonight, he too should have been washed down the sewers. Blind, dumb luck had saved him. Sloan admitted it.

The Doors cut came to an end. Wanderin' was the song he wanted to hear. It was the first cut on Side Two. He switched records, poured some more rum, and sat back down. With the first notes, he took a long, easy swallow. The rum's rough warmth and

Van Ronk's rough wail blended seamlessly, like two entwining chemicals with a need to bond. What was there about the blues that gave you comfort? You'd think it'd be the other way around. If you read the words in a book, they'd depress you even more. Instead, the blues gave you strength. Was this self-pity? That didn't make sense, that self-pity could be a source of strength. Was it the making of a human connection, hearing someone suffering with you, knowing that you weren't alone? Maybe. Who knows? One thing for sure, if you let them, the blues could carry you away to a better place. His own thoughts made him uneasy. 'Who cares how?' Maybe that was what he wanted from dope, a barrier against introspection. No way, not with marijuana. Grass was instant introspection. Yet he hardly ever smoked weed when he was doing pills. Maybe he did the pills to get away from the weed. Hey, maybe weed did lead to the stronger stuff.

Sloan did not want to think about that either, not right now. He wanted to listen to Van Ronk, to submerge himself within the rhythm, the words, the feeling in the voice.

> Been workin' in the army, workin' on a farm
> All I got to show is this muscle in my arm.

Sloan thought, 'All I got to show is this needle in my arm.' He smiled to himself. No, there was no needle in his arm, not yet anyway. He had never shot up anything. 'Big fucking deal!' You didn't need to shoot up to OD. And that's where he had been headed, to OD oblivion. Why the hell didn't he get out of Berkeley? There were only three people in the whole fucking town he could stand — Rob, Screw, and Smitty. And it wasn't the same with Rob. Still his best friend, Rob was married now. That changes things.

Sloan thought about all the great guys he had met in the Marine Corps. Never had he made so many decent friends in such a short time. Then again, never had he lost so many. Hell, if Smitty didn't come back with his bush cover, he'd reenlist to get another one. Sloan did more than smile, he laughed at that thought, then took another good swallow of rum.

'Reenlist,' he thought again, smiled again. What a ridiculous idea. Yet why was the idea so ridiculous? Sure, he could end up getting blown away in Nam, but if he kept doing what he was doing, he'd end up dead in Berkeley, maybe even sooner. Some faces from the Marine Corps came back to him. He missed them, both the dead and the alive. 'I'd go to Hell with those fuckers.' Reenlisting, at the very least, he'd be around decent people for a change. And he knew things he could pass along to the "boots", kids like Screw, things that had kept him alive and might do the same for them. He could save some money too, maybe enough to buy a sailboat when he got out. Plus pick up some unemployment insurance. Maybe he would reenlist. Sloan thought hard about it, finally saying to himself, slightly more seriously, 'Smitty don't come back with my hat, I reenlist to get another one.'

The album side finished, still with no sign of Smitty. The rum helped, but Sloan was uneasy, becoming uneasier. He now regretted involving Smitty. The dude could end up an accessory after the fact, liable to the same sentence as Sloan. And what could that be? Beating up a cop, stealing pistols. Five years? Ten? Three, at least. Who knows, maybe even twenty? That was one more thing Sloan didn't want to think about. He did anyway. He couldn't help it. Worst case, he may end up having to cop a plea just to get Smitty off.

Sloan had intended to flip the record over, yet he just sat there in the silence. Any trace of adrenaline had drained away. The rum was exactly what he had needed. One more shot would set him just right. He decided to forgo that, to tough things out. His head was getting heavy. Where the hell was Smitty?

Attempting to get to his feet, Sloan held his side as he rose. A sharp pain and some tightness came from somewhere else, his knee. He collapsed back down on the couch. Sloan gently placed his hand on his knee, only now realizing how swollen it was. He did not even remember the cop stomping on it. This time he got to his feet with the help of the couch's arm rest. He scribbled Smitty a note, locked up, and went down to his own apartment.

Sloan entered determined to go cold turkey, to get himself in shape, real shape, hard. And not for the hell of it, not just to see if he could. No, this time he'd stay clean. Sloan headed straight for his stash, ready to do something he had never done before. He poured all the variously colored pills into his palm, gave them a long, hard stare, knowing that he was holding over two week's wages. No matter. He closed his hand tight around them and headed for the bathroom. Sloan held his fist high over the toilet and slowly opened it. The colorful pills cascaded down. The few left stuck to his palm followed one at a time, reluctantly. Sloan decided to give them a royal send off. He whipped out his prick to piss them away. The color of his urine shocked him. There was blood in it. 'This is not good.' Again he felt the pain of the cop's flashlight to his kidney. Sloan was too tired and exhausted to leave his apartment. He would wait a day or two. Sloan flushed away the blood, the urine, and the pills, thinking, 'Hell, if I gave up women, I can give up dope.'

A hard, no nonsense knock on his door brought all of Sloan's senses to attention. 'Cops!' He went to door, thinking, 'Face the music.' What he faced was Smitty standing in the threshold, holding out his hat. Sloan's surprise and relief at seeing it was tempered by the angry glint in Smitty's eyes. Was he pissed-off at him? If so, why? Sloan smiled anyway as he took the hat, saying, "Thanks, Man. Owe you one."

Smitty merely nodded and headed upstairs.

*****

Straughton lay between his black satin sheets. For the last half hour he had been working up the energy to get out of bed and roll a joint. An unexpected sound managed to get him sitting up. It was somewhere between a very hard knock on his door and a battering ram trying to splinter it. Screw's voice got him to his feet. "Straughton! Straughton! Open up."

When he did open up, he found an excited Screw urging him, "C'mon, let's go! A shootout between the cops and the SLA is on TV."

"What happened?" asked Straughton.

"It ain't over yet. It's live, on TV."

A live shootout on TV was just reason enough to forego your morning joint and hit your local bar. "I'll get dressed."

Screw checked his wallet, making sure he had his phony ID. "I'll get Smitty."

He got Sloan too. All four of them rushed to the nearest bar. The TV was blasting away, an excited narration over bursts of gunfire. Not surprisingly, the bar had only a few customers. Surprisingly, one of them was Marco, sitting right in front of the television.

There was an untouched beer in front of Marco. His stomach couldn't stomach beer. He had ordered it anyway, after the bartender took as a personal insult his request for buttermilk. A nauseous expression had come to his face, as if he were about to spew all over the top of Marco's head. Marco would not have been in the bar, if not for the three people who had stopped him on the street, conveying the joyous news that his wife was in a shootout. Even if he weren't afraid of missing something before he could make it home, Marco would have holed up at the bar to avoid someone else telling him the news. Now, just his luck, in walk four people who knew him. Worse yet, one of them was Straughton.

Smitty and Sloan took barstools to one side of Marco. Straughton and Screw sat on the other side. Straughton could not believe his luck. Not only would he see Marco's reactions firsthand, he should be able to get an interview out of him too. A few comments, minimum.

The television camera, showing a small, frame house, panned away to a cop behind a wall shooting at it. It then panned up to a roof, showing a police sniper taking a position.

"I don't fucking believe it," said Sloan. "If there's a TV on in that house, they're giving away the cops' positions."

The camera then panned back to the house, with the announcer saying, "For some reason, we've just been advised not to show you the police."

Sloan mumbled, "I told you the damn reason."

As the firing continued, Screw asked aloud, "Isn't this neat?"

An angry glance from Marco told him to be more careful about what he said.

Screw decided to mollify Marco with a compliment. "That wife of yours sure is making a name for herself."

'That she is,' Marco admitted, to himself. Despite the idiocy of what she was doing, and the incompetence with which she was doing it, Susan was having one hell of an impact, at least on the media. Marco assured himself that he didn't envy her a bit, which was the surest sign that he did.

Sloan predicted, "They keep firing tracer rounds, they're gonna set that house on fire."

A few minutes later the camera zeroed in on some smoke. The announcer said, "The house seems to be on fire."

"Two for two," Smitty mumbled, glancing at Sloan.

The lower corner of the television screen showed, one after the other, pictures of all the suspected SLA members. The first was Genghis Khan, with his birth name printed below his picture. The second photo was of Susan. No one glanced at Marco. He looked straight ahead, as if the picture was of a stranger. Smoke was now coming out of both sides of the house. Marco thought to himself that it must be hard to breathe inside. Soon a white flag, or bed sheet, or whatever, would appear in one of the windows. Then the SLA would file out the front door one at a time with their hands up. Susan would make a beautiful defendant. She'd get all the publicity, become a hero, a martyr. If the trial took place in the Bay Area, Sylvia O'Reilly could probably get her off. Angela Davis got away with murder, no problem. They made a martyr out of her. Now she's a hero, who can get a job teaching at any big university. Susan has ten times the brains of Angela Davis, and she's a hundred times better looking. Marco wondered if he would take her back, knowing without admitting that he would do it in an instant.

Marco watched mesmerized as the smoke billowed out of the house. 'How could Susan breathe in there?' He himself could not seem to get enough air. Flames appeared at the edge of the roof, and in minutes engulfed it entirely. Marco sat with his mouth agape. Where was the white flag? The heat inside must be unbearable. Yet they were bearing it. When were they coming out?

The walls too were burning now. The sound of gunfire from the house just kept increasing, and the announcer asked in disbelief, "How can they keep firing?"

Marco sat marveling at the insane courage of those inside. They were going out in a literal blaze of glory. Susan, his beautiful wife, was being burned alive. He would never see her again, her striking face, her gorgeous white body, still wet as she came out of the shower. No, he would never get another chance to make her happy, to make her proud of him. How he wanted that chance. Yet Susan, who had shared his bed, was fighting to the death, was sure to be burned alive.

The newsman sounded anguished as he said, "They're still firing. How can they survive in that inferno?"

Sloan leaned back and looked at the screen in disbelief, saying, "You fucking idiot!"

Straughton found Sloan's comment music to his ears, though he had no idea to what Sloan was referring, just the who of it. In the excitement of the moment, Straughton had forgotten how much he loathed TV's blow dried pretty boy newsmen. Sloan had reminded him, and he now felt a camaraderie with Sloan he had never experienced before.

"You fucking idiot," Sloan repeated. "There's no one alive in that house. It's the fire setting off those rounds."

'Three for three,' thought Smitty. Why hadn't he realized that?

Marco fought the idea, refusing to accept it.

The bartender was standing to the side, watching the TV and absentmindedly rubbing the soap stains from a glass with cloth napkin. He leaned closer to the television, "Yeah, anybody inside that house is a Krispy Kritter now."

'The ignorant fascist," thought Marco. His hand squeezed tighter around his still full glass of beer. How he'd like to fling it in the bartender's big brutal mug. Only his survival instincts stopped him.

*****

As usual, Screw had been in a good mood all day, and without chemical enhancement. Now he was in a better one. Timothy Leary, who had been broken out of a federal penitentiary by the Weather Underground, had somehow escaped to Algeria. The Black Panther Party in Exile had immediately granted him political asylum at their embassy. "Read all about it. Leary escapes to Algeria." Screw had sold even more papers than when Leary broke out of jail — three loads, minus the one paper he had left.

A brand new Cadillac completely filled the parking space in front of him. With his pockets full of coins, Screw had been picturing himself cruising the streets of Berkeley in it. That was the way to go. After a few miles in that Cadillac, switching back to a John Deere tractor just might feel like a comedown. A few more days like today, and he'd have the down payment on a Caddy.

Show up back at the farm in style. Intruding into Screw's fantasy came a very pissed-off looking guy in a business suit. He flung his briefcase into the trunk, and slammed it shut. 'What's he got to sweat?' As the man headed for the driver's side door, Screw stood thinking, 'Must be true — money ain't everything.' Then he noticed what looked like a baggy of marijuana in the street where the guy had been standing. Casually walking over and picking it up, Screw discovered that that was exactly what it was.

By the time the guy had started the car, Screw was already at the driver's side window. "Mister, you dropped something."

The guy flinched, saying defensively, "Never saw it before." Yet he surely had seen this scene before, more than once, in film comedies. Now, happening to him, it wasn't the least bit funny.

Screw laughed. "I'll be glad to take care of it for you."

The guy gave Screw a suspicious once-over, finally smiling as he said, "Don't waste your matches, Kid. It's garbage. I got burned."

Screw straightened up and was about to walk away, when he changed his mind. "You wanna score something good, Mister?"

Five minutes later, they were at a dealer's. The guy was sifting some grass through his fingers, asking suspiciously, "You sure this is quality?"

"Guaranteed," said the dealer, as if a dealer's guarantee was worth something.

Screw stepped in, asking, "Is this is the same Panama Red as the last time?"

The dealer nodded.

Screw turned toward the guy. "If it is, and I think it is, this is dynamite."

The guy liked the way Screw only said "I think", but not enough to take a chance. "I've been burned once today. Let's do a joint." He took his second drag thinking about how Screw had returned what he thought to be a lid of grass, and had told him up front that he would get a cut from the dealer. Dope had a way of turning people into thieving whores, but this kid seemed surprisingly straight, with the emphasis on surprisingly. As he thought this, the guy glanced down at his watch. "Shit! I've got a meeting in twenty minutes." He rose to his feet. Looking at Screw, he said, "I'll take a chance on you, Kid." He turned to the dealer.

"Give me $100's worth."

The dealer smiled. "Five lids coming up."

As they walked outside, the guy said, "You know, I'm already stoned...from two tokes." He brought out his wallet, handing Screw a twenty. "Here, Kid, buy yourself some shoes."

Now shoes were something Screw already had if he cared to wear them. The Panama Red and the cash he received as his cut, plus the twenty dollar tip, were a completely convincing argument to take the rest of the day off. Screw was well aware that incidents such as this were not restricted to Berkeley, but he doubted there existed a place on the globe where they happened more often. Yet a problem remained, one he was always willing to take on. How should he spend the rest of this pleasantly successful day? Going over to Smitty's to smoke a joint and listen to some music would be just the thing. Just the thing if Smitty weren't such a drag since Marcia dumped him. All Smitty did now was sit around drinking beer and listening to the blues. A potent joint would do him good if you could get a few tokes down his throat. Fat chance of that.

Screw found himself walking by a record store. This gave him an idea. A new album might get Smitty tokin', jokin', and out of his rut. Screw asked the clerk, "Got anything new by The Doors or Stones or Hendrix?"

"Naw. Heard The Stones are coming out with one in a month or two."

Just then, a freak walked up to the clerk, asking with the intonation of a confirmed stoner, "Hey Man, where's that new album by Rabbi Shenker?"

The clerk appeared stumped. "Rabbi Shenker?"

"Yeah Man, Rabbi Shenker. It's for my woman. She says it's the hottest album in Berkeley now."

The clerk said, "In Berkeley, Israel, maybe. In Berkeley, California, I guarantee you it ain't."

"That's what my old lady says."

"Maybe your old lady knows more about music that I do. Maybe she ought to open a record store."

The freak gave this some thought. "You really think so?"

"Would I lie to you?" the clerk asked.

"Hey Man, I didn't accuse you of that."

Screw, having nothing better to do, decided to get in on the conversation, perhaps clarify things and solve everybody's problems. "Hey Man, what type of music does this Rabbi play?"

"Guitar music, she says."

The clerk was willing to waste another half minute or so. "Tell me how he spells his name, and I'll look him up for you."

"Hey Man, how would I know? I'm no Jew."

The clerk had had enough, and was about to send the stoner packing when he got a brainstorm. He would ask the other clerk, who did happen to be a Jew. "Hey Steve," he called across the store, "Do we have an album of guitar music by Rabbi Shenker?"

Steve called back, "Are you fucking serious?" Even in Berkeley, the word fucking yelled across a record store draws the attention of at least half of the customers, which it did.

"Yeah," the clerk replied. "This dude says it's the hottest selling album in Berkeley."

Steve was just about to make a very insulting remark about "this dude" when a thought came to him. "Are you sure he didn't say an album of sitar music by Ravi Shankar?"

Things were beginning to make sense to the clerk. He turned back to his customer. "Is that what your old lady said?…It's Indian music, India Indian, not American Indian."

The customer thought hard on this. "You know, I was a little stoned when she said it."

The clerk saw no reason to doubt this, and a hell of a lot of reasons to accept it. He reached over a couple of bins and pulled out two albums. "This is about the hottest selling album in Berkeley. I've got two left. If it ain't what your old lady wants, don't open it. I'll give you a refund."

Screw reached for the remaining album, saying, "Let me see that?"

One of the customers who couldn't have helped but hear the cross store conversation came over. "Where are those Ravi Shankar albums."

Screw made up his mind. "Sorry, I got the last."

As he was paying for it, another customer walked in the door asking for the album. This gave Screw even more confidence in his decision. He had the music. He had the dope. The only remaining necessities for an afternoon of toking were the munchies. He quickly acquired the Clark Bars, M & M Peanuts, Screaming

Yellow Zonkers, and Twinkies. Then he dragged Sloan and Straughton out of their apartments and banged on Smitty's door. If all this dynamite couldn't blow Smitty out of the doldrums, nothing could.

Smitty took his time getting to the door, and he didn't ask who was there before opening it. As was lately his custom, he met his guests with a solemn expression and an open beer in his fist.

Screw, still waiting for the words, "Come in", held out the album. "Happy birthday."

The solemn look still on his face, Smitty said, "Today ain't my birthday."

"It'll do," Sloan assured him. He himself was having second thoughts about partying. Off and on, Sloan had been enduring some mild symptoms of withdrawal — headaches, sinus trouble, nausea, even tremors. At the moment, except for slightly nervous hands, he was feeling alright. Not right, but alright. Grass or booze did not fit his rehab regimen, more retox than detox. Still, he owed Smitty a favor. Cheering him up would be Sloan's good deed for the day, for the month in fact. Hell, for the last few years.

Smitty, without inviting them in, looked over the album. He finally mumbled with no enthusiasm, "Yeah, this is supposed to be good."

Sloan said, "If not, you can exchange it for a Leonard Cohen album — music to slit your wrists by."

Smitty had to chuckle. "Music to slit your wrists by, so there is a use for Leonard Cohen." He swung open the door. "We'll try this first."

It took less than a minute before they had the album on, a joint circulating, and the munchies broken out. Smitty had heard all the raving about Ravi Shankar and his sitar music. It was like hearing everybody talk about the foxy new babe in high school. You're dying to see for yourself. Well, not quite that bad. Still, the album didn't instantly grab him. In fact, the conversation drew him away from it.

As Screw exhaled, he said, "You know, there's a third way." Being stoned, he felt no great need to make any sense, so he left the thought right there.

Smitty sat thinking how a little dope brings out the philosophical in people. "Let's not get into that."

449

"What?" Screw asked.

Smitty replied, "I ain't in the mood for any oriental bullshit."

"What?…I meant there's a third way for me besides the Marine Corps or enrolling at Berkeley." The sitar music intruded on Screw's thoughts. He had never heard anything like it, not anything considered music. Screw decided you had to get used to it. He hoped to get used to it fast, because the racket was getting on his nerves. Still, time was no problem. Neither was dope. They had enough grass to wear out the damn album. And the munchies were good for at least another hour or two.

Straughton broke a long silence by asking, "Screw, My Man, did you intend to enlighten us about this third way, or merely announce you had found one?"

Screw, feeling no pain, was amenable to either. In that Straughton seemed to be nudging him towards the former, he saw no reason to resist. "I could join a commune."

Smitty would not have seen anything wrong with this, even if he weren't stoned.

Sloan did, despite the fact that he was pleasantly stoned. "Are you fucking batshit?"

Straughton thought, 'Batshit, in the sense of crazy.' It was not an expression he himself would ever use, but one that he should remember to make use of, to spice up a quote, or add verisimilitude to a completely manufactured one.

Screw took Sloan's question literally, answering, "No". He certainly didn't feel batshit. "Why shouldn't I join a commune? I've been a farmer all my life."

This made sense to Smitty.

Not to Sloan. "Those worthless bums don't grow anything you can't smoke. They survive on food stamps.…Drugs and fucking is all they do."

Smitty sat wondering if he was the only one who caught the irony of farmers living on food stamps.

"'Drugs and fucking is all they do,"?' thought Screw. 'Sounds good to me.' He studied Sloan a while before saying, "If you're trying to dissuade me, you're going about it the wrong way."

Smitty, impressed, felt obligated to let Screw know. "'Dissuade', excellent, Screw. You can definitely make it as an English major."

Straughton, no great lover of music, was usually able to filter it out effortlessly. However, this sitar music seemed to have a nasty way of overwhelming his filters. He decided to talk through it, putting his superior language skills at Sloan's service. "Our ex-Marine is trying to enlighten you that a working commune is a conflict of terms."

"Former Marine," Sloan corrected, then turned to Screw. "The only communes that last are the ones that grow enough dope to sell the surplus....And the competition is cutthroat, literally."

Straughton said to Screw, "My man, if you intend to try your hand at farming, may I suggest a place called Nebraska."

"Heard of it," said Screw.

Sloan added, "Unless you yourself want to get planted in an unmarked grave, keep out of these canyons around here." Despite the excellent dope and mouth-watering munchies, Sloan felt surprisingly irritable. He suddenly realized why. "If an unmarked grave is what you're after, let me catch you buying another Ravi Shankar album. This shit is torture."

Smitty stood immediately and headed for the turntable. "God, I thought it was just me. They call this air pollution music?"

Straughton said, "Air pollution would be a more precise description."

Sloan added, "I don't want to sound paranoid, but Ravi Shankar has to be a communist plot to destroy 'Peace, justice, and the American Way'."

Screw found all eyes upon him. "Hey Mothers, I ain't in on no plot. I bought it without even hearing it."

Smitty already had the album off the turntable.

Sloan said, "I wish I hadn't heard it either."

Smitty returned the album to its jacket and handed it to Screw. "Here, get your money back, plus damages."

Straughton cautioned, "If that album is returned to the record store, it can be used again, against other innocent people."

Smitty said, "We'll leave that up to Screw's conscience."

"Hey, don't forget I brought the grass too. Nobody's complaining about that." Screw scanned the room, thinking, 'These guys are getting to be a drag.'

Sloan said, "Screw, if the dope wasn't dynamite, you'd probably gotten that album broken over your head."

Smitty pointed out, "Your dope ain't strong enough to make Ravi Shankar bearable."

Straughton said, "I doubt such dope exists."

"So crucify me, fuckers, for getting rooked buying a friend a present."

Smitty felt mercy in his heart. "Okay, Screw, considering it's my birthday, and you supplied the dynamite dope and munchies, you're forgiven.

Screw said irritably, "If the dope wasn't dynamite, you'd know it ain't your birthday."

'He's right,' Smitty admitted to himself. Yet this did not stop him from putting up a defense. "Well, it's my birthday party."

"Gentlemen, contemplate this," said Straughton, "All over Berkeley, at this very moment, there are hundreds and hundreds of people sitting around stereos, pretending to enjoy sitar music."

Smitty winced. "That's too painful to contemplate."

"They deserve the pain," said Sloan.

Screw added, "Academy Awards is what they deserve."

Smitty wasn't so sure. "Some of them are just masochists."

Sloan saw Smitty shuffling through the albums. "Hey, put on Tim Buckley for a change."

Just as he heard Sloan say it, Smitty found himself looking at the album. He put it on, and the first few notes brought with them a sense of relief. "That's more like it."

Sloan felt relief too, even though the cut was No Man Can Find the War. That had him glancing at Screw, who did not look the least bit relieved. His almost permanent smile was gone, the result of all the ribbing. Right now, the poor kid looked exactly like a kid. Sloan's protective instincts kicked in. Uneasy that Screw was still considering joining the Marines, Sloan slipped into his mentoring mode.

"Screw, you know what you should do?"

Screw was in no mood to hear what he should do. He was tired of being treated like a kid, especially by Sloan. With a rare, irritated look on his face, he said, "Yeah, I should get some new friends."

Smitty nodded, thinking to himself that this would be an excellent idea.

Sloan too was impressed by Screw's insight. "Couldn't do

worse."

Screw was far from mollified, and tired of being the subject of the conversation. He asked Sloan in an accusatory tone, "How come you lied to me about Kathleen?"

Sloan had no memory of saying a word about Kathleen to anyone.

Screw continued, "You said she was a Jesus Freak."

Sloan realized he must have said something, and must have been ripped on drugs at the time. Sloan had nothing against Jesus Freaks. It was cults of any type that he despised. They were evil. He still hadn't decided whether Kathleen was one of the brainwashed or the brainwashers. Yet he was long past caring.

Screw still wanted to know why Sloan had lied to him. "She's no Jesus Freak. She's a witch."

"She was a Jesus Freak when I knew her." As soon as the words were out of his mouth, Sloan made the connection. Kathleen had disappeared the day after he had taken her to Salome's. Though she had dragged him away the night before, Kathleen might have been drawn back the next day. Instead of running from Salome, Kathleen had run towards her. He couldn't help but be amused.

"She a witch now," Screw insisted.

Smitty stared at Sloan with added respect. Sleeping with a witch as decent looking as Kathleen, that would look good on anyone's résumé.

It occurred to Sloan that that made Kathleen the second witch he had slept with. Well, technically, they weren't witches until afterwards. Still, the accomplishment was impressive. Maybe he turned women into witches. Hell, he might have done it to others. Just never found out.

Straughton, sensing the seeds of an article, wondered if Screw had seen Kathleen in action. "What makes you say that?"

"She told me straight out, and invited me to her cavern."

"What was it like?" asked Straughton.

"I didn't want to go to any cavern…full of bats and all that."

Smitty thought, 'Hell, I would have gone.'

Straughton asked, "Are you sure she said 'cavern', not 'coven'?

Screw thought this over. "Yeah, she might have said that. What's a coven?"

"A coven, My Man, is a witch-style fraternity."

It occurred to Smitty that covens came first. So that was where fraternities got all their nonsense.

From what Screw knew about fraternities, and what he thought he knew about witches, this description made little sense. Rather than show his ignorance, he decided to let the matter drop. Fortunately, out of nowhere, Sloan changed the subject, even if it meant he was being treated like a kid again.

"Screw, be smart, go to college first. You can always quit and join the Corps."

Screw said grudgingly, "That's probably what I'll do."

Sloan added, "Just don't fall for the bullshit."

"What do you mean?"

"College is a left handed circle jerk."

"What do I care," asked Screw, "as long as I've got a half decent women on each side of me?"

This reply threw Sloan.

Smitty gladly stepped into the breach. "Circle jerks are not coed. You need a dick to join."

Screw asked, "Well what do you call it when it's boy-girl, boy-girl?"

"That's a daisy chain," Smitty informed him.

"In which case," Straughton added, "the technique switches from manual to oral."

Both Smitty and Sloan nodded to Straughton, acknowledging his input.

Screw pictured a daisy chain, and a question came to mind. "Does it stay in the same direction, or does someone yell, 'Switch!'"

Being very stoned, Smitty found this an interesting question. He saw no reason why switching directions wouldn't work.

Sloan asked, "How the fuck would I know?"

Screw had assumed he would. "You never done it?"

"Not that I remember...and I damn sure would."

Screw looked towards Straughton.

"Unfortunately not," said Straughton, thinking that he wouldn't be adverse to some research on the subject. An article on a daisy chain would surely be of public interest. And no personal waste of time either.

That left Smitty, who shook his head No.

"Then why not try one?"

He drew no arguments from anybody, but Sloan pointed out, "We're minus the female links, four of them."

Despite the grass, Smitty went into problem solving mode. "We could put an ad in The Badger."

There were nods of agreement and smiles of satisfaction all around. It was amazing the way the human mind could come up with such brilliant plans when stoned, and no less amazing how quickly these plans were forgotten when the dope wore off.

Screw had a vague feeling that they had been talking about something else, something more important, before they took off on this tangent. In fact, he suspected the subject was he himself. "Hey, what were we talking about before daisy chains?"

Smitty had no idea, and it took Sloan a long moment to remember. "You, going to Berkeley. Take it easy on the dope....Stay away from politics."

"Desert The Revolution?" Screw asked, half seriously.

"That'd be a start," said Sloan. He decided to hammer home his point with a little test. "Smitty, who are the most ignorant, arrogant people on the face of the earth?"

Smitty's first reaction was to wonder why he had been anointed the resident expert on this subject. Still, the marijuana had put him in too accommodating a mood to wonder long. 'A crowded field,' he thought. Yet there was one group that stood out. "College students!"

"Right-on," Sloan replied, proud of himself for choosing Smitty as his straight man. He turned back to Screw. "And watch out for the faculty too. Never trust anyone who pretends he can stand college students."

Screw shrugged. He had had enough of being preached to. In an attempt to change the subject, he asked the first question he could think of. "Smitty, you looking for a new roommate?"

This question, out of nowhere, hit Smitty like a slap across the face. "No!" Sure, he needed a roommate, and fast. But the only roommate he wanted was his old one, Marcia.

"Must have been rough," said Straughton sympathetically.

Smitty's back stiffened. He wasn't looking for sympathy.

Straughton added, "Dividing up the record collection."

This remark, whether intended as a joke or not, angered Smitty.

His feelings were only slightly tempered by the realization that Marcia had not come back for her records, thus giving him reason to hope. Glaring at Straughton, Smitty realized that he probably was serious.

Catching Smitty's glare, Straughton quickly explained, "Dividing up the record collection is the tragedy of the Sixties, a misfortune that can strike anyone — like cancer."

It was now clear to Smitty that Straughton was dead serious, probably talking from experience.

Screw, also dead serious, pointed out, "More like a venereal disease than a cancer."

Smitty glanced at Sloan as if to ask, "What planet are these two aliens from?"

Sloan was tempted to commiserate with Smitty, but his sense of humor got the best of him. "Yeah, it used to be about the kids. These days, it's who gets which Doors album."

Screw said, "I'd buy Marcia every Doors album that ever was."

Straughton said to Smitty, in all seriousness, "I always wondered what she saw in you."

Smitty wondered what it would feel like to coldcock Straughton.

Screw added, "You ain't gonna find another girl that good looking, not around here."

About to blow his top, Smitty had a question of his own. "Why don't you two jerks just shut the fuck up?"

"'You two"?' thought Sloan, realizing that he had not been doing his part. "Take it easy, Man. They're just trying to help you accept the fact that the rest of your life is downhill from here."

"Yeah, Man, face it," Screw agreed.

Smitty decided to just keep his mouth shut and ignore them.

Sloan tried to get a laugh, or at least a smile out of Smitty. "Seriously, Man, have you considered turning queer?"

He failed, and Smitty asked, "Is that an offer?"

"Sure, I can set you up."

Something close to a smile appeared on Smitty's face. "I'll think it over." The smile left his face when—

Screw asked in all innocence, "Hey, what is the story between you and Marcia?"

Smitty thought, 'The story starts with that fucking wine bottle you opened.' Still, as much as Screw was sticking his nose where it didn't belong, Smitty wouldn't feel right laying the blame on the kid. About to offer the appropriate reply, "None of your fucking business", Smitty suddenly remembered catching Screw the previous day with the ultimate hard-on test, sneaking her into his apartment and then back out a few minutes later. "What's the story with that dumpy little hippy chick?" While Smitty took pride in the clever way he had changed the subject—

Screw replied casually, "She tagged me out at third base."

This reply was too casual for Smitty. Still irritated, he asked, "Your dick too small?"

"Naw," Screw answered, just as casually. "The opposite....I don't want to blow my own trombone, but if I did, I could."

"'My own trombone,'" thought Smitty, amused, his irritation dissipating. Was it the grass, or had he underappreciated Screw's sense of humor?

Then Screw chose to ask, again in all innocence, "Did you and Marcia have a fight, or just get tired of each other?"

Re-irritated, even worse than before, Smitty turned to Sloan for back-up. "What do you think of a question like that?" He had turned to the wrong person.

"Answer it, and I'll tell you afterwards."

Smitty knew this question did not deserve an answer. Yet something inside him refused to leave the impression that they had tired of each other. "A fight," he said grudgingly, determined that this would be the last question he would answer.

Screw, not being a mind reader, asked, again in all innocence, "About what?"

"Get fucked!" Smitty said angrily.

Sloan asked in a tone so deadpan that it had to be a joke, "You didn't tell Marcia that, did you?"

Smitty could not believe what he had heard. He wanted to do two things — to take a swing at Sloan and to keep from laughing. He did neither.

Straughton said to him, "That, My Good Man, would have been a poor choice of words."

Sloan agreed, "They don't need no encouragement."

*****

Sarah awoke in the middle of the night. She was tired, not having slept well the previous night. Even with her eyes closed, she could tell that Rob's reading lamp was still on. If she opened her eyes she would have trouble getting back to sleep. Perhaps he passed out with the light on. She doubted this. "What's wrong?" she mumbled.

"It's embarrassing," was his reply.

"'It's embarrassing?'" she wondered. 'Strange thing to say.' Could she be dreaming? Not likely. And it wasn't likely she would get back to sleep, not until she found out what that cryptic reply meant. "What's embarrassing?"

"Being a Jew," he replied distractedly.

This answer got her completely, though unwillingly, awake. She sat up, and wriggled backwards until her neck was against the headboard. "Would you mind repeating that?"

Thoughts about his kid coming into the restaurant crying, not wanting to be a Jew anymore had been keeping him awake. "I mean it's embarrassing how many Jews are protesting this war."

"Embarrassing?…I'm not embarrassed by it. I wish they'd bring every soldier home tomorrow. Don't you?"

"I don't know anymore."

"What!"

"Mike was actually there. Most of the people he met have no love for the communists. They want our help."

"Help destroying the whole country."

"He does say we're not gonna win doing what we're doing .…I'll take Sloan over any of those protestors."

"A junkie?"

"…Yeah.…It just bugs me that such a disproportionate number of protesters are Jewish?"

"Not so disproportionate," she replied, "not for middleclass college educated people, and liberals, which most Jews are.…Or alienated people, which most Jews are, alienated by anti-Semitism.…I'll bet the number of Jews in Washington helping fight this war is every bit as disproportionate."

"Probably," Rob admitted, "and that's even worse.…Why do we have to be so visible?"

"No more visible than as judges, artists…or

scientists....Nowhere near as visible as at winning Nobel Prizes for this country....You want Jews to be invisible?"

Rob admitted to himself that she had a point, but only to himself. "Tell me it doesn't make you cringe when you see that disgrace of a lawyer Pussler on TV."

"He's a communist, not a Jew. He never fought for a Jewish cause in his life."

"To the goyim, he's a Jew," Rob insisted. "To some of them, he's all Jews."

"Then they're ignorant bigots."

"Some of them didn't know what a Jew was till they saw that scumbag Pussler on TV."

Sarah asked, "Meir Kahane and his Jewish Defense League are just as visible. He's for the war, and hates the Communists."

"Nobody hates the Jews because of anything he does."

"Exactly! People don't hate Jews because of Jews who are Jews. They hate Jews because they need something to hate, someone to blame. The Pusslers and the Abbie Hoffmans just make it easier for them....The hell with the self-hating Jews and anti-Semites. Ignore them."

His wife could always hold her own in an argument, but Rob was surprised how combative she was tonight. He guessed it had something to do with keeping her from sleeping. "When they're after my six-year-old kid?" Rob was regretting this low blow when—

"Five-year-old."

"You know it's not the anti-Semitism that gets to me. It's the responsibility." He switched off his reading light.

She felt as if she were missing something. "For David?"

"Not just for him. A goy does something and gets away with it, that's it. A Jew gets away with something, some other Jew is sure to pay for it."

Rob's voice told her that he would be asleep in a minute. She resented this, knowing that she herself would probably be awake till dawn. "That's what it is to be a minority."

Rob yawned his reply. "Seems like there should be one place on the face of this earth where Jews don't have to walk on eggshells."

"There is," she replied.

It was the middle of the night, and Sloan couldn't sleep. He was doing pushups to exhaustion. A thin elastic mucus string ran from his nose to the floor. Four o'clock in the morning, and this was his fifth workout that day. The torture of exercise blunted the torture of withdrawal, but it took all his will to keep working out. Sloan's will soon drained out of him. His chest hit the floor with a loud, wet slap.

Sloan had thought he had beaten them, yet the tremors, headaches, and nausea had come back with a vengeance. He wondered if the previous day's marijuana was the cause. Sloan doubted it. Still, he decided to take it easy on the grass for awhile, and the beer too. But right now he did not have the luxury of thinking about the things he wasn't going to do. He had to find something to do, to occupy himself, to keep his mind off how lousy he felt.

Sloan took a quick shower. Afterward, he decided to wash his bush cover. That afternoon, he had bought some mild hand washing detergent just for the job. Sloan turned on the water in the bathroom sink. Waiting for it to fill, he checked out his hat. It surely needed something mild. The pathetic rag was close to falling apart. It actually saddened Sloan to conclude that his trusty bush cover was living on borrowed time. What was there about it that eased his mind? Sloan laughed to himself. Some people carried around their security blankets. He wore his on his head. He dipped the hat into the soapy water and gently, almost lovingly, kneaded it. The water quickly turned embarrassingly dark. He took his time washing the hat, then carefully hung it in the shower.

A hard, angry knock on the door shot through Sloan like a jolt of electricity. 'Shit!' Somehow the cops had found him. He waited for the inevitable, "Police. Open up." He kept waiting. It didn't come. A repeat of the hard, angry knock did. Sloan walked towards his door, now more conscious of and fighting to control the nausea and dizziness afflicting him. He straightened up, telling himself that maybe it wasn't the cops.

It wasn't. It was Smitty. He looked angrier than Sloan had ever seen him. Something must have happened, maybe something to do with the hat, something that really pissed him off.

Smitty asked angrily, "You got a pistol?" He had seen Sloan in worse shape, most of the time he had known him. Still, he did not look good. Smitty wondered how strung-out he was, if he were wasting his time.

Sloan was not in the habit of answering questions without knowing exactly why they were being asked. How the hell had Smitty found out about the pistols? How had the cops found Smitty? Had they put him through the wringer? Still, there was no reason Sloan couldn't give an honest answer. "No."

"Know where I can get one, fast?"

Sloan felt relief, realizing that Smitty had not been referring to the cop pistols he had tossed down the sewer. Rob had his father's Luger from WWII. No way would Sloan borrow it to put into Smitty's pissed-off hands. "What do you need one for?"

"Marcia's father just called. He hasn't heard from her in two weeks. He says she quit going to class."

"What do you need a pistol for?"

Smitty explained how Muhammad and his thugs would not let him see her.

"Do they have a gun?"

Smitty shook his head. "Not that I know."

"Then you don't need a pistol."

Smitty had no patience for Sloan telling him what he did and did not need. "These ain't frat boys. If they don't have guns, they've got shivs."

"We'll get something better than shivs. I'll go with you."

Smitty felt a weight lifted off of him. Sloan would know what to do. What he did was have Smitty drive them over to Rob's, who was not glad to see them at that hour of the night. Sloan had explained over the phone that if Rob wanted his dishwasher in on time, he better help get some business out of the way. They returned to Smitty's apartment with two baseball bats, two gloves, and a ball. It was still dark out. Aware that Muhammad and Friends knew The People's Crash Pad better than they did, Sloan wanted to wait until light. Bat in hand, Smitty paced the apartment like a newly caged animal.

Sloan found this worrying. Smitty might be too stoked to think straight, prone to make a mistake. "What do you say we smooth things out with a shot of something?"

"If you want to."

Sloan didn't. His withdrawal symptoms had all but disappeared, except for a mild headache. The sudden pressure and need to focus had done him good. Still, he wanted to calm down Smitty, and kill some time to boot. Their drinks were soon finished, and there was still some time to kill. "How 'bout some pre-game."

"Huh?" Smitty asked.

"Put on Spoonful, by Cream, the long version."

Smitty did so, feeling better immediately. To the music, he practiced swinging the bat, not as a weapon, but as if trying to hit a baseball, yet viciously. He imagined the hollow sound it would make crushing Muhammad's skull. When Spoonful finished, he put on Living Loving Maid by Led Zeppelin. They could have left after that, but Sloan insisted on finishing the pre-game with I'm Ready by Muddy Waters. When the song ended, they too were ready. Smitty glanced around the apartment. He walked over to the couch, and took an all-out swing at the front of it. A surprisingly thick cloud of dust arose. It had them both laughing and Smitty coughing as they headed out the door.

Sloan and Smitty arrived at The People's Crash Pad just after dawn. Sloan's headache had faded into the background. Nothing like a job with baseball bats to marginalize the small stuff. He experienced a forgotten focus and calm, for the first time in a very long time. A pleasant feeling this was. It gave him added confidence. Smitty opened the door to get out, but Sloan stopped him. "Wait. It's still too dark inside the house." Sloan did not want any mistakes, and he wasn't just worried about the punks they would have to face, and face down. If the cops got involved, they might connect him to the beating he gave their two buddies. Luckily, his camouflage hat was hanging wet in his shower. Still, without it, Sloan felt like Samson with his hair shorn, and he felt ridiculous for feeling that way.

Sloan wanted to picture in his mind what was going to take place. "You know exactly where her room is?"

"First one at the top of the stairs. The lights were off when we went by."

"Okay," said Sloan, "I'll go first."

"No!" said Smitty with determination, feeling like a coward desperate to make amends. He should have come back here the day after Muhammad refused to let him in. As if he had needed "a plan". The plan he needed was to do whatever he had to do to get Marcia out.

Sloan caught the determination in Smitty's tone. There was no point in arguing with him. Besides, with Smitty in front, he could better keep an eye on him. "Okay, but get up there fast. And that bat's not for show. Use it."

Smitty nodded.

"Let's go." They walked casually towards the crash pad, bats resting on their shoulders, as if headed for a game. The walkway was strewn with garbage. The People's Crash Pad was on the way back to what it had been. Sloan pointed Smitty to the hinge side of the door. He took the knob side. Smitty went into a slight crouch. Sloan turned his back to the door and gave it a mule kick just below the knob. The door flew open as fast and as cleanly as if that was the way it was supposed to be opened. Smitty hit the stairs full speed, Sloan right behind him. He tried to concentrate on bursting through Marcia's door, but something would not let him.

Sloan smelled it too — the worst stench in the world. Worse than sweat, worse than garbage, worse than shit. It was the choking, overpowering stink of putrefying flesh — the stench of death.

Smitty knew what it was before he was halfway up the stairs. His heart sank and his mind panicked, saying to himself, 'No. No!' Marcia's door was ajar, but he burst through it anyway. The room was a mess. Her things — clothes, books, writing, hairbrush — were scattered on the floor, all trashed and picked though. The stench was literally suffocating. He couldn't get enough air down into his lungs, and his heart was pounding so hard he could feel it in his throat. Smitty fought back the vomit.

Sloan rushed by him. He went for the window, trying to open it for a second. 'Fuck it!' He took the thick end of the bat to half the panes. Sloan sucked in the outside air. Smitty did the same. Sloan glanced back into the room, eyes settling on a closed door, probably to a closet. That had to be the source of the smell. He glanced over to see Smitty, white with fear and nausea, staring at it too. "Go down stairs," Sloan ordered him.

Smitty shook his head No.

Sloan pulled up his T-shirt over his mouth and nose. Smitty

copied him. It did little good. Sloan yanked open the closet door. The stench that couldn't be worse, got ten times worse. Despite it, they both stepped forward to get a look at its source. Smitty barely pulled his shirt down in time before retching all over the floor. He continued to retch as he staggered out the door. Sloan took another quick glance in the closet. Close to retching himself, he ran for the stairs, doing his best to avoid stepping in Smitty's vomit.

Smitty stood bent over in the yard, dry heaving.

Sloan asked, "You know it's not her?"

Smitty knew. The dead girl was blond, petite. She was upside down, her neck grotesquely twisted so her open eyed face had looked right up at him. She had probably been pretty. Not anymore. Discolored and bloated, her flesh seemed ready to burst open her clothing in an explosion of putrescence. One of her legs had been straight up, a little butterfly tattoo visible against the purple flesh of her ankle. The other leg was bent painfully against the wall beneath her. Her only showing arm was also tattooed, with needle bruises. Someone must have picked her up by the ankles to carry her into the closet, must have carelessly dropped her on her head. Smitty saw her as clearly as if she were still in front of him, a sight like none he had ever seen. Soon, with time to think, he would realize that it was a sight he would see again, many, many times, until the end of his life.

"I have to check the other rooms," said Sloan.

Smitty wanted with all his strength to say, "Wait, I'll go with you." Yet all his strength was not enough. He knew seeing Marcia in that state would break him. His knees almost buckled just thinking about it. He nodded to Sloan.

Sloan made quick work of the job. He came down to find Smitty sitting head-in-hands on the porch. "There's nobody else up there."

Smitty said out loud something he rarely said, even to himself — "Thank God." He looked up to see Sloan standing with two baseball bats over one shoulder, as if ready for a game. This struck Smitty as absurd. In no ways humorous, just absurd. Feeling as if he had to do something, at a loss as to what that was, Smitty asked, "Should we call the cops?"

"If you like cops, wanna spend a few hours with 'em."

On the way home, Smitty did not utter a word. Halfway there, the picture of that putrid, upside down little corpse in the closet came to him. It refused to fade. Somehow, the remembered picture was far, far clearer than the actual sight had been. That's when it hit him, stunned Smitty like ice cold water across his face. He had seen more than he had realized. That bloated, distorted, ghoulishly tinted face, he knew it, had seen it on his very own couch, when it looked like the face of an angel, belonging to the little stereo thief who still slept with her teddy bear, the streetwise inspiration for The People's Crash Pad — Donna. 'A shame,' he thought to himself, feeling soft and weak. He knew the cure for that — a little sarcasm. 'The People's Crash Pad did Donna a lotta good.'

*****

Marco was out of popcorn. He craved some, but not enough to make him leave the house. That would involve shaving, taking a shower, and putting on some clean clothes, which also meant doing a wash. Most of all, leaving the house meant seeing people who now knew that Susan had abandoned him and chosen death. All this was out of the question. He didn't have the energy. Ever since the Siamese Liberation Army had been incinerated, cremated in that god-awful fire, Marco found himself falling into a deeper and deeper daze. He'd sit in his underwear in front of the television all day, and often all night, mesmerized by that flickering little screen without really seeing it.

Susan was dead. He would never find another woman who could come close to her. People who hadn't known her would not believe he ever had such a wife. Susan had the guts to act upon her beliefs. She was a martyr, a bona fide martyr. Marco told himself that his place should have been next to her, that he should have gone off with her, ignoring the fact that Susan hadn't even let him in on her plans. He should have been there to comfort her at the very end, put his arm around her as the flames engulfed them. Marco could not imagine the pain she must have endured. Just thinking about it, he could feel the heat. How he loved her and wanted her back. Marco swallowed, his throat dry. Some buttermilk would taste good now.

Marco was out of buttermilk too. Aside from water, the only thing in the house left to drink was a half bottle of Bailey's Irish

Cream. He had bought it a week ago, on the advice of a liquor store clerk — something that would go down easy and still get him drunk. Marco had only been drunk twice in his life, once in high school and once during his freshman year. The high school drunk had been a one hundred percent disaster. He had found himself sick and puking even before the drunkenness came on to make things worse. His freshman year drunk had been a great time, giving him a joyful feeling he would always remember. Unfortunately, he also remembered making a complete fool of himself. That joyful feeling was what he was looking for with the Irish Cream, only this time he would be alone with no one to judge him a fool. The Irish Cream went down smooth all right, but it didn't stay there. In less time than he needed to get drunk, less time than seemed possible, it was already bursting out his other end. No drunk was worth that experience. Marco berated himself for not sticking with the hard stuff, like the Southern Comfort he drank his freshman year. So what if it was rough going down.

Marco's stomach growled, but not from anything he drank. It was empty, demanding something, anything. Except for some dry cat food, the cupboard was bare. The last human food in it had been yesterday's box of macaroni. It had come with the envelope of powdered cheese, and was pretty good and easy to make. Marco told himself he should buy some more, when and if he ever left the house. Of course he would soon leave the house. Yet not just yet, not until what was left in the refrigerator ran out, or maybe a day or two after that. Under no conditions would he eat the cat food. Marco's stomach growled again. He got to his feet and headed for the kitchen.

The refrigerator shelves were as remembered — bare except for a jar of strawberry jam. He had checked that out days earlier, when he still had some bread. There was a layer of mold on top. He knew he could scrape it off to get to the jelly below, but hadn't yet worked up the will. Marco hoped he could leave the house first. The freezer offered no pleasant surprises. There were three packages left, one wrapped in butcher paper and two in plastic. Ice crystals inside the plastic made these packages as much of a mystery as the one wrapped in butcher paper. Marco pondered a long moment before tossing the paper wrapped package onto the counter and the other two back into the freezer. His stomach rumbled again, telling him to find a way to defrost the package now. To do that, he would first have to know what was inside. Marco peeled off the outer paper, but the rest was stuck tight. It could take five or six hours for the mystery package to defrost. Again his stomach grumbled. Marco found a pot, threw in the package, wrapper and all, and covered it with water.

He headed back to the television. Marco was not surprised to see a full-screen picture of Susan, that is, he was not surprised until he realized he was seeing an actual news bulletin and not his own thoughts. The announcer repeated what Marco had missed — the coroner had stated that only the remains of Genghis Kahn and five members of the Siamese Liberation Army had been recovered from the ashes and identified. The police were positive that the other members, including Pamela Kane, the newspaper heiress, were still alive and on the loose. Susan's picture appeared again, not only as the presumed new leader of the Siamese Liberation Army, but also as the new number one on the FBI's Most Wanted List.

"The rotten bitch," said Marco aloud. There was no relief in his heart or his head. The bitch was alive. She was the reason the FBI had humiliated him, had bugged his house and made a joke out of him. Killing Berkeley's first black Superintendent of Public Schools and its first oriental cop made her the most dangerous revolutionary in the country, the idol of the New Left. After all he'd done, all he'd accomplished, he was now nothing more than Susan's abandoned husband — a trod upon footnote to The Revolution. "The rotten bitch," Marco repeated. He told himself that if Susan were there right now, he would strangle her to death. That's what he told himself, but even he didn't believe it.

*****

Smitty sat on the steps of the Student Union, across the plaza from Sproul Hall. Back at his apartment, myriad confused thoughts had fought for his attention. He had no answers, didn't want to think about any of them. His mind had felt as stuffed and overflowing with junk as his closet back home. Worse. If he opened the door, half of it would fall on top of him. Somehow, soon, he had to sort through that junk, rid himself of much of it.

Instead, he had dealt with most immediate and easiest problem —
the need to just get the hell out of his apartment.

Smitty, with a half hour to kill before class, had treated himself
to two French crullers, and chosen the Student Union steps to eat
them and watch the world go by. As was his habit now, he did a
careful double take on every girl even slightly resembling Marcia.
Once more he admitted to himself that she had gotten to him like
no woman ever had. Rachel had been hinting around that they
should shack-up together. So far, he'd pretended not to hear, which
wouldn't have fooled a girl with half Rachel's brains. Marcia still
had most of her stuff at the apartment. Smitty, worried she would
come and get it while he wasn't there, had changed the lock. The
peace of mind this suddenly brought him left him feeling like a
genius. He only wished he were genius enough to figure out how
to cover the rent by himself. This month would be all right, but
after that he'd be in dire straits. No money meant no school. No
school meant no draft deferment. Next stop Vietnam. Letting
Rachel move in would prevent that. Still, there was no way he
could live in fear of Marcia coming home to find Rachel sleeping
in her bed. Marcia might even show up just to pay her half of the
rent. Possible. In any case, instead of sitting here eating donuts, he
should be checking out the student employment office. Hell, he'd
put that off for another day.

As Smitty sat watching the world go by, he saw a part of it he
had come to know quite well lately. Rachel walked by right in
front of him. Smitty was very surprised by two things. First of all,
she failed to notice him. More surprisingly, the reason she hadn't
was that she and this complete freak were as joyously wrapped up
in each other as physically and mentally as possible. 'Sonofabitch,'
Smitty said to himself, 'A girl can get knocked up walking with a
guy like that.' Smitty's emotions were so mixed, they were
mixed-up. His ego had taken a kick. 'Well, always knew I wasn't
the world's greatest lover....Guess I proved it....Again.' Yet his
life sure had been simplified. Still, Rachel was a complication he
valued and would gladly welcome back. They had yet to really hit
their stride. Too bad. Maybe he just wasn't freaky enough for her.
Not that she was so freaky herself. Still, Smitty knew that Rachel
had never really gotten to him, not the way Marcia had. She must
have realized that too. 'Maybe he loves her more.'

Smitty wondered if things would have been different if he had known Rachel first. He concluded, as he often did, Yes and No. Now at least, he would not feel as guilty every time he thought about Marcia, feel as if he were cheating on her, as he sure as hell wasn't. Smitty sat weighing the pros and cons of being dumped when he felt a hand on his shoulder and heard a voice from behind him.

"Sorry about that." Rachel sat down on the steps next to and right up against him.

Smitty found these three words ambiguous enough to be the subject of a PhD thesis. He sure as hell hoped she wasn't feeling sorry for him. He could damn well take care of himself. If Rachel was no more sorry than she sounded, she wasn't very sorry. And if she was sorry, was it about cheating or being caught? And, considering their relationship, as far as it went, does the word cheating even apply? And—

Rachel continued, "He was my boyfriend for a year. I'm giving him another chance."

Smitty found her tone a little too sympathetic. He shifted into Take It Like A Man Mode. "What'd he do to blow his first chance?" he asked, not the least bit interested in her answer.

"He was sort of distant, cold...conservative and uptight."

'Distant, cold,' thought Smitty. He himself had been accused of both of those. Then again, most men probably had. Smitty remembered how her former and current boyfriend had been dressed. "Looked like a complete freak to me."

"He's trying," said Rachel. "He would have never gone to that Sexual Liberation Front meeting with me."

Smitty almost said, "Maybe you mean too much to him." He had caught himself, and was relieved that he had.

Rachel filled the silence. "You hear the news on the Sexual Liberation Front?"

Smitty shook his head.

"It split into two factions. One faction is taking their fight to the streets....Whatever that means."

Smitty said without emotion, "Traffic jams, probably."

"You mad at me?"

Smitty, without looking at Rachel, placed his hand just above her knee and squeezed. At the same time, he shook his head No.

What right did he have to be mad? He'd been the selfish one, stringing her along in hopes that Marcia would return. She deserved better. He looked over at Rachel and found her still smiling at his answer. She was cool. So he had never really gotten to her either. "I'm late for class." He stood and went down a step, then turned and took Rachel's face in his hands. She stretched up towards him, exactly as he wanted her to do. The kiss made up for in feeling what it lacked in passion. Smitty walked away savoring it. 'So that's what they mean by "bitter sweet".' Bitter sweet wasn't bad.

*****

Rob and Sarah had no illusions that the presentation would be a fair one. They came for the discussion afterwards, to lend support to the pro-Israel faction, if one magically appeared, or to be the pro-Israel faction if one didn't. Sarah could not believe the tension in the auditorium. Three hundred people were packed into it. A brawl seemed both imminent and inconceivable. The lecture, sponsored by Berkeley's Middle Eastern Studies Department, had been billed as a discussion of the refugee problems caused by the 1948 Arab Israeli War. While exhaustively covering the plight of the Arab refugees, the lecturer completely ignored the larger number of Jewish refugees kicked out of Arab countries. Even if he had wanted to, and he gave no indication that he had, the lecturer probably would have been dissuaded from doing so by the ominous rumble every time he uttered the word Israel.

The lecturer left the stage to a standing ovation as he handed the microphone to the moderator. "Thank you, Mr. Carrington. Now it's time for a discussion on how to end this conflict." He pointed into the audience. "Yes, Madam."

"Thank, you. I would just like to say, as a Jewish woman, that when the Israelis understand the damage they have done to the Palestinian people, and the Palestinians understand the Jewish People's need for a country in their homeland, then there will be peace, and that can only come about if the Israelis and Palestinians listen to each other the way we are listening to each other here tonight." Three people clapped. Even that was short lived.

Numerous hands shot up. The most agitated of these belonged

to a woman. The moderator pointed at her. In a venomous tone and a Middle Eastern accent, she said, "You can't make peace with Jews...I mean Israelis. They're murderers. They're bloodthirsty murderers." The auditorium erupted in applause. As it died down, she added, "Send them back to Europe! Let the.m go back to Germany." This ignited a new round of applause, louder than the first.

Sarah mumbled, "To Auschwitz."

Rob held up his hand, wanting to say something so bad, he felt as if he were about to burst. Surprisingly, the narrator pointed at him. "If I may point out to the lovely woman, the majority of the Jews in Israel did not come from Europe. They were kicked out of Arab countries."

As the audience erupted in grumbles and boos, Sarah put her arm around him. He put his arm around her.

The next speaker said, "I am a Palestinian refugee. The Jews will never leave Palestine voluntarily. The only way to free Palestine is to defeat them militarily. And that's exactly what will happen if the United States stays out of it. Then Palestine will be free, and there will be peace." Again there was loud applause, this time accompanied by cheering. The sentiments of the next half dozen speakers were similar, the two most venomous coming from professed Jews.

Sarah had been holding her hand up to no effect. Finally the moderator called on her. Rob sat certain that she would do him proud. "I don't claim the Israelis are angels,—"

The boos started.

"—but it's time we gave them their due....Hatred for Israel is the only thing the Arabs can agree upon. To a substantial degree, Israel distracts them from killing each other. This has saved thousands of Arab lives." The chorus of boos had reached a crescendo by the time she finished. Rob and Sarah were now encircled by people with daggers in their eyes. Rob smiled broadly back at them as he proudly put his arm across Sarah's shoulders. Yet in his mind, he was thinking, 'What a waste of time and effort.'

The moderator recognized a young man who looked like a college student. He spoke with a deep southern drawl. "I didn't come here thinking I had a dog in this fight. I'm a Christian who wants to spend his life working for peace, and not just in the Middle East. I came here to learn. What I knew about the Middle East was that my savior Jesus Christ, the Prince of Peace, was born there. I also knew, that however important the Holy Land is to anyone — Christian, Muslim, or Jew — is because it was the home of Jewish People and ancient Israel. I didn't learn anything new tonight. I doubt I will, and I doubt you all will bring the Middle East any closer to peace. I'm leaving. Peace to you all."

*****

Straughton replaced the receiver. The line was still busy. This idea was so brilliant, he could not fathom why he hadn't thought of it himself. The New York Review of Books had just phoned. His Cleaver interview was drawing such a positive response, "phenomenal" they said, that they wanted to know if he could get to Timothy Leary, do an interview with him too. Straughton saw no problem. Leary couldn't live without making a spectacle of himself. On the miniscule chance that he refused to cooperate, Cleaver, as a favor to Straughton, could pressure him. After all, Cleaver was generously granting Leary political asylum with the Black Panther Government in Exile.

There was one serious little issue. The interview would have to actually take place. Even Straughton's ego was not large enough to incite an attempt at faking Leary's flakiness or vocabulary. Also, he would have to get Leary to repeat his little known prediction that Governor Ronald Reagan would soon fade away into oblivion. For that one quote, The New York Times might even outbid the NYRB. It hated Reagan.

Straughton then had a disturbing thought. The phone charges were sure to make those from Cleaver's interview look like petty change. 'Phone charges be damned!' Straughton felt irritated with himself for even considering them. Onward he'd march, carrying the banner of journalism across uncharted oceans to unknown lands. And what more convenient way than by telephone? If only that idiot jabbering away on the Black Panther Government in Exile's telephone would hang up for a minute.

Straughton dialed again, dreading the sound of another busy signal. He didn't get much of any signal before the receiver was lifted and a man said, "Black Panther Government in Exile, Algeria."

Straughton felt a tinge of irritation at this strange voice poised to throw obstacles in his course. "Roger Basil Straughton VI, here. May I please speak with Eldridge Cleaver?"

The same voice, only with far more excitement, said, "Roger, My Brother! What's hap'nin'?"

So Eldridge was answering his own phone. How low the mighty have fallen. Though in Cleaver's case, not from any great height. "Good news, Eldridge. The entire country's abuzz about our interview."

"Great! Call my publisher and agent. Make sure those crooks are taking advantage of this....I need the bread."

"Rest assured. Your royalties will skyrocket."

"Will it get me a plea deal?"

"It should help. What does your lawyer say?"

"That skunk won't even answer my calls. Did you talk to Holy Joe about getting me another one?"

"I have not seen him around," Straughton lied.

There was irritation in Cleaver's tone as he said, "Go to the entrance to the university and you will see him around."

"For you, I'll do that."

"And did you send my mother a copy of our last interview?"

"You never gave me her address."

"Well don't hang up till I do. And send her a copy of the new interview. Momma's feelin' poorly lately."

"Before I forget, have you got another number there?"

"No, why?"

"You are a hard man to get through to. I got a busy signal for over an hour."

"Oh, yeah, that's 'cause I was ordering a pizza."

Straughton could not quite picture the Black Panther Party in Exile, Algeria Branch, telephoning out to their neighborhood pizza parlor for a delivery. "My Man, they have pizza in Algeria?"

"Naw, it's sorta pizza, without the cheese and tomato sauce, with something else on top."

Straughton could not picture this either. "What on top?"

There was irritation in Cleaver's tone. "Now how the hell would I know?...Chick peas, prob'ly. These clowns make everything outa chick peas. Prob'ly built this building out of 'em. Prob'ly run their donkeys and their cars on 'em too. Man, you gotta get me out of here."

"I am working on it, Eldridge."

"Hey, you don't happen to know anyone that could get me into the Israeli army?"

Straughton found himself really thrown for a loop. "No. Why?"

"I wouldn't mind coming back here in a tank."

This was something else Straughton could not picture. Then again, Eldridge Cleaver street thug turned rapist turned murderer turned convict turned Black Muslim turned ex-con turned revolutionary turned Black Panther turned award winning author turned intellectual icon of the New Left turned presidential candidate turned indicted felon turned fugitive turned Head of the Black Panther Government in Exile turned car thief turned smuggler turned born again Christian turned granter of asylum to Timothy Leary finally turned into an Israeli tank gunner. Hell, it was practically a natural progression.

Straughton suddenly realized how far off course they had gotten, and more important, the phone charges this must have entailed. "Eldridge, I would appreciate greatly it if you would facilitate my interviewing Timothy Leary."

Cleaver's surprising answer came with surprising speed. "Impossible."

So unexpected a response resulted in a question Straughton rarely asked. "Why?"

"His brain's fried on drugs."

"It always was. That's why he's Timothy Leary."

"No way, Roger. He'd just give you a headache, rapping about getting your consciousness into harmony with your cells and molecules, spaced-out shit like that. He'll call you a mutant, and tell you that's a compliment."

Straughton felt the career and wallet enhancing interview slipping away. He glanced at his list of prepared questions, marveling at the out of character preparation he had done. There was even one answer he was dying to know for himself. When Leary was arrested by the Feds, he was almost certainly forced to take a battery of tests to gauge his sanity. Ironically, while teaching at Harvard, he himself had authored a few of these tests.

Straughton was dying to know how Leary thought he scored on them. "Eldridge, please, I am asking you a favor."

There was a long pause before Cleaver answered, "Roger, I can't afford that zonked-out acid head doing or saying anything that will get me kicked out of this dump of a country. Not yet."

"Eldridge, please."

"Roger, you get me out of here, and I'll give the keys to Leary. He can turn this rats' nest into the LSD Trippers Government in Exile. Then you can talk to him all you want. You can even ask him for asylum."

Straughton felt as if he had hit a wall, at fifty miles an hour, without a car. "Eldridge, give me one practical reason why you cannot put Timothy Leary on the phone with me for fifteen minutes."

"Because there is no phone line to the cellar, where the Black Panther Government in Exile, for its own protection, has Timothy Leary locked up under house arrest."

*****

Smitty had spent almost an hour trying to read the first page of an English assignment, and that had been two hours ago. Rachel sure had simplified his life by dumping him. He was grateful for that, in theory. In reality, he could not remember ever being so depressed.

The sight of Marcia's record collection still gave him hope. Once he had felt it anchored her to him. He still did, yet by a thread not a chain. Smitty again relived the night he had left her to go to Sausalito. That was the clutch and he blew it. He owed Straughton at least a broken jaw for dragging him away. Just as he thought this, came what sounded like Straughton's knock on his door. Smitty made a fist, thinking it better not be Straughton. He walked towards the door tightening that fist, ready to give 'that leach' the ride of his life.

Straughton had been worried about Smitty, the best amateur chauffer he had ever had. The young oaf seemed to be getting a little more brutish every time they met. Having just scored three complimentary lids of grass, he decided to blow one on mellowing out his Director of Transportation. Little did he know that holding out a Baggy of grass was the perfect defense against a straight right hand. "Panama Red, great for your head."

Seeing Straughton bearing gifts proved something of a shock. Smitty was not in the mood to smoke, hadn't been for a while. He took the Baggy anyway, in case he ever was in the mood again. Still, suspicion set in. 'The leach wants me to drive him back to Connecticut.' About to send Straughton away, Smitty was distracted by some commotion downstairs.

Screw was banging on Sloan's door. Instead of his usual, "I brought the dope," Screw said, "I brought the ice cream." When Sloan opened up, he added, "C'mon, we'll go up to Smitty's for some sounds."

Smitty shook his head and waited at the open door to give Screw the bad news.

Screw arrived at the top of the stairs with both arms wrapped around a brown, three gallon restaurant container of ice cream.

Straughton sensed a possible article. "My Man, how did you score that."

"Oh, the usual way."

With a defeated expression and a jerk of his head, Smitty motioned everyone inside. He headed for his record collection. Music for booze or dope, no problem. Music for ice cream had him stumped. Smitty decided that Fats Domino goes with anything, especially ice cream. Just looking at the Fat Man always put a smile on his face. Yet he came to a Huey "Piano" Smith album first, and put that on instead. Don't You Just Know It was a feel good song he hadn't heard in years. Smitty then headed for the overflowing sink of dirty dishes. It was a lot of work and a lot of noise, but he dug out four dishes for the ice cream, three of them off the bottom.

When he came back with the cleaned dishes, Screw was asking Sloan, of all things, "Did you ever read The Art of War, by Sun Zhu?"

Smitty himself hadn't, and found it hard to believe that Screw had.

Sloan just laughed.

Smitty asked, "What made you read that?"

"My girlfriend gave it to me as a going away present."

Sloan laughed harder.

Screw did not enjoy being the subject of laughter. "I told her I was joining the Marines."

Sloan said, "Believe me, it won't help you in Nam."

"You read it?"

"Yeah, after I got back....It was on a used book table outside a store. Ten cents, and worth ever cent of it."

Smitty sat thinking that he would read it too, especially if he saw it for ten cents."

"You didn't like it?" Screw asked.

"No, it was hilarious."

"Hilarious?"

Sloan explained, "You have to read it after Nam, to get all the jokes."

"What jokes?"

"You'll see. Read it stoned, like I did....It's really just common sense."

Smitty sat thinking that some common sense just might keep Screw from joining the Marines and going to Vietnam in the first place.

Sloan said, "Look, Screw, to the generals, war may be an art. To a rifleman, it's just the dirtiest, most insane job he'll ever do."

"Dirtier than cleaning out a hog pen?"

"Dirtier than swimming in a hog pen."

Screw asked, "What about Hemingway?"

Straughton ears perked up, seeing an opportunity to exhibit his erudition. "Grace under fire."

Screw looked towards Straughton. "Yeah."

Sloan shook his head, asking, "Your girl give you one of his books too?"

Screw shrugged.

"In Nam, you'll find Hemingway just about as useful as Sun Zhu....You'll probably see guts under fire. If you see anything that looks like grace under fire, you'll be looking at some phony showboat that deserves to get his ass blown away.'

Screw appeared insulted.

Sloan said, "Screw, writers are jack-off artists."

Unnoticed, Smitty too appeared insulted. 'Me, a jack-off artist?' Though he kept it to himself, Smitty had vague pretentions of some day putting pen to paper. He flashed back to an incident in his eighth grade English class. One of his friends had raised his hand and asked, "Miss LaPlume—" Not just her name, she herself could also have come straight out of a Dickens novel. —"I was looking at the biographies in the back of our literature book. How come so many of these writers were drunks, or drug addicts, or just plain crazy?" Exactly as Dickens would have had her do, Miss LaPlume hesitated thoughtfully before answering, "Arnold, it seems that genius is often accompanied by madness." Now, recalling this incident, Smitty wondered if he were crazy enough to be a good writer. Among he and his friends, striving for craziness was something of a competition. Unfortunately, he, the only aspiring writer, was probably the sanest of the lot. Neuroticism didn't happen to be a part of this competition. None of them seemed to aspire to that.

Sloan didn't notice that he had insulted Smitty, only Screw. "Look, what do you know about Hemingway?"

"He was wounded in the war."

"Doing what?"

"Driving an ambulance."

"Nothing to be ashamed of, but did you ever hear of an ambulance driver showing grace under fire?"

Screw felt bullied. "There must have been some."

"Probably," Sloan admitted, "but you never heard or read about any….If Hemingway himself was a Hemingway hero, he would have damn well found a way to get to the front and stay there."

Screw said, "I don't know about that."

"Would you join the Marines to be an ambulance driver?"

Screw didn't answer.

Straughton, feeling left out, asked Sloan, "You were at the front?"

Sloan shook his head. "I was in the bush. If there was a front in Nam, I never found it." He turned back towards Screw. "What else do you know about Hemingway?"

"He was a big game hunter. That took guts."

"You hunt deer, don't you? Does that take guts?"

"No," Screw admitted, "but it takes skill….Killing a lion or an elephant must take some guts."

"Maybe," Sloan admitted, "but here's how Hemingway did it. He hired a big game hunter, and the big game hunter hired a cook and a bunch of African porters to carry all the gear, which included cots to sleep on and stand-up tents to sleep in. The big game hunter would then lead Hemingway by the nose to whatever he wanted to blow away. When big, brave Hemingway aimed his rifle at that lion, you think the big game hunter stood there behind him scratching his ass. Not a chance. He had that lion in his sights too, in case Hemingway missed, like half his clients did....You wanna call that big game hunting, go ahead. I call it camping."

Screw sat chastened, yet a thought came to him. "He was a good boxer."

"He was six-foot-three."

Smitty, impressed, wondered how Sloan knew so much about Hemingway.

Sloan continued, "Middleweights don't fight Heavyweights because Middleweights can't hurt Heavyweights. I don't know for sure, but I doubt there were many guys around who were Hemingway's size, and if any of them really knew how to fight, I doubt he fought them."

Screw, for the sake of argument, said, "But you don't know."

"No," Sloan agreed, "but I know he was an drunk, a bully, and supposedly a bullshit artist."

Screw said grudgingly, "I heard he was an alcoholic."

This was a fact known to Smitty too. He flashed back on a Creative Writing course he had sat in on at Ohio State. Half the students in it set their alarm clocks an hour or two early so they could write in the morning, just like Hemingway. It never occurred to them that Hemingway wrote in the morning because that was the only time he was sober enough to hold a pen steady. Or that Joyce refused to use quotation marks because he was as blind as a bat, and couldn't see them with a telescope, forget about a magnifying glass.

Sloan said to Screw, "Say you're trying to size someone up, someone you don't know. But you know he is an alcoholic, a bully, and a bullshit artist. Would you think he's more likely to have guts, be a tough son-of-a-bitch you could depend on, or a coward you should avoid?"

Again, Screw shrugged. "Someone to avoid, I guess."

Smitty had never realized any of this. He did admire some of Hemingway's writing, especially The Old Man And The Sea. Yet the short sentence style sometimes seemed just as pretentious as Faulkner's worst purple prose. And the "He said, She said" Greek Chorus business seemed even worse. Smitty remembered how at first his death was attributed to an accident, and later how his English teacher had told his class that Hemingway had killed himself because he had cancer, a false rumor that persisted for years. People wanted to believe it because Hemingway himself was such a hero, an idol even. Smitty's opinion of Sloan was rising markedly. He decided to get in on the conversation. "How about the way he killed himself?"

"Yeah," Sloan agreed. "He blew his own head off with a shotgun, inside his own house."

"He went nuts," Screw objected.

"Nuts or not, he could have gone outside. Or used a .38 pistol. Instead he painted the inside of his house with his own brains and blood....You call that 'grace under fire'?"

Screw resented Sloan's rubbing it in. He felt irritated. "What do you got against Hemingway?"

Smitty wondered too.

"I told you, writers are jack-off artists."

Smitty winced again. 'Guess that explains it.'

Yet Screw sensed otherwise. "That's not it. What do you got against Hemingway?"

Sloan was surprised by Screw's insight. He was a good kid and deserved the truth. A faint, embarrassed smile came to his face, one he couldn't hide. "Before Nam, Hemingway was a hero mine too."

*****

The lunch hour was over. It had been an easy one, and Rob felt good. He felt even better when he looked over and saw his wife Sarah sitting at a table by the window. In order to spend some time with him, she had left early on her way to pick up David from school. Sarah used to come by almost every school day. Then, gradually, she started coming less often. The last few weeks, she hadn't come at all. Rob missed those few relaxing minutes talking to her. Worse yet, he knew he was to blame for their absence.

He walked over with two cups of coffee, determined to be a

'good boy', let her know how much he appreciated her, get her to start coming again. Rob sat down wearing a big smile. She returned it with a sweet one of her own. Yet he noticed her eyes were a little red. About to ask her why, he realized she had been crying. "Sarah, what's the matter?"

"I received some bad news today."

Rob's heart sank. He could tell this was serious. His first thoughts were about David, but he brushed them aside. No, this had to be about his wife.

"I called my mother today," she continued, "to tell her some good news."

'It's her mother,' thought Rob with a sense of relief, one he immediately felt guilty for experiencing.

Sarah teared up. "She has cancer."

"…How serious?"

"What could be more serious?…But the doctors say she has a chance."

"How did she sound?"

"Strong, but not as strong as she used to be. Watching my father die took a lot out of her."

"If anyone can beat it, she can. She survived Auschwitz…one of the few."

"I'm not so sure she did."

Rob found this remark disturbingly strange. "What do you mean?"

"Do you know where they can find the cure to cancer?"

"No, but they'll find it someday, hopefully in time for your mother."

"Rob, I've thought about this when my father was dying of cancer….Do you know where you can find the cure?"

Rob could not fathom what Sarah was getting at, and her tone worried him. "No."

"The cure to cancer, and to hundreds of other diseases, is in the ashes at Auschwitz."

The truth in Sarah's words stunned him. Still, he had to say, "Others will find it."

"And millions will die needlessly in the meantime."

"You're right. It'll take longer." Something else occurred to Rob. Hitler didn't kill just 6 million Jews. He cut off their seed for all time. He killed their descendents, untold millions of them, ended forever family lines that had existed for at least 4000 years, turned 6 million Jews not just into ashes, but into dead ends. How many beautiful paintings will never be seen? How many magnificent symphonies will never be heard? How many literary masterpieces will never be written? The Nazis realized all this, yet to them, exterminating the Jews was well worth the price. Rob pictured The Six Million — men, women, and children — walking to their deaths into the gas chambers, so many of them thinking that this could not be happening, no, their fellow human beings could not be so cruel. Yet their fellow human beings proved them wrong.

Sarah broke into his thoughts. "Rob, I want to go back to the Midwest, take care of my mother."

He nodded, still thinking about the unfathomable, awesome damage Hitler had done to this world — fifty millions worth.

"David will do her good....Rob, I want you to come too."

He felt off balance. That would be a serious move. "Sell the restaurant?"

"Why not?"

He tried to think of a reason. He couldn't. "You know, when we got married, we never considered living anywhere except Berkeley. It seemed like the center of the universe....Now, it seems like some crazy, insignificant asteroid flying off by itself into space....Sure, let's jump off while we can?"

Sarah nodded.

"You want to live in the Midwest?"

"Not particularly....When Mom gets better, God willing," Sarah hesitated, unsure of his reaction, "I want to live in Israel."

Rob, again surprised and caught off balance, felt as if he had received a stiff kick in the pants, yet one that he sorely needed. A phrase from long ago returned to him, one that had haunted his adolescence. He had not thought of it in years. Rob wondered why. It was a phrase that should haunt the thoughts of every Jew, every Jew who was worth a shit — "If I forget thee, O Jerusalem, let my right hand lose its cunning." He searched his wife's face. Sarah was a fighter. The fight was in Israel. He was proud to be her husband. "Whatever...you...want."

Just then a waitress walked over. "We're almost out of rolls."

Sarah checked her watch. "I've got time to go by the market before I pick up David." She stood, took one step away from the table, then turned back to him wearing a faint smile. She shook her head. "I almost forgot the good news."

Not expecting much, Rob said absentmindedly, "The reason you phoned your mother?"

Sarah nodded and her smile broadened. "God willing, you don't have to worry anymore about David being an only child."

*****

Sloan sat bemused, sipping a Coke, at the counter of Rob's Cosmic Organic Fried Chicken. Twice, Rob had passed right in front of him without the slightest acknowledgment. The first time Sloan had asked himself, 'Is he pissed-off at me?' The second time, due to Rob's distracted expression, Sloan decided No. The third time he did a double-take so unintentionally comic, Sloan couldn't help but laugh.

Rob now stood astonished. The stranger sitting at his lunch counter was Sloan. The fact that he was not wearing his hat was the least of it. He wasn't wearing much hair either, just enough to cover his scalp. He was wearing a white, button-down, job interview dress shirt that had to date back to his freshman year.

"You're lookin' good. Who stepped on yah?"

"Lately, nobody," Sloan replied.

"You go to Oakland to get that haircut?"

"Uh-huh. Had to find a very old barber, one with a good memory."

Rob had always told himself that Sloan would pull out of his nose dive, that he was just waiting until the last possible instant. Still, Rob often wondered if he were fooling himself. Now, he saw his vindication in Sloan's still bloodshot eyes. There was both hunger and determination in them. Despite this, he asked, "How long you gonna stay straight this time?"

Sloan shook his head. "For good....Dope wasn't gettin' it done....If I decide to kill myself, I'll use a gun."

Rob now noticed that Sloan was still fighting off some slight withdrawal tremors, doing a fair job of it. "This mean I need another dishwasher today?"

Sloan shook his head. "Naw, I'll give it a try." No way did he want to sweat out this withdrawal on a mattress. Besides, it was nowhere near as bad now. "You'll need a new dishwasher soon, though."

Rob was glad to hear it. "Giving up all this job security?"

"Have to."

"Why's that?"

"I'm fleeing this town."

Rob nodded, impressed. "You didn't fry all your brain cells."

"Got a few left."

"Where you going?"

"Wherever the Marine Corps sends me."

Rob flinched, not really believing what he had heard. "You got a death wish?"

Sloan laughed. "I got a sailboat wish."

"C'mon, you can find a faster way to scrape up some coins, safer too."

"I could."

"Then why the Marine Corps?"

Sloan remembered the cliché answer for pledging a fraternity. "I liked the guys."

Rob, also remembering, laughed. He decided to tell Sloan something he had intended to keep to himself for a while. "I got news for you too."

"What's that?" Sloan asked.

"I've had it with Berkeley too. No way I'm raising my kid here."

"Drugs?"

"Naw, drugs are everywhere. Berkeley is no place for any Jew, except the gutless, self-hating kind."

Sloan laughed. "Enough of those here."

"Thousands....Guess where I'm going."

Sloan said immediately, "Israel."

Surprised, Rob said, "Your brain really did survive....How'd you figure that?"

"If I were a Jew, that's where I'd be."

"Seriously?"

"Yeah....Just before I left Nam, I got a letter from my first squad leader, the guy who kept me alive until I learned the score.

He said Israel was blowing his mind....You see in Nam, we knew that except for the guys we were with, and a few relatives and friends back home, no one gave a shit about us. We were just numbers. He said, in Israel, every soldier lost was a national tragedy. In the rice paddies, that seemed hard to believe. I wanted to see for myself."

"When I get settled, you can."

"I just may sail over and do that....I have another buddy from Nam there too." Sloan thought a moment. "But he's in jail."

"For you, that's a handy place to have a friend."

Sloan nodded. "Let's hope he's still in when I get busted."

*****

"I can't do it at the Berkeley office?" Sloan asked. He was talking on Smitty's telephone. "Where in San Francisco?" Smitty walked over and handed Sloan an opened beer. They clicked bottles as Sloan said into the receiver, "Okay, thanks."

Sloan sat down near the stereo as Smitty turned it back up. The album was the Stones' Aftermath.

"One of their best," said Sloan.

"Yeah," Smitty agreed. "Goes good with beer or weed."

Sloan nodded. "All purpose."

The cut playing was Under My Thumb, Smitty's favorite on the album. Yet he didn't like it as much as he used to, not since Marcia had walked out on him. The lyrics had turned into a sarcastic taunt. He tried not to think about them, asking Sloan, "The Marine Corps has a recruiting office in Berkeley?"

Sloan nodded, already deep into the music.

"What for?" asked Smitty.

Sloan surfaced from the music and pondered a moment before answering, "Marines don't run."

Smitty could understand that. "Then why can't they enlist you."

"I got broken time. I'm supposed to lose everything except my ribbons and medals."

"So?"

"They want me back in. The San Francisco office might get me a better deal."

"You got medals."

Sloan nodded, trying to get back into the music.

"I'll drive you over there now, if you want."

"Naw, thanks. I wanna be cleaned up, in good shape when I go....Maybe tomorrow."

"No problem."

"After this, can we hear that Van Ronk album with Wanderin' on it?"

"Sure." Smitty replied. "I'm always up for Van Ronk."

Sloan was already flipping through the albums. "You know you're right. That may be the greatest song ever recorded."

Sloan finished going through all the albums, then went through them again. "It ain't here."

"It's gotta be," said Smitty, taking over the search.

There was a knock on the door.

"Come in," said Smitty. That was one advantage to beer. Even in Berkeley, you didn't just say, "Come in," if you were smoking a joint. Well, some people did, but Smitty was not one of them.

This time, it wouldn't have made any difference. Screw had done the knocking. "Hey Dudes, got any roaches? Need two or three more for a joint."

Smitty said, "I got grass."

"I don't mix," said Screw.

"Roaches ain't that much stronger," said Sloan.

"Yeah," Screw agreed, "But it's the principle of the thing."

Smitty, curious as to which possible principle this involved, was not curious enough to ask. "Check the ashtrays."

"Have a beer," Sloan suggested.

"Booze is for pigs."

Sloan stared at the beer in his hand. "Thanks for the compliment."

Screw added, "It's counterrevolutionary."

"How so?" asked Smitty.

"I never puked on my shoes from smoking weed."

Sloan experienced a epiphany. "So that's what happened to your shoes!"

Smitty did too. "I've never seen you in shoes."

Screw, roaches on his mind, kneeled down and spotted an ashtray under the couch, way under it. "Jackpot." He lay on his belly and put his cheek to the floor. Soon his entire head and one shoulder had disappeared under the couch. Strange sounds emerged as he reached with all he had. A muffled, "Aw right!" emerged from under the couch, followed shortly by Screw himself.

Smitty glanced over and recognized the ashtray as one that had been on the run for at least two weeks. He was glad to have it back in the fold. "Good work, Man."

"Eureka," said Screw, counting the four fat joint butts it contained. He carefully picked them out and added them to some others roaches already in his hand.

Smitty said to Sloan in an irritated, disbelieving tone, "You're right, it ain't here."

"What ain't there?" asked Screw.

"My Van Ronk album with Wanderin' on it."

"It'll turn up," said Screw.

"Yeah, right after I buy a new one."

"Ain't that the truth," said Sloan. "Fuck! Now I want to hear that damn song more than ever."

Screw laid down his roach collection on the table. "Relax, Guys. I'll borrow Straughton's copy."

"He wouldn't have that album," said Smitty.

"I saw it yesterday," Screw insisted. He pointed to the joint butts on the table. "Guard my roaches with your lives."

Screw was back in three minutes with the album. He handed it to Sloan who cued it up.

Smitty thought to himself, 'Straughton has better taste in music than I figured.' The sound of Van Ronk wailing Wanderin' felt good. If he had to pay twice for an album, Smitty admitted to himself that this would be the one he'd choose. Besides, his copy had some scratches on it, similar in fact to the scratches he was now hearing. Smitty sat up, saying to Sloan, "Hey! Flip me that album cover."

Sloan did.

"This is my album!"

Screw had laid down a new cigarette paper to catch the grass remaining in the resin soaked butts of the smoked joints. "What makes you so sure?"

"My name on the album cover, for one."

Sloan said, "That'll hold up in court."

"And possession, which I got….That worthless fucker ain't

never getting his hands on this album again."

"You must have lent it to him," said Screw.

"No," Smitty replied, certain that he hadn't. Yet he couldn't picture Straughton just stealing it out of the apartment. Then again, neither could he picture the album walking over to Straughton's by itself. Smitty, at the moment, lacked the concentration needed to solve this mystery. He set it aside for another time, instead saying to Screw, "Sloan here is reenlisting in the Marines."

There was surprise in Screw's tone. "You talked me out of it, and you're going back in yourself?"

Sloan remained silent. What could he say, that he thought Screw would get blown away in Nam?

Screw had completed his joint-from-roaches project. "Why you doing it, Man?" He lit it and sucked out a long drag as he walked over to offer Sloan the joint.

Sloan waved it off. "Can't stand the people here."

Smitty found Sloan's answer jarring, but decided not to take it personally.

Screw asked, "You have to join the Marines to find people you like?" He headed for Smitty, taking another drag along the way.

Sloan replied, "Easiest way I know....Better to be in a bad place with good people, than a good place with bad people."

Before he took the joint, Smitty said, "Then you think Berkeley's a good place?"

"Compared to Nam, it's paradise...except for the people." Sloan then realized that Vietnam had its good points. "Well, compared to Nam as seen courtesy of the Marine Corps."

Screw pointed to the center of the floor. "A roach."

"Then pick it up," said Sloan.

"No, a real roach."

"Then step on it," said Smitty, stoned and comfortably seated.

Screw stood and approached the roach, which sent it scurrying under a chair. He moved the chair and jumped into action, doing something close the Mexican Hat Dance, with the roach as the hat. Screw stomped all around it without stomping on it. The roach made a successful dash under the couch.

Sloan sat thinking, 'A natural born killer he ain't.'

Screw started to move the couch, when—

Smitty said, "Forget it, Screw....I'll phone Chicago. Bring in some mob boys to do the job."

Screw accepted defeat and sat down. He returned to the question he had been asking himself before being bested by a roach. Why had Sloan dissuaded him from enlisting. An uncomfortable possibility came to mind. "You don't think I'm crazy enough to be a Marine?"

Sloan had no idea what Screw was getting at. Being straight when talking to two stoners seemed to be putting him at a disadvantage. "Who said you had to be crazy?"

"You did, the first day I met you. You told that guy that it wasn't just that Marines were tough, they were crazy too."

"I was just shutting the scumbag up, intimidating him....But it's true, most of us were at least half crazy even before we enlisted.

That made sense to Smitty. You had to be crazy to join the Marines with Nam going on. Yet this didn't explain why or how Marines were supposedly so different. "In what way?"

Screw found the question itself enlightening. There were different ways of being crazy. Now he too wondered in which way.

Sloan, not sure himself, tried to answer by taking a different tack. "The Marine Corps has its own sense of humor."

Screw said what Smitty was thinking, "Huh?"

"Its own way of looking at things," Sloan added. "For example, here in Berkeley, you have all these freaks and politicos, thinking that they're really doing something, that they're changing the world, when they're really just making a lot of background noise. In Nam, where it's all for real, you got Marines knowing it don't mean a thing."

This made some sense to Smitty, but he wasn't sure how.

Sloan's words made no sense to Screw. "What about People's Park?"

"Exactly," said Sloan.

Sloan's words were making more and more sense to Smitty.

Yet not to Screw. "Huh?"

Sloan regretted, wondered why he was trying to explain. He felt stoned even though he had waved off the joint. All Sloan wanted now was to get back into the music. He tried to end the conversation with, "The Marine Corps gets it."

"Gets what?" Screw asked with irritation.

Sloan had no desire to answer. He held his tongue a moment

before finally blurting out, "The joke!"

Screw became even more exasperated. "What joke?"

Sloan had already tried hard enough. He now refused to answer.

"What joke?" Screw repeated angrily.

It was left to Smitty to finally answer. "Life."

✶✶✶✶✶

There was one sound Straughton hated above all others — the sound of an alarm clock. It took hours to get the god-awful ringing out of your head, and then a Herculean effort to salvage the rest of the day. Straughton's knack for shallow empathy, the skill that helped him write from all angles, was often turned on by the grinding, metallic screech of an alarm clock. During those excruciatingly painful and degrading moments, he felt he knew exactly what it was like to suffer under slavery. The sound assaulted his ears exactly the way overseers' whips must have assaulted the backs of slaves.

In fact, to Straughton, setting an alarm clock was almost as discomforting as hearing one. It was like rigging a time bomb, then placing it upon your night table. How were you to sleep dreading that imminent explosion? Still, in the world as is, one has sometimes to compromise. Straughton had long ago made his peace, an uneasy one, with alarm clocks. If they would allow him a minimum of three hours sleep, he'd go ahead and set them. If not, he would just stay up, any way he could.

Fortunately, when he had gone to bed two hours previously, Straughton had had no need to set his alarm clock. He could sleep until recharged, rejuvenated, and refreshed — or so he thought. Little did he suspect that he would be awakened by the second worst sound in the world, by that of a telephone. "Straughton, here," he answered groggily, despite his pain.

A voice he did not recognize said, "The pigs are taking back People's Park". Immediately, there was a "click", followed by a dial tone.

A number of questions came to Straughton's mind, the first being, "Am I dreaming?" No, he decided. This led to his next question, "Was I dreaming?" Again the answer was No. He then asked himself who the caller could have been. 'What difference does it make?', was his own reply. Could the call have been a prank? Certainly. The Chancellor of the university system had promised not to take any unilateral action concerning People's Park. Should he check out the call anyway? Straughton, on two hours sleep, was not in the mood to do an interview, even with himself. Now that he was wide awake, he decided to end the present one. Straughton reluctantly got out of bed.

Smitty was shuffling around his apartment, in a mood even worse than Straughton's. He had dragged himself to the grocery store the night before because he was out of mayonnaise. There were a dozen other things he had also needed, and he had purchased those. Of course he had forgotten to buy the mayonnaise, the most essential staple in his diet, the necessity that had gotten him off his ass and down to the store in the first place. Now, every time he opened the refrigerator, a half pound of sliced turkey mocked his stupidity, or absentmindedness, or both.

A knock on the door, sounding like Straughton's, didn't help his mood any. The only person he really wanted to see when he opened it would be Marcia. Smitty figured the odds of that were slim and getting slimmer. Yet this would not keep him from hoping, and then almost certainly having those hopes dashed. That is exactly what happened when he found himself face to face with Straughton's phony smile.

"The cops are taking back People's Park. Do you want to go?"

Smitty realized that the question was actually, "Do you want to chauffer me?" People's Park was less than a ten minute walk, and Smitty would not have considered bothering to drive himself, even forgetting the hassle of finding a parking spot. Staring at Straughton, he pictured him as a baby bonneted teenager, being wheeled around by a nanny in a big baby carriage. Amused by the thought, Smitty told himself that a good riot might be just what he needed. At the very least, it would get him out of his damn apartment.

On the ride to People's Park, Berkeley seemed normal to Smitty. 'Normal?' he wondered? There had to be a more precise description. Then he thought of it — 'Berkeley was Berkeley as usual'.

Berkeley looked like Berkeley to Straughton too. That meant the telephone tip about People's Park was probably a hoax. His mind wandered to Moe's dislike of Smitty's book review. Straughton could look for someone else to do the next one. Yet that might involve some actual effort, and Smitty lived conveniently right down the hall. Why not give his neighbor another chance?

"My editor was not happy with your book review."

Smitty, like anyone who had ever written anything, found this hard to believe. "What didn't he like about it?"

Straughton had only read the first paragraph. It seemed surprisingly readable. Paying out half the money that Moe gave him to someone else to write a review, and then having to go to the trouble of reading it seemed self-defeating, and anti-capitalist to boot. One thing that Straughton firmly believed in the instant he heard about it was the division of labor. And the task he most preferred was no more than the actual dividing. He gratefully considered this one of his God given talents. "Moe claims it was more like a book report than a book review."

Smitty was not one to pretend he understood something when he didn't. "What the fuck is that supposed to mean?"

Straughton had not the slightest idea. For the first time, he wondered about it himself. Fruitlessly. After all, what did he know about reviewing books? His mind fell back on his conversation with someone who did, Chelsea Sinclair. "Perhaps you could have included in your review a defense of socialist realism."

Smitty gave Straughton a quick, suspicious glance, wondering if he had even read the review. "It was a book on how to grow marijuana."

Straughton could see Smitty's point. "I do not claim this would have been easy."

Smitty knew he had to find a part-time job, yet the will to actually get out and do so had not yet reached critical mass. Money from doing book reviews was a pittance, yet every dollar helped. "Look, explain to me the difference between a book report and a book review, and next time you'll get a review."

'Right back where we started,' thought Straughton. If he got someone else to do the next book review, it might turn out even worse. Straughton fell back on his tactic of first and last resort — bluffing his way through. There was another thing he remembered from his conversation with Chelsea Sinclair. Maybe it would make more sense to Smitty than it did to him. "Think of it this way. A book report is a camel with one hump. When you're writing a book review, then what you have to aim for is a camel with two humps." Straughton glanced over at Smitty to see if he were going to get away with this.

Smitty looked back at him as if he were nuts.

Straughton knew he had to think fast. He reached back into his quiver, finding only a single suspect arrow. Well, he might as well shoot it. Straughton spoke with the groundless self-assurance that had gotten him out of many a jam. "I'll go over that in simpler terms.—

Smitty sat thinking, 'That might be a good idea,' yet completely lacking any confidence that it would.

"—If you think of a book report as a zebra, then a book review is a horse."

Smitty was seriously trying to figure out whether Straughton was ripped on dope or merely insane when he found himself stomping on the brakes hard enough to set his tires squealing, his rear end fishtailing, Straughton crashing into the dashboard, and his front end inches from demolishing a surprisingly placed roadblock. Smitty had no time to take pride in his quick reflexes. On the other side of the roadblock, six very seriously looking cops in full riot gear were staring him down. And that wasn't the worst of it. One had his pistol drawn, and another had a shotgun pointed right in his face. Smitty recognized it as a twelve gauge, but from where he was sitting, the barrel looked fit for a tank. What the hell had he gotten himself into?

"I'll handle this," Straughton said with confidence.

It was a confidence that Smitty envied, though he certainly didn't share it. He shifted into reverse, so all he would have to do was floor it if Straughton started babbling to the cops about camels and zebras.

"Press," Straughton said, holding up a card.

The nearest cop lifted his face shield and said sympathetically, "In that case, we'll give you ten seconds instead of five to get the hell out of here."

"I'm with the—" Straughton managed to get out before Smitty had the car flying backwards. He calmly told Smitty, "I'm not certain that was necessary."

493

Still in reverse, Smitty pointed out, "You would have been, if the shotgun was pointed in your face....Those babies ain't loaded with ping-pong balls." He had the car turned around in record time.

Straughton said, "Check out the next street. See if there's a roadblock there too." There was, and the street after that, and the next two.

Smitty said, "They must have every cop in the county here."

"My Man," said Straughton, "So far, we have seen Berkeley cops, Oakland Cops, California State Troopers, even the Alameda County Blue Meanies. I am quite curious to know what is happening on the other side of those roadblocks."

Smitty was too. "What do you want to do?"

"Go one more street and park. I have an idea." Straughton led Smitty through the front door of an old office building, then out the back, down an alley, and across the next street. They cut between two houses, then two more.

The scene Smitty and Straughton came upon stopped them cold. Across the street was People's Park, or what was left of it. A bulldozer was toppling the last few trees. Another was scooping up the bright green grass and piling it in large mounds. Workers, dozens of them, were erecting a tall, chain link fence around the remains. Guarding the workers and equipment were more cops than either Smitty or Straughton had ever seen in one place, hundreds of them.

Smitty knew that the street people and students had no right to "liberate" the land in the first place. He knew their basic motivation was to stick their thumbs in the eyes of the authorities, to cause trouble. Still, the results of their actions had been a surprisingly pleasant, attractive, in some ways self-justified oasis. Now, all he saw before him was a sickening waste.

*****

Screw sat at the counter of Rob's Cosmic making short work of a tall glass of milk and a double slice of apple pie. He was one of only three customers in the place.

Rob walked over and said, "Thanks for coming in today. We needed you."

"Everybody's at Sproul Plaza."

"About People's Park?"

"Naw, some anti-Israel bullshit."

Rob now remembered hearing something about this. "A lot of people?"

"Yeah, at least a thousand, maybe two."

This surprised Rob. "For an Arab-Israeli teach-in?"

"Yeah, Man. I left right away. Boring as hell."

"Wish I'd known."

"Why, you an Arab or a Jew?"

Rob shook his head, laughing to himself. Screw had been coming in for months, and didn't know he was a Jew. Maybe it wasn't quite as obvious as he had thought.

"Which one?" asked Screw.

"Jew."

"We ain't got any Jews in our county, far as I know....I hear they got all kinds a Jews in Omaha."

"All kinds," Rob repeated.

As if to make up for the lack of Jews, Screw came up with, "We got two families a Japanese."

Sloan came out of the kitchen and sat down next to Screw. "Not a dirty dish in the place."

Rob slid Screw's now empty plate in front of Sloan. "Here's one....There's an Arab-Israeli teach-in at Sproul. I'd have liked to hear it."

"I'll summarize it for you — the Israelis make Nazis look like pacifists, and the Palestinians are blowing up men, women, and children for world peace."

"Yeah," said Rob, "The peace that comes when all Jews are dead....Wish I'd gone."

This did not make sense to Sloan. "To hear that bullshit?"

"Damn right. It's fuel to get me out of this town...without looking back."

Sloan said, "Go. This place is dead. I'll cover for you."

Rob had his apron off and was out the door immediately. He found himself walking faster than he had in years. Reaching Sproul Plaza, he could not believe the size of the crowd. Screw was right, two thousand people, or close to it. Could there be that many Israel haters around? In Berkeley there could, obviously, as evidenced by the prevalence of Palestinian flags and keffiyahs. Nearly all the keffiyahed crowd appeared to be waspy Arab wannabes. There had to be some Jews among them too. Anti-Semites were a fact he could stomach. It was the gutless, masochistic, self-hating Jews trying to prove that they really weren't like other Jews who disgusted him. Rob doubted there was a city in the US, a country in the world, where you couldn't easily drum up an equally repulsive crowd — millions and millions of people to draw from, with nothing better to do than try to destroy the one tiny Jewish country on the face of this earth.

Among the ubiquitous waving placards, Rob spotted the one he loathed the most — a Jewish star and a swastika connected by an equals sign. Nobody called the Russians Nazis, or the Red Chinese, or even the South American dictators who actually were Nazis or their imitators. Even the "new" Germans of the Sixties, so many of them unrepentant Nazis, were never called Nazis anymore. No, only the Jews, the Nazis' main victims, were now slandered as Nazis. It wasn't enough that the world could not forgive the Jews for being born Jews, the world could not forgive the Jews for being victims of the world's abiding hatred for Jews. No, the Jews deserved whatever they got.

The entire crowd seemed to erupt into bloodthirsty boos every time the word Israel was mentioned. Rob scanned the mean, angry faces surrounding him. This wasn't a teach-in. It was a hate-in. Why did the world hate Israel like they hated no other country, except perhaps the United States? Well, at least Israel was in good company, in fact, the best possible company. This so-called teach-in seemed to consist of speaker after speaker bashing that Colonialist-Fascist-Zionist-Entity ruthlessly oppressing the Poor-Defenseless-Peace-Loving-Palestinian-People. Rob could not believe the crowd's, the mob's joyful acceptance of such outright lies and ridiculous conspiracy theories. It occurred to him, this being Berkeley, that he was gazing upon a huge cult. Anti-Semitism, and its anti-Israel face, were uniquely part-time cults. They were sets of deranged ideas you could dive off the deep end on anytime you found a need for a hate-filled escape from reality. It explained almost everything wrong with you and the world around you. When your need for hatred had been sated, you could resurface completely refreshed as a supposedly sane, normal Palestinian-loving human being.

Though Rob had expected what he was experiencing, as much as he needed it to reinforce his decision to leave Berkeley, still, inside, he yearned for someone to stand up and state Israel's case, to introduce a few facts to counter the conspiratorial fantasies and name-calling slanders. Yet though he yearned, he knew this would be a useless exercise in front of the self-deceiving mob surrounding him. It was as if all these people had gathered to tell Rob, "This town ain't for you. Get out." Yet more than anything, these people were proof positive that there had to be one country on the face of this earth where a Jew, if he chose not to, did not have to live as a minority; one country where he could say, "You don't like Jews, then get the fuck out"; one country, where if it came down to it, a Jew would have the choice dying with or without a rifle in his hand. Rob scanned the educated, self-righteous, bloodthirsty horde before him, knowing that this was the stuff pogroms were made of. No, Hitler was far from the first and he would not be the last. This mob proved to Rob, and should to any Jew with even an ounce of guts, that Jews needed and deserved their own country more, far more, than any other people on the face of this earth, that if this world was not big enough for one tiny country called Israel, then this world just wasn't big enough.

Rob assumed he had missed the "pro-Israel" speaker, when the moderator said, "Now, giving us the Israeli point of view, Rabbi Michael Lomed. Rob felt blood rushing to his temples. He knew that if Israel's case were going to be made that day, it would not be by this flake. Michael Lomed was, for all intents and media events, Berkeley's Rabbi, a rabbi who would only be considered one in a place such as Berkeley. He was your generic feet off the ground head in the clouds type of clergyman, who by chance had been born of Jewish parents. His acceptance of Judaism was quite selective and subservient to the current leftwing zeitgeist. He ran a touchy-feely synagogue which was in fact an introduction to Unitarianism, Buddhism, or the next trendy hocus-pocus spiritualism to come along. His specialty was those mixed marriage weddings officiated by both a Rabbi and a Christian clergyman, those mish-mash ceremonies which managed to make a complete mockery of both religions. In fact, this Hebrew holy man had once been credited with breaking new ground. He co-officiated a wedding with a Buddhist monk, despite the fact that both bride and groom were nominally Jewish.

Rob expected nothing from Rabbi Michael Lomed's "defense" of Israel. He was not disappointed. Lomed did stick his neck way out in front of the lynch mob by stating that Israel had a right to exist. Weathering an immediate storm of boos and verbal abuse, he went on to say that Israeli Jews and Palestinian Arabs must learn to get along just as harmoniously as the Arabs and Jews in Berkeley. Lomed's major point in defense of Israel was his plea to all members of the audience to put pressure on the United States government to abandon its "unconditional" support of Israel, and to force Israel to make peace with its Arab neighbors. Lomed seemed to have hardly started before he had finished, and for Rob he could not have finished soon enough.

As Rabbi Michael Lomed left the podium, Rob stood thinking, 'With defenders like that—' Again he pictured the mish-mash wedding ceremonies that were Lomed's specialty, certain that they barely scratched the surface of this Rabbi's potential, thinking, 'Someday that flake will marry a horse to a cow.'

*****

Sloan had not gotten up from his seat at the counter since Rob had left. No need had arisen. Not a single customer had entered, and aside from Screw, only one remained.

Screw said, "I can't believe they took it away from us so easy, without a fight."

"It was never yours," Sloan pointed out.

Just then, Smitty entered and sat down on the other side of Screw. "Man, you guys wouldn't believe what they did to the park."

Sloan asked, "You want something to eat?"

Screw asked, "You saw?"

Smitty found Sloan's question somewhat odd, being that he had just sat down in a restaurant. "You must be psychic."

"I'm still alive, ain't I?"

Screw tried again. "How'd you get by the roadblocks?"

"Went through some alleys and backyards." Smitty leaned forward, saying to Sloan, "Well if you're psychic, you know I want a hamburger medium rare, lettuce, tomato, mayonnaise, and onion."

Screw asked, "Did they really mess it up?"

"Obliterated it."

Sloan said to Smitty, "If you were psychic, you'd know that the night grill man doesn't come in for another hour, Rob ain't here, and I'm beat from washing dishes all day."

Screw found it hard to imagine. "You mean there's nothing there now?"

"There's something there all right — a cop jamboree on a vacant lot," Smitty replied, then asked Sloan, "Where's Rob?"

Screw answered instead. "Sproul Plaza, at some Death to Israel rally."

This did not make much sense to Smitty. "What's Rob's grudge against Israel?"

"None," said Sloan.

Screw added, "He's on the other side."

This still didn't make any sense to Smitty. "Then why's he at a Death to Israel rally?"

Sloan replied, "He's got this Freedom Rider complex….Wants to get lynched or something."

This made less sense to Smitty, but pursuing the matter seemed to make no sense at all. "Whatever happened to my hamburger?"

"Pick it up tomorrow."

Screw, in the middle, was not enjoying being there. "Why don't you two take this argument outside."

Smitty said to Sloan, "C'mon, Man."

Sloan said, "I'm not getting up to make you no hamburger lettuce, tomato, mayonnaise, and onion."

Smitty took on a more reasonable tone. "Okay, leave off the onion."

Screw decided to play the peacemaker, saying to Smitty, "Have a slice of that apple pie and some milk."

"Milk? Never touch the stuff…except to float my Frosted Flakes."

"I'll get you Frosted Flakes, no problem," Sloan offered.

"Forget it. I'll take a piece of that pie and a glass of water."

Sloan got up to get it as Straughton walked in. He handed Smitty his pie while asking Straughton, "What would you like?"

"I'll have a piece of pie too."

"What kind?"

"Pumpkin."

Sloan made a face before coming back with another piece of apple pie."

"This isn't pumpkin," Straughton objected.

"Who the hell eats pumpkin pie except on Halloween?"

"We do," said Straughton, meaning the Straughtons.

"We do too," Screw cut in. "My mother always plants a few pumpkins for Halloween jack-o'-lanterns, and we have to eat the pies left over."

Sloan said, "Here at Rob's Cosmic, you don't."

"I can live with that," said Screw. "You know what my father says about pumpkin pie?"

Sloan replied, "If I did, I forgot."

Smitty sat thinking he had underestimated both Sloan's sense of sarcasm and humor.

Screw continued, "My father says that the best thing about pumpkin pie is that even the worst piece of it you'll ever eat really isn't that much worse than the best piece of it."

Smitty almost choked on his apple pie. "That's funny."

Screw said innocently, "You know, that's the only funny thing I ever remembering him saying."

Smitty laughed even harder.

Screw asked, "What's that noise?"

It was a faint, distant rumble, slowly getting louder. They all froze for a moment to listen, then Screw headed outside and they followed. The noise was coming from the university. It continued to get louder. The traffic heading towards campus slowed to a stop. The opposite lane emptied. Then some cars closer to the university started filling it, making U-turns. Soon people were walking towards them, clogging the sidewalks, street, and the spaces between the stopped cars. They were chanting, "We want the park!"

Sloan rushed inside and came back out with a ring of keys. He yelled to Smitty and Screw, "Hurry, help me get these grates." Smitty and Screw pulled them closed and Sloan barely got them locked before the crowd was upon them like a killer wave. People were squeezed shoulder to shoulder, as if marching through a funnel. The chant, "We want the park!" was deafening. Some of the people in the stopped cars sat petrified as demonstrators squeezed by, often banging on the metal in time to the chant. Straughton took off with the marchers. Sloan, Smitty, and Screw headed inside the restaurant to get out of the way. Rob rushed in behind them before they could close the door.

"What's happening?" Screw asked.

Rob, out of breath, gasped, "They gave the microphone to Marco to say a few words…and the few words were, "Let's take back People's Park!" At this, Screw had the door open and was halfway out it.

Sloan did not like the look in his eye. He grabbed Screw by his upper arm. "Where you going?"

"To get our park back," Screw said excitedly.

"From cops in riot gear, behind roadblocks."

"Cops with shotguns," Smitty added.

"I don't care," Screw said with determination.

Sloan still had Screw's arm, and he had no intention of letting him go alone. Turning towards Rob, he asked, "You need me?"

"No, I'm closing."

"Should we wait for you?"

"Hell no! Fuck that bullshit!"

Sloan looked towards Smitty.

Smitty nodded, damn curious to see what was happening.

"Okay," said Sloan. "Let's stay together."

Heading outside, they were immediately swept away by the crowd. Sloan squeezed between Screw and Smitty. The force of those behind pushed them forward. It was as if they were not walking, but rather surfing on a wave of humanity. Smitty was excited, but Screw was exhilarated. Sloan did not like the look on the kid's face.

Screw was feeling the adrenaline rush of his life. It even topped playing high school football. The chant, "We want the park!" was a deafening mantra. He lived that final chase scene of a cowboy movie, the way, as a kid, he had ridden along vicariously with the good guys, urging on his horse, running the bad guys to ground. He experienced the power of the torch carrying mob, rushing through the cobblestone streets to Dr. Frankenstein's castle. Screw was part of a stampeding herd. No cowboy, no living thing, wanted to be in its way. He had never experienced such power, such confidence, and the sense of invulnerability this brought on — all put to one purpose, one noble cause. "We want the park!"

Smitty kept thinking to himself, 'This sure beats any football riot.' He heard the sound of shattering glass storefronts. People squeezed tighter around him. He felt like a fullback that no brick wall could stop. Smitty then had visions of something that could stop him — that big barreled shotgun he'd been looking down a few hours earlier. There was enough lead at the other end of that barrel to knock down an entire backfield. Still, this didn't worry Smitty that much, not yet. There were plenty of people in front of him to absorb the birdshot first. Besides, this was exciting. To him, the park was just an excuse. What he wanted was to be where the action was, up front where he could see what was happening.

One thought kept repeating itself in Sloan's mind — 'Somebody is gonna get killed today.' He doubted it would be a cop, or only a cop. Scanning the faces around him, Sloan saw no shortage of prime candidates, Screw among them. He would keep a good eye on the kid. In fact, that was the only reason he'd come along, and he still felt like a sucker for doing so. A few words from a phony agitator such as Marco, and the mindless minions of Berkeley were on the march. As if Marco cared about any People's Park, or The People's Crash Pad, or The People's Anything. Sloan doubted he cared about people at all. All he cared about was manipulating them and the sense of power that this afforded him. It occurred to Sloan that Marco must see himself, not just as a leader, but as some sort of People's General, marching his troops around. Sloan wanted to laugh at the thought, but it wasn't really funny. There was something pathetic about it, about both Marco and his willing minions. General Marco. Sloan pictured him starting his military career the same place Sloan had — Parris Island. Marco in Marine Corps boot camp, nose to nose with three drill instructors. Now that was a funny thought, one Sloan could laugh at. Sloan doubted those drill instructors would judge General Marco as impressive as this Berkeley mob seemed to.

Smitty had tensed up, sure he was approaching one of those roadblocks he had seen that morning. In his thoughts, he was again looking down the business end of a shotgun — a once is enough experience. Instead he found himself looking at the top of a chain-link fence, not fifteen yards away. How could that be? They had reached the park without passing any roadblocks. His relief turned to glee. 'The cops, shotguns and all, had run for it!'

Smitty's glee was short-lived. He found himself being pressed forward, against those in front of him who were being pressed against the fence. Cries of pain came from the front. He heard Sloan yell, "Spread out!" Surprisingly, the crowd took heed, spreading out along the fence as the chant, "Spread out! Spread out!" replaced, "We want the park!" Soon protestors lined one entire side of the fence. The chanting faded as more and more protestors got a glimpse of what remained of the park — nothing. You could not tell it had been there. Cops, hundreds of them, were gathered in the middle of the lot, well away from the fence. They eyed the demonstrators, just waiting.

Screw clung stunned to the fence, peering through it with disbelief. What yesterday had been his park, his playground, was now piled high upon scraped raw ground. "Why?" he asked out loud to himself, and then to Sloan. "Why?"

"That's what they wanted," Sloan mumbled.

It took a moment for Screw to realize that Sloan's "they" were the instigators of the park, not those who destroyed it. "The hell with that!"

Sloan saw no point in arguing. Screw appeared close to tears. Obviously, People's Park had really meant something to the kid.

"I planted five trees right here," he shouted. Screw looked to the rear to check his bearings. "Right here!" he shouted even louder. "Beautiful trees," he mumbled. "One already bloomed."

The chant, "We want the park!" started again, every bit as loud as before, now with an added vehemence and meanness. Screw climbed halfway up the fence. He started shaking it. Others joined in. Soon their entire section of the fence was modulating in a wave, forward and back.

Sloan thought to himself, 'That fence is gonna go.' When it did, there would be nothing between cop and demonstrator. They would come together — 'And not for a love-in.' For sure there would be blood. Again, Sloan thought, 'Someone's gonna get killed.'

Screw worked on the fence like a crazed chimpanzee rattling its cage. Sloan shook his head at the sight, noticing that Smitty too was working on the fence, though with less passion. He walked over to him, asking calmly, "You want the fence down?"

Smitty thought about this for the first time. The best answer he could come up with was, "Why not?"

"Why?" Sloan asked him.

Smitty did not have an answer.

But Sloan had another question. "What are you gonna do when it's down, rush those cops?"

Smitty looked over at the cops, holding enough shotguns to open duck season. They were spreading out and heading determinedly towards the now violently undulating fence. "It's coming down with or without me."

Sloan jerked his head towards the approaching cops. "And when it does, that birdshot is gonna fly with or without you."

Smitty nodded agreement.

"How do you want it?" Sloan asked, "With or without you?"

"Birdshot do smart," Smitty had to admit.

Sloan jerked his head towards Screw, who had climbed to the top of the fence, swaying it back and forth. "What do you say we peel Cheetah down, find a safer place to watch this train wreck?"

Smitty nodded agreement.

Sloan reached up and grabbed Screw's arm, only to have Screw angrily jerk it from his grasp. Sloan looked over at Smitty. Smitty climbed up even with Screw and tapped him on the shoulder. Screw, intent on finishing his demolition job, shook his head angrily. He refused to look at Smitty. Sloan and Smitty each grabbed an arm, though neither tried to pry him off the fence. Screw ignored them, facing forward, eyes focused on the approaching cops.

The chant changed to a taunt. "No pigs in the park! NO PIGS IN THE PARK!"

A shotgun blasted to their left. As their heads turned in that direction, one went off directly to their front. That was enough. Sloan and Smitty both yanked down on Screw. He came off the fence without much resistance. Amidst additional shotgun blasts, and the screams accompanying them, they turned and ran across the street, heading for a three story building. Someone had opened the hydrant next to it, and they had to plow through a deep puddle. Screw, still in tow, glanced back over his shoulder. Sloan angrily jerked his arm, asking, "You want to get blinded?"

As they made it into the building, the firing quickened, the screams grew more frantic and louder. They stood panting in the hallway when Screw opened the door. Sloan kicked it shut, asking angrily, "You crazy?"

Equaling Sloan's anger, Screw replied, "I wanna see what's going on."

"Fuck that!" said Sloan.

"Hey," said Smitty, "Let's go up on the roof, where we can really see?"

Neither Screw nor Sloan could argue with that. They followed Smitty up the stairs in silence. As he opened the door onto the roof, Smitty was surprised to see someone already there, looking down at the park. The figure appeared familiar, even from the rear. Before Smitty could think much about this, Straughton turned around in surprise. "Gentlemen, how did you find me?"

"We searched everywhere," Sloan replied.

Straughton didn't doubt this. "You succeeded."

"Oh, yeah," Smitty agreed.

Straughton held out a burning joint to Screw, who shook it off. He was in no mood for marijuana, or conversation. He went straight to the edge of the roof to see what was happening. People's Park, or what had been People's Park, appeared even worse from three stories up. The fence was down in two places, but no demonstrators were inside it. There were none against the fence either. The cops were now strung out along the inside of it, especially at the breeches. The demonstrators were cautiously returning from wherever they had run to. They walked slowly, tentatively back towards the fence. The gunfire had ended the chanting, leaving behind an eerie and ominous silence.

Again Straughton held out the joint to Screw.

Again Screw shook it off.

"Take a toke," said Sloan. "Put an edge on."

Screw shook his head, still looking out at the park.

Straughton offered the joint to Sloan.

Sloan too shook it off.

That left Smitty, who could not think of a reason for passing up a toke or two. He took the joint and a deep one. Smitty scanned the streets, looking for casualties. He saw none. "Wonder if anyone got hit by the birdshot."

Straughton said, "They're not using birdshot."

"Rock salt?" asked Sloan.

"No," Straughton replied, "Buckshot."

"Bullshit!" said Smitty.

One person could be heard chanting, "No pigs in the park."

"You ain't serious?" asked Sloan.

Straughton, whose father had failed to take him along when hunting, asked, "What's the difference?"

Sloan answered, "Birdshot'll blind you, but buckshot'll kill you."

"Oh," said Straughton, writing this down.

As the crowd re-gathered along the fence, the chanting grew louder. "No pigs in the park!"

"So, it's birdshot, right?" asked Screw.

"No, when they were handing out the ammunition, an officer of the law said, 'Hey, this is buckshot'. They told him to keep loading. They didn't have any more birdshot."

The crowd along the fence was even larger than before. The volume of the chanting increased with it.

"Shiiit, buckshot," said Screw. He looked back at Sloan. "Thanks for dragging me outa there."

Sloan said, "You got to keep a cooler head."

"Man, I helped build that park. Worked my ass off."

"Smoked your ass off," Smitty pointed out.

"That too."

Sloan looked upon Screw as someone being used, which could prove hazardous to his health. "You got to realize, Marco wants police brutality. To make the cops look bad, to get headlines, and more fools for his next riot."

In a tone mean enough to be completely out of character, Screw said, "You really are a fascist."

The kid was way out of line, and Sloan was tired of cutting him slack.

"Then so am I," said Smitty. "Listen to them baiting the cops down there."

Screw did, but it was to Sloan that Smitty's words really hit home. No pigs in the park! wasn't exactly endearing the counterculture to law enforcement. Sloan thought back on his run-in with the cops. There was still some satisfaction in those memories, but he began to question them. To those two fuckups he had been worthless, repulsive, less than human, just another half dead junkie bound for the sewers, dirt they didn't want under their fingernails. Someone who broke the law when he bought dope, and again when he used it. Someone who probably broke the law to pay for his dope. To those cops, Sloan also admitted, he was a freak who hated their guts not for who they were, but for being cops. He thought of them as, even called them pigs, sometimes to their faces. He was their enemy. Sloan could understand why those cops had harassed him. Still, he couldn't and didn't want to justify what they had done. They deserved an ass-kicking, for their incompetence as much as their brutality. Still, he understood them.

Straughton broke into Sloan's thoughts with, "Are you gentlemen aware that People's Park wasn't originally intended as a park?"

"This gentleman wasn't," said Smitty.

It was intended as a place for political rallies, protests, and debates.…The landscaping came later."

"I did not know that," said Sloan, filing this fact away under the heading Info of Dubious Value.

The crowd below had grown unbelievably large, twice the size it had originally been. There was the faint sound of approaching helicopters. Even three stories up, the chanting was louder than ever. As the crowd grew in size, it grew in courage. It pressed against the fence, and began shaking it again. Another section went down. The crowd froze, except for one man who rushed forward. A few people followed him, then the entire mob. A barrage of gunfire stopped them dead. A few protestors fell to the ground, and many more dived to it. The cops rushed forward, through the breech, chasing the protestors in three directions — left, right, and straight ahead. The protestors could not flee any faster, but the cops continued to fire, their shotguns almost drowned out by the whir of helicopters.

"They've gone rogue!" Screw yelled in disbelief.

Straughton, calm and detached, said as a point of interest, "I have never seen anything like this."

Sloan had, but not exactly. Fleeing rioters were falling wounded, but not as many as you would think, not from all that

507

firing. Clearly, most of the cops were firing above the fleeing protestors. Yet not all. His eye caught one woman, writhing on her stomach in the street. Her white blouse turned bright, wet red, every visible inch of it. Seeing all this, to the sound of helicopters overhead, brought on paralyzing flashbacks from far more dangerous times.

"They've gone rogue!" Screw repeated.

Smitty, mouth wide open, stood thinking, 'He's right.'

"Why?" Screw shouted, arms outstretched, looking up at the sky. He kept shouting, "Why?" Again and again.

"They're out of control," Sloan mumbled. "No excuse for it. No fucking ex—" Before he could finish the word, Sloan heard a sound from out of his past. It was a distinct, unique sound that could only mean one thing. It was a sickening, debilitating sound that defined you as helpless and impotent. It was the "THWAP" of a round piercing and sinking into the flesh of someone nearby. Sloan, diving backwards before he knew it, shouted in midair, "GET DOWN!", just as his eye caught sight of Screw, already flat on his back. Sloan propped himself up high enough to see the sparse pattern of buckshot across Screw's chest. He yanked Screw's T-shirt up past the wounds, at the same time seeing his wide-open, lifeless eyes.

Sloan heard Smitty, lying prone on the other side of Screw, ask, "What can we do?"

From above, he heard Straughton, who still did not have the presence to get down, say, against the roar of the chopper blades, in a dazed, bewildered, hopeful tone, "He's not bleeding bad."

'That's right,' thought Sloan. For if Screw were bleeding really bad, that would mean that his heart was still pumping.

*****

Marco, his eyes burning, snot hanging from his nostrils, walked in a daze through the haze and stink of tear gas. He was headed home. Yet if asked where he was going, he would have been unable to answer, would have been too distracted by the vivid, blood-red flashbacks of what he had just experienced. He had seen riots before, numberless riots. He had seen police brutality, many times. Not just seen it, experienced it. Or thought he had. Today,

508

he'd seen the real thing. Unarmed demonstrators had been slaughtered in the streets, shot-gunned to death. He himself had seen a dozen people wounded and bloodied. There must have been dozens more. Who knows, the cops might have killed over a hundred. This sunny day, unlike most days, taught Marco something. He now knew what it was like to face the Czar's army, to be shot down and trampled under the hooves of charging Cossack horses. Every word Marco had ever said about the ruthless, fascist rulers of The United States of Amerika had been proven true today. The cops had proved them. Yet Marco was too shocked by this revelation to feel vindicated.

Through the fog of his thoughts, he heard someone say, "Stop. Stop! I can't hold on." He turned to see a motorcycle pull up to the curb. A woman was driving it, and a man, a much larger man, sat behind her. They both wore Hells Angels jackets. The man staggered off the back of the motorcycle holding his side. Brilliantly bright red blood seeped through his finger and dripped from his hand. He lay down on the sidewalk, saying to his woman, "Get me an ambulance."

The woman did not seem all that alarmed, not compared to Marco himself. The biker might die, might bleed to death right there on the sidewalk. It did not occur to Marco to try to help. What could he do? Still, this was not the reason he kept walking. Since The People's Park riot, he had been experiencing the world around him as something separate from himself. Though he was in it, right in the damn middle of it, he was not of it. To Marco, at the moment, the world around him was a panoramic 3-D movie, an unreal, all-encompassing illusion that followed him as he walked.

Marco did not return to and take his place in the world around him until hours later. First he stripped off his tear gas suffused clothing. He left them in a pile on his bathroom floor, only half aware of the way they had been irritating his skin. Then he took a hot shower, followed by a long, even hotter bath. Wearing no more than a towel, he headed for the refrigerator and poured himself a tall, cold glass of buttermilk. Boy, was that refreshing. Again he was struck by the ignorant tastes of the masses, guzzling their beer and coke and orange juice. Then he turned on the television and watched a parade, or more correctly a hand puppet show, of talking heads, interspersed with clips of the day's riot. They kept repeating that while scores of people had been shot, only one person had been killed, some kid he never heard of named Jake Pedersen. Marco, having witnessed the mass slaughter with his own eyes, realized that a cover-up was in effect, that the fascist conspiracy was again at work.

Slowly, re-experiencing the riot through television news clips, Marco returned to the present. A revelation came to him — an unbelievable opportunity lay at hand. The People's Park massacre had provided a means to catapult himself forward at such speed, that he became light headed just thinking about it. Marco realized exactly what he had to do. There was not a doubt in his mind that he could and would do it. This day had been a turning point, the most important day of his life.

*****

John Pedersen, Screw's father, felt a strange sense of relief when he could not find a parking place near the apartment. He dreaded what he might find there. He could have arranged for somebody else to gather up Jake's belongings and ship them home. Sure, but then there would be even more that he'd never know. He had to at least see Jake's apartment, the way he had left it. Maybe he'd find a clue to what had happened. The cops had told him next to nothing, would not even admit to firing the shots. They knew. They had to know. Mr. Pedersen had always been on their side. He felt betrayed.

What had changed the son, his firstborn son, of whom he had always been so proud? He now wondered if Jake sensed this pride. He never came out and said anything, not even the time Jake ran seventy yards after that scat back, falling farther behind at first, yet not giving up like the other two boys, running his heart out, then seeing that running back slow a step, sucking wind around the twenty yard line, Jake giving one last burst that nobody thought he had in him, tackling that scat back on the two yard line, saving the team a nothing-nothing tie. No one carried Jake off the field for that play. The newspaper, those jerks, didn't even say who made the tackle. 'And I never came right out and told him how proud I was,' thought Jake's father. 'No.' Len Arneson had slapped him on the back, saying, "That boy of yours, he's no quitter." Yet John

Pedersen had never once mentioned that play to Jake. 'Not our way,' he thought. 'That's what women are for, I guess.'

To John Pedersen from his pickup truck, Berkeley looked strange — a rich man's place near overrun with hippies. He'd seen hippies up close before, a few at a time. Yet now he was surrounded by them. Not until he parked the truck and got down onto the sidewalk, did he really feel their presence. Now it wasn't one or two out of place hippies, among him and his neighbors. No, now he was out of place amid circling hordes of them. This was their town. And there were more of them in every town, maybe taking over the whole country.

To John Pedersen, hippies didn't look like people you would want to be around either, grinning like they weren't right in the head, or like they thought they were so smart. 'Must be stupid in the water.' Back in Nebraska, they'd still have one hard time getting away with it. 'Out here, guess you can.'

John Pedersen's didn't like the look of anything he saw — blankets spread all over the sidewalks like some Arab bazaar. 'Is that what this country's coming to?' And the things they were selling, jewelry and clothes the lowest whore in Nebraska wouldn't wear. 'Junk. Was this what my boy liked about Berkeley?'

Jake was a hard worker. These hippies, not one of them looked like he could give you an honest day's, even an hour's work. Is this our next generation? Is this what the United States of America, that feeds the world, is coming to? He hoped not — 'We'll all end up starving to death, like in India and China.' Maybe what these kids need is a good depression. 'Good depression?' he wondered. 'Well, it might do them some good.' He figured that worrying about their empty stomachs wouldn't leave much time for rioting, for waving Viet Cong flags. 'A man with an empty stomach ain't worried about being happy.'

John Pedersen reached his son's apartment building before he realized it. From the outside, it didn't look that bad. He climbed the steps to check the mailboxes. He'd need a key. There wasn't a box marked "manager". This did not surprise him. He heard someone climbing the steps behind him and turned to see.

Smitty was headed for his mailbox, key in hand. 'Never saw this guy before.' He'd seen quite a few like him, hippies dressed like farmers. Smitty gave a slight nod and Pedersen returned it. He inserted his key.

Mr. Pedersen put his finger on Jake's mailbox. "I need the key to Jacob Pedersen's apartment."

'Hands like a real farmer.' The name was still strange to Smitty, though he had been hearing it on TV and reading it in the newspapers. Smitty now understood. "Screw," he said, more to himself than to Mr. Pedersen,

Pedersen stared at Smitty, trying to decide if he were cursing or crazy.

Smitty felt like an idiot. "Jacob Pedersen," he said, then more softly, regretfully, "Jacob Pedersen…he was a friend of mine."

Pedersen nodded solemnly, still wondering what the hell Smitty had meant by, "Screw."

"We'll call the landlord to bring the key over. Come in."

Pedersen followed him up the stairs, thinking, 'Screw?' He decided not to waste any more time wondering. 'Heck with it.' Smitty looked all right to him. There were kids in Nebraska running around with hair just as long. At least this kid didn't have one of those goofy grins.

As soon as he entered his apartment, Smitty asked Mr. Pedersen to sit down and went into the bedroom to phone the landlord. He came out saying, "He says he'll be here in an hour." There was a knock at the door.

It was Sloan. "Can I use the phone?"

"Sure," said Smitty. He tilted his head towards Mr. Pedersen. "Jake's father. He's come to get his things."

'Jake.' A sense of guilt overwhelmed Sloan and he forgot about his phone call. Maybe if he had left him 'Jake' instead of branding him 'Screw', the kid would still be alive. Yet he had worn the nickname like a badge of honor, had taken pride in it, just like the original Screw. So what? Sloan deeply regretted tagging the kid with that nickname, and the bad karma that apparently came with it. Now, choosing words Mr. Pedersen would find appropriate, Sloan said, "Jake was a fine young man. He would have made something of himself," while thinking, 'If I had looked out for him.'

These words gave Mr. Pedersen some comfort. Clean-cut and serious looking, Sloan impressed him as possibly worthy of Jake's friendship.

512

Smitty asked, "Can I get you something to drink?"

Looking sad and tired, Pedersen shook his head.

Smitty wanted a beer for himself, but decided to get three cokes out of the refrigerator. Pedersen changed his mind. They drank slowly, talking little, especially after Sloan answered Pedersen's question about exactly what had happened.

Pedersen's face was usually good at masking emotions, but not this time. The anger showed through. "No reason for it." Again he thought about how the cops had treated him, resenting them even more. "Seems like somebody should pay."

Smitty shook his head. "No one will."

Sloan said, "Family, friends, we'll pay for it. That's all."

Mr. Pedersen just shook his head. From then on, there wasn't much to say, until over an hour later when Smitty came back from the phone. "He says he may be another hour."

Pedersen, burning up inside, looked at his watch. "He said an hour an hour and a half ago. Is that the way people are in this town?"

Sloan said, "Most of 'em. Ain't many you'd want to depend on."

Pedersen said, "I've got a long ride ahead of me."

Smitty asked, "You're not going back tonight?"

Pedersen nodded solemnly.

"You can crash here," Smitty offered.

"Crash?"

"Sleep," Sloan explained.

Pedersen shook his head. "No thanks."

It was clear to Sloan that Pedersen just wanted to get his boy's things and get the hell out of Berkeley. "Look, it wouldn't take much of a shoulder to get that door open."

"Wouldn't be right," said Pedersen.

"Is it right keeping you waiting two and half hours?" Smitty asked.

Sloan said, "Heins is an asshole. He may not show up at all."

Pedersen couldn't take it anymore. He didn't want just out of Berkeley. He wanted away from it, far away. "Okay."

Sloan had the door flying open with what seemed like a slight bump from his shoulder. He was relieved by the condition of Screw's apartment. Though a mess, he had seen it much worse.

Pedersen and Smitty followed him in.

Straughton, hearing Sloan's entry, exited his apartment. He scoped out Screw's room from the hall. He and Smitty spotted each other at the same time. Smitty walked to the door to whisper, "Screw's father."

Sloan heard this, and looked back in time to see Straughton's eyes light up. Before Smitty realized what was happening, Straughton was past him and headed straight for an interview with the bereaved parent. Sloan met him halfway, with a look on his face that could have stopped a train. "Out....Now!"

Straughton recoiled as if faced by a cobra. He backed out the door.

The sight of Jake's one-room apartment pained Pedersen like a blow to the heart. Smitty's apartment had been just as dilapidated, but it wouldn't be the last place he would ever live. This rat hole had been Jake's last home. The sight of it hurt Pedersen all the more because Jake had seemed so happy on the phone when telling them he had rented it. And what the hell was that on the wall? Pedersen wasn't wondering about the pretentious, framed, poster-sized sketch of a naked woman, nor about The Doors poster, nor the Che Guevera poster he didn't recognize. What he couldn't take his eyes off of was the hammer and sickle poster, and the Chairman Mao poster next to it.

Sloan saw exactly what was bothering Pedersen. Wincing, he waited for the man to get over it.

Pedersen didn't. He just kept staring in disbelief. What was this doing in Jake's room? For God's sake, he had gone to Berkeley with plans to join the Marines.

Sloan went up to him. "Mr. Pedersen, that don't mean a thing — Berkeley wallpaper." After a pause, he added the lie, "Those posters were here when Jake moved in." This broke the spell, and Pedersen began to walk slowly around the room. "Maybe you'd like to be alone for awhile."

Pedersen nodded without looking back at Sloan.

Sloan said, "We'll round up some boxes, help you get Jake's stuff down to your car....It'll be a good idea if we get you out of here before that fucking landlord shows up....Fifteen minutes enough time?"

Again Pedersen nodded without looking back at Sloan.

Once alone, Pedersen reminded himself that he hadn't come just to pick up Jake's things. He had also come to see, to understand. Well, he was seeing, but he wasn't understanding. The top of Jake's dust covered dresser had coins spread upon it, mostly pennies. Some receipts. There were a half dozen packs of rolling papers, all of them empty or almost. Well, even in Nebraska, kids were growing marijuana all over the place. Adults too. Arthur Latimore once tried to get him to smoke some. He almost did. To see what it was like. There was also a roach clip on the table. Mr. Pedersen couldn't figure out the purpose of such a fancy alligator clip. He picked up a kaleidoscope, the type without stones, which broke up and multiplied actual images. Looking through it at the blank wall, he saw nothing. Pedersen put it back down, figuring the stones had somehow fallen out.

Jake's father pulled open the top drawer. All it contained were socks, underwear, and a lot of empty space. He sifted through them. 'Rags.' He couldn't very well bring these home. It would break his mother's heart to see them. As if her heart weren't already broken. He sifted through the drawer again, determined to find one pair of socks or underwear he could take home. He failed. Mr. Pedersen opened the next drawer. It held Jake's shirts. Most of those were rags too. He did find a couple. In the next drawer he found a few more half decent pieces of clothing, and beneath them two small framed photos. One pictured the entire family except Jake, who must have taken it. Mr. Pedersen was sure he had never seen the photo before. He felt himself on the verge of tears, but fought them back. The other photo was of Jake, when he was twelve, next to a prize hog he raised for a 4-H competition. His mother had a larger copy. It had hung in the living room, like similar photos in half the houses of rural Nebraska. Yet only for a few weeks. Then the boy had done something, given the impression that he was getting too high an opinion of himself. Pedersen had taken down the picture. It had stayed down since then. Well, he wouldn't have to worry any more about Jake getting a swelled head. Probably never did have to.

In the bottom drawer there was something wrapped in tissue paper. Mr. Pedersen opened it and was glad to see some new clothes, something less sad to bring home. There were a half dozen of those fancy tie-dyed T-shirts, a little too fancy for Mr.

Pedersen's taste. Yet Jake could wear them. He would have looked good in them, with his friendly smile. The collar on the top one was awfully small. He then realized they must be presents that Jake had bought for the family. The one on the bottom was extra extra large, more conservative, no rainbow colors, just a tie-dyed design in dark, dark blue. Mr. Pedersen knew who that one was for. This time he couldn't hold back the tears.

Mr. Pedersen put down the shirts and went to the window. The view it offered was of an alley, as ugly a garbage can filled alley as he had ever seen. He just couldn't understand. It didn't make sense. Any of it. He wanted a reason for Jake's death, a person to blame, he himself would do. But he had no one to blame, because he didn't even know why it had happened. He never would. Mr. Pedersen was not as religious as he would like to have been. Still, he did believe. He wanted also to believe there was a reason for everything, even if it was one of God's unfathomable reasons. Yet the older he grew, the more fearful he became, that some things, too many things, were just blind, dumb luck.

Yet luck alone could not explain why he had lost his firstborn son at eighteen years. There were the drugs, the clothes he wore, and what was that damn poster of Chairman Mao supposed to mean? Something had happened to Jake. And Jake was nothing like the scum he saw on the news, burning flags, blowing up buildings, making heroes out of the commies. Again he thought, 'A good depression, that's what they need....Keep their minds on filling their own damn bellies....Wouldn't have time for nothing else.' What got into them? What right did they have to complain, call their own government fascists? He knew what fascists were, real fascists. He'd fought them. Where did these spoiled brats come from? Whose children were they? Were they his? No, Mr. Pedersen refused to believe it. Jake was a good kid, an All American Boy. Well what happened to him? Why did he have to die like he did? 'Vietnam, better if he'd died there.' Then there'd be someone to blame — the commies, our own worthless politicians, himself. But to lose a son like Jake the way he lost him, it just did not make sense. Mr. Pedersen knew that he would never know the answer to the question that kept repeating itself in his mind — 'What did they do to my boy?'

It was John Pedersen who had encouraged Screw to travel for

six months before joining the Marines. He himself, a farmer's only son, had never traveled at all, except in the Navy, WWII. And that sure wasn't the way to do it. He didn't want his son to live his life with the same vague, uneasy feeling that had come upon him the day Jake had been born — the feeling that part of his life was over before it began, that he had missed something, and that he would never even know what it was. Not that John Pedersen complained, nor would he have been willing to trade his troubles for anyone else's, however slight. No, Jake's father was grateful for what he had, and that he could provide for those who depended upon him. He figured that when Jake finished his hitch, he'd come back to the farm because he wanted to. Or else he'd find some other job he did want, leaving the farm to one of his brothers. And in the very back of Pedersen's mind, there had been another reason he wanted his son to travel instead of going right into the service. Though he wanted the type of son willing to fight for his country, he did not want his son actually doing that fighting, not halfway around the world.

Mr. Pedersen picked a receipt up off the dresser, just to glance at it. He didn't. What was beneath it stopped him — a small old-fashioned pen knife. Jake had had it since he was eight or nine years old. Of all his possessions, this one, for some reason, he had chosen as his lucky piece. He carried it everywhere. He even hid it inside his football uniform. Jake once had the whole family in the barn looking for it. When the rest gave up, he stayed another three or four hours by himself, until he finally found it. His grandfather was dead by then. It was he who had given it to him. Jake had promised his grandfather that he would take good care of that little pen knife, that some day he would pass it on, just as it had been passed on to him. Now he never would. And his lucky pen knife lay on his dresser, left behind on the one day he really needed it.

*****

Smitty headed down Telegraph Avenue towards the university. The carnival had returned to the streets of Berkeley. He was in no mood for it. Screw was dead. The scent of marijuana again drifted across stoned and smiling faces, just as if Screw had never lived, never died.

Smitty passed a storefront displaying a poster with a phrase he had seen many times, in many places — "Revolution For The Hell Of It". This time he read it differently, thinking, 'That sums it up.' Brushing by the freaks surrounding him, he felt a cold, hard separation from them. In no need to hurry, he began hurrying anyway, plowing through the crowd with little regard for those in his way. It took the sight of a panhandler to stop him, a healthy looking one, his own age, who had suckered him for numerous quarters. Not this time. The panhandler gave a smile of recognition. Smitty returned it. "Hey Man, you want some real money?

"Do I," said the panhandler with an even larger smile.

"Then, c'mon. I have some work for you."

"Whoa." The panhandler took a step back, raised his open hands as if to fend off Smitty. "This is my thing, right here."

Smitty was already walking, the mean smile on his face matching his foul mood. It turned into a real smile when he saw the cart across Bancroft Way. Yes, there was at least one thing he still liked about Berkeley — the French crullers. There had been other things he had liked just as much if not more — the action, the sex, the dope. Yet these amusements proved to have their hidden costs. The complete cost of a huge, fluffy, melt in your mouth French cruller was twenty-five cents.

As usual, there was no line. The other carts were doing a brisk business, selling organic this and stone ground that. Smitty had tried them all at least once. 'Organic stone ground cardboard, hardly distinguishable from ordinary cardboard. This isn't to say that Smitty had become all that particular about what he ate. He could still chow down right out of a can, just as easily as he could drink right out of one. Yet he wasn't any junk food junkie either, except perhaps as diagnosed in Berkeley. In fact, it seemed the only junkies actually labeled as such in Berkeley were the junk food variety. Smitty himself would never admit to being one. Certainly not. He merely experimented with French crullers. Yet not today. Smitty had no desire to put anything sweet in his mouth.

Beside the gate, Holy Joe erupted in fire and brimstone upon the sinners surrounding him. He wore the same ill fitting black suit and tieless white shirt, open at the collar. His faithful scion was heckling and harassing him. How bad could Holy Joe be? He not only got along with his son, he took him into the business. So the argument, the harassment was just an act, a conflict to draw a crowd when no one was in an arguing mood. Almost as sneaky and slimy as all the television commercials America takes for granted. Could this be a case of ends justifying means? His motives appeared pure. He had probably even saved a few souls, though Smitty had never seen any evidence of this, not around campus.

The sinners gathered closer, smugly smiling down upon or outright laughing at this fulminating Christian relic. Holy Joe wasn't merely looking for followers, Smitty was sure of that. He could have raised an army in no time, half of them Ph.D.'s, by preaching some type of astrological numerological pharmacological transcendental organic holistic psycho babble Christianity, with of course some I Ching, Yoga, and Zen thrown in to boot. And if that didn't have the multitudes marching in step after him, all Holy Joe would have to do is spice up his sacraments with a little bio-feedback, free love, and herbal enemas. Who of Berkeley's oh so clever self-important religious skeptics could resist the Lord in that form?

"In this den of iniquity," Holy Joe fulminated, pointing towards the campus, "They teach you that man descended from the apes. Nonsense! Lies!"

"A proven fact!" yelled his foil and scion.

Smitty's ears perked up. He sensed an imminent attack upon Darwin. This brought back proud memories of his own groundbreaking work in defense of the man. Smitty's First Corollary to Darwin's Theory of Evolution states; "Anyone who refuses to accept the obvious fact that we have evolved from apes, has obviously failed to evolve as far as the rest of us."

Holy Joe continued, "Every year they dig up another monkey, and call it the missing link."

His foil called out, "Proof!"

"Proof of nothing! If this year's monkey bones are the missing link, then what were last year's monkey bones? Next year, they'll find another missing link to prove that this year's link is just monkey bones. Man created the missing link! God created man! God created Darwin!"

His foil yelled out, "Darwin created The Theory of Evolution."

"Look around you, Sinners! Do you see evolution? Do you see

perfection of the species? No! You see corruption of the species. You see sin and filth and self-degradation."

Smitty glanced around, admitting to himself that Holy Joe had a point. If Darwin were right, you would think the old human gene pool would have far fewer throwbacks flopping around in it. Hell, Holy Joe himself was Exhibit A. His genes should have been flushed out of the pool generations ago. And just look at the skeptical freaks standing around laughing at him. There was no excuse for half of them, not according to Darwin. Smitty glanced around again, this time uneasily, to see if anyone was staring at him and thinking the same thing. Sure enough, an intelligent looking girl was giving him the Skunk Eye. Discomfited, he turned and walked away.

Smitty hurried across Sproul Plaza. His long hair bounced on the back of his sweaty neck, making him itchy. Still, there was no way he would cut it. A glance here and there told him that all the plaza regulars, or their clones, seemed to be present. As usual, a speaker on the steps of Sproul Hall was trying to incite a riot. He had found that one tiny spot on the globe where the odds would be most favorable. Fledgling inciters must flock to Berkeley from all over the planet, many on scholarship, harboring fantasies of victorious perches upon the shoulders of the all conquering masses.

Further on was another would-be Joan Baez, today joined by an aspiring Bob Dylan, whose voice was a clear improvement on the original. There were the usual petition mongers — legalize marijuana, support the Viet Cong, gay rights, boycott grapes, free the Presidio Six. Once again, Smitty took it all in, now with eyes more squinted than wide.

Thoughts of Darwin came back to him. The behavior of so many of the people surrounding him must have a genetic component. Yet mutations could not explain it all. Then it dawned upon him — Smitty's Second Corollary to Darwin's Theory of Evolution; "Not only does environment, through natural selection, enhance the survivability of certain traits, species themselves can enhance their own survivability by finding a safer environment. What else could explain the survivability of your average college faculty? If it weren't for the safety of the campus, half, a third minimum, would be living out on the street, or already starved to death. And Smitty wasn't thinking about just those Bozos who still claimed to be communists. Hell, if their lives depended upon jumping on a bicycle and riding away, your average college instructor wouldn't have more than a 50/50 chance of jumping on facing in the right direction. Still thinking about environments, hostile ones this time, it occurred to Smitty that there was one particular environment that had succeeded exceptionally well in cleansing true communists from the gene pool, through both capital punishment and behavior modification — communist countries themselves. The only communists they suffered were the sham variety. Smitty felt as if he were really on to something. It seemed amazing how a college campus could turn Darwin on his head — location, location, location — turn survival of the fittest into survival of the weirdest and most helpless. Smitty saw himself on the very cusp of perfecting Smitty's Third Corollary to Darwin's Theory of Evolution. Maybe even a fourth, if hypocrisy could be proved to have a genetic component. He felt quite proud, better about himself than he had in a long time. It even occurred to him that maybe he should change his major to biology.

It wasn't that Smitty had come to dislike English. He had merely come to dislike the posers who pontificated upon it. Take Breslen, who taught the class he was headed for. He was a big guy, who probably could have had a decent physique if he didn't camouflage it under forty pounds of useless flab. This flab, where exposed to the world, mainly above his neck, had a blotchy, unhealthy, even unclean look to it. His curly red hair covered only and stood out from the sides and back of his head. The man's clothes were a slovenly, misguided attempt at being hip. Now Smitty had nothing against slobs. Some of his best friends were slobs, in fact most of them. Yet all of these friends understood, subconsciously, that slobdom demands a certain degree of humility, usually in the form of a don't give a shit take me or leave me it's your choice and you're welcome to it attitude. Breslen had never caught on to this. There is no more repellant slob than an arrogant one.

Breslen was a full professor, and a relatively young one at that. He could rarely complete a lecture without referring to his acclaimed book of criticism, the one that earned him his professorship — Literature as Ambiguity. Though not required reading for the course, Smitty had read it in self-defense. Grades mattered to him, in themselves and as protection from the draft. His marks would not be helped by inadvertently attacking the ideas of the learned man who would grade his papers. Breslen's thesis was that writing which clearly conveyed the author's intentions was no more than writing. Literature must be ambiguous, and the more ambiguity the greater the literary value. A truly great novel must open an infinite number of conflicting interpretations. The overriding intention of any worthwhile novelist was to make the reader think and imagine, force him or her to delve into his own or her own psyche, to interpret the work in his or her own individual way, no matter how extreme that interpretation.

Smitty didn't buy this. Not at all. In his as yet unwritten tome of criticism, Literature as Smitty Reads It, people who write books had to be, by definition, an egotistical lot who wanted you to think exactly as they thought, or oddly enough, wanted merely to tell a good story, and possibly both. A specific example Breslen used in his book served only to reinforce Smitty's skepticism. Breslen proffered that it was equally valid to argue that Melville made Moby Dick white as a symbol of the pure force of nature set upon by voracious destructive human nature, or as a symbol for sperm and the force of life set upon by a ruthless, destructive, capitalist culture. Now Smitty was perfectly willing to grant that both interpretations were equally valid, in that they were equally ridiculous. The second interpretation was even suspect on scientific grounds. Though Melville surely knew that cum was white, how could he know the color of sperm, of which even Smitty was not sure, and this despite handling it many, many times, perhaps more often than even Melville. Both interpretations were suspect on a practical level too. Whales could only be ordered up, even by the most gifted of authors, in three solid colors — the predominant shades of blue and grey, and the extremely rare albino white. Melville obviously made Moby Dick a white whale so that Ahab could later recognize and hunt down the leviathan that amputated his leg. Smitty would have liked to point out to Breslen that the novel would not have worked quite as well if Moby Dick were a grey whale with a speech impediment, or a specimen with one blue and one brown eye. However, Smitty did have to admit that ambiguity in literature held great value to critics and teachers such as Breslen whom it kept employed.

Fortunately, even Breslen could not totally destroy a course on William Faulkner. In Smitty's critical judgment as an English major, he rated Faulkner as "definitely cool". And it wasn't just those couple of novels that Smitty considered masterpieces. The dude had a pair of brass balls you could bowl with. He took chances, outrageous ones. What other Nobel Prize winner would have the guts to write a novel set in WWI, in which Private Jesus Christ gets blown away and eventually buried in The Tomb of the Unknown Soldier. It was one of the most ridiculous messes that Smitty had ever read, but how could any reader, suddenly realizing what Faulkner was trying to do, keep from exclaiming in awe, "Jesus Christ!" Faulting the man for that novel would be like faulting your buddy for getting shot down by Faye Dunaway while trying to pick her up in a bar. Hell, you should be cheering him on, or up as need be. Faulkner had an ego that could have made the gods envious. It probably did.

Though Breslen's ego was slightly smaller than Faulkner's, Smitty had much less tolerance for it. He took his seat in class determined not to let anything said or done really bother him. He failed immediately. This ass kissing girl was already at Breslen's desk, looking up at him like an adoring puppy. She usually waited until after class, so as to walk him out the door. Smitty wondered if she walked him all the way to bed. What some people won't do for a grade. And what some people won't do for a lay. Hell, he couldn't fault that asshole Breslen for that, unless he really was jacking up the slut's grade, which he probably was, so Smitty could fault the asshole after all.

Breslen began his lecture standing, as he usually did. The man liked to walk around looking well above the heads of his students. His words came slowly, his tone contemplative, as if he were speaking completely off the cuff, working things out, drawing his ideas from thin air, or perhaps from divine inspiration. The creep was on a power trip. Smitty noticed the strange way Breslen held his hands. Though hardly ever used for emphasis, they did not hang at his sides. He held them to the front of and above his waist, very close to his paunch. The fingers were spread. It was as if he thought everything around him was made of shit, and he was being careful not to get any on his hands.

For almost an hour, Breslen's words faded in and out of

Smitty's consciousness, only reaching the center of it when he asked a question. Then the stimulus of disgust would half awaken Smitty. 'Don't ask me your dumb question....You're dead and don't even know it.' Yet today, the name "Thomas Wolfe" did jolt him to full attention. Smitty's half written term paper compared Wolfe and Faulkner. Breslen had never before mentioned him. Smitty feared hearing some nonsense that would force him to junk his paper.

"Faulkner was once asked to rank America's best writers. Not surprisingly," Breslen continued, "Faulkner placed Hemingway well down the list. Surprisingly, he placed Wolfe at the top of it and himself second....Do any of you think you know what this means?"

Smitty thought he knew exactly what Faulkner meant. It was all in his now probably worthless term paper. Faulkner had borrowed, or stolen, much from Wolfe. Among other things, their sentence structure was often strikingly similar, especially their common and frequent use of run-on sentences. They even shared some pet words and phrases. The big difference was that Faulkner saved the histrionics for a shooting or a throat slashing. Wolfe went into hysterics over traffic tickets. It was possible that Faulkner really thought that Wolfe was the best American writer. More likely, he was merely acknowledging a debt.

Smitty sat listening to his classmates' explanations. None came close. The doofus broad Breslen was or was not screwing said something that was outright laughable. Smitty was more tempted than he had ever been to speak up in class, yet not tempted enough.

Finally, Breslen said, "Faulkner knew that no one else would rank Wolfe at the top, so by doing so, and placing himself second, he was actually ranking himself first."

Smitty thought what he would have liked to say aloud, 'Horse shit!'

Breslen continued, "During our next class, we'll discuss whether or not Faulkner was a racist. See you then."

'How charmingly relevant,' thought Smitty.

As the students gathered their things, one of them called out, "Professor Breslen."

"Yes."

There was a very slight hint of the wise guy in his tone.

"Professor, if this were a course on Shakespeare, would we devote an hour to discussing whether or not he was an anti-Semite?"

'That took guts,' thought Smitty, surprised to hear such a question, especially at Berkeley. How come he never had the guts?

Breslen at first appeared stung, then irritated. Finally, he accepted the challenge. "If I thought it relevant….Especially if this were the Thirties."

Smitty left the room in a lousy mood. He blamed Breslen. And himself. He never should have chosen the asshole's course. The Slate had warned him not to, but he had done so anyway, just for an extra hour of sleep. From now on he better be more careful when choosing professors, something he would need to do soon. Smitty scanned the plaza, searching for someone selling the new Slate. He saw something else that made him forget about The Slate. There was a girl with hair like Marcia's. She was too far away from him to make out her face. Certain, even at that distance, that she wasn't Marcia, he still hurried towards her. How many times lately had he done this? How many corners had he turned with hope in his heart? How many times had he been disappointed, like right now, as he got close enough to see that the girl's face was nothing like the one always in his thoughts?

'What the hell am I doing?' Smitty asked himself. 'Looking for The Slate,' he lied to himself. This thought brought back a memory — the first girl in Berkeley to catch his eye, the one who turned him on to The Slate, she of the fishnet sweater and snorkeling nipple — "It helps me sell." Whatever happened to her? 'Probably working on her second million by now….Ah, she could give a dead queer a hard-on.'

Not ten yards away, someone selling The Slate magically appeared. Not so magically, he was a ratty looking student-freak. 'You can't always get what you want, especially lately….Get used to it.' Then again, if he did eventually run into his fantasy vendor, he could just buy another Slate.

Smitty needed English courses. He also needed a sadistic laugh or two at the expense of his tormentors, those high and mighty professorial poppets, rightfully ridiculed in The Slate as banal and anal. He bought the Slate and scanned the list of English instructors. Some new rating categories had been added after their names — "Political Relevance", "Radical Sensibility", "Oneness with Students", "Concern for Spaceship Earth". Smitty read the new categories with disdain. He was interested in the old categories — how they graded and how they grated. He turned the pages, and kept turning them with increasing irritation. Where the hell was the useful shit? Starting again from page one, he ripped out all pages filled with political bullshit. He kept on ripping them out until the entire Slate was ripped apart. Smitty couldn't believe it. Yes, he could. Another putsch by the radicals. They had destroyed The Slate in the same way they were destroying everything he thought he liked about Berkeley. No doubt about it, the worthless fuckers wouldn't stop until Berkeley was nothing but a huge steaming cow pie of political bullshit. 'Berkeley, where it happens first,' thought Smitty, 'Every new form of self-delusion.' If Berkeley was where it happens first, the entire U S of A really was in very deep shit, deeper than even the radicals claimed.

Standing alone and angry, Smitty was pondering just how to choose his instructors when a brainstorm struck. It blew him across the plaza at a very fast walk. He wanted answers, and he knew where to get them. Actually, he wanted more than answers, even more than an argument. Looking for a fight, he headed straight for the English Department Office.

Some of Smitty's anger had worn off by the time he had climbed the stairs. Yet not enough of it. He entered the office and strode right up to the front counter. No one was in sight except for the young lady behind it. She rose from her desk, asking sweetly, "How can I help you?"

Smitty replied with a straight forward, no nonsense, "I'd like to talk to the Chairman of the English Department."

"I'm sorry, you'll have to make an appointment."

Only now did Smitty realize that it was lunchtime, and that the young girl was probably alone in the office. If he made an appointment, he would end up talking to some flunky two weeks from now. And if he told her why he wanted an appointment, he would end up talking to a psychiatrist. "I'd like to talk to him right now."

"Perhaps I can help you."

'No fucking chance,' thought Smitty. He felt crazy, literally. Not quite insane, but crazy. Hell, he must have been crazy to think he would talk to a department chairman, to anybody who was anybody around here. A voice in his head said, 'You're wasting your fucking time.' Another said, 'This is gonna end bad. Split while you can.' Smitty did not enjoy hearing voices in his head. They angered him even more. He vented this anger at the only available target. "I don't think you can help me!"

A hurt, insulted expression replaced her smile. "How would you know if you don't ask?"

Smitty felt like a bully and realized that a choice lay before him. The smart, decent, not to mention sane thing to do would be to politely take his leave. The foolish, the crazy thing to do would be to abuse this innocent young lady further. Having already gone too far, Smitty chose the latter. "Okay....I need some courses for next semester. Give me the name of one instructor who isn't trying to save the world through English literature, who isn't trying to be relevant, who isn't competing in UC Berkeley's ass kissing popularity contest judged by the radicals." He stood daring her to do so.

The young girl, mute and visibly shaken, stared questioningly at Smitty, gauging the extent of his insanity, and the likelihood it was leading towards violence. Behind her, an elderly man stepped out of a back office. "Claire, I'll take care of this."

Smitty watched the man approach, thinking, 'No shit! Chairman of the English Department....Goodbye, Berkeley. Hello, Vietnam.'

Dr. Butler studied Smitty, for a long and silent moment.

Smitty felt himself being judged the craziest freak this man had ever seen. A preposterously unjust opinion, considering that they were both in Berkeley. Deeply insulted, Smitty mulled over the many times of late he had suffered similar looks, had chosen to brush them off. That was another thing about this fucked up town. He never got that sideways look back in Cleveland. Fully aware of the belligerent expression now on his own face, Smitty made no attempt to soften it.

When the elderly gentleman reached the counter, he said evenly to Smitty, "You're a very demanding young man."

"Only in Berkeley, where it seems too much to ask for one English Lit class that actually has something to do with English Lit."

"Then may I suggest Jackson Burgess' course on Dickens?"

Smitty had in no way expected any answer, not to mention a

civil one. Having received exactly what he supposedly wanted left him even more frustrated, and with no recourse but to offer a grudging, mumbled, "Thanks". Thoroughly defeated, he was halfway out the door as Dr. Butler added, "Richardson's course on Shakespeare, that would be another one."

Though Smitty's anger had dissipated, so had his strength. Yet his frustration remained. 'What good did that do?' And then another question occurred to him. 'Did I just do that?...Am I going nuts?' Smitty decided that he better get hold of himself, fast. A sugar fix might help. Frustrated and dejected, he headed straight for the donut pushcart and its French crullers.

*****

Marco, in his mind, pictured a vista both limitless and awe inspiring. He envisioned a demonstration that would be the culmination of the entire Sixties protest movement. Finally, the establishment would be dealt a mortal blow. It would flee in terror, bellowing and bleeding like a wounded beast. The People's Park massacre had shown him the way. That wounded Hells Angel lying on the sidewalk had opened his eyes, not then and there but in retrospect. At People's Park, the fascists had declared war upon The People. Now it was up to him, to unite The People, to take all the oppressed, trod upon minorities, and to forge them into a majority. Marco had no doubt that he could.

"We are going to stop that troop train, that conveyer belt feeding naïve young men into the Vietnam meat grinder," he said with confidence.

Chandler nodded, wondering what exactly Marco wanted from him. Why had he asked him over with such urgency?

"This time it is going to be different," Marco continued. "Every segment of the counterculture will take part. I've sent out word. Thousands are coming from out of town, even from the east coast."

"You're confident you can pull this off?" asked Chandler.

"Completely." Marco wondered why all blacks couldn't be as cultured and clear thinking as Chandler, people you could talk to. So what if Chandler sometimes got that arrogant, dismissive look on his face. Marco smiled. "With your help."

"With my help," Chandler repeated evenly.

"Yes, I want you to be my liaison to the black community."

Chandler studied Marco. "You mean the counterculture elements of the black community?"

Marco nodded. "The Black Panthers, the Black Muslims."

"I have no connection to those thugs and con men," he replied testily, thinking, 'except the color of my skin.'

Surprised, Marco thought this over. "Well, you can make a connection. After all, you're a bona fide member of the counterculture."

Chandler stared at Marco as if he were crazy. "What makes you say that?"

"Well, you haven't missed one of my meetings for over a year."

Chandler saw no reason not to tell Marco, "I'm writing a book about radical politics in Berkeley."

This surprised Marco, and his expression showed it. He felt flattered. "A sympathetic book?"

"Not exactly. I wouldn't even claim it's objective. I happen to be a Republican, a conservative one at that."

Marco, feeling more fooled than betrayed, was at a loss for words.

Chandler continued, with no lack of irony, "If you still care to have me as your liaison, I can be your liaison to Governor Reagan. During the last campaign, I was his liaison to the black community. That's the black community, not the black counterculture."

*****

Sloan sat at the end of the dock, legs dangling over the side. He watched as dawn's first light broke slowly over the mainland. He had been waiting for just that for over an hour now. A heavy sadness weighed down upon him. Yet somehow, inexplicably, there was a sweetness to it, one of acceptance and understanding. For just that quiet moment, he was at peace.

A tiny arc of the sun now cleared the horizon across from him. With it, came memories of Vietnam. Even when it was pouring rain, even if he were shivering, there was something so comforting and rewarding about the end of last watch. That's when you took account, said to yourself, 'Survived another day.' More important, that was when you could now make out, scattered around you in that dim first light, those ugly, stinking piles of filthy rags which camouflaged the men who were your fire team, your fellow Marines. That was when you could take the credit and satisfaction for keeping them alive. It was a feeling of fulfillment, that gave you a sense of warmth within. Sloan missed it. Though he would never admit it, sometimes he missed Vietnam too.

Sloan hadn't had the slightest urge for dope, or even a beer, since Screw's murder. The word murder did not seem right. A death so random, so senseless, so undeserved and unexplainable could not be described as murder. Sloan had never believed in bad karma, but Screw's death seemed close, some kind of karma anyway. Sloan was not superstitious, but he had a feeling that Screw would not have survived Vietnam either. Still, one recurring thought gave him comfort, a thought he truly believed — 'It's not how long you live.' And what exactly was Life? He had not a clue.

Sloan watched the sun float higher into the haze, feeling that this was the very last time he would be seeing it from the Berkeley Marina. Well, the world was full of marinas — larger, smaller, more picturesque. The only strong attachment he had to this one was a woman he couldn't seem to forget, a woman who had surely forgotten him. Their last contact was a postcard she had sent him while he was in Vietnam — the only picture he ever had of her. Rob's good sense had kept him from forwarding it, just describing it instead. In Nam, it would not have lasted long. Yet it hadn't lasted long in Berkeley either, soon disappearing in some drugged-out fog.

The card was the commercial type you find on hotel racks. A professional photographer must have asked her to pose, maybe even paid her a few bucks. She was on her sailboat in a Hawaii marina, leaning over the railing. She wore a beautiful smile and a beautiful lei to match it. Sloan had never thought of her as the model type, or strikingly beautiful. She wasn't. It was just that confident glint in her eye that made her so cool, so very, very cool. The photographer must have seen it too. He sure caught it in that postcard. What Sloan would not give to have that photo now, see that look one more time. Yet something told him that he was better off without it.

The only word printed on the front of the postcard was,

"Aloha". On the back was the only human touch — his old address and her first name. Not Hi nor Hello nor Love, certainly no return address. What secrets did that photo hide? What kind of woman splits without leaving a forwarding address, cutting off everyone she knew? She sure lived in the moment, one of the very few luxuries Nam had afforded him, one that both she and Nam taught him to value. The past was unchangeable, set in stone, and it defined the present. Yet the present was fluid, and the present defined the future.

About her past, he never learned a thing. Perhaps he himself had preferred not to. Possible. Sloan sensed that she appreciated the fact that he never asked. One thing for sure, she was the type of person you could go to war with. Since Nam, that was pretty much the measure of things. One question did matter to Sloan, one that really bothered him. What was she telling him with that cut and dried postcard? "Come to Hawaii and find me."? Possibly. More likely, "I gave you your chance and you blew it." Would he ever meet another woman so capable, so justifiably confident? Little chance of that. All these questions were further proof to Sloan that, in this life, 'There's a lot of things you'll never know.'

Facing the now bright sun, Sloan rose to his feet. One of the reasons he had come to the marina was to be farther away from Screw's memorial service. He didn't even want to think about that, and about Marco and his whole sick crew. There remained plenty of time to kill before that steaming, stinking pile of political bullshit was over.

'What the hell.' For one last time, he'd walk the sailboat quays, not even looking for the woman who used to draw him there. Sloan now judged himself an expert in wasting time. Exhibit A, the year plus he'd squandered in a drug induced fog. He was painfully aware of his life full of mistakes. Yet wasn't everybody's? 'Life's a road you walk just one way down.' And during his own short meandering, staggering walk, Sloan felt that he had learned things, moved closer and closer to the truth, even if it was a truth he doubted existed. No, Sloan had never met even one man he'd trade places with, not his past, not his present, and not his future. He saw his road leading him back to Vietnam. That could be another mistake, one hell of one, perhaps his last. Sloan had gone to Nam the first time convinced that he was a survivor. Now he no longer believed in survivors. Too many times he had seen Life for the crap shoot it is. Survival, like everything else, was just a temporary state. Still, he believed in instincts for survival. Some people had strong ones. He figured that he had damn well proved that he was one of them. 'Well, whatever happens happens.' The Reaper loomed over him. Yet the Reaper loomed over everyone, and can never be appeased. Vietnam or no Vietnam, life was short and fragile. It was about time, past time, he got the fuck on with his.

Sloan scanned the sailboats as if he were choosing one to purchase. He even pictured himself at a few of their helms. Problem was, there weren't enough boats to keep him occupied until Screw's memorial was over. He'd have to find another way to kill some time. Maybe get something to eat. He could depend upon Rob having enough sense to skip Marco's phony memorial. Sloan sniffed his armpit, made a face. He'd need a shower first. That meant going back to his 'shithole' of an apartment. He'd get in and get out as fast as he could. Since Screw's death, the place was driving him nuts. He could hardly get any sleep there. That was the main reason he had found himself at the marina an hour before dawn. He'd lock the door, turn off the light, and lie down. Then, alone in the darkness, just as he was about to nod off, he'd hear it, a relentless, eerie sound, gradually amplified by the walls as they closed in upon him, a sound that kept him from sleeping — the sound of a heart not beating.

*****

There was a knock on Smitty's door. He went to answer it, knowing, 'Gotta be Straughton.' He would want a ride to Screw's memorial service. Smitty didn't mind. He was going there anyway, and preferred doing so with someone he knew. Sloan, for some reason, refused to go.

It was Straughton. He did want a ride. Not surprisingly, he wanted more. "If possible, I would prefer to arrive a half hour early to speak with Marco."

Smitty could not see where this would cost him anything. Straughton wasn't exactly dragging him away from an orgy, and, as he had learned, orgies weren't all they were made out to be. In truth, Smitty was again grateful for an excuse to get out of his dreary apartment. Once outside the building and into the sun, Smitty asked Straughton to wait as he went back in and knocked on Sloan's door.

Sloan met him in somber silence. He was shirtless, his short hair still wet, obviously just out of the shower.

To Smitty, he looked fit and formidable — 'Like a Marine.' "C'mon, Man, we gotta pay our respects to Screw."

"It ain't about Screw," Sloan said coldly. He was almost ready to leave his apartment again. A minute more and he could have avoided this. "It's about using Screw…even after he's dead."

"How do you know until you've seen it?" asked Smitty.

"I've seen it before."

"I haven't. C'mon, as a favor."

Sloan did owe Smitty a favor — 'Got my hat back.' Who knows, the memorial could turn out all right. 'Fat chance of that.'

Smitty just stood there.

"Okay, give me a minute."

On the ride over, Straughton asked, "Did you hear about the bank robbery."

"Pamela Kane again?" Smitty asked.

"No, two Berkeley students and two convicts they tutored got caught in a shootout with the cops."

'Figures,' thought Smitty.

Straughton added, "Apparently the convicts were better tutors than the students."

'Least I saved Marcia from that.' Smitty felt as if this news should have made him feel better. It didn't. In fact, it added to his depression.

They arrived at the park early, yet a large crowd had already gathered. Straughton searched out Marco.

Marco was even more interested in talking to Straughton, and spotted him first.

When Straughton saw Marco coming towards him with a big smile on his face, he glanced behind, curious to know who Marco was so glad to see. By the time he glanced back, Marco, still smiling, was standing right in front of him.

"Straughton, great to see you."

Straughton smiled back. 'Little Lenin' had finally come to appreciate all the free publicity.

"I need some personal anecdote for my speech. This Pedersen supposedly sold The Badger. You ever run into him?"

Smitty and Sloan glanced at each other, surprised by Marco's question.

Straughton was equally surprised. "Certainly, I did. You knew him too."

Marco was sure that Straughton was mistaken. Since high school, when he had read How to Win Friends and Influence People, he had never broken its most important rule — Don't ever forget a person's name. There was indignation in his tone as he replied, "I never knew any Jake Pedersen."

"My Dear Man, Jake Pedersen was Screw."

A look of surprise flashed across Marco's face, immediately replaced by a smile of satisfaction. "Great! Pedersen was Screw. I know just what to say." Marco turned and walked away, his lips moving as he revised his speech.

Smitty had wanted to strangle Marco. Anger still on his face, he snuck a glance at Sloan, who's expression said, "I told you so."

Smitty turned away and scanned the growing crowd. Screw was not his only reason for coming. If Marcia was still in Berkeley, she would be here. For the last two days he had been fantasizing about spotting her, apologizing, saying whatever he had to say to get her back. Now, as the crowd grew larger, he feared she could get lost in it. People were already sitting down on the grass. Sloan was one of them. He looked very pissed-off that some idiot had talked him into coming.

Smitty, identifying with that idiot, was in no hurry to sit down next to him. "Save me a place." Sitting, he would have been unable to spot Marcia. Smitty walked back through the audience, scanning each face. Every one that wasn't Marcia's depressed him a little more. Finally, he ran out of faces.

Smitty made his way back to the front. Screw's memorial was taking on a party atmosphere. He flashed back on Marcia's demonstration for The People's Crash Pad, how it had turned into a ten ring circus, a grass and ice cream fueled strip show. Smitty dreaded Screw's memorial degenerating into something similar. When he reached Sloan, before sitting down, he glanced back over his shoulder to search the crowd one more time. Again, no luck. No Marcia.

Marco was already at the podium, tapping the microphone. "Thank you for coming today. Please excuse us for not starting this memorial with The Pledge to the Flag, The National Anthem, or a prayer." Scattered chuckles came from the crowd. "No, we are here today to pay our respects to Jake Pedersen, our friend, known to many of us as Screw."

Smitty and Sloan exchanged glances, no sense of amusement in them.

Marco continued, "We'll start with a poem. Please welcome Michael McKlur."

McKlur stepped to the podium holding a large stack of papers and wearing the exact same military field jacket as Sloan. Except on the left front pocket, where Sloan's had a faded Marine Corps emblem, McKlur's had a meticulously stenciled peace sign. The jacket itself, unlike Sloan's, was without a single stain. And it looked recently ironed. So did McKlur's Levis, with a straight crease down the front. His shoulder length hair was no less meticulously cut and parted.

McKlur started, "I have copies of the poem I wrote for Jake. Unfortunately...or fortunately, not enough for everyone. Janet, will you please hand these out." A tall, attractive woman took the stack from McKlur. She didn't start distributing them until she was a few rows back.

Smitty turned to Sloan. "Did he know Screw?"

"Wouldn't have wanted to," Sloan assured him.

Some people sitting in front, alongside Smitty and Sloan, called out for a copy of the poem. Finally, someone, obviously a friend of McKlur, yelled out, "Hey Michael, what about us?"

McKlur himself caught up with the woman distributing his poem. He took some copies and began handing them out himself. He passed Smitty by trying to separate the pieces of paper. When in front of Sloan, still looking at and fiddling with the papers, McKlur held out a copy of his poem.

Sloan reached up for it.

McKlur glanced down at him, and immediately jerked the poem back and handed it to the next guy.

Smitty, baffled, looked questioningly at Sloan. "He knows you?"

Sloan shook his head and pointed to his temple.

Smitty still didn't understand. "Why'd he take it away?"

Sloan couldn't believe Smitty hadn't figured this out. Again he pointed. "My new haircut."

"Are you shittin' me?"

"No, my hair's too short for the fucking phony."

Sloan's explanation seemed absurd to Smitty, but he could not think of a better one, or any other explanation at all. Smitty again regretted dragging Sloan along.

McKlur confidently, smugly scanned his audience. He started reciting his poem, and Smitty started gritting his teeth. After slighting Screw's best friend in Berkeley, the prick was reciting line after line after line of pretentious, self-righteous bullshit, supposedly about the life and death of Jake Pedersen, whom he hadn't even known. McKlur finished with a self-congratulatory smile, followed by adulation and loud applause from the crowd.

Smitty squirmed in embarrassment, telling himself, 'Can't get worse.' Then, watching Marco return to the podium, he had his doubts.

"A few short days ago, Jake Pedersen, a friend of ours, was shot down and murdered in cold blood because he had the courage to stand up to the fascist military-industrial complex that calls itself the government of the United States of America, that runs and ruins our lives. I promise you now, Jake Pedersen did not die in vain." Marco paused, and was duly rewarded with applause and shouts of encouragement.

"Jake was a marked man ever since he fought for and helped establish The People's Crash Pad. I remember so clearly the day he came to me with that idea. That was the day he became more than just a friend, a lot more. That was the day it was clear for all to see, the courage and intellect he possessed. That was day we all realized that Jake Pedersen was a leader."

Smitty found himself squirming at almost every word. He was afraid to even glance at Sloan, hoping his surely murderous thoughts were directed at Marco.

"Years from now, when they try to decide which event sparked the revolution that brought down the police state now oppressing us, they are going to look back to the day that what we call our government, slaughtered a brave, unarmed Jake Pedersen. Yes, that was the moment our fascist government made a fatal mistake.

They didn't just attack the vanguard of The People. They attacked all the people. Now all the people are ready to fight back.

"This time our target won't be local, won't be People's Park, or what's left of it. No, our target will be national. Our brothers are coming not just from the Bay Area, not just from California. No, our comrades are coming, leaving today and tomorrow and the next day and the days after that, from all over the United States, to stand side by side with us. Thousands and thousands of them. On the first of next month, a train is leaving the Bay Area, the same train that leaves every month. It will be full of young Americans, from all over the west coast, headed for basic training, young Americans about to be transformed into psychopathic killing machines. WE...WILL NOT...ALLOW...THAT...TO HAPPEN!

"If we want to stop the war, if we want to stop the oppression, if we want to stop fascism, then we must not stop, NOT UNTIL WE STOP THAT TRAIN!"

Not only did the audience applaud loudly, they stood to do so. Smitty and Sloan were two of the few exceptions.

Marco motioned for the crowd to sit down again. "We will stop that train! We will stop those iron wheels that crushed our friend Jake Pedersen. We will do so because there will be thousands and thousands of us. The tyranny trying to destroy us serves only to inspire us. Yes, Jake alone was murdered that day, but scores were wounded. Blacks were wounded. Every black organization in the Bay Area will be there, and many times their numbers are coming from all over the country. Gays were wounded. Every gay organization in the area has promised me that they will be there, plus affiliated groups from all fifty states. There were Hells Angels wounded. For the first time, HELLS ANGELS MARCH WITH US!"

At this the crowd literally jumped to its feet and applauded.

Sloan stood with them, shaking his head and shouting to Smitty, "I can't take any more."

Smitty got to his feet, replying, "Neither can I."

Sloan started to leave by walking forward.

Smitty grabbed his arm, indicating that he wanted to leave by going back through the crowd. It was the shorter way, but would be more trouble and take longer.

Sloan asked, "Why?"

No way was Smitty going to explain. He merely jerked his head towards the back and started walking.

Sloan had no desire to walk over and between 'these fucking androids'. He was about to turn and go his own way when struck by a flash of insight. Smitty was looking for Marcia. The poor kid could not accept that he would never see her again, that she would remain a missing piece in the puzzle that was his life. Sloan hurried to catch up, without being too careful about who he stepped over. He experienced an urge to let Smitty know that he was on to him, to ride him a little, to set him straight. Sloan fought off that urge. Who was he to ride anybody? Soon enough, Smitty would find out that life leaves you with a hell of a lot more questions than answers. 'So many things you'll never know.'

When they cleared the last of the crowd, Sloan glanced back, then asked out of nowhere, "You feel like going to San Francisco?"

No, Smitty did not feel like going to San Francisco. Yet he didn't feel like not going either. He did feel curious enough to find out why Sloan had such a determined expression on his face and what the hell he had in mind. "What for?"

"You know that troop train Marco wants to stop?"

Smitty nodded.

"I wanna be on it."

*****

Rob was dead tired. He had caught the dishwasher downing a beer in the storeroom, and had no choice but to get rid of him. That meant cleaning up alone, an extra hour of work. Now, finally done, he wanted a cup of coffee as much as he had ever wanted one. What was left in the pot had to be too bitter to drink. No way was he going to brew another pot. He'd have to wait until he got home to make some.

There was tapping on the window. Rob was too tired to even turn around. The tapping turned into rapping he could not ignore. He looked over to see Sloan and Smitty banging on the plate glass. They both had big, idiotic grins on their faces — a sight that did not exactly fit his mood. Rob had neither the time nor patience to deal with them. He rudely waved them away from where he stood.

They banged harder, grinned harder, and finally burst out laughing. Rob didn't have the time or patience for a broken front window either, not tonight. Now irritated as well as tired, his expression showed it. Rob walked briskly to the front door.

Sloan slurred through it, "Let us in!"

Rob opened the door just wide enough to ask, in an unfriendly tone, "What the hell do you want?"

"Something to eat," he slurred, trying to push by him.

Rob's reply was an angry one. "Eat shit. I closed an hour ago."

"Hey Man," Smitty said from behind Sloan, "He just joined the Marines."

"Reenlisted," Sloan corrected him. He held up a bottle of wine. "C'mon, let's party."

Rob, stunned Sloan had really done it, just shook his head. Then he noticed the label on the bottle. "Thunderbird?"

"Hell, yeah," Sloan assured him, "Drink with us, you go first class."

"Only the best," Smitty slurred over Sloan's shoulder.

"It's understood," Sloan added.

Rob, now smiling and shaking his head, backed up and held open the door. "No fucking mess, understand that."

"Understood," said Sloan

"Understood," Smitty agreed.

Rob pointed to a table. "Sit down before you fall down."

Smitty and Sloan did so, while Rob went for three glasses, some rolls, and cold cuts. He came back saying, "Haven't touched that rotgut since high school. Let's see if I can still get it down."

"It can be done," Sloan assured him.

Smitty nodded agreement.

Rob said, "Obviously." He gave Sloan a look in the eye. "So you really did it."

"Oh, did I do it," said Sloan, filling the glasses with wine.

"He did it," Smitty testified.

"You dumb fuck," said Rob. Then, in a more sympathetic tone, he asked, "You didn't come back crazy enough the first time?"

Sloan leaned forward, whispering conspiratorially, "Tell you a secret; most of us were crazy before we enlisted."

Rob said, "You weren't a fucking dishwasher before you enlisted. You came back one!"

"No!"

Rob was taken aback by Sloan's certainty. "Oh, dishwashing was just your path to enlightenment, some sort of spiritual quest?"

"No! I been thinking about how I got the way I was."

"'Was'?' thought Rob. Sloan wasn't looking too great at the moment.

"I came back all right...for a while....The thing that really fucked me up was coming back to Berkeley."

Rob thought this over. "Maybe....But now you're headed straight back to Nam."

"All the way," said Sloan. "You gonna do something, do it all the way."

Rob held up his glass. Sloan and Smitty did the same, catching on fairly fast considering their condition. "Here's to you getting all the way back to the U S of A, and in one piece, you fucker." He swallowed half of it, then looked down at what was left. "Thunderbird...brings back memories...not all good." Rob stared at Sloan and Smitty. "How many bottles of this piss you drink?"

"That's the second," said Smitty.

"You pansies got this shit-faced on that?"

"Hell, no," said Sloan.

Smitty said, "We were drunk on beer before we started on Thunderbird. Looking for my car, we found this great bar in San Francisco."

Rob's face showed disbelief. "You drove back from San Francisco this drunk?"

"No, no," said Sloan. "Couldn't find the car. Took the bus back."

Smitty said, "We better find it tomorrow."

"We will," Sloan assured him. "It's five minutes from the recruiting center, somewhere. Hell, we start there and do a circular search. Can't take more than an hour."

"Circular search," Smitty repeated. "You learn that in the Marines?"

"Uh-uh, sailing." He noticed that Rob had poured himself another glass of Thunderbird, and was now studying him. "You think I'm crazy?"

Rob shrugged.

Sloan told him, "I admit it. You have to be a little crazy, but that helps you stay alive once you're in the Marines."

Rob said, "To join up twice, you have to be more than a little crazy!"

Sloan nodded agreement. It then occurred to him that the first time he really didn't "join" the Marine Corps. The wise ass he was more or less challenged it to a fight, a fight which the Marine Corps won. There was no smile on his face as he said,

"I'll tell you something I thought about on the bus ride back. You know, one of my worst memories from the Corps wasn't from Nam. It was from before Nam, infantry training at Camp Geiger, in North Carolina. We used to go on these forced marches, starting in the dark, before dawn. The column was like an accordion, the farther back you were, the worse it was. You'd have to run to catch up, only to fall behind again, having to run again as soon as you did. You could run for an hour or more straight, with a full pack and gear. It was torture. But you got used to it.

"Something I never got used to was crossing this same two-lane highway five minutes after we'd start. It'd be dark, sometimes foggy too. And there'd be a lot of traffic on the highway, people driving to work, probably fifty, maybe a hundred miles. You couldn't see a thing but their headlights coming at you and their taillights going away. Still, you knew that some of them were headed for shit work for shit pay. And a lot of them were miserable, about where they were coming from and where they were going. But seeing those lights, you were more miserable, 'cause they were free, at least compared to you. If they really wanted to, they could just keep going down that highway, and some other highway after that. You, you couldn't go nowhere except on a forced march. The Marine Corps owned your sorry ass, intending to ship it to a place it could get shot off. Parris Island was no picnic, but for me, it was a joke compared to crossing that two-lane highway, watching those headlights come at me and those tail lights disappear.

"And the thing that kills me, when I signed my ass back over to the Marine Corps today, I felt freer than I ever felt in my life except for one time, the time I got my discharge....Go figure."

Rob said, "I figure you felt free of Berkeley."

A thought surprised Sloan. "Guess freedom's just a state of mind."

Smitty said, "Man, when you were talking about that highway and the headlights, I saw it all. Sloan, you could make it as an English major."

Sloan did not appear flattered. "Rather get blown away in Nam."

"Enough of this shit," said Rob. "I gotta get home." He noticed some Thunderbird remaining in the bottle. Rob divided it up, and was just about to down his portion when he remembered something. Turning to Smitty, he asked, "You ever see that pretty girl you were shacking-up with?"

Marcia was the last thing Smitty wanted to be reminded about. Since leaving Screw's memorial, he hadn't thought of her once — a new record, or close to it. His displeasure with Rob was obvious as he shook his head.

Rob caught it, and it caught him off guard. He thought about dropping the matter. Yet for Smitty's information more than his own curiosity, he asked, "You don't know where she is?"

Again Smitty shook his head, wanting Rob to spit out whatever he was getting at.

"I think I saw her yesterday."

"Where?" Smitty asked, shocked half sober. He leaned forward, his eyes boring into Rob.

Rob pointed to the front window. "She might of walked right by here." He hesitated before asking, "Could she be a Hare Krishna now?"

Smitty, stunned into silence, could not picture Marcia as a Hare Krishna. He shook his head. Then his fear took over and he could picture her.

Sloan felt irritated with Rob. It took his inebriated mind a moment to figure out why. Rob should have told him, when Smitty wasn't around, so he could have checked things out himself first. "God damn it, you've seen the girl enough times to know whether it was her or not."

Surprised by Sloan's irritation, Rob's tone showed some of his own. "How the hell could I be sure, with a robe on and her head shaved?"

'Head shaved?' thought Smitty. This really knocked him for a loop. Again he couldn't imagine it until he suddenly did. 'Fuck!' Smitty felt dizzy. Trying to think, he wished he were sober and doing a better job of it. Did all the Hare Krishna women shave their heads? He didn't think so. But what the fuck did that matter? He didn't care about all of them, just Marcia. And Rob said Marcia had shaved her head. The thought made him nauseous, more nauseous than he would have been if sober. 'Oh, no. Fuck.' Maybe Rob was wrong. Slightly relieved by this thought, he immediately felt like shit. Finding her bald would be a hell of lot better than not finding her with her hair down to her ass. He got to his feet, grabbing the table for balance. Though drunk, he wasn't anywhere near as smashed as he had been a minute ago. "You coming?"

"Sit down a minute," Sloan ordered.

"Fuck that! I'm going over to that Buddhist temple."

"We don't even have a car," Sloan pointed out.

"Fuck it, I'll take a taxi."

Sloan also stood, saying angrily, "Think a God damn minute! They got dozens of zombies over there. You'd never get near her, even with me and Rob running interference."

These words jolted Rob. He hadn't considered helping out. Now he couldn't see why he shouldn't — except perhaps a kidnapping charge.

"I can try," Smitty insisted.

"And if you don't get Marcia," Sloan replied, "They'll ship her who knows where within an hour."

Smitty collapsed into his chair with resignation, but his tone was still hostile as he asked, "Then what's your fucking plan?"

"First we find out if she's there."

"How?"

Rob cut in, "Send Straughton, saying he wants to do a story on them."

Smitty and Sloan both nodded, but Smitty asked, "If he doesn't want to go?"

"You'll kick his ass," Sloan suggested.

Smitty saw no problem with that suggestion, and it lightened the mood considerably.

Rob said, "He'll do it just for the story, as if he doesn't know us, no names."

Smitty had to act. "We'll talk to him right now."

"We better," said Sloan, not telling Smitty why. The Hare Krishnas were known to pair-up their zombies and marry them off to each other. Sloan hoped they weren't too late.

*****

"What connections do you have with the Black Panthers?" asked Marco.

"Excellent," Straughton replied, feeling slighted. "You've surely read my interview with Eldridge Cleaver?"

"But he's in Algeria."

"Yes," Straughton answered with pride.

"Do you know any of the locals?"

Straughton hated to admit it. "In truth, I find them a rather disagreeable lot."

"How about the local Hells Angels?"

"Relatively less disagreeable....Yet in no ways charming."

"Can you get me a meeting with their leader?"

"Probably."

"I need their participation in a demonstration, the biggest ever." Marco had already publicized that they were on board, but his original intermediary had proved worthless.

"I doubt their leader would be of much help to you."

Marco did not appreciate being told his business. "You set up the meeting. I'll worry about getting his help."

"Certainly, but the meeting will have to take place in San Quentin...where he's doing eight to ten."

Marco sometimes found conversing with Straughton irritating. This was one of those times. "Can you get me a meeting with any Hells Angel who can guarantee a turnout for the demonstration?"

A half hour later they were sitting in Twelve Gauge's living room. He had sat scratching himself during Marco's entire spiel. "Why the fuck would we be interested in your candyass demonstration?"

Marco stated with determination, "Because, for the first time, the entire counterculture will be there." For Twelve Gauge's benefit, he added, "Flexing our muscles."

Fat Rat couldn't see where Marco's muscles would be much of a contribution. "Hells Angels got nothing in common with your crew."

Marco was ready for that reply. "Yes you do....Because we all believe in freedom."

Twelve Gauge thought this over silently. Freedom for Hells Angels, you bet your sweet ass. Freedom for anyone else, who gives a shit?

Marco, refusing to give up, played his Ace in the hole. "At People's Park, two of your men were wounded."

Twelve Gauge laughed. "Marxo, if we took it personal every time a cop shot a Hells Angel, we'd a been outa ammo years ago."

"You're the only element of the counterculture that won't be there."

"Look, Marxo, we're not the demonstratin' types."

"You won't be there to demonstrate. Your job is to keep riding up and down the edges of the march, to keep it moving, to make sure there is no looting or rioting along the way. We have to get to the train tracks. We need you to supply the necessary discipline to make sure that we do."

"Why not?" Twelve Gauge replied, surprising Fat Rat even more than Marco.

After Marco and Straughton left, Fat Rat asked, "Why'd you do that? Those pinko fairies make me puke."

"To get rid of them."

"So we ain't going?"

"We might."

"Why?" Fat Rat asked irritably.

Twelve Gauge smiled. "'Cause it'll be a riot, a real riot."

*****

Sloan, somber and silent, sat in the back seat of Smitty's car. This little op could turn into a fiasco. He had planned and set it up by himself. That was not the part that worried him. One little mistake by his team of amateurs, or just some bad luck, could prove disastrous. If the cops showed, they might connect him to the beating he gave their two buddies. Merely staying in Berkeley was tempting Fate. This little op was kicking Fate in the ass.

Sloan had stolen a license plate off a white van just like Rob's, then switched it with one from another white van, and then put that plate on Rob's van. It had been so easy, he swiped a plate for Smitty's car too. That proved not so easy. Finding a wreck similar to Smitty's was hard enough. Finding one the exact color seemed impossible. Well, in the end, he'd accomplished the impossible. Couldn't ask for a better omen than that. Hell, if he were handling this job alone, he wouldn't have even gone to the trouble of switching plates. Sloan turned and looked out the rear window. Rob's van was there all right, a car or two farther back than it should have been, but close enough.

Rob was more worried about losing Smitty's car than Sloan was worried about losing him. Sure enough, a big UPS van pulled out in front of him, completely obstructing his view. 'Shit!' A half block later, to Rob's relief, the van pulled over, out of the way. Smitty's car was in view again. If only he could get one or two cars closer.

Rob wondered if the others realized that legally they were kidnapping someone — a capital crime. Still, for helping a man get back his own daughter, he doubted anyone would end up in jail, forget about the gas chamber. Then again, in Berkeley, there were no certainties. Even taking a crap could have legal, not to mention political, implications. Yet surprisingly, all and all, Rob was enjoying this little adventure. Aside from drugs, he had not done anything illegal since high school. Speeding, yeah, he'd done some of that, but not by much over the limit. Some illegal parking too. Who hasn't? Even in high school, he'd never done anything that would have impressed Al Capone. It was past time that he did. Rob was actually flattered that Sloan had asked him to sign on for this caper. Of course, if they hadn't needed a van, Sloan might not have. He probably would have though. Two cars traveling in front of Rob made right turns, and he found himself one car back from Smitty's. 'Going like clockwork...so far.'

Sloan saw Rob pull closer. Yet it was not Rob he was worried about, nor Straughton either. Straughton would do whatever he had to do to get his story. It was the guys in the front seat who worried him — Smitty and Marcia's father. They were both too emotionally involved. He doubted either of them could think straight. No telling what they might do. Sloan figured, that when the action started, he'd have his hands full making sure they both did the right thing.

Smitty stared grimly through the windshield. He wanted to beat the shit out of every Hare Krishna in the world. They'd turned

Marcia into a zombie, shaved her head. What a shame that was, all her beautiful hair. He could picture it on the floor, in the garbage. What a crime. Her hair would grow back soon enough. Getting her deprogrammed, how long would that take? How long before she was back to normal? Would she ever be back to normal? From now on, he'd have to weigh every word he said to her, everything he did, for fear that she'd go running back to her Krishna slave masters. Oh, how he'd like to beat them bloody, every fucking one of them.

Blood was something Smitty had been thinking about all day. Soon, he expected to see some. Those "pacifists" were not going to let Marcia get away without a fight, and they had the numbers. He had wanted so much to wear his favorite shirt, the one Marcia had embroidered for him. Seeing it, she would remember how much it meant to him. Yet it meant too much to him. He would not take a chance getting that shirt ruined, nor did he trust himself with the life of anyone who damaged it.

Smitty had to drive through the ghetto to get to the Buddhist temple. Marcia's father sat next to him. Thirty yards up ahead, a few dozen black teenagers lined opposite sidewalks. Two kids on bicycles burst from among them, from either side of the street, heading on a collision course. Marcia's father watched to see what they were up to, assuming they would turn away at the last instant. They didn't. To the cheering delight of the crowd, the bikes crashed loudly in the middle of the street. One bike came to a dead, cartoon-like stop. Its rider managed to keep both himself and the bike upright. The other bike spun in a violent circle. Its thrown rider rolled over and over in the street and halfway under a parked car. The excited spectators rushed to his aid, pulling him smiling out from under the car and to his feet. Skinned, bleeding elbows seemed the extent of his injuries.

Marcia's father, stunned, asked, "What was that?"

Smitty weaved the car around the bikes.

"Bike fights," said Sloan.

'Ghetto jousting,' thought Smitty.

Marcia's father looked back to see the bikes pulled from the street, and two more jousters ready to go. He kept watching, until the bikes collided, knocking both riders to the pavement, thinking, 'As if their chances weren't bad enough.'

He turned forward and saw another kid on a bike, the same color bike. "How come all these kids paint their bikes blue and yellow?"

'A long story,' thought Smitty, one that he was not in the mood to tell. He waited, hoping Sloan would answer. And waited. Finally, answering himself, "Some Berkeley students fixed up a few hundred bikes, and painted them the university's colors."

Marcia's father smiled. "And gave them to the poor kids? That was a nice idea."

'Not exactly,' thought Smitty. He smiled, now finding amusement in how it all turned out, better than it should have. He thought about Marcia, glad that Honor Bikes had not been a complete waste. "You know," he said to her father, "Marcia was one of the first to do it. She got me to help out."

Her father smiled. "Really, Marcia fixing bicycles?"

"Yeah, she got to be pretty good with a wrench," he exaggerated. "Bet you thought she was wasting her time at college." Smitty realized immediately these careless words had been a mistake.

"No," her father said somberly. "Never."

Marcia's father wasn't even thinking about what was to come. The idea of it was all too surreal, like a dream he knew was a dream and struggled to wake from. He had wanted to blame the kid sitting next to him. He couldn't. The first time he had met Smitty — 'the way he looks right into your eyes' — Marcia's father had assumed that he was stoned. The fact sickened him, and when he realized that the fact was fiction, this sickened him even more. He, an oncology surgeon, should have been used to people searching his eyes as if he were God, as if their fate were in his hands, praying to hear that magical word cured, or, failing that, to hear how much longer they had left to live. His own wife had not searched his eyes. He had never had a patient more stoic. Perhaps she had known that he would fail her.

The determined kid sitting next to him looked stoic too. He also looked streetwise, as if he could handle himself. He didn't look anything like the smooth, over privileged Santa Monica boys Marcia had brought home. Yet he didn't look particularly intelligent either. Still, he must be. He got into Berkeley. Marcia's father glanced at Smitty again. He had to admit, that if Marcia had brought him home, despite the kid's rough edges, he would have thought that this is someone I can trust to take care of my daughter. 'How wrong I would have been.'

Marcia's father couldn't keep his eyes off all of the black kids, too many to count. Most of them looked as happy and innocent as any other children in the world. Yet a few appeared hard and mean beyond their years. What chance did they have to make it out of this ghetto alive? He wondered how many had fathers to help raise them. How many didn't, stacking the odds against them?

Yet he had raised Marcia alone. And that was why he could not blame Smitty. A year or so after her mother died, he had asked Marcia if she wanted another mother. No, she told him, she wanted her own mother back. And he had let a little girl decide. Not really. He had known she needed a mother. His first wife, his first love, had spoiled him. He could not make himself go through that again, even for Marcia. And she was always the perfect daughter, from the time her mother passed away until the time she disappeared. It hurt when he found out she was living with a boy. Still, that was inevitable. That was what went on these days. Being brainwashed by cults went on these days too. That wasn't inevitable. If only he had had the strength and determination to find Marcia a mother, he was positive that he would not now be riding in this car with a hypodermic needle in his pocket.

*****

Straughton sat astride one of his trusty Honor Bikes, catty-corner to the Buddhist temple. The afternoon parade of Hare Krishna's hadn't exited yet. According to the intelligence he had gathered, they were a few minutes late. This surprised him. With all their gongs, he had assumed they were a rather punctual cult. Still, when they exited was less important than the route they would take. The kidnappers were waiting in ambush. If Straughton had guessed wrong about the route, he would have to ride over fast to inform them. This complication could mean trouble. A new ambush site would have to be set up on the fly, and it would take some luck to find a good one. Of course the ambush turning into a complete disaster, that might make a good story too. Still, considering the pride he took in his skillful espionage, his sympathies were with Sloan's Raiders.

Straughton did not mind waiting, not for a good story. It added to the suspense and got his hormones going. Hormones helped when it came to the writing. Even if they wore off before he reached his typewriter, the story would already be written in his head. Then it was just a matter of tapping some keys. His adrenalin level always got an additional boost when he himself had helped instigate the incident. Straughton knew that all this self-righteous hypocrisy about manufactured news was mere carping and backbiting by those lacking the foresight, talent, and imagination that staging required.

Sure enough, today's parade began to exit the temple. Here came the marchers in their bright saffron robes, or sheets, or whatever they were. They immediately started their joyful dancing and hopping around single file to the beat of drums and tambourines, and of course the numbing lyrics:

Hare Krishna
Hare Krishna
Hare Krishna
Hare Ramah

Straughton spotted Marcia towards the end of the line. Even with her head shaved, she was quite sexy. Marcia apparently didn't rate a drum or tambourine. She merely clapped her hands as she hopped around. Even so, her timing was slightly off. The poor kid lacked the musical talent to be a showcase Hare Krishna. This further justified her rescue, made the act even more commendable, if not lawful.

Straughton was proud to see that the Krishnas were taking the exact route his intelligence had predicted. No time to waste. He took off on his Honor Bike for Rob's van. Straughton found it exactly where it should be, stopped along a residential street. The van was double-parked in front of an open spot between two parked cars. This left a conveniently large, clear gap between van and sidewalk. Pulling into it, Straughton saw Sloan leaning against the sliding side door. Smitty and someone he guessed to be Marcia's father stood slightly bent over just inside. "Everything according to plan," he reported to Sloan.

"Good," Sloan replied. "How many are there?"

"About twelve, most of them men."

"Where's Marcia."

Straughton thought a moment. "Third from the end, if I remember correctly."

"Get back and trail them, in case they change their route."

Straughton took off with a serious expression on his face. He saw himself as a World War II spy bicycling through occupied France. The Huns were no fools. If he fell into their hands, he faced torture and certain death. To outsmart these uncouth barbarians, he would need to summon all the courage and wits he could muster. Straughton pedaled faster, creating a crisp breeze against his face. War was exhilarating.

*****

Sloan, relieved that things were going as planned, was still wary. Something always went wrong. The sooner it did, the more time you had to fix it. He had forgotten to tell Rob to clean out his van. Usually you couldn't open any of the doors without suffering an avalanche of junk burying you up to the ankles. Luckily, Rob had had enough sense to take care of this without being told.

Sloan decided to go over the plan one more time. Turning to Marcia's father, he saw him checking a little leather case, big enough for a few cigars. Sloan figured it contained chloroform or a hypodermic. As her father put it in his shirt pocket, Sloan warned, "Just grab Marcia and carry her into the van. I guarantee you, she's so brainwashed talking won't work." He turned to Smitty. "Look, don't get in a fight. We haven't got time for that." He pointed towards the sidewalk. "See that hedge?" It was solid, but only about three feet high. "I'm gonna knock the guy in front of Marcia right over it. You do the same to the guy in back of her. Don't go over with him. Then we block off anyone who tries to help Marcia. If I can't get to the door, then you slam it shut." He turned to Rob. "Okay, start the motor and keep it running." Then Sloan added, enunciating each word separately, "And don't get out." Once again he turned to Marcia's father. "The quicker you can get her in the van, the quicker we're outa here." Sloan wondered if he had forgotten anything important.

Whatever fears and doubts Smitty had, none concerned Sloan's plan. Smitty had complete confidence in him, and was thankful Sloan had taken charge. The man covered every angle, planned for every contingency. Smitty glanced back at his car, half a block down and on the other side of the street. Parking it there had been Sloan's idea. He figured if it were too close, he and Smitty would not be able to get in it without the Krishna's swarming all over them. Who knows, maybe lying down in front of it? Sloan had said, "If we can't outrun some Hare Krishnas, we deserve to get caught."

'Military precision,' thought Smitty, with new respect for the term.

He looked over at Marcia's father, 'The poor fucker'. He appeared so sad, so lost in thought. 'How should he look?' They had spoken very little since Smitty had telephoned him. Smitty blamed himself for what had happened to Marcia, and he assumed her father blamed him too. Smitty hadn't told him anything about Muhammad, and certainly nothing about Donna. He wondered what Marcia had told him over the phone, if he knew anything Smitty did not know. He was dying to ask, but he couldn't make himself. Her father would be taking her straight back to Santa Monica today. There was another, more important thing, Smitty wanted to know and hadn't been able to make himself ask. It was now or never, and it looked like never. Then Marcia's father turned towards him, as if sensing Smitty's gaze.

Immediately, before he could lose the nerve, Smitty asked, "When will I see her again?"

Her father's reply was calm, almost gentle. There was no sense of bitterness or accusation in it. "You won't."

These two, simple words stabbed Smitty like a knife in his side. He merely nodded, understanding that he deserved no better. 'Hates my guts.' With added respect, Smitty stared at the man who had wounded him. 'He's honest'. This sad, serious man had kept Marcia safe for twenty years. He hadn't been able to keep her safe for a measly few months. Smitty steeled himself not to fail again. He'd return Marcia to someone who could keep her safe. 'The least I can do.'

Sloan said, "I hear them."

Smitty did too, somewhere deep in the back of his mind.

"Okay," said Sloan, "Face the van." Smitty and Marcia's father stepped out and turned toward the open side door. Sloan did too, but he kept scanning the street. "Don't look until I tell you, and start running first."

The drums, tambourines, and chanting grew louder, but, along this residential street, without an audience, remained more subdued than it would have been along a busy city sidewalk. Sloan copped a quick glance, seeing the first few Hare Krishna's pass. Everything was set. Everything was perfect. There was plenty of room between the two parked cars for all three men to rush through side by side.

Sloan found himself trying to get mean and serious as he whispered, "Get ready....GO!"

As all three men took off, rushing for the sidewalk, Sloan spied a problem. The Hare Krishna behind Marcia was female. Too late to tell Smitty to knock her flat, Sloan hoped he had the sense to do so.

Smitty, half a step behind Sloan, lost another half step when he saw Marcia and her shaved head. Regaining focus, he noticed the woman behind her. 'Shit!' Tall. Heavy. Should he level a woman? The Krishna behind her was even larger. He looked familiar. Smitty went after him.

Marcia's father froze. Could that poor shavedheaded girl in the saffron robe, hopping around and clapping in front of him, could she really be his beautiful daughter?

Sloan's Krishna was rail thin, frail, and wearing glasses. For an instant, and only an instant, out of fear of breaking him in half, Sloan considered easing up on the kid. This thought was chased away by the motto he lived by — "If you're gonna do it, do it all the way." The kid disappeared behind the other side of the hedge in a flying heels over head saffron blur.

Just as Smitty leaned a shoulder into his Krishna, he realized that this was the one he had seen at the Battle of the Honor Bike, sitting atop and squeezing the life out of the undersqueak. No way did Smitty want to find himself in the same position. He applied some extra shoulder into this Sumo-wannabe, who went over fast and hard. Not over the hedge by any means. No, he landed on top of it, with enough force to obliterate the bush beneath him with a loud crack. Unfortunately for Smitty, Jumbo was able to grab hold and take him along for the trip down. Fortunately for Smitty, he landed on top.

Straughton, astride his bike, watched in awe from the sidewalk. Matters had taken a surprisingly physical turn — 'Better than a movie'. His journalistic detachment had kicked in, and he was perfectly content to play the role of eyewitness.

Marcia's father had quickly regained enough presence of mind to go after her. She was petrified, trapped between him and the hedge. He reached for her hand, but she drew it back in horror. No time. No choice. He put Marcia in a bear hug, lifted her up, and headed for the van. "No! No!" she screamed, pounding him hard with closed fists. The Krishna girl who had been behind her came up and grabbed Marcia's arm, pulling her away from the van.

Sloan was on her in an instant, yanking her backwards with a take no prisoners stranglehold. He let go as she fell fast and hard on her ass, coughing and grasping her throat. Sloan winced, mumbling, 'Sorry, Mamasan.' He glanced backwards to see—

Smitty freed himself and climbed off the Sumo-wannabe, who was now a semi-permanent part of the hedge.

Another saffron robed kamikaze slammed right into Sloan from behind.

Marcia screamed, "Help! Help!"

The sumo fought to regain his feet.

Smitty whipped the sumo's legs out from under, while Marcia's cries cut him to the bone. He fought the urge to run to her, or even look in her direction.

Rob leaned out the driver's window to see—

Marcia's father struggled to push her into the van while she fought back, refusing to let go of the door handle. "Help! Help!"

Rob wanted out of there, fast. 'The hell with Sloan.' Disobeying orders, he exited the van, first pulling on a red and green ski mask with a big white pom-pom on top. Rob yanked Marcia's hand off the door, at the same time shoving her father and her inside. They landed on the floor, legs still sticking outside. A quick forceful lift from Rob and they were rolling to the other side of the van. He slid the door shut with a bang. Rob jumped behind the wheel and stomped on the gas, sending out a blue, foul-smelling fog thick enough to get lost in. Only after escaping it, did he slow down to legal speed, while still expecting to hear a police siren any second.

A driver coming from the opposite direction rubbernecked him as if he were Public Enemy #1. Justified as the driver was, Rob couldn't figure out how the hell he knew. Another oncoming driver pulled off the road in fear. 'What's going on?' Rob asked himself, as he went to scratch his chin. This told him exactly what was going on. He was still wearing the ski mask.

Smitty and Sloan were now running for their car. No Krishna's were after them, but they ran as if there were.

Smitty reached it first, and dug into his pocket for the keys.

Sloan, running to the passenger side, couldn't believe Smitty had done something so stupid.

Smitty jumped in and unlocked Sloan's door.

Sliding in, Sloan asked angrily, "Are you an idiot?"

Smitty, concentrating on pulling out, said, "I must be."

"What the fuck you lock the doors for?"

Stomping on the gas, Smitty answered indignantly, "You want someone to steal my 8-track?"

Sloan, feeling lucky they had accomplished their mission with no casualties, decided to let the matter drop. He then heard something between a wheeze and a laugh coming out of Smitty's mouth. "What the hell you laughing at?"

Smitty hesitated, not wanting to insult the military genius behind this commando operation. Yet the more he thought about it, the more he did want to needle Sloan. "So much for military precision."

Sloan did not take the remark personally. "Don't tell anybody I told you, but there ain't no such thing."

"Now you level with me."

"Didn't want rattle you. Military precision is an oxymoron."

"You know, you really could make it as an English major."

Smitty began to laugh harder, but it wasn't at his own joke. "Did you see Rob's fearsome ski mask?"

Sloan finally joined him in laughter. "With that pom-pom on top!"

*****

Straughton was headed for The Badger office, telling himself he wanted to say goodbye to Moe. Actually, he wanted to see Moe's reaction upon hearing that he was now working for The New York Times or The Washington Post. He still hadn't decided which. As an excuse to break the news, Straughton had come up with the ingratiating idea of asking Moe's advice. Of course he'd ignore this advice. What did Moe know? Well, Straughton had to admit, Moe did know something about writing, and about the newspaper business. He had picked up some very useful tricks from him. And Moe wasn't a bad guy, a peasant, a Jewish peasant, yet not a bad guy. He had treated Straughton relatively well. In fact, Straughton realized, that in all the time he had worked for Moe, he had never attempted to throw him down the stairs. That qualified Straughton as one of the Chosen Few, something in which to take pride. Not something one could add to one's portfolio, yet still an accomplishment.

Straughton scanned the bustling sidewalks of Berkeley. Yes, he would miss them. Still, the truth was, he had seen just about all the sights they could offer. Lately, Straughton could compare each noteworthy event to the previous times it had occurred. His writing had begun to suffer. Berkeley was still an interesting, exciting place, but less so, at least to him. Every new day brought diminishing returns. His horizon, and a new dawn, awaited him in the East.

Straughton, for probably the last time, climbed the worn, narrow stairs up to The Badger's office. Moe stood a few yards away, only half conscious of him. Straughton had seen this more often lately, Moe almost in a trance, as if trying to remember something.

Moe acknowledged him with a suspicious, corner of the eye stare. Straughton's smile was not one that he had seen before, and he did not like it. "You got something for me?"

Straughton's smile widened. "News…of the personal variety."

"Personal news don't interest me."

"Moe, I have been offered a job, back East." Straughton held out his hand. "I've come to say goodbye."

Moe began to nod his head. "Well, you stuck with me when those fuckups started The Clan." Moe then did something completely out of character. He stuck out his own hand and shook Straughton's. "Newspaper?"

Straughton nodded, still smiling.

"Which one?"

"I have yet to decide — The New York Times or The Washington Post."

Moe was impressed, but he managed to hide this. Of course Straughton's old man probably pulled some strings. Still, he had what it takes to work for any major newspaper in the country. Straughton was unburdened by those handicaps that separated the journeyman from the truly accomplished reporter — character, honesty, or a working conscience. Moe had no doubt that he had not heard the last of Straughton. He'd make it big — in newspapers, television, or both.

Straughton was surprised by what he now saw on Moe's face. There was a tiredness he had never before noticed. Much of his strength had deserted him. In most people, this sight would have brought out sympathy. In Straughton, it merely brought out amazement, enough to reinforce the smile on his own face. "What would you advise, Moe — New York or Washington?"

Moe thought about the staffs at both papers. "You'll fit in fine at either place, Kid....In Washington, you can get very rich or very powerful very fast. But it ain't much of a town. New York's a hell of a town. And that's where the real money and the real power are. It's harder to get to it, but it's there....You'll do okay wherever you go."

Straughton was more than shocked, he was disarmed by Moe's tone, one far more fatherly than he had ever heard from anyone, including Roger Basil Straughton V. Though his own father's tone was not the same one he used with the stable boys, it was never far removed from it. Straughton was feeling a surprising closeness to Moe. That's when Moe did something really fatherly. He placed his arm across Straughton's shoulders.

It was then that Straughton realized that Moe was leading him towards the stairs. He stiffened in fear. The only times Moe had ever put his hands on anyone, was to throw them down the stairs.

This was exactly Moe's intention when he had placed his hand on Straughton's shoulder. After all, what could be more natural, obligatory even. The false modesty and phony expression Straughton had used to give him the news were reasons enough. Yet as they reached the top of the stairs, Moe's arm grew heavy and, to his own surprise, it dropped to his side. Moe wasn't sure what had happened or why.

The fear left Straughton, and he took a deep breath in relief.

Moe watched him go down the first step, with the vague feeling that he had missed an opportunity that would haunt him the rest of his life. Still, Moe had neither the strength nor inclination to act.

Straughton realized that he was accomplishing something extraordinary, that he was leaving The Badger office for the last time, without ever having been thrown down the stairs. And then he realized that this was impossible. A vision flashed through his mind. At that instant, Moe must be lifting up his foot, ready to kick him, ready to send him down the stairs more viciously then he had ever sent anyone. Straughton envisioned himself on the landing below, his neck bent horribly to one side, obviously broken. Straughton glanced back up at Moe in fear, only to see him gazing down with a sad, questioning expression on his face.

Straughton was puzzled by Moe's look, but not for long. It was then, still looking back, that Straughton tripped over his own feet. Caught completely unawares, he found himself, like some cartoon character, peddling thin air. An instant later, he was descending the stairs on his knees, which immediately proved impossible. When Straughton reached the landing, his head hit the wall with a loud, hollow thud.

Straughton was treated to a spectacular fireworks show, starbursts of green and red, originating from within his very own skull. He felt no pain. The blow to his noggin had anesthetized him. What he did feel was stoned, more pleasantly than on many of the trips he had experienced. Yet why was he staring down unfocused at a worn, dirty floor? Why was his nose pressed against it? He struggled to his hands and knees like a crawling infant. Straughton saw more stairs below and realized where he was — on the landing. It even occurred to him, 'That's why it's called a landing…a rather hard one at that.' Straughton was dazed enough to assume that Moe had caused his fall. He raised his gaze to find him still at the top of the stairs, a calm, unreadable expression on his face. Straughton opened his mouth, about to ask the one word question — "Why?" Yet even in his dazed state, he realized the folly in this. You don't ask a fish why it swims, or a bird why it flies. Sprawled out on the landing, looking up at Moe, Straughton realized that the answer was no more complicated than Moe's nature.

Moe, looking down at Straughton, was the more confused of the two. Fate alone could not explain such fortuitous clumsiness. For the first time in his life, Moe had the feeling that there was a certain logic beneath all the chaos that is our world. It now made little difference that he had not thrown so deserving a slimeball down the stairs. His failure to do so would never haunt him. No, it was as if an invisible hand had closed the circle, had added the last punctuation mark to their relationship. This minor miracle he had just witnessed was almost enough to make Moe believe that somewhere in this universe there existed a God, a benevolent one.

Charity swelled in Moe's heart. "Good luck, Kid."

'Good luck?' Straughton asked himself. He struggled to his feet, still woozy from the knock on his head. Holding the railing tight, he made it down the rest of the stairs. The people on the sidewalk seemed to be moving faster than usual, too fast. Straughton joined them, walking to who knows where. Still stoned from the blow, slightly unsteady on his feet, yet in no pain, he felt calm and relaxed. He remembered what he had seen upon banging his head — the green and red star bursts. Straughton had had no idea that that actually occurred outside of cartoons. 'Educational', he said to himself. Yes, Berkeley had been quite an education, and he wasn't thinking about the classroom element. Still, he had had enough. Certainly enough of getting thrown down the stairs. 'Another first....And last...I should hope.' Straughton glanced around dreamily as he walked. Where was he going? 'Perhaps for something to eat,' he suggested to himself. Yes. He could get some chicken at Cosmic Rob's. Or the Power to The People Pizza Parlor, only a block away. No, maybe later. Right now he had a yen for a fresher, sharper taste. He would satisfy this hunger by walking to campus, perhaps for the last time — a sort of farewell tour. There he would find an Honor Apple stand. His mouth began to water as he walked, contemplating just one of the many treasures this town had offered him, one of the endearing reasons he would forever think fondly of Berkeley — 'The free apples'.

*****

Smitty headed towards the office with determination in his

stride. His thoughts focused upon his destination, his mind oblivious to his surroundings along the way. He felt not the slightest interest in them. To Smitty, Berkeley was a city gone stale. For a few days now, he had thought about taking this walk. Yet the first steps there had always proved too easy to delay. This morning he had considered taking a entirely different walk, one with Marco and most of Berkeley, as they tried to stop the troop train. Yet his usual fear of missing any action had quickly waned into a sense of shame. He had had enough of Marco and his delusional minions. Smitty didn't even want to think about them. Worse yet, there was not one damn face in this town that he did want to see. This, and the mood it put him in, supplied the impetus to finally take the walk he was now taking.

Smitty had only been noticing the office since Sloan had mentioned it. 'What a joke.' A smirk came to his face every time he saw it. No other storefront on the block had a brick façade in place of the original plate glass window. Though the front door was glass, a grate of expanded steel protected it. Even ignoring its looks, the storefront seemed, not just out of place in Berkeley, but out of sync with the times. It was an affront to, a foreign body within the city. If the United States Marine Corps could commit the blunder of putting a recruiting office in the middle of this insane town, Smitty could not even imagine what blunders the Marine Corps must be committing in Vietnam. Surprisingly, these very thoughts now fueled his reckless determination. Not only would the Marine Corps Recruiting Office provide asylum from this asylum known as Berkeley, it would provide a ticket out, an escape that would make a statement about Berkeley itself and about all that he had witnessed herein.

Smitty pulled on the door handle. It would not budge. He peered through the grate and glass. Two uniformed Marines looked up from their desks and stared at him. Smitty checked his watch against the "Office Hours" sign on the door. He pulled again. The door still wouldn't budge. Neither would the two seated Marines. Apparently recruiters were choosier than their reputations. He wondered, half seriously, if this were some sort of test, the question being, "Are you good enough (at opening doors) to be a Marine?" Hell, he'd pull harder. Smitty did. Again he failed. His bad mood was getting worse. Smitty rattled the door. One of the

Marines stood and came towards it. He was a muscular six-foot-four black man in his late twenties. As he cracked open the door, his expression was dead serious and suspicious. "What can we do for you?"

'What's going on?' Smitty wondered, sure that he must have missed some clues. There was irritation in his tone as he replied, "I want to find out about joining the Marines."

The black Marine's expression became even more suspicious. He turned his head back towards the other, still seated Marine. "Staff Sergeant, this— he says he wants to find out about enlisting."

The Staff Sergeant rose slowly to his feet and walked to the door. Smitty stared transfixed at his Enemy of The People haircut — sides shaved clean and no more than a thin fuzz on top. Twenty pounds overweight and a head shorter than his partner, the corporal, he relieved him at the crack in the door. Staring at Smitty even more suspiciously than the other Marine, he asked, "What can we do for you?"

"I want to find out about joining."

The Staff Sergeant took a moment to size up Smitty, then asked to make sure, "The Marine Corps?"

Smitty, his temper simmering, not trusting his voice, kept his lips tight as he nodded Yes. The Staff Sergeant's name tag was filled with letters from one edge to the other. The name started with a C and ended with a "SKI". In between there were a lot of I's and two Z's. Smitty, skeptical that the spelling gave even a clue as to the pronunciation, didn't bother trying to figure it out.

The Staff Sergeant looked over at the corporal, only to receive a blank stare. He then turned back towards Smitty, warning, "You better not be another of those freaks, here to talk us into deserting."

Doubting that his patience would hold up much longer, Smitty shook his head in silent exasperation.

"I'm warnin' yah, you better not be."

The corporal leaned towards the crack in the door, adding slowly and convincingly, "We'll beat the living shit out of you."

Smitty just stared at them.

The Staff Sergeant, staring back, was surprised to see the makings of a Marine.

"Come in and sit down."

Smitty entered with a sense of accomplishment, though far from certain about what.

The recruiters' expressions continued to show suspicion as they directed Smitty to the chair in front of the Staff Sergeant's desk. The Corporal sat down at his own desk, directly behind Smitty, never taking his eyes off him.

The Staff Sergeant said to the Corporal, "Get me the Oakland office on the phone." He then asked Smitty, "You in any trouble with the cops?"

Smitty solemnly shook his head.

The Sergeant's tone became friendlier. "Even if you are, we may be able to straighten it out."

"I'm not."

The Sergeant leaned forward, saying in a quieter, conspiratorial tone, "Let's just say that if someone had a police record or something, he'd be smart to leave it off the forms. If it's found out, it won't be till you're in boot camp, and if you're doing okay there, they'll probably just forget about it."

Smitty, weary of protesting his innocence, accepted his outlaw status with a nod.

The Corporal said, "Oakland, Sarge."

The Sergeant picked up the phone, saying into it, "This is the Berkeley office. We have a prospective recruit here and— Yes Sir, the Berkeley office." The Sergeant paused, listening to the receiver, then gave Smitty the once over. "He looks all right...especially for around here." The Sergeant listened to the receiver again before asking Smitty, "You an American citizen?"

Again Smitty nodded.

The Sergeant spoke into the telephone, "He says Yes." After listening a moment, he asked Smitty, "Where were you born?"

"Cleveland."

The Sergeant said into the phone, "He says, 'Cleveland'." After another moment listening to the receiver, he checked with Smitty. "United States?"

"Ohio."

The Sergeant said Yes into the receiver, then warned Smitty, "You have to be able to prove it." Back to the receiver again, he said, "That's what I wanted to know, what forms?"

Smitty was well acquainted with all the Polish jokes and the term "dumb Polack". Yet the Polish people he had known not only seemed to be a good bit smarter than your average Smitty or Jones, they seemed to be sharper too. Now, finally, he found himself sitting directly across a desk from, putting his life in the hands of, that notorious exception to the rule who was giving all the other Skis a bad name.

The Sergeant opens his desk and starts shuffling around in it, still listening to the receiver. He pulled out a piece of paper. "I've got that one right here," he said, proud of the ease with which he had found it. He laid it carefully on top of the desk, smoothing it out with his palm before resuming his search. He pulled out some other papers. "I've got the test too." Then he started to really dig around in the drawer. "I don't see it....No, it's not here." To Smitty he says, "This is the slow time of year, what with everybody in school and all," then back into the receiver, uneasily, "Ask him to come back? Send him to you?" His voiced stiffened. "There's gotta be a way to sign him up here." The Sergeant's face lit up. "I got it. While he's taking the test, I'll send the corporal over to you for the form....Yes, right now."

The Sergeant hangs up the phone and faces Smitty with a smile. "You'll have a half hour to finish this test....If you need a few more minutes, we can see to that....And if you don't understand a question," he gives Smitty a wink, "I'll explain it to you."

*****

Even Marco, who had planned the march, could not believe the awesome sight before him. In his wildest political fantasies, he had never imagined the electricity now coursing through him. All of Berkeley, San Francisco, Oakland, and thousands from beyond had turned out. They jammed the street, stretching as far as he could see. He wondered with awe just how far back they went, and about how many people must be clogging the side streets, waiting anxiously to squeeze themselves in.

Today, history was not just something to be read about in books. No, Marco assured himself, today history was alive and being made. "Power to The People", once merely a slogan, was today a fact, proof of the strength in numbers. The cops and the National Guard would never be able to stand up to the masses he had assembled.

Marco had proved all the skeptics wrong, and also all the taunters who populated his childhood. He, Marco, had finally empowered The People, and they in turn now empowered him. Through reason and psychology, organization and manipulation, cajoling and badgering, he had proved there was no lack of commitment among The People. All they had ever lacked was a leader. Today he had proved himself that leader. The chant was constant and deafening — "Stop the troop train! Stop the war!" Shouted with such unity and clarity, it took on the certainty of a Commandment. Gazing at the multitude, Marco too believed it. Above the crowd waved a sea of placards, indicating the participation of every segment of the counterculture, from Vietnam Veterans Opposing the War to the Sexual Liberation Front, from the Venceramos to the Gay and Lesbian Alliance, from the Black Panthers to the NAACP. He had united them. Only the university custodians had refused to be swayed. Marco told himself that they still resented his failure to help them unionize. Despite all he had done for the grape pickers. They were Chicanos too. The custodians had cited other reasons — anti-communism, sons fighting in Vietnam, the economic opportunity this country afforded them. Even in retrospect, their stubborn ignorance frustrated him. Little wonder Mexicans found themselves so ruthlessly exploited by the establishment.

Revving motorcycles heralded the arrival of another group Marco had all but given up on. He set out towards the sound, waving on a few of his flunkies to follow. Twelve Gauge met him with a quick, surly glance before looking away.

Marco stepped into his line of sight before speaking.

Twelve Gauge still managed to look past him, keeping his surly expression.

Marco asked, "You understand what you need to do?"

Still not looking at him, Twelve Gauge nodded, though barely.

Marco continued, "You have to keep the marchers in line, literally and figuratively." Remembering to whom he was speaking, Marco decided to go over that again in simpler terms. "No attacking policemen, not on the way. No looting either. When a store window gets broken, place some of your men in front of it." Marco forced himself to stomach Twelve Gauge's disparaging attitude. He needed him and his men to control the crowd. This march could only succeed if it made it all the way to the railroad tracks. Marco thought of one more thing to add. "Keep your eye on the Sexual Liberation Front. Make sure the women keep their clothes on. Nothing can stall a march like a strip show."

Marco walked away congratulating himself for recruiting the Hells Angels. Today, The People could only be defeated by The People themselves — through a lack of discipline. If any group could ensure that needed discipline, it was the Hells Angels. Marco again gazed back at the massive crowd jamming the street. It seemed to sway this way and that, like some restless beast, ready to prove itself indomitable. Marco checked his watch. It was time to unleash that beast. Without a word, with a mere jerk of his head, he sent one of his lieutenants forward to do just that.

*****

Moe walked along the sidewalk with conflicting emotions. He had told himself that this was one demonstration he would sit out. Yet here he was, on his way to another fiasco of incompetence and aimless rioting by the arrogant pishers of the New Left. They were fuck-ups, led by fuck-ups, intent upon getting fucked-up and fucking up. The fascists had handed them the ultimate cause célèbre — the Vietnam War. Any left except the New Left would have used it to turn this country upside down and on the path to social justice. What did they do with it? They transformed an anti-war movement into an excuse for self-righteous temper tantrums, an opportunity to stick out their childish tongues at anyone older than themselves. Burning American flags and blowing up buildings, they made far more enemies than converts. When the war finally ends — they all do — they'll take the credit. In truth, they probably prolonged it, by years. What had they accomplished so far, besides replacing the exploiters and crooks who ran this country with bona fide fascists elected for the sole purpose of crushing them? If they ultimately succeed in getting a Hitler elected president, they'll file into to the gas chambers shouting, "This proves it. We were right. Admit it."

'So why the hell am I here?' Moe asked himself. There were numerous reasons, and Moe knew them all. For one, these days the

New Left was the only left. If he didn't belong to it, he didn't belong to anything. There was also force of habit. He was too old to change. Moe had never lost his taste for political action. Today's action was this march. He had sat alone in The Badger's office determined to stay there. The streets were so quiet it was eerie. He felt left out. And this just might be the biggest demonstration in the history of the Bay Area. It wasn't mere posturing, a self-righteous temper tantrum likely to morph into a riot. This demonstration was a throwback to the old days. It actually had a rational, direct, attainable purpose — to stop a troop train.

Moe could hear the chanting long before he reached the marchers — "Stop the train! Stop the war!" Even Marco And His Morons might pull this off. He'll have enough people to line the tracks for miles. A few of them with the guts to lay across those tracks, and that troop train ain't going nowhere. Stopping it could set a precedent. And there are more than enough protestors to stop every troop train in this country. No troops, no war. Moe marveled at the simplicity of the plan. 'How the hell did an incompetent jerk like Marco come up with it?…By accident, that's for sure.'

The march had already started by the time Moe reached it. Used to being at the front, he searched for it. All he saw up ahead were people without end. Moe looked back to see the same. Regrets about coming were forgotten. Never before had he witnessed a demonstration this massive, not in Berkeley, not anywhere. Instead of joining immediately, Moe chose to stand on the sidewalk and just take it all in. A hippie marched by with a placard proclaiming that ubiquitous cliché, "Make Love, Not War". Moe shook his head — 'Ignorant brats think they invented sex.…Did as well as any of them.' Yet Moe then admitted to himself that that had been a long time ago. He glanced down at his crotch, seeing no farther than his huge pot belly. It had been almost as long since he had seen his own dick. 'Least it doesn't keep me up at night,' he thought, then thought again. It sure did, but for another reason.

Moe scanned the marchers. Reading the placards as they passed, he came across one that astounded him — "BERKELEY CHAMBER OF COMMERCE". While admitting grudgingly that this time Marco deserved some credit, he saw a placard that surprised him even more — "BERKELEY PTA AGAINST THE WAR". And the next placard topped even that one —

"BERKELEY WICCAN COVEN". It didn't say anything else, against this or for that, but there was an eye drawn beneath the words. Moe wondered if it was supposed to represent the eye of a newt, then immediately asked himself, 'What fucking difference does it make?' So Berkeley had a Wiccan coven. Who the hell wasn't here? 'No one,' he thought, then thought again. Where were the workers, the blue collar union members? The ones who built the buildings that the radicals were blowing up? The ones who liked to wave the flag, not burn it. If they were here, he didn't see them.

Moe heard the roar of a Harley. 'Hells Angels?', he asked himself. 'Here to break up a hippie march?' They loved nothing better.

Instead, the Harley stopped right next to him and its rider ordered, "Off the sidewalk, Fats!"

As a card carrying member of The Left, the ignominy of being ordered around at a leftist demonstration by a fascist, drug dealing, murdering Hells Angel was too much for Moe. "Fuck you," he replied.

The Hells Angel smiled and calmly raised his right arm and undid his jacket cuff.

Moe, unsure what this portended, was sure it portended no good.

The Hells Angel lowered his right arm, and a weighted pool cue butt-section the length of his forearm slid down and out. He caught the thinner end of it. Most of the other Hells Angels had come similarly equipped. The idea had been Twelve Gauge's, a nonlethal, just barely nonlethal, method of crowd control.

Moe realized immediately that this was no time to stand upon principle. He turned to step off the curb, yet not quite fast enough.

The Hells Angel aimed for Moe's kidney. He missed, a little high. Still, the blow was a solid one.

Moe staggered forward in pain, off the sidewalk and right into the marchers, taking one down with him. A few more fell over him. A fall that would have merely proved painful, now turned excruciating with some newly broken ribs. The pain was so intense he could hardly breathe. Moe, as best he could, crawled gasping up onto the sidewalk. He lay on his stomach waiting for the pain to abate. It wouldn't. All he now wanted was to get the hell away.

That meant getting to his feet, which would increase his agony. Moe grabbed on to a street sign and slowly, fitfully pulled himself up. He'd had ribs broken before, twice, at the hands of management goons. As he caught his breath, he warned himself that this pain was something he had better get used to for a while, a long while. Bent slightly forward and to the side, he took agonizing baby steps down the sidewalk.

So that self-important twerp Marco had turned to the Hells Angels. This did not surprise Moe. The pain now torturing him forced him to finally admit that the New Left itself was predominantly fascist, from their self-defeating in-your-face arrogance and self-righteous hypocrisy, to their might makes right philosophy, to their worship of other practicing fascists such as the Hells Angels, Black Panthers, Black Muslims, and brutal, sadistic, psychopathic ex-cons, their gonzo journalists and snotty, elitist comic strip artists. He thought about their leaders and their followers, and there wasn't one that he would trust covering his back. Moe thought about the Old Left, and all the people he had and would have trusted. Sure, the Old Left had it faults, especially the two-faced trickery — disguised agendas, liberal and progressive fronts, dissimulation, infiltration, cooption. Yet, at the moment, holding his ribs, he was in no mood for a confession and cut it short.

Moe had to finally admit something else, something he had been mulling over in the back of his mind for months — 'That fucking traitor was right,' meaning Eric Hoffer. Even Premier Khrushchev affirmed this, saying, "The left and the right in the US were so far apart that they were almost touching." If anybody ever deserved to lose it was the New Left. Moe, bent double, hobbling along the sidewalk, said to himself with certainty, 'They'll find a way.'

This thought brought Moe no satisfaction. He had never felt so old. Moe had stood up to goons tougher than that Hells Angel. More than once. Yet those days were over. For good.

*****

'Flawlessly,' Marco thought to himself. That's how the march was going. He would have preferred to take this as a given, the expected result of all his planning. He couldn't. Marco had planned before. Too often these plans had ended in fiascos. Never had his planning come to fruition as flawlessly as today. The mood around him was joyous, the atmosphere intoxicating.

Marco, intoxicated, grew more confident with every step. He was hardly conscious of walking. The multitudes he led fed him their energy and strength. Marco felt as if he were riding the neck of a huge dragon, one that would soon, upon his command, breathe awesome fire. His feelings of potency brought with them a sense of exhilaration far surpassing any he had ever felt. Then, suddenly, unexpectedly, an epiphany clobbered him — the meaning of what was happening. It hit him like a brick, numbing his senses and making him dizzy. He saw in an instant how all the books he had read, all the demonstrations he had organized, all the riots he had instigated had led directly to this one moment. More astonishingly, he saw to where this moment would lead. The People had been unleashed. He, Marco, had rendered their chains asunder. Soon the entire country would be on the march. No police force would dare get in The People's way. No army could stop them. The military-industrial establishment was doomed. The United States government itself would be brought down by The People, and without the firing of a single shot! He now saw so clearly that the only real weapon this government possessed was intimidation. The entire oppressive establishment was no more than the façade of a Potemkin Village. All it would take to send it crashing down into the dust was a fog of chaos and a little pressure. Marco now felt that needed pressure, far more than enough, marching behind him through the streets of Berkeley. From this day forward, The People would not be intimidated. He himself would see to that. Today would change the world.

Marco felt like a man of tempered steel, indestructible and destined for that glory reserved only for the true leaders. He stared confidently forward, feeling ten feet tall. The fact that he was so much closer than usual to the front of the march amplified his exhilaration. The only people ahead of him were Vietnam Veterans Opposing the War. No cop could get to him without going first through them. The veterans would not make this easy. Though he had fully expected them to be disciplined and self-assured, Marco was surprised by their intelligence. Hard as it was to admit, much of the march's success so far was due to them. Marco had always relied upon bullhorns or runners to control his demonstrators. The veterans had not only suggested walkie-talkies, they had supplied them. They also gave Marco the idea to have a few of his lieutenants monitoring the local radio stations. This might tip him off about what the cops were doing, thus enabling him to keep the march one step ahead. He congratulated himself on making good use of the veterans, vowing to do so again in the future.

Marco glanced over at his assistant who marched alongside him. She pressed tighter on the earphone to her transistor radio. Her expression lent gravity to whatever she was hearing. "What?" he asked.

The woman held up her finger to silence him.

Marco sensed something serious happening somewhere. Unfazed, he was confident that he could handle whatever it was. Today was going to be his day.

"They stopped the train!" she blurted out, still listening intently and holding her first finger up to keep him quiet.

Marco smiled, triumph in his expression. He had so terrified them that they had stopped the train. Then it hit him. 'Wait!' The bastards had robbed him of the sight of it, surrendering before the battle, before he had even arrived. 'Little matter,' he tried unsuccessfully to convince himself. 'A victory is a victory.'

She continued excitedly, "They took the guy to the hospital, his legs too."

"His legs too?"

"The train cut them off," she explained, still listening intently to the earphone.

Numerous thoughts fought it out for Marco's attention. Someone had lain upon the tracks. What courage this had taken. The train must have left early — two whole hours early! Marco could picture the martyr's determination, refusing to move, refusing the pleas of bystanders, as the locomotive sliced off his legs. Yet this brought on a question that Marco had to ask out loud. "What the hell was he doing there before us?"

"Shush," the woman warned, not willing to rely upon her first finger alone. "There's thousands of people there."

"Thousands?" Marco asked himself out loud. How could there be thousands of people at the station already? The veterans were leading the march, and there they were right in front of him. The word shortcut came to mind. He brushed it aside, thinking, 'Ridiculous.' The obvious finally occurred to him. Some people, apparently thousands of them, had decided to opt out of the marching and head directly to the real show — stopping the train. His confidence draining, Marco berated himself for not anticipating this. Fortunately, he still retained the presence of mind to cut short any self-accusation by redirecting his berating. Turning back to the woman monitoring the radio, he shouted. "Why the hell didn't you tell me there were thousands of people already there?"

Startled by his volume and his tone, she forgot about listening to the radio. "I thought you knew."

"HOW THE HELL WOULD I KNOW?" he screamed.

She stared stunned at Marco, unable to answer.

By now she was not the only person staring at Marco. Everyone within hearing was doing the same. Marco, embarrassed by his lack of self-control, at a loss how to regain face, felt his power draining away. Yet the march was continuing as smoothly as planned. Then again, if the troop train had already been stopped, there remained no reason for the march to continue, smoothly or otherwise. He might as well grab a walkie-talkie to tell his army, "Never mind. Go home." What a disgrace, what a letdown, what a bummer. Marco glanced back at the multitudes behind him. And would they all go home? Who knows what they would do? Marco imagined them rushing forward in anger and trampling him to death. Suddenly his flawless march had turned into a farce. He glanced over and noticed—

His 'idiot' assistant was staring at him, an angry pout on her face.

Marco glared back at her.

She refused to turn away.

Finally, he shouted, "What?"

Her pout turned from angry to mean. "The train that ran over the protestor's legs…it was the wrong train."

*****

"What the fuck we doing?" asked Fat Rat. He had turned his motorcycle sideways to stop Twelve Gauge from passing.

"What the fuck you mean?" asked Twelve Gauge, feeling like a cop working a funeral procession and knowing exactly what Fat Rat had meant.

"We're Hells Angels, not the Mickey Mouse Club."

Twelve Gauge saw Fat Rat's point, but this did not mean he had to concede it. Instead, he echoed Marco. "Look at it this way, today, Hells Angels joined a combined action."

"The Hells Angel I joined don't fuckin' join nobody. Hells Angels is Hells Angels, and everybody else ain't shit."

Twelve Gauge had joined the same Hells Angels, which wasn't a debating society either. All of a sudden Fat Rat had turned into a lawyer or a philosopher or something. He was begging to get his lights punched out.

Fat Rat dismounted from his chopper. He motioned with his arm towards the marchers in front of him, who at the moment were the gay and lesbian contingent. "Look at these cunt holes. You join 'em?"

"You first!" said Twelve Gauge, shoving him as hard as he could.

Fat Rat plowed through the marchers like a bowling ball, knocking down a half dozen before he also lost his balance. Three more marchers tripped over him, then a fourth and fifth over them. "Hold up! Hold up!" yelled the demonstrators directly behind them. They struggled to keep from being trampled while pulling the fallen to their feet. Two lesbians, one as big as a bear, helped Fat Rat halfway up before he fought them off. Noticing Twelve Gauge on the sidewalk laughing at him did not improve his mood. A king-sized hula dancer — grass skirt, coconut shell halter, two day beard — came up behind Fat Rat. Figuring he was a member of the club, the hairy hula dancer placed one of his leis on him. Fat Rat spun around in surprise, just in time to receive a smooch on the lips. Before the kiss could get passionate, Fat Rat had one hand squeezing Hula Boy's throat shut while the other hand pounded his face. The Gay and Lesbian Alliance immediately shoved Fat Rat back down on to the pavement, calling a meeting on top of him.

Twelve Gauge rushed to the rescue, swinging his pool cue butt section. Quarters were too close to take full advantage of this weapon. He barely managed to shove and fight his way to Fat Rat before joining him beneath a kicking, biting, scratching pile of gays and lesbians.

*****

Marco stared ahead with renewed confidence. Those incompetent protestors already at the station, the ones who had stopped the wrong train, had surely made obvious how indispensable he was to the anti-war movement. At least they should have. He hoped those bumbling idiots had learned their lesson, and were now awaiting patiently for his crucial leadership. The pace of the march had quickened. Marco awarded himself credit for this just as he received word of a bottleneck behind him.

Reluctantly, yet calmly, he halted the march. The fact that the trouble's source was the Gay and Lesbian Alliance did not surprise him. He had begged their leaders to keep the vamping to a minimum, and now assumed their failure to do so was the problem. He refused to take chances, walking back to handle this matter personally. On the way there, Marco reminded himself to inspire confidence by keeping calm, this no easy task on a day such as today when the stakes could not be higher, A few hours earlier, he had felt invincible, as if riding the neck of a dragon. Well, his fire breathing dragon had turned into a roller coaster, with all its ups and downs. Now he had to hold up the entire march because the gays and lesbians thought they were at Mardi Gras. Big deal. Marco calmly, determinedly decided to stop letting the highs raise him so high and the lows bring him so low. Doing so was merely a matter of self-control.

To Marco's relief, he arrived to find calm. His relief lasted only until he had made his way to the center of everyone's attention. Calm had obviously been achieved by the beating senseless of two Hells Angels. Fat Rat was sitting in the middle of the street in a daze. Twelve Gauge, laid out next to him, was only half conscious at the most. A strutting man or woman, Marco wasn't quite sure which, circled them threatening even more of a beating with the butt of a pool cue. Marco stood thinking, 'This is not good, not good.' That was even before he heard the roar of approaching motorcycles.

The gays and lesbians stood their ground, even with the arrival of a half dozen Hells Angels, even with the sound of more approaching in the distance. The Hells Angels headed instinctively for the obscured Twelve Gauge and Fat Rat. The gays and lesbians grudgingly opened no more than a narrow path before closing in again behind them. The Hells Angels formed a protective circle around their comrades. The gays and lesbians, instead of backing off, crowded in closer. Marco realized that the march's success lay in the balance. He would have to act fast and decisively. This would take all his powers of persuasion. Determined and confident, Marco took a step towards the lead biker just as another of those pool cue sections magically appeared in his hand.

Marco said, "Gentlemen, there's no need—"

"Fuck you, faggot!" the lead biker cut him off.

Marco opened his mouth again, intending to diffuse this little misunderstanding with logic and reason. His mouth stayed open, yet he never got a word out. Instead, he stood mesmerized, watching, seemingly in slow motion, as—

The lead biker, with the thick end of his pool cue butt, applied a clean blow to the side of Marco's neck. Marco doubled over compliantly, thus allowing a clobbering follow-up blow, this time to the back of his neck. Marco, in a less than graceful swoon, fell flat on his face.

The gays and lesbians, far from cowed, charged with a fury. They drove the bikers off their feet and into a remarkably compact pile, directly on top of Marco. This proved lucky for him, as he lay shielded from the kicking and stomping that ensued. That's when two dozen more Hells Angels arrived. Most of these reinforcements chose to forgo the use of pool cues in favor of their more traditional means of mayhem — knives and motorcycle chains. Only a few protestors, mostly lesbians, were foolish enough to stand up to them. They too soon found themselves running or staggering after their friends.

Panic took hold all along the line of march. Ignorant of exactly what was taking place, naturally assuming something apocalyptic, the protestors stampeded like wild beasts into the side streets. Most ran in fear, yet some ran in freedom, fragmenting in all directions, down boulevards and through alleys, plowing around, over, and through whatever and whoever stood or lay in their way, often meeting again head-on, all this amidst a crashing of broken glass and the wail of distant sirens.

*****

Smitty stepped out of the recruiting office feeling surprisingly and completely stoned. He hadn't smoked a joint in days. And for God's sake, he had just signed his ass over to the United States Marine Corps for two years. Two…long…years! This seemed like a lifetime. Where he was headed, a dumb mistake or some bad luck might mean a much shorter time, yet a lifetime all the same. How the fuck did it happen? That question Smitty chose not to ponder at the moment. He wasn't sorry. Yes, his life had taken one hell of a sharp turn, yet by his own damn choice. To his amazement, irrationally, he felt free. Two long years of bondage lay ahead, yet he felt free. This seemed insane until he remembered what Sloan had said the night he reenlisted, "Guess freedom's just a state of mind." Stoned to the point of sedation, baffled as to why, he decided that he might as well just enjoy the high.

As Smitty walked, he was conscious of, yet unconcerned about, something strange in the air, something besides the wail of distant sirens. Part of the strangeness was a thicker than usual West Coast haze. No, it was smoke, there was a smell to it, that of burning rubber. Smitty turned the corner to see the source — a police car, upside down, on fire and billowing very black smoke. You didn't see that every day. This was no accident. Many of the storefront windows were smashed. Eerily, there was not another person in sight. The adjective apocalyptic came to mind. No smile appeared on his face as he thought, 'Fuck, I could have made it as an English major.'

No longer sedated, his high dissipating, a sense of unease began taking hold of Smitty. The sirens seemed to be getting closer. Considering that, there were surely smarter places to be than standing near a burning police car. He turned and headed in the opposite direction. The sound of breaking glass came from up ahead, not directly, but off to one side. He began to hear faint shouts too. These sounds were far enough in the distance to keep him headed away from the burning police car. Obviously, somewhere, there was a riot — 'What's new?' Smitty had no interest in it. Probably wasn't the naked hippie girl type anyway. Even if it were, he wouldn't have walked a block to see it. Hell, just looking never did him much good. The opposite, in fact.

Signing up for the Marine Corps had increased his emotional distance from Berkeley. Whatever the hell was happening here, or would be happening in the future, no longer concerned him. Walking its streets, he might as well be looking down at Berkeley from a hot air balloon. The feeling was odd, yet in no way bad.

Smitty turned a corner to see hundreds of people, not two blocks away, charging frantically towards him. Their desperation was obvious. Cops must be chasing them, cops with nightsticks, at the very least. The fleeing mob still found time to smash a few storefronts along the way. 'What the hell for?' he asked himself, a question he would not have thought to ask a few months earlier.

Smitty watched the rioters approach with a feeling of revulsion. Despite the fear on their faces, he had no more sympathy for them than for the cops chasing them. 'It's their problem,' he thought, suddenly realizing that it might not be their problem alone. No, how would the cops chasing them know that he was just some innocent bystander? The rioters stampeding towards him were now little more than forty yards away.

His hot air balloon landed with a thud, right in the middle of some serious mayhem. Now experiencing the riot at eye level, all sense of detached observation deserted Smitty. He too took off running, twenty yards in front of the mob. A voice in his head said, 'This is ridiculous.' Why should he have to run? He ran anyway, berating himself for not taking off sooner. Still, no sweat. He could run all day if he had to. Running felt good, exhilarating. His senses awoke. He felt alive.

Up ahead, he spied an alley. Using his legs and his brains, he cut into the alley with the speed and agility of a scatback, this to an extent he himself found surprising. 'Wow! Safe!' Now he could walk the rest of the way home. The mob behind him would keep going straight. Yet it didn't. Most of it followed Smitty, its newly anointed though less than willing leader. The alley quickly proved too narrow. Behind him, garbage cans went flying as the rush of rioters fought to squeeze between them. Smitty, leading his suddenly acquired pack, turned to glance back, a decision he would immediately regret. Smitty tripped over something, something very small, yet large enough to send him body surfing on his stomach down the center of the alley. The first thing that had hit was his knee. The pain was excruciating. His knee locked. Despite this, he immediately staggered to his feet. Smitty hobbled forward in agony as a rioter passed him, then a few more. A glance back revealed a human wave rushing to envelop and push him under. His knee unlocked. It had to. Panicked, he took off running again. Yet he had lost some speed, a lot of it. The human wave slammed into him. He barely managed to keep his balance as it propelled him forward. Rioters to his sides surged ahead, enveloping him in the mob. The wave had become a river, eddying around and sometimes carrying along with it garbage cans and the refuse they once contained. Smitty feared his injured leg would suddenly give out. A slip, a misstep, and he would be flat on his stomach, possibly trampled to death. Now, while being pushed aside, towards the edge of this human river, he pictured himself bent double over a trash can, both he and the can then driven into the ground. Smitty spied a sudden opening to his side. Hardly taking time to think, he darted through it towards a small alcove. He crashed, hands first cheek next, hard into a door. Luckily, he kept his balance.

Smitty, cheek still flush against the door, mouth wide open, struggled to catch his breath. Before he could, now even more conscious of the pain in his knee, he forced himself to turn and face the entrance of the alcove. Rioters streamed by. Cops with nightsticks had to be pursuing them. He stood trapped, cornered. He tried the door. No luck — locked. In pain, Smitty backed himself against the near edge of the alcove. Maybe the cops would pass by without seeing him. 'Possible.' The first few did exactly that, right on the heels of the rioters. They swung their nightsticks in a frenzy, sending a few unfortunates to the pavement. Smitty, with all his strength, pressed himself tighter against the side of the alcove. A half dozen more cops rushed by. Focused on catching up with their comrades, none glanced back to spot him. After a few seconds that seemed to last for minutes, one of their stragglers huffed and puffed after them. Smitty stood waiting a very long few moments, dying to make his getaway, dying to stick his head out to check if the coast were clear. Still, he forced himself to wait a little longer. Sure enough, one more cop — out of breath and exhausted, ready to drop — limped by. For some reason, perhaps Smitty's bad luck, this one glanced back.

This cop was overweight, his face way too old and drawn for that of a beat cop. An oddly relieved expression came to it. Smitty had offered him a welcome excuse to stop running. The cop limped forward, within six feet of Smitty. Yet he just stood there panting, sizing up his foe. His expression slowly, relentlessly transformed into that of an animal moving in on its prey, moving in for the kill. The cop's sharply focused eyes told Smitty that he better make the first move. If he could get by him, he could outrun him, bad knee and all. Or he could jump him before he caught his breath. Smitty did neither. The cop did have a revolver, holstered as it was. Something told Smitty to hold off a moment, keep his cool. The cop took another step forward and stopped, still trying to catch his breath. The insane grin finally faded, replaced by a somber stare. The cop straightened up and moved another step forward.

Smitty held his arms up in front of himself, palms open, as if to say, "Now wait a minute."

A look of pure, overpowering loathing came to the cop's face.

Smitty had never in his life seen an expression of such hatred directed at him. This had to be a mistake. Why did the cop hate him? The rage on the cop's face was mesmerizing. Smitty, immobilized, kept his arms up in front, hoping for a miracle. An urge to explain was followed immediately by a realization that any attempt would be not just futile, but ridiculous.

The cop took another step forward, this time viciously swinging his nightstick, knocking Smitty's arms out of the way, then immediately bringing it down hard upon his head with a hollow, vibrating crack.

Smitty, cornered, cowering, moved in the only direction he could. Lunging forward in a crouch, he took a glancing blow to his lower back. The cop jumped aside. Smitty grabbed the arm holding the nightstick. Instinctively, he stuck out his leg and rolled the cop over it. The cop's head hit the pavement with an hollow crack. He was conscious yet stunned. Smitty, left holding the nightstick, reached back with it but froze. The cop stared wide-eyed up at the nightstick. Smitty glanced down the alley in both directions. It was deserted. He raised the nightstick higher, hesitated, then tossed it aside. Pain from his knee shot through him like a bolt of lightning. Throwing the cop over that injured leg had done it no good at all. Hadn't done the cop any good either. He lay immobilized with blood all over him. His wide, questioning eyes stared up at Smitty. He appeared baffled and confused, trying to figure out what was happening to him.

Smitty could not believe he had hurt the cop so bad. Was he dying? Smitty hoped not. Still, he had no intention of sticking around to find out. Smitty dragged him by his feet farther out into the alley. The other cops would be back looking for him. What a bloody sight they'd see. Noticing new drops of blood all over the place, Smitty finally realized, 'Fuck! It's my blood.' He felt the top of his head, quickly finding the gash. It hurt, yet not like his knee. He tore off his shirt, pressing it on the wound as he staggered away.

Smitty knew he needed some stitches in his skull, quite a few. He'd head for the university's hospital, get his money's worth out of that insane asylum. Then, as soon as he damn well could, he'd flee the place, get the hell back to Cleveland, spend some time with his family and friends, real live sane human beings. Berkeley, he'd had enough of Berkeley. And all the phony bullshit Berkeley had to offer. Staggering down the street, he thought hard about this. Nothing here was worth it, nothing came close — 'Nothing!'

Cleveland — "better than most places" — was good enough for him. Then Smitty got a really uncomfortable thought. How the hell was he going to explain it all back home? Berkeley? The Marine Corps? The scar on his noggin? 'Impossible.' He wouldn't even try. No way. It was all too, 'Unbelievable'.